WRATH
of EMPIRE

By Brian McClellan

GODS OF BLOOD AND POWDER
Sins of Empire
Wrath of Empire

THE POWDER MAGE TRILOGY
Promise of Blood
The Crimson Campaign
The Autumn Republic

Forsworn (novella)
Servant of the Crown (novella)
Murder at the Kinnen Hotel (novella)
Ghosts of the Tristan Basin (novella)
In the Field Marshal's Shadow (collection)

WRATH of EMPIRE

GODS OF BLOOD
AND POWDER

BRIAN
McCLELLAN

www.orbitbooks.net

Copyright © 2018 by Brian McClellan

Author photograph by Emily Bischoff
Cover design by Lauren Panepinto
Cover art by Thom Tenery
Cover copyright © 2018 by Hachette Book Group, Inc.
Map by Isaac Stewart

Orbit
Hachette Book Group
1290 Avenue of the Americas
New York, NY 10104
orbitbooks.net

First Edition: May 2018

Orbit is an imprint of Hachette Book Group.
The Orbit name and logo are trademarks of Little, Brown Book Group Limited.

The publisher is not responsible for websites (or their content) that are not owned by the publisher.

The Hachette Speakers Bureau provides a wide range of authors for speaking events. To find out more, go to www.hachettespeakersbureau.com or call (866) 376-6591.

Library of Congress Cataloging-in-Publication Data has been applied for.

ISBNs: 978-0-316-40726-7 (hardcover), 978-0-316-40724-3 (ebook)

Printed in the United States of America

LSC-C

10 9 8 7 6 5 4 3 2 1

For Zina Petersen and Grant "The Boz" Boswell.
My two favorite college professors, both of whom managed to teach
stress-free but interesting classes about subjects I still think about ten
years later.

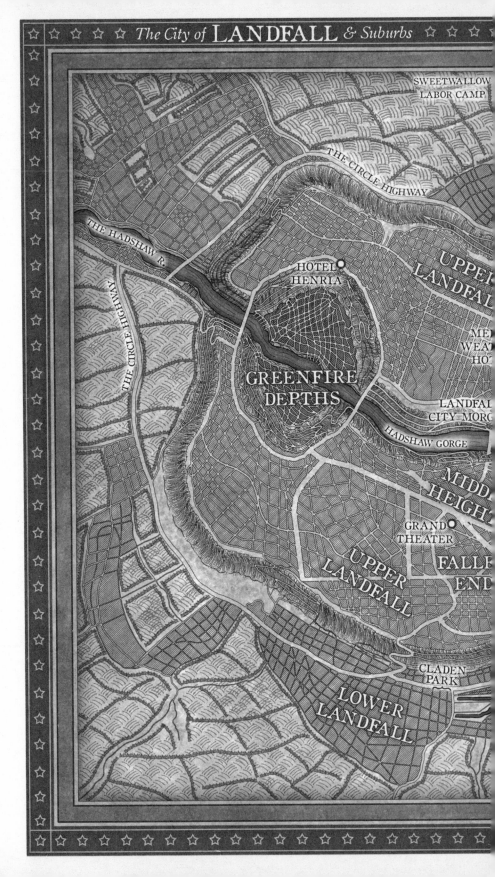

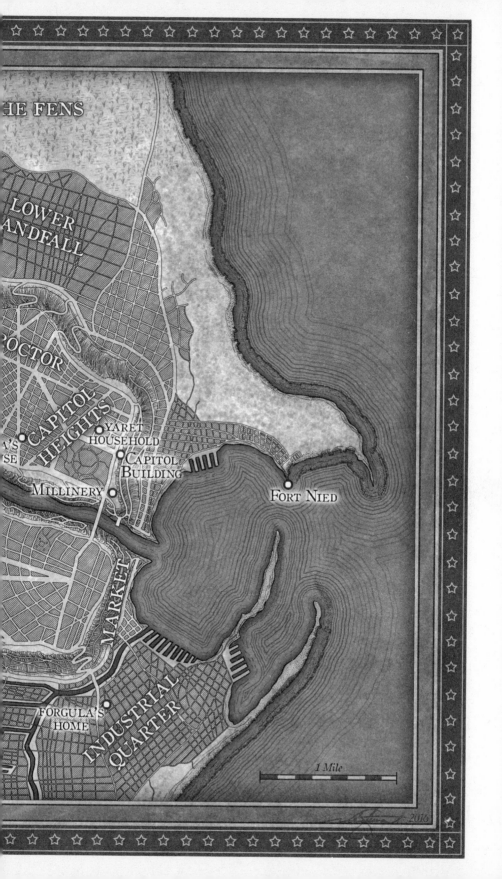

THE FENS

LOWER
LANDFALL

PROCTOR

CAPITOL
HEIGHTS

YARET
HOUSEHOLD

V'S
SE

CAPITOL
BUILDING

MILLINERY

FORT NIED

MARKET

FORGULA'S
HOME

INDUSTRIAL
QUARTER

1 Mile

2016

WRATH
of EMPIRE

PROLOGUE

Orz stood at the bottom of a narrow flight of steps, head tilted toward the light streaming in from the open hatch above him. He could hear gulls calling above and feel the gentle rocking of the ship as it sat in harbor. Both sensations had become ubiquitous to him these last few months.

"Go on," a voice said.

Orz looked over his shoulder at the morion-helmed soldier standing just behind him. The soldier held a short pike, a ceremonial weapon carried by some of the bone-eye bodyguards. Orz wondered where they were—what port had the floating prison sailed into this time. More importantly, he wondered which bone-eye had come to gawk at him now.

Bone-eyes were not unlike Privileged; their vast power was contained within fragile human bodies that could be broken as easily as any ceramic vase. Bone-eyes could die. This bodyguard could die. Orz envisioned himself stalking through the ship, murdering everyone in his path before swimming to shore and disappearing into the countryside.

"We don't have all day," the soldier behind him said, thrusting the blade of the pike against the small of Orz's back. "Move."

Orz snorted and took the first heavy step, careful lest the weight of his chains cause him to lose his balance and tumble backward onto the soldier's blade. He jangled as he climbed, feeling the iron shackles scrape against his bare skin, and within a few moments he stepped out into the light of day for the first time in months.

He blinked, trying to let his eyes adjust, but was shoved along in front of the soldier. Several other guards arrived, forming a cordon around him, pushing and prodding him along the deck, half-blind, and then up another flight of stairs to the ship's forecastle.

Orz felt a hand on his shoulder and jerked away, turning toward the railing and gazing through the pain of the light at an unfamiliar shore. A city rose above him, high on an immense plateau covered in strange buildings. He felt his breath catch in his throat; during the long, secluded journey he had *thought* they were taking him to a new prison somewhere in Dynize.

This was not Dynize. This city, this plateau—he knew only one like it in the storybooks: Landfall.

He was not given further opportunity to wonder. Hands grasped him by the chains and pulled him forward, driving him to the other edge of the forecastle, where he was kicked to his knees. He fell without a sound, ignoring the pain as he had been taught, and instead raised his eyes to find the bone-eye he'd already guessed had called for him.

Orz had never met the old man sitting straight-backed on a stool, sipping from a tiny porcelain cup, but he knew him by description and reputation. Ka-Sedial was the emperor's second cousin and chief adviser, and most people in Dynize knew him as the true power behind the crown. He was a bone-eye who had risen to power on a tide of blood and taken credit for ending the Dynize civil war.

Orz was not impressed. As a dragonman, he was not impressed by much.

Ka-Sedial finished his tea and handed the cup to an attendant, then placed his hands palms-down on his knees and stared out to sea. Orz began to think that he was being purposefully ignored when he heard a commotion behind him: another person, wrapped in chains similarly to Orz, was dragged up to the forecastle and thrown to her knees.

Then another was brought up, and then another, until six men and women knelt before Ka-Sedial. Orz examined his companions. He only recognized two of them, but all five were covered in inky black tattoos, their bodies hard as granite. They were like him.

Six dragonmen, all in one place.

"This is an auspicious gathering," Orz said softly.

Ka-Sedial finally turned his head, sweeping his gaze across all the prisoners. When he spoke, his voice was gentle, forcing Orz to strain to hear him over the creaking of the ship and the squawking of the gulls. "Do you know what you all have in common?"

They were all dragonmen, but Orz suspected that was not the answer Ka-Sedial sought. Orz looked one way, then the other, at his five companions. The woman to his left had long, dirty red hair that covered most of her face, but he remembered the scar across her left eye. Her name was Ji-Karnari, and seven years ago she desecrated a bone-eye temple for reasons he never learned. The man to his right, willowy and small of stature, was named Ji-Matle. Nine years ago he was assigned to guard one of the emperor's cousins, whom he bedded.

No one spoke up, so Orz cleared his throat. "We have all disgraced ourselves in the eyes of the emperor."

"Very good." Ka-Sedial stood up, and Orz couldn't help but smile at how old and frail he looked. He could snap Ka-Sedial like a twig, if not for these chains. Ka-Sedial noticed the smile and his brow wrinkled. He took a step over to Orz. "Tell me, Ji-Orz, what was your crime?"

Orz closed his eyes, thinking of the last few years spent in this dungeon or that, every movement restricted, always watched, like a prize dog gone rabid whose masters could not bear to put him down. "I did not bow during an audience with the emperor."

"And why did you not bow?"

"Because he is not *my* emperor."

Ka-Sedial gave an almost grandfatherly sigh and gestured toward the shoreline and the city on the plateau. "The civil war is over. Your false emperor is dead and the governments of both sides have reconciled. We have turned our wars outward—as is proper—and we have come to Fatrasta to reclaim land that was once ours. We have come to find our god, and we have done so *together*. United." He sighed once more, shaking his head like a disappointed teacher, and Orz found himself annoyed that after all he and his companions had suffered, Ka-Sedial would treat them all like children.

"Why are we here?" Orz asked.

Ka-Sedial looked down at him, a hint of disgust in his eyes, then raised his hands toward the chained dragonmen. "You have all disgraced yourselves in the eyes of the emperor, and your positions as dragonmen prevent us from spilling your blood. Every one of you will live long lives alone in the darkness, left to rot away."

"Or?" Orz asked. He could smell it now—the scent of an option, a way out. He tried to think of what he knew about Ka-Sedial. The Ka was a driven man, cold and thoughtful but given, from time to time, to rage. He'd built his power by destroying or subjugating all that opposed him. He was a man who did not take no for an answer, and did not leave any enemy standing.

Annoyance flashed briefly across Ka-Sedial's face at Orz's interruption. He lowered his hands. "Or you can redeem yourselves. My armies have taken Landfall. We will take Fatrasta in due time. Meanwhile, I have an errand that needs to be run and

I cannot spare any of the dragonmen, Privileged, or bone-eyes in my army."

The invasion of Fatrasta had been planned for almost a decade, but Orz still found himself surprised that it had actually happened—that the treaty between the two sides of the civil war had managed to hold long enough for this to happen. He needed more information about the invasion—what kind of people had been found in Fatrasta, their weapons and their warriors. But that would come later, he was sure of it.

Ji-Karnari, the scarred woman beside Orz, finally raised her head. Orz could see the eagerness in her eyes and couldn't help but judge her. Dragonmen should hide their emotions better.

"What is this errand, Great Ka?" Ji-Karnari asked. "How can we be redeemed?"

Ka-Sedial put his hand out, brushing his fingertips along Ji-Karnari's forehead. She shuddered at the sensation. He said, "There were…humiliations suffered in the taking of Landfall. Humiliations against the army, and humiliations against the dragonmen. I have already sent soldiers to deal with the former, but the latter…" He trailed off, smiling coldly. "One of your order—one of the very best dragonmen by the name of Ji-Kushel—was murdered in Landfall by a common soldier."

"So?" Orz asked. He felt emboldened. This was a way out now, and Ka-Sedial was going to give it to him. But he did not trust Ka-Sedial, and he *would* ask questions. "Many common soldiers have killed dragonmen. There are overwhelming numbers or lucky shots, or—"

"In single combat," Ka-Sedial cut him off.

Orz heard his teeth click together as he quickly shut his mouth. The hair on the back of his neck stood on end. He'd heard rumors of powder mages, sorcerers who might have the speed and strength to kill a dragonman with the aid of their magic. But Ka-Sedial would have said so if it was one of those. For a common soldier to kill a dragonman in single combat? That *was* a humiliation.

Ka-Sedial looked toward the land again, one hand twitching as if in impatience. "I do not stand for such humiliation. This soldier is an old warrior and, if given time, may attract followers. He may become even more dangerous than he already is. I am cutting you loose. All six of you. I want you to work together, with Ji-Karnari in command."

A smile crossed Ji-Karnari's face. Orz resisted the urge to roll his eyes. A small part of him wanted to spit on Ka-Sedial's feet and tell him off, but a much larger part had no interest in spending the rest of his life in chains. He would accomplish Ka-Sedial's task, and then he would revel in his freedom.

"Who is this soldier?" Orz asked.

"He is a lancer by the name of Ben Styke," Ka-Sedial replied. "Find him and bring me his head."

CHAPTER 1

As a child, General Vlora Flint had heard stories of refugee camps formed during the Gurlish Wars. Whole cities displaced, a million people on the run from enemy armies, or even forced from their homes by their own soldiers. The camps, she'd been told, were places of untold suffering and misery. Disease and starvation were rampant, bodies left unburied, and the people living in constant fear of the next army to come upon them.

Vlora, in all her nightmares, had never imagined herself de facto leader of such a camp.

She stood on a gentle rise overlooking the Hadshaw River Valley and surveyed the long, winding string of wagons, tents, and cook-fires that stretched into the distance. It was early morning, the air heavy and humid, and all she could think about was the numbers that her quartermasters had brought her just an hour ago. They'd finished their counts and estimated that over three hundred thousand people had fled Landfall—just over a third of the city—and that of those, some two hundred and twenty thousand were following this river valley toward Redstone.

Her own men, including the Mad Lancers and the Landfall garrison, had been badly mauled during the defense of the city. She had less than ten thousand men under her command, just one soldier for every twenty-two people.

How in Adom's name was she going to organize this mess, let alone protect it?

She pulled herself out of her own head and looked at the camp below her. She could pick out her soldiers walking up and down the river, waking people up, telling everyone it was time to get moving. Three weeks since the Battle of Landfall and disease was already beginning to spread; many of her own soldiers had contracted dysentery. Food and medicine were in short supply. Most people had left the city in a panic, grabbing valuables rather than necessities, and fled without plan or destination.

She inclined her head slightly toward the man waiting patiently beside her. Olem was of middle height, a few inches taller than her, with sandy hair and a graying beard. He walked with a slight limp, and his right arm was still in a sling from a bullet wound from Landfall. He was a Knacked—possessing a singular sorcerous talent that kept him from needing sleep—but even he looked tired as piss, with crow's-feet in the corners of his eyes and his face gaunt with worry. She wanted to order him to rest, but knew he'd ignore her.

She wasn't entirely sure what she'd do without him.

"Any sign of the Dynize?" she asked, turning from her view of the refugees to look back down the river the way they'd come. Landfall was about sixty miles to their southeast, and the road that direction was dotted with stragglers. Her own army was camped here, guarding the rear of the refugee convoy.

Olem sucked on a cigarette, smoke curling out of his nostrils, before giving a measured response. "Scouting parties," he said.

"They're watching us leave. But I imagine they're too busy solidifying their hold on Landfall to bother coming after us. *For now.*"

"You know," Vlora said, shooting him a sour look, "you could leave off the 'for now.' It just sounds ominous."

"I never try to give you anything but the facts," Olem responded, straight-faced. "And the fact is they're leaving us alone. I can't imagine it'll last forever. I've got our dragoons sweeping our rear, trying to catch one of those scouting parties, but they've come up with nothing so far."

Vlora swore inwardly. She needed to know the state of the city. She and her men had won the Battle of Landfall, only to be forced to abandon it at word of an even bigger Dynize army on the way. Last she knew, that army had begun to land near the city, and she had no intelligence since then. How big was that army? Were they pushing outward aggressively? Were they taking their time to fortify the city? Did they have more Privileged sorcerers and bone-eyes?

Beyond food and supplies for so many people, the next most valuable commodity was information. She needed to know whether the Dynize were hot on her heels. She also needed to know if the Fatrastan Army was heading this direction, because that offered its own set of complications. "Any word from Lindet?"

Olem pursed his lips. "Nothing official. We've taken in nearly two thousand Blackhats. None of them seem to have orders, or know of the falling out between you and their Lady Chancellor. I've put them to work as a police force among the refugees."

Olem's ability to keep even the biggest army occupied and organized never failed to amaze her. "You're a saint, but keep a close eye on those Blackhats. Any of them could be Lindet's spies. She may have left town two steps ahead of us, but if she didn't leave eyes and ears to keep track of me, I'll eat my hat."

"And I, mine," Olem agreed. "But I've got my own men among them. I'll keep things sorted as best as I can. Did you know Styke is openly recruiting from the Blackhats to fill out the ranks of his lancers?"

Vlora snorted. "With success?"

"More than I expected. He's making them renounce their loyalty to the Lady Chancellor before they can sign on. The Blackhats are damned angry she abandoned so many of them without orders. He's got over a hundred already."

"And may Adom help any spies he catches," Vlora said. She hesitated, her eyes on a string of horsemen riding single file along the other side of the river. They were a company of hers, wearing their tall dragoon helmets and crimson uniforms with blue trim, straight swords and carbines lashed to the saddles. "Did I make a mistake giving Styke command of my cavalry?"

"I don't think so," Olem replied.

"You hesitated."

"Did I?"

Vlora clasped her hands behind her back to keep from fiddling with her lapels. "Lindet told me he's an uncontrollable monster."

"I get the feeling," Olem responded, dropping his cigarette butt and crushing it beneath the heel of his boot, "that Lindet's version of the truth is whatever is convenient at the time. Besides, right now he's *our* monster."

"Again, that's not reassuring." Vlora tried to get a rein on her thoughts. They were unfocused, scattered, and the sheer number of uncertainties running through her head was enough to drive her mad. There was so much to attend to within her own army—Blackhat stragglers, the city garrison, the Mad Lancers, and the core of the brigade of mercenaries she brought with her from Adro. She had over five thousand picked men, many of them wounded, half a world away from their homes, without an employer. A desperate bark of a laugh escaped her lips, and Olem shot her a worried glance.

"You all right?" he asked in a low voice.

"I'm fine," she said reassuringly. "There's just...a lot to take in."

"You know these refugees aren't your responsibility," Olem said, not for the first time.

"Yes, they are."

"Why?"

Vlora tried to find a satisfactory answer. She wondered what Field Marshal Tamas would have done in such a situation, and realized that he would have marched to the nearest unoccupied city and booked passage home for his troops the moment his contract became null. But she was not Tamas. Besides, there were more reasons to stay in this land than a quarter of a million refugees. "Because," she finally answered, "no one else will do it."

"The men are beginning to wonder where their next stack of krana will come from."

Another of a thousand worries. A little bitter part of her wanted to tell the men that they should be more concerned about getting out of Fatrasta alive than their next payment, but she couldn't be too hard on them. They were mercenaries, after all. "Give them promissory notes against my own holdings."

"I already did."

"Without asking me?"

Olem gave her a small smile and dug in his pocket for a pouch of tobacco and some rolling papers. "I figured you'd give the order at some point. But not even you can pay them indefinitely."

"I'll figure out something." Vlora waved him off as if she wasn't concerned, but it was a worry that kept her up at night. A thought suddenly hit her and she squinted down into the camp. "You know, I haven't seen Taniel or Ka-poel for a while. Where the pit are they?"

"They remained in the city when we left."

Vlora scowled. "And you didn't think to tell me?"

"I did, actually. Twice. You assured me both times that you'd heard every word I was saying."

"I lied." Vlora felt a sudden stab of despair. Despite their rocky history, Taniel was a reassuring man to have around, and not just because he was a one-man army. "Why would they stay in the city? Are they gathering intelligence?"

Olem shrugged, then hesitated before saying, "I know you and Taniel have known each other a long time. But don't forget that those two have their own agenda."

It was not a reminder Vlora needed—or wanted. Taniel was more than an old lover; he was an adopted sibling and a childhood friend. Instinct told her to trust him, but years of military and political training reminded her that shared history was a long time ago. So much had changed.

With everything going on right now, his disappearance was the least of her worries. She ran her fingers through her tangled hair, wondering how long it had been since she'd had a proper bath. Setting aside her discomfort, she said, "I need information."

"Well, we might have something." Olem pointed toward a uniformed messenger hurrying his way up the hill toward them.

"It won't be useful," Vlora responded, annoyed. "It's going to be some asshole city commissioner trying to hassle me for supplies he thinks we're hoarding from the refugees. Again."

"I bet it's something important."

"I bet it's not."

"I'll bet you that spare pouch of tobacco you keep in the left cuff of your jacket," Olem said.

"Deal," Vlora said, watching the messenger approach. It was a young woman with a private's insignia on her lapel, and she saluted smartly as she came to a stop.

"Ma'am," the messenger said, "I've got word from Captain Davd."

Vlora shot Olem a look. "Is it important?"

"Yes, ma'am. He said he's spotted a Dynize pursuit force."

Vlora took a deep, shaky breath as a wave of trepidation swept through her. This would mean a battle. It would mean men dead and the lives of all these refugees at stake. But at least she could finally see her enemy.

She dug into her sleeve and pulled out her pouch of emergency tobacco, handing it to Olem without looking at him. Smug bastard. "Take me to Captain Davd."

The Hadshaw River Valley was heavily trafficked, the old-growth forests that had once sprawled across this part of Fatrasta logged into extinction over the last couple hundred years. The land was rocky and unforgiving, very unlike the floodplains closer to the city or the plantations to the west. Farmsteads dotted the hilly landscape, surrounded by walls built from the stones the farmers dug from their fields.

The occasional rocky precipice was topped by a stand of scraggly honey locusts, and it was in such a vantage point that she found two of her soldiers hunkered on their knees between the boulders.

Captain Davd was in his early twenties, with black hair and a soft, beardless face. He tapped powder-stained fingernails against the stock of an ancient blunderbuss and nodded as Vlora crept up beside him.

His companion was an older woman with graying, dirty-blond hair. Norrine lay with her head against a stone, her rifle propped on a branch, sighting along it as she watched some target only she could see.

Anyone else might find it odd to discover two captains out on a scouting mission, but Vlora took it in stride. Like her, they were both powder mages. By ingesting a bit of black powder, they could run faster, see farther, and hear better than any normal soldier. It made them ideal scouts for an army on the run. She had taken a page out of her mentor's book and given powder mages under her command a middling rank and an auxiliary role. They answered only to her.

In addition to scouting, they could also use their sorcery to fire a musket or rifle over fantastic distances, picking off the most difficult targets.

"Norrine has an officer in her sights," Davd said in an excited whisper. "Say the word, and they'll be down a ranking metalhead."

Vlora snorted. Her men had begun to refer to Dynize soldiers as "metalheads" because of the conical helmets they wore. She laid a hand gently on Norrine's shoulder. "How about you fill me in on what's going on before you start killing people."

Davd looked crestfallen. Norrine gave Vlora a thumbs-up and kept her bead on her target.

"Well?" Vlora urged Davd.

Davd shifted to make room for Vlora to hunker down between him and Norrine in the rocky crag. She crawled up beside them, looking over the edge of their vantage point, and fished a powder charge from her breast pocket. She cut through the paper with her thumbnail and held it to her right nostril, snorting gently.

Her senses flared, giving her an immediate high as sounds, colors, and smells all became brighter. The world came into focus, and she squinted down the length of the Hadshaw River Highway toward a small party of soldiers in the distance. The powder trance allowed her to see details as if she were a mere fifty yards away, and she took quick stock of the enemy. Long experience at this sort of thing gave her an estimate of five hundred or so soldiers, at about two miles distance. They wore the silver breastplates and bright blue uniforms of the Dynize soldiery. About half of them rode horses, which was new to Vlora—the Dynize who had attacked Landfall had no calvary.

The troop was on the move, the horses trotting while the soldiers marched double time. Every so often they were joined by a rider coming over the ridge from the east or fording the river from the west. Messages were exchanged, and then a dispatch was sent south.

"It's a vanguard," Vlora concluded.

"Making regular reports," Davd added. "I'm willing to bet they're no more than a couple of miles ahead of the main army. They're probing, checking the lay of the land and trying to draw out our rear guard."

"They're moving awfully fast for a vanguard."

"Huh," Davd commented. "So they are."

Vlora took a shaky breath. Her army—and the refugees they were guarding—were less than five miles from the pursuing Dynize. If the army was traveling as fast as the vanguard, they could force a battle before nightfall. If they took their time, Vlora might have two days to prepare. She wondered whether she should attempt to gain a few more miles before nightfall, pushing the refugees ahead of her, or choose a defensive position immediately. "You two, get me information. I want eyes on the enemy army. I want to know their strength and how fast they're moving. No guns, and don't be seen."

She crawled out of the thicket of honey locusts and returned to the messenger who'd shown her the way. "We have enemy contact. Have someone prepare my rifles, then go find Major Gustar. He and Colonel Styke have an enemy vanguard to crush."

CHAPTER 2

Ben Styke sat at the crest of a hill, his scarred face turned toward the morning sun, the ground damp and cool beneath him. He leaned against his saddle while his warhorse, Amrec, grazed nearby. The sun warmed Styke's bones, allowed him to test the limits imposed upon him by old wounds. He squeezed a handful of pebbles to strengthen the tendons in his arm that had once been cut, then healed, by sorcery.

A little girl, Celine, played on a crumbling dry-stone wall. She skipped from stone to stone, barely seeming to pay her surroundings any mind until one stone slipped out from beneath her and she switched feet deftly, finding purchase before she could fall. She continued down the wall a hundred yards or so and turned around, doubling her speed for the trip back.

Somewhere over the nearby hills was Lady Vlora Flint—Styke's new commanding officer—along with her tiny mercenary army and hundreds of thousands of refugees from Landfall. Styke kept his own men away from the column, preferring to flank the refugees and handle the scouting. Refugees weren't his problem. Killing—when it had to be done—was.

Styke squeezed the pebbles until a bead of sweat trickled down his forehead. He searched the back of his mind for his birthday—one of the many things forgotten after so long in the labor camps—and decided he was just a few months away from his forty-sixth. Almost old enough to be Celine's grandfather. Certainly old enough to be her real father, if he'd gotten a late start.

Celine reached the end of the wall nearby and leapt to the grass. She wasn't wearing shoes, despite having two new pairs, and her jacket and loose trousers were muddy from three weeks on the road. She had a girl's long hair and a soft face, but her bearing left her mistaken for a boy more times than not. She was at once skittish and confident, the daughter of a thief and toughened by years in the labor camps.

She grasped Amrec fearlessly by the bridle, stroking his nose. He snorted at her but did not kick her to oblivion as he would anyone else so daring.

Styke discarded the pebbles and brushed the grit from his hands. The release of pressure on his tendons made him swallow a gasp, and he took a deep breath before calling to Celine.

"How do you decide which stone to step on?" he asked her.

Celine seemed surprised by the question. She left Amrec and came over to Styke's side, throwing herself down against the saddle in the mock exaggeration of a tired soldier. She was, Styke decided, spending too much time with the lancers. Not that that would change any time soon.

"I just step on whichever one looks secure."

"And how do you know which is secure?"

"I just know," Celine said with a small shrug.

"Hmm. Think, girl," Styke replied. "Think about *how* you know."

Celine opened her mouth, closed it again, and furrowed her brow. "I don't step on the flat ones. They're the worst, because they wobble. The ones that are shaped like…" She made a triangle with her hands.

"Like a wedge?" Styke urged.

Her face brightened. "Yeah, like a wedge. Those are the strongest, because they rest on two other stones."

"Very good." Styke searched in his saddlebag and found a bag of wrapped caramels that he'd discovered while looting a Blackhat supply depot before leaving Landfall. He placed one in Celine's hand.

Celine regarded the sweet seriously before looking up at Styke. "Why does it matter? Didn't you tell me that instinct is a lancer's best weapon? That's what I use to find the stones, isn't it?"

Styke considered his answer and glanced down the hill. Far below them, several hundred lancers practiced drills on horseback, riding back and forth across the small valley until it was a muddy cesspit. He listened to the shouts of his officers as they barked corrections and orders. "Instinct is just a word we use to describe all the little bits of information your senses collect and how your brain interprets them. Instincts can be improved."

"So, when you make me inter…inter…"

"Interpret."

"Interpret my instincts, you're exercising my brain? Like what you're doing with your wrists?"

Styke grunted, stifling a smirk. "You're a clever little shit, you know that?"

"Ibana says that's why you like me," Celine responded, sticking her chin in the air.

"Ibana says a lot of things. Most of them are bullshit." Styke climbed to his feet, leaning down to tousle Celine's hair, then turning a critical eye on the lancers training down below. The training lasted hours each day as Ibana whipped old lancers and new recruits alike into shape. Both men and horses had to be trained, and Styke didn't know of any army on this continent that drilled as hard as the Mad Lancers.

But that's part of what made them the best.

Styke felt an ache deep in his back, in his thighs, and in his shoulders. He took a few breaths and stretched. There was a time when he was just shy of seven feet tall, and not a man in Fatrasta would have looked him in the eye. He was the biggest, strongest, and meanest—a hero of the Fatrastan revolution with a lover in every town between the coasts.

Now he was a broken man, and though mended by sorcery he was still bent from years in the labor camps, gnarled from wounds left by the firing squad.

"I'm still Ben Styke," he whispered to himself. He thought about going down there, participating in the drills. He was out of practice himself, and he'd had Amrec for less than a month. Any warhorse big enough to carry Styke would need plenty of time learning the maneuvers of a lancer battalion. But that could wait. Half the lancers were old comrades, gathered from Landfall before it ended up in the hands of the Dynize. The other half were raw recruits. Best to remain aloof and let Ibana train them on the legend of Mad Ben Styke, rather than see the broken soul he'd become.

He turned to find Celine staring at the side of his face—at the scar where a bullet had bounced off his cheekbone a decade ago. Celine had grown bold since leaving the labor camps at his side. She was bigger, stronger, responding well to a healthy diet. In ten years she would be a stout woman with fists of iron, and Styke pitied the men who might think her an easy tail to chase.

"Ibana says not to let you feel sorry for yourself."

Styke narrowed his eyes at Celine. "What is that supposed to mean?"

"She says you're not as strong as you once were, and she catches you staring at your hands all the time. She says self-pity makes you a dog, and she needs you to be a man."

What the *pit* was Ibana doing telling all this to a little girl? *Styke's* little girl, particularly. "Ibana needs to shut her bloody mouth."

Celine stretched out against Amrec's saddle and stared up at the sky. "The boys have been telling me stories about you during the war."

"Shit." Styke sighed. As much as he tried to avoid it, Celine had become something of a favorite in the camp. Everyone who'd lost a daughter or a cousin or a sister back during the war took it upon themselves to tell her stories and "raise her up right." Aloof or not, Styke was going to have to start cracking heads.

"Did you really kill a Warden with your bare hands?"

Styke snorted. "I told you that story."

"Yeah, but I didn't believe it before. I thought you were making stuff up. My da used to make stuff up all the time so his friends thought he was tough. But Jackal said you *did* kill a Warden. Did you?"

"I did. Broke his back, then cut his throat."

Celine nodded seriously, as if this were the response she expected. "Then Ibana's right. You shouldn't pity yourself. You're too strong to pity yourself."

"Okay," Styke said, pushing her off his saddle with one toe. "That's it. I'm not letting you spend time with Ibana anymore. Or Jackal. Or Sunin. I don't need everyone thinking they can heal me. I'm fine." His final insistence rang a little too forceful, even to his ears. "That was over ten years ago. You weren't even a twinkle in your daddy's eye back then. I'm not strong enough to kill a Warden anymore. People change. That's the nature of life."

"You killed a dragonman. I saw the body after."

Styke looked down at his hands. If he focused hard enough, he could still feel the slick, warm blood up to his elbows, the bits of brain between his knuckles. "Yeah," he said uncertainly. The memory felt like a dream. "I did, didn't I?" He shook his head. "All right, enough of this. Help me get Amrec's saddle on him. He and I need to go through some paces before Ibana lets everyone go for the day."

Styke was tightening the straps on the saddle while Celine fed

Amrec an apple, when he heard the sound of approaching hooves. He looked up to find Major Gustar, commander of Lady Flint's cuirassier and dragoon companies. Gustar rode with the comfortable slouch of a natural horseman, and he gave Amrec an appreciative glance as he reined in. "Afternoon, Colonel."

Gustar was a tall man, thin and bowlegged with the shoulders of a saber-swinging cuirassier. He had brown hair, perfectly trimmed muttonchops, and a clean-shaven face. He struck Styke as the type of man who'd joined the cavalry to impress women and was surprised to find he was a capable officer.

"Gustar. Word from Lady Flint?"

"Indeed. We've spotted a Dynize vanguard."

"How large?"

"Five hundred. Mixed horse and infantry."

"Any idea what kind of an army is coming up behind them?"

"We do. Five brigades of infantry, and they're marching recklessly fast. Flint expects to engage them this evening."

Styke played with his big lancers' ring, looking down toward the drilling lancers. The words to an old lancers' hymn came to him, and he sang under his breath, "Ride, lancers, ride, through the meadows, against the tide. Let your hooves ring, steel ring; break your lances, break their bones, break their spirit against the stones." He took a deep breath. "What are our orders?"

"You have command of me and my cavalry again. Lady Flint is preparing a welcome for the Dynize. We're to crush their vanguard and then sweep their eastern flank to keep their scouts from seeing her preparations."

"Cavalry?"

"Not that we've seen. We suspect that their horses are simply what they could scrounge from Landfall."

Styke smirked. "We took all the good ones when we left. They'll have nothing but fourth-rate mounts. You said they'll be here this evening?"

"That's what we expect."

Styke looked up. It was still early in the morning, but he could tell it would be a pleasant day. It was hot, but not too hot, and the humidity was bearable. As good a day as any for killing. "Ride, lancers, ride," he sang to himself. Louder, to Gustar, he said, "Pass on the orders to Ibana. We head out within the hour."

Styke and Celine watched the arrival of the Riflejack cavalry—a force of over a thousand that included a few hundred cuirassiers in their steel breastplates and bearskin hats, along with a larger contingent of dragoons, all riding under the Riflejacks' flag of a shako over crossed rifles. Styke waited until they had streamed into the Mad Lancers' camp and then rode down to join them.

He found his second-in-command, Ibana ja Fles, standing next to a makeshift headquarters—a tent flying the skull and lance of the Mad Lancers—issuing orders and reviewing inventory reports. Major Gustar stood nearby, his jacket resting loosely over his shoulders, hand on the butt of his saber, eyeing his men in silence. Styke lowered Celine from the saddle and followed her down, tying Amrec to a post before heading over to join the officers.

Ibana finished with a set of reports and handed them off to a soldier. "Flint has no idea how big that Dynize army is, and she's still preparing to dig in and fight."

"I don't think she has much of a choice," Styke responded, nodding to Gustar. "She can withdraw and let them ravage the refugees, or she can pick her ground." He asked Gustar, "What's this surprise she's preparing for them?"

"No idea. All I know is we need to keep them from getting a good look at her formations."

"Do they have cavalry beyond those in the vanguard?"

Gustar spread his hands. "Sorry."

"Pit. We need better information than this."

Ibana snorted. "Yeah, well. This whole venture was your idea. So what do we do?"

"How are the new recruits?" Styke responded with his own question.

"They'll do." Ibana sucked on her teeth. "I'd like another three months to train them, but that's not going to happen."

Gustar gestured toward her. "Same here. We've been trying to fill out our numbers from Adran ex-pats and retired cavalry officers among the refugees. They're a willing bunch, but very rusty."

Like Ibana said, they would have to do. Almost a third of their number would be green or out-of-practice riders with just a few weeks of training under their belts. "Make a buddy system," he said.

"A what?" Ibana replied.

"A buddy system." Styke smiled grimly. "They used to do that in the labor camps when a new batch of prisoners came in. Pair one of the new guys with two or three old hands. The old convicts were responsible for the new—teach them the ropes, the guard signals, the schedule."

"And that worked?" Ibana asked doubtfully.

"Seemed to. I knew the camp quartermaster, and she said the buddy system extended life expectancy and reduced injuries." He tapped his finger on the side of his leg thoughtfully, fiddling with his big lancers' ring. "Of course, every once in a while the old convicts would just murder the new one for his shoes."

"That," Major Gustar said, "is not reassuring."

Styke ignored him. "We do as we're told. Smash the vanguard and then go looking for trouble." He pictured a mental map of the area, considering the refugees, the river, and Flint's forces. "The river is too deep for them to flank us, but they may send scouts. Gustar, I want you to take a hundred and fifty of your dragoons and sweep the west bank. Keep eyes off of Flint."

"Yes, sir."

Styke flexed his fingers, feeling that twinge in his wrist. He wasn't the young, strapping cavalry officer he'd once been. But he was the best Flint was going to get. "Ibana, take the rest of the Riflejacks down the road. I'll swing wide with the lancers and we'll hit that vanguard before they know what's happening."

Styke walked among the dead on the banks of the Hadshaw after a short, bloody battle. The Dynize vanguard had tried to withdraw when they saw the Riflejacks bearing down, and had run straight into the lancers. Some fled, some fought, but he'd caught them all in his pincer movement and they'd been ground into dust in an appalling slaughter.

He searched through the corpses until he found his lance, buried through the chest of a Dynize scout. The scout was a middle-aged woman, and her eyes shot open when Styke grasped the handle of his lance. She made a deep sucking sound, her mouth bubbling blood. She tried to reach toward him. He drew his boz knife and ended her suffering with a single stroke before reclaiming his lance, leaving the body where it lay.

He wiped the gore off the tip and examined the corpses of the vanguard. The horsemen wore turquoise uniforms and carried a light kit with nothing more than a knife and an outdated carbine for defense. The infantry still carried the same short bayonets that they'd used in the assault on Landfall and had been unprepared for a flanking maneuver by cavalry. Styke was unsurprised to see only a few bodies belonging to Riflejack dragoons, and none to his lancers.

Ibana approached on horseback, her roan picking its way through the bodies with an almost dainty affection. "We got them all," she reported. "It'll take the main Dynize army a few hours to figure out something is wrong. I've got boys set up all along the road to ambush any messengers who come looking for the vanguard."

Styke lifted his eyes from his lance and looked across the river, where Gustar and his dragoons hugged the shoreline and cleaned up the handful of Dynize who'd braved the depths of the river to flee. He tapped his ring against the lance, frowning. "Why do I feel uneasy?"

"Too clean of a kill?" Ibana suggested. "They barely put up a fight."

Styke grunted an answer and put his lance over his shoulder and headed back to where Amrec stood nibbling at the grass on the riverbank. He patted Amrec's nose, speaking over his shoulder. "Gather the horses. Send any prisoners back to Flint. She'll want to interrogate them. I think that..." He trailed off, turning around to examine the field of slaughter.

The dead lay scattered in a radius of about ninety yards. Riderless horses had already been captured by attentive lancers, though some had fled in the confusion.

Ibana seemed to sense something was amiss. "What is it?"

Styke climbed into Amrec's saddle and searched among his own men until he found Sunintiel—an ancient woman who looked like she'd be unhorsed by a breeze. Celine sat behind Sunin in the saddle, and waved when Styke gestured her over to a captured Dynize horse.

"Tell me what's wrong with this horse," Styke said when the two approached. Sunin opened her mouth, but Styke made a shushing motion. "Celine."

The girl's forehead wrinkled. "Nothing is wrong with it," she said.

"Its health is fine, sure," Styke said. "But what about it is out of place?"

By this time several of his officers had arrived. Looks of understanding began to dawn on their faces. They remained silent. Celine glanced around nervously. Styke watched her trying to work out the solution. "Don't worry about them. Worry about that horse. What can you tell me about it?"

"Small," she said. "Probably pretty quick. Not particularly strong. It was spooked by the battle. By the hindquarters I'd say it was bred for endurance over other qualities."

Proud smirks spread among the officers, and Styke had no doubt each of them would take credit for teaching Celine about horses. But he knew where she really learned it, and stifled his own smile. "What kind is it?"

"It might..." She hesitated. "It might be a Unice desert racer. But I haven't seen a horse with those markings before."

"Neither have I," Styke said. "Neither has any of us." He swung down from Amrec and gave the captured horse a quick walk-around, treating it to a whisper and a light touch to calm its nerves. He returned to Amrec and pulled himself into the saddle. "I'll bet my saddle this is a Dynisian." Mutters followed the proclamation.

"I've never heard of that," Celine said.

"That's because the Dynize have been a closed nation for over a hundred years, and before that they weren't exactly friendly." Styke searched his memory. "Supposedly, Dynisians were bred for, as you said, endurance. They're an all-purpose horse, meant to be docile, obedient, generic, and easily interchangeable. Just about every Fatrastan breed has a bit of Dynisian in them, going back to when the Dynize actually ruled this damned place."

"So, what's so special about this one?" Celine asked.

"Nothing more than any of the others," Styke said, gesturing toward a group of lancers attempting to run down riderless horses up on the ridge.

Ibana snorted. "We don't have time for this, Ben. Tell the girl what you're getting at."

"Right, right," Styke said. He stretched his fingers and adjusted his lance before climbing back into Amrec's saddle. "A Dynisian here means that the Dynize have cavalry—they're not just using scrounged fourth-rate Fatrastan horses." He meditated on the possibilities for a moment. "We're not just sweeping for scouts now. We're looking for an enemy cavalry force, and we have no idea how big it will be." He looked around at his officers. "Strip the bodies of anything useful."

They were on the move again within fifteen minutes. Captured horses trailed behind their column, and Styke made sure that his "buddy system" was still in place. They'd had more injuries during that quick battle from green riders getting fingers tangled in the reins than they had from actual enemy combatants, and he needed to keep those kinds of accidents to a minimum.

They headed east away from the river, then cut south to flank it, being sure to keep at least two hills between themselves and the river valley at all times. His own scouting parties fanned out to watch for contact with the enemy army.

Styke couldn't help but shake a feeling of uneasiness. He shouldn't be surprised by Dynize cavalry, not really. Lancers would make quick work of any force riding Dynisian mounts. So what was bothering him? The prospect of greater numbers? Disappointment that he had more to worry about than flanking enemy infantry?

He was still pondering this question almost an hour later when Ibana joined him at a gallop.

"We have contact!" she shouted.

Styke snapped out of his reverie. "Where? To the west? From the river?"

"No, south. Directly south!" Ibana was flushed, and she immediately began barking orders.

Styke was about to ask for an explanation when he topped a small rise in the landscape and inhaled sharply. Directly in front of them, riding in their direction, was a wide column of Dynize cavalry. Breastplates shone in the evening sun, and at half a mile he could see that they were armed with sabers and pistols. Their column was spread out, moving at a walk with no real cohesion, and he could see a sudden flurry of excitement ripple through them.

Ibana raised her looking glass to her eye for a moment, then stowed it in her packs with a curse. "They're as surprised as we are. God damn it, we must have taken out each other's scouts."

It didn't take a genius to realize why they were here. The Dynize cavalry were going to attempt the same thing as the lancers—flank the enemy. But instead of a handful of ill-equipped riders on fourth-rate horses, these were Dynize cuirassiers, and there appeared to be almost two thousand of them.

"Orders, sir?" Ibana asked. "We're outnumbered and have no element of surprise. All things being equal, they've got us."

Styke rocked back and forth in his stirrups. Beneath him, Amrec began to stomp, pawing at the ground in anticipation. Styke had to think quickly. They could outrun the weaker Dynisian horses. But a retreat would only give the Dynize extra ground and the time to assess Styke's forces. Best-case scenario: Draw them all the way back to the Riflejack infantry and set up some sort of ambush. But Flint could not afford the men to deal with Dynize cavalry. He needed to handle this on his own.

"Orders!" Ibana snapped.

"Send a runner to Flint. Tell her we've met a superior force."

"And?"

"And we have engaged. Split the column. Arrow formation. Lancers will tip, Riflejack cuirassiers just behind. Send our dragoons in two columns to harass their flanks but do *not* let them engage hand-to-hand." Styke was beginning to wish he hadn't sent Gustar and those hundred and fifty extra horses across the river.

"You want us to split into three groups against a superior force? Are you mad?"

"Do you really need to ask? Now give the orders, Major Fles, or I'll do it myself."

Ibana fumed for a few moments. "No withdrawal?"

"No." Styke loosened his carbine and urged Amrec forward. "We hit them now, and we hit them hard, before they can tighten their formation." He glanced over his shoulder, to where Jackal rode with the Mad Lancer banner fluttering over him. "With me!" he bellowed.

The orders spread quickly, and the whole group sprang forward, rushing toward the startlingly close Dynize. Styke prodded Amrec faster and faster. Within moments he could see the confused expressions on the enemy's faces, no doubt wondering why they were being charged by a smaller force.

He knew that confusion, and he knew the doubt that it would sow. *Are we about to be flanked?* the enemy would wonder. *Is a large force about to hit us from just over that ridge? Where are our scout reports?*

Styke had no interest in giving them the chance to recover. He breathed deeply, searching with his senses, and could not smell any sorcery on the wind. Good.

At forty yards he fired his carbine, then shoved it into its holster. Powder smoke streamed behind his whole arrow-shaped company, and then hundreds of white lances lowered toward the enemy. A scattering of pistol shots responded from the confused enemy vanguard, before they drew their sabers and attempted to meet the charge.

The concussion of the two lines meeting was audible, and Styke was soon enveloped in the enemy force. The clash of steel surrounded him, powder smoke filling his nostrils. Not even cuirassiers could break a Mad Lancer charge, and their momentum carried them into the heart of the Dynize force before Styke could sense their speed ebbing. He shouted, urging them on, when he felt the jolt of his lance catching something more than flesh.

The tip snagged on the groove of a Dynize breastplate without punching through. The Dynize cavalryman jerked from his saddle, but his reins were wrapped around his wrist and his horse continued to gallop past Styke, pulling its rider—and the tip of Styke's lance—along with it.

Styke felt the movement, but his twingy hand did not respond quickly enough to drop the lance. He was ripped from the saddle, spinning, and could do nothing but brace himself as the earth rushed up toward him.

CHAPTER 3

W hy wasn't this given to me immediately?" Vlora
demanded.

She stood in the trampled grass of the river valley, her jacket
soaked with sweat from an afternoon of riding back and forth
across the valley, making sure her defensive line was properly prepared. It was almost six in the evening. Behind her, roughly two
thousand men waited behind a narrow strip of raised earth they'd
spent the entire afternoon constructing. They crouched against the
muddy earthwork anticipating her orders.

A messenger stood in front of Vlora. He wore a black jacket with
a yellow scarf, indicating that he was one of the Blackhats the Mad
Lancers had recruited into their fold. She could smell the whiskey
on his breath.

"Are you going to answer me, soldier?" Vlora asked in a low tone.

The Blackhat opened his mouth, closed it, then opened it again.
Behind him, Olem stood with one hand on his pistol, his face grim,
head turned to examine the southern horizon.

Vlora held a message between her fingers. All it said, in a hasty scrawl, was, *Superior force encountered. Engaging.* It was stamped with a skull and lance, and said the date and time. Nearly five hours ago. Vlora's hand began to tremble with anger. "If you gasp at me like a fish one more time I will throw you in that goddamn river with a cannonball chained to your ankle."

"General," Olem said quietly.

"I—I—I—" the messenger stuttered.

"You what? Took a message of utmost importance from a colonel in my army and rushed it back to camp? You were in such a state that you thought you'd have a drink to calm your nerves before you brought this to me? And then you had some more to drink, with a bloody urgent military correspondence in your pocket?"

The messenger gave a shaky nod.

Vlora drew a powder charge from her pocket and cut the paper with her thumb. She held it up to one nostril, snorting once, then followed suit with the other. Her rage became distant, more controlled, like the sound of a river far away, and after a few deep breaths she decided she would *not* kill a man in front of her infantry. Sights and sounds became sharper. The world made more sense.

"General," Olem repeated in a gentle but firm tone.

"I'm fine," she said evenly. "Tell me," she asked the messenger, "do you know what you've done?"

Another shaky nod.

"Do you really? Do you know the scope of this?"

"I...I think so." Sweat poured down the man's face and neck.

She leaned forward until their faces were almost touching. "I don't kill men for incompetence, even when I want to. Even when they deserve it. Even when they may have just lost us a forthcoming battle. When the enemy comes, I expect you to be on the front line fighting like a man possessed. Now get out of my sight."

The messenger turned and fled.

Vlora took a few moments to calm down, her mind racing as she attempted to adjust all her stratagems. "We spent all afternoon preparing for enemy infantry. Now we find out that they have proper cavalry as well."

"That seems to be the gist of things," Olem agreed.

"Have we had any messages from Styke since?"

"None."

"Shit," Vlora breathed. "He may be dead. Captured. For all we know, we'll have five thousand enemy horses on our flank in an hour." She closed her eyes. "He could have damn well said *how* superior their force was."

"I can't imagine it was much bigger, if he engaged," Olem said hopefully.

"Mad Ben Styke charged forces several times his size during the Fatrastan War. You think he's mellowed with age?"

Olem pursed his lips. "I don't think he has."

"Send out our scouts. Anyone we have left with a horse. I want to know where Styke is, and I want to know where the enemy cavalry are."

"I already sent them."

"Good. What's our last report on the Dynize main army?"

"They're still coming in quickly. Marching like a force possessed."

Vlora hesitated. She didn't know *why* the Dynize were moving so fast, but she would use it to her benefit.

"Did you get a confirmation on their numbers?"

"Twenty-five thousand, give or take." Olem hesitated. "But again, we have no knowledge of their cavalry. I suggest we send five hundred of our reserves up to the ridge with sword-bayonets fixed. If they try to flank us with cavalry, that might give them pause."

Vlora paced back and forth. The powder trance was helping, but she still wanted to hiss and spit and swear. She had to keep reminding herself that things could be worse. These odds—this Dynize army—it was still something she could beat. She *had* to beat it. "Give the order," she confirmed.

Olem didn't move. Something to the south had grabbed his attention.

Vlora's pacing continued for a few more moments. "Well?" she asked. "What are you waiting for?"

"They're here."

The Dynize Army came around a bend in the river, marching in the footsteps of the vast migration of refugees. Vlora saw their advance force first—a few dozen cuirassiers decked out in enough silver, jade, and gold that they *had* to be a general's bodyguard. The infantry fanned out, and within thirty minutes the glitter of breastplates filled the river valley. The cadence of their march drifted to her across the wind and she could see that they were deploying with an almost reckless speed.

She didn't have time to wonder why.

Vlora took a deep breath and opened her third eye, fighting a wave of nausea. Her vision became awash with glowing pastels as she looked into a sorcerous mirror of the real world. She stared into the Else for almost a minute, ignoring the rising tension of the approaching army, searching for little flickers of light.

"I don't see any Privileged or bone-eyes," Vlora finally said, closing her third eye. "Just the usual smattering of Knacked."

"Same here," Olem confirmed. "Nothing from Davd or Norrine, either." He sent a runner for the flanking defensive force Vlora had ordered, and brought up extra messengers to handle the stream of orders they would no doubt soon be giving. Vlora called for her horse and mounted up, remaining about fifty yards in front of her army, watching as the Dynize finished their deployment.

Her powder trance allowed her to examine the enemy as if she were standing right in front of them. She looked into the eyes of the men, examined their stances, their armor, their faces. It was obvious that they were tired from a long, forced march up from Landfall. Some shoulders slumped and eyelids fluttered, but there was a resolve there she didn't expect. They were ready for a fight.

The absence of bone-eyes meant that Vlora could break them. But she didn't have experience fighting Dynize. She did not know how well their discipline would hold, or what actions would break their spirit.

And she did not know where her—or their—cavalry were at this moment. She needed a little more time.

"I'm going to seek terms," she told Olem. "Gather a few men."

Vlora rode out across the valley with a small bodyguard and Olem at her side. A mile or so separated the two forces, giving them ample space to size each other up. She wondered why they hadn't tried to take the high ground of the ridge, trapping the Riflejacks against the river. Perhaps they knew that their cavalry would cover that flank. Perhaps they didn't want to risk Vlora pulling back while they maneuvered.

Or perhaps Styke had managed to tie up their cavalry, and the Dynize were just as uncertain as she was. She barely dared to hope.

They reached the center point between the two armies, and watched while the gaudily dressed cuirassiers rode toward them. Vlora let Olem watch the enemy bodyguard and kept her eyes on the ridge. She knew it was a fruitless exercise with Olem's scouts up there now, but she couldn't help but watch for the arrival of cavalry.

The Dynize came to a stop about a dozen yards away and a single horse rode out in front of the group. It was ridden by a middle-aged man with an orange-lacquered breastplate and teal uniform. He sat rigidly in the saddle, a distant expression on a gaunt face. Gold hoops and small feathers hung from his ears, and he wore silver rings mounted with human teeth. His fingernails were painted with gold.

"Lady Flint," he said in thick, if understandable, Adran.

"I don't believe we've had the pleasure," Vlora said, eyeing the army over the general's shoulder, then shifting her gaze to the man himself.

"My name is General Bar-Levial. I command the Shrike Brigades of the Emperor's Immortal Army."

"That's a mouthful," Olem muttered. He tucked a cigarette between his lips and lit a match.

Bar-Levial's eyes did not leave Vlora's face. "You seek terms?"

"I want to know why you're here. You hold Landfall, and the Fatrastans are no doubt pulling their armies in from the frontier, yet you're here chasing the Landfall refugees as if they are important to your plans."

"Refugees?" Bar-Levial seemed surprised. "We don't care about the refugees. We're here for you, Lady Flint."

Vlora scoffed. "Me?"

"I'm here to satisfy the honor of my emperor and his appointed emissary."

"Ka-Sedial?"

"Yes."

"I..." Vlora couldn't quite believe what she was hearing. "You're here because I made you look like assholes at Landfall? You're here for revenge?"

Bar-Levial's eyes narrowed. He straightened in his saddle. "I am here to satisfy the honor of my emperor..."

"Yes, yes, you mentioned that already. But you marched an entire army out here to find me just for revenge? Don't you have better things to do with your soldiers?" She wondered where Lindet's field armies were at this moment—Fatrasta was a young power, but they would have gathered themselves by now and prepared to strike back.

"The emperor's armies will not stand degradation," Bar-Levial said coldly.

Beside Vlora, Olem ashed his cigarette. "You shouldn't take it so hard. Yours isn't the first army humiliated by an Adran general. It won't be the last."

"Silence your man, Lady Flint."

"Shut up." Vlora found herself getting angry. She would meet an enemy on any field of battle, but the idea that Ka-Sedial had sent an army after *her*—not the refugees, not to sow chaos, but specifically after *her* just because she'd beaten him in battle—was infuriating. "I'm a mercenary, and the Fatrastans don't even want me anymore. What about this? How about I tell you that I'm leaving the continent, and I don't give a shit about your bloody war? Will you turn around and go back to Landfall, and let me and my men walk away without a fight?"

"That changes nothing."

"Why?"

"Because Ka-Sedial does not take defeat lightly. He believes that allowing a victorious enemy to remain victorious spells doom for an entire theater of war."

"I'm a loose end he wants tied up?" The fact that Sedial had enough soldiers he could send an entire army to deal with a loose end was rather terrifying.

Bar-Levial's lip curled. "Are you afraid, Lady Flint?"

These Dynize were new to her—their dress and customs as alien as anything she'd ever seen. But she'd spent her life with arrogant generals, and Bar-Levial would fit in at a military ball anywhere in the Nine. "Like any good general, I would prefer my men live to see their homes again."

"The words of a coward."

Vlora seethed inwardly. "Why are you in such a hurry? Why force a battle tonight?"

"A friendly contest." Bar-Levial smiled. "I shall see you on the field of battle, Lady Flint, and I will take your head back to my emperor."

"No," Vlora replied. "You will do no such thing." She turned her horse around and rode back to her line, trying to calm herself.

Olem caught up to her a moment later. "That was abrupt."

"Levial's not going to budge, and their scouts are heading toward our lines. Besides, he was pissing me off."

She glanced over her shoulder at those scouts. She could guess what they saw from their vantage point—around two thousand riflemen, dug in and braced for the onslaught of a superior force. The Dynize would take heavy initial losses before rolling over those riflemen with ease.

It was precisely what Vlora *wanted* them to see. But if the scouts moved forward another half mile, it would force her to change her entire battle plan.

"Do we have eyes over the ridge?" she asked.

"We do," Olem said. "They'll let us know the moment anyone attempts to move on our flank."

"Good."

Vlora had not yet reached her own lines when she heard the sound of a trumpet. Glancing over her shoulder, she saw the entire Dynize Army shift, the lines spreading out even farther to fill the entire valley, before lurching forward at another signal.

"He really is in a hurry," Olem commented.

"He said something about a friendly contest. Any idea what that means?"

Olem shook his head.

Vlora reined in her horse and turned in the saddle. She raised her arm high, pointing toward the ridge and the Dynize scouts moving along it. "I think it's time we blind them."

A shot rang out, quickly followed by another. Smoke rose from a copse of honey locusts near the ridgeline behind her own forces, and two Dynize scouts toppled from their horses. Two more followed, then another two. The shots continued every fifteen seconds or so, and Vlora watched with some satisfaction as the remaining scouts realized they were being picked off and fled toward the main body.

Vlora finally reached her line, retreating behind the earthworks that suddenly seemed so insignificant. She eyed the two thousand men she'd picked to hold this first line of defense. Their faces squinted against the morning sun, looking to her for leadership. That in itself always seemed more intimidating than the enemy armies.

"Aim for the center of the chest," she shouted. "Those breastplates might be able to deflect a glancing shot, but they're designed to stand up to softer bullets fired with inferior powder. These poor fools weren't at the Battle of Landfall. Let's show them what they missed, shall we?"

A cheer went up, rifles lifted into the air, then the line went deadly silent as the men crouched behind their earthworks and double-checked their weapons.

Vlora remained on horseback, pulling even farther behind the line, while Olem rode along the ranks shouting encouragement. The Dynize plodded onward, and every so often an officer would fall into the dirt, a victim of Vlora's powder mages firing at will from their vantage.

Vlora searched for the general's bodyguard as the front lines reached a quarter of a mile away from hers. She found the gaudy cuirassiers and Bar-Levial and had a brief moment of morbid curiosity. In an age of canister shot and sorcery, was it poor sportsmanship to aim for the enemy officers? Perhaps. But this was war. Kill or be killed. Bar-Levial wanted so badly to take her head to his emperor, and Vlora decided not to risk giving *him* that chance. With a single thought, she set off the powder of every one of the cuirassiers. The sorcerous kickback nearly knocked her off her horse, and she bent double to catch her breath.

The conflagration caused the Dynize lines to waver as the sight of their general's bodyguard being blown to pieces by their own powder no doubt made a few mouths go dry. Cheers rose from Vlora's own men, but she just smiled coldly and hoped that one of those charred corpses belonged to that orange-lacquered prick.

The Dynize kept on. A disciplined army didn't run just because their general died. This was just the beginning.

At two hundred yards, sergeants along Vlora's lines gave the order to open fire. Dynize fell to the hail of bullets, but soldiers just moved up to take their place, and the army churned forward.

Another volley followed, then another. The Dynize reached a hundred yards. Vlora drew her pistol, aimed at a random officer, and put a bullet in his brain with a nudge of her sorcery. Seventy-five yards. Fifty yards. The Dynize stopped, the front line knelt, and they opened fire.

Anyone not hunkered behind their earthworks was cut down. A second Dynize volley fired and then a trumpet sounded, and like a slow wave rushing toward the beach, the Dynize infantry charged.

"Fall back!" Olem bellowed.

The Riflejacks leapt to their feet and fled, running flat out from the Dynize charge. Vlora watched, amused at the sight of the Dynize chasing her men, as if the two armies were playing out some coordinated game. As her men approached, she kicked her horse into a gallop, rushing along ahead of them. Her horse leapt a shallow ditch and she turned once again to face the enemy.

The valley was eerily quiet. Riflejacks ran. Dynize charged. The smoke cleared and no bullets were fired. Her men, fresher than the Dynize, widened the gap and then suddenly began to disappear, leaping into the same shallow trench that she'd just crossed. When they'd all reached that spot of safety, a voice cut the silence. "Companies, ready!"

A second line—two thousand more riflemen—rose from behind an earthwork of sod collected from the valley floor. A few yards behind them a third line emerged from hiding, and then a fourth and fifth behind that, composed of the Landfall garrison and volunteers from the refugee militia. Each line braced itself, aiming carefully as the enemy closed the distance.

"Fire!" Olem bellowed as his own horse cleared the ditch.

The first line fired and ducked. There was a pause of six or seven seconds, then the command came again. The second line fired and ducked, and the orders continued until ten thousand bullets had been sent into the enemy in the course of less than thirty seconds. Thousands of the Dynize were swept beneath the hail. Vlora leaned forward in her saddle, silently urging the enemy to break. The field was suddenly obscured by powder smoke, and when it cleared, she leaned back in her saddle, shaken, as she watched the Dynize flood forward, climbing over the corpses of their companions.

Olem returned to her, choking on powder smoke. "Even without sorcery, these bastards are tough," he coughed.

Another volley hit the Dynize lines, and a few moments later they finally reached Vlora's ditch, only to be met with a wall of fixed bayonets from her original front line.

The field dissolved into chaos. On her side, individual captains tried to keep some sort of sustained volley fire, while others gave a "fire at will" order. On the Dynize side, soldiers crouched behind piles of corpses to shoot back, their captains rallying them with swinging sabers and then falling when a powder mage shot them in the head.

"Kresimir," Vlora breathed. "They're still not breaking."

"Even after that pummeling they outnumber us," Olem said. He squinted toward the ridge. "Only a handful of their companies are wavering. No sign of either of our cavalry. Should we bring our reserves to bear and try to crack them?"

For a split second, Vlora waffled. Committing the last of her troops might tip the balance. But she wanted those men free in case the Dynize had something else up their sleeves. "Not yet," she said.

The center of the battle became more chaotic as both sides dissolved into a bloody melee. The Riflejacks had longer bayonets, but the Dynize breastplates proved more effective against those than they did against rifle shot, and the Dynize soon drove her front line out of the ditch. She watched, snapping off a string of orders between shots from her pistol. "Bring up the Fifty-Third to relieve the Eighth Company. Commit three platoons of the Landfall garrison to our eastern flank. Pull back those volunteers; they're not doing anything but shooting our own men in the back."

Vlora set off powder when she could, blowing holes in the Dynize lines, but each effort hit her hard, threatening to overwhelm and exhaust her.

Despite the early slaughter, the battle slowly began to shift to the Dynize. Even with their officer corps cut to ribbons, they continued to push forward. An hour passed, then two. The light over the field began to wane. Soon her men had fallen back to the third line, and the volunteers on her right flank collapsed beneath a Dynize charge. Vlora called up the last of her reserves—two companies of Riflejacks wounded in the Battle of Landfall—and reluctantly sent them into the fray.

She leaned back in her saddle, breathing deeply of the powder smoke. This was it. This was all she had. The Dynize had faced an early slaughter and endured, and now their more numerous troops held the battle in balance.

"Contact on the Dynize rear!" a voice shouted behind her.

Vlora tried to squint through the haze, over the sea of infantry and corpses. Bleary-eyed, she spotted the movement and tried to make sense of it.

Cavalry. Breastplates glittered in the sun, and her breath caught in her throat. Dynize cuirassiers, at least five hundred of them. They were moving up to assist the infantry.

She desperately searched for some way to counter them, hoping that her powder mages could at least put a dent in their morale before they arrived. Her eyes swept the battle, looking for the freshest company of troops she could put in their path with a bayonet wall. She came up with nothing and turned back to the enemy, watching them helplessly. She shook her head, sensing something amiss. Why were they charging from the Dynize rear? Why didn't they flank her army? Beside her, Olem stood in his stirrups, stock-still, squinting through an eyeglass. Vlora said to him, "They'll break our ranks when they get here. Pull together some of our least wounded. We need to form a bayonet line."

Olem remained still.

"Now, Olem!"

"I don't think that will be necessary," he said.

"Why not?"

"Because I don't think Dynize cuirassiers carry lances. Or ride down their own troops. Or have a big, ugly bastard leading the charge."

Vlora felt her chest suddenly lighten and she let out an involuntary breath, something between a gasp and a sigh. She sat back in her saddle.

Mad Ben Styke had arrived.

CHAPTER 4

Styke limped slowly across the river valley as the sun set, stepping over corpses, ignoring the cries of the wounded all around him. He bled from a dozen wounds, some of which would need stitches, and fought the exhaustion brought on by two tough battles in less than ten hours. His back and head hurt; his left shoulder had been sliced to ribbons. He wore a captured Dynize cuirass from the biggest corpse he could find, and it was still a little too small around the chest, buckles poking him in the ribs.

And the corpse he dragged along behind him wasn't light.

His eyes passed over the bodies: Friend, foe—even some of his own lancers—they gave him as little pause as so much meat at a butcher. He wondered if there was ever a time when the sight of so much gore shocked him. If there was, he couldn't remember. He thought of Celine, hiding back with the refugees, and wondered if for her sake he should get out of this business. Then he thought of the wind in his hair and the thrill of the charge, Amrec at a full gallop and his lance smashing through the breastbone of an enemy.

He *should* get out of this business. But not yet.

Styke caught sight of Ibana on horseback, watching passively as a Riflejack surgeon put a screaming Dynize soldier out of his misery. Styke changed directions, heading toward her, still dragging the body. He raised one hand in greeting.

"There you are," Ibana said, scowling down at him. "Where's Amrec?"

Styke waved vaguely toward the river. "Last I saw, he went to get a drink."

"You've been unhorsed twice in a single day. And back in Landfall, too. Pit, Ben, it's a wonder you haven't broken your back. You've got to get used to riding again."

Styke bit back a reply. She was right, of course. "It's all about knowing how to fall."

"Who's that?" Ibana asked, jerking her chin toward the corpse Styke was pulling along.

The body belonged to a middle-aged man with a gaunt face, wearing what little was left of a charred teal uniform and an orange-lacquered breastplate. "Dynize general," Styke grunted. He poked the body with his toe. It was missing a chunk out of its side, right where he might have been wearing a pistol and a few spare powder charges. "He must have pissed off Flint. She's the only one of her mages who can detonate powder at any significant range, and this guy was blown almost in half by it."

Ibana barked a laugh. "I find myself liking Flint more and more."

"And here I thought you were going to kill each other sooner or later."

"She's been growing on me," Ibana replied. "But things can still change. Where is she?"

Styke pointed to a squat bit of squared stone rising from the valley floor a few hundred yards away. A few weeks ago, he imagined it had been a small stable and waypoint for the Fatrastan messenger service, but the building had been stripped down to the foundation by refugees looking for firewood. It was currently occupied by a dozen soldiers in the crimson coats of the Riflejacks, with just two blue coats standing out among them—Vlora and Olem.

Styke resumed his journey, dragging the corpse along behind him. It would be easier, he mused, to leave the body where it lay and come find it later, preferably with Amrec in tow. But there was a statement to be made by dragging the enemy general across the bloody field. What it was, he hadn't yet decided, but he was certain it was there.

When he reached the makeshift headquarters, he was surprised to find Major Gustar had returned from his expedition across the river looking a little rough around the edges, and wondered if he'd managed to find an enemy force. The major was the first one to notice Styke, and touched the brim of his bearskin hat. "Good evening, Colonel."

"Evening, Major. How was your ride across the river?"

"Eventful. Your ride into the country?"

"Same."

Styke lifted the body and draped it over the old foundation stones. The assembled officers fell silent, staring at Styke. Most were wounded, red-eyed from exhaustion and powder smoke. Night was coming on quickly, and they all knew there would be little sleep in the aftermath of such a battle. Styke was not the first Mad Lancer to arrive—Jackal stood next to Lady Flint, his old yellow jacket hanging open to reveal a shirtless, tattooed torso. The damned Palo didn't have a cut on him.

Eyes moved from Styke to the body behind him and back.

"Brought you a present, General," Styke told Flint, jerking his thumb at the body. "I believe that's your handiwork."

Someone gave Styke a congratulatory thump on the shoulder, and conversation resumed as quickly as it had stopped. He let out a small sigh, thankful for the familiarity. He'd spent enough of his life as a curiosity—a horror, even—that he didn't need everyone staring whenever he walked up. Of course, he realized wryly, dragging around a corpse probably didn't help him fit in. He limped over to Flint at her beckoning. Someone had set up her table and maps, along with her personal trunks.

"Colonel Styke," Flint said with a reserved air, bent over the table with both palms flat on a map of the Hadshaw River Valley. "I want to commend you on your timely arrival. I've been told not to inflate your ego, but it's quite possible you saved the battle."

Styke raised his eyebrows. He'd charged the enemy rear with just seven hundred cavalry, most of them wounded from the fray earlier in the afternoon. He wouldn't have done that if he didn't think Flint needed it. "Looked like you had everything in hand."

Flint gave him a long, cool look that told him a thousand words. She knew he'd saved the battle. She knew that *he* knew he'd saved the battle. But it was all the praise he was going to get. "Jackal here was just telling us of your contact with the enemy cuirassiers. I understand you charged a force twice your size."

"They had inferior horses and were more surprised to find us than we were them."

"Your losses?"

"Acceptable."

"Good."

A new voice cut into the conversation. "Should I tell her how you were unhorsed less than two minutes into the fight?" Styke looked over his shoulder to find that Ibana had ridden up and now leaned on her saddle horn, a grin on her face.

"I'd rather you not," he told her.

Ibana and Flint exchanged a look, and a smile flickered at the corners of Flint's mouth. Styke was surprised to find himself braced for a fight, and even more surprised that it never came. Officers had questioned his judgment his whole career, though few of them liked to give credit for his results. Flint seemed unconcerned with the former as long as she got the latter.

She said, "We're going over Major Gustar's report right now, but first I think you should know how the battle went." Her tone lowered, growing more serious. "We have nine hundred dead, and over seven thousand wounded—many of the wounded will join the dead by the end of the week. We estimate those numbers account for roughly equal numbers of Riflejacks, the Landfall Garrison, Blackhat volunteers, and the refugee militia."

Styke let out a low whistle. All things considered, if three or four thousand wound up dead, it was still a resounding victory. "We had a good look at the battlefield as we ran them down. I think ninety-five percent of the Dynize are dead or wounded."

"That's our guess."

"Congratulations, General." Styke found himself legitimately impressed. "That's a slaughter."

Flint didn't seem to share his optimism, waving off the compliment. "I might enjoy it if not for the information Major Gustar just brought us. Gustar, if you please?"

"Thank you, ma'am." Gustar stepped over to the map, pointing at the river and addressing Styke. "As you know, you sent me over the river early this morning to scout and counter any flanking force. This is where I crossed. And this is where we are now." He pointed to a third spot. "This is where I encountered an enemy force."

"Dynize cavalry?"

"Yes. About fifty of them. Lightly armed, but wearing cuirasses and not so spongy like that vanguard we crushed. My men and I engaged. We tried to trap them, but they managed to slip away, and led us on a merry chase." He dragged his finger along the west side of the river, southward. "Every time I ordered my men to pull back, they returned to harry our flanks, so we ended up skirmishing with them for miles."

Styke scowled. "They tried to lead you into a trap."

"That's what worried me, but we kept our wits about us, eyes out for traps and flanking forces, and played their game. Didn't manage to finally crush them until down here." Gustar pointed to the map again.

"So?" Styke asked.

"Here's the thing—I think they *were* trying to lead us back to their main force, but we managed to catch them just in time. Pure luck, I'll admit, but—"

"Wait," Styke cut in. "What do you mean *main force*?"

A flicker of a grim smile crossed Flint's face. "The Second Dynize Army."

"Shit," Styke grunted. "A *second* army? Where?"

"They were seven miles to our south," Gustar said. "By our guess, around thirty-two thousand men, including around four thousand cavalry."

Styke caught his breath. No wonder Flint was so grim. Another, bigger army marching on their position and over half of her force was wounded. "So they could be here tomorrow?" he asked.

"Thank you, Major," Flint said, resting a hand on Gustar's shoulder. "Go check in with your men and get some rest. Come back to me in an hour for a new assignment."

Gustar snapped a salute and slipped away, leaving Styke with Flint. Over his shoulder, he could sense Ibana waiting and watching the conversation, no doubt trying to make her own plans based on that information. Jackal still stood at Flint's side, silent and watchful, and Styke wondered what the Palo's spirits would say about all this.

"Yes," Flint finally said, "they'll be here tomorrow. I've been wondering all day why the enemy was in such a hurry; according to several officers we captured, Ka-Sedial ordered two different enemy generals to track down the Riflejacks and eliminate them. They were racing each other—trying to get here first, take our heads, and claim the prize."

"The Dynize commander ordered it?"

"Yes. Turns out he takes defeat *very* personally. The general we faced today forsook sorcerous support and marched his troops double time to get here. The general we face tomorrow is ... not so foolhardy." Flint was silent for several moments, looking at her maps, before finally saying in a low voice, "We can't fight that."

"Do you have a plan?"

"At this point? Not much of one. The Dynize are here to avenge the humiliation we gave them at Landfall. This second general will be more cautious than the first, but once he finds out how few fighting men we have left, he's going to pounce. If he takes his time to scout us out, we have just three days to prepare."

Styke resisted the urge to repeat his question. He could sense Ibana's eyes on him, and he knew what she'd say—cut our losses and run. Get the Mad Lancers out of here before they encountered something they couldn't cut through with brute force.

Flint continued. "We're going to pull our men back to the refugee camp. Assuming the Dynize take their time, that'll put a few more miles between us. We're going to leave their dead and wounded for them to clean up. Maybe give them some pause." She shrugged.

"But you intend to fight?"

Flint lifted her gaze, looking Styke in the eye. "If I have to. I'm open to other options, but with so many wounded I don't think we could slip away even if we got the opportunity. The only good news in all of this is that the Dynize aren't really interested in the refugees. So at least we needn't worry too much about shielding them." There was a sour note in her voice, and Styke realized that for all her heroics she was not pleased with the idea of dying on foreign soil protecting foreign refugees.

Mercenaries were, of course, paid to die on enemy soil. Flint didn't seem to think that applied to her—not because she could weasel out of assignments, like so many mercenaries, but because she genuinely believed she would win every fight. Styke wondered if it was confidence or arrogance. Probably a bit of both. But he was the last person in the world in a position to make that judgment.

Flint fell into a sullen silence, staring at the map beneath her hands. Styke touched his forehead and backed away. "I'm going to find my horse and regather the lancers. We captured a lot of Dynize horses. We'll get to work making sledges and do what we can to move wounded back to the refugee camp."

"Very good," Flint said absently.

He left her to brood and returned to Ibana, who looked none too pleased herself. "We have to talk," Ibana said.

Styke lifted the body of the enemy general onto his shoulder and began to walk. "I have to get my horse."

Ibana rode along beside him until they were well out of earshot of Flint, then said, "We should get out while we still can."

"I think we're past that point already."

"We're not Riflejacks. We're not Adrans. We can slip away tonight and no one left alive by the end of the week will even remember."

The thought was both repellent and attractive to Styke. Ibana was right that they weren't precisely Riflejacks. The Mad Lancers had ties to Fatrasta, even after all Fidelis Jes had done to destroy them, and if the Riflejacks managed to slip away and head back to the Nine, the Mad Lancers would likely remain here.

"We've fought beside them for three weeks. We've taken Flint's money. That's enough for us to see this through."

"And see us all dead," Ibana retorted.

Styke stopped, looking up the river, then back down it. He kicked at the muddy, bloody ground with one toe and decided he was close enough to the highway. "Give me your spare lance."

"Excuse me?"

Styke reached up to her saddle and took it. He placed it handle-first against the ground and pushed, leaning on it until it was buried almost two feet into the soft mud. Once it was in place, he lifted the corpse of the Dynize general under the armpits, like lifting a child onto horseback, and then dropped it. The tip of the lance entered the small of his back and easily slid up the neck and out the top of his head, leaving the body with arms slumped like a scarecrow over a bloody field.

"Macabre," Ibana noted.

"Give the soldiers of that new army something to think about."

"You're really going to stick around for Flint, are you?"

Styke admired his handiwork, wiping his hands off on his pants. "Where is Celine?" he asked.

"You're avoiding the question."

"And I want to know where Celine is."

"She's with Sunin. I saw the two of them up on the ridge half an hour ago. Now answer my question."

Styke searched the ridgeline. "I need to find a horse for Celine," he mused. "She's plenty old enough."

"Ben..."

He waved her off. "I'll think about it. We're sticking around for now. Attend to our wounded, and keep everyone on their toes in case I change my mind."

Ibana finally nodded, seemingly content with the idea of a contingency plan. "We lost twenty or so of old bodies and maybe sixty of the new ones. More are wounded. You want me to try to fill our numbers from the refugees?"

"Sure."

"Okay, I'll..." Ibana trailed off. "Who is that?"

Styke turned to follow her gaze, and was surprised to see a dozen horses swimming across the current of the Hadshaw River. It was almost dark, and it was difficult to see their riders clearly until they reached the close bank of the river. The riders wore sunflower-yellow cavalry jackets just like Ibana and Styke, but Styke had never seen these men before. He was suddenly apprehensive, resting his hand on the hilt of his boz knife as they made their way toward Styke, coming to a stop with horses dripping.

The man at their front wore a colonel's stars at his lapel. He was young and fresh-faced, no more than twenty-five, and he examined Styke's old cavalry jacket with a troubled expression. After a few moments of silence, he finally cleared his throat. "I'm looking for General Vlora Flint."

"Who are you?"

"Colonel Willis of the Eighteenth Brigade."

Styke shared a long look with Ibana. "Did Lindet finally send some soldiers to help us fight this thing?"

"She did," Colonel Willis said, stiffening.

"I hope it's more than a brigade," Ibana said.

Willis scoffed. "A brigade? The Second Field Army of Fatrasta is camped about ten miles from here."

Styke felt a laugh bubble up from his stomach and escape his lips. He bent over, slapping his knee.

"I'm not sure what's so funny," Willis said.

"What's funny," Styke said, wiping his face, "is that we could have used you twenty-four hours ago." He couldn't help but wonder if this field army had *planned* on being late, hoping the Dynize would wipe out the Riflejacks. It was something Lindet would do.

"I can see that," Willis said, sparing a decidedly haughty glance for the battlefield.

"Did you know there's another thirty thousand Dynize camped just south of here?"

Willis pursed his lips. "We've been informed, yes. But that's not my concern."

"Then what is?"

"I'm here to arrest General Flint."

CHAPTER 5

Michel Bravis crouched in the doorway of a boarded-up shop in the northern suburbs of the city of Landfall. His eyes were blurry from lack of sleep and more than a few too many swigs from the flask in his jacket pocket. The air reeked of the dead morass of the nearby fens, and somewhere in the distance a pack of dogs began to bay and yip. A single pistol shot rang out, and they were silenced.

The city was eerily quiet, and he wondered just how many of the residents had managed to flee before the Dynize Army occupation. It seemed as though half the homes and businesses on any given street were abandoned. It was too quiet, even for this late hour of the night, and Michel had a constant, twisting pain in the pit of his stomach from the realization that this was no longer the city he had grown up in—the city he had sworn to two different masters that he would protect.

He tried to tell himself that Fatrasta had recovered from their war for independence from the Kez. They'd lost Landfall before, and regained it. But a voice in the back of his head told him that this was different—that everything had changed—and he had to constantly fight a rising terror.

Michel took a swig from his flask, grimacing at the bitter taste of the whiskey, and gave it a shake. Just a few more swallows, and he'd be out of liquid courage for the night.

"You don't have time to be a coward, Michel," he told himself.

"Easy for you to say," he whispered back. "You're getting drunk."

"No, I am perfectly sober."

He squeezed his eyes shut. "No one should have to be perfectly sober in a city occupied by an enemy force." He opened one eye hesitantly, squinting into the street, where the only light came from a single gas lantern fifty yards down the cobbles. His ears picked up a sound and he tilted his head toward the street, trying to make it out.

He was soon able to recognize the tramp of boots, and he willed himself farther into the darkness of the doorway of the boarded-up store. He heard an authoritative shout in a foreign language, and a few moments later a platoon of Dynize soldiers marched into view, bathed in the light of that single lantern.

It was a strange procession: men and women with fire-red hair, pale skin, and ashen freckles, armed with outdated muskets and curved breastplates, wearing old-fashioned morion helms with their finned, kettle-hat shape. Their uniforms were turquoise, decorated with colorful feathers and bleached-white human and animal bones. The word "exotic" came to mind, but it was a word often associated with "quaint," and the army that had occupied Landfall was anything but that.

A soldier at the front, his breastplate decorated with a lacquered crimson stripe, called out an order and the platoon turned left at the lantern, heading down the street toward Michel. He inhaled sharply, fighting the urge to reach for his flask, knowing that any movement might attract the eye of a passing soldier.

As the Dynize patrol drew closer, Michel whispered to himself under his breath. "My name is Pasi. I am an Adran immigrant whose wife and children left the city before the invasion. I came down from the plateau to scavenge and was caught out after curfew. I am waiting out the night so I can return home in the morning." He repeated the alibi to himself twice more and fell silent, hugging the arms of his threadbare wool jacket and waiting for one of the soldiers to spot him.

They marched by, close enough he could have reached them in three strides. Soldiers glanced in alleyways, doors, and toward dark windows, but no one cried out, and the platoon did not stop.

Michel waited until they had turned the next corner before he allowed himself a sigh of relief and the tiniest sip from his flask. "Bloody pit," he whispered. "That was a heart attack I didn't need." He put his hand on his chest until he could feel the thumping of his heart steady out. He settled into a more comfortable position to wait.

He remained in the doorway for over forty minutes, frequently squinting through the dark at his pocket watch, until a figure emerged from the shadows of the alleyway across the street.

"Bloskin!" a voice called out, wavering.

Michel tensed, ready to run if his rendezvous had somehow turned into an ambush. "It's a good night to see a friend," Michel responded. The figure hesitated, as if checking the code words against her memory, then came far enough into the street so that Michel could make out some of her features. She had long, dirty-blond hair and a heavy brow, her nose and cheeks broad. Michel wouldn't have wanted to meet her in a dark alley.

And yet, he realized with in inward laugh, here he was doing just that. "Over here," he called.

The woman joined him in the doorway, pressing herself into the darkness. "You're Bloskin?" she asked.

Another of Michel's aliases. He wondered how many he'd gained just in the last three weeks since the occupation, and hoped that he'd be able to keep them all straight. "I am."

"Hendres sent me. My name is Kazi Fo—"

"Wait," Michel said, pressing a finger to her lips. "Don't tell me your full name. In fact, don't tell anyone your real name, if you can help it. Not on a night like this. Where are they?"

"I left them across the street. I wanted to make sure it was safe."

"Well done. You told them my name?"

"I told them you are Bloskin, a Blackhat Bronze Rose. I told them you knew their mother."

Michel squinted at her. "Are *you* a Blackhat?"

"An Iron Rose. But I don't have it with me. It's hidden."

"Good. Don't show that Rose to anyone. It's too dangerous. Why didn't you leave the city during the invasion?"

Kazi glanced back into the street, taking a half step away from Michel. He could practically feel her distrust. Blackhats were the Lady Chancellor's secret police. They were inherently distrustful but should always be able to count on each other. The invasion and subsequent occupation had changed all the old rules. "You don't have to tell me anything about yourself," Michel reassured. "I was just curious. We all have our reasons."

"Yes, we do," Kazi said, her tone standoffish.

Michel *needed* trust right now, people he could depend on. But his list of trusted contacts was pitifully small, so why should hers be any longer? If he wanted to know more about Kazi, he'd have to ask their mutual contact. "Get out of here," he said. "Get some sleep. There will be more families tomorrow." He grabbed her sleeve as she turned to go. "Cover your head. Your hair stands out in the darkness. Also, careful of the patrols. They're changing up their routes."

He waited until Kazi had headed back toward the secret paths up to the Landfall plateau, before crossing the street and entering the alley she'd emerged from a few minutes prior. The alley was littered with old crates, barrels, and other refuse, and he couldn't immediately pick out anyone hiding there.

"I'm Bloskin," he said in a loud whisper. "Kazi has gone home. You're with me now."

Slowly, figures emerged from their hiding places. The first was a man, medium height with long, dark hair under a flatcap. He held a bundle in his arms, which Michel quickly realized was a child, no more than a year old. Five more children of various ages followed.

"Kazi said you know my wife," the man whispered urgently.

Part of Michel's job as a spy had always been knowing when to tell the truth and when to lie—and when to walk the gray places in between. "I don't, actually. I don't know who you are, except that your wife is a Silver Rose, and we need to get you out of the city. That'll have to be good enough, unless you want to risk the Dynize purges."

The children huddled around their father, who seemed at a loss. He looked around at the waiting faces before finally nodding at Michel. "We don't have any choice but to trust you. But this is my family. If you so much as—"

"Don't threaten me," Michel said with a tired sigh. "It's childish. You can either let me do my job, or I can go find somewhere to sleep. Now, are we getting you out of the city or not?"

"Is Bloskin even your real name?" the father asked. Michel could hear the tension in his voice, and he wished that for once this process could be simple.

"No, and I suggest you not tell me yours." Michel squinted at his pocket watch, trying to discern the time in the darkness. "Kazi got you here late, so if we're going to go, we need to do it now. Make a decision."

The father's mouth formed a hard line. "We'll go."

"Right, follow me. And no one make a peep."

Michel led the family back the way they'd come and began to cross streets and duck through alleys in a pattern that might look to an observer to be entirely random. They crisscrossed their own path several times, but he led them steadily north through the suburbs until the streets began to widen and the tenements and stores began to thin. They were soon among small, two-story houses, ducking through one of the many Palo quarters of the city, where the streets weren't cobbled, the gutters were filled with trash, and the Dynize patrols were fewer.

For eight nights Michel had done a variation of the same route—carefully planned out during the day—and managed not to cross paths with a single Dynize patrol. On this night, however, the patrols were constant and the group was forced to hide almost every hour.

They waited for the third of the patrols to pass by, crouching beneath one of the stilted houses on the floodplains north of the city. Over a hundred strong, and led by a soldier whose breastplate was lacquered black, the patrol carried torches, which they thrust into the alleys and under the houses as they went, and Michel quietly urged the children to move farther into the darkness.

"They've changed the routes," Michel whispered to the father. He swore to himself and listened to the ticking of his watch in his breast pocket, knowing time was running short.

"What does that mean?"

"I don't know. Could be they're getting wise to people leaving the city. Could be that they just change their routine every week or so. Either way, it's going to be more and more dangerous to leave the city from here on out."

"Are we going to be able to get out?" There was a tinge of desperation to the father's voice.

Michel hesitated. If he was smart, he'd leave the seven of them here to try and make it on their own. He'd flush his safe house in Upper Landfall, cut off his contacts with Hendres, Kazi, and anyone else, and find the deepest hole in Greenfire Depths to wait out this occupation.

He didn't *need* to help these people. His own mother was safely out of the city, and as a spy he'd never been close to anyone else.

But despite his alternate loyalties, he didn't believe anyone deserved to be snatched up by foreign occupiers, least of all children.

"You'll get out," Michel finally said. "But we have to move fast." The patrol passed, and Michel led the family out from beneath the stilted houses. He picked up the smallest of the children, cradling her face against his neck, then began to hurry them all along at a quicker pace. They crossed the sandiest, deepest part of the floodplains and entered the fens. The wetlands were bisected by hundreds of drainage ditches built by convicts in the labor camps. The ditches made poor highways, but it kept them out of sight of the road as they moved farther and farther away from the city.

Wet, muddy, and stinking, the group emerged on the opposite side of the fens and crossed the final highway before the coastal plains became cotton and tobacco fields for as far as the eye could see. As in the city, patrol frequency out here had increased, and it wasn't until Michel and his charges were hiding in a farmer's shed on the northern side of the highway that he allowed himself to breathe a sigh of relief.

Outside, the sky was beginning to lighten. It would be daybreak soon, and that would complicate his return to the city. He glanced at the small faces huddled in the shed, and then at the father, whose eyes were tired and his expression bleak. "How much farther?" the father asked.

"Until what?" Michel responded. "Safety? Long time until then." He heard the bitter note in his voice and silently scolded himself. He was here to help, not deepen the man's fears. "Sorry," he said in a gentler voice. "This is as far as I take you. I've got to get back before it's light. You'll head about two miles due north. There's a farmhouse with distinct yellow paint on the east wall. They'll hide you for a day, and tomorrow night get you to a carriage that will take you along the back roads and safely out of range of the Dynize patrols."

There was a long silence, and Michel could see the man steeling himself to try and herd six children across two miles of open land before the sun came up. Michel didn't envy him the task.

"How can I thank you?" the father asked.

The question surprised Michel. Most of these smuggled families were so exhausted by the trek that good-bye was a simple nod and then disappearance into the dark. "Just... if you find your wife, or reach the armies, or the Lady Chancellor or anyone, you can tell them that people are still fighting in Landfall. And we'd rather not be abandoned."

"Come with us," the father said. "If an escape route can take seven, it can surely take eight."

The offer was tempting. But Michel had made his decision. He was going to stay in Landfall through this thing, for good or ill. There were more people to keep out of Dynize hands. He slapped the father on the shoulder. "Get moving. If daylight hits you, find a ditch to hide in. Watch the horizon for patrols. Remember that the farmhouse you're looking for has a yellow wall."

The father nodded, and Michel opened the shed door and watched the silent, frightened children file out and follow their father into the cotton fields. Michel watched them merge into the night, then turned back toward Landfall.

From here, the massive Landfall Plateau and the city that covered its face and skirted its knees seemed almost peaceful. There was no sign of the bombardment that had scarred the eastern face of the plateau, or the rancid smoke of the fires to the south where bodies were still being dumped. The only sign of the battle was a trickle of smoke rising from Greenfire Depths, where the fires were still not out from the Palo riots.

Michel almost turned and ran to catch up with the father and his children. Better to escape now, while escape was still an option, a small voice told him. "Stop being a coward," he told it. Taking his last swallow of whiskey, he crossed the highway and headed back into the fens to make his way toward the city.

CHAPTER 6

Michel jerked awake, reaching for the pistol on the bed-side table, knocking an empty wine bottle and his pocket watch to the floor with a clatter that made his head hurt. He fumbled for a grip and sat up in bed, pointing the pistol toward the doorway, his head hammering in his chest and his eyes crossed badly.

"It's me," a voice said gently.

Michel took several deep breaths and lowered the pistol. "Sorry," he said. "Nerves a little frayed."

Hendres stepped inside the tiny room that she and Michel shared in a tenement on the south side of the gorge in Upper Landfall. Hendres was young—or at least what Michel thought of as young, though in her midtwenties she was probably just as old as he. She had brown hair, cut short beneath a bowler cap, and wore a reddish-brown day laborer's suit much the same as Michel's. Her face had old pockmarks down the left side. She had intelligent eyes and a military bearing about her, and had somehow managed to make the rank of Silver Rose in the secret police despite her young age.

Michel knew how hard that was from experience.

Hendres closed the door behind her and touched the empty wine bottle with her toe. "I have no idea how you keep finding something to drink. The Dynize have put the squeeze on everything going in and out of the city, and the booze seems to have disappeared first."

"I, uh, know a lot of bartenders," Michel responded. "Most of them owe me a favor or two. He squinted at the pistol in his hand. The pan wasn't even primed. He sighed and set it on the bedside table.

"You're a bit shaky with a pistol," Hendres observed.

"Guns aren't really my thing," he said, trying to rub the sleep from his eyes and the headache from his brain. He looked at his empty flask sitting on the washstand across the room. "Pit, you're a terrible spy," he muttered. "You should not be drinking."

"What's that?"

"Nothing, nothing."

Hendres moved to sit on the edge of the bed, then suddenly recoiled. "By Adom, what's that smell?"

"Had to go across the fens last night to get that family out."

"I thought we agreed you were going to wash before coming to bed. You know I have to sleep here too, right?"

"Sorry," Michel said, though he didn't feel it. "Got caught out near dawn because your courier showed up forty minutes late. And the bloody Dynize changed their patrol routes."

Hendres pulled a face and finally sat down beside him. They'd known each other for all of three weeks—Hendres was one of the regiment of Blackhats that had stayed behind to help hold the city after the Grand Master was killed by Styke. She'd returned with Michel to try and make a difference during the Dynize occupation.

They'd spent the first week hiding—and screwing—in a Blackhat safe house before the occupying forces finally instilled order on the city. Since then their relationship had cooled to purely professional, and Michel was glad for it. He already liked Hendres for her competence and her lack of questions. He didn't need to get any more attached.

"Someone threw a bunch of grenades into a crowd of Dynize soldiers," Hendres said.

"So?"

"That's probably why they changed the routes. It killed three of them, injured twenty more."

"Pit." Michel scratched his head vigorously with both hands, trying to wake up. "Someone" could be other Blackhats, or partisan Fatrastans, or just Palo trying to stir up chaos. It meant bad things for his and Hendres's efforts. "What time is it?"

"Half past one."

"Where have you been all morning?"

Hendres sighed, picking at something on her sleeve. "Setting up the next family to get out. And trying to find out how many of us are left."

By "us," she meant Blackhats. "Yeah? Any progress?" Michel didn't *want* to make contact with any more Blackhats. Someone higher up the food chain might know about his betrayal. But he couldn't very well tell Hendres that.

"Some. There's rumors, but everyone is laying low. As far as I can tell, most of the higher-ranking Roses left the city with Lindet."

"And abandoned their families in the process," Michel said, unable to help the note of bitterness in his voice. He shouldn't blame everyone who abandoned the defense of the city. They were only following orders. But he wasn't inclined to feel kindly toward men and women who'd left their families to the mercy of an enemy army.

Hendres remained silent. They'd had this discussion several times, and she was obviously conflicted regarding her loyalty to the Lady Chancellor. Loyalty was meant to come unquestioning to a Blackhat. This war made things...complicated.

Michel waved the thought away. "But we're here to take care of those families," he said, throwing back the thin covers and sitting up. He caught a whiff of himself—and the fens he'd dragged himself through to get home this morning—and almost passed out again. Hendres dashed to the doorway, covering her nose.

"Go wash. Now!"

"I will, I will!" Michel searched for his pants. "You sound like my mother," he muttered.

"I what?"

"Nothing!" Michel dressed quickly and headed into the hall, ready to go find a public bath. He leaned against the wall, trying not to get dizzy, and wondered where he'd find some breakfast. Food was already becoming a problem, what with the Dynize closing the port, and it would only get worse as the occupation went on.

Hendres joined him, keeping her distance. He opened one eye and caught her staring at him. "What?"

She shifted her feet. "You're being careful, right?"

"At night? Of course."

"You're changing your route out of the city every time?"

He hadn't been. "I am. I mean, I will tonight. Best not to take any risks with the patrol routes changing."

There was a long moment of silence, and Hendres continued to stare. "You're being followed."

"Excuse me?"

Hendres reached into her breast pocket and produced an envelope. It was sealed with wax. "A Palo kid was waiting outside the building this morning. He handed me this, and said to give it to you."

"By name?" Michel asked, his heart jumping into his throat. He had been careful—very careful—every time he returned to the safe house. There was no way he was followed.

"By name," Hendres confirmed, watching his face intently.

Michel took the envelope and broke the seal. He was fully awake now, like he'd downed six cups of iced coffee, and he bit his lip as he read the note. It was just an address, followed by a time. Two o'clock. At the bottom was a single letter "T." Michel took a deep breath to calm himself.

"Are we found?" Hendres asked.

"We're fine," Michel responded. "What time did you say it was?"

"A little past one."

His chest feeling tight, Michel headed down the hall. "I've got to go," he called over his shoulder. "If I'm not back in a couple hours, you should leave the city."

"Do you need backup?" Hendres asked, a note of concern in her voice.

"Wouldn't help!" Michel reached the street, looking for a hackney cab, then remembered they were few and far between since the occupation. He shaded his eyes against the hot afternoon sun, pulled his collar up, and went to see Taniel.

Michel crossed the city on foot. With no functional government to pay the pig keepers or the sweepers, the gutters overflowed with shit and trash. Every third person seemed to be a Dynize soldier, while the citizens who would not—or could not—flee with Lady Flint's army went about their days with eyes cast toward the ground, fear writ plain on their faces. The entire city felt subdued.

Rubble spilled into the street, and whole blocks had burned down in the fires caused by rioters and shelling. Only a concerted effort by volunteer fire brigades had kept the entire city from going up in smoke, though there were places where the smell of soot was so thick no one dared go out without a handkerchief over their face.

Michel lowered his eyes and tipped his hat to every passing Dynize patrol. The strangely armored soldiers rarely took an interest in one man, and moved through the city as a show of force, rather than any real policing action. He was able to reach Greenfire Depths without incident and he rounded the rim of the great old quarry, eyeing the smoke that still rose from the charred remains of the slum.

Over half the tenements in the Depths had been destroyed by fire. Surviving Palo huddled in the few open spaces at the bottom of the quarry, some even spilling out on the rim. Rumors swirled about desperate Palo looting the homes and businesses of the people who had fled, and Michel could not find the energy to be surprised—or to blame them.

These were not times, he decided, that he would judge any man for acting in fear.

Around the northern rim of the Depths, he reached the address indicated in the note. Instead of finding the Hotel Henria—which had stood for over a hundred years and was ancient by the standards of the young country—he found only its charred stone foundation.

Michel passed the blackened stone, confused, and wondered if perhaps he'd read the address wrong. There was barely anything left of the place, and the little passing traffic paid it no mind. No one had any time for a burned relic.

He checked the note in his pocket, then glanced at his watch. Five minutes after two. And yes, this was the right address. Perhaps, he decided, the note had been delivered a couple of weeks late? This kind of communication was not always reliable.

He hid in the shadows of the ruin while a squad of Dynize soldiers marched past, their breastplates gleaming in the sun, colorful feathers hanging from their shouldered muskets. Once they'd gone, he decided to have one quick look around before heading back to the safe house.

He'd only climbed onto the lowest of the foundation stones when a figure caught his eye. He let a half smile cross his face and carefully picked his way through the unstable ruin to where the former southern wall of the hotel perched on the very edge of Greenfire Depths.

A man sat on the burned-out foundation, the back of an expensive suit pressed carelessly against bricks blackened by smoke and soot. He was tall, worn but handsome, with hawkish features and striking blue-gray eyes. His black hair was hidden beneath a top hat, and one leg dangled carelessly off the two-hundred-foot drop into the quarry. He held a weathered old sketchbook in one hand and a bit of charcoal in the other, and as Michel approached, he could see a rather good rendition of the Depths.

The man was fair-skinned, but the hand clutching the charcoal was a bright red, the skin hairless and smooth like a child's.

"I didn't know you still kept a sketchbook," Michel said.

Taniel Two-shot, the Red Hand terror of the Fatrastan frontier, squinted down into the fire-ravaged slums of the Depths and made a few quick marks in his sketchbook before flipping it closed and stowing it in a leather valise. He pulled a glove over his right hand, then picked up a silver-headed cane and pointed it at Michel. "You're late." He crinkled his nose. "And you smell."

"Everyone's a critic," Michel muttered. Louder, he said, "I wasn't expecting to meet in a ruin."

"Ah, right." Taniel grimaced. "I wasn't expecting that either, to be honest. You know, Pole and I stayed here for several months when we first came back to Fatrasta. Third floor, corner suite."

Michel glanced around, half expecting to find Taniel's silent companion lurking in the ruins of the hotel. "Where is she?"

"Hiding outside the city. Landfall is crawling with bone-eyes. Pole may be able to turn a god inside out with raw power, but she's all self-taught. We don't want to risk the Dynize finding her until we're ready for a serious fight."

The thought both scared and exhilarated Michel. "Makes sense. So what brings you back? I thought you two left with Lady Flint."

Taniel stood up, balancing on the foundation stones, hopping from one foot to the other before glancing down at the long drop and stepping into the safety of the ruin of the hotel. He brushed a bit of soot off his sleeve—a wasted effort, because he was covered in it. "Never left."

Michel made a noise in the back of his throat and pursed his lips. "You've been here for three weeks? You're joking."

"Afraid not. Lindet abandoned the city. The Dynize, despite all their spies, really have no idea what they're getting into. It was too good an opportunity for me to do some poking around."

Michel paced back and forth, kicking a loose brick into the ruins of what had once been the hotel's wine cellar. The brick clanked twice, then shattered a bottle. Three weeks of flailing around, helping the Blackhats because those were the only allies he knew, worried one of them would find out who he really was and put a knife in his back. All while his real master was wandering around the very same city. Michel talked himself down from shouting and simply said, "You could have told me."

Taniel eyed him. Two-shot could be warm as a brother, or very very cold. This time he offered a neutral shrug. "I had no idea where you were. I could have used your help sorting through Blackhat files. It wasn't until yesterday that one of my contacts was able to track you down."

"Right." Michel wondered whether to believe him. Master or not, Taniel had his own agenda. It was kept secret for good reason, but it didn't make it any easier when Michel was left in the dark. "So what happens now?"

"I understand you're still with the Blackhats?"

"I've bunked up with a Silver Rose. We've spent the last week or so trying to get Blackhat families out of the city before the Dynize agents find and kill them."

"Commendable." Taniel stared at him for several moments, until the silence grew awkward. "Do the Blackhats know you betrayed them?" he finally asked.

"I don't think so," Michel responded hesitantly. "Hendres—the Silver Rose I'm working with—knows that Fidelis Jes wanted me dead before Styke cut off his head. But I don't think she knows why. The fact that I'm here, helping the Blackhats, seems to be enough for her. It seems I'm still a Gold Rose."

The silence returned, punctuated only by the sound of Taniel tapping his cane against a brick. After half a minute, he seemed to come to some sort of decision. "Are you still my man?" he asked.

Michel opened his mouth, but found himself unable to respond. He worked his lips for several moments, fighting back the urge to punch Taniel in the mouth. "I spent six years dirtying my hands for the Blackhats on your orders." His voice rose in pitch. "I betrayed the most dangerous man in the country for the Red Hand. I..."

"Ah," Taniel said gently. "I'm not trying to offend you, honestly. I needed to ask. The world is...volatile right now."

"I'm still your man," Michel answered sharply. "And I'll ask you kindly not to question that again." The fact that Taniel even felt the need to ask smarted, but he tried to remember that this was a game much bigger than either of them. Infiltrating the Blackhats had been the greatest accomplishment—and danger—of Michel's life. Now with the Dynize in play, well...Taniel was right. Everything had changed.

"I won't. I need you to remain in the city."

Michel had planned on staying in the city to help the Blackhats, but the request still surprised him. "For what?"

Taniel pursed his lips thoughtfully, staring off into the distance for a few moments. "I need you to do something dangerous."

"You'll have to be more specific."

"There's a...woman. Ka-poel and I have been in contact with her off and on throughout the last few years, and she's fed us information regarding the Dynize."

Michel turned his head. "What do you mean by that? No one knows anything about the Dynize, not before they arrived on our shores. Any information you can dig up in Fatrasta is from before they closed their borders—at least a hundred years old. How could you...?" The dots connected in his head and he found his mouth hanging open. "You had a spy *in* Dynize?"

Taniel idly tapped his cane against a blackened foundation stone. "We did. Only Ka-poel and I know, and I'd like it to stay that way."

"Kresimir on a stick, Taniel. If you had a spy in Dynize, how the pit didn't you know that there was an invasion coming?"

"We suspected the invasion."

"And didn't tell me."

"Couldn't risk distracting you."

First Taniel questioned his loyalty, and now this. "You didn't answer my question."

"She's not..." Taniel sighed. "She's fed us information, but she's not a spy—not in the same way you are. She's still a loyal Dynize. She didn't tell us when, exactly, the invasion would happen because she hasn't been in contact for over a year. But over the last few weeks she's gotten back in touch with us."

"And?"

Taniel held up two fingers. "A couple things. One, she knows an immense amount about the Dynize hierarchy. She knows some of their plans, and most of their strengths and weaknesses, which makes her wildly valuable. Two, we think she's in danger. I need you to find her, convince her to leave, and extract her from the city."

Michel ran his hands through his hair. "Excuse me?"

"Find her and extract her."

"Yes, I heard the first and third things you said. I'd like you to repeat the second."

"I told you, she's still a loyal Dynize."

"So..." Michel said, drawing the word out, "you want me to extract a spy who isn't a spy who probably doesn't want to come with me?"

"That's about the size of it."

"Why don't you do it? You're still here."

Taniel snorted in frustration. "Despite our best efforts, we haven't been able to find her. And we have to leave."

Michel resisted the urge to ask where Taniel and Ka-poel were heading next. Taniel wouldn't tell him anyway. Compartmentalization, after all. "And the Blackhats?"

"If they're useful, use them," Taniel said with a shrug. "But I have the feeling you'll be in over your head. Anyone from Fidelis Jes's inner circle might know more about your betrayal and try to kill you."

"I thought all the Gold Roses left Landfall with Lindet."

"At least one remained behind, but I don't know which."

A shiver went down Michel's spine. Every rumor had pointed to the fact that the high-ranking Roses had left with Lindet. He was still using Blackhat resources—safe houses, caches, message drops. After the first week he'd decided that no one left in the city knew his true role in betraying Fidelis Jes, and he had not been cautious enough with those resources. "Pit," he breathed. He took a moment to walk around the ruin, trying to shake loose his own sense of dread. Extracting an informant could be tricky at the best of times, but finding a foreigner in an occupied city could be next to impossible—especially if she didn't want to be found. He summoned an inner calm, trying to come at the problem logically.

If he was cautious, he could continue to use Blackhat resources. He could moonlight with Hendres and spend his days tracking down this Dynize informant. Once he found her, he'd have to deal with convincing her to leave. Getting her out of the city—as long as his escape routes were still open—would be the easy part.

"Right," he said, returning to Taniel. "I'll do it. What help can you give me, and what can you tell me about this woman?"

Taniel produced an envelope and handed it over. "These are the addresses of my personal safe houses. Memorize them and burn the paper. You'll find money, gold, weapons, food, and a safe place to sleep. Some of them may have been destroyed or compromised during the riots. I don't know which ones. There are also a handful of names in there—loyal agents of mine who have remained behind. I suggest using them . . . sparingly, and only in an emergency."

"This will help," Michel said, taking the envelope. "And the woman?"

"Her name is Mara. I don't know what she looks like, beyond the fact that she's Dynize. She's embedded with the Dynize higher-ups, so reaching her might be difficult."

"In what way?"

"She's attached to the retinue of one of their ministers. I don't know which one."

"Anything else?"

Taniel clearly hesitated. "That's all I know that can help you."

"You're certain?"

"Yes."

Michel knew Taniel well enough to know when he was holding something back. And that he wouldn't spill the beans if he didn't want to. "Right. I'll see what I can do."

Taniel stood up, adjusting his gloves and cuffs and straightening his jacket. "Be cautious, my friend. If the Blackhats find out what you are, they'll torture and kill you. The Dynize will do worse."

Michel scoffed outwardly, while his stomach twisted in a knot. What could possibly be worse than torture and death?

Taniel offered a hand, and Michel shook it. Without another word, Taniel picked his way through the ruins of the hotel and disappeared into the street. The warning echoed in Michel's head, raising goose bumps on his arms. How the pit was he supposed to find this woman, let alone convince her to leave Dynize? He might have to resort to a kidnapping, which posed its own set of problems.

This was going to get him killed, and he knew it. Taniel probably knew it, too.

Michel took his time returning to the safe house. He stopped by one of the few remaining coffeehouses in the city and traded a few coins for a pitifully small amount of coffee that didn't even have ice. He drank it slowly, considering, trying to come up with a plan to accomplish this impossible task Taniel had just asked of him. He would have to widen his operation, recruiting other Blackhats and old contacts—perhaps even risk contacting the remaining Gold Roses that Taniel had warned him about. That would be a last resort, of course, but the option was there.

Michel finished his coffee. He would have just enough time to reach the safe house before curfew. He'd get a couple hours of rest and then there'd be another night of smuggling families out of the city. He could meditate on the problem during the mission.

A short time later he walked down the street toward the safe house, tipping his hat to a passing Dynize soldier, who told him, in broken Adran, that the curfew was fifteen minutes away. As he rounded the last corner, he felt his feet slow involuntarily, his senses responding to the long instinct of a spy rather than any particular stimuli. He came to a stop, eyeballing the street, looking for something out of place, and then stepped onto a nearby stoop to continue his examination.

It took him several seconds to see what his instincts had responded to: Three Dynize soldiers loitered near the entrance of the tenement containing the safe house. Michel focused on them for a moment, trying to decide if their presence was a coincidence, when a movement caught the corner of his eye.

Another Dynize soldier peeked over the rooftop of the tenement, his face barely visible beneath the morion helm. Michel felt his pulse quicken, and now that he knew what to look for, he quickly spotted the extra soldier at the opposite intersection, and then another lurking in the window of the apartment two doors down from his safe house. Michel's mouth went dry, his legs twitching with the desire to run.

The safe house was compromised. Hendres was either dead, captured, or had gone underground. Michel ran through a checklist of items he'd left in the safe house to make sure there was nothing he couldn't abandon, then cursed himself for a fool. He should have realized earlier; if Taniel could find him, so could the Dynize.

CHAPTER 7

Vlora stood on the dark slopes of the Hadshaw River Valley with a half-empty skin of watered wine dangling from one hand. She hugged herself, Olem's jacket thrown over her shoulders, and stared into the darkness. The garment, smelling of Olem's sweat, cologne, and favorite tobacco, had a comforting effect that allowed her to think about the last few weeks without becoming overwhelmed.

Two days had passed since what the soldiers had taken to calling the Battle of Windy River. Two days since the Second Dynize Army had been spotted, and two days since a Fatrastan colonel had served her with a warrant of arrest from Lady Chancellor Lindet.

It was a stupid gesture, of course. Both Vlora and Lindet knew she wasn't going to accept the warrant and come along quietly. The colonel had given her the papers and returned to his own army, and Vlora suspected that the paper was simple ceremony—something to tell the Fatrastan soldiers that the mercenary defender of Landfall had done something to lose Lindet's favor.

Vlora sipped her wine. She'd not slept well for almost a month. Her eyes were tired, her body sagging. She refused to take powder until she actually needed it, forcing her body to accept the fatigue rather than give in to addiction. The last thing she wanted was powder blindness.

"Are you all right?" a voice asked through the darkness.

Vlora felt Olem's hand slip into hers and gave it a little squeeze. He came to stand beside her, wearing the same blood-soaked shirt he'd had on since the battle, an unlit, half-smoked cigarette hanging from his lip. He wore a bandage around his left forearm to protect the stitches of a deep cut he'd received from a Dynize bayonet.

"Not really," she answered.

Olem stared off into the night for a few moments. "Normally, people just lie and say yes when they're asked that question."

Vlora took a half step closer to him and put her head on his shoulder. "They're burying another forty-three soldiers." She let her gaze fall to a small gathering of torches about a hundred yards down the side of the valley, where her men threw the last few shovels of dirt on the graves of soldiers who'd given in to their wounds during the course of the day.

"Still bothers you, does it?" Olem asked.

She looked up at him, barely able to see his bearded profile in the darkness. "It doesn't bother you?"

"I..." He was silent for a few moments. "One of the women they just put in the ground has played cards with me for twelve years. I'm going to miss her. But I'm a soldier, and I can't stop and think about all the death or I won't be able to function tomorrow."

Vlora shivered, though the air still retained much of the damp heat of the day. "I've built up plenty of calluses toward death. But some days..." She lifted her eyes past the burial, over the fires of the Riflejack camp, and across the river to a sea of flickering lights that spread out in the distance on the other side of the river. The Fatrastan Second Field Army had arrived yesterday. It was enormous, over fifty thousand men plus auxiliaries and camp support, and as much as Vlora would like to have taken comfort in their presence, she was all too aware of that warrant of arrest sitting on the table in her tent.

Olem searched his pockets, giving up after a few moments. He seemed to sense the direction of her gaze. "I'm not entirely pleased," he said, "that they decided to camp there."

"I don't think we're meant to be pleased." For the first time since coming to this damned country, Vlora felt small. Her brigade of mercenaries—just over four thousand left after this last battle, and most of those wounded—was barely a footnote in the eighty thousand or more soldiers assembled within shouting distance here on the banks of the Hadshaw. If she walked up to the ridge, she could see the Dynize camp to the south, watching her and the Fatrastan Army with a caution that their brethren had lacked. She felt as if they were a hammer poised above her, and the Fatrastans were the anvil. "I gave the order releasing the Landfall Garrison and the Blackhat volunteers over to the Fatrastans."

"I heard. Are you sure that's wise?"

"If we get sandwiched between these two armies, as I suspect we will, five or six thousand men won't make a difference. Besides, they're Fatrastan. Having them tell the tale of the Battle of Landfall might gain us some goodwill."

"We must have made a good impression, because about a thousand of them have asked to sign on."

"Even knowing about the arrest warrant?" Vlora asked. She raised her eyebrows in surprise. Soldiers could be loyal to the death, or they could blow away with the next foul breeze. She expected anyone willing to join a mercenary company to be the latter.

"They're mostly Adran expatriates asking to join. Even here, so far away, Adran patriotism has run high since the Adran-Kez War."

"I'll take it, I suppose," Vlora said reluctantly. "Sign them up and spread them out among the companies. We'll need to fill out our numbers if we get out of this situation."

"And if we don't get out?"

"Then they'll learn firsthand about the risks of being a soldier of fortune."

"I see the calluses have grown back already."

Vlora gave him a tight smile, though he probably couldn't see it in the dark. "Have our scouts reported anything from either camp?"

"Nothing of particular note. The Dynize are probing both sides of the river with quite a lot of caution. So far they haven't made any move to set up on our flanks. Seems that the Mad Lancer desecrated a few hundred of those Dynize cuirassiers and left the bodies where they'd be found. I have no idea what the Dynize are used to, but that probably turned a few stomachs."

"Including mine. One of these days I'm going to have to rein Styke in, and I'm not looking forward to it."

"Neither am I." Olem turned his head toward her. "Is that my jacket?"

"Yes."

He reached into the breast pocket. A matched flared to life a moment later, lighting his cigarette and illuminating a pleased smile. "There's some communication between us and the Fatrastans, but mostly trade. Our boys are making good use of their camp followers while they have them."

"And spending all the money Lindet paid us to defend Landfall. Soldiers have no sense of planning for the future, do they?"

"If they did, they wouldn't be soldiers. I say let them enjoy themselves while they can. We might be fighting those Fatrastans soon."

Vlora's stomach clenched, and she instinctively glanced south toward the Dynize camp. Hammer and anvil. The arrival of the Fatrastans had only delayed the inevitable. How much more time did she have to plan until the enemy decided to strike? How long could this standoff last? Hours? Days? Weeks? And when it finally happened, which army would turn on her first? "We could turn them against each other," she murmured.

"Eh?"

"The Dynize and Fatrastans. If they didn't both want my head, they'd focus entirely on each other. They'd barely even notice us."

"We could fake your death," Olem suggested.

"I've never been good at such crass deception," Vlora said with a grimace. "Besides, it's too obvious. We need something more subtle."

"Distract them and slip away?"

Vlora caught sight of a figure walking up the slope toward them, and she thought she recognized the shadowy form. "Perhaps," she said slowly. The figure stopped some twenty yards away.

"General? Colonel?" a voice called.

"Up here," Vlora responded.

Olem squinted into the night. "Is that Gustar? I haven't seen him since the battle."

Vlora waited to answer until Gustar had reached them, snapping off a shadowy salute. "Ma'am, sir. Major Gustar reporting in."

"Gustar," Vlora explained to Olem, "was one of just a handful of officers who wasn't wounded the other day."

"Pure luck, ma'am," Gustar interjected.

She continued. "Right after the battle, I sent him and a squad of dragoons as far north as they could go in twenty-four hours. I'm glad you made it back in one piece, Major. What can you tell us of the road to the north?"

Gustar removed his hat, dragging a sleeve across his brow. "The short version, or the long version?"

"The short, for now."

"Very good. I can tell you that the Second Field Army came down the Hadshaw from the Ironhook Mountains via keelboats. They stripped everything on their way—supplies, conscripts, local militias. From what we could discover, every town for a hundred miles in that direction pooled everything they had into the Second Army."

"Leaving them defenseless," Olem said flatly.

"Yes, sir."

"If only I were the pillaging type," Vlora murmured. "Go on."

"Supposedly there are two more armies on their way down from Thorn Point and Brannon Bay, but with the seas compromised, they could take weeks to arrive. No one knows anything about the armies recalled from the frontier to the northwest."

"They'll come down the Tristan River," Vlora said. "I'm not worried about them. Just what's north of us."

"That's it," Gustar said. "If we head northeast, we're not going to run into anything. There's no word of the Dynize landing this far north, and everything Lindet has between us and New Adopest is contained in that army across the river."

"Excellent," Vlora said. "You and your men help yourself to a double ration and hit your bunks. You deserve to sleep in tomorrow."

"Thank you, ma'am."

Another salute, and the major headed back down the hill.

Vlora waited until he was out of earshot, and said, "Gustar fought in two battles and didn't blink an eye when I ordered him to ride for forty-eight hours straight. The man deserves a promotion."

"Agreed," Olem said. The tip of his cigarette flared. "Were you going to tell me about this scouting mission?"

"I . . ." Vlora wasn't entirely sure *why* she hadn't told Olem. "It didn't seem important at the time, and we've been more than a little busy the last two days. I sent Gustar on a whim. I didn't expect the path from here to New Adopest to actually be clear."

"So we are going to try and slip away, then beeline it to the coast and head for home?"

"It's not elegant," Vlora admitted. "But yes, that's my backup plan. It may be our best bet of getting out of Fatrasta alive."

"*If* we can give two major armies the slip."

"Exactly." Vlora scowled at the sea of campfires across the river. "Did you ever tell me who's in command over there?"

"A woman named Zine Holm."

"Never heard of her."

"She's a Starlish noblewoman. Fought in the Fatrastan War for Independence as a soldier of fortune, and has been commanding armies against the Palo since."

"Competent?"

"As far as I know, though I think this is the biggest army she's ever commanded."

Vlora considered this for several quiet minutes, working through the various plans in her head and trying to create something coherent enough to actually work. "Get me a meeting with her. Also with the Dynize general, whoever the pit that is."

"When?"

"Tomorrow. No, wait. Tonight. As soon as possible. Tell them it's urgent, and we'll meet at a neutral location."

She could practically hear Olem grimace. "I'll try, but..."

"Make it happen." She tugged on the shoulders of his jacket, feeling a real chill for the first time tonight. "I'm going to try to sleep for a couple hours. Wake me up as soon as you've set up those meetings."

Three hours later, Vlora rode north along the Hadshaw River Highway with Olem and a dozen handpicked bodyguards. She half listened to a corporal droning on about supplies and yesterday's casualties, sniffing a few granules of powder at a time just to stay awake. Across the river, most of the Fatrastan fires were out and the night was all but silent. Occasionally her sorcery-enhanced senses spotted sentries along either ridge of the river valley—Fatrastan on the west side, and hers on the east.

They reached a crossroads and small keelboat landing, where a party of equal size awaited them on the dusty shore. Torches flickered in the light breeze, casting shadows on sunflower-yellow uniforms.

"Did you hear back from the Dynize?" Vlora asked quietly as they dismounted. She kept her eyes on a forty-something-year-old woman in the center of the waiting group, uniform decked out with medals and the black epaulets of a Fatrastan general.

"I did," Olem responded. "The Dynize general refuses to see you. He's convinced it's a trap, and that you hope to get him alone for an assassination."

"He's smarter than his colleague we met a couple days ago," Vlora said. "Which is unfortunate. I need to size him up. For now I'll have to satisfy myself with Holm." She handed her reins to one of her bodyguards and crossed the distance between her and the Fatrastans without preamble.

"General Holm." Vlora held out her hand. "Thank you for meeting me on such short notice."

"General Flint." Holm took the offered hand, shaking it firmly. She was a stocky woman, broad at the chest with hands as big as a grenadier's. She had smile lines at the corners of her mouth and friendly eyes that Vlora was more likely to see in a tavern owner. "I'm a big admirer. This is an odd time to meet, but I'm a night owl anyway and I figured you had something important to say."

Vlora tried to gauge the Fatrastan general, but found herself lacking. Holm didn't seem like the hard-bitten type forged on the frontier, nor the soldier of fortune Olem described. "To be honest, I thought we should meet as soon as possible, and this is the first time I've been able to pull myself away from my duties."

"I see." Holm clicked her tongue as if mildly annoyed. "Well, we're here now. I'd like to congratulate you on your victory the other day. My scouts arrived just at the tail end, but I'm told it was rather something—holding the line against a superior force until your cavalry could hit them from behind. Exactly what I'd expect from Lady Flint."

"I'm flattered, General. But I either win or die. I prefer to do the former."

Holm chuckled. "And that's exactly what I expect an Adran general to say. Imminently practical." She clapped her hands together. "Excuse my delight, Lady Flint, but this is just too much. I've always wanted to meet you. I wish I could show you the hospitality of my camp."

"You'll forgive my refusal, considering the arrest warrant I was served by your colonel the other day. A Fatrastan Army camp seems less than welcoming right now."

Holm's eyes tightened. "Ah, yes. That. I'm . . . unaware of the circumstances of the warrant, and will freely say I disagree with arresting a foreign war hero who's fighting Fatrastan battles on our behalf."

"Does this mean you're going to ignore it?" Vlora asked hopefully. "You outnumber the Dynize, but I understand your army was hastily assembled, and I think you could use our experience when you go to retake Landfall. You *are* going to retake Landfall, aren't you?"

"That is my ultimate mission," Holm said. "Unfortunately, I have every intention of arresting you. I'm a great admirer, but Lady Chancellor Lindet has won my loyalty too many times for me to disobey a direct order."

Vlora wondered if Holm knew about Lindet's abandonment of Landfall, but bit her tongue. Throwing mud over Lindet's name was not going to win Holm's friendship. "You're aware that my men have no intention of allowing me to be arrested."

"I'd hoped that you'd come along quietly." Holm paused thoughtfully, then continued. "I am convinced this is a misunderstanding. If you're willing to accept my hospitality, you will be treated as a guest in my camp until we are able to meet with Lindet in person. Your wounded will be cared for, your men given safe passage back to Adro—or allowed to fight with the Fatrastan Foreign Legion if they'd like. You'd have my word that no harm would come to you under my care, and I would be an advocate in whatever dispute you have with the Lady Chancellor."

Olem leaned forward, whispering, "That's a better offer than the Dynize gave you."

"Much," Vlora murmured. She considered her run-in with Lindet back in Landfall. "Unfortunately, I don't think you can promise my safety, General Holm."

Holm's eyebrows rose. "Why is that?"

"I tried to arrest Lindet for crimes against her own country right before the Dynize arrived. We put our differences aside just long enough to defend Landfall." *And then,* Vlora added silently, *that bitch fled without lifting a finger to help hold the city.*

"Well," Holm scoffed. "You certainly have a pair of balls worthy of your reputation." She held up a hand as if she needed a moment to digest this new information. "I'm aware that Lindet is far from perfect, but crimes against her own country?"

Vlora considered telling her about the godstones and Lindet's ambitions, but decided against it. The story was too far-fetched, and even if Holm believed it, she might very well think Lindet deserved to get her hands on them. Instead, Vlora offered a small shrug. "I believe that Lindet will have me executed the moment she gets a chance. And so I must refuse your offer."

Holm's brow furrowed, and Vlora was surprised to hear a note of genuine sadness in her voice. "I'm sorry to hear that, Lady Flint. Am I to understand that I should consider your army that of an enemy?"

The implications of that were immediately clear. Vlora's men would be shot on sight, and Holm would probably begin the morning by crossing the river in a flanking action to encircle Vlora's army—at which point she could either force a fight, or simply wait for Vlora's men to run out of rations and surrender.

The question of the Dynize Army made the entire situation much murkier.

"Tell me," Vlora said, "did you bring Privileged?"

Holm's reply was frosty. "That is not information I will tell you if we are enemies."

"Our scouts say they have three Privileged," Olem cut in.

Holm opened her mouth, a scowl on her face, but Vlora simply held up her hand. "I'm not threatening you—and I have no intention of murdering your Privileged unless we engage in combat. I just wanted to warn you that the Dynize do *not* have either bone-eyes or Privileged with them. But they are bloody disciplined, and breaking them will take more than overwhelming force."

"Why are you telling me this?"

"Because whatever happens to me, you're going to fight those Dynize sometime in the next few days. And I'd rather you win than them. Frankly, I think the battle will be more in their favor than you expect."

Holm chewed on this information, a worried frown on her face, eyeing Vlora. "I'll take this information under advisement."

"I—" Vlora was cut off by the sound of hooves galloping toward them from the direction of her camp. "Excuse me," she told Holm, striding back toward her bodyguard. She found one of her messengers waiting with them, his chest heaving from a hard ride. "Is it the Dynize?" Vlora demanded. "A night attack?"

"No, ma'am," the messenger said in a hushed tone. "You told me to let you know the moment Taniel and Ka-poel arrived." He gestured into the darkness behind him, and Vlora was able to make out two figures on horseback hanging back in the darkness. She could suddenly sense Taniel's powder magic, as if it had appeared from nothing—as if he were letting her know about his presence.

Vlora looked at Olem. "They're here."

"Should we return to camp?" Olem asked.

"No," she said, jerking her head toward the road. "They're *here*."

"Oh."

Vlora returned to Holm. "General, I'm afraid I have to cut this meeting short. Will you allow me to reconsider your offer?"

"Has something changed?" Holm asked, peering over Vlora's shoulder toward the messenger.

"Maybe."

"I can give you until tomorrow afternoon. Then I will consider the Riflejacks an enemy army."

"Thank you." Vlora turned to leave, then paused. "Am I to be assured the Landfall refugees have your protection?"

"We've already begun to pass out what supplies we can spare. I will take care of them the best I can—and I will not let the Dynize have them."

"Again, thank you," Vlora said. "I will answer you tomorrow." She left the general at the keelboat landing and headed back to her bodyguard to fetch her horse. She and Olem rode ahead, toward the two figures waiting in the darkness.

She could see that both Taniel and Ka-poel were tired. Their horses were haggard, their clothes covered with the dust of the road. They both wore greatcoats over frontier buckskins, with rifles, swords, and pistols strapped to their saddles. They looked like a pair of bounty hunters chasing an outlaw.

"Good evening," Olem said, tipping his hat.

"Morning, more like it," Taniel responded. "Good to see you again, Olem. Glad you've healed up since Landfall." Ka-poel waved. "We would have been here yesterday," Taniel explained, "but the Dynize have the roads south of their army buttoned up pretty tight."

"What news?" Vlora asked.

Taniel shared a look with Ka-poel, then gave Vlora a tight, tired smile. "We found them. We know where the other two god-stones are."

CHAPTER 8

B en, wake up."
Styke stared at the stars, his saddle beneath his head as a pillow while he stretched out on a bedroll tossed sloppily on the damp grass to keep him dry. He waited to answer until a boot nudged his ribs. "I'm awake."

Ibana leaned over him, peering into his eyes, and gave him a gentle slap on one cheek. "Then answer when I call."

"It's the middle of the night," Styke replied. He'd never had a problem sleeping until the labor camps. The pain of his old wounds, the uncertainty he felt toward the guards and the other inmates; he'd gained the ability to take catnaps but still had difficulty with real, deep sleep. Since he got out, his rest had been inconsistent—some nights as easy as lying down, while other nights sleep was elusive until late in the morning. This night was one of the latter.

"I damn well know it's the middle of the night. But there's something you should see."

"Is it important?"

"It is for you."

Reluctantly, Styke found his boots and climbed to his feet, glaring at Ibana through the darkness. "I was enjoying the quiet."

"It's not going to be quiet much longer. Rumor has it Flint has a plan up her sleeve, and it includes us making a move before sunup."

"Is that why you woke me up?" Styke made a fist, then stretched out his fingers, repeating the motion to loosen the muscles.

"No. Something else."

"Pit." He thought about ignoring her and throwing himself back to the ground in a futile effort to get a few more hours of sleep. If this was *really* important, Ibana would have woken up everyone. "Okay, fine. What do you want to show me?"

Ibana led him through the lancer camp and out through their eastern pickets. They didn't exchange another word until they were well beyond earshot of the guards; then she said, "How is your hand?"

"Fine." Styke, midstretch, buried his left hand in his pocket. "Why? Celine telling you stories?"

"She's worried about you."

"Yeah? Well, I'm more worried about you telling a little girl that I need to stop feeling sorry for myself."

Ibana paused briefly before continuing their walk. "And I need to teach her how to keep secrets."

"Not from me, you don't."

"Every girl keeps secrets from her dad," Ibana said with a note of bemusement. "Just like every boy keeps them from his mom."

Dad. What an odd notion. Styke had no way of knowing if he had a few bastards scattered around Fatrasta, but he'd certainly never thought of himself as a father. But with Celine, it felt right. "I wouldn't know."

Another pause. "Sorry."

Styke rolled his eyes. Thirty years or more since his father murdered his mother. It was underhanded to play that card, but he was tired and irritable and Ibana hadn't yet told him why she was dragging him all the way out here. "It's fine. What's going on here, anyway? You didn't wake me up to ask after my health."

"No," Ibana said, "I didn't." She gestured ahead of them, and Styke looked up to see the distant outline of a small farmhouse with a light flickering in the single window. He scowled, curious, but allowed Ibana to lead him onward until they were almost to the house. It was an old farmsteaders' plot, a one-room home with rotting timber walls and a low sod roof.

"Who lives here?" Styke asked.

"No idea. We found it empty, but it seemed apt for our needs."

"What needs were...?" Styke trailed off as Ibana opened the door and they both stepped inside. Everything of value had been cleared out of the house, leaving bare walls and a dirt floor. A single lantern hung from the rafters and illuminated three men. Styke recognized two of them: Markus and Zac were a pair of Brudanian brothers in their midthirties, ugly as sin and dressed in rags that helped them blend in when they were out scouting. The brothers were old Mad Lancers, two of the original group that had helped Styke terrorize the Kez Army all those years ago.

The third figure was a bigger man, kneeling between the brothers with a burlap sack over his head and hands bound behind his back.

"Afternoon, Colonel!" Markus said cheerily, snapping a salute.

"It's the middle of the night, you twit," Zac told him.

"Don't make no difference. Night, afternoon, all just a construct of the modern man."

"Oh, don't start this shit again."

"It's true! If it weren't for man, the sun in the sky wouldn't care what we called each particular time of day. Why, I bet—"

Styke cleared his throat and Markus's mouth shut. Styke glanced at Ibana, who'd taken up a spot by the window and now stood watching the small group impassively. "What's all this?" Styke asked her.

Ibana nodded at the two brothers. They exchanged a glance, and Zac spoke up. "It's a little bit of a story, Colonel, sir, if you don't mind me telling it."

"Make it short," Styke said, though his curiosity was piqued. He squinted at the kneeling man, wondering who was hidden beneath that burlap. He had the distinct impression he knew the prisoner.

"You remember the day they took you to the firing squad?"

Markus punched his brother in the shoulder. He hissed, "Of course he remembers, fool. Don't be insensitive!"

"Right, well..." Zac cleared his throat. "Markie and I, we've spent a lot of time thinking about that day."

"Me too," Styke said slowly.

"On that day, the Blackhats came and took our weapons, then carried you away. They put you to the firing squad before we could organize ourselves and afterward they didn't even leave us a body. We had a funeral for you the next day."

"That's touching," Styke interrupted, "but I don't know what you're getting at."

"He said short, you prick," Markus whispered. He cleared his throat and took up where his brother left off. "What he's getting at is this, sir: There were four of us missing from the funeral."

Styke felt his eyes narrow and now he couldn't take his gaze from the kneeling form. He was beginning to have his suspicions about who was under that burlap bag, and about where this story was going. It was not a direction he wanted to follow.

"Thing is, sir, we gave up our weapons because four of us convinced the rest that the Blackhats were going to give them right back. And those four that made that argument... well, they weren't at your funeral. So a couple years ago, me and Zac decided to track them down. Did some asking, dug around a little bit in back channels. All four of them wound up with a windfall from Lindet's regime right after the war. They got paid off for something, sir."

"You're saying they betrayed me?" Styke asked bluntly. He resisted the idea—he didn't want to consider that any of his lancers would turn on him—but slowly, it began to make sense. His memories of the day were fuzzy at best, but he remembered an argument among the lancers before they were disarmed. There was no way Fidelis Jes could have managed that without inside help.

"They betrayed *us*," Ibana said.

The brothers looked at Ibana for a long few moments before Markus ducked his head toward Styke. "Three of them weren't hard to track down. We've been keeping an eye on them since. But this one"—he nudged the kneeling figure with one boot—"he hasn't been seen since. We found him with the refugees yesterday."

Styke took a step toward the kneeling man and jerked the sack off his head, discarding it in the corner. The face that blinked up at him was familiar, if aged a decade. He was in his forties, roughly the same age as Styke, and had graying brown hair and a wispy beard. He had a thick neck and muscular shoulders, which had made him a fantastic lancer, and he blinked up at Styke's face impassively. His left eye was swollen nearly shut by a recent shiner, and Styke wondered which of the brothers had given it to him.

"Sergeant Agoston."

Styke remembered Agoston as an implacable figure, unruffled by burned villages and slaughtered enemies. He'd been a sword-for-hire before the war and joined up with the lancers for the spoils, always ready to go through the pockets of the dead after a battlefield. Styke had considered Agoston a friend—not close enough for secrets, but a man he'd share a beer with at the end of the day.

Agoston glanced at Ibana, more irritated than afraid, and gave a deep sigh. "Styke," he replied. "I'm not a sergeant anymore. Haven't been since the war."

"Yeah? And what have you been up to since the war?"

"A little bit of this, a little of that."

Agoston's nonchalance suddenly touched something within Styke, and he could feel a rage building deep in his stomach. "And this story the brothers are telling me? What do you make of that?"

"A bunch of rubbish."

Ibana snorted. "He's lying."

"I am not," Agoston protested.

"I played cards with you for eighteen months, asshole. You look down and to your left when you bluff."

"I do not..." Agoston looked down and to his left, then grimaced. He sniffed, his mouth forming into a hard line.

When it became clear he would say no more, Styke began to pace. The anger was building, and he forced his voice to remain neutral, matching Agoston's calm demeanor. "You betrayed the lancers, Agoston. You got me sent to the firing squad. Did you know what Fidelis Jes was planning?" There was a long, empty pause, and Styke added, "Don't pull this silent bullshit on me. You can either answer the question or we can take a few minutes and bury you alive beneath this hovel."

Agoston glanced around the room once more, and Styke could see the calculations going through his head: his chances of escaping, or putting up a good fight, or at least making them finish him off quickly. The corner of his lip curled, and Styke remembered something about his own experience playing cards with Agoston: He always got surly when he was losing. "Two million krana."

Styke raised his eyebrows. "Pit. You're joking, right?"

"Fidelis Jes really wanted you dead."

"I *knew* that. But two million?" Styke scoffed. "I would have damned well just retired if he'd come to me first."

"No you wouldn't," Agoston spat. "You like killing too much."

"Maybe." Styke acted careless, but on the inside he continued to boil. Agoston had been a comrade-in-arms, even a friend. To sell

Styke out, even for so much money...He felt his facade crack and turned away for a moment so that Agoston couldn't see the emotions playing out across his face. "Why didn't you just put a knife between my ribs yourself?"

"Because I'm not stupid. These assholes would have hunted me down no matter where I went. There's not enough money to knife Ben Styke."

Styke almost gave Agoston credit for that underlying assumption that he could have finished the job. *Almost.* "And that money? Did you spend it well?"

"Bought a townhouse in Upper Landfall. Changed my name. Kept my head down. Spent the last decade whoring and gambling in places so expensive I was never likely to see a lancer again." Agoston gave him a shallow smile. "So, yeah, I spent it well."

Styke looked at his hand and flexed his fingers. Ten years in the labor camp, when only a couple miles away one of the people who put him there lived a life of luxury and excess. He'd *known* about Fidelis Jes, of course, and his hatred was one of the things that kept him alive. But Jes had always been an enemy. Agoston...not so much. Styke remained looking at the wall, facing away from Agoston. "Cut his bonds," he said.

Ibana started. "What?"

"You heard me."

Hesitantly, Ibana nodded to the brothers.

"You sure, sir?" Markus asked.

Styke nodded, not trusting himself to speak. He flexed his fingers, feeling that twinge, churning that rage. "Zac, do you have a pistol on you?"

"Yes, sir."

"Is it loaded?"

"Yes."

"Give it to Agoston."

"Sir?"

"Now!" Styke turned around and glared at Zac, who licked his lips and glanced warily at Ibana. Styke held a hand toward her. "Don't say a damned word. Zac, give him your pistol."

Zac drew his pistol and handed it to Agoston as he climbed to his feet. Agoston brushed himself off and took the pistol, staring at Styke intently. "What's this?" His tone said that he sensed a trap, but he didn't know where it was.

Styke took a step toward him and spread his hands. "You wanted me dead. You were *paid* to help put me in a grave. It didn't work, so here's your shot to earn that two million. Put a bullet in my head."

Without hesitation, Agoston lifted the pistol and took a half step forward, pressing the barrel against Styke's forehead. He pulled the trigger, and Styke heard the click-and-snap of the flintlock.

Nothing happened.

"You think you're hot shit, Agoston," Styke said, finally letting his fury unfurl. "But you never paid attention. Zac still carries the same shitty, leaky powder horn he has for fifteen years. Powder gets wet and his pistol misfires two times out of three."

As Styke finished the sentence, a look of panic spread across Agoston's face. He backpedaled and tried to flip the pistol around to use it as a weapon, but Styke was on him before he could take a second step. Styke drew his boz knife, dragged the blade along Agoston's sternum, and rammed it into the soft spot beneath his jaw until the crosspiece touched skin and the tip jutted from the top of his skull. Agoston's eyes bugged, a rasping came from his mouth, and his body convulsed. Styke allowed his momentum to carry them against the far wall of the hovel and slammed Agoston's body against the rotted timbers. The whole house shook.

His hands soaked with warm blood, Styke stared into Agoston's dead eyes. "Who else betrayed me?" he asked the brothers quietly.

"Bad Tenny Wiles, Valyaine, and Dvory," Markus answered.

"Where are they?"

"Tenny Wiles owns a plantation about a hundred miles west of here; Valyaine is a boxer in Belltower; and Dvory is a general in the Fatrastan Army."

Styke let Agoston's body fall. "Toss him in the rubbish heap out back. He doesn't deserve a real burial." He took a deep breath and clapped Markus, then Zac on the shoulder, leaving a bloody handprint on each. "Thank you. I needed that. Whatever happens these next few months, I'm going to find the rest of those assholes and kill them." He looked at Ibana. "Let's go find out what Flint is up to."

CHAPTER 9

V lora drank cold coffee at the table in the middle of her tent. She stared absently at the maps laid out in front of her and noticed that her hand was trembling. Olem sat on the corner of her cot, fiddling with the metal tin he kept his matches in. His face mirrored her expression: absent, lost—shell-shocked. He licked his lips, opened his mouth as if to speak, but closed it again. She hadn't seen him this out of sorts since the Adran-Kez War. Taniel and Ka-poel were standing just outside their tent, waiting for Vlora's decision on the news they'd brought from Landfall.

"Taniel wants us to go find these other two godstones," Vlora said. "Is it our responsibility?"

Olem looked up, blinking away his own thoughts.

Vlora continued before he could reply. "We're Adrans. We have no horse in this race. The Fatrastans, Dynize, and Palo are going to spend the next few months—maybe even years—killing each other over these things. Why should we get involved?" She slapped her palm on the table, almost spilling her coffee, feeling a sudden swell of anger. "We're in this damned situation because I couldn't just keep my head down and do a job. I tried to arrest Lindet over these stupid things, and I managed to lose our allies on this continent in the process."

Olem clicked his match tin against the wooden frame of her cot, his expression conflicted. "We've seen what gods can do to a country," he said.

"This isn't our country. We're mercenaries, and after a year in the swamps and two major battles the men are almost spent. I'm not going to appeal to their patriotism, because this isn't an Adran matter."

"I agree with that."

"Then answer me this: *Is this our responsibility?*"

"No," Olem said. He tilted his head, as if pained, and said, "And...yes."

"Explain."

"Less responsibility," Olem said, "and more necessity. Back in Landfall you said that the world doesn't need any more gods, and I think you're still right about that. These consequences that you and I understand—I think it makes us responsible, even if our men are not. This world is not as large as it once was. You're still a member of the Adran Cabal, and we're both still Adran generals. We can either deal with a new god once this continent has finished warring over the stones, or we can try to prevent one from being born in the first place."

"So you'd argue that it *is* an Adran matter?"

"I'd argue that it will be. Unfortunately, we aren't accompanied by the Adran Army. We're accompanied by mercenaries."

"So what do we do? Send the men home and you and I offer to join whatever it is Taniel is stirring up?"

"It's an option," Olem said. "But these things will probably be much easier with an army at our back, even if it's a little mauled right now."

Vlora finished off her coffee, spitting the dregs out on the ground and returning her gaze to the map on her table. Taniel had left two pins in the map. One of them was located on the edge of the Iron-hook Mountains, not all that far from here. The other was located on the west coast of Fatrasta. Vlora tapped her finger on the tip of each pin, and then on New Adopest—the closest large port not in the hands of the Dynize, and the best chance she had of getting an army back to Adro.

"Taniel!" she shouted.

A moment passed before the tent flap was thrown back. Taniel and Ka-poel entered. Ka-poel immediately rounded the table to examine the map in silence, while Taniel looked from Vlora to Olem with an irritating air of expectation.

Vlora said, "You told me once that you still have Tamas's foreign wealth at your command."

"I do," Taniel said, pulling back somewhat. This was not the question he had expected.

"Good. Because Olem and I are in. This is a matter for the Adran Army and the Adran Cabal, and we're the only representatives on the continent. However, this isn't the responsibility of my men." She paused for a beat. "But I'm not going to do this without an army. You're going to hire the Riflejacks. I expect every soldier out there who survives, and all the widows and widowers of the ones who don't, to leave this conflict as wealthy people. Understand?"

Taniel cocked an eyebrow. Across the table, Ka-poel grinned and nodded. *Done.*

"I offered to hire you before," Taniel said.

"That was before I grasped the stakes. Besides, I'm serious when I say 'wealthy.' Our prices went up significantly since we last spoke."

Ka-poel shrugged and twirled her finger, as if saying the conversation was already finished and she was ready to move on. "All right," Taniel said. "We'll hammer out details on the road."

"One other thing," Vlora added. "You will give us objectives, but

I will decide how they're carried out. You're not going to dictate what happens to the godstones once we find them. Understand?"

"I see." Taniel's eyes narrowed, and Vlora could tell he was rethinking the idea.

She leaned on the table, looking him in the eye. "I intend to destroy those things. That is my goal—no, that is the goal of the Adran Republic Cabal. No new gods."

"You're making a lot of demands for a mercenary."

"You didn't hear what I just said. I have a mercenary army, but I represent Adro in this matter. And you have a look on your face that seems awfully uncertain for someone hoping for my help. I'm ready to go home right now, Taniel. Take it or leave it."

Taniel looked to Ka-poel, and the two shared a long, silent gaze. "Taken," Taniel said with finality.

Vlora swallowed, her throat suddenly dry. She wished she had a few days to sleep on the decision. She wished she had a bigger, healthier army. And she wished she didn't feel like events were about to spiral out of her control.

"What are you going to do about these armies we're pinned between?" Taniel asked.

"Olem," Vlora said, "when is dawn?"

"Two hours or so."

"And what will the weather be like?"

"We've had a chilly night. Same as last night, and yesterday morning we had a thick fog until ten. I don't see things being different today."

Vlora took the pins out of her maps and began to roll them up carefully. "Get everyone moving. I want us on track to be gone within two hours."

"And you think the Fatrastans and Dynize are just going to let you leave?" Taniel asked flatly. "I understand both are looking for your head."

"Fog will give us a head start," Vlora said. "The rest...well, I have an idea. Olem, I want to see Styke, Gustar, and my senior officer corps. Vallencian, too. I think he crossed the river, so you'll have to do that quietly. Now, get out of here so I can write some letters."

Dawn was almost upon them, and Vlora stood by her horse and watched as the rest of her camp vanished before her eyes. Soldiers finished packing their kit, officers kept things orderly, and quartermasters examined the wagons of supplies they'd managed to bring over from the Fatrastan camp followers in the darkness.

The fog Olem had predicted was thinner than she would have liked. It would mask their movements, but for only so long—within hours both the Dynize and Fatrastans would know that she'd given them the slip. The question Vlora needed answered most of all was whether they would turn their focus on one another, or whether either general was dogmatic enough to come for her.

A familiar figure appeared through the gloom, torch held high over his head, the scrap of bearskin still clinging to his shoulders. Vallencian Habbabberden, known more widely as the Ice Baron, was nothing short of a walking miracle. He'd saved the Battle of Landfall by riding his merchant ships out on the tide to crash into and sow chaos among the Dynize fleet. Somehow, he'd managed to swim back to shore against the currents and recover from half drowning, only to be on his feet again to help with the evacuation of the city. He'd spent every moment since then as a whirlwind through the refugee camp, redistributing supplies, breaking up fights, tending to the sick, and organizing former small-time politicians into a genuine leadership for the refugees.

Vallencian had grown gaunt since they'd first met in Landfall a couple of months ago. He'd lost weight, his hair had grayed at the edges and remained uncombed, and his face seemed fixed by a frustrated scowl.

"You're leaving," he said brusquely.

"We are."

"Does General Holm know? I've been a guest of hers for the last day and she is very intent on presenting you to Lindet."

Vlora produced a letter she had written less than an hour ago and offered it to Vallencian. "She will when you give her this letter."

Vallencian stared down his nose at the paper and did not reach for it. After a long moment's consideration, he said in a low voice, "Don't leave me with them."

"Excuse me?" Vlora was shocked to hear genuine dismay in his tone. "Are they mistreating you?"

"Quite the opposite. Holm has assigned me an entourage. I think she's having me watched. I had to pretend I needed a shit just to sneak out of my tent when your summons came. They're making me sleep in a real bed. And these damned refugees are trying to elect me as mayor of this moving city we have gathered."

Despite her frayed nerves, Vlora had to stifle a smile. "I can't think of anyone better suited."

"I could name a dozen in a single breath. Probably a hundred if you give me the chance to think." Vallencian paced, gesturing as he spoke. "These refugees don't need a mayor, and Holm has no intention of allowing it. They'll be split up and sent to whatever towns and cities can take them, as quickly as can be managed. I have no interest in being the general's guest and I have no interest in being bullied into a position of leadership."

"I thought you had taken well to helping..."

Vallencian stopped his pacing long enough to shake a thick finger beneath her nose. "*Helping!*" he exclaimed. "Not leading. I'm a reluctant businessman at best. I will not be a politician."

"You're very good with people," Vlora ventured. "They could use your help, at least until this refugee camp has been dissolved."

"Absolutely not. I will come with you, Lady Flint."

Vlora resisted the urge to point out he hadn't been invited. "You won't stay with them? At least for a few weeks?"

"No."

"Even if I request it personally?"

Vallencian came to a stop and turned toward her cautiously. "Why would you want me to stay with them? Are you trying to get rid of me?"

Vlora could think of nothing more pleasurable or frustrating than the idea of having Vallencian along on Taniel's mission. "I swear I am not. I know that you have done much for me—you damned well ended the Battle of Landfall—but I need a personal favor."

"I sacrificed my ships for Fatrasta," Vallencian declared. "I would not humble myself to claim a favor for such an act. In fact, I intend on charging Lindet for those ships, and the revenue I've lost from their destruction."

"Reluctant businessman indeed," Vlora murmured. "Vallencian, I have about seven hundred men who are too wounded to march. I have discharged them from the company so they won't be treated as enemy combatants, but I need someone to care for them—to advocate for them—and if need be, to protect them."

Vallencian drew himself up, chest puffing out. "And you would trust me with such a task?"

"If it's not too . . ."

"Too much? It would be an honor!"

Vlora saw the movement too late. "Vallencian, don't . . . hug me." She found herself crushed against his broad chest, then thrust back at arm's length like a father examining his daughter on her wedding day. His face was red, his lips pressed in a tight line.

"Please don't cry," Vlora said.

"I won't." Vallencian's voice cracked, and he dabbed at the corners of his eyes with his bearskin. Vlora tried to reconcile the avenging angel piloting burning ships into the enemy fleet with the man standing before her on the edge of tears. "I won't," he said with more confidence. "But I will have you know that I accept this task, and I will take it very seriously. Your wounded soldiers will

not be neglected or used as bargaining chips or in any way mis-
treated while I still live."

Vlora wondered if there was a more genuine man in the entire
world, and had no doubt that he would do as promised. "Some will
die from their wounds," she said quietly. "Some will be cripples for
life. Hopefully more will recover fully. You can send them on to
New Adopest to take a ship home where they can claim their pen-
sion. If they are hale, they can come find me."

"You're not going back to Adro?" Vallencian's eyes narrowed
curiously.

"It's best I not tell you where we're headed."

"I understand." Vallencian reached out and plucked the letter
from Vlora's fingers. "I will deliver this to Holm immediately."

Vlora held up a hand. "If you would wait two hours, actually."

"Exactly?" Vallencian produced a pocket watch. "It will be done.
Good-bye, Lady Flint. May we meet again under more favorable
circumstances." He gave a flourishing bow and backed away, then
turned and disappeared into the fog.

Vlora watched him go, then turned to find Ben Styke waiting
for her. She took a deep breath, letting it out slowly.

"What a strange person," Styke said.

"He's a good one," Vlora said, somewhat more defensively than
she'd intended.

Styke spread his hands. "I heard what he did with his ships at
Landfall. 'Strange' isn't an insult coming from me. You wanted to
see me, Flint?"

"I expect you figured out we're leaving."

"I gathered. My lancers are ready to ride, but no one knows
where to."

Vlora stood on her toes, peering into the dark fog for some sign
of Olem. She spotted him nearby, his jacket discarded while he and
a trio of soldiers replaced a wagon wheel. "Where is Taniel?" she
called to him.

"One, two…" Olem grunted as he helped lift the wagon, and replied in a strained voice and the jerk of his head. "Last I saw, he was getting a new horse."

"Come with me," Vlora told Styke. They walked over to a corral of captured Dynize horses, and found Taniel and Ka-poel going through the herd with a critical eye. She beckoned them over. While she waited, she turned to Styke. "You remember the godstone, correct?"

"The thing we fought the Dynize for south of Landfall?" He rubbed his nose vigorously. "That thing reeked of old sorcery. I didn't like it."

"I'll give you the short version," Vlora said. "That godstone is an artifact of immense sorcerous power. It is one of three that in conjunction can be used to create a new god. Taniel has hired us to find, secure, and hopefully destroy the other two godstones before either Lindet or the Dynize can find and use them."

Styke stuck a tongue into his cheek. "Huh."

"I don't really care if you believe me. You and your lancers will be paid the same as my own Adrans—and Taniel is going to bleed gold for this."

"I've heard weirder things," Styke grunted.

"Are you in?"

"Perhaps. Where is our objective?"

"The western coast of Fatrasta, at the end of the Hammer."

Styke lifted his eyes to the sky, his lips moving silently, as if he were examining a map in his head. A small, strange smile touched the corners of his mouth. "The money sounds good, and keeping Lindet away from her prize will delight the pit out of my lancers. So yes, I'm in." Taniel and Ka-poel joined them, and Styke gave each a nod. He eyed Ka-poel for several seconds before turning his attention back to Vlora.

"Excellent," Vlora said. She had expected more questions, defiance, or…she didn't really know. Styke's legend never included him being easy to work with, so his quick answer was a relief. "Taniel and Ka-poel managed to dig through the archives Lindet was forced to abandon in Landfall."

"Her personal archives," Taniel interjected.

Styke gave a low whistle. "I bet those were full of fun."

"You have no idea."

"I think I do," Styke said with a tight smile.

Vlora continued. "Lindet has the approximate location of both of the other godstones, but as far as we know, she hasn't actually found them yet. We don't know if they're hidden, or buried by time, or what. One of them is located in the Ironhook Mountains near a gold-mining town called Yellow Creek. I'm taking my army up to try and find it."

"And you want the lancers to find the other one?"

"Our information on the other one is more vague," Taniel spoke up. "We know it's out on the Hammer, probably in the vicinity of Starlight. We need someone mobile to go looking for it."

Styke looked from Taniel, to Ka-poel, to Vlora. Slowly, he took off his big ring and breathed on it, polishing the skull on the breast of his faded cavalry jacket. "Have the Dynize landed on the west coast?"

"That's what Taniel's intelligence says," Vlora said. "Though not in as big numbers as at Landfall." She watched Styke's face for some hint of hesitation. She needed to go after both stones, but splitting her infantry was the worst possible scenario.

"And Lindet will no doubt have troops in the area," Styke added.

"Without a doubt," Vlora said. "I intend on putting Major Gustar and the remnants of his cuirassiers and dragoons under your command. You'll be riding with close to a thousand seasoned cavalry."

Styke replaced his ring and opened and closed his hand, eyes on a thin white scar over the tendons of his wrist. "Fewer might be better in this situation," he said. "But Gustar knows what he's doing. I'll take them." He nodded to himself, and Vlora let out a soft sigh of relief. Losing her cavalry would be rough, but Styke could use them more fully on the coast than she could up in the mountains. Styke opened his mouth, and Vlora tensed in the face of protestations. He said, "I can smell sorcery. I have a few other Knacked in my company. But if Lindet's Privileged haven't found it yet, how do you expect a bunch of lancers to do it?"

Vlora glanced at Taniel, who snorted out a laugh. "You remember that favor you owe me, Colonel?" Taniel asked.

"I do," Styke said slowly.

Ka-poel grinned, and Taniel put his arm around her waist. "Well, I'm calling it in. You're not going to find the godstone. She is, and you're going to make sure she survives, even if it costs the lives of you and every one of your men."

Vlora dismissed Styke and left Ka-poel and Taniel to pick out their horses for the journey ahead, hoping she'd made the right decision in giving Styke her cavalry. Something nagged at the back of her mind, something that she couldn't quite put her finger on. She put it aside and found Olem just as the first company of Riflejack infantry began their march out of camp.

"Everything set with Styke?" Olem asked.

"He's in," Vlora said. "He'll take Ka-poel and go cause havoc in the west. Taniel will come with us to find and secure the other godstone."

"Does Styke know he's a distraction?"

Vlora grimaced. " 'Distraction' is a harsh word. He has his orders, and he has Ka-poel. I daresay he has a better chance of finding and destroying his godstone than we do ours."

"But sending him out across Fatrasta will draw attention away from us."

"Styke is not a subtle man. I think he's well aware of that and the dangers it entails. What's done is done. Oh, I gave Vallencian a letter for Holm." Vlora dug into her pocket and produced a second letter, handing it to Olem. "Wait an hour, then send a runner to the Dynize camp."

Olem took the letter and held it with both hands, as if weighing it. "What do they say?"

"The first letter," Vlora said, watching the last vestiges of the camp disappear as soldiers fell into marching formation, "tells General Holm that I'm leaving. It also tells her that the Dynize general has orders to take my head and will march after me. She can either give chase, or she can use the opportunity to press on toward Landfall."

"And this letter?" Olem hefted the other note.

"It tells the Dynize general that I'm leaving, and that the Fatrastans also want my head and will give chase and that he can deal with whichever he deems to be the largest threat."

Olem stared curiously at the letter. "So you told them both the truth, more or less."

"A half-truth, yes. The difference is that I expect Holm to believe me. I don't expect the Dynize to believe me. The Dynize will shore up their defenses, maybe even send a couple brigades after us, while Holm—being a competent general—will not want an enemy force behind her. She'll attack the Dynize as soon as possible."

"We should have done this two days ago."

"I didn't know the character of the enemy generals then," Vlora said. "Find me my horse and let's get going. I hope this works."

CHAPTER 10

Styke sat astride Amrec a mile northeast of where the Riflejacks had made camp the last few nights and watched the column of infantry marching double time through the thinning morning fog. They'd left the river highway in favor of a dirt road through rougher terrain where they could stay ahead of any pursuers, and Styke guessed that the two enemy armies would figure out their disappearance any time now.

Supposedly, Flint had some trickery up her sleeve to keep the two armies occupied with each other. Styke didn't know. He didn't particularly care. It wasn't his problem anymore.

In front of him in the saddle, Celine slept with her head against the crook of Styke's arm, snoring softly. He thought about waking her to watch the troops go by, but figured she'd had enough of soldiers for one lifetime. He adjusted her head to lay against his chest so he could lift his arms, and turned around to find Jackal waiting nearby. The Palo bannerman sat easy in his saddle atop a captured Dynize horse, watching the columns pass. Styke nudged Amrec gently around to join him.

"What do your spirits say about all this?" Styke asked.

Jackal didn't take his eyes off the passing soldiers. "That we're all going to die."

"Oh." Styke felt the hair on the back of his neck stand on end.

"But," Jackal added, "they always say that. They don't actually know *when* we're going to die—just that it will happen. Which is pretty obvious. Spirits are preoccupied with death."

Styke swallowed a lump in his throat. "Was that a joke, Jackal?"

"I've been working with street children for the last few years," he said without smiling. "It helped me develop my sense of humor." He finally looked up from the Riflejack column and gazed at Celine for a few moments. "She's good for you, I think. Tempers your fury."

"I think ten years in the camps tempered my fury."

"That's not what the spirits say," Jackal replied.

Styke smoothed Celine's hair gently with one hand. "I have no idea whether to take you seriously."

"You added another to their number a couple hours ago. Agoston, I believe. He is hiding from me, but the spirits say he betrayed you." As crazy as Jackal sounded sometimes, he always came up with bits of information he had no other way of knowing. It made Styke more than a little uncomfortable. Jackal continued. "The spirits say you're a man of madness. They say Death walks in your footsteps just to find an easier road. Some of them fear you. Some hate you. Some like you." Jackal's eyes narrowed. "The ones that like you are not sound of mind."

"Thanks for that."

"They also think this is a terrible idea."

"The spirits? What idea?"

"Searching for the godstones."

Goose bumps spread on the back of Styke's arms. Another piece of information Jackal hadn't—or shouldn't have—been told. "Have you been spying on us?"

"The spirits bring me a lot of information to sort through. One of the braver ones happened to overhear your conversation with Flint and the other two."

"Taniel and Ka-poel."

"The spirits just call them Black and Fire. But yes, them. The spirits want nothing to do with the godstones, and think we shouldn't, either. The stones are surrounded by a cacophony of death so thick that it drives spirits to madness."

"I didn't know the dead *could* go mad."

"Madness can follow them from life. But for a spirit to be driven to insanity *after* death? That's something."

Styke turned toward Jackal and sniffed, trying to sense any sorcery about him. He thought he detected something—a hint of grave moss and fresh-turned dirt—but it was so minuscule it might be his imagination. Was Jackal using some kind of strange new sorcery? Had a Knack manifested itself late in life? Styke should be able to smell it, but he hadn't used his sorcerous senses for ten years, and had never considered the fact he was out of practice.

They sat in silence for several minutes. In a nearby field, Ibana was gathering the Mad Lancers and the Riflejack cavalry for their briefing—minus the scouts keeping an eye on the nearby armies. Styke wondered if he made Ibana do too much of his footwork. But that's what a junior officer was for, was it not? As the senior officer, he sat around, made important decisions. Maybe he'd do some paperwork once in a while, though upon reflection he realized he made Ibana do that as well.

He glanced sidelong at Jackal. "Can the spirits help us find the godstones?"

Jackal made a sour face. "I asked. It took almost an hour to get them to talk to me again."

"So that's a no."

"Definitely no."

"Well," Styke said, lifting his reins. "Tell me if they're good for anything."

He turned Amrec away from the road and headed off across a shallow gully to where the cavalry was assembled with Ibana. Halfway to Ibana, Ka-poel met him on horseback. He pulled up, eyeing her for several long moments. Ka-poel smiled at him, and though he was almost two feet taller than her, he found something incredibly terrifying about the casual intensity in her eyes. To his Knack, she smelled of coppery old blood.

"So we're to be your bodyguard, are we?"

She nodded.

"Do you ride well?"

Another nod.

"I don't know your signing language. Is there a better way we can communicate?"

She hesitated, then tapped the side of her head.

"You'll think of something?"

A nod.

"Try to do it soon." Styke adjusted Celine in his saddle and wondered how she could sleep so well. Even after three weeks on horseback, his thighs and balls still hurt too bad to so much as snooze. To be young again, he mused. "Tell me," he said to Ka-poel. "Did I dream you in that town north of Landfall? Did I dream that you wiped blood on my face and disappeared?"

She smiled.

"You can be coy with Taniel and Flint and everyone else. But I'm going to keep you alive the next few months. Don't play with me. Did I dream that?"

She snorted, her face growing serious, then shook her head.

"No, I didn't dream it, or no, you didn't do it?"

She smiled again.

"God damn it."

"Styke!" Ibana called.

Styke pointed at Ka-poel. "We'll talk about this again later." He rode over to where Ibana waited at the head of the assembled cavalry and ran his eyes across them. Most wore the crimson and blue of the Riflejacks—some volunteers wore whatever they happened to have on them, and the rest wore the old, sunflower-yellow jackets of the Mad Lancers. Everyone was mounted, facing toward Ibana and Gustar at the front, and each had the reins of an extra horse tied to their saddle.

The Mad Lancers had each taken the breastplate of a dead Dynize cuirassier. Styke's hung from his saddle—he needed a smith to hammer it out to fit him. Their breastplates weren't as strong as those of the Riflejack cuirassiers, but they were much lighter, and he decided he'd have the Riflejack dragoons fitted with them the next time they slaughtered a Dynize army.

"Some of you know me from old," Styke began, shouting to be heard across the field. "Some of you have already ridden under my command at Landfall. And some of you signed on just in the last few days, in which case you will come to know me soon. But for every one of you here today my name is Ben Styke, and I am your new colonel."

A thousand pairs of eyes watched him silently. Someone in the back cheered, but quickly fell silent.

"I understand that most of you are here for the money, that you followed Lady Flint across the ocean in return for riches, so she is the one who holds your loyalty." Styke held up a finger. "Flint has given us one mission, and has cut us loose. Your soul belongs to her, but your bodies belong to me. When I tell you to slaughter, you slaughter. When I tell you to burn, you burn. When I say charge, you charge. Anyone who has a problem with that can slink back to her right now and explain that you don't want to follow orders."

No one moved.

"Good." Styke continued. "We will ride hard every day. We will train every day. We will treat our horses with respect. If you fall behind, we will not coddle you—but we will not abandon you, either. You will be *taught* to keep up. It doesn't matter whether you are a cuirassier or a dragoon or a lancer, or a farmer, or an accountant. From this day forward, you are a Mad Lancer.

"Mad Lancers are as kind to our allies as we are cruel to our enemies. We take in the broken and we turn them into warriors. We crush those who think themselves invincible. We thrive on the ravages of war. The Mad Lancers protect Fatrasta—even from itself. When all this is over, Lady Flint has assured me that all the survivors will be rich. But mark my words: If you disobey my orders, I will kill you myself."

Styke took a long moment to enjoy the irony of a man famous for ignoring his superiors expecting unquestioning obedience from his own cavalry, before continuing on in a shout: "Welcome to the Mad Lancers. We ride as brothers and sisters. We die as brothers and sisters. Let's move out!"

He turned immediately to Ibana and Gustar, noting that Celine had woken up during his speech and was looking around groggily. "How was that?"

"Could have been better," Ibana said.

"Go to the pit," Styke told her.

"A bit more violent than my boys are used to," Gustar commented. "But I like it."

"They'll learn," Styke warned. "We aren't knights in shining armor. We're killers."

"Adrans have few hang-ups about war," Gustar assured him.

Ibana sighed. "I miss my old armor." She thumped her Dynize breastplate. "This won't even stop a good rifle shot."

"Quit your whining. It'll turn a sword or a bayonet. Until we can find out where Lindet stashed our armor, this is the best we've got."

Ibana perked up. "We're going looking for it?"

"It's on my list," Styke said. He didn't want to get anyone's hopes up—he wasn't entirely certain that Lindet hadn't destroyed it like she said—but he also had a feeling it was floating around in a Blackhat armory somewhere. If it was on the west coast, he was going to find it. "Get the men moving," he told Gustar. "We'll head north two more miles, then cut through the refugee camp and go west. I'd like to skirt them entirely but that would take too long, so we'll have to be well on our way before Holm has any idea we passed through."

Gustar snapped a salute and rode off, shouting for the men to form columns.

"We've got a lot of new volunteers," Styke said, looking over the cavalry. "Are you sure you're going to be able to whip them into shape?"

Ibana scoffed. "You may be an old cripple, but I'm in the prime of my life. If we turned farmers and dockhands into cavalry during the Fatrastan War, we can do it now." She paused for a moment. "I'm surprised you said yes to this. That eager to be cut loose?"

Styke considered the question for several moments, looking down at Celine, who was content to watch the activity without comment. "The longer we stick around, the more likely it'll be that Flint and I come to blows. I don't want that to happen."

"Sure."

"But it's not just that. Flint has sent us west. What's to the west?"

Ibana shrugged.

Styke held up three fingers. "Bad Tenny Wiles, Valayine, and Dvory."

A wicked little smile crossed Ibana's face.

Styke continued. "I figure there's a pretty good chance we come across those bastards while we look for this thing for Lady Flint— and I really like the idea of mixing business and revenge."

CHAPTER 11

Michel spent the next few days after losing his safe house trying to ascertain just how much damage had been done. He left notes for Hendres at preordained drop points, tried to chase down a handful of trusted contacts, and stewed in his own frustration at a small hovel on the edge of Greenfire Depths—the first address on Taniel's list of resources.

He was just about to give up hope that Hendres had escaped the Dynize when he found a note at one of the drop points. *Still alive. Safe house compromised. Meet at 14 Laural Way, 2 p.m. Will wait for two days.* Hendres's neat handwriting was unmistakable.

The meeting spot was in a posh area of Landfall called Middle Heights. Before the invasion, it was the favored locale of the Fatrastan elite. The streets were wide and cobbled, lined with immense townhouses, with every street corner lit by gaslight during the night. There were museums, theaters, and fine restaurants—even Michel's favorite whorehouse was in Middle Heights, though he could rarely afford it.

Since the invasion, everything had changed. Middle Heights was practically a ghost town. Homes and businesses were boarded up in a vain attempt to prevent looting. Only about one in ten residences was still occupied, and the big public buildings were either guarded by Dynize soldiers or had been taken over by squatters.

Rumor had it that the Dynize planned on moving their own low-level bureaucracy into the mansions of Middle Heights, but so far there was only an average Dynize presence in the area.

Michel headed to the indicated meeting spot an hour early and did a slow walk around the block. Fourteen Laural Way was a big theater—only a few years old, it was the pride of some Brudanian investors, with an immense stone facade decorated by gargoyles and columns. The newspapers spoke much about the mazelike tunnels beneath the main stage with state-of-the-art lever-and-pulley systems that would allow actors to descend from the catwalks or pop up from the floor anywhere onstage.

There was graffiti on the outside walls admonishing the Dynize invaders in Palo, and the tents of homeless squatters covered the immense floor of the columned front portico.

Michel walked through the tents, glancing in at the faces. They were mostly Palo—refugees from the fires in Greenfire Depths— and no one questioned him as he passed. He tried the front door to find it barricaded from inside, then headed around to the alleyways, his eyes sharp for Dynize soldiers, though it soon became clear that he needn't worry. The Dynize had clearly decided to ignore this place, at least for now.

Michel did a second circuit of the block, eyeing the squatters and checking the windows and roofs of the nearby townhouses before heading back around to the front steps and settling down to wait. Thirty minutes passed, then an hour, and it was almost two thirty before he finally spotted Hendres hurrying down the street toward him.

He stood up, hands clasped behind his back, and frowned. She walked hurriedly, her eyes on the doorways of the townhouses as she passed them, constantly searching. She seemed...off. "Ignore it," he whispered to himself. "She's had a rough couple of days, too."

"She's carrying a pistol beneath her jacket," he retorted. "You better damn well keep your eyes peeled." He still glanced over his shoulder, checking his escape route around the back of the theater.

She spotted him and crossed the street, picking her way slowly through the tents, her face worried. He tried to give her a reassuring smile and raised his hand in greeting. "Glad to see you in one piece," he said.

Hendres flashed a quick smile, and Michel felt that same gut response he'd gotten outside of the safe house a few days ago. Something was wrong. He could see it in her gait and in her face. He did a quick glance around, looking for any sign of Dynize soldiers, but came up with nothing.

"What's wrong?" he asked.

"I'm fine," she said. "Still a little shaken up. I...went out after you did the other day. It was pure luck that I wasn't there when the Dynize showed up."

Michel ran a hand through his hair. "Shit. I was hoping you'd be able to tell me why they were there."

"Why would I be able to tell you?" The words were a little too quick, accompanied by a look full of suspicion.

Two and two clicked together in Michel's head, and he held up his hands. "You don't think I tipped them off, do you?"

Hendres hesitated. She did. She definitely did, and that had Michel worried. "I don't know," she said.

"I didn't tip anyone off," Michel assured her. "I came back that evening and spotted them staking out the safe house. I'm glad you did the same. Shit, shit." He began to pace, his mind racing. Not only did he have to figure out why the Dynize were at his safe house, but he also had to convince Hendres he hadn't betrayed her. "Look, one of us might have been followed. We might have been sold out, or we might have just gotten unlucky—the Dynize are cracking down more than ever since those grenades the other day. We need to find another safe house and regroup. We have to make sure our routes out of the city haven't been compromised, too."

"I . . ." Hendres seemed to consider his words, the corners of her eyes tightening. Her mouth formed into a firm line, and she said, "I don't think so."

"What do you mean?" The last word had barely left Michel's mouth when he heard footsteps behind him. He glanced over his shoulder to see a tall woman with black hair cut short on the sides in the style of the Starlish military. Her name was Aethel, and he recognized her as an Iron Rose who had worked beneath him on occasion the last few years. She ambled up behind him, her jaw set. Michel forced down a rising panic and shoved his hands into his pockets. "What's going on, Hendres?"

"You betrayed us," Hendres said, her tone flat. "You betrayed *me*."

"I didn't tip off those Dynize," Michel hissed.

"Don't lie to me."

"I'm not! This is a damned big misunderstanding. We need to go somewhere and talk this out."

Hendres gave a resigned sigh, her lip curling. "I saw you with him, Michel."

"Who?"

"The other day. The day the Dynize found our safe house? I saw you meeting with the Red Hand."

Michel felt the bottom of his stomach drop out. He swallowed hard, searching for words.

Hendres continued. "I came back to find the safe house being watched. I'm not a spy, Michel, but I'm not an idiot, either. I did a little asking around. You were with the Red Hand when Fidelis Jes died. You met with him again the other day. You're a damned traitor. You're going to come with us now and tell us everything you know, or this is going to get very painful for you. Don't make it worse."

Michel's mouth was dry. He knew Blackhats better than most, and he knew the line she'd just fed him was bullshit—if he went with them, it wouldn't matter what he said. Things would get painful either way. He squeezed his eyes closed for a moment, feeling every bit of control slip away from him. This . . . this wasn't how it was supposed to go.

The fingers of his right hand slipped into his knuckle-dusters. "Look," he said, pulling his hands slowly out of his pockets. He heard another footstep behind him, judged the distance, and turned around, cocking Aethel in the side of the jaw.

It took the Iron Rose completely by surprise. Aethel crumpled, and Michel stumbled past her and broke into a run, heading for the alley around the back of the theater.

"You piece of shit," he heard Hendres shout. The words were followed by the blast of a pistol, and he ducked as a bullet ricocheted off the stone facade of the theater just above his head. Hendres swore again, louder, and he heard her footsteps pound after him.

He rounded the side of the theater and headed down the alley, leaping trash and dodging the tents of squatters. Faces watched with concern as he raced by, no doubt drawn out by the sound of the pistol shot. Michel was a couple dozen yards from the next street when a figure loomed in the mouth of the alley.

It was Geddi, a short, stocky Iron Rose with black hair and a beard. Michel skidded to a stop, glancing over his shoulder to see Hendres bearing down on him, fury in her eyes. She held the pistol by the barrel, raised above her head to strike.

Michel's only option was the chimney sweep's ladder going up the side of the theater. He slipped the knuckle-dusters back into his pants pocket and leapt for the lowest rung, pulling himself up. He scrambled up the ladder, only stopping when he reached a window ledge about forty feet up. He hooked his toe between the ladder rung and the wall and took off his jacket, wrapping it around his fist in one swift motion and punching it through the window. He swept off the jagged edges and leapt inside.

He entered through an office that had obviously been ransacked. Papers lay scattered on every surface and a large safe stood open in one corner. Michel dashed across the room and out into the hall, racing through the darkness and down a flight of stairs. He twisted his ankle as he reached the landing, swearing to himself quietly and pausing just long enough to listen for sound of pursuit.

Nothing.

He continued on down to the next floor and then along another hallway, this one pitch-black. He navigated by feel and the memory of a previous visit, when he'd come here to do a favor for one of the theater investors. Within moments he burst out a door, around a narrow turn, and out into the lobby.

The lobby had seen better days. A few squatters had taken up residence below the enormous stained-glass skylight, and they looked up at him as he entered. The front door was blocked by a chair from one of the offices. Michel dismissed it as an exit, worried about running into Aethel or Hendres. He looked down to the other side of the lobby, where he knew that a hidden door allowed performers to pass beneath the theater seats and pop up to entertain guests before a show.

He was just a few steps down the main staircase when there was a sudden crash. The front door burst open, the chair flying, and a very angry-looking Aethel strode through the opening. Michel grabbed the banister and spun himself around, heading back up. He reached the main theater and threw the curtain aside, running recklessly down the aisle with little regard for his twisted ankle or the possibility of breaking something during his descent. Aside from the little light coming in through the way he'd just entered, the theater was pitch-black.

He reached the bottom and threw himself to the floor. Back up at the lobby entrance, he saw a tall silhouette, and Aethel called out, "We're going to find you, traitor. And I'm going to kill you myself."

"So much for talking my way out of this," Michel muttered to himself. He crawled quickly along the floor, around the orchestra pit, and up onto the stage.

"He's down here," he heard Aethel call. A moment later there was a second silhouette briefly outlined by the light from the lobby. Hendres.

"Geddi," Hendres shouted, "see if you can find the gas line for the main theater. Turn on the lights, and he's ours."

Aethel responded with something that Michel could not understand, but he used it to pinpoint her position about halfway up the theater seating. Quietly, he slipped his shoes off and soft-footed his way across the stage and into the wings. He tried to see something—anything—in the inky darkness behind the curtains. His memory of a brief tour of the backstage was fuzzy, and he followed it haphazardly into the darkness, barking his shins on crates and running into stage props.

Michel finally found an empty hall and followed it down a flight of stairs and through two curtains before emerging into the storage area beneath the stage. A dim light coming from street-level windows at the far end of the long room allowed him to pick out the dressing areas and the enormous set pieces. Everything was set up as if for a performance—likely forgotten when news came of the invasion.

Michel paused long enough to put his shoes back on, then began to head to the far side of the room, where he thought he remembered an exit that came out on the other side of the street behind the theater.

The figure that emerged from the next stairwell took him entirely by surprise. He only got a quick glance—enough to see the stocky figure of Geddi coming out of the shadows—before he was grabbed by the shoulders and thrown through an enormous canvas painting of a wooded countryside.

Michel stumbled and fell on the other side, crashing into an array of pulleys with enough force to rattle his teeth. He pulled himself up, only in time to catch Geddi's fist in his kidneys.

He'd seen Geddi work before. Geddi was considered, even among Iron Roses, to be the go-to man for roughing up an enemy of the Chancellor's office. The blow doubled Michel over and sent him reeling into a wooden set piece, gasping for breath and holding up one hand in the vain hope of stalling Geddi's approach.

"He's down here!" Geddi shouted. He reached out and snagged Michel by the arm.

To Michel's surprise, he managed to slip right out of Geddi's grip, allowing him a precious few seconds to backpedal. He snatched his knuckle-dusters from his pocket and forced himself into a boxer's stance, only then noticing that his left arm was coated with blood. Michel didn't have time to consider it. Geddi came on quickly, fists swinging.

Michel stepped to one side, taking a glancing blow to the shoulder, and slammed his fist into Geddi's temple as hard as he could. Geddi took two wobbly steps to one side, touching his cheek, fingers coming away bloody. Michel didn't give him the time to focus. He grabbed one of Geddi's thick forearms and smashed his knuckle-dusters into Geddi's elbow until Geddi began to scream. He pulled back, punched him one more time in the side of the head, and turned and ran.

Michel backtracked, past the stairway he'd descended from and all the way to the wall of the under-stage, where he found a narrow corridor leading into the darkness. Hoping he knew what he was doing, he placed his palms on both walls of the corridor to keep his balance and hurried down it.

He emerged a short time later through a trapdoor into the lobby. The door boomed against the floor as Michel came through it, and he didn't bother to pause as he scrambled out the front door and into the street.

In the light of day, he found his left arm deeply gouged by the glass of the window he'd broken. There was blood on his face from hitting the pulleys, and a deep pain in his side from Geddi's punches. The self-examination took him just a few seconds. He spotted a curious Palo looking out from his tent on the front steps of the theater. "You," Michel said, searching his pockets. He came up with a booklet of meal vouchers for the Dynize market out by the docks. He shoved it into the Palo's hands. "Sell me your jacket. Quickly! And if someone comes out that door, tell them I went that way."

Michel practically pulled the jacket off the poor Palo and hurried across the street and down an alley. He zigzagged through afternoon traffic, hoping his bloody face and arm didn't attract too much attention. He was half a dozen blocks from the theater before he finally allowed himself to rest in a dirty alleyway outside a baker's shop. He stared at the blood dripping from his fingers and the knuckle-dusters still on his other hand, and felt true despair for the first time since the Dynize had invaded.

Hendres knew who he really was. The Blackhats left in the city would come for him.

Michel was now truly alone.

CHAPTER 12

The Fatrastans and Dynize have engaged."

Vlora knelt by a creek and splashed water on her face, cleaning off the grime of the road. She relished the shock of the cold water coming out of the foothills, scrubbing her cheeks, enjoying the moment of respite. She climbed to her feet and dried off with a handkerchief, turning to find the scout standing a few feet behind her. It was late in the afternoon and she knew she would have to give the order to make camp soon, but she wanted her infantry to eke out another mile or two before nightfall.

"What happened?" she asked the scout.

"The Dynize turned to follow us when we left," the scout reported. "They sent a brigade in our tracks, but the Fatrastans engaged around noon and the brigade was forced to pull back."

"Full engagement?" Vlora asked hopefully. "Did you see the battle?"

"No, ma'am. Just skirmishing. Last I saw before coming to report was the Dynize consolidating."

"Very good." Vlora wiped her hands on her handkerchief and returned it to her pocket, dismissing the scout. She turned her face toward the sun and closed her eyes, listening to the tramp of marching soldiers making their way along the winding road of the foothills just a few hundred yards down the creek. A pair of swallows chased each other overhead.

"That was a clever bit of maneuvering."

Vlora jumped, her pistol halfway out of her belt before she spotted Taniel sitting just above her on the hillside. He wore his buckskins, matching satchels hanging from his shoulders, and leaned on his Hrusch rifle with a casual air as if he'd been there for an hour. She felt a spike of annoyance, and couldn't help but think that she wouldn't be in this mess if not for him. "Don't sneak up on me."

"Sorry."

"Don't be sorry. Just don't do it." Vlora returned to her horse for her canteens and filled them at the creek. She was suddenly self-conscious, aware of Taniel's gaze following her. "Did Ka-poel get away fine with the Mad Lancers?"

Taniel spread his legs, laying his rifle across them and checking the flint and pan. "She did. They're southwest of us right now and riding hard. As far as we know, they're not being followed."

This information surprised Vlora. "You can speak with her at a distance?"

"Not exactly." Taniel looked suddenly uncomfortable. "We can sense each other—feel each other's pains and attitudes. It's very rudimentary, but it's a sort of communication."

"That sounds convenient."

"It's a pain in the ass, actually. If she feels pain a hundred miles from me, there's nothing I can do about it, and vice versa. It can be comforting, but it can also make me anxious as pit."

Vlora tried to dredge up some sympathy. There wasn't much to find, so she walked up the side of the hill and sat down next to him. "Tell me about where we're going."

"I don't know much myself," Taniel admitted. "All I could find in Lindet's private archives was a reference to a place called Yellow Creek. As far as I could tell, she'd been working off old Dynize texts to pinpoint the location of the other godstones using translations and some sort of mathematical formula her Privileged had cooked up."

Vlora felt a sudden weight in her stomach. "You mean this could be a wild-goose chase?"

Taniel lifted his hands defensively. "If I thought it was a wild-goose chase, I wouldn't have offered to pay you a rather large fortune for your help. Lindet's not the only one who's been looking for all three godstones, and the two guesses she's mapped out for our missing artifacts are in the same area as my own estimates. That can't be coincidence."

"That doesn't make me feel any better." Vlora mulled it over. No use wishing to be somewhere else—the deal was struck, and she and her men were in this for the long haul. "Yellow Creek. The name sounds familiar."

"It's a mining town," Taniel said. "They—"

Vlora cut him off, remembering an article she'd read in the newspaper almost a year ago. "They struck gold there, right? A big-time haul. Thousands of prospectors from all over the world have gathered there."

"Right."

"What else?"

"That's about all I know." Taniel grimaced. "Well, maybe not *all* I know."

"What?" Vlora asked, her eyes narrowing involuntarily. Taniel himself was enough of a surprise and a mystery that she didn't need anything else. She wanted this job to be as straightforward as possible; track down the godstone, smash anything or anyone who gets in the way, then figure out how to destroy the thing. The moment it was in a thousand pieces she intended to be on a boat back to Adro.

"There's a complication with Yellow Creek. Technically, the land it's on is claimed by three different countries."

"Who?"

"Fatrasta, Brudania, and the Palo Nation."

Vlora wasn't surprised about the first two. Lindet had claimed the entire continent for her country and was fighting for the legality of her claim with half a dozen colonial powers who still held some land in Fatrasta. But the other? She tried to search her memories. The Palo were spread out in a thousand tribes over a landmass almost as large as the Nine. The actual nation of Fatrasta claimed the whole continent of the same name, but in reality only controlled pieces on the eastern and southern coasts. There were millions of square miles of dense forest northwest of the Ironhook Mountains that only a few Kressians had ever managed to penetrate.

The Palo Nation was a coalition of those northern tribes, but she'd never heard anything about them beyond conjecture. To Vlora's knowledge, Lindet's frontier armies had only ever fought tribes who themselves had opposed the Palo Nation, bringing back rumors of walled cities, farmland, and even organized government. It seemed like a fairy tale back when Vlora was putting down insurrections by tribes still living in huts in the swamps.

"I didn't know the Palo Nation claimed land. In fact, I don't know much about them at all."

"No one does," Taniel said, kicking at a clod of dirt with his heel. "Which makes them dangerous. Last I heard, they were contesting gold claims in the Ironhook Mountains. I'm not actually sure what that means, though."

"So we might reach Yellow Creek and find a Palo army waiting for us?"

"I'm guessing we're more likely to find the town being harassed by a skirmishing party. Either way, we should be ready for violence."

Vlora pursed her lips. "I suppose that's my job, anyway." She considered the facts for a few moments, realizing how little she knew.

"I don't want to march into contested territory without scouting it first."

"I wouldn't expect you to," Taniel said. "But if you want to make camp and scout out Yellow Creek, you can't take long."

"Why not?"

"Because at some point, Lindet is going to find out what we're up to and send a whole field army to come bury us."

"Or," Vlora mused, "the Dynize will crush Lindet's troops and try to figure out where we went."

"Either one."

Vlora got to her feet, dusting off her trousers. "It's settled, then."

She had the brief satisfaction of seeing Taniel surprised as she got on her horse. "What is?" he asked.

"We have to get moving. I'm going to find Olem."

Olem was at the rear of the army, riding along behind the last few carts of provisions in the long and winding column. He wore a thoughtful expression, leaning back in his saddle with a hand gently patting his horse's flank as he hummed a tune.

"I just sent someone to find you," he said by way of greeting.

Vlora waited by the road and then nudged her horse up next to his, letting them walk together. "Anything important?" she asked.

"Another of our rear scouts just reported in. The Dynize and Fatrastan field armies skirmished all afternoon, but it looks like they've made camp on either side of the river and are content to feel each other out—for now."

"That could be ideal for us."

"Could be," Olem agreed. "Both armies have a handful of scouts following us. They want to know where we're headed."

That was decidedly *not* ideal. They couldn't hide a whole army, of course, not even up in the Ironhook foothills, but she'd hoped to make a clean break that would keep their location a mystery for at least a few weeks. "How many horses did we keep for ourselves?"

"Sixty dragoons," Olem said. "Everyone else went with Styke."

Vlora chewed on the number, watching as Taniel rode over a nearby hill and joined them. "Leave twenty of them behind to set some ambushes," she told Olem. "Scare off the scouts or delay them; just buy us a little more time until they figure out where we're heading. I don't want either the Fatrastans or Dynize following us to Yellow Creek."

"Will do."

"With any luck, the two armies will be so tied up with each other that we're an afterthought. At least for now." She glanced at Taniel, who'd hung his rifle from his saddle and pulled out a sketchbook. He began to sketch quickly, his eyes on the hillside to their left, expertly dashing bits of charcoal against the paper along with the cadence of his horse's gait. "We have a problem," she said to Olem.

"Which is?"

"We know nothing about what we're walking into."

"Yellow Creek?" Olem produced a prerolled cigarette from his pocket and offered it to Vlora, then to Taniel. They both shook their heads. He shrugged and lit it for himself. "It's a gold-rush town. I've got nothing more than that."

"That's what Taniel said, too," Vlora said, jerking her thumb at Taniel, who'd covered half the page of his sketchbook in charcoal markings in less than a minute. "But that doesn't really help us."

"What do you propose?" Olem asked.

Vlora hesitated. "You're not going to like this."

"You want to go ahead and scout it yourself, don't you?" Olem ashed his cigarette and scowled at Vlora. "I definitely won't like that."

"We can't just ride in at the head of an army. At best the locals will send runners to all the closest cities asking for help, thinking we're trying to move in on their claims. At worst, we'll run into a stubborn militia and won't even be able to get into the town without bloodshed."

Olem fixed her with a long, steady gaze. "And sending me with a squad isn't an option?"

"Even in plain clothes, you'll stand out," Vlora replied. "A squad of soldiers always *looks* like a squad of soldiers, even when dressing down."

Taniel suddenly put away his charcoal, flipping the leather cover over his sketchbook before she could see what he'd been drawing. He looked from Vlora to Olem, then said, "There isn't anything in Yellow Creek that Vlora and I can't handle."

"I don't remember inviting you," Vlora said, turning to Taniel.

"Do *you* know what we're looking for?" Taniel asked.

"An obelisk seeped in sorcery and covered in Dynize writing."

"Maybe."

"What do you mean, *maybe*?"

"We have no idea if the godstones all look the same," Taniel said. "Until Michel told me about the one outside Landfall, I thought I was looking for an artifact the size of a pair of saddlebags. We still might be. Besides, my senses are more highly tuned than yours. If we get within a hundred yards or so of the godstone, I should be able to find it."

Vlora and Olem exchanged a glance. "Give us a minute," she told Taniel. She pulled gently on her reins, coming to a stop while Olem did the same. They waited for almost a minute as the column marched on, until they wouldn't be overheard even by Taniel's powder-mage senses.

"Do you trust him?" Olem asked.

It was a question Vlora had been mulling over for weeks. "I trust him to not get me killed."

"And beyond that?"

"I have no idea," she confessed. "I'm still not even sure what he is. Bo told me he's become something more than just a powder mage—he's transcended into something new." She considered Borbador—her and Taniel's mutual adopted brother—wishing briefly that he was riding alongside her. *He* would know what to make of Taniel.

Olem took a drag on his cigarette. "That doesn't give me a lot of confidence. You should at least take our mages with you."

"And leave the army undefended against Privileged or bone-eyes?" Vlora shook her head. "Not a chance."

"Just one," Olem pressed. "Take Norrine. She's known Taniel for longer than you have. She'll watch both of your backs, and can pull you out of trouble if Taniel gets himself into something only he can handle."

"No. You need her here. Look, I can handle Taniel. I can handle a gold-rush town. You've got to trust me on this. I'm going to leave you in command and I need to know that you're focused on that and not spending all your energy worrying about me."

Olem looked at her glumly. He spat into the weeds and let out a sigh. "Fine."

"Good. As long as no one is on our tail, you can let the army take it easy from here to Yellow Creek. Find somewhere a dozen miles outside the city to camp and send someone in to find us. With any luck we'll have already destroyed the godstone and be ready to leave."

"You don't have that much luck."

"No," Vlora agreed. "I don't." She paused, thinking about Bo again. "Do me another favor."

"What's that?"

"Dispatch a letter to Adopest. Send three copies with three different couriers so you know it gets there."

"From here? It'll be six weeks on the fastest ship."

"Send it anyway. I want Bo to know what's going on here. Tell him about the godstones, and that both Lindet and the Dynize want to use them."

Olem barked a laugh. "That sounds like a trail of catnip for a kitten. Do you really want Bo to come here? I'm not entirely certain he won't throw his own hat in the ring to become a god."

"Bo is a lot of things, but power hungry is not one of them. He may show up with the intent to study the damn things, but..." She trailed off.

"But what?"

"But I think having him here would do more good than harm. If only slightly." She paused. "Oh, and tell him to bring his better half. I wouldn't mind having the strongest Privileged in the Nine standing over my shoulder."

"I know they're your friends," Olem said softly, "but involving them could be dangerous."

"Then I better hurry," Vlora replied. "So that this whole business is finished before Bo can even set sail." She flipped her reins, riding to catch up with the army and calling over her shoulder, "I leave first thing in the morning. I expect to see you in my tent at sundown, Colonel."

CHAPTER 13

After twenty-four hours, Michel still couldn't stop the bleeding.

There were three long slices down his left arm, all from the glass at the theater. One was manageable, but the other two were far worse than he'd first expected. His one-handed stitch job was sloppy at best—constantly pulling out—and it seemed as if the cuts began to bleed again every time he moved.

He stayed in Taniel's hovel of a safe house for the entire morning, trying to fix the stitches while he considered his next course of action. He started by cursing himself for allowing Hendres to follow him that afternoon he met with Taniel. He hadn't even considered that she might, and the oversight had cost him both her friendship and whatever resources were still left to the Blackhats in Landfall. Manpower, food, and safe houses were all compromised.

He wondered if, perhaps, he could still use Blackhat resources sparingly. Hendres couldn't spread the word *that* far, not with the Dynize hunting down any Blackhat left in the city. He might be able to get to some of his contacts first, throwing suspicion on Hendres. If he found the Gold Roses that Taniel said had stayed behind... well, that would be something.

Michel made a list of the contacts he knew had remained in the city. It was pitifully short, and even shorter when he crossed off the ones that Hendres knew about. Despair began to set in—quietly at first, nagging at the back of his mind, then slowly growing. The pain from his arm made it difficult to think straight.

The more he considered that he was in an occupied city, cut off from Taniel and now friendless, the more he considered abandoning Taniel's mission and fleeing Landfall. Was this Dynize informant really important enough to face these odds?

He forced himself to breathe deeply, drinking straight from a bottle of whiskey to dull the pain.

He wasn't completely friendless. Taniel had left him with a number of contacts. They were only to be used in an emergency, but this was beginning to feel as if it qualified. Michel needed information, resources, and best of all—someone who could stitch up his arm. He picked a name from his mental list of Taniel's contacts. It had been marked specifically as someone Michel could trust to speak freely around, which sounded like a damned good start.

Michel wrapped his left arm tightly and put on a shirt and jacket, then headed out into the street. He wore a flatcap and a high-collared style of jacket he had not worn around Hendres. The journey was uneventful, and he soon found himself entering a small building on the northern side of the Hadshaw Gorge, marked with the single word MORGUE.

"This isn't a good idea," he whispered to himself.

"Taniel said he could be trusted."

Michel licked his lips. "I'm not talking about that. The morgue is underground. I don't know all the exits."

"Don't be a baby," he responded to himself. "It's not a doctor, but a mortician is going to be able to stitch you up better than you can yourself. Get in there."

Reluctantly, he obeyed his own promptings. There was an empty reception desk and little else but a stairway that led down into the plateau, so Michel followed it down, thankful for the gas lamps that lit every landing. The air grew cool, and he soon picked up the butcher-like smell of corpses and the harsh, chemical scent of embalming fluid. The staircase finally ended, leaving him in a long, wide hallway cut into the rock. Open doors led off either side of the hall, and as he passed them, he saw dozens of bodies in various states of undress and of obviously diverse deaths laid out on marble slabs.

He had yet to spot anyone living, when he heard the gentle sound of humming coming from the final doorway on the left.

Michel approached the open door and took a moment to examine the man standing inside. He was an albino, tall and slim with a receding hairline in a shock of fine white hair. He stood straight, chin lifted, peering down his nose through a pair of green-tinted glasses at a body laid out in front of him. As Michel watched, the albino painted black dotted lines on the corpse with a tiny brush, stopping occasionally to examine his work and rub out one of the lines with his thumb before correcting it.

Michel cleared his throat.

The albino looked up at him, blinking in surprise behind those green-tinted glasses. "Ah, hello? I'm sorry, I didn't see you there. If you're dropping off, we're almost out of space, but you can put up to three more bodies in room seven."

"I'm not dropping off," Michel responded. "I'm looking for someone."

"I see." The albino spoke in clean, crisp Adran, and Michel immediately pegged him as well studied. It was the accent of someone with the best education. "I am the only one here, unfortunately. Unless you're looking for me, I'm afraid I'll have to ask you to go. The morgue is not open to the public."

"Are you Emerald?"

The albino examined Michel for a moment before making a gentle *hmm* sound and setting down his paintbrush. He tapped his green-tinted glasses. "Emerald is a nickname. My real name is Kevi Karivenrian, and I am the chief mortician at the Landfall City Morgue."

"Right. You're the one I'm looking for." Michel took off his jacket and rolled up his sleeve to reveal blood-soaked bandages. "If it's not too much trouble, I need you to stitch this up for me."

Emerald looked taken aback. "You want a doctor, sir. I think someone has sent you to me as a joke." His eyes narrowed. "Tell me, who gave you that name? Emerald? Only my friends know me by that."

"Look, I don't know you, but we have a mutual friend. His name is Taniel."

Emerald made that *hmm* sound again. "I see. And you are?"

"Michel Bravis, at your service. Or rather, I'm hoping you'll be at mine." Michel indicated his wounded arm with a hopefully charming smile.

"Do you have a password?"

" 'Touch the noontime bells,' " Michel responded. It was the last password he'd used with any of Taniel's people. He hoped it was current.

" 'And listen to them ring,' " Emerald finished. "Well, then, Michel Bravis, give me your arm." He took Michel gently by the shoulder and led him to a workbench in the corner, where he quickly began to unwrap Michel's bandages. "I was told you'd only contact me in the event of an emergency," he spoke as he worked, a flash of annoyance crossing his face. "Taniel left town just five days ago. Has it all gone wrong so quickly?"

Michel considered how to answer. Taniel had expressed complete trust in his contacts, but he hadn't actually told Michel how much information they knew. Emerald knew both Taniel *and* Michel's real names, so that was a start. "It hasn't gone...well."

"I would say it hasn't." Emerald finished unwrapping the arm and turned it one way, then the other, to examine the three cuts. "I have seen rheumatic blind men make tighter stitches than these."

"Thanks," Michel said flatly. "Can you fix them?"

"I have doctorates from four different medical colleges. If I can't do a better job than this, I should kill myself now." He rummaged through his workbench before coming up with a needle and thread. Without warning, he began to pick out Michel's stitches.

"Ow."

"Oh, yes. This will sting a little. Tell me, Michel, does Taniel know that the Blackhats have turned on you? Or was that after he left?" Michel tried to pull his arm away, but Emerald snatched him by the bicep with his free hand. "Hold still, please."

Michel swore under his breath. "How much do you know?"

"You don't know whether to trust me," Emerald stated. He finished pulling the stitches from one cut and began to redo them, working quickly and precisely.

"That's about the size of it."

"I know a lot," Emerald said. "I have been friends with Taniel and Ka-poel for about eight years now. Ka-poel uses my spare mortuary rooms to practice her blood magic. I know about the Red Hand and your infiltration of the Blackhats—though he only filled me in on that last week. I do not know why you are still in the city, and I will not ask."

Michel didn't know how to respond. He winced as Emerald tightened a stitch. "Well. That's . . . a lot more than I expected."

"I am Taniel's eyes and ears within Landfall."

"You're a spy."

"Indeed I am."

Michel processed this information. He had expected to be sent to "a guy who knows a guy," not directly to Taniel's spymaster. He realized immediately how dangerous it was for them to meet directly like this and why Taniel had instructed to only meet his contacts in an emergency. If either Michel or Emerald were caught and tortured, they could reveal the whereabouts of the other. "He didn't tell me," Michel said quietly.

"He wouldn't have."

"You were the only contact on his list that he said could be trusted implicitly."

Emerald paused his stitching and rested his elbows on the workbench before looking at Michel over his glasses and letting out a soft sigh. "I apologize for being cold. You're not a stupid man, so I'm guessing you've already realized the risks you took coming here."

"I have."

"But since my job is to know things, I am well aware of your break with the Blackhats."

Michel hesitated. Every bit of information that Emerald shared could be a weapon against either of them. "You have eyes in the Blackhats?"

"I do."

"I'm not sure myself how bad it is," Michel admitted. "My companion—Hendres—followed me to my meeting with Taniel. Then the Dynize found our safe house, and she assumed that I'm working for both the Red Hand and the Dynize."

"Sloppy."

"I know."

"No, I meant these stitches." Emerald paused. "But yes, allowing her to follow you was sloppy as well. I know this: There is a Gold Rose remaining in the city."

"Taniel told me."

Emerald went on as if he'd not been interrupted. "I'm not sure which Gold Rose was left behind, but they are attempting to re-form the Blackhats as a spy network to funnel information back to Lindet. Hendres has made contact with them. Most of the Blackhats are now on the alert, and know to look out for you."

"Shit." There went Michel's possibility of creating a schism within the Blackhats. He couldn't risk using their caches or safe houses now, either. One chance meeting could get him killed—or worse, captured. "Do I have any chance of getting back in with them?"

"That's not for me to judge," Emerald said. "But I do know that several Blackhats who remained behind were with Fidelis Jes when he died. They corroborated Hendres's story. They are very confident that you are a traitor."

"So much for that." Michel closed his eyes, trying to ignore the stab-and-pull of Emerald's needle. He had a whole boatload of new enemies, many of whom knew what he looked like. The escape routes he and Hendres had put together could no longer be risked, which meant he'd have to figure out another way of getting Taniel's informant out of the city. If he could find her. "Hendres thought I tipped off the Dynize, but I didn't. Any idea who did?"

Emerald shook his head.

"Maybe it was just bad luck," Michel grunted.

"Probably," Emerald said. "The Dynize have managed to capture or turn a few Bronze Roses, which compromises safe houses. They've also increased their patrols and random searches since the bombing."

"So, who is responsible for the bombings?"

"I'm afraid I haven't found out yet. There was another this morning—a café was destroyed when someone lit a fused artillery shell and rolled it among a group of Dynize officers. Managed to kill about half of them, along with nine civilians."

Michel swore. It was probably some misguided Blackhat cell, attempting to use force to scare the Dynize out. It was also stupid; random killings would turn the population against the Blackhats and only serve to increase Dynize aggression. That wasn't his problem anymore, though. His mind raced as he moved on, mentally writing off the Blackhats and trying to shift his way of thinking.

He had to focus on staying alive while he found this Mara woman whom Taniel needed moved. "Do you have any resources you can lend me?"

Emerald finished the stitches on one of the cuts. He dabbed away the blood gently with a wet cloth and smiled at his handiwork. "I will give you whatever information I can, but I'm afraid information is all I can give you. I will not risk allowing you access to anything that will jeopardize my position here."

"Understood," Michel said tightly. He swore on the inside. Emerald likely had contacts, escape routes, supplies, safe houses. All of that was closed to Michel, and it annoyed the pit out of him. But he understood why. "How the pit are you able to run Taniel's spy ring from a public morgue?"

Emerald gave him a coy smile. "I've run the Landfall City Morgue for over twenty years, under three governments. The occupying administration did the exact same thing Lindet did when she took over the country a decade ago: They saw that I was running a tight ship and left me to my own devices."

"That's it?"

"Public morgues aren't so different from sewage systems. People only notice them when they're run badly. Besides, I'm a widely published physician who's never had a drop of politics in his writing. I take care of the messy business of bodies and in exchange, the government leaves me to my work. Why should any administration look closer than that?"

Michel decided not to ask what, exactly, his work entailed. "Hiding in plain sight. Intriguing. What can you tell me about the Dynize?"

"What do you want to know?" Emerald started on the next cut.

"Who is in charge? Wait, no. Who is in charge of their counterespionage? Who is the one giving out rewards for any Blackhat who comes over to their side?"

Emerald gave Michel a considering glance, his lips pursed.

"You're not thinking about doing something stupid, are you? If the bone-eyes get ahold of you ..."

"I know the risks. Right now, I just need to know what I'm up against."

Emerald clearly didn't believe him. "His name is Meln-Yaret. His title translates to something roughly akin to 'minister of scrolls.'"

"Scrolls?"

"The connotation is probably closer to 'minister of information.' I haven't been able to find out much about him beyond the fact that he exists. I have no idea how much power his title actually holds, or where he stands in the Dynize hierarchy. He is, apparently, well liked by his underlings. Other than that ...?" Emerald shrugged.

"Right." Michel thought over the archaic-sounding title and tried to picture the man who would hold it. In his mind's eye, this Meln-Yaret looked like a stern librarian or the headmaster of a religious school. Tall, with graying hair and angular features. He realized after a moment that he was picturing a redhead Fidelis Jes. "Anything else you can tell me about the Dynize?"

Emerald didn't answer until he'd finished up the next set of stitches. "They are very efficient. They are preparing a census of the city to find out how many people remain and who they are. Their finest minds are studying Kressian technology. They want to upgrade their gunsmithing and metallurgy to compete with ours, and I suspect that they'll begin retooling Landfall's factories by the end of summer to upgrade their armies."

Michel reeled. "They're really moving that quickly?"

"They've planned for this," Emerald said. "I don't know for how long, but it may be decades. They prepared for Fatrasta's armies and sorcery and even for Lindet. One of the few things they underestimated was the military-technology gap. They assumed that rifling and sword bayonets wouldn't play as big of a part as it did. If they eliminate that gap, they believe the war will be won by the end of next year."

"Pit," Michel breathed.

"Don't get me wrong," Emerald continued. "They're also almost stupidly cocky. Most of their generals believe this war will be over by winter, and then they can take their time figuring out the god-stones and preparing their armies for anything the Nine decides to throw at them." He finished one last tug at the stitches. "However, I'm just passing on what whispers I've heard. I'm not a military man myself."

Michel examined his arm. The stitches felt tight and uncomfortable, but they were as precise as if they'd been done by a machine. "I'm not, either. I'll leave all that to Taniel."

"And in the meantime?"

"In the meantime," Michel said, thinking of Taniel's informant, "I have my own tasks to accomplish." He wondered how quickly he could even find this woman, and if the war would already be lost by then. Strictly speaking, the war wasn't between the Dynize and Taniel's faction of Palo. But if Fatrasta fell, Michel had little doubt that the Dynize would crush any other opposition to their rule. The longer Lindet managed to hold out, the longer Michel had to accomplish his task. "I appreciate the help," Michel told Emerald. "I need to get out and clear my head."

Emerald politely inclined his head. "I hope I was of some use. Just remember that in the future..."

"Only in an emergency."

"Precisely."

Michel left the morgue, stewing on all this new information, and headed to one of the few remaining markets in the city, where he procured wood ash and vinegar. He returned to his safe house, where he created a mixture of the two and let it sit in his hair for part of the afternoon. When he washed it out, his hair was a shocking dirty blond. He carefully shaved the stubble from his face, leaving only a mustache.

He practiced holding faces in the mirror, subtly changing the depths of his cheeks and the squint of his eyes until he found something that he could keep up steadily in public. When he finally looked at the finished transformation, he barely recognized himself.

He leaned over the washbasin, staring at himself in the mirror, taking several long, deep breaths before fetching his shoes. Removing the sole of the left shoe, he produced both his own Gold Rose and the Platinum Rose he took off Fidelis Jes's body a month ago. He practiced his best confident smile in the mirror.

Wearing a new jacket, he headed for the capitol building.

He approached the guards out front, asking several before he found one who spoke passable Palo. "I'm looking for Meln-Yaret," Michel said. "Can I see him?"

"Only with an appointment."

"I understand he wants information."

"That is true."

"And he'll pay for it?"

"Yes."

"Good. Take him a message for me. Tell him my name is Michel Bravis, and I would like to help him dismantle the Blackhat presence in Landfall." Michel produced the Gold Rose and gave it to the guard. "When you tell him, show him this."

CHAPTER 14

The Mad Lancers rode hard after splitting with the Riflejacks, circumventing the Fatrastan Army and heading southwest across the countryside. Plantations seemed to stretch forever in every direction, broken only by the slight roll of the land and lines of willow and birch that divided the fields. Every plantation they passed told the same story—laborers scurrying in the fields to try to get in an early harvest, while the households packed up everything of value and prepared to head toward safety.

Styke wondered if safety was even an option at this point. Each new town was filled with panicked rumors—that the Dynize had landed on the west, south, and east coasts. That nothing within fifty miles of the ocean was safe from their barbarity. A passing farmer claimed that Swinshire had been burned to the ground, while a cobbler said that Redstone itself was under siege.

The lancers took roads when they could and forged their own paths across the vast plantation fields when they couldn't. At this point, Styke wanted nothing more than speed. They had a thousand men and three times as many horses. Subtlety was not an option, and he had an itch between his shoulders that told him they were being followed.

He called a stop on the afternoon of the third day to let their horses rest and graze, regrouping in a field next to one of the thousands of nameless roads that crisscrossed Fatrasta.

Styke leaned on his saddle just off the road, letting Amrec graze without a harness. Celine lay on her stomach in the grass, feet bare, picking the heads off flowers with her toes. Normally, Styke would enjoy watching her foolery for a few quiet minutes, but he found his gaze drawn to the bone-eye witch wandering among the men and horses.

Ka-poel hadn't communicated in three days, sticking to herself at the back of the column, stopping frequently to scramble in the dust and then riding hard to catch up. Sometimes she ranged on ahead with the scouts, sniffing the air like a bloodhound, her fingers pressing against the wind as if touching a pane of glass.

Styke found himself drawn to her—she was amusing to watch in much the same way as Celine—but he had an inkling that her antics had a much darker purpose than childlike wonder, and he didn't like it.

"Have you found me a horse?"

Styke pulled himself away from watching Ka-poel and turned his attention to Celine. "Still looking," he said. "Anyone catch your eye from our reserves?"

Celine plucked a piece of grass and stuck it between her teeth. "You said I can't have any of the horses that someone is already riding."

"Right. Don't take a man's horse. Not unless you've paid him, killed him, or stolen it fair and square."

Celine pouted. "And I can't steal from our men."

"No, you cannot."

"Then, no. I haven't found a horse I like."

The problem, Styke found, was that first-rate horses were rare.

Most of the men in his cavalry were riding second-rate horses already, and there wasn't a single first-rate horse left that didn't have a saddle on it.

Now, there was nothing wrong with a second-rate horse. They could be strong, fast, smart, dependable, but not all of the above. He wanted Celine to have a creature that wouldn't let her down, one she could bond with. He'd find it one of these days, but not among the horses they had with them.

Until then, she'd ride with either him or Sunin.

"Colonel," a voice called. Styke looked up to find Zac and Markus riding up the column toward him. The two brothers, in addition to their normal rags, tended to ride junk horses that none of his other lancers would spare a glance. Perhaps it was part of their scouting disguise, but Styke didn't understand it himself. A good horse was worth more than any amount of blending in.

Styke nodded to the pair as they approached.

Zac snapped a sloppy salute. "Colonel, we had a question, sir."

"What's that?"

"Are we heading on a fixed course?"

Styke cocked an eyebrow. "What do you mean?"

"This direction we've been going. We continuing on for the next few days?"

"Why?"

Markus cleared his throat. "Because, sir, you're going to miss Bad Tenny Wiles."

Styke perked up. "That's right. He's nearby, isn't he?"

"Yes, sir. He owns a plantation about forty miles south of here. Big ol' building right next to a bend in a stream, surrounded by birches. You know the Cottonseed tributary?"

Styke pictured a map in his head, considering the location. He nodded.

"The plantation sits on the land near the spring that feeds the tributary."

"Ah. I think I might know the plantation itself. Not far from where we picked up Little Gamble during the war?"

"That's right."

Styke nodded to himself, thoughts turning. "Thanks for that. Where's Ibana?"

"Bit farther back, sir."

Styke headed that direction and soon found Ibana dismounted by an old stump. Her warhorse grazed nearby, and she and Jackal bent over a map. "Since when do you use a map?" he asked Ibana.

"It's been almost six years since I've crossed this part of the country," Ibana retorted. "I'd like to know what we're looking at the next few hundred miles."

Styke couldn't fault that logic. He shouldered his way in to stand between them and squinted at the tiny roads and town names. It took a few moments for his eyes to adjust to the way the map was drawn, and he was soon picking out old haunts and prominent landmarks, orienting himself to their location.

"We're here," Ibana said. She pointed to their location, then drew an imaginary line with her finger cutting north of Little Starland and going straight to the Hammer on the west coast of Fatrasta. "Ka-poel says that our search is going to start somewhere around here. You still want to head straight across the middle of the continent?"

Styke considered the question. "Jackal, are your spirits telling you anything useful?"

"Hard to keep up a good conversation with the dead while we ride," Jackal responded, his voice matter-of-fact. Ibana gave Styke an irritated look, as if to say, *Don't encourage him.* She was not, she had made it clear, a believer in Jackal's ability to talk to spirits. "However," Jackal continued, "there are a lot of dead coming from the coasts—all the coasts. There's fighting in every direction. Swinshire is almost certainly gone. Maybe Little Starland, too."

"That's not good. Are we going to run into any serious enemies?"

Neither Ibana nor Jackal seemed to know the answer to the question. Hesitantly, Ibana said, "*If* the fighting is still on the coasts, then we shouldn't have too much of a problem till we reach the Hammer. We might run into a Fatrastan field army, but they should be pretty preoccupied with reaching the front line. I think we're safe making a beeline to the Hammer." She tapped on a dot on the map. "Once we reach Belltower, though, things will get tricky. And if Lindet finds out what we're up to..."

The idea did not please Styke. "We'll just have to keep her in the dark as long as possible. Pit, our own men don't even know what we're really up to. How is she going to find out?"

"Since when has Lindet *not* known exactly what was going on?" Ibana countered.

"Right. You remember our talk with Agoston?"

"I remember cleaning his blood spatter off of my jacket."

"Markus and Zac say that Bad Tenny Wiles is about forty miles south of our current position."

Ibana's eyes narrowed. "You want us to change directions."

"Nah. This is something I'm going to handle myself. I want you to keep heading toward our objective." He turned his attention back to the map, poring over the roads and towns before pointing to one about eighty miles to their southwest. "I'll catch up with you here," he said. "In a week. Shouldn't take longer. If things get hairy, you can keep moving and I'll find you farther down the road."

"All right. Make it quick."

"Have you ever known me to linger over a kill?" Styke ended the conversation by rolling up the map and handing it to Jackal. He returned to Amrec and began to put the saddle back on while Celine still lay in the grass nearby.

"You're going to ride with Sunin for the next few days," Styke told her.

Celine rolled over, staring at him. "Why?"

"Because I've got an errand to run. I'll catch up with you later."

"Oh?" Celine sat up. "You going to kill someone?"

"What gives you that idea?"

"Rumors going around the lancers that you found out about some traitors—the ones who sent you to the firing squad."

Markus and Zac and their damned loose lips. Styke swore under his breath. "Yeah," he answered half-heartedly. "I'm going to kill someone."

"I want to come."

"You can't."

"You took me into battle, but you won't take me to kill one man?"

Styke finished with the buckles and ran his hand along Amrec's flank, then patted him on the nose. He thought through a dozen reasons why this was different, knowing that Celine would fight him about each one. Truthfully, he could move quicker and quieter without her. On the other hand, she was his responsibility. Handing her to Sunin every time he wanted her out of the way felt a lot like how his father had treated him as a boy.

The thought caused a sour feeling in Styke's stomach.

"Fine," he said. "Let's go."

They slipped away from the lancers and turned south, quickly putting a hill between them and the cavalry. Styke preferred to be away before anyone noticed, and back before anyone had the courage to ask Ibana questions, and they were almost a mile down the road before a horse caught up with them at a gallop.

It was Ka-poel. She put her horse in front of Amrec, forcing Styke to pull on the reins.

Her hands moved in a quick, demanding flurry. He could guess what she wanted to know, but instead he just sighed. "I have no idea what you're saying."

Ka-poel snorted at him. She produced a piece of slate, like children in a schoolhouse might use to practice sums, and wrote out a sentence, showing it to him. *Where are you going?*

"Business," Styke said. "I'll meet up with you again next week. Stay with Ibana and the lancers."

No.

"What do you mean?"

I'm coming, Ka-poel scribbled.

Styke looked down at Celine. "What is this? Are the two of you in cahoots? I've got work to do, and I can't protect you by myself. Stay with the lancers."

I don't need a bodyguard.

"Damn it." Styke rubbed his eyes, wishing she'd just turn around and go away. She made him uneasy at best, and he needed his mind clear for this. Having Celine along was already trying enough. "Ibana thinks you're with her."

I told her I'm going with you.

"I don't take orders from you, girl," Styke warned.

Most people shied away when Styke became visibly annoyed. Ka-poel just smiled at him coldly. She wrote, *I ride with you or I follow. Choose.*

Styke stared at her for a few moments, then ran his hand through his hair. "Have it your way. Let's move."

CHAPTER 15

Michel waited just inside the capitol building for nearly an hour, trying to look nonchalant under the watchful eye of three Dynize soldiers. He found a blank piece of paper in one of his pockets and practiced folding it into various shapes, holding each one up for the purview of his silent guards. They continued to watch, unmoving, unresponsive, though Michel swore that he saw a hint of bemusement in the eyes of one of them.

His patience was finally rewarded by the arrival of a middle-aged woman wearing a soldier's uniform without the customary Dynize breastplate. She had fire-red hair and a gentle face that Michel immediately associated with an indulgent governess. She was unarmed, and her turquoise uniform was adorned with the stylized symbol of a dagger poised above a cup just above her heart. Crow's feathers dangled from her earrings.

When she arrived, Michel's guards seemed to stiffen, and she examined Michel with a detached, unimpressed gaze. "You are the one who brought the Rose?" she asked in passable Palo.

"I am."

"Follow me."

Michel glanced over his shoulder toward the door, trying not to let his misgivings get the best of him. This was *probably* a terrible idea. He didn't know the Dynize—not their hierarchy or customs or laws. He didn't know how to navigate their world, and he was stepping in blind hoping that this Meln-Yaret was smart enough to see the value in Michel's willing cooperation.

After a few more seconds of hesitation, he followed the woman down the hall.

They walked side by side past rows of offices. They passed soldiers and bureaucrats, officers and errand boys. It was a strange sight, seeing redheads—whom Michel had so long associated only with the Palo—in the government offices, but other than that change everything looked much the same as it did before the occupation. If there had been any particular chaos here after Lindet fled, it had long since been cleaned up, and it appeared that no damage had been done during the fighting.

The woman led him down the first flight of stairs and past several turns, then a whole other set of stairs down into the bowels of the building. Michel began to grow concerned as they left daylight behind and now had to depend on gas lanterns, and was about to ask their destination when the woman stopped and opened a door, indicating with a gentle smile that Michel should step inside.

"I want to see Meln-Yaret," Michel said.

"I know."

"Will I?"

"Please." She gestured to the door once more, and Michel cautiously stepped into the doorway. The room inside was lit by a single lamp. It was small, almost claustrophobic, and it had a drain in the center of the floor.

"Look," Michel said, "I—" He was suddenly driven to his knees, a pain erupting from his left shoulder. His entire left arm went numb, his vision spotty, and he gasped out loud as he fell. He turned, attempting to scramble away—and farther into the dank room—only to see the woman standing above him with a blackjack held casually in one hand and a wan smile on her face. "Wha...?" Michel tried to ask.

The woman lashed out at his chest with one foot, connecting painfully, and Michel tried to retreat farther, only to come up against the wall. He tried to yell or speak, but all that came out was a breathless whimper.

She came at him with the blackjack, and he raised his numb left arm, only to remember too late that it was the same arm that Emerald had stitched mere hours ago. The blow landed hard, causing him to gasp once more. He dug into his pocket with his right hand, but had left his knuckle-dusters back at the safe house. When she drew back to kick him again, he moved to one side to cause a glancing blow, then attempted to tackle her by the legs.

The woman stumbled, nearly fell, then almost casually swatted Michel just above the ear with the blackjack. It wasn't even a hard blow, but Michel saw darkness for several seconds before his vision returned, and a horrifying pain shot through his head. He let go of her legs, wrapping his arms around his head, and attempted to curl into a ball to await the next blow.

"Devin-Forgula!" a man's voice barked.

The next blow never came. Michel hazarded a glance through blurry vision. He saw the woman standing over him, turned toward the hallway, where two men had appeared. One of them was young—probably about Michel's age, in his midtwenties—and had a bald head and a short, lean frame. This one stared at the woman with outright antagonism. The second man was old, probably in his forties, with a beer belly and two fingers missing on his right hand.

The older man spoke, and it was obvious it was he who'd called out the name. "Devin-Forgula," he said again, his voice quiet but reprimanding. "Get out." The words were in Dynize, but close enough to their Palo counterparts that Michel understood.

The woman answered too quickly for Michel to follow.

"Get out," the older man repeated.

The woman wiped her blackjack off on her sleeve and left at a brisk stride without looking back.

Michel eyed his saviors, trying to focus on them rather than on the immense pain in his arm, head, and shoulder. The older man watched Forgula go, then gave an exasperated sigh and stepped into the room. He bent over Michel, pulling Michel's arm gently but firmly out of the way and examining the side of his head. "His head is bleeding," he said in Palo. "And his arm. Can you stand?" The question was directed at Michel, but it took his addled brain a moment to register it. Slowly, he crawled to his knees and then, with the help of the younger man, up to his feet.

He limped after the two men. Neither helped him when he moved slowly on the stairs, but they did not hurry him, either. They headed to the next floor, where they found an empty room. They were still in the basement of the capitol building, but natural light came in through a high window and there was a rug and chairs here— probably the office of a low-level bureaucrat under Lindet's regime.

Michel sat in one chair, head in his hands, watching blood drip from his arm onto the rug. He felt the eyes of both his new companions but did not look up at them. He was doing all he could not to throw up.

"Forgula says that you are a Blackhat spy," the older man said. "Is that true?"

"I was," Michel responded, stressing the second word.

"But no more?"

"I...understand that you are offering rewards and amnesty to Blackhats who switch sides."

"Switch sides." The man laughed. "That's one way of putting it. Yes, that is the offer."

"That woman—"

"Forgula is not a member of my Household," the man said, his tone shifting to anger. "She serves another master—one who believes that enemies should be slaughtered rather than turned into allies. Someone told her about this little trinket, and she decided to take matters into her own hands before I could respond."

Michel finally looked up to find the older man holding his Gold Rose, turning it in his fingers to examine the details in the light. "You're Meln-Yaret?" Michel asked.

"I am." The man smiled, and Michel could see that it was both tired and genuine—the smile of, as Silver Rose Blasdell used to say, *a man who had to work for a living.* "I apologize for letting Forgula get her claws into you. That had to have been"—he eyed Michel's arm—"unpleasant."

"That's one way of putting it."

Meln-Yaret gave a bemused snort. "Forgive me," he said, gesturing to his younger companion. "This is Devin-Tenik. He is one of my cupbearers." Michel took a longer look at Devin-Tenik, his eyes finally starting to clear, and realized something strange: Devin-Tenik didn't have the subtle facial markers that differentiated the Dynize from the Palo. His face was softer, his eyebrows farther apart, and his chin slightly weaker. If he hadn't been wearing a turquoise uniform, Michel would have immediately assumed he was a Palo. "What do you think of our new friend, Tenik?" Meln-Yaret asked.

"He admits he is a spy." Tenik had a startlingly deep voice that belied his slim, short stature.

"He admits he *was* a spy."

"Once a spy, always a spy."

"Perhaps."

Michel squeezed his eyes closed. The pain in his head was a dull throb now, which was only slightly easier to think through than the sharp pain from earlier. He knew that there were layers to this meeting—Forgula, Tenik, Meln-Yaret, Households, and cupbearers. There was more going on than was immediately apparent, but in his current state he could not guess what it was. "I was a Blackhat spy," he said. "Before the invasion, I was elevated to Gold Rose, which is the highest order within the Blackhats. The invasion came, the Grand Master was murdered, and then Lindet fled the city without warning."

"And now..." Meln-Yaret made a tutting sound. "What did you tell the soldier to whom you gave this Rose? That you would hand me the Blackhats within Landfall?"

"That's right. I can help you dismantle their efforts here."

Meln-Yaret nodded. "You certainly have my attention. Let us start with this: What can you offer me, and what do you want in return?"

Michel forced himself to sit up straight, looking Meln-Yaret in the eye. This was now a negotiation, and he couldn't conduct a negotiation from a point of such weakness. He needed to appear strong, even if that appearance was obviously a sham. "I can offer you the locations of caches and safe houses. I can help you track down Blackhats who have remained in the city. I can tell you how they work and how they think. I'll admit that I wasn't a Gold Rose long, but I spent years as a Silver Rose. I saw far more than the average Blackhat."

"And what reward do you expect for your aid?"

"People."

"What do you mean, *people*?" Tenik cut in. "Slaves?"

The casual way Tenik said the word reminded Michel how foreign the Dynize still were. He shook his head. "Not slaves." This was something he'd thought about a lot since the occupation. "You've been rounding up Fatrastan citizens, the families of Blackhats who left the city with Lindet. It's part of war, I understand. But those people were abandoned by their government and their loved ones. They don't deserve to be hunted, tortured, and forced into labor camps or worse. In exchange for my help, I want you to let those people go."

Meln-Yaret leaned back in his chair, thoughtfully stroking his chin. He glanced at Tenik. "You don't want riches? Power?"

"I don't have ambition for power. Riches..." Michel allowed himself a smile. "I intend on proving myself very useful to the Dynize government. The riches can come later. For now, I want those people released."

"You ask too much," Tenik said bluntly.

Meln-Yaret held up a hand to silence his companion. "It's true, you ask a great deal. We gather these people because they themselves may be spies, but they are also useful as hostages and forced labor. We have hundreds already, and I imagine we'll end up with a few thousand by the end of the year, even without your help."

"Probably," Michel admitted, "but the hostages themselves have little value. The spouses and children of low-level Blackhats? Lindet doesn't care about them. Eject them from your territory. Hand them over to the closest Fatrastan army. Let them be a hindrance to your enemies and disguise it as an act of goodwill. There are already rumors that you're treating the Palo better than Lindet ever did. The people might begin to see you as a benevolent conqueror. If this war draws on, that itself will be a dangerous weapon."

Meln-Yaret smirked. "You make a very persuasive argument, Michel Bravis. But what you ask... it would be very difficult."

Michel gingerly touched the side of his head. It hadn't occurred to him that the minister of scrolls might not actually be that powerful of a position. If Meln-Yaret was simply a hound used to find enemy spies rather than a spymaster in his own right, Michel may have badly misplaced his bets. He needed a powerful patron if he was going to find Taniel's informant.

"On the other hand," Meln-Yaret continued after a moment's silence, "I may be able to work with your demands. Tell me, why should I trust you? You've already admitted to being a spy.

Shouldn't I assume you're still working for the Fatrastans? This could simply be your way to get into my good graces."

There was a glint in Meln-Yaret's eyes that Michel didn't particularly like. He swallowed, holding Yaret's gaze. "Give me the chance to earn that trust."

"Why? Why shouldn't I just torture you for your information? Or hand you over to the bone-eyes?"

Michel tried not to let his fear show at the mention of bone-eyes. He knew what a bone-eye was capable of, but that information was something he didn't want to let on. "Because I came to you in good faith. You offer a reward for service. Is this the reward of which you speak? Because if it is, word will get out sooner or later. Even sympathizers will grow wary of you, and rumors will spread that the Dynize ministers are not true to their word."

Yaret exchanged a glance with Tenik, tongue in cheek.

"He has balls," Tenik said with a shrug. "But he's still a spy. What good is goodwill if it is used against us?"

"Goodwill is a double-edged sword," Yaret admitted.

Michel leaned forward, ignoring the blood dripping from his chin. "Do I seem like someone who would be more useful as a willing participant, or forced to aid you under duress?"

Meln-Yaret did not answer the question. "Can you tell me where Lindet keeps her personal files?"

The question caught Michel off guard. "I can't."

"Can you tell me where the gunsmiths fled, so that we might capture them and use their expertise to improve our armies?"

"I can't," Michel answered again. For all his bravado, he knew he was on shaky ground. Meln-Yaret obviously had goals. If Michel couldn't help him with those, then Meln-Yaret might just hand him off to someone else. Someone like Forgula.

With each answer, Meln-Yaret looked increasingly doubtful. He sighed, shaking his head. "Caches and safe houses are not enough. You're asking me to put a lot of trust in you, and in return all

I receive are promises. Give me something, Michel, and we can begin a relationship. Until then..." Meln-Yaret trailed off.

Michel wracked his brain. His bluster about seeing a lot as a spy had been mostly that—bluster. He certainly knew some secrets, and he had no doubt that he could be useful to the Dynize in the long term. But immediate evidence of his good intentions? His eyes fell on the Gold Rose as Meln-Yaret turned it over and over again between his fingers.

"Tell me," Michel said, "did Lindet destroy the third floor of the Blackhat Archives when she left?"

Meln-Yaret stopped twirling the Gold Rose and looked up sharply. Michel had hit upon something. "She did not."

"Do you know what's up there?"

"We have...an inkling."

"Secrets. A lot of them. I assume it's heavily warded. It will take your Privileged months, if not years, to break into it without destroying the contents. You want goodwill? You want trust?" Michel took a fraction of a second to study Yaret. His expressions and composure reminded him once more of Captain Blasdell, and Michel decided to take a gamble. "The Gold Rose is a key," he said simply. "It'll open the gate to the third floor. It worked for me. I don't see why it wouldn't work for you." He silently prayed that Lindet's Privileged hadn't had time to change the wards before they fled the city.

Meln-Yaret looked down at the Rose in his hand. "Well. As simple as that?"

"As simple as that."

The two Dynize exchanged a glance, and Meln-Yaret addressed Tenik with a clever smile. "Sedial will be furious. All right, Michel. Assuming this works, I will put you on a leash and let you go to work. You'll have freedom of movement, a Household, protection, and the backing of my name. I'll see what I can do about the families that we have rounded up. The more results you get me, the more likely I'll be able to free noncombatants."

As simple as that. Michel barely allowed himself to breathe. "Is there anywhere you want me to start?"

"There is. I have several hundred men combing the city to find out who's responsible for the recent bombings. We've captured countless Blackhats and partisans, and not a single person can tell me who carried out or ordered them. A Household Captain of the Guard was killed less than an hour ago, and it has the ministers nervous."

"I'm not an investigator," Michel warned. "If it's not the Blackhats, I won't be able to help you."

"Then rule them out," Yaret responded.

Michel hesitated. He already suspected that the perpetrators were a Blackhat cell, but he didn't have the slightest idea where they were holed up or who they were led by. Perhaps the mysterious Gold Rose? Regardless, he had to say yes. Michel needed to gain stature within the Dynize as quickly as possible—lengthen that leash and get to know the Dynize officials. The more he infiltrated their government, the more likely he was to find Taniel's informant.

"I'll see what I can do," Michel promised.

CHAPTER 16

I s spying always this boring?" Tenik asked.

Michel stood at a window in a stuffy tenement room in the industrial quarter of Lower Landfall. He gazed through a slit in the curtains, watching the entrance of a tenement across the street while he listened to the sound of the midafternoon traffic. Before the war, this whole district was choked with smoke and the sound of carts, people, and factories. Now it was almost quiet with the factories empty and the traffic sparse.

Michel turned away from the window just long enough to glance at the man sitting in the corner behind him. Devin-Tenik looked even more like a Palo once he had shed his turquoise uniform for a brown cotton suit and flatcap, and he lounged on the floor as if it were more comfortable there than in a chair. Michel answered the question, "Most of being a spy is waiting, watching, and listening. So yes, it's always this boring."

Tenik flipped a coin in the air and caught it. He slapped it on the back of his wrist but didn't bother looking at the result before flipping it again. He'd been doing so for about four hours, and Michel wasn't sure whether to strangle him or find something to take his own mind off the tedium.

"Are you supposed to follow me everywhere?" Michel asked.

Tenik smiled. "That's the idea. Your Gold Rose opened the third floor of the Millinery. You have earned Yaret's trust, and you are now part of his Household. But you're still a foreigner. For your safety, I am to be your bodyguard, guide, and assistant."

"Bodyguard, eh?" Michel muttered. Tenik didn't appear to be a soldier, but he was lean and fit and walked with the confidence of someone who knew how to handle a fight. Michel suspected that his job was less "bodyguard" and more "guard." Michel wondered how long it would take for him to become fully trusted. Years, perhaps. He didn't have that much time. Until then, he could make use of an assistant and guide.

"What do you mean when you say 'part of Yaret's Household'?"

"Dynize society is based around Households," Tenik explained. "A Household revolves around a Name." He flipped his coin, caught it, and pointed a finger at Michel. "You are the newest member of Yaret's Household."

"Yaret is the Name of the Household?" Michel asked. He kept his attention on the road and the entrance to the tenement across the street, but he listened carefully. He suspected that much of his downtime the next few weeks would be spent learning about Dynize society. He needed to enter and climb it as quickly as possible.

"It is. Ah!" Tenik felt around in his jacket pockets for a moment, then withdrew a card and handed it to Michel. "This belongs to you. It marks you as a member of Yaret's Household and entitled to the protection of Yaret's Name. If we are ever separated and you are questioned by soldiers, you can show them this and they will escort you to Yaret's home."

Michel took the card and turned it over in his hand. It was on a heavy stock, coated in wax and decorated with a stylized golden trim. There were words in Dynize at the bottom and a red thumb-print in the center. He immediately wondered how hard it would be to counterfeit. If he'd gotten hold of one of these as a Blackhat, doing so would be his first concern.

"Handy," he said.

"It is, but you should be careful."

Michel glanced at Tenik sharply. "Of?"

"Remember Forgula? She belongs to a rival Household. Yaret's protection is meant to be sacred, but in reality it is only as good as the power of his Name. Forgula attempted to snatch you out from under us, and it's possible that she will do so again if she thinks it's worth angering Yaret."

"Her Household Name is stronger than Yaret's?"

"Her Household is stronger than everyone's."

"And whose is that?"

"Sedial." Tenik's expression darkened. "Ka-Sedial is the emperor's appointed ruler on this continent. Be wary of him. Be wary of the bone-eyes."

"Why?"

"I…" Tenik hesitated, as if remembering that he was talking to someone he shouldn't completely trust. "Just be wary of them. Prove yourself to Yaret and in return you'll be taught all you need to know to be a useful member of his Household."

Michel was surprised to receive such a warning from a Dynize. They seemed so organized and in-step that he had expected the division among them to be minimal. Household rivalries sounded like something he could use. He would have to learn more about them.

"Do people ever change Households?" he asked.

Tenik's penetrating stare told Michel a great deal. After a moment, Tenik answered, "All the time. Marriages. Trades. Formal requests. Both Household Names must agree for it to be done formally."

"And informally?"

Tenik's expression softened and he resumed flipping his coin, as if carefree, but there was a glint in his eye. "Concern yourself with finding this Gold Rose you promised your new master."

Michel slowly turned back to the curtain. "Right."

A few minutes later he heard Tenik get up and cross the room, coming to stand just behind Michel and craning his neck to look outside. Michel stepped to one side, allowing him the view.

Tenik asked, "How does starting here help you find the person responsible for the bombings?"

"I thought you worked for the minister of scrolls," Michel responded, pulling away to get a good look at Tenik's face.

"I do. What of it?"

"And you don't know *anything* about being a spy?"

Tenik let out a soft laugh. "You think Yaret is some kind of spy?"

"That..." Michel hesitated, thinking of his conversation with Emerald. "That's what I was led to believe. Well, not a spy himself. But a spymaster."

"I don't know that word."

Tenik knew far more Adran and Palo than Michel had expected, and their conversations took place in both those languages as well as Dynize. Michel tried to think of a Palo word for "spymaster," but settled on "one who commands those who watch your enemies."

"Ah, I see," Tenik said. "Yes, I suppose that works. The minister of scrolls traditionally oversees government information—history, census data, that sort of thing—but Yaret wanted to be involved in the invasion. He worked to expand his position so that Sedial didn't have complete control of the war."

Census data could be useful, if it included the names of Dynize citizens here in Fatrasta. "The emperor doesn't have a designated spymaster?"

"I believe he does," Tenik recalled, "but they only oversee threats against the emperor's person. Government spies were purged after the end of the civil war, and we needed something new when we turned our eyes outward."

Michel considered the information. He had a thousand questions about the things he was just told, but he couldn't risk being *too* curious. He needed to pick his questions carefully. For now, it was enough to know that Yaret was more akin to a record keeper than a spymaster. Shrewd, perhaps, but not seasoned. "So what are you? A census taker?"

"No, no," Tenik said, "I am one of Yaret's cupbearers."

The term sounded archaic, and it was not the first time Michel had heard a Dynize use it. He seemed to remember that it was an honorarium in the court of Kressian kings. "I'm not familiar with the term. What is your role?"

"I have no role—and I have every role," Tenik said, spreading his arms. "A cupbearer is a trusted member of the Household who takes on whatever the Name needs doing. I have been many things. For now, I am your bodyguard and assistant."

"It's an honored position?"

"Very."

"Looking after me seems . . . beneath you."

"Not at all. You were a high-ranking member of the Blackhats. Your place within the Household has yet to be determined, but you are not a slave." He paused. "No, what is the word for the lowliest member?" He said something in Dynize, then "commoner? Is that the word?"

"I think I get your meaning," Michel said.

"Good. By the way, you never answered my question."

"Which one?"

"How does this help us catch the culprit behind the bombings?"

Michel pulled himself away from his myriad of questions and nodded to the tenement across the street. "I'm waiting for someone."

"Who?"

"A woman named Hendres. We worked together for a brief time after the war started."

"How will she be useful?"

"Because she knows that I turned. I'm willing to bet that with me gone, she will have spent the last couple of days tracking down the highest-ranking Blackhat in the city. With any luck, it's a Gold Rose who, if not personally responsible for the bombings, will probably have a good idea who is."

"You were friends with this Hendres woman?"

Michel decided not to mention their time as lovers. "Partners. We were trying to figure out how to save the families of Blackhats from your purges."

"And why did you stop being partners?"

"Because I decided that joining you was more efficient." Michel didn't much like this line of questioning, and hoped that it came across in his voice.

Tenik didn't seem to notice. "How do you know she'll come here?"

"I don't," Michel said. A glance at Tenik's face revealed the other's skepticism, and he continued. "Hendres isn't a spy. She was an enforcer, then a bureaucrat. Everything she knows about sneaking around she learned from me in the last month."

"And?"

"And we worked from the same list of safe houses. The safe house across the street is one of the few we never discussed using as a backup. Hendres is smart enough to have ditched our backup safe houses and will only use those she thinks I'm less likely to search. If she doesn't show up at this one tonight, we'll check one of the others tomorrow."

Michel gave the explanation offhand, and it didn't occur to him until he'd finished speaking what, exactly, he'd just revealed. He risked a quick glance at Tenik, whose eyes were still focused on the street. He was just beginning to think Tenik hadn't noticed the slip, when Tenik asked, "How does Hendres know that you're working for us?" The question was posed in a quiet, thoughtful tone.

Michel licked his lips. "It's complicated."

"I think I could follow an explanation."

Michel grew even more cognizant of the fact that Tenik had been sent to keep an eye on him. Everything he shared with Tenik would be revealed to Yaret, and might affect Michel's standing. Carelessly giving away information, he decided, would be a stupid way to end his short stint with the Dynize.

"Hendres accused me of being a spy for the Dynize," Michel said. "She tried to kill me."

"You became a traitor because you were falsely accused of being a traitor?"

Michel didn't like the word "traitor." It ignored the complexities of what being a spy actually meant. "Yes," he said.

"And why did she think you were a traitor?"

"Because one of our safe houses was raided by Dynize soldiers while I was away. She barely escaped, and only the two of us knew about the safe house." It was close enough to the truth for Michel. He added a twist of anger to his words—also real—and clicked his tongue. "Speaking of which, do you see that woman with the brown hair down at the end of the street?"

"I do."

"That's her."

Michel took a deep breath to calm himself as he watched Hendres mill about the intersection at the end of the street, checking subtly for a possible ambush. Her body language was tense and she checked the street, rooftops, and tenement doorway several times before finally coming down the street and heading inside. It seemed she was still spooked from coming back to the Dynize stakeout last week.

"She didn't see us," Tenik observed.

"She didn't check the windows at all," Michel said. "She really needs to learn to do that."

"What next?"

"You don't have to whisper," Michel responded. "Even if she was still in the street, she wouldn't hear us."

Tenik cleared his throat and his cheeks flushed. "So what next?" he asked in a normal voice.

"Now we wait."

Tenik rolled his eyes and returned to the corner of the room, slumping down on the floor. The familiar flicking sound of him flipping a coin soon began. Michel waited, nearly stepping back from the window when he saw a curtain flutter in Hendres's safehouse room.

"Now we know where she's staying," Michel said over his shoulder. "We can come back tomorrow morning and wait until she goes out, and then..." He paused as Hendres suddenly appeared in the tenement doorway. "Shit, never mind. Come with me, now!"

Michel left the room at a run, heading down the hallway without waiting to see if Tenik had followed him. He went up two floors, then climbed out the window of an abandoned apartment and around the ledge, then hiked himself up onto the roof. He crossed it in a few moments and crouched down, searching the traffic below.

It wasn't long until he spotted Hendres heading north. He heard a clatter behind him, and Tenik joined him a moment later with a string of words in Dynize that were definitely curses.

"Come on," Michel told him, heading to the other side of the roof and quickly climbing down the chimney sweep's ladder. He caught up to Hendres a few blocks later, falling into step a hundred paces back and pulling his hat down over his face. He indicated that Tenik do the same.

"The trick to following someone," Michel explained in a low

voice, "is to stay far enough away that they won't suspect you're on their tail—but close enough that you won't lose them when they inevitably turn corners or go into buildings."

"What happens when they go into buildings?"

"Depends. If you're trying to catch them, you make sure it's not a trap, then set your own. It helps to have some thugs with you."

"And if you're not trying to catch them?"

"Then you wait until they come out again."

Tenik groaned.

"Hold up," Michel said, turning to face a shop window as Hendres stopped at an intersection and checked behind her. He watched her out of the corner of his eye while pretending to study a hat, then turned to follow her again once she'd kept going. "I dyed my hair after I last saw her," Michel explained. "It won't hold up to a close examination, but it's enough to fool her at a distance."

"Is she that stupid?"

"*People* are that stupid," Michel responded. "You'd be surprised at what even a cautious person will overlook."

They soon left the industrial quarter, and passed the old dock-side market and the ruins of the eastern face of the plateau. Out in the harbor, Fort Nied sat pitted and forlorn, mostly ignored by the occupying force. Hendres crossed the river and rounded the plateau to head into the northern suburbs.

She stopped at two different buildings, both times briefly, before continuing her journey. One of the stops was at the bar of a known Blackhat contact, and the second was unfamiliar to Michel. He tried to put himself in her shoes, working through her route, trying to figure out what she was doing.

"How do we know when we've followed her to the right place?" Tenik asked quietly while they waited for her outside yet a third stop.

"We don't," Michel responded. "It might be obvious, or we might have to stake out all of these places."

"We're trying to find this other Gold Rose?"

"Exactly. If we're lucky, she'll have already made contact with him since my departure and she'll lead us right to him."

"If we're unlucky?"

"If we're unlucky, she's spotted us and is leading us into a trap." With those words, Michel double-checked his pocket to make sure his knuckle-dusters were still there. They were. He didn't want to be caught unawares again like he had with Forgula.

He stopped at an intersection to wait for a column of Dynize soldiers to walk by, tipping his hat to them. Tenik gave him a questioning look.

"Force of habit," Michel said. "You're less likely to notice someone with good manners. Not great manners, mind you. Just good ones." The column passed by and he swore under his breath.

"I don't see her," Tenik said.

"Me neither. Pit. Head down, keep walking. Watch to your right out of the corner of your eye. I'll watch the left."

They continued straight down the street past a row of shops, half of which were boarded up. This was a residential area, lower middle class, and had maintained much of its population after the evacuation. No one paid them any mind, and after they'd gone two blocks Michel whispered to Tenik to turn around.

They did a second sweep, coming up with nothing.

"She's got to be in one of these buildings," Michel said. "But the longer we linger, the more chance she'll look out a window and notice us standing around. Over here." Michel headed into a nearby bakery, following his nose into the front of the shop where hot loaves had just come out of the oven. "Don't stand out," he said quietly. "Buy something."

Tenik went up to the counter while Michel turned to watch out the front window.

"We don't take those," a voice said loudly.

Michel turned to find Tenik offering the baker a Dynize rations card. Tenik opened his mouth, but Michel stepped in to intercede, handing over a couple of Fatrastan coins. He thanked the baker and pulled Tenik back outside, where he tore the loaf in half.

Tenik scowled back at the door. "These are valid," he said, shaking the rations card under Michel's nose. "The government has ordered that all businesses accept them."

"Don't worry too much about it," Michel said, bemused by Tenik's indignation. "You look like a Palo and dress like a Palo. They're going to treat you like one. Which means they won't let you pay with a currency that might not be any good in a few months."

"He thinks Dynize will lose the war?" Tenik looked like he was ready to march back inside. Michel took him by the arm and led him away.

"Hedging his bets, probably. Like I said, don't worry about..." Michel trailed off as he spotted someone over Tenik's shoulder. "Don't turn around," he said in a low voice, lifting his half a loaf of bread up to his face but keeping his eyes fixed down the street. "Loosen up," he told Tenik. "Your shoulders are hunched and your body tense. That's going to be obvious to anyone who knows what to look for. Now, I see Hendres just over your left shoulder. She just came out of that alleyway next to the cobbler's. We're going to stay here until she moves again. If I say turn, I want you to casually look at that playbill plastered on the wall to your left. Understand?"

"Yes."

"Good." Michel watched for several moments as Hendres spoke with someone just around the corner. He silently urged them to step out into the street so he could see the other party, but Hendres was suddenly on the move again. "Turn!" he hissed at Tenik.

They waited as Hendres walked past them. Michel forced himself to breathe evenly, watching out of the corner of his eye until she rounded a corner. He glanced over Tenik's shoulder once and then took one step after Hendres before freezing in place.

"Should we follow her?" Tenik asked.

Michel didn't answer. Slowly, casually, he swept his gaze back across that alley Hendres had been standing in a moment ago. A man had emerged to chat with one of the shopkeeps, smoking a cigarette carelessly.

"She's getting away!"

"Forget about her," Michel said. "We got lucky. Damned lucky."

"How?"

Michel took Tenik by the arm and led him down a nearby alley without answering the question.

"Where are we going?" Tenik asked.

"To find a lookout spot. The man who Hendres just met with is named Marhoush. He's a Silver Rose, and he's the right-hand man of Val je Tura. Not only is je Tura Lindet's personal enforcer, but he also spent most of the Fatrastan revolution killing Kez soldiers and civilians with explosives. I'm willing to bet je Tura is the one bombing your soldiers, and Marhoush will lead us right to him."

CHAPTER 17

Styke, Celine, and Ka-poel rode for three days in near silence, broken only by Celine's occasional questions about the people and horses they passed on the road. They traveled against the flow of traffic as thousands of refugees left their homes and businesses and fled northwest in an attempt to stay ahead of the Dynize invaders.

Stories traveled with them: a thousand rumors that painted the Dynize as everything from blood-drinking monsters who snatched away Kressian youths, to liberators who brought with them freedom from the oppressive rule of Lindet and her Blackhats. Regardless of which rumor was carried by the passing travelers, everyone seemed to prefer taking their chances with the evil they knew—Lindet—rather than the evil they did not.

By the third day, Styke found the spring that gave birth to the Cottonseed tributary, a small river that meandered between plantation fields for about thirty miles, growing bigger until it joined the Cottonseed River and eventually poured into the Hadshaw.

Styke stopped at the spring, washing the road dust off his face and instructing Celine to do the same before making sure his carbines were loaded and his knife was sharp. After a brief lunch, he lifted Celine back into the saddle and followed the banks of the tributary.

"What are we looking for?" Celine asked.

"The closest plantation." Styke handed the reins to Celine and removed a skull-and-lance banner from his saddlebags before tying it to the tip of his lance and raising it above him.

They crossed several streams and a mile of plantation fields full of bonded Palo working desperately to harvest the half-grown fields. No one challenged Styke as he rode past, but Ka-poel received more than a few curious glances.

"Who are we going to kill?" Celine asked.

"Try not to sound so eager when you ask a question like that," Styke retorted. "*I'm* going to kill a man named Bad Tenny Wiles."

"And who is that?"

"One of the Mad Lancers," Styke answered. "At least, he used to be. Sometimes he was a clerk, sometimes did some cooking. A mean son of a bitch—mean enough to keep the men from pilfering the rations when times were lean. But we were all mean back then."

"Why do you want to kill him?"

He felt a knot tighten in his stomach. Over the years people had called him a brute, a murderer, even a monster. He'd been all those things and more, but the idea of killing someone who'd once ridden at his side was distasteful. Murdering Agoston had sated his rage the other night, but it had also left him feeling queasy. He supposed he could just forget the whole thing, but...vengeance needed having. "It's complicated."

"So?" She looked up at him expectantly.

"Do you know what 'precocious' means?"

"I know I'm one. Ibana said so."

Ka-poel grinned openly at Styke.

"Of course she did." Styke checked his knife and drew the blade down his whetstone a few times before stowing them both, taking the reins from Celine's hands. He wondered if he was getting such a young child too used to the idea of blood and death, and had to remind himself that she'd seen men gut each other over a biscuit in the labor camps, and she'd watched her own father drown in the fens. He pointed to the sorcery-healed scar on his left hand between the knuckles of his third and fourth finger. "This," he said, then pointed to his leg, then his face. "This, and this. All from the firing squad ten years ago." The sorcerous healing of his wounds had come ten years too late, and they all still ached every day—and those two fingers still didn't like to obey him.

Celine took Styke's hand in hers, running her fingers over the wound, then across his knuckles. Her hands were tiny compared to his. "Did Tenny Wiles shoot at you?"

"Not exactly."

Styke ignored Celine's further questions as he spotted a nearby driveway and directed Amrec away from the riverbank. The drive ran beside the river for a few hundred yards and then across an open lawn to a manor house. The manor had the typical flat facade in the common style of Fatrastan plantations. As far as those went, it wasn't immense—though it was obviously the home of a rich man. The fountain out front was in disrepair, the paint on the shutters peeling, but otherwise the house and grounds were in decent condition for an older home.

Styke felt his queasiness increase, and he thought about Agoston's blood on his hands and arms and pictured the look on Tenny Wiles's face as he gutted him. Killing old comrades. A dirty business, even for him.

A carriage and a dozen wagons filled the drive just outside the front door, and a flurry of activity filled the vestibule as servants rushed to load the wagons with furniture and supplies.

Styke caught sight of Bad Tenny Wiles standing on the front step, directing the whole thing. Tenny was probably five years younger than Styke, and hadn't borne the rigors of the labor camps, but he did not look good. His split nose was red and runny, and the side of his face with the missing ear was covered in the scars of a past infection. But it was definitely Tenny—just wearing expensive clothes.

Everyone was so focused on packing the house that they didn't seem to notice Styke as he came up the drive, rounded the fountain, and dismounted. He pulled Celine down and set her next to Amrec, handing her the reins. "Stay here," he said. The knot in his stomach was still there, but he could feel it loosening beneath the resolute feeling of a job that needed doing.

"I could come with."

"You don't need to watch me skin a man." He pointed at Ka-poel. "You stay here, too."

He left Celine scowling at his back as he headed through the bustle of the servants and toward the front door, stopping just a few feet from the bottom step. He sighed, a hand on the hilt of his knife, and let his weight fall on his good leg as he waited for Tenny to notice him.

It didn't take long. Tenny directed two servants maneuvering a feather mattress out the door, pointing to one of the wagons. On noticing Styke, his mouth opened and he blinked in confusion. Slowly, the blood drained from his face.

"Hello, Tenny," Styke said.

Bad Tenny Wiles, the scourge of unwary Kez infantry, began to tremble. It started in his hands, then moved through his body until Styke thought he might convulse and fall to the ground in a fit. He waited for a weapon to appear in Tenny's hands, and the quick exchange of blood to follow. He did not expect Tenny to turn and flee into the house.

The pounding of retreating footsteps surprised Styke, and it took him a moment to follow. He passed startled servants, listening to Tenny's shouts, and followed them up the grand staircase to the second floor. He paused for a moment on the landing, the house suddenly silent.

"You there!" a servant called, mounting the stairs below Styke with a firepoker in his hand.

Styke pointed his knife at the man, then continued upward. No one followed.

He prowled the second floor, glancing in each room, moving with slow, deliberate steps. He expected the blast of a blunderbuss as he opened every door, or the ring of a pistol shot. But he found the master bedroom without encountering an ambush.

Tenny stood in the center of the room alone, supporting himself on one corner of a four-poster bed. He'd stilled his trembles, and he held a pistol in one hand, pointed at Styke. "Not another step," he growled. "I don't care if you're a ghost or the real thing, but I will pull this trigger."

"Do you think you can finish with one bullet what a firing squad couldn't with twenty?" Styke asked. He entered the room, glancing around for a bevy of servants waiting to jump him. There was no one else, so he let himself relax slightly, glancing around at the furniture and ceiling as if he meant to buy the place. "What was your price, Tenny?" he asked. "How much did Fidelis Jes pay you to betray me? Was it this place? A whole plantation? I'll admit you got a good deal. I hope you enjoyed the last ten years more than I did."

Tenny's pistol didn't waver. "How did you know? Pit, how are you still alive? Jes told me they finished the job!"

Styke had once watched Tenny kill a whole squad of grenadiers with a broken sword after one of them cut off his ear. He'd never heard that edge of panic in Bad Tenny Wiles's voice. But seeing a ghost will do that to a man.

"I spent ten years in the labor camps thinking that Fidelis Jes had arranged my failed execution—then disappearance—without any of my men knowing. I shouldn't have been so naive. I got out two months ago, re-formed the Mad Lancers, and helped defend

Landfall. So how do I know? Turns out you didn't come to my funeral. Markus and Zac noticed, and they found out that you and a few others got paid off by the Blackhats. Doesn't take much math to figure out why."

"I didn't—"

Styke cut him off. "I *know*, Tenny. I killed Agoston a few days ago."

"Does everyone else know?" Tenny whispered.

"Me, Ibana, Jackal. Markus and Zac," Styke said. "I haven't decided whether to take your head back to show the rest. You're lucky Ibana isn't here. She would—"

As Styke spoke, the muzzle of Tenny's pistol suddenly dipped, then jerked up toward his mouth. Tenny grabbed the muzzle in his lips and squeezed his eyes shut.

Styke crossed the room in two quick strides and jerked the pistol out of Tenny's hand. He tossed it on the bed, grasping Tenny by the front of his suit and shaking him hard enough to rattle his teeth. Tenny reached for a knife at his belt, but Styke slapped it away and lifted Tenny off the ground. He drew his boz knife and held the tip to Tenny's throat. A quick jerk, and Styke would have another traitor's lifeblood spilling down his arms.

"You don't get to take your own life," Styke snarled. "You gave up that privilege the moment you betrayed me and the lancers."

"I didn't want to, damn it! Agoston and Dvory talked me into it. They said we were better without you, and Fidelis Jes, he—"

Styke shook him again. "Don't mention that piece of shit. You know what I did after Landfall last month? I found Jes and cut his damned head off and sent it to Lindet." He looked around the room, feeling angry and sick. "You traded me for this, Tenny. Don't worry, because you only have to live with it for a few more minutes."

Finish the job, he told himself silently. Have it done and be gone. He thought of Agoston's blood and squeezed his eyes shut.

"You don't have to do it, Ben," Tenny whispered.

"Oh, shut up." Styke carried Tenny across the room and threw him out the big bay window.

Glass shattered, and Tenny's scream was undercut by a shrill one from the closet. Styke whirled as the closet opened, and a woman in her early twenties burst forth. Two young children hid among the clothes inside, frightened, staring at Styke—a crippled giant of a man with a fighting knife as long as a sword. The woman looked from him to the window and took a step back, her eyes rolling like those of a frightened horse.

"Stay here," Styke ordered. He strode into the hall to find a crowd of worried servants. Shoving them aside, he headed downstairs and out to the side of the house, where he found Tenny lying on the lawn among broken glass and fragments of a windowsill. Tenny's eyes were closed, his arm bent beneath him and obviously broken, but his chest rose and fell. He gnashed his teeth against the pain, trying to move.

Tenny's eyes shot open as Styke approached. "Why are you still alive?" he whispered between gritted teeth.

Styke squatted beside him, knife loose in his hand. Above them both, the woman stood at the window, wailing. "Because none of the gods have invented anything to kill me yet," he replied. "Don't pretend this is a surprise. You knew who and what I was when you decided to sell me to Fidelis Jes." He tapped the tip of his knife against Tenny's collarbone.

Tenny trembled, but Styke could tell that it was from pain, and no longer fear. He could see the acceptance of a dead man in Tenny's eyes. "Gut me," Tenny said. "Flay me. Do what you need to do. I deserve it. But leave these people out of it. Don't do it in the sight of my wife and children. I know who and what you are, Colonel, and I know you *are* better than that."

Styke glanced up at the window again. The woman had disappeared, and only servants stared down at him. He could still hear her wailing. He wondered if begging had ever stalled the blade of the old Ben Styke—if the invocation of a wife and children had ever kept him from a bloody deed. If it had, it was a long time ago.

He felt eyes on him, and glanced over his shoulder to find Celine standing by the corner of the house. She still clutched Amrec's reins, and the big horse nibbled at the grass without a care in the world. Stone-faced, Celine watched Styke, eyeing the knife in his hand and the man at his feet. Ka-poel stood behind her with an appraising look in her eye.

"Finish it, Styke," Tenny said. "Don't make me linger. It's not your style. Drag me into those woods over there. Finish the job. Just don't do it in front of them."

Styke frowned at Celine. The girl's head was cocked to the side as if she were watching a butcher about to cut up a side of beef. He felt conflicted, that war between his lust for vengeance and the sickness brought on by killing his own men. Celine scowled at him, clearly finding something amiss.

Styke bowed his head. Tenny deserved to die, no question about that. But Styke couldn't help but hesitate. He took a deep breath, let out a sigh, and tapped Tenny's collarbone with the tip of his knife again.

"Get that arm set and wrapped," he heard himself say softly as he stood. "The Dynize are close by. If you leave by sundown, you might outrun their scouts. The river valley is choked with refugees, so you'll want to go southwest."

"What are you doing?" Tenny gasped. He tried to sit up, voice dripping with suspicion.

"I'm not gonna skin an old comrade in front of his own household. Even if you deserve it. Get out of here, Tenny. Change your name. You should probably leave the country. If Ibana ever finds you, she'll turn you into a rug." Styke sheathed his knife and headed back to Celine. He took Amrec's reins.

"I thought you were gonna skin him," Celine said.

"Nobody likes a bloodthirsty little git," Styke said, swinging into the saddle. Celine climbed up in front of him.

"I'm not bloodthirsty," she protested. "I was just curious. Why didn't you kill him?"

Styke took her by the shoulder. He searched her eyes for eagerness or disappointment. Finding neither, he flipped the reins. "Hardest thing a soldier can do is leave the killing behind him. Tenny didn't sell me out for money or power. He sold me out for a better life. Shitty thing to do, but he went somewhere he couldn't hear the hooves and the cannons and became a good husband to a fat little country girl. He did what I should have done twenty-five years ago."

"So you're just gonna let him go?"

"I'm just gonna let him go," Styke confirmed. The rage still burned in his chest, but that queasiness was now gone. "I've got plenty of killing to do. One less mark on my knife handle won't make a difference. Just don't tell Ibana."

CHAPTER 18

The rolling plains of southern Fatrasta turned into the foothills of the Ironhook Mountains as Vlora and Taniel rode north ahead of the army. They followed the banks of the Hadshaw for nearly three hundred miles, pushing themselves and their spare horses hard before cutting west and heading into the mountains.

The roads became narrower, climbing steep hills and crossing deep ravines over bridges that became increasingly untrustworthy. Farmsteads gave way to forests of towering pines as they left behind the regular villages.

Progress grew slower and slower as the terrain sharpened. The depth of the forest gave Vlora a sense of foreboding. More than swamps of the Tristan Basin, this land felt as if it were on the edge of civilization, isolated and wild, a place where she could scream for ten miles of road and no one would hear her. They bought supplies from the infrequent logging camps and express depots, and it took them almost seven days to reach the outskirts of Yellow Creek.

The county limits were marked by a flatboard nailed to a stick, written in charcoal, and guarded by a rough-cut log tower with two men armed with rifles. The guards watched them approach, but did not hail them or comment on their passing.

Vlora turned in her saddle to look back at them as she passed. "Not much of a guard post."

"They aren't looking for Kressians," Taniel said.

This should have surprised Vlora. "Palo?"

"Definitely Palo. Kressians out here stick together—they have to, or the Palo war parties will pick them apart."

"I didn't know there still were aggressive tribes this close to the coast. We're just a few hundred miles from Landfall."

Taniel looked up to watch a circling buzzard. "There are a handful of independent tribes on this side of the Ironhook, but they all have treaties with Lindet in order to ensure their survival. The problem is expeditions from the other side of the mountains."

"Then why was that guard post way down here? Why wasn't it up in the mountains?"

Taniel grinned at her. "You ever try to explain the difference between groups of Palo to the average Fatrastan?"

"No."

"That kind of nuance is lost on most people. A Palo is a Palo, regardless of where they come from. If Palo from across the mountains attack the trade routes to and from Yellow Creek, the townspeople just assume it was one of the neighboring tribes." Taniel tapped the side of his head. "People desperate enough to come out here to settle the frontier don't always have the best critical-thinking skills. It's easier to shoot first and ask questions later."

Vlora spotted a cabin at the top of a nearby gully—the first sign of settlement she'd seen in twenty miles. A few minutes later, she spotted another one. "Damn near getting crowded now," she muttered to herself. "So these Palo coming across the mountains...are they from the Palo Nation?"

"Almost certainly."

"I thought you said they were different. More civilized."

Taniel considered this for a moment. "The Palo Nation is complicated. They have no interest in having what happened to the southern Palo happen to them. So they sit behind the mountains and send raids. They scout, they kill and steal. They do what's expected of them, because they don't want Lindet to suspect that they are anything more than an upstart tribe."

"Then, what are they?"

Taniel looked at her seriously. "You wouldn't believe me if I told you."

"Try me."

"They're a republic."

Vlora scoffed. "You're joking."

"Not at all."

"A bona fide republic?"

Taniel nodded, and Vlora found herself struggling with the idea. She'd fought the Palo up in the Tristan Basin. They weren't stupid by any means, but their tribal societies didn't have room for a concept like republicanism. They lived year to year, fighting among themselves, in a place where survival of the strongest was the rule. She'd always considered advanced forms of government a "civilized" luxury.

"How do you know?" she asked.

"I lived with them for a while." He pulled off his glove, showing her the reddened skin of his right hand. "Who do you think funds the Red Hand?"

"I assumed it was leftists in Landfall."

"Some of it, sure. But the Palo Nation loves having Lindet run around after freedom fighters instead of pushing closer to their territory."

"Does she have any idea about any of this?"

"Honestly, I can say that this is one of the few things Lindet doesn't actually know."

Vlora imagined the look on Lindet's face when she found out that there was a literal Palo Nation just on the other side of the Ironhooks. "Aren't there explorers?"

"Plenty. But Kressians don't last long beyond the Ironhooks."

"Oh? Then how did you?"

Taniel's face soured. "I was with Ka-poel, for one. For another..." He trailed off.

"Yeah?"

"I had to murder a small army in self-defense to get them to leave me alone."

Vlora quickly dropped that line of questioning. Her attention shifted to the larger number of paths diverging off the main road into the forest, and then a small family they passed driving a wagon the opposite direction. The one wagon became two, then four, then ten. It was the most traffic they'd seen since leaving the Riflejacks behind.

"There's a lot of Palo," she commented to Taniel, watching a woman pass by with a yoke over her shoulders, suspending two pails of water.

"They're good labor."

"I thought you said the Kressian settlers don't like Palo."

"They don't like sharing an address or a drink with them. They *do* like how hard they work."

"How the pit are those guards back there supposed to tell the difference between a good Palo and a bad Palo?"

"The way they're dressed," Taniel said. He tugged at the front of his buckskin jacket. "If they're dressed like me, they're bad." He pointed to her jacket and tricorn hat. "If they're dressed like you, they're good."

"That's stupid."

"Like I said, no time for critical thinking on the frontier."

They finally reached the outskirts of town—a muddy track that suddenly turned muddier and led under an enormous wooden sign that said WELCOME TO YELLOW CREEK. The canyon opened up into a large valley a couple of miles across, clear-cut and organized, and filled with wooden buildings of all sorts—hardware stores, whorehouses, banks, letter-writing services, cobblers, and everything in between.

The town itself was dense and claustrophobic, trash and shit trod underfoot and filling Vlora's nostrils with a vile stench. The scenery around them, however, was gorgeous. Mountains rose in every direction, shooting up from the pine-forested foothills to bare rock that towered impossibly high into a ribbon of clouds.

"I miss Adro," Taniel said quietly.

Vlora turned toward him sharply, but his face was impassive. "So do I," she said.

They rode deeper into the town in companionable silence, and Vlora realized that she would be shocked if the town housed fewer than ten thousand people. Not a proper city, certainly, but a veritable metropolis this far out on the frontier. "This is much bigger than I expected," she said over the din of the traffic.

Taniel's eyebrows rose. "I'll admit, I'm a little surprised. I've never been in a gold-rush town bigger than a few hundred people. There must be a damn huge amount of gold in these mountains." He raised his hand. "This'll do."

Vlora followed him across the street to a large building on the corner of an intersection. Large letters over the roof proclaimed HOTEL while a sign beside the door said VACANCIES. NO PALO. NO GURLISH. Vlora nearly objected, before realizing that every proper-looking building on the street had a similar sign. Some rejected Kez. Others rejected Stren or Rosveleans. There was even one that said in bold letters ADRANS NOT ADMITTED.

"I see this is a happy, inclusive place," she commented, tying her horse to a hitching post. "I thought you said the Kressians stick together."

Taniel looked uncertain for the first time since the Dynize had arrived. "It's been a while since I've been up this direction. It seems old hatreds are cropping back up."

Vlora bit back a comment about Taniel not knowing as much as he thought he knew. She was still uncertain about his ulterior motives in this whole endeavor, but she *did* trust him. There was no reason to upset him if she didn't have to.

The hotel great room was two stories, highlighting a winding staircase and a row of rooms that looked down from the balcony above them with hallways going off to the side. Most of the main area was taken up with a bar and tables. At this hour they were empty but for a pair of drunks bemoaning some awful fate over in the corner.

Vlora and Taniel were greeted by a wormy little man in a faded purple jacket and flatcap. He called to them from behind a podium that said in block letters HOTEL MANAGER. He said something quickly in Brudanian.

"We need two rooms," Vlora told him.

The manager switched to Adran. "Two rooms will be tight, I'm afraid. The city is very crowded right now and most of the guests are doubling or even quadrupling up!" He followed the sentence with a simpering laugh.

Vlora looked at Taniel, who just shrugged at her, and decided she had no interest in sharing a bed—no matter how platonic— with an ex-lover. "How much?" she asked.

"Forty for the week. Sixty includes lunch and dinner. Drinks are extra."

Vlora plunked a handful of large coins on the podium, sorting through them carelessly and then sliding two across to the manager. "Two rooms." She slid another two across to him.

The manager licked his lips. "I think we've just had a vacancy."

"Good."

The manager hurried away, and Vlora turned to look across the great room. It wasn't much, but it would be home for the next couple of weeks. Taniel slid up next to her, leaning in so that only she could hear him.

"You haven't really learned subtlety, have you?" he asked.

She felt her already dubious mood sour. "I'm a goddamn Adran general. I don't do subtlety."

"You're not an Adran general *here*," Taniel said. "We've got to stay low until we find this thing. You saw those postal relays on the highway. Word could reach Lindet about our presence within a week. The notes I found in her personal library indicated she was already snooping around in this neck of the woods, so she doubtlessly has spies in the city. The Dynize might, too."

Vlora grunted. As much as she hated to admit it, Taniel was right. Their whole purpose here—coming without her army—was to get in and get out without being detected by enemy agents. Handing the manager enough money to buy a horse just to get an extra hotel room was probably ill-advised.

The manager returned with their keys and a pallid smile. "If there's anything else I can do for you, please let me know." His eyes ran across Vlora and Taniel's weapons; then he leaned across the podium conspiratorially. "You'll do well here, I think."

Vlora, whose attention had wandered from the dislikable man, turned to him sharply. "What do you mean by that?"

The manager recoiled. "I mean, with the troubles brewing. You're soldiers of fortune, aren't you? Mercenaries?"

Taniel didn't look any happier than Vlora. "What kind of trouble?" he asked.

"The Picks and the Shovels," the manager explained. "I assumed you came because of the newspaper advertisements."

"Happenstance, actually," Vlora assured him. She looked at Taniel, then continued on cautiously. "We just thought we'd find work guarding some caravans or mines."

"A happy coincidence, in your line of work," the manager said with the tone of voice that implied he expected a large tip. "Trouble's been heating up the last few months. There's two groups in town that own most of the big mines around here, and they've been trying to buy each other out. The Picks own most of the eastern side of the valley." He waved vaguely over his shoulder. "And the Shovels own the west side. Their big bosses have been bringing in more and more muscle to try and make a point. If one of them doesn't agree to sell, it'll be bloodshed by the end of the month."

Vlora prayed they'd be gone by then. The last thing she needed was their presence being complicated with a war over prospecting rights. She thought back to the Palo in the Tristan Basin and then in Greenfire Depths, and realized local politics had been plaguing her entire time in Fatrasta.

She plastered a thankful smile on her face and palmed a five-krana coin, shaking the manager's hand. "Have those rooms cleaned out by supper. Fresh linen, and flip the mattresses." She retreated to the front stoop of the hotel, feeling suddenly claustrophobic. The pungent smell of the mining town didn't help, but turning her face to the sun allowed her to breathe more easily. A few minutes passed before Taniel joined her.

"You're getting posh in your old age."

Vlora opened one eye and glanced sidelong at Taniel. "And you're still just a bit of a smug asshole, you know that?" There was more bite in her words than she'd meant, but she let them stand.

Instead of getting angry, Taniel laughed. "I won't argue that. You and Dad were really the only ones that ever seemed to notice."

"Everyone noticed. But they were scared of either you or Tamas. That famous family temper. Come to think of it, I haven't seen it come out since you resurfaced."

Taniel's smile disappeared, his forehead creased. "I don't want to be my father."

Vlora bit back a remark. Taniel had fled from his father's legacy, faking his own death. Vlora had embraced that legacy and become the renowned general—but at the end of the day she didn't have

Tamas's political skills to deal with the Adran government. Coming here with a mercenary army had been her own sort of running away, so calling Taniel out on his seemed more than a little hypocritical.

Vlora let the silence stretch, taking in the city. It was much dryer up here in the mountains than it had been in either Landfall or the Tristan Basin, and she was glad for it. The heat was more bearable, too, but she imagined the bugs would be just as bad come nightfall.

"I'm going to go for a…walk," she said, eyeing a nearby bar. "Get the bearings of the city."

"Good thinking. I'll do the same."

They split up, heading in different directions down the street. Vlora waited until she was out of sight and ducked into one of the dozens of bars that seemed so prolific along the main thoroughfare. It was barely a building—not much bigger than a good hotel room with three tables and a single barkeep pouring drinks for the miners heading toward or coming back from the hills.

She ordered a beer and took a seat facing the open door, watching the faces pass her in the street, and put her feet up on the chair opposite to discourage company. The beer was terrible, but it was cold, and she downed it quickly and went for another. It took a *lot* for a powder mage to get drunk, but she wasn't looking for that— just the slightest buzz to take the edge off the soreness from a week in the saddle, and a week with Taniel.

She wondered why it bothered her so much. They'd parted on good terms, and she hadn't seen him for ten long years. In the years since, she'd thought long and hard about whether she had any residual feelings for him, and decided it wasn't that, either.

Perhaps it was because they'd been practically siblings before becoming lovers. Taniel and Tamas had saved her from the streets and given her purpose, and Taniel had been her closest friend and confidant. She wondered if there was a part of her that wanted that back. Taniel's murky ambitions, and her own growth over the last decade, made that an impossibility.

Vlora's contemplations—and her fourth beer—were cut off by a figure passing through the street outside the bar. She frowned, tilting her head to the side and glancing at the glass in front of her. She almost ignored the figure, but curiosity got her to her feet and out onto the stoop. She caught another glimpse, and hurried along the walkway to try and get another one, pausing for a moment at the next intersection as the figure finally turned to give her a view.

It was a tall, distinct-looking woman with the shoulders of a boxer and long brown hair in a ponytail. She carried a blunderbuss casually on one shoulder and the right side of her face was reddened by an old blast wound that left her eye milky white. Vlora was certain she knew the woman, yet hesitated for long enough that her quarry slipped down a side alley.

Vlora hurried across the street and turned down the alley, only to come face-to-face with the flared muzzle of a blunderbuss. "Follow me one more step and I will blow your ... Vlora?"

"I'll be damned," Vlora said, raising her hands, open palms outward. "It *is* you. How are you, Little Flerring?"

"*You'll* be damned? By Adom, Vlora, what the pit are you doing in Yellow Creek?" Flerring lowered the blunderbuss and thrust a hand toward Vlora, which she shook happily.

"It's a long story, but I could ask you the same thing." The conversation was interrupted by the arrival of Taniel, who stepped into the alleyway behind Flerring, his sword drawn. Vlora turned to him sharply. "Were you following me?"

"I was just trying to catch up."

"I thought we'd split up for the night?"

Taniel stared at Flerring, clearly unwilling to say more in front of her. He eyed her blunderbuss for a moment before putting up his sword. He did not answer her question.

Flerring looked back and forth between Vlora and Taniel, finding herself boxed in, and scowled at Taniel. "Who the pit is this? Aren't you still with Olem?"

"It's not like that," Vlora explained, gesturing Taniel to join her. He slipped past Flerring and came to stand beside Vlora. He leaned in, speaking in a whisper that only she could hear.

"So you know each other?"

"We do," Vlora said. "She's a longtime contractor for the Adran Army." She smiled reassuringly at Flerring and said in a low voice, "Should we tell her who you are?"

"You trust her?"

"Yes."

"Then go ahead." Taniel shrugged, dropping the whisper. "Your men already know. Word will get out eventually that I'm still alive."

"All right." Vlora spoke up. "Little Flerring, this is Taniel Two-shot."

Flerring scoffed. "No shitting?"

"No shitting," Taniel said, offering his hand.

Vlora continued. "Taniel, this is Little Flerring. She makes powder. She sold the Adran Army enough gunpowder to get us through the Kez Civil War, and then some."

Flerring took Taniel's hand. "Two damn powder mages out here on the frontier. *Adran* powder mages, and one of you is supposed to be dead. What are you doing here?"

Taniel whispered softly, "You're *sure* you trust her?"

"I do," Vlora responded. "She's an Adran hero after the Kez Civil War, and we worked together closely."

"You better trust her," Taniel said, still in a whisper, "because it's here."

"The stone?"

"Yes. I sensed it moments after we split up. I've been trying to find you to tell you. It's definitely here, but I don't know where. We might need help finding it."

Vlora had no idea why Taniel could sense the thing and she could not. It probably had something to do with Ka-poel's sorcery. But confirming it was actually here was the first step in their mission. "Flerring," she said, "do you have somewhere we could talk?"

CHAPTER 19

Michel spent nearly a week following Marhoush before finally losing patience.

He and Tenik sat on the rooftop of an abandoned store about a block from the cobbler's, where their target had been holed up this entire time. It was a blisteringly hot afternoon, the roofing tar sticking to the bottom of their shoes, but Michel wanted the vantage point to be able to see down into the street both in front of and behind Marhoush's hiding spot. He sat near the edge of the flat roof, hidden behind a cluster of chimney stacks, and watched the street while he and Tenik sweltered.

A week, he knew, was a long time. There'd been two other bombings. A perpetrator had been caught after the second, but she'd managed to commit suicide before being questioned. Michel had recognized the body as that of a Bronze Rose who worked for je Tura.

Beyond that one lead, none of Yaret's Household had managed to get any closer to tracking down the source of the bombings.

"Marhoush hasn't come outside for over a day," Tenik observed. The Dynize had his feet up, his shirt off and wrapped around his head to shade it from the sun.

"He might have a secret entrance," Michel responded. He'd spent the first two days scouring the area and consulting old maps to find out if that were the case. The basement of the cobbler's shop *might* connect with the catacombs within the plateau, but he didn't think they did. More likely, Marhoush had slipped out sometime the night before last when Michel was catching a little sleep and just hadn't come back. He'd left one of Yaret's Household layabouts to keep watch but didn't know if they were at all reliable.

Michel would soon find out. He consulted his pocket watch, then glanced down the street, where he saw a squad of Dynize soldiers milling about in the intersection. They took their helmets off, exchanged skins of tea, and spoke freely among themselves. A similar scene was playing out in two other nearby intersections, and Michel couldn't help but smile.

In the short time he'd been among the Dynize, he'd found out a great many things. One was that Yaret's Household had access to hundreds, perhaps thousands of loyal soldiers that could be called upon in a pinch. Another thing he'd learned was that Dynize soldiers took orders *very* well. Give them a battle plan and they'd follow it. Explain how to properly stage a raid, and they'd follow your instructions to the letter.

"What happens if we don't catch the Silver Rose?" Tenik asked. He took out his coin for the first time in two days and flipped it, caught it, then flipped it again.

"Depends on the size of the safe house and the number of Blackhats we pull out of it. If we catch even two of them, we'll be able to start asking questions. They might put us back on Marhoush's track or even help us find the Gold Rose." He didn't bother adding *if we're lucky*. He was incredibly frustrated that Marhoush had slipped past him, and if this raid came up with nothing useful, he'd be out a week's worth of work.

Which wouldn't inspire confidence in his new boss.

Tenik lifted his hands, ticking off fingers as he spoke. "Iron Roses are the lowest rung—then Bronze, Brass, Silver, and Gold?"

"That's right."

"And you were a Gold Rose?"

"Only briefly. I earned my Gold Rose just before the invasion by tracking down a Palo freedom fighter. I was a Silver Rose for a couple years."

"This Marhoush . . . how well do you know him?"

"Only by sight. We've met twice, I think."

"You have a good memory?"

"When you're a spy, you have to develop a talent for names and faces. It'll save your life."

"And how well do you know the Gold Rose he works for?"

"Je Tura?" Michel thought for a moment, picturing je Tura in his mind. "I saw him at the Millinery once. He's a mean, stocky little bastard. Shorter than you and twice as wide. Carries a broadsword around with him."

Tenik snorted. "Does he use it?"

"Often, from what I've heard. Chops off the hands of people who anger him, the feet of people who betray him, and the heads of his enemies."

"And your people call us savages?" Tenik tilted his head to get a view of the street before getting comfortable once more. "There are always rumors about powerful people. Are any of them true?"

"I'm not sure. I didn't believe half the rumors about Fidelis Jes until I began to work directly under him."

"I've heard of this Fidelis Jes," Tenik said. "He was one of the people our informants told us to be wary of as we tried to take the city. Was he a good master?"

Michel considered the threats and the morning duels. "I believe he was good at his job."

"That is not the same as being a good master."

"He was an asshole and I'm not sad that Ben Styke cut his head off."

Tenik grinned broadly. "That is the answer I was looking for. You will find Yaret a much better master than that. When he dies, I'll grieve as much as any of his family."

Tenik had referenced Yaret as a good person or a considerate master on several occasions throughout the last week. Michel hadn't spent any time with him since that first day, so he didn't have a point of reference, but he doubted that Yaret could live up to the hype. Michel had worked under decent people and even competent Roses, but in his experience, the higher up the chain of command, the less room there was for basic humanity.

Michel kept facing the street but watched Tenik out of the corner of his eye. He'd come to rather like the man over the course of the week. Tenik was a wealth of knowledge about his people but seemed just as interested in learning about Fatrasta and the Nine as Michel was about the Dynize. He rarely turned Michel away from a question and had a quiet sense of humor that belied his sharp eyes and ability to grasp a concept or situation easily. He was also, Michel had found, oddly naive in certain ways.

The situation between the Palo and the Kressians was one of those.

As if he could hear Michel's thoughts, Tenik suddenly said, "Are the Palo always treated like that?"

Michel glanced over to see Tenik watching the street. He followed Tenik's gaze down to a Kressian man openly beating a Palo laborer about the shoulders with his cane, only retreating when one of the Dynize soldiers seemed to take interest in the altercation.

"Yes," Michel said, returning to his examination of the cobbler's shop. The Dynize soldiers relaxing at the various intersections began to put their helmets back on, saying good-byes as if they had finished a quiet afternoon break.

"You're Palo, aren't you?"

"Part," Michel responded. He leaned forward, watching as the soldiers fixed their bayonets and shouldered their weapons, then began to walk swiftly toward the cobbler's shop. Their counterparts on three different intersections began to do the same, forming a pincer movement that would cut off all four possible avenues of escape from the safe house.

Tenik didn't seem to notice that the raid was going forward. "If you're half Palo, and the Kressians treat the Palo so poorly, why do you fight for them?"

Michel had no interest in explaining the ulterior motives he had for joining the Blackhats and climbing their ranks. For one, it would raise too many questions. For another—well, the whole situation was a sore point, to say the least. He wondered briefly where Taniel's people had hidden his mother and hoped she was well out of harm's way. "Because," Michel answered glibly, "I can still take advantage of being half Kressian to live a better life." He directed Tenik's attention to the raid. "Here we go."

Dynize soldiers flooded the cobbler's shop, the alley next to it, and the buildings on either side. They cut off every possible exit and kicked in the doors, rushing inside with bayonets ready. The raid was a complete surprise—Michel could tell from the lack of gunfire and the surprised look of the Roses as they were dragged into the street and held at musket-point. Michel examined each as they were brought out, praying that Marhoush would be one of the faces.

He wasn't. Thirteen in total were pulled from the cobbler's shop. Michel guessed that only seven of those were actual Roses—the rest sympathizers. A small crowd of onlookers began to assemble. The soldiers ignored them, dragging off their captives, and the traffic soon returned to normal. Michel waited for about five minutes before he signaled to Tenik.

"Let's go see what kind of a catch we got."

The captives had been taken to an abandoned warehouse about half a mile away. Michel and Tenik joined the captain of the soldiers just outside.

"We found Roses on four of them," the captain said, dropping the medallions into Tenik's outstretched hand. There were three Irons and a Bronze. "Two others seem to be Blackhats as well. The rest claim ignorance."

"The cobbler?" Michel asked.

"He says he had no idea Blackhats were hiding in his attic." The captain did not sound convinced.

"Did they tell you where Marhoush is?" Michel asked.

She shook her head. "The lot claim to have never heard the name."

"Let me see them."

Michel entered the warehouse through a side door and climbed up to an iron catwalk that crossed above the middle of the large, dusty space. He proceeded to a spot just above the group of prisoners. They sat on the dirt floor, hands tied, heads down, with a group of soldiers keeping watch. Michel leaned on the catwalk railing and examined them for several minutes.

"That one," he finally said in a quiet voice, pointing to a woman whose lip bled from being smacked around by a soldier. "She's a Bronze Rose. She used to be a Silver Rose. A year ago she was caught taking protection money from a family who had personal ties to Lindet. She was demoted."

Tenik frowned at the information. "What does that mean?"

"It means she's a greedy little piggy," Michel responded. "Bring her."

Tenik nodded to the captain. He and Michel headed into one of the second-floor offices on the opposite side of the warehouse, where Michel paced while he waited. Tenik leaned comfortably in the corner, flipping his coin, obviously pleased to be out of the heat. "You're going to try to turn her?"

"I am."

"For over a month, we've been offering rewards for anyone who will turn. Why would she do so now?"

"People don't give up when they think they have options. Our dear Bronze Rose is down to just two, and I'm going to make sure she knows it."

Their conversation was interrupted by the door opening and a soldier coming in with the Bronze Rose, whom he pushed to her knees in the middle of the floor. Her eyes went first to Tenik, then to Michel. She seemed confused to find a Palo and a mutt, rather than a Dynize torture squad.

Michel smiled at her gently, trying to recall her name. "Soreana, was it?" he asked.

"How do you know my name?"

"Because I used to be a Blackhat."

The information took a moment to process before her eyes widened. "You're him, aren't you? Michel. How the pit did you find us already?"

"Because Lindet left a bunch of thugs behind, rather than spies."

"You're a damned traitor."

She wasn't wrong. Michel kept his smile and tutted. "Let's not be so judgmental this early on, shall we?"

Soreana looked around the room, her eyes lingering on the Dynize soldiers standing by the door. Michel could see the same thoughts ticking through her head that had gone through his own in a few tight situations—*How well tied are my bonds? How closely are they watching? Can I fight or talk my way out of this?* He didn't give her a chance to consider those options.

"Soreana, do you know where I can find either Marhoush or je Tura?" he asked.

She drew herself up—as best as she could while kneeling with hands tied behind her back. "I have no idea what you're talking about."

Michel rolled his eyes. "Let's have a quick rundown of your options, Soreana. If you'd like, you can play the good little Blackhat. If you do that, I'll be forced to hand you over to the fine gentlemen outside, who will torture you for every scrap of information and then execute you."

Soreana swallowed hard. The average Blackhat signed on to rough up neighborhood malcontents, not to embroil themselves in dangerous guerrilla warfare.

"Or," Michel continued, "you can tell me what I want and I'll make sure your pockets are filled with gold. We'll give you a job or put you on the next ship to the Nine or give you a whole slew of other options." Michel removed his pocket watch and looked at the hands. "I'll give you thirty seconds to decide."

Soreana looked from Michel to Tenik to the guard. She licked her lips.

"Ten seconds left," Michel told her.

"I'll be safe?" she asked.

Michel smiled kindly. "I've eaten better since I switched sides than I ever did under the Blackhats. The brothels are better, the pay is better." Not precisely true, but a good enough set of lies for the moment. "Five seconds."

He could see her waffling. He watched the last few seconds tick by, silently willing her to talk, then dropped his watch back into his pocket without bothering to hide his annoyance. "Sorry, Soreana. Take her away."

"Wait!" She awkwardly surged to her feet, stumbling into the wall. "I'll take the offer. Please."

Michel glanced at Tenik, who shrugged as if to say, *This is your game.* "Yes?"

"Just promise me that no one will find out I talked."

"I think that can be arranged. Where is je Tura?"

"I don't know where je Tura is, but I can tell you about Marhoush."

"Go on."

"He switched safe houses two nights ago. He moved to the house on King's Street in Lower Landfall. But you won't find him there, not now. He's supposed to be meeting with someone important in an hour."

Tenik visibly perked up. Michel took a step closer to her. "Who? Je Tura?"

"I'm not sure. I just know it's supposed to be in Claden Park at four o'clock. He's been going to these meetings every other day for two weeks."

"All right." Michel took a deep breath. This was the next link in the chain, but he'd have to move fast. Claden Park was clear on the other side of the plateau. "I'm going to find you later and get everything you know about the Blackhats. For now, we're going to make sure everyone downstairs thinks you've been executed. Give me your best scream."

The fastest route across the plateau turned out to be surrounded by a dozen Dynize soldiers on the backs of galloping horses. Michel clung to his saddle in terror as they rounded the western base of the plateau and then cut southeast. They arrived at Claden Park with just minutes to spare, which Michel used to get his feet back under him before borrowing a looking glass from one of the soldiers and scouting out the north end of the park.

Claden was a bit of marshland that had, at one point, been part of a Brudanian lady's estate. Early on in her life she'd filled in the marsh and had it planted with willows and beech as a garden for her sickly husband. Their great-grandson had bequeathed the land to the public—along with a generous endowment for policing and upkeep. Rumors had swirled for years that local industrialists were leaning on Lindet to develop it, and Michel wondered what would happen to the land under Dynize rule.

For now, it was still a park about the size of six city blocks. Traffic passed through a narrow road running down the middle, and a few squatters' tents had popped up in the overgrown lawns. Michel swept the looking glass back and forth until he saw a middle-aged man sitting on one of the benches, surreptitiously reading a newspaper.

"Heads down," he told the soldiers. "You need to look like you're just passing by and not like you're waiting for something. Do a circuit around the park, then head down that street there"—he pointed to a street leading to the industrial quarter—"and post someone at the corner to wait for my signal."

Michel split from the group, Tenik in tow, and headed in the opposite direction around the park.

"Marhoush is waiting on the bench there—don't look!" Michel told Tenik. "Whoever he's meeting hasn't arrived yet, and will probably wait for your soldiers to go before they approach." Michel kept walking at a leisurely stroll. After he reached the midpoint, he stopped behind a tree and kicked at a rock, hands in his pockets like any loitering Palo on a hot afternoon. "Flip your coin," he told Tenik.

They had to wait only a few moments before a figure approached Marhoush, sitting down on the bench next to him. Michel watched out of the corner of his eye for a moment, then moved a few dozen yards down the road to get a profile look of Marhoush's contact. He slid the soldier's looking glass from his sleeve and held it up to his eye. He blinked, rubbed the lens, and looked again.

Without a word, he handed the glass to Tenik.

The figure sitting next to Marhoush was one who had burned herself into Michel's memory a week earlier. She had a soft face and medium-length red hair, and she lounged with a casual ease next to

Marhoush. She was dressed like a Palo in a low-quality brown cotton suit. It was, without a doubt, Devin-Forgula.

"Why is she meeting with a Silver Rose?" Michel whispered.

"I have no idea."

"Do we bring her in?" Michel asked.

Tenik lingered with the looking glass to his eye for an uncomfortably long time before finally lowering it. His face looked like he'd just eaten an unripe lime. "You're certain that this Marhoush is still a loyal Blackhat?"

"Mostly certain," Michel replied.

"*Mostly.*" Tenik chewed on the word. After a few moments, he said, "No. She is one of Sedial's and if we make accusations we must be prepared to back them up. We take this to Yaret as soon as he can see us."

CHAPTER 20

Styke, Ka-poel, and Celine arrived in a tiny town called Grana-lia a few days after leaving Tenny Wiles. Granalia was nestled between two forested hills in eastern Fatrasta, and though it was a long way from Landfall, it appeared to be abandoned as they came over the hill and rode down the main street.

"Ka-poel is going to teach me her sign language," Celine told Styke proudly.

"Oh?"

"Yeah. That way she won't have to write everything down. I can translate for her."

"And when did you decide that?"

"This morning, when you were taking a piss."

Styke rolled his eyes. It would, he admitted, be useful to have a translator. Celine was a quick girl—she already knew Adran, plus a lot of Palo and Kez and a smattering of half a dozen other languages. He had little doubt she would be able to pick up a sign language in no time.

As they drew closer, Styke was surprised to find signs of violence: doors hanging from broken hinges, smashed locks. He dismounted to examine a few of the buildings, only to find the inside of the pub a mess of broken bottles. The general store was cleared of anything useful, as were all the houses and shops. He found a half-eaten meal on more than one table and sniffed at the fly-covered contents. Whatever had happened here was recent.

"They haven't been gone for more than a couple of days," Styke said as Celine followed him into one of the houses.

She frowned at the contents of the table. "I don't like this town. I gives me the creeps."

"It's just empty," Styke told her. "Nothing here is going to hurt you."

"I didn't say anything would hurt me," Celine replied defiantly. "I just said it gives me the creeps." She rubbed her arms, looking around, and followed closely when Styke went back outside. "How long do we have to stay?"

"Until the Mad Lancers catch up. They should be here today, tomorrow at the latest."

"What if they already passed?"

"I'd see signs of a thousand cavalry having passed through town." Styke returned to Amrec and rubbed his nose. He wouldn't admit it, but the empty town had unsettled him. They were far from Landfall—much closer to Little Starland—and if the Dynize were raiding all the way up here, it meant that Jackal's spirits were right about the fall of the other big coastal cities.

If things were serious enough, it might spell trouble for the Mad Lancers.

He turned his attention to Ka-poel, who squatted in the dirt road, running her fingers through the ruts from a wagon wheel.

"Any idea what happened here?" he asked.

She shook her head.

"The Dynize obviously took the people who lived here," Styke said. "But we haven't seen any evidence of that anywhere else. Why take *these* people?"

Only silence answered his question. Ka-poel touched her fingers to a spot on the ground and crossed over to Styke, showing him the gooey blackness on her fingertips. Blood, a couple days old. She seemed to feel at the air with those two fingers, then led them around the back of the church to a small, fenced-off graveyard, where someone had neatly stacked half a dozen bodies like firewood.

The smell hit them as soon as they rounded the building, and Styke was surprised he hadn't caught it earlier. The corpses stank of shit and death, coated in flies as thick as molasses. Piling them unburied in a graveyard seemed like someone's idea of a twisted joke.

Styke appreciated that kind of humor.

Ka-poel wiped the old blood off her hands on the grass, then cleaned her fingers with a handkerchief and pulled out her chalkboard. *They did not resist,* she wrote.

That was Styke's first impression as well. He stepped over the graveyard fence to get a closer look and was surprised when Celine followed him. Maybe the place genuinely *did* spook her. Bodies, on the other hand, were something she'd grown used to.

He squatted beside the pile, running his eyes over them. If this had been a normal raid, or a looting gone bad, the bodies would have been left where they'd fallen, not stacked here in a bizarrely orderly fashion. These men and women had been executed—some with musket blasts to the back of the head and others bayoneted to death. They hadn't fought back.

It had to be the Dynize. But this town was much bigger than six people. Why lead off the rest, but not these?

Ka-poel joined him, writing something on her slate. *This is a Palo town.*

"So?" Styke asked.

She pointed at the corpses, forcing him to look once more. Slowly, it dawned on him. The dead were all Kressians. "So they killed the Kressians but led away the Palo?"

Ka-poel nodded.

"Why?"

She shook her head. A few moments passed, and she headed off on her own, poking around in the grass and walking into one of the nearby houses—no doubt looking for clues as to the fate of the town. Styke remained with the bodies for a moment, studying them thoughtfully, then did a circuit of the church.

He wandered through several more buildings in a half-hearted bid to discover a survivor before finally giving up and returning to the front stoop of the general store with an overlooked bottle of gin and a fresh horngum root from the apothecary's garden at the end of the street.

He broke off a piece of horngum and chewed it thoughtfully, feeling the numbness spread through his jaw. After a swig of gin the numbness spread to his back, hips, and ass to happily relieve so many weeks of riding tension. He leaned back on the stoop and offered the gin to Celine. She took a sniff of the bottle, shaking her head.

The silence was interrupted by the sound of hooves in the distance. He listened to them approach, waiting for the shout of one of Ibana's scouts.

But there was no shout, and the hoofbeats grew louder. He frowned, looking over at Celine. The sound was coming from the east. Unless Ibana had found a shorter route, she should be coming from the north. "What kind of horse is that?" he asked Celine.

She tilted her head to listen. "It's light," she said. "Maybe an Angland racer?"

"It's not an Angland." Styke got to his feet. The road from the east was on the other side of the church. The problem that unsettled him was that he did not recognize that hoofbeat, not entirely. It sounded like...

He rounded the church to spot a small group coming toward him on Dynizian mounts. There were six of them—four men and two women—wearing regular Fatrastan traveling clothes and not outwardly armed. They had the red hair and freckles, but their horses precluded them from being Palo. Styke felt the hair on the back of his head stand on end as they came to a stop on the other side of the graveyard, barely sparing a glance for the pile of corpses.

"Who are they?" Celine asked.

"Go back to the horses," Styke said. "Find Ka-poel. Both of you go to the edge of town and wait for me."

"What do you...?"

"Now!"

Celine set off at a run. One of the horsemen broke off from the others and began to trot after her. Styke put himself in the man's path. That seemed to be enough, as the rider simply switched his attention from Celine to Styke. All of the riders were staring at him.

"Are you Ben Styke?" one of them asked in heavily accented Adran. The woman speaking had a scar across her left eye. Whatever had caused it had barely missed leaving her half-blind.

"Who wants to know?" Styke slowly reached for his knife.

The man whose horse Styke had blocked pointed at Styke's chest. He spoke in Dynize, but it was close enough to Palo that Styke could understand most of it. "Look at his size. He's a crippled giant with gunshot wounds. Has to be him."

"Ji-Orz, go keep watch," the woman with the scar said. One of the men broke off and headed back the way they'd come, remaining on horseback on a nearby hillock. "You *are* the man they call Ben Styke, correct?" she asked.

Styke's feeling about these Dynize grew worse and worse. He took a half step back. The group was far too at ease to be soldiers. Styke could see the bulge of knives beneath their coats, but none of them carried a firearm. He tried to remember the Dynize title "Ji," but he didn't think he'd ever heard it before. "I am."

The nearest one leaned over in his saddle, peering at Styke. "You think it was just a story? I can't imagine an old cripple like him killing Ji-Kushel."

Styke's blood ran cold as he remembered the name. Kushel. The dragonman he'd killed in Lady Flint's muster yard. "Ji" was the title for dragonmen. He felt a small bead of sweat break out on the back of his neck and wrapped his fingers around the hilt of his knife. Six dragonmen. Styke nearly died fighting *one*.

"We were sent by Ka-Sedial," the woman said, "to kill the man who murdered one of our brothers in single combat. You killed Ji-Kushel?"

Styke had the sinking feeling that he was about to die. He fought the feeling, flinging it from his mind with a growing annoyance. *Six* dragonmen. Whoever this Ka-Sedial was, he had no intention of underestimating Styke. "Yeah," he said. "I killed him. I popped his head like a zit."

One of the other dragonmen snorted in derision. They glanced from one to the other, barely suppressing smirks. They didn't seem all that worried that Styke had murdered one of their comrades.

"Ji-Matle," the woman said, "go secure that girl."

Ji-Matle flipped his reins, urging his mount forward into a casual trot that belied any kind of urgency. He came abreast of Styke and looked down at him, shaking his head. "I still don't believe it."

Styke stepped sidelong in front of the horse, jerking his head back from Ji-Matle's quickly drawn blade, and rammed his boz knife through the neck and up into the brain of the horse. It spasmed, and blood fountained from the wound to cover Styke's arms. He shoved, pushing the dying creature over as Ji-Matle leapt free with startling dexterity.

The dragonman landed in a crouch, looking at his horse in dismay. "You're strong," he noted, looking over his shoulder at his companions.

"Finish him quickly," the woman said, "and we can be back in Dynize by the end of the month."

"You really think they're going to let us go home with a war on?" Ji-Matle asked.

"We have Ka-Sedial's word. Would you question that?"

"Of course not."

Despite Styke's display of strength, none of the dragonmen seemed at all concerned about the danger. While they spoke, Styke circled around to the horse and knelt by it, sawing at the neck with his blade as if making sure the creature was dead. The warmth of its blood felt slick between his fingers, and he whispered an apology.

"Come now, Ben Styke, you have already killed my horse," Ji-Matle said, gesturing with a bone knife.

"I've got a knife like that," Styke said, still kneeling by the horse. "It belonged to your friend Kushel."

The woman's eyes narrowed. Ji-Matle looked to her once again, as if for guidance. "Where is that knife?" she asked.

"Left it with a friend on the other side of the country," Styke lied. "I just want you to know that I used it to cut out Kushel's tongue and eyes before he died, then I took a shit in his mouth."

The woman spat. "These Kressians are all damned savages. Kill him, Ji-Matle, and we will be gone."

Ji-Matle frowned, appraising Styke for several seconds before darting forward and drawing a second knife. Styke caught sight of the dragonskin armor beneath his duster just as Ji-Matle leapt over the dead horse, swinging his knife downward.

Styke whipped his left hand out of the horse's neck, flinging warm blood into Ji-Matle's eyes and then rolling out of the way of the swipe. He came out of his roll and reversed directions as Ji-Matle barely managed to stick his landing and stumble toward the graves. He dropped one of his knives, pawing at his eyes. Styke ran at him on the balls of his feet, boz knife forward. Ji-Matle swiped blindly, slashing through the left arm of Styke's jacket, the blade biting into his skin. Styke did not slow, ramming his own knife into Ji-Matle's groin and plowing him over.

Ji-Matle continued to struggle despite the life flowing out of him, reversing the grip on his knife and swinging for Styke's side. Styke caught him by the wrist and slammed Ji-Matle's elbow against a marble gravestone, bone erupting from the skin. Ji-Matle refused to scream, still attempting to fight until Styke grabbed him by the face and smashed his head against the same stone.

The fight was over in seconds. Styke dropped the crumpled figure at his feet, fingers covered with blood, brain, and bits of skull. It seemed like his whole body was slick with warm blood—from the horse and from Ji-Matle—and he turned to face the dragonmen.

They stared at him as if in disbelief, looking at him and at the corpse of their dead companion. The woman spoke. "Ka-Sedial was right not to underestimate you, Ben Styke," she said quietly. "Kill him."

The word had barely left her mouth when a blast went off nearby and the top of her head exploded. Her mouth remained open, her face fixed in an expression of mild annoyance, before she toppled off her mount and to the ground.

Both Styke and the remaining dragonmen looked for the source of the blast, only to see Celine sitting astride Amrec less than twenty yards away, partially hidden by a nearby house. She held Styke's carbine in both of her hands. She trembled visibly, and immediately began to reload the carbine.

Several things happened at once. First, the dragonmen began to move—one toward Celine and two toward Styke. Celine dropped the carbine, and Styke began to run toward her, shouting over his shoulder, "Ka-poel, if you're done hiding, I could use some of that blood magic!"

The nearest dragonman froze. "What did he say? What name did you speak?"

The dragonman keeping watch from nearby shouted, taking the attention of all three of his remaining companions. They suddenly turned their horses and beat a fast retreat toward the east, leaving Styke standing in bloody clothes to try and figure out what had scared them off.

He didn't have to wait long. The sound of approaching riders came swiftly, and soon behind them the Mad Lancers rode out of the forest to the north with Ibana and Jackal at their front. Ibana joined Styke quickly, staring at his clothes and the bodies of the dragonmen. "What happened? Do you want us to run them down?"

"Not a great idea," Styke said. The lancers might have a better chance against dragonmen with carbines at a distance, but he did not want them to get tied up in a forest against those bastards. "Keep everyone tight, and triple the scout patrols."

"Who the pit were they?" Ibana asked. "And what happened to you?"

Styke hurried toward Celine, calling over his shoulder, "They're dragonmen, and they've been following us since Landfall. Apparently they've been sent to kill me." He reached Amrec and picked up his carbine, returning it to the saddle. Celine looked distant and frightened.

He pulled her down, taking her in his arms. "It's all right," he told her.

"I killed her."

"You did. It was a very good thing."

Celine blinked at the sky. "I didn't like it."

Styke squeezed her gently and set her on her feet, only then realizing she was now *also* covered in blood. He lifted her chin with one finger, laying his other hand on her shoulder. "It's okay. You never have to kill anyone when I'm around. Never again."

"But she would have killed you." Her face hardened. "I didn't like it, but I won't let anyone kill you, Ben."

"I know," Styke said gently.

She looked down at his arm. "You're bleeding."

"That's just horse blood. And human. But it's his."

She poked him, sending a jolt of pain up that arm. "It's also yours."

"Right. I'll get cleaned up in the river. Go find Sunintiel. Tell her you killed a dragonman. She'll be very proud." He pushed her away and headed back to the bodies, only to find Ka-poel had beaten him there. She frowned down at the dragonmen's corpses. He said, "If they had rushed me, could you have done anything?"

She shook her head.

"That's not very reassuring." He paced from one end of the graveyard to the other, walking off the adrenaline rush. Part of him knew that he very easily could have died. Another part rejoiced at fighting another real warrior like that. The fight with Kushel had been drawn out. This had been short, brutal, and satisfying. "Did you find out anything about the town?" he asked Ka-poel.

She shook her head.

Frustrated, Styke paced the graveyard again. Maybe he *should* have sent the lancers after those dragonmen. Losing even a hundred men would be worth not having four dragonmen prowling the countryside. He thought about the woman Celine had shot and turned to Ka-poel.

" 'Ka' is the title for the bone-eyes, right?"

Of the royal family, she wrote on her slate.

The implication was not lost on him. "So what are you, some kind of princess?"

Another head shake.

"Then what?"

I don't know, she wrote.

Styke stared at her for several long seconds, hoping she'd give at least some sort of elaboration. When none was forthcoming, he finally turned away to examine the passing column of lancers. None of them looked worse for wear, which meant they hadn't run into any trouble the last week. But that, he was certain, was about to change.

CHAPTER 21

Vlora, Taniel, and Little Flerring relocated to a small complex of cabins deep in the forest on a gently sloped hillside. Flerring pointed at each of the buildings as they passed, explaining their uses. Most of the buildings were used for the creation and storage of black powder, but a few stone huts way up the hillside away from all the others were set aside for the substance that had made the Flerring family a household name throughout the Nine: blasting oil.

"We do everything explosive," she explained to Taniel as they headed up a path to a cabin sheltered from all the others by a large boulder. "Black powder was our original trade, and still makes up the volume of our production. You'd be surprised at how many different mixes there are for mining applications. Explosive velocity, temperature, humidity—all these things have to be taken into account when we decide the formula and granule size."

"Just like mixing powder for military use," Taniel said.

"But far more complex!" Flerring declared. "Out here in the

mountains, you've got to be more careful. I'm handing explosives over to idiots from all over the world, most of whom have never even fired a gun, let alone drilled into solid rock and detonated explosives in the hole. I've got to know what kind of rock it is, the altitude, the depth of the mine." She scoffed. "I do everything I can to make it simple for the miners, but people still die every day."

"Is that why you're here?" Vlora said. "I'm surprised you're on-site, rather than one of your people."

Flerring made a sound in the back of her throat. "I'm on-site because I'm making a damned fortune selling these miners blasting oil. Transportation has been banned all over the Nine due to . . . accidents . . . so the damned stuff has to be mixed in person. I wanted to do a little traveling anyway, so . . ." She shrugged and unlocked the cabin, ushering them inside. It was cozy without being cramped, with space enough for perhaps a dozen people to gather around a potbellied stove or half that many to enjoy a game of cards.

Flerring stoked the fire and put on a kettle, then kicked her boots off. "So that's why *I'm* here. You going to tell me what a dead war hero and a decorated Adran general are doing in the armpit of Fatrasta?"

Vlora had been struggling with how much to actually tell Flerring. She was perfectly trustworthy—after all, someone in the explosives business has to know how to keep secrets to keep a leg up on her competitors—but this wasn't the kind of information she wanted spread around.

Taniel gestured toward Vlora, as if to say, *She's your friend.*

"We're looking for an artifact," Vlora said. "You've heard about the war?"

"Everyone has," Flerring replied. "Word just arrived the other day that Landfall fell. We're so far off the beaten path that no one here wants to abandon their claim, but if the fighting swerves this way, my bags are packed."

"Right. Well, we're looking for an artifact, an ancient bit of Dynize sorcery that should be floating around nearby."

"*Is* floating around nearby," Taniel corrected.

Vlora went on. "This artifact is the reason the Dynize are invading. It has both Lindet and the Dynize scrambling to find it."

"And you want to get to it first?"

Vlora glanced at Taniel, whose expression was unreadable. "We want to destroy it," she said.

"Huh." Flerring moved a few bits around on the table next to her until she found a boning knife and began to pick her teeth with it. "What does it do?"

"It grants power," Taniel said quickly. "Sorcerous power. The kind we don't want *anyone* to get their hands on."

"So you're here to find it and blow it up?"

"Maybe," Vlora said hesitantly. "We have to find it, but we might have to figure out how to steal it. We tried blowing up a matching artifact outside of Landfall with enough black powder to level a city and it didn't do shit."

Flerring snorted. "You military types think you know how to blow things up properly."

"I'd like to see you do better," Taniel said.

Flerring sat forward as if intrigued. "I'm guessing by your presence that this is a matter of the Adran Cabal?"

"It is," Vlora said.

"Well, then, as a representative of the Adran government and for a small consulting fee, I would be delighted to try."

Vlora realized, without even knowing it, that she'd been hoping Flerring would make the offer. The thought pleased her to no end, but there was a niggling feeling in the back of her head that not even Flerring's blasting oil could damage the powerful sorceries protecting the godstone. "Consider yourself hired. But we still have to find the thing."

"Not sure if I can help with that," Flerring said. The kettle began to boil, and she got up and poured them each a cup of tea, then disappeared beneath the floor and returned a moment later with a handful of shaved ice, plunking a bit in each cup. "I've been here a while. If someone had found a sorcerous artifact, I think I would have heard about it by now."

"Perhaps," Taniel said. "It might be buried. It might be actively hidden. If you're willing to help us find it, we can do more than whatever the fee the Adran government will give you."

"Fascinating." Flerring continued to pick at her teeth with the knife, her face thoughtful. "It's a bad time to ask questions, but I'll see what I can do."

"What *is* going on?" Vlora asked, sipping her tea. "We got a little of it from the hotel manager. Some kind of power struggle?"

"You could say that. Everyone wants the gold, but not everyone wants to work for it. Now, when we talk about gold sniffers in Yellow Creek, you've got freelance fools digging their own holes or panning for gold in the streams, and you've got hired fellas. The hired fellas work for one of two bosses, and those bosses own all the big claims in the surrounding hills." She held up two fingers. "There's Jezzy, the owner of the Pink Saloon. Her boys are called the Shovels. Then there's Brown Bear Burt. He's a Palo out of Redstone who made a fortune selling family land to Lindet after his whole tribe died to disease. Burt's hired fellas call themselves the Picks."

Vlora leaned back, trying to take it all in, rubbing her eyes. "Don't these guys know there's a war on?"

"You try to tell a desperate man he should abandon his claim to possible riches and he will gut you seven ways from sundown." Flerring sighed. "Some of the independent miners are getting smart—selling their claims or closing things off to wait out the war. But not Jezzy and Burt. Those two are locked in a feud for control of the mines and won't let up till one of them is dead or the Dynize roll into town to claim the whole lot."

"We might be able to use this to our advantage," Taniel said thoughtfully. "With all this chaos, we need to find the artifact and get out of here before Lindet even knows where we are."

"Seems like a good call." Flerring spat on the floor. "You know that bitch tried to kidnap me? Had some muscle up here six months ago trying to take me to Landfall. Had to run them off with a couple vials of blasting oil, then make it clear to her that if she ever wants to do business with the Flerring Company, she will wait until I come to her."

"I've met Lindet," Vlora said. "I can't imagine she took that well."

Flerring spat again, then finished her tea. "I don't care how she took it. Brute force has no place in the business of explosives, no matter how incongruous that may seem. It's all careful, planned, and gentle." She squinted toward the window, nodding to herself. "Sun's going down. I need to do my rounds before dark, and you should get back to town."

She walked them to their horses and then said good-bye before heading to one of the outbuildings.

Vlora and Taniel returned to their hotel just at dark and had dinner in the great room. The food was better than road rations— barely—with watered-down beer and unidentifiable meat. They spoke quietly about Flerring and their search for the stone.

"I figure," Vlora said as they finished eating, "we have two or three weeks until Olem gets here with the army. Those hills and narrow roads are going to slow them down, and I told him to take it easy. If luck is with us, we can find the stone and figure out a way to destroy or move it before they arrive. We sneak in a group of men and we can be out of here without having to bring in the army."

Taniel's eyes roamed the great room. "Lots of armed men," he said. "If it comes to a fight, they won't stand a chance against the Riflejacks, but the last thing we need is locals seeing an army and digging in. They'll slow us down. We keep our own heads down while we search. Don't let anyone know who we are. And we've got to stay out of this Picks and Shovels nonsense."

"You won't hear an argument from me," Vlora said.

Taniel put aside his plate and produced a leather satchel, flipping it open to reveal a sketchbook. Vlora felt the corner of her mouth tug upward, and she found herself happy to see that Taniel still enjoyed his old hobby. She remembered posing with Bo and Tamas as a child, while Taniel—face serious—forced them all to sit still for hours while he perfected his charcoal drawings.

She didn't pry, but a glimpse at the pages as he flipped them told her that he'd gotten much better since then.

"That," Taniel said, nodding across the room, "is a funny-looking man." He opened to a fresh page and began to sketch.

Vlora would have loved to stay and watch him work, but she needed some time alone to think—and a full night's sleep would do her damned good. She fetched a bottle of wine from the barkeep and headed upstairs, gently tapping each door as she passed it until she reached the number that matched her room key. Rubbing her eyes, she stepped inside and closed the door behind her.

She was surprised, when she blinked through her tired haze, to find the room already occupied. Three men waited in the room—all of them big, all of them heavily armed, and all of them with the kind of grizzled faces that looked like they'd been run over by a brigade of cuirassiers. One stood by the window, one leaned against the wall, and one reclined on her bed, grinning at her in what he must have thought was a friendly manner.

Vlora took them all in sourly. Her saddlebags sat next to the bed, so this wasn't the wrong room. "I paid for clean linens, asshole," she told the one on the bed.

The man's grin faded and he stood up, crossing the small room to tower above her. "What's your name?" he demanded.

Vlora looked up at him and resisted the urge to cut his throat. People didn't loom like that unless they were trying to intimidate, and her height meant she had to deal with confident, tall idiots all the time. She could kill all three of them before they could draw their swords, but now was not the time or the place. "Can I help you gentlemen with something?"

"Back off, Dorner," the man by the wall said. Dorner, Vlora noted, was a Brudanian name. The man continued. "We were told a pair of mercenaries had checked into the hotel this afternoon, and were unaware of the circumstances surrounding the, uh, local politics."

The last two words made Vlora want to punch him really hard. Instead, she forced a smile on her face. "And what are you doing in my room?"

"Recruiting," the one called Dorner said in a deep growl. "You're unaligned, and nobody in this town with a sword is allowed to be unaligned."

"And which one of these clubs do you idiots belong to?" Vlora asked. She leaned back against the door, slumping casually, her hands within easy reach of both her weapons.

Dorner drew himself up. "We're Jezzy's Shovels, and if you know what's good for you, you'll sign up with us tonight."

"What Dorner means," the man leaning on the wall said, "is that Jezzy pays the best, and she's not a greasy Palo. We'll pay a hundred a week for your sword and we'll give you a place to bunk."

Vlora pretended to consider. "Not interested," she finally said.

Dorner loomed closer. "Excuse me?"

"I said I'm not interested. I came up here for some easy work guarding a mine or a caravan. This city is hot as a powder barrel over a fire and I'm not interested in getting into some stupid turf war."

"Listen, bitch," Dorner growled, "you're either with us or against us. You can—"

Vlora's palm hit him beneath the chin, snapping his neck back and spraying her face with blood. He stumbled back, crimson pouring out of his mouth. He spat half his tongue onto the floor and immediately began to scream, pawing at his face.

The man by the window rounded the bed, drawing a cudgel, but even without a powder trance Vlora was faster. She punched him hard in the gut, doubling him over, then slammed his head against the wall hard enough to put him out cold. In the same motion she drew her pistol, pointing it at the man leaning against the wall. His hand fell away from his sword.

"You tell your boss," Vlora said, "that I'm not interested in playing in a turf war. I don't give a shit about your sides, and I'd like to be left alone until I see fit to check out of this fine establishment. Is that civilized enough for you?"

The man raised his hands, palms out. "I get it, I get it."

"You were polite, so I'm not gonna smash your face in. Take your asshole friends and get out."

The man pushed his now tongueless companion out the door, leaving so quickly that they forgot their third member lying unconscious on the floor. Vlora stared down at the prone figure and sighed, putting her pistol back in her belt. She reached down and took him by the hair, dragging him out the door and down the hall, then down the stairs while the entire great hall watched in silence.

Taniel sat in the corner, head in his hands, while Vlora dragged the body up to the manager's podium. The squirrelly little man stared at her, eyes wide. "Is...is...is...there something I can do for you, ma'am?" he stuttered.

"You can leave this guy somewhere until he wakes up," Vlora said. "He shouldn't be out more than a minute or two. Send someone up to my room with fresh linens and to clean the blood and the bit of tongue off my floor." Vlora took a handkerchief out of her pocket and wiped the red spatter off her face.

"Did you say 'tongue'?"

"I did. And if you'd be so kind as to not sell my comings and goings to the town big bosses, I'll be kind enough not to feed you your own toes. Good night."

CHAPTER 22

Styke pored over a map by the light of a single oil lantern while the camp around him settled into the silence of an army at rest. They were several miles north of Granalia and he'd finally gotten the chance to wash the blood from his skin and clothes, but the dragonman ambush was still fresh in his mind.

If the Mad Lancers had not arrived, those dragonmen would have killed him, Celine, and Ka-poel no matter how hard he fought. While he'd never particularly feared death, he knew from experience that dragonmen had no problem with harming children, and the idea that they would murder Celine without a second thought made him sick to his stomach. It was a disquieting feeling, fueling an indignant rage that kept him from being able to sleep.

The flaps of his tent were thrown back, breaking him out of his meditation, and Ibana's face appeared in the opening. "Have a minute?" she asked.

Styke joined her by the coals of the fire, map still in hand. "You should sleep," he said.

"Too much to do. You?"

"Harder to sleep since the labor camps." Styke tapped one finger on the back of his Lancers' ring and changed the subject. "How did your ride go? Doesn't look like you saw any action." It was the first time they'd had a chance to talk since their arrival had saved him from the dragonmen, and he needed to catch up.

"We didn't," Ibana confirmed. "We saw three armies—two Fatrastan and one Dynize—and a dozen scouting parties. But we managed to steer clear of any trouble. One thing of note: Lindet's armies are stripping the land. Every town between here and Land-fall that hasn't been looted by the Dynize is being hit by Fatrastans. They're taking harvests, emptying granaries, stealing wagons, weapons, and animals. Anything of use to the war effort is being swept up."

"Conscription?"

"Everyone healthy between fourteen and sixty."

"Pit." Styke didn't like the idea of conscription. Forcing someone to fight didn't make them a warrior. But beyond his personal ide-als, the fact that Lindet had already turned to conscription meant that she was worried about this war. "Next time you see soldiers stealing from Fatrastan citizens, string them up."

Ibana's eyebrows rose.

"What's the point in fighting for people who will starve before winter?"

Ibana responded, "Lindet would argue that every resource left behind is one the Dynize will snatch up."

"Then Lindet damn well needs to guard her citizens better." Styke had a small sense of understanding: The Dynize landing all along the coast meant Lindet had to pick her battles. This was as bad or worse than the Revolution. But that didn't make it right. "You're recruiting?"

"Anyone who is strong enough to ride and hold a lance."

"They know what we're really up to?"

"They know that they'll be left behind if they don't follow orders. We added about a hundred and fifty to our numbers since you left to deal with Tenny Wiles."

"Good enough, I suppose," Styke said.

Ibana watched him sidelong. "How did that go, by the way?"

"It went well."

Ibana opened her mouth as if to ask further, but something in Styke's tone must have warned her away. She took the map, rolling it out on her lap. "We've got some news from our scouts."

"Yeah?"

She paused, looking Styke in the eye. "Do you really believe Jackal and his muttering about spirits?"

"What does that have to do with our scouts?"

"Just answer the question."

"I have more evidence to believe him than not," Styke replied.

"Well, I don't. It's a lot of horseshit."

"Then why do you ask?"

She hesitated again, clearly frustrated. "Because he was right." She drew her finger along the map. "The coasts are in flames. Every major city and most of the small ones are either captured or under siege. Little Starland is definitely gone, just like Jackal told us a week ago. Swinshire is captured, too."

"Shit," Styke said. Swinshire was on one of two major routes from the center of Fatrasta out onto the sliver of land on the west coast they called the Hammer. They'd planned on swinging through Swinshire to pick up news, a day of rest, some recruitment, and a major resupply before their final push toward whatever awaited them near the godstone.

That meant they had one option left—Bellport—and Styke wasn't sure he was ready for that. Valayine, the third of the men who'd betrayed him to Fidelis Jes, was rumored to be in Bellport. Since letting Tenny Wiles go, Styke had wanted more time to consider his actions before another confrontation.

"Bellport it is, then," he said.

"Bellport it is," Ibana agreed, rolling up the map. "You figure out what you want to do about those dragonmen?"

Styke cursed them under his breath. Their mere presence complicated things, let alone the fact that they wanted to kill him. "Did you triple the size of our scouting patrols?"

"I did, but no one has seen hide nor hair of them since they fled Granalia."

Styke remembered the dragonman in Landfall. He'd been an arrogant prick, acting like he could take on an army and win. Styke had now seen two of them fight, and his victories had come from brute force that few could match. He had no doubt that four dragonmen, if they were so inclined, could make life miserable for the lancers.

But would they? They'd taken great pains to come after him when he was isolated. Perhaps they didn't want the risk of fighting a whole army.

"Not much we can do until they show their faces again," Styke said. "Drill the men and make sure they know exactly what we're dealing with. I don't need dozens dead because they underestimate the enemy. With any luck, they'll keep their distance when we reach Bellport." Styke ran a hand through his hair, listening to Celine's snoring in the next tent over. "Drill the men for an extra hour tomorrow. You're still using that buddy system?"

"It's working pretty well, I think," Ibana answered.

"Good. I'm going to try to get some sleep. If you see Ka-poel, tell her we're going through Bellport instead of Swinshire."

Styke watched Ibana drill the men the next morning, enjoying the way the horses raced back and forth across the meadow. He waffled between frustration and amusement when volunteers fell from their saddles or dropped their lances, but was definitely annoyed to see Major Gustar and the Riflejacks were showing up the old lancers.

They rode out of their camp just after noon with a wind at their backs and the sun high in the sky. Smoke rose in a pillar above some town far to their south, and the road was clear for as far as the eye could see.

Styke paused on Amrec, looking back toward the place they'd spent the night, and spotted figures in the distance. Curiosity got the better of him and he removed his looking glass, directing it toward the strangers. They were far enough away that he couldn't make out any details beyond the fact that there were four of them and they were on horseback. They weren't wearing Dynize breastplates or yellow Fatrastan jackets.

They sat still, watching as the Mad Lancers marched down the road before slowly beginning to follow. Styke briefly considered sending a platoon to run them down, but rejected the idea. He'd either wind up with a slaughtered platoon of lancers or waste everyone's time. The dragonmen weren't going to be seen unless they wanted to be seen.

The Dynize bastards, Styke decided, would be harder to lose than he hoped. Troubled, he put away his looking glass and urged Amrec to catch up with the rest of the lancers.

CHAPTER 23

Michel wasn't able to see Yaret until the day after he spotted Forgula meeting with Marhoush. Michel expected to return to the capitol building, where he'd meet with Yaret in one of the enormous offices upstairs. Instead, Tenik led him to a street a few blocks over from the capitol building, where a row of townhouse mansions lay within an easy walk of the engine of government.

The street was full and lively, packed with Dynize dressed in military uniforms and civilian clothing, and it quickly became apparent that the Dynize elite had simply moved into the homes formerly owned by their Fatrastan counterparts.

The Yaret Household was headquartered in one of the smaller townhouses at the far end of the street. It was a strange sight: Soldiers flanked the front doorway, while a pair of redheaded children played in the narrow garden out front and restless teenagers loitered on the sidewalk. Tenik scattered the teens with a sharp word and led Michel past the soldiers to the front hall, where Michel found a bustling household.

"Household," it turned out, was an apt word for Yaret's power base. Dynize of all ages filled the halls and rooms. Michel, with his limited Dynize vocabulary, overheard conversations involving political strategy, economic speculation, war projections, and plenty of gossip as he was led down the halls and up to a door on the second floor.

"Is this Yaret's family?" Michel asked in a low voice as Tenik rapped on the door.

They both looked back down the hall at a pair of thirty-somethings sharing a cigarette and openly lambasting a rival family whose name Michel hadn't caught. "Yaret's Household," Tenik corrected. "Family has importance in our culture, but Household comes first. Everyone in this building is loyal to Yaret through blood, action, or political ties."

"How big is the Household?"

"Here? A few hundred, if you don't include active soldiers."

"And back in Dynize?"

"Tens of thousands."

Michel let out a low whistle and wondered if every other house on this street had the same flurry of activity. He couldn't voice the question before he heard a muffled sound from inside the room and Tenik swung the door open.

Yaret's office seemed to be the only room in the house with a single occupant. It was a large room constructed in the current Fatrastan fashion with deep, built-in bookshelves, a wide window, and an immense desk. The window was open to allow a southerly breeze and the desk had been shoved to one side and replaced in the center of the room with a pair of lounging couches.

Yaret stood in front of one of the bookshelves. He spared Michel a glance, then removed a book from the shelf and flipped through it for a moment before tossing it on a large pile in the corner. "I'm amazed at the rubbish you people stack on your shelves just to look intelligent," he commented. "There are histories, encyclopedias, medical texts, sex manuals. Very few of these books have ever been cracked, let alone studied."

"You should see my mother's house," Michel said offhand. He immediately bit his tongue, wishing he hadn't said that. Admitting to a living mother was a piece of information that enemies could use against him.

Yaret raised an eyebrow. "She likes books?"

"Loves them, sir." Michel cleared his throat. "Mostly penny novels. She likes adventures."

"Does she read them?"

"Every single one. Many times."

"Then she chooses better books than the fool who owned this library." Yaret tossed another book on the pile. "I don't keep books unless I intend on reading them. Seems like a waste of money, space, and resources." He gestured at Tenik. "You're welcome to look through those and see if there's anything you want for the Household library back home."

"Thank you," Tenik said with a nod. He seemed pleased with the allowance, and Michel wondered if such an act was a special privilege. At this point, he understood just enough about Household dynamics to know how little he actually grasped.

Yaret discarded one more book and walked to one of the couches. He lay down, propping his head up with one arm, and examined Michel with a sort of idle curiosity that nearly made him squirm. After a few moments Yaret said, "I understand you have information for me. Have you found the Gold Rose?"

Michel cleared his throat, trying to collect the proper words to explain a week of watching a building with nothing to show for it. He decided to tell it straight. "We've been following a man named Marhoush for a week," he reported. "Marhoush is the second-in-command to a Gold Rose named Val je Tura, who I believe has remained in the city."

"And you hoped Marhoush would lead you to this Tura?"

"Je Tura," Michel corrected the vernacular gently. "Yes, that is what we hoped."

"And has it?"

"It hasn't," Michel answered.

Yaret's eyes flicked to Tenik with a clear unspoken question. Michel took that as his cue to forge ahead before Yaret could make assumptions about complete failure.

Michel said, "Marhoush didn't lead us to je Tura, but he did lead us to someone equally intriguing."

"Intriguing or useful?" Yaret asked, using the Adran word for both.

"'Intriguing' is the best term," Tenik said, stepping in. "But I think it could be useful."

"Well?" Yaret asked Michel.

Michel hesitated. In the Blackhats, he would have done his due diligence before such a meeting. He would have found out Forgula's friends and enemies, whom she was useful to, and why. He would have known ahead of time whether her meeting with an enemy of the state was a surprise, a given, or something else. In short, he'd have a pretty good idea how Yaret would react to the news and whether it needed to be sugarcoated or spun. But Dynize politics was still an unknown, as was Yaret himself.

"We saw Marhoush meeting with Forgula," Michel said. "We weren't close enough to overhear the conversation, and Tenik didn't think we should bring them in for questioning."

Yaret glanced at Tenik, who gave a small nod. "Well." Yaret tapped his chin. "One of Sedial's cupbearers meeting with an enemy of the state. That *is* intriguing." Yaret paused to sweep his eyes across the half-empty bookshelf on the other side of the room. "You were right not to bring them in. What do you make of this, Michel?"

Michel was surprised to be asked. This was no longer his territory. He simply didn't know enough about the Dynize to create an informed opinion. But that wouldn't keep him from trying.

"I'm not certain," he began. "It's possible that Ka-Sedial has turned Marhoush and that Forgula is the intermediary. It's also possible that je Tura is negotiating some kind of deal—again with Forgula as the intermediary."

"Or...?" Yaret asked. The question was a single word, but it held, at least in Michel's mind, a world full of menace.

How, he wondered, did the Dynize react to accusations of treason among their own people? "Or," he finally said, "Forgula has been turned by the Blackhats."

"Forgula is Sedial's creature through and through," Tenik said quietly. "I don't think she would betray either him or the emperor."

"I agree," Yaret said, sitting up and leaning toward Michel. "But it's also a possibility that we can't entirely eliminate."

Michel found himself nodding along.

Yaret continued. "Ka-Sedial's Household is not supposed to concern themselves with spies and enemy agents. Sedial oversees the military and the temporary government on the emperor's behalf. I do not—"

Yaret was cut off by a rap on the door. He nodded to Tenik, who opened it to reveal one of the youths Michel had noticed loitering in the hall earlier. "Pardon, Minister," the girl said, "but Ka-Sedial is here to see you."

"Now?" Yaret asked with some surprise.

"He is at the door, sir."

"Send him in." As soon as the door closed, Yaret stood and straightened his pants and jacket, rolling his eyes. "Do you have demons in any of the Kressian religions?" he asked.

"We do," Michel answered curiously. "Uh, should we go, sir?"

"There's an old saying in Dynize: Speak a demon's name and he will appear. No, I'd like you to remain." Yaret cleared his throat and clasped his hands behind his back, smiling at the door. Tenik took Michel by the arm and pulled him to one side just as the door opened.

Michel had heard more than a few things about Ka-Sedial's singular meeting with Lindet just before the invasion began. Sedial was rumored to be an old man, but Michel had not expected him to be in his late seventies, wearing a teal cloak over a comfortable-looking maroon tunic. Sedial walked with a cane, though it was not clear if he actually needed it, and he had a grandfatherly but slightly hawkish face, with sharp eyes and smile lines in the corners of his mouth.

If Ka-Sedial noticed Michel and Tenik standing to the side, he did not give any indication. "My friend," he said warmly to Yaret, taking Yaret's offered hand in both of his.

"Good afternoon, Sedial," Yaret said in a gentle tone. "I didn't expect your visit. I apologize for the mess."

"Oh, no need. I've been cleaning the bookshelves in my own new home. So much Kressian and Fatrastan rubbish. It's a pity they wasted so much paper!"

The two men shared a laugh as if they were old friends. Michel watched the sides of their faces carefully, and despite the warmth of their conversation he thought he spotted a glint in the eyes of each man.

"My friend," Sedial said, wiping an imaginary tear from his eye, "I was just passing by, but the truth is that a grave matter has been weighing on me for several days."

Yaret spread his arms. "If there's anything I can do…"

"There is." Ka-Sedial's face hardened. The change was almost immediate, like an actor switching masks in the middle of a street performance. The grandfatherly look was gone, replaced by severity chiseled out of marble. "I want the Gold Rose."

Michel couldn't help but frown. He wasn't certain how much communication went on between the Dynize ministers and their Households, but it made sense that Ka-Sedial would know about Yaret's quest for Lindet's spies. Did he really micromanage this badly, or was there something more sinister going on?

Michel saw Yaret's body tense slightly, but Yaret continued as if he had not noticed the change in Ka-Sedial's expression. "We're making progress on our search," he said assuringly. "We believe we're looking for a man named Val je Tura. Unless..." He paused. "If you're looking for the item we used to open the third floor of the Blackhat archives, I believe the minister of artifacts has it now."

"I'm not interested in the artifact," Ka-Sedial said, "nor this supposed je Tura. I want your pet Blackhat. The one who gave you the Rose."

Michel heard his own sharp intake of breath and fought to suppress the sudden hammering of his heart. Out of the corner of his eye, he saw Tenik glance at him with concern, while Yaret and Sedial ignored the noise as if he were a piece of furniture. Michel barely trusted himself to breathe, waiting for the moment Yaret pointed in his direction and ordered Sedial's bodyguards to haul Michel off. Michel did not know much about Sedial, but Taniel's warnings about the bone-eyes still echoed in his mind. And he still had the bruises from Forgula's beating.

"Whatever for?" Yaret asked curiously.

"Because he's a spy," Ka-Sedial replied, as if that were all the reason in the world.

"Yes, I'm aware he's a spy. That's why he's valuable."

"He's *still* a spy."

"Ah." Yaret seemed to consider this as if it were new information. "I think I see where the confusion is. You believe he's still working for the enemy?"

Ka-Sedial gave the cold smile of someone who knew that Yaret was acting a fool but could not think of a way to politely break the facade. "I believe that is the case, yes. Some of my Household are concerned that you've given him too much trust too quickly."

"Oh? I had no idea that the way I run my Household was under scrutiny."

"I—"

Yaret continued before Ka-Sedial could interject. "If my Household is under imperial review, I would like to know immediately. If it is not, I would like to know why your underlings are watching me. The amount of trust I put in someone I've welcomed into my Household is entirely up to me." Yaret's voice continued in a gentle manner, but there was a new bite to his words.

"You're not under imperial review," Ka-Sedial reassured him.

"I'm glad to hear that."

"But I'd like you to consider handing over the Gold Rose for questioning."

"He gave us entry to the Blackhat library."

"True. But we have no idea what other secrets his head may hold."

Michel felt his hackles rise while the two discussed him. He wondered whether Ka-Sedial knew that the man they were discussing was literally in the room. Sedial had given no indication. The thought concerned Michel, and he wondered if Yaret had known this conversation was coming—and if so, why Yaret wished him to stay in the room for it.

Yaret's genteel facade finally broke. "I will not hand over a member of my Household to be tortured."

"He's hardly a member of your Household already," Ka-Sedial scoffed.

"He is," Yaret insisted. "He proved his usefulness when he gave us the Millinery library. He is one of dozens of Blackhats that my people have managed to turn over the last month. Not only is he already the most valuable of those, but he has given me no reason to suspect that he's a double agent. He's actively working with my people to hunt down his former companions."

"And you truly trust him?"

"'Truly'? Trust is a sliding scale, Sedial. He has begun the journey of earning my trust in good faith. I will not break that faith."

Ka-Sedial's hardened expression took on an air of annoyance. He was clearly a man used to being given what he asked for. For his own part, Michel was shocked that he hadn't been handed over already. "He need not be tortured," Sedial said.

"I won't give him to the bone-eyes, either," Yaret said.

Michel tried not to panic at the idea. Ka-Sedial said, "You could oversee the questioning. All we have to do is make sure he's spilled *all* his secrets. If he has, he can return to your Household. No harm done."

"You and I have very different definitions of 'harm,'" Yaret said quietly. "But I think you already knew that."

Ka-Sedial watched Yaret for several moments. His face was still merely stern, but his eyes spoke of a bottled fury. "Don't let our past disagreements cloud your judgment, my friend."

"And don't let your reliance on your sorcery cloud yours," Yaret retorted. He spread his arms. "You control the military and the government. If you try to manage even more, you will run yourself into an early grave. None of us wants that, so I suggest you leave the espionage to me."

Ka-Sedial snorted. "Think on my request," he said before turning toward the door. He paused halfway through his turn, eyes locking on Michel and Tenik as if noticing their presence for the first time. He gave a slight frown and opened the door. Before he could go, Michel spotted a figure standing down the hallway—a striking young woman wearing Privileged's gloves. She was obviously waiting for Ka-Sedial, greeting him with a nod as he emerged. For some reason her presence seemed to drive the danger of this situation home to Michel; the realization that he could be destroyed by two different sorceries or any number of mundane ways made everything just a little more terrifying.

The door closed and Michel found himself alone with Yaret and Tenik again. He glanced between the two of them, his throat dry. No one spoke.

After nearly a minute, Michel cleared his throat. "Thank you," he said.

Yaret looked up from his own deep thoughts. "Hmm?"

"Thank you for not turning me over to them. I have no desire to be tortured, or subjected to sorcery."

"Ah, yes." Yaret waved off the thanks. "You are a member of my Household, no matter how early or tenuous. If I make a precedent of handing my people over to a rival Household, it will make it clear to everyone that I am no longer fit to be a Minister."

Michel waited for an ominous follow-up. Something like, *Don't make me regret this decision,* or *Betray me and I will kill you myself.* It never came. Instead, Yaret frowned at the door for a few more moments before saying, "Do you know why I asked you to remain in the room?"

"You wanted to show me that you protect the people who work for you?"

Yaret gave a genuine chuckle. "Nothing so serious, though I do make a point of doing so...No, I did it to annoy Sedial. He's a prick, Michel, and I don't really give a shit who knows it."

A long, awkward silence filled the room. Michel had the sudden realization that he'd just backed the underdog in a struggle he hadn't known was going on. Yaret might have resources, but Sedial was in charge. This...couldn't be good. "I think he's up to something, sir."

"Sedial is always up to something."

Michel tried to piece together the fragments he had gleaned from his week with Tenik. "His underlings are meeting with a Silver Rose in secret. They tried to intercept me when I defected. I... sir, I know it's not my place to say it, but if spying and counterespionage is your purview, Sedial is definitely making a play for your power."

Yaret and Tenik shared a long look, and Yaret gave a sigh. "You're not saying anything I don't already know."

"Doesn't he have enough power?" Tenik asked. "He is emperor in all but name."

"It is not quite that bad," Yaret said with a gentle rebuke. He turned to Michel with an apologetic smile. "I realize you are getting a very swift—and possibly dangerous—introduction to our world. If you would like to remain with my Household but avoid the current scheming, I can send you back to Dynize."

Michel was surprised at the offer. He'd never had a superior extend an offer of safety before—every day was always about what Michel could do to further the cause, no matter the danger. Yaret seemed to have a different respect for human life than Michel was used to. Funny enough, safety in Dynize would destroy Michel's plans completely. "I believe I can handle it, sir. I promised to be useful in exchange for hostages. I'm not going to give that up."

"Good," Yaret said, giving Michel a tight smile. "Unfortunately, there are too many tasks and too few people to do them. I don't mind telling you that I need someone with your skills right now."

"Tell me how I can help," Michel said. *The farther I climb, the better chance I have of getting access to your records*, he added to himself silently.

"I need you to keep looking for this je Tura, but I also want to know why Forgula is meeting with the Blackhats. Tenik will give you whatever assistance we can spare, including men to follow the Silver Rose."

"I'll get right on it, sir," Michel promised. He waited for a nod of dismissal, then headed toward the door. He stopped with one hand on the knob, turning back. "Sir, I don't mean to question fortune, but this seems…important. Why do you trust me with this already?"

Yaret chewed on the inside of his cheek, once again looking at the bookshelf he'd been in the midst of cleaning out. "Like I said, there are too few people to do too many tasks."

Tenik took Michel by the elbow and pulled him out into the

hall, which had emptied since Sedial's departure. Michel scowled at the door as it closed, wondering what he'd gotten himself into.

"He's trusting you," Tenik said quietly, "because he knows having a high-ranking foreignor in his Household will annoy the pit out of Ka-Sedial."

Michel swallowed. He *liked* Yaret, but something about his relationship with Sedial was personal. He knew enough about Households to realize that if Sedial decided to destroy Yaret, Michel would go down with him. It was not a pleasant thought—and more reason to find Taniel's informant and extract her as quickly as possible.

"Where do you want to start?" Tenik asked him.

Michel thought for a moment. "I'm going to give you a list of Blackhat safe houses. I want them all watched—and I want Marhoush followed. In the meantime, I need to get closer to Forgula."

"How?"

"I'm not sure. Do the Dynize have social entertainment?"

Tenik raised an eyebrow.

"Something like boxing or horse races—a place where Households can intermix?"

"We have...well, the best translation is war games. Very popular among all castes."

"And Forgula?"

"She supports one of the players."

"Can you take me to one of these games? I don't need to meet her—I just want to observe her."

"Is tomorrow soon enough?"

Michel took a deep breath. He didn't need to just climb the ranks of Yaret's Household. He needed to enter Dynize society. Anything that let him mix with more people would give him a better shot at finding Taniel's informant. "I'm looking forward to it."

CHAPTER 24

Vlora met Taniel in the hotel great room for breakfast. He sat in the same place as the night before, in the one quiet corner with his back against the wall, sketchbook on his lap and two plates of eggs and hash in front of them. He pushed one over to Vlora without looking up from his sketch.

She dropped down across from him and craned her neck. Taniel was drawing the hotel manager.

"Do you remember that discussion we had last night about being circumspect in our mission here?" he asked quietly.

Vlora dug into the eggs and hash. "Do you remember when I told you not to be a smug prick?" she replied between bites.

Taniel sucked on his teeth and finally looked up. His face was serious, brows knit in worry.

"Sorry," Vlora muttered into her meal.

"Everyone's been talking about your fight with Jezzy's men," Taniel said. "In here, out there. It's the latest fun bit of gossip. Our only saving grace is apparently there are so many fights every day that people will have forgotten about yours by tonight."

"They tried to recruit me for their club brawl," Vlora said defensively. "And they weren't being nice about it. What would you have me do? I didn't take it far enough to give away who I am."

"But you did draw attention." Taniel nodded across the room to an older woman leaning against the hotel bar. She had an easy manner, with a quality pistol and sword at her belt and epaulets on a faux uniform jacket. She was staring at Vlora and Taniel. "That," Taniel said, "is the Yellow Creek sheriff. The good news is that she's apparently the only impartial bit of law in this town—and she's given you a pass because Jezzy's boys have a habit of coming on too strong. The bad news is she's now going to watch us closely."

"Until something else draws her attention." Vlora sniffed the tin mug in front of Taniel and found watered wine. She lifted it to the sheriff and downed the rest.

"Hopefully soon," Taniel said.

Vlora fetched beer for the two of them, not trusting the water in a place like this, and returned to her seat. "You're in a mood today," she said.

"I spent half the night wandering the town," Taniel said. "I don't sleep much these days."

"Can't?"

"Don't need it."

Vlora felt the hair on the back of her neck stand on end, and was reminded that as much as she wanted to think Taniel was still the boy she'd befriended two decades ago, he was now something more than human. "And?"

"And I can't find the damned thing." Taniel flipped his sketchbook closed in frustration, as if he'd expected to waltz into town and discover the godstone within hours. "I can sense it, and that should be enough. Once Pole knew what we were looking for, she tuned me into the same sorcery as the godstone in Landfall.

I should be like a bloodhound to this thing, but instead I'm just walking in circles."

Vlora sipped her beer. He *did* expect to find it immediately. "Why do you think that is?"

"No idea. It's like trying to follow sound in a fog." He got up and stashed his sketchbook, his eyes focused inward on thoughts he did not share. "I'm going to head back out and—"

Taniel was interrupted by the sound of a crash, and the front door of the hotel suddenly burst open. Vlora turned to look for the commotion and her heart fell. It was that asshole Dorner from the night before and the friend whom she'd dragged down the stairs. Dorner stumbled around the room, clearly drunk, trying to speak with his half tongue. His companion steadied him and pointed at Vlora.

The sheriff perked up. "Boys," she said warningly.

They ignored her and came straight toward Vlora. Vlora stood up and lay one hand on the pistol in her belt. Neither man had a weapon in hand, but both had swords on them.

Taniel stepped between Vlora and the two, barring them both with his arm. "Can I help you fellas?" he asked.

Dorner stabbed a drunken finger toward Vlora, mumbling something. His companion translated. "My brother here lost his tongue to this bitch. We're gonna take hers and see if it fits."

"Everyone needs to calm down!" the sheriff said loudly. She was still ignored.

"I think that's unnecessary," Taniel said. "Let me buy the two of you a few rounds and we'll talk about some way less violent to solve this whole thing. I think that—"

Dorner shoved Taniel hard in the chest, and both men went for their swords. Taniel crashed into Vlora's table, and before either she or the sheriff could respond, his sword was in his hand.

"Calm down before someone gets—" Taniel began.

Dorner leapt forward, sword flashing, his companion on his

heels. Taniel thrust once, pivoted, and pushed before either man could take two steps. The movement was so quick that Vlora could barely follow it. The two men twitched and tumbled, stuck together by Taniel's sword like chickens on a skewer, dead before they hit the floor.

The room was deathly silent, all eyes on Taniel. "So much for keeping things quiet," Vlora muttered under her breath.

The sheriff approached, pistol in hand, circling the two bodies and leaning over to put her fingers to their necks one at a time. "Dead," she proclaimed.

Slowly, Taniel pulled his sword out of the two and faced the sheriff. Vlora could see the fight in his stance, the tension in his legs like a snake coiled to strike. She had no doubt that he could wipe out the whole room before anyone made it to the door, and the thought frightened her.

"Sir, I'm going to have to ask you to disarm yourself," the sheriff said.

"It was self-defense, ma'am," Taniel said.

"I saw that," she replied, "but we're gonna have to put it in front of a judge. You need to disarm and come with me." The sheriff's voice wavered. She could see that same tension in his legs that Vlora could, and she was scared.

Vlora waited for him to move. Whatever he did, she would have no choice but to back him up. Things had panned out about as badly as was possible and she couldn't think of a way to turn it around.

"Tan," she said quietly.

"I know." Taniel took a deep breath and bent to wipe his sword on Dorner's body before handing it and his pistol to Vlora. "Get my rifle and pack out of my room," he said to her. He showed his empty hands and belt to the sheriff and looked down at the bodies, dismayed. "I guess I am a smug prick. And you're on your own until we can get this sorted out."

The sheriff slowly put up her pistol. "You two are just a load of trouble, aren't you?"

"Just trying to live our lives, ma'am," Vlora said.

"We'll get this sorted out before a judge," the sheriff repeated, "and then I'll ask you kindly to live those lives somewhere else. Understand?"

Vlora swore to herself, meeting Taniel's gaze. This was going to be a problem, and both of them knew it. "How long will this take?" Taniel asked.

"Couple weeks." The sheriff sniffed. "We've got just one judge and a damned lot of violence."

Vlora could see in Taniel's eyes that he was reconsidering his offer to go quietly. But the options were slim: Either he could sit in a cell for two weeks while Vlora searched on her own, or they could cut their way out through a lot of innocent people and end up being run out of town. She looked meaningfully at the sheriff and nodded.

"So be it," Taniel said coldly.

The sheriff escorted Taniel out of the building, leaving Vlora alone with two corpses and a whole bunch of eyes staring at her. She left the rest of her wine and took Taniel's weapons upstairs, then fetched his pack and stowed it in her own room.

She slipped out the back of the building, hoping to avoid any more unwanted attention. Halfway down the street she stopped and swore to herself, realizing that without that damned magical compass in Taniel's head, she didn't have a chance of finding anything. She muttered and swore to herself and continued on, trying to formulate a plan.

She found a secluded street in the Gurlish quarter and sat down in an alley to try and focus. She closed her eyes, and took a deep sniff of powder to enhance her senses and focus her mind. Once she was in a deep trance, she opened her third eye.

The world became a hazy, colorless place. Buildings and people seemed almost translucent, and she swept her gaze all around her looking for color. There was a little of it—small flames, like candles burning in windows, that she knew belonged to Knacked throughout the city. There were a few dozen of them, which was unsurprising considering the amount of money involved in such a town. Knacked, after all, were useful people.

There was nothing else, though. No bright flames of a Privileged, and none of the customary pastel smudges that indicated leftover sorcery. She tried to remember what the godstone in Landfall looked like in the Else, and realized that she'd never bothered to check. In the chaos of the battle and subsequent retreat, it had never even crossed her mind.

She cursed herself for her foolishness, and closed her third eye.

"I can't do this on my own," she said quietly to herself.

She returned to the main street and walked along, eyes on the signs above the storefronts. It wasn't long until she found one that said EXPRESS MESSENGERS: YOUR LETTERS, CONFIDENTIAL AND GUARANTEED.

It was a company that she'd seen in Landfall, and she had made use of their services before. She went inside, where a single clerk waited behind a dusty desk, half-asleep with his chin resting on his fist. He roused himself as Vlora entered.

"Paper," Vlora demanded.

She sat in the corner and penned a letter in Adran military code. She sprinkled the wet ink with black powder and then sealed it in wax with a signet ring she kept in her pocket. It was marked with the old symbol of the Riflejacks—a chevron over a powder horn. She gave the letter to the clerk.

"Where to?" he asked.

"That," Vlora said, placing several coins on his desk, "might be difficult."

She gave the clerk her hotel and room number in case of an answer and stepped out into the midmorning air, breathing in the stench. She wanted nothing more than to crawl into a bottle until Olem arrived with the army, but that didn't seem like a very good use of her time. She needed a plan—any plan—that would keep her moving and looking.

Without Taniel's sorcerous compass, she was going to have to depend on footwork. Luckily, she'd already done some thinking on the matter. She would walk each valley and examine each mine, combing the landscape under the pretense of looking for an employer who wasn't the two big-boss fools here in town. It would be slow going, and there was a very real risk of attracting attention, but it was the best plan she had.

She would look for anything suspicious in this world and in the Else.

"Ma'am?"

Vlora was pulled out of her thoughts by a voice at her elbow. She turned and immediately stiffened, her hand falling to her sword arm. There was a Palo woman by her side, wearing a duster and tricorn, and the tight pants and loose shirt of a duelist. She was accompanied by seven men and women, most of them Palo, all wearing similar outfits and also armed with small swords.

Vlora ordered them in her mind, body prepared to work through the motions as she cut her way free of imminent violence. The process took her mere seconds, but it was interrupted by a friendly clearing of the woman's throat.

She looked at Vlora's sword hand. "No need for that, ma'am," she said. "We're here to talk."

"About what?"

"Our boss wants to meet you."

"And who is your boss?" She thought she had a pretty good idea.

"His name is Burt."

Brown Bear Burt. Jezzy's competition. Vlora considered her options. Eight against one were steep odds in a fair fight. She still had a buzz from her earlier sniff of powder, so she could probably take them without too much risk. But if even one was a skilled swordsman, she could be in trouble.

Her eyes narrowed as she realized that not one of them was carrying an ounce of powder. Odd, that. A coincidence? Or something else?

She thought of Taniel sitting in a cell in the Yellow Creek sheriff's office, and decided that the mission had already taken a big enough hit. "When?" she asked.

"Right now, if that's convenient."

Vlora took her hand off her sword. "Then let's get this over with."

The Yellow Creek Picks, as they called themselves, were headquartered at a brothel not more than a few blocks from Vlora's own hotel. It was on the edge of the Gurlish quarter, a sprawling, three-story wooden building with an enormous barroom and numerous hallways leading into the bowels of the establishment. Men and women of every nationality in various states of undress circled the room, chatting up the few miners who hadn't yet left to tend to their claims.

Whores of both sexes eyed Vlora as she walked in, but she was spared the sales pitches and escorted straight upstairs to a spacious room that looked down onto the main floor of the brothel. The center of the room was taken up by a wide desk on top of the biggest bearskin Vlora had ever seen.

The man behind it, despite his name, looked nothing like a bear. Burt was only an inch or so taller than Vlora. He had flaming-red hair and muttonchops and a wiry build. He wore the kind of expensive suit Vlora only saw in the best parts of Landfall, with a gold chain hanging from the breast pocket and a pair of spectacles perched on the tip of his nose. He had papers in one hand, reading them while toying with a big boz knife, the tip of which was buried in his gouged desk.

He set the paper down and looked up as Vlora came up the stairs. She waited for her escorts to take her weapons and frisk her, but instead the Palo guards retreated back down to the bar.

Burt leaned forward, grinning at her, and opened a box on his desk. "Cigar?"

"I would, thanks." Vlora took one, figuring that she might as well enjoy a few minutes before the bastard tried to have her killed, and allowed him to light the end.

"Your name is…"

"Verundish," Vlora said, using the name of an old military colleague. "I'm guessing you're Brown Bear Burt."

"That's me," Burt said cheerfully.

"You're not very bearlike."

"Just *Burt* will do," he said. "Kill one big Ironhook grizzly with a lucky shot and suddenly people make it a nickname." He spoke Adran without an accent—suspiciously so. A lot of Palo spoke Adran, but he sounded like he'd been born there.

Vlora puffed on the cigar. The tobacco was good—very good. She held it out, looking along the length for a tobacconist's mark. It was a small spear with a circle around it. Nothing she recognized. She waved away a face full of smoke. "That's a good cigar."

"Little place off the coast I invested in a while back. Things go well, they'll be selling them as far away as Strenland in a couple years."

Vlora took another puff, then set the cigar carefully on the ashtray on Burt's desk. She couldn't let herself relax, not here. She'd already been introduced to the way people do business here by Jezzy's Shovels, and even someone as skilled as she could wind up facedown in a ditch if she wasn't careful. "Is there something I can help you with, Burt?"

"Hmm. Verundish, you said?"

"That's right."

Burt got to his feet, still puffing on his cigar, and walked over to the balcony to look down to the bar below. He returned to his desk, pouring a glass of whiskey and offering it to her. She declined, and Burt shrugged and took a sip. "Why are you here, Verundish?"

"Came looking for work."

"That's what you say. Yet you've already turned down my competitor, Jezzy."

"I'm not looking for that kind of work," Vlora said. "This town is going to explode one of these days—anyone can feel it—and I have no interest in being in the middle. I'd like something a little quieter."

Burt took a seat, throwing his feet up on his desk. "Your companion, too? He's looking for something quiet?"

"That's the plan."

Burt shifted in his seat. "See, now, that's what's so strange to me. Your kind doesn't really attract quiet, do they? You're too valuable for quiet work."

"My kind?" Vlora was genuinely puzzled. Did he mean Adrans?

"Powder mages."

Vlora stiffened, forcing herself not to reach for her pistol and blow Burt's head off right here and now. *She*, Vlora Flint, was a celebrity and a renowned general. But there were still a lot of people in the world who had it out for powder mages without a name. "I'm not sure what you're talking about."

Burt rolled his eyes. "Don't play coy, Verundish. I've got a Knacked on my payroll that can sense powder mages. Not a very useful Knack, but he's a smart man, so I keep him around. He earned his pay when you walked into town."

Vlora's fingers crept toward her pistol. Behind the desk, with his line of sight, he wouldn't be able to tell.

Burt continued before she could respond. "Don't get me wrong. I'm not threatening you or your companion. I'm not an idiot. Nor do

I *actually* want to know what two powder mages are doing out here on the frontier looking for quiet work. If you're keeping your heads down, I'm not the type of fool to bring that to anyone's attention."

"So what do you want?" Vlora asked coldly.

"Same as Jezzy wants. I just happen to know what you're worth." Burt took his feet down and leaned forward. "Come work for me—the two of you—and I'll pay you five thousand krana up front and fifty thousand the first day of next spring. *Each*."

Vlora couldn't help but raise her eyebrows. He actually *did* know what a powder mage was worth, though he wasn't sure who Vlora really was. That was an immense amount of money for a hired gun for six months of work. She wasn't interested, of course, but at least she didn't have to kill him. Yet.

She shook her head.

Burt frowned. "Eighty thousand."

"Pardon?"

"Same offer. Eighty thousand krana."

Vlora swore inwardly. If she was really a hired gun, she would jump on the offer in an instant. "It's not about the money, I'm afraid."

"What's it about?"

She tried to come up with a better excuse, but found herself grasping at straws. *Nobody* turned down that kind of money. "I don't want to get involved," she said emphatically. "I want *quiet* work. Easy work. I'm not here to show off."

"Ah." Burt puffed on his cigar, examining her through half-closed eyes. "You're hiding from something." He raised his hands in a peaceful gesture. "Again, I'm making no threats. Just an observation."

Vlora knew the risk of such an excuse. If Burt wanted, he could try to blackmail her. But if he was as smart as he seemed, threatening a powder mage was probably low on his to-do list. "It's not personal. If it makes you feel any better, your competitor isn't going to get a rise out of either me or my companion, no matter how much she offers to pay. There are things worth more than money."

"We agree on that, at least. A little quiet is priceless," Burt said thoughtfully. He stood up again, clearly frustrated, and paced behind his desk. "If you're not getting involved, you should probably get out of town."

"I'm not going anywhere until a judge clears my companion."

"I'd suggest you reconsider," Burt said.

"Is *that* a threat?" Vlora asked, keeping her tone neutral.

"Not at all. It's a friendly warning. You're right when you say this town is hot. Fighting will break out eventually, and when it does, anyone with a weapon will be a target. What's more, Jezzy doesn't take no for an answer. You're going to be a liability for her and, frankly, for me. I've got your assurances that you won't get involved, but I don't know you. You could be lying. Or things could just change."

"That sounds like a threat."

Burt showed her his empty hands. "Cross my heart. Just friendly advice."

"I don't know you, either."

"*Touché.*" Burt chuckled. "I think we each know where the other stands now, so I'm not going to waste any more of your time. One last offer: Come work for me." Vlora tensed, looking over her shoulder. The sentence was too ominous not to be the precursor to some sort of retaliation if she said no. But the two of them were alone. Burt continued. "How about this: You sleep on it tonight. Talk to your friend at the town jail, and chew on this bit of information: Jezzy already has herself a powder mage. I'll pay you two whatever you want to kill the bastard."

Vlora rocked back. So *that's* why Burt was so anxious to hire her and Taniel. Two powder mages to counter one. It was surprising information, and more helpful than Burt knew. A powder mage could sense another, so if Jezzy didn't know what she and Taniel were yet, she would soon. And that complicated the pit out of their mission.

Things just kept getting worse and worse.

Vlora stood up, straightening her jacket. "I'll take that under advisement. Thank you for being... polite."

"Of course," Burt said, raising his cigar. "But lest you think I'm too polite: I have people I trust who know what you are. If a bullet happens to find my brain, they'll make sure that whatever you're running from is able to find you. Understand?"

Vlora smiled at him tightly. This man was not an idiot. Unfortunately. "Good afternoon," she told him.

CHAPTER 25

Michel followed Tenik into the capitol building at about noon. It was a weekend and the halls were mostly empty, with just a few couriers and soldiers present. Other than when he handed himself over to Yaret at the beginning of this mess, it was the first time Michel had been back in the building since the occupation, and he allowed himself to take in the small details that had changed along with the government: Red-on-black Dynize flags flew from banisters and high windows, while much of the upholstery on hallway benches had been changed to match. Everything that had the old regime symbols and colors had been either replaced or defaced.

As a spy, Michel was used to being an outsider in enemy territory, but it still felt very strange not to see the familiar sunflower yellow of the Fatrastan flags or the rose symbol of the Blackhats. He knew that they were just cosmetic changes, but they troubled him more than he'd expected.

He did not allow his unease to show on his face as he followed

Tenik down the long main hall. "Who will I meet at this war game?" he asked.

Tenik flipped his coin without breaking stride, catching it every time. "It's hard to say. Most of us haven't been able to attend a game since we left home. This one was put together by the Tchellasi Household—Tchellasi is the minister of finance."

"I'm guessing since we're in the capitol building that it's not exactly open to the public."

"You guess right. It'll be mostly government bureaucrats, senior Household members who make some excuse to get away from their duties for a few hours. I'll stake my ration card on Forgula attending—one of the players is her cousin."

They stopped once as a Privileged and his retinue passed by. Michel mimicked Tenik's bowed head before they continued their trip down the hall. "Will there be any of those?" Michel asked, glancing over his shoulder.

"Privileged? I doubt it. I'll be surprised if we even see any of the minor Names. It'll be mostly cupbearers, Captains of the Guard, stewards, and doormen."

"The people who *really* run the empire, you mean?" This could be a very good experience for Michel. He needed to keep his eyes and ears open—but not lose focus on the current issue with Forgula.

Tenik gave him a sly smile. "We would never presume."

"I'm sure you wouldn't. What role do the Privileged play in Households, by the way?"

"They don't belong to Households," Tenik said. "Technically, all Privileged are property of the emperor."

"I saw a Privileged with Ka-Sedial yesterday."

Tenik wrinkled his nose. "Sedial is different. He speaks with the emperor's voice on this expedition, so the Privileged report to him. I didn't see this Privileged, but I'm surprised Sedial openly has one as an escort. Emperor's voice or not, he has so far been careful not to flaunt his power on this expedition lest he encourage several of the lesser Households to ally against him." Tenik shook his head. "I'll look into the matter."

They rounded a corner and continued on for another hundred paces, where they reached a double set of ornate doors. Tenik pushed one open without knocking, revealing a room that belied the quiet of the rest of the building.

What had once been the foreign dignitary room had been, at first glance, converted into a boxing arena. It was already well suited to observation, with high banks of windows and tiered seating where bureaucrats could observe important meetings. More chairs and another set of tiered seating had been added all around the room, and the enormous table where Lindet had met with Ka-Sedial had been removed.

The arena-like feel was what reminded Michel of boxing. The room was filled with people, stinking from so many bodies, filled with the noise of their cheers, jeers, and the placing of wagers. Tenik shouldered his way through the crowd, pulling Michel along behind him until they reached the object of everyone's attention.

In the center of the room, where the enormous meeting table had once stood, was an octagon over twenty feet across and filled with smaller octagonal tiles of various colors. Carved ivory and jade figurines stood on some of those tiles. It was, to Michel's eyes, the likeness of a general's war map, and it didn't take him long to realize that the two people standing beside the octagon were the "generals" in this war game.

The players moved around the map freely, using long sticks to carefully adjust the positions of the figurines in a seemingly pre-ordained order. A third person, like the referee in a boxing match, occasionally would reach out with a long pincer stick to remove one of the pieces.

Michel was immediately taken with the game. Tenik had

explained the basics the night before, and he'd thought the concept sounded slow and boring. But this moved quickly, each player taking their turn in a matter of seconds while the crowd's noise grew from silence, to whispers, to a roar—all depending on the actions of the players.

He tore his eyes away from the game as Tenik tugged on his sleeve. They moved back through the crowd to the edge of the room, climbing up into an open spot on the tiered seating where they could get a decent look at the room.

Michel took one look around and immediately realized how out of place he looked. His blond-dyed hair and his part-Kressian, part-Palo features made him stand out in a room full of redheads. Even his suit—brown cotton trousers and jacket—seemed drab and strange among all the teal and ivory worn by the Dynize.

More than a few were watching him as he did a slower examination of the room. Some whispered to each other curiously, while others were obviously annoyed at his presence.

"Tell me," Michel said out of the corner of his mouth, "do foreigners often attend these games?"

"Not that I can recall."

Michel cursed himself for not thinking about how out of place he would be—and Tenik for not warning him. He needed to stay in the shadows while he looked for Taniel's informant, not damn well stand on a stage.

He forced himself to ignore the glares and the whispers. "Names," he told Tenik. "I need to know who these people are."

"There's a lot of people here."

"I'm going to have to learn them eventually."

"Where do you want me to start?" Tenik asked.

Michel's wandering gaze finally found his target. Forgula stood about twenty yards away, down at the other end of the tiered seating with her neck craned to see over the heads of people in front of her. To his surprise, he recognized the woman just behind her.

"I thought you said there wouldn't be a Privileged here," Michel said.

"Eh?" Tenik looked around. "Where do you see a Privileged?"

"Behind Forgula. That's the woman I mentioned earlier."

Tenik searched for a moment. "Ah. Saen-Ichtracia. I should have known."

"About what?"

"A Privileged with Sedial? She's his granddaughter."

Michel made a mental note that this was not someone he wanted to cross paths with. "She's pretty."

Tenik laughed softly. "They call her 'the people eater.'"

"Do I want to know why?"

"She's survived seventeen separate assassination attempts. The first was when she was seven. She strangled the assassin with the string from one of her nursery toys."

Michel let out a soft whistle. "Because of her grandfather?"

"She's a member of the imperial family and a Privileged. She gained enemies simply by being born." Tenik clicked his tongue thoughtfully. "Her nickname, it also has a double meaning. You know about Privileged, right?"

"They're damned dangerous."

"Not that. The sorcery, it makes them ravenous."

"For sex?" Michel scoffed. "I thought that was a myth."

"No myth," Tenik said. "As far as I've been able to tell, our Privileged are less... discerning than yours. Try not to catch her eye. If you do, she will use you like a damp rag and discard you. Whether you survive the encounter will be left up to chance." Michel turned to look at Tenik, expecting a tongue-in-cheek smile, but the cupbearer was dead serious.

"You're joking."

"A friendly warning," Tenik said. He went on. "The man beside her is a cupbearer for the Jerotl Household—minister of public works. The woman behind her is a captain of the Sedial Household guard."

Tenik spent the next ten minutes pointing out people and telling Michel their names, Households, and their occupations. Michel repeated each name that was told to him, trying to get the pronunciations down and casting them to memory. Within minutes he was trying to juggle two dozen names. Soon that number doubled. The game below them carried on, and the noise in the room began to grow in pitch, suggesting to Michel that some sort of conclusion was forthcoming.

Michel's eyes kept returning to Forgula. Tenik had described her as a capable woman, and as Michel examined her, he began to see through the deception of his first impression that she had a gentle face. While it was true that some baby fat still clung to her cheeks, she had the thin, hard body of an athlete and her eyes were just as intense as those of the Privileged standing behind her. She grimaced at the game, occasionally smiled, and once bore her teeth toward the players with an open malice.

There was a weight to her right sleeve, suggesting to Michel that she carried a blackjack—the same weapon she'd beaten him with last week. His forehead and arm were finally beginning to heal, and he reminded himself not to allow this to get personal. He was here, he told himself, just until he could find Taniel's informant. The opportunity to have some vengeance on Forgula by disrupting whatever she was doing with Marhoush was a secondary concern.

Unfortunately, the informant's name, Mara, was not among those that Tenik shared with him by the time the roar of the spectators suddenly drowned out the next name that Tenik whispered into Michel's ear. Roughly half of the room broke out into a cheer, while others looked away with disgust and disappointment.

Michel felt his own disappointment, swearing under his breath. He tried to remember what little Taniel had told him about Mara, that she was part of a Dynize higher-up's retinue. "Retinue," he decided, meant "Household." But now that he knew roughly how big a Household could be, that information was practically useless.

There had to be a more efficient way to do this.

Michel discarded the thought and turned to Forgula, whom he saw shaking hands with the crowd.

"Her cousin won," Michel said.

Tenik nodded. "He's a very good player, but he got lucky."

"You were watching the game?"

"Weren't you?"

"I was listening to you."

Tenik slapped him on the shoulder. "If you come to more games, you'll have to learn to talk and watch. Good morning!" he called to someone a few rows down the seating, waving a greeting. He whispered the person's name in Michel's ear, which Michel promptly forgot.

Michel's attention was still on Forgula as she began to move through the crowd, exchanging a few words here, touching an arm there, then a longer conversation. She snubbed one woman, warmly greeted another, then put her arm around a man who spoke in her ear.

Michel noted the faces of each of the people she spoke with, and how they interacted. "This room smells like politics," he said to Tenik. "These games are the political underbelly of Dynize, aren't they?"

A moment of silence passed, and Michel turned to find Tenik watching him carefully. "You're very perceptive."

"It's my job," Michel answered. "I have to know just enough about everything to keep from getting killed. And instinct tells me to get out of here as quickly as possible."

"Instinct?"

"Instinct, and the looks your compatriots are giving me. I'm unwelcome here."

"That is true."

Michel wondered again if coming here had been a mistake. He was a spy, and he should be operating from the shadows. Let the

Dynize upper crust wonder about the foreign spy in Yaret's Household, but keep himself hidden.

But not all spying, he reminded himself, was from the shadows. Hiding in plain sight was a useful strategy. If it didn't get you killed.

Someone passed him on their way down the tiered seating, knocking hard into his shoulder and almost throwing him to the ground. A word was hissed as Tenik caught him. Michel regained his balance. "What did that mean?" Michel asked.

"He called you a dirty foreigner." Tenik's eyes narrowed at the assailant's back.

"Is he an enemy of the Household?" Michel asked.

"An ally, unfortunately. He's a footman for the minister of agriculture. I will speak to him later."

"Let it go," Michel suggested.

Tenik shook his head firmly. "You're a member of Yaret's Household now, whether our allies like it or not. And someone like him"—he nodded to the assailant—"is not high enough a station to get away with insulting you. His minister isn't even here. She's back in Dynize, schmoozing the emperor instead of helping with the cause."

"Just out of curiosity, who *is* high enough station to get away with insulting me?" Michel asked, eyeing Forgula as she continued to wind her way through the crowd. He studied everyone she made contact with—who knew about her contact with the Blackhats? Was there a conspiracy? Was she a traitor? Was her master vying for more power?

Tenik considered the question for a moment before answering. "That is a complicated answer. If you are insulted, *you* should let it go. *I* can deal with it."

"That sounds like my mother telling me to ignore the boys who beat me up in school," Michel responded. He caught the eye of another Dynize staring in his direction, and realized with a start that it was Ichtracia. The Privileged was watching him with open curiosity, and Michel felt a shiver run down his spine. "I think I've learned enough for one day," he said to Tenik. "We should go."

He began to head down the tiered seating, only to see Forgula directly below him, speaking urgently with a young woman in a soldier's uniform. Michel turned to work his way around her just as she looked up toward him. He swore silently, resisting the urge to slink away, and decided to walk directly past her on his way out. He decided Forgula was someone to whom he shouldn't show weakness.

Michel looked her in the eye and gave her his most charming smile.

A look of disgust crossed her face. "Tenik," she said sharply.

Tenik was just one step above and behind Michel. "Good morning, Devin-Forgula," he said, touching his forehead in greeting.

"Don't 'good morning' me, Tenik. I've just received news of another explosion. At least thirteen soldiers dead or wounded down in Lower Landfall."

Tenik stepped down beside Michel and scowled. "I'm sure that Yaret has been informed."

"Has he?" Forgula took a half step toward Tenik. "Because his cupbearer is attending a game with a foreigner instead of out there looking for the men killing our troops."

Michel bit his tongue. She had no idea she'd been followed the other day, and he had to resist the urge to throw her meeting with Marhoush back in her face. He could see the same struggle on Tenik's face. "You've no right to question Tenik's actions," Michel said.

"Why is he talking to me?" Forgula asked Tenik.

Michel felt his heat rising, and before Tenik could answer, he said, "Why can't you ask me? You were good enough to attack an unarmed man, but too good to talk to him?" His jaw snapped shut at the end of the sentence and he immediately regretted opening his mouth. But, as his mother liked to say, in for a penny, in for a krana.

Forgula's nostrils flared. "Silence your new pet, Tenik."

"Silence yourself," Tenik said. Michel, it seemed, wasn't the only one sick of Forgula's shit. Tenik crossed his arms, staring her down. "He's right. You've no place questioning what I do and how I do it. My Household is combing the city for the empire's enemies while Sedial ignores our pleas for more soldiers. This *foreigner* has handed us more enemy agents in the last few days than anyone in your Household."

"You have no idea the sacrifices my Household makes to hold this city," Forgula hissed. She turned her nose up. "I won't speak another word in the foreigner's presence."

Michel noted that the room had grown silent. Well over a hundred sets of eyes were watching the confrontation. Whispers had already begun, and he thought he saw money change hands somewhere in the crowd. The Dynize, it seemed, enjoyed a good show as much as any Kressian.

"You're a damned coward," Michel told her.

Forgula's eyes widened slightly. In Fatrasta, "coward" was a trigger word to start a fight. She glared at him, but did not move. "Slime," she retorted.

Michel sought his memory for the worst Palo insults his mother had taught him as a boy. "Horse eater," he threw back at her.

There was a sharp intake of breath from the watching Dynize. Someone behind Michel swore, while a woman in the crowd laughed out loud. Forgula's arm jerked stiffly, and the moment Michel had been waiting for arrived—her blackjack came to hand and she swung her arm.

Michel barely got his own arm up in time to keep the blow from hitting him below the eye. His forearm went numb, and he couldn't help but gasp at the pain that shot down his arm. He stumbled into her, his numb hand grasping without feeling at her jacket. With the other hand, he dipped into his pocket and slipped his fingers into his knuckle-dusters. She shoved him backward, then raised her blackjack one more time.

Michel's jab with his knuckle-dusters was hurried and sloppy, but he still managed to catch her a glancing blow on the chin that sent her wide-eyed and reeling into the arms of her companions.

Someone to Michel's right kicked him hard in the side of the knee. He nearly toppled to the ground, not letting himself take his eyes off Forgula as Tenik suddenly dove into the middle of the chaos and shouted for silence. Michel felt Tenik grab him by the sleeves and jerk him along, half pulling, half dragging him through the crowd and out a side door into a narrow corridor. He was shoved into a chair and left while Tenik ran back inside.

Tenik returned a moment later. "What the pit did you think you were doing provoking her like that?" he hissed.

It was the first time Michel had seen Tenik genuinely angry. They were alone in this corridor, and Michel let himself lean back and test his numb arm, wincing in pain. "Ow," he responded.

"You're lucky she didn't stave your head in," Tenik said. "You're lucky you—" Tenik stopped, looked closely at Michel, then gasped. "You did that on purpose."

Michel forced himself to chuckle. He didn't feel it, not with the pain shooting up his left arm.

"Why?" Tenik demanded.

"I wanted to see how easily she was provoked," Michel answered.

"I could have told you that!"

"I also wanted to make it very clear to her that I hit back." Michel worked the knuckle-dusters off his fingers and waved them at Tenik before putting them back in his pocket. He reached into the opposite pocket with the numb fingers of the other hand and showed Tenik a thick leather booklet. "And I wanted the chance to steal her pocketbook."

"Like pit..." Tenik stared at him for several moments. "How did you know she carried one?"

"I saw her write in it earlier."

"If she realizes that you—"

"She already wants to kill me," Michel said. "I can see it in her eyes. She's not going to admit to anyone that I stole from her, so what's the harm?"

"Forgula can do a lot of harm," Tenik warned.

Michel leaned back on the bench, cradling his damaged arm, hoping the feeling would come back soon. "I haven't picked a pocket for a couple years. Still have the talent for it, though, even with numb fingers."

"You disgust me." There was a note of respect in Tenik's voice. Michel decided he only half meant it.

Before Michel could retort, the door to the foreign-dignitary room opened and Michel swallowed whatever he had to say. Saen-Ichtracia, the granddaughter of Yaret's political enemy and a damned Privileged sorcerer, stepped into the hall and closed the door behind her. She tilted her head to one side, pulling a wry face, and stared at Michel.

Michel glanced at Tenik, hoping he'd step in with some excuse, and when no such help was forthcoming, attempted a furtive glance toward the closest exit.

"Michel Bravis, was it?" Ichtracia asked. She spoke in perfect Adran, catching Michel off guard.

Michel's mouth was dry. "That's me."

Ichtracia let out a giggle—a damned giggle—and Michel realized she'd been the one to laugh when he called Forgula a horse eater. "I haven't seen someone hit Forgula since I was a little girl." She clapped her hands slowly, the grin on her face speaking volumes of both respect and pity. "I think the woman who struck her ended up strangled in the bath."

Tenik cleared his throat. "Saen, we're sorry for causing such a commotion. We—"

Ichtracia held up a finger toward Tenik without even looking at him. He snapped his mouth shut. "Michel," Ichtracia said, "I won't keep you any longer. I just wanted you to know that you made me laugh. Good afternoon." She turned and swept down the hall without another word, leaving Michel with a hammering heart—and a good view of her hips as she walked away.

She was well gone when Tenik said in a low voice, "I warned you about catching her attention."

"Believe me when I say I had no intention of doing so. Shit, shit, shit." Michel got to his feet, trying to shake the numbness out of his arm and only receiving another jolt of pain for his efforts. Between Hendres and Forgula, his damned arm had taken a beating the last two weeks. He forced himself to put Ichtracia out of his mind and held up Forgula's wallet. "Let's go somewhere private and see what we can find out about our friend."

CHAPTER 26

Vlora spent the next several days scouting up and down the numerous valleys that led into the mountains from Yellow Creek. They varied in size, from immense canyons big enough to march a field army through, to little crags and gullies that were hard to spot unless you were right on top of them. The biggest were filled to the brim with prospectors—larger mines up the side of the canyon belonging to either Jezzy or Burt—and the streams filled with independent panners hoping to make it rich on gold dust.

Vlora created a system in her head, starting with the largest and busiest canyon and then working clockwise around Yellow Creek. It was slow going, searching everywhere without *looking* like she was searching everywhere, and then doing the whole thing again with her sorcerous senses. So much time spent in the Else exhausted her, leaving her strung out at the end of each day with barely enough wits about her to keep an eye out for Jezzy and Burt's goons, or for the powder mage Burt had warned her about.

She talked to a hundred prospectors each day under the guise of looking for a quiet, but well-paying job, and had heard enough gossip from them to fill an entire lifetime. Everyone had news of the distant war—that the loss of Landfall was enemy propaganda, that Lindet had been captured and hanged by the Dynize—and everyone had an opinion on Burt and Jezzy. Between the two, everyone agreed, Jezzy was the more heavy-handed but had more money. People seemed to like Burt, but in most Kressians' eyes he was still a filthy Palo.

She returned from the hills on the fourth day with her eyes bloodshot and her feet hurting. Seventeen prospectors had offered her a job—most of them on behalf of the two big bosses—and no less than twice that many had offered graphic descriptions of what their sex life would be like if she followed them back to their tent.

She was irritable and coming up empty-handed, and it did not improve her mood when a man of about thirty fell into step beside her as she headed toward her hotel through the Palo district.

He was nearly six feet tall, with blond hair and blue eyes; a wide, pleasant face wrinkled from scars and smile lines; and a broad-shouldered build that made her think of Rosvelean sailors. He carried a pistol and sword, and wore a bicorn and red bandanna with a loose-fitting white shirt, sailor's boots, and a long-tailed dressing coat that had seen better days. He looked like a damned storybook pirate.

But what caught Vlora's attention was not the way he was dressed but rather the way he smelled—he reeked of black powder, and she barely had to touch her sorcerous senses to know that this man was a powder mage.

She kept walking, pretending she hadn't noticed him, and let her hand fall on the pommel of her sword. She pushed away her exhaustion, senses prepared, her heart beating quickly. She'd never fought a powder mage before—not for real. She'd sparred and practiced, and she'd considered all the theories about what a fight between two mages would entail, but never before engaged in true combat. As she looked up from her thoughts, she found herself shocked that he was walking beside her instead of putting a bullet in her head from across town.

"It's a lovely evening," he said, clearing his throat.

Vlora stopped, turning toward him, putting her best card-playing face forward. "What do you want?"

He offered his hand. "My name is Nohan. Pleased to meet you."

Hesitantly, expecting a trap, Vlora took his hand. He squeezed a bit too hard, with too broad of a smile, and Vlora snatched back her hand and watched him cautiously. "Verundish. What do you want?"

"Can I buy you a drink?"

It was not a question Vlora expected, but her immediate thought was to get this man off the street and out of the open. If this came to a fight, she would have to do things that would not easily be explained to onlookers. "Sure," she said, nodding to a bar across the street. "There."

The bar was obviously a Palo establishment, but it was small and nearly empty, and the proprietor didn't question them when they ordered drinks.

"You're Adran," Nohan observed after they'd been served.

Vlora tried to guess his accent. "And you're Starlish."

He nodded. "Very good. I wouldn't have expected to see an Adran powder mage in this part of the world. You here with those mercenaries down south?" His tone was light, even friendly, and Vlora tried to loosen the knot in between her shoulder blades. Tensing up would not help things if this came to a fight.

"Avoiding them, more like," she answered.

"Understandable. That General Flint is a real bitch. You don't want to cross her. She'll try to recruit you, and kill you if she can't."

Vlora barely resisted laughing in his face. "Is that so? I've never met her."

"I have," Nohan said, using the opportunity to lower his voice and move a little closer. "Her goons chased me halfway across Adro a few years ago when I told them I wasn't interested in joining her cabal."

"No kidding?" Vlora's mind raced, trying to remember if any such thing had ever happened. She'd never seen this man before in her life, but the name was vaguely familiar. Had one of her underlings gotten into a scrap with him?

"No kidding," Nohan confirmed. He put money on the bar, enough for both their drinks, and clinked his against hers. "But I gotta stay independent, if you know what I mean. More money in that."

Vlora fiddled with her drink, hoping that he wasn't smart enough to plan ahead and have her poisoned. She *had* picked the bar, so she doubted that. "So you're the other mage in town, eh?"

"Aside from you and your boyfriend, yeah."

"He's just my partner," Vlora said. She realized her mistake too late as Nohan's eyes moved up and down her body. His nose twitched, and he none too subtly removed a powder charge from his breast pocket and cut the end with his thumb, sniffing delicately. Vlora did the same, almost laughing at the thought of a powder mage after-dinner club where they all sat around drinking and running powder trances.

She could see the thoughts turning in his head, and decided to press her own questions before he could come on to her. "I'm told you're working for Jezzy."

"That's right."

"I spoke with Burt a few nights ago. I think he pays a lot more than Jezzy."

"He might," Nohan admitted. "I didn't check. But Jezzy's got the upper hand. I like to get paid *and* end up on the winning side."

"I'm guessing you know that I already turned Jezzy down, right?" Vlora asked.

Nohan barked a laugh. "Heard what you did to poor Dorner.

Your partner did him a favor skewering him. Living a life with no tongue?" He clicked his tongue twice, then laughed again. The sound was tinged with cruelty.

"I turned down Burt, too, if that's why you're here. I'm not interested in working for either of them, so you can go back to your boss and tell her." Vlora finished her glass and raised it to Nohan. "I appreciate the drink, but I'm not for sale." She turned to go, deciding it was best to withdraw from this before he could get a chance to try for blood.

Nohan snatched her by the arm. "That's not why I'm here, lover."

"Excuse me?" Vlora felt her chest grow tight. His grip was too firm, his tone too familiar.

"I'm here to offer you and your partner something a little different."

"Which is?"

Nohan leaned forward until their faces were almost touching and spoke in a low, conspiratorial tone. "We've got three powder mages here. Three of us, we could gut this whole damned town. Pick 'em off, cut 'em down. Doesn't matter how, we've got the strength."

"I'm not sure what you're suggesting," Vlora said, though she had an inkling. The sparkle in Nohan's eye when he said "cut 'em down" was just a little too obvious.

"I'm talking a slaughter. We take out the big bosses, get their two armies fighting each other, and we set fire to the town and go a-hunting. We kill everything with two legs and there'll be no one to stop us from loading up a mule train with gold and heading for the coast. We'll be in Gurla, living like kings, before anyone knows what's happened."

Vlora's fingers itched for her sword. "That's...quite an offer."

"I know," he said with a grin.

"You already took Jezzy's coin."

"So?"

"If you're willing to betray one partner, why the pit would I trust you?"

Nohan tightened his grip on her arm. "Because you're strong. You're a mage, like me. I'm not stupid. I won't betray someone who can fight back."

Vlora looked down at his hand on her arm for several long seconds. When she decided she'd calmed down, she jerked away from his grasp. "That's about the most cowardly thing I've ever heard someone say."

Nohan's grin disappeared. His expression changed to baffled, then disgusted in an instant. "What are you, some kind of hero? Nobody gets anything in this life they don't take with force. And we've got the force to take it."

"I work for my money, thank you," Vlora said quietly. "I'm not a cowardly dog, biting the hand and stealing the scraps."

"Bitch," Nohan snarled.

"I've been called worse by better."

It didn't surprise her when Nohan took a swing. Vlora caught his wrist, but was forced back a step by the power of the blow. He was running a powder trance just like her, and was physically much larger. Her sorcery wasn't an advantage here.

He moved quickly, swinging his other hand with the glass still in it. She ducked, kicking out his leg, the glass catching her a glancing blow across the back of the head. She heard the sound of glass shattering and brought her fist up hard and fast, connecting with his chin with enough force to lift him off the ground and lay any grown man out cold.

He caught himself on a table, shaking off a daze, and came at her quick. Only preternatural senses allowed her to sense the movement of his sorcery, leaping out to set off her powder like a finger on a hair trigger. She fought back mentally, suppressing his ability to detonate powder with her mind while fending off a series of powerful blows that sent her retreating across the bar.

The bartender leapt into a backroom, slamming the door, while the few occupants cleared out. Nohan's fingers went for her throat, and Vlora kneed him between the legs and grabbed the lapels of his jacket, swinging him around and into the beam holding up the roof with enough force that there was an audible crack.

Once again, Nohan shook it off. He regained his feet and fell into a boxer's stance, one fist forward. "I gave you a chance," he said, jabbing. Vlora jerked back from the blow, imitating his stance and slamming her fist into his gut three times before he could get an arm around her head and throw her away from him. She hit the bar headfirst, seeing stars, and barely recovered before he came at her again.

She held her arms up in defensive posture, taking a pummeling before getting an opening of her own and grabbing him by the throat. She lifted him over her head, powering forward, and slammed him through a table with all her strength.

She didn't bother going for her pistol. Both of them could prevent powder from igniting a spark. Instead, she drew her sword and leapt toward him, intent on putting a blade through his eye. He was quick, snapping away from the thrust and rolling to his feet. He struggled to draw his own sword as he dodged Vlora's thrusts.

Vlora became more frustrated. She'd fought a lot of quick people, and sparred with powder mages, but the frustration of having someone dodge your attack so easily mounted quickly. The irony, she realized in the back of her head, was not enjoyable.

She missed on a thrust, and Nohan kicked her hard in the chest, sending her reeling across the bar. He finally drew his own sword but made no motion to advance.

They both panted from the fight. "I was a member of the Starlish Cabal," he said. "We could have worked well together, but you passed up a chance at real riches." He spat at her feet. "Watch your back." Without warning, he suddenly broke and ran, pushing his way out the door and into the street.

Vlora considered giving chase, but her leg hurt from a kick to her shin, and her vision was slightly blurry. She felt the back of her head where the glass had broken, only for her fingers to come away covered in crimson. Finding her hat in the ruin of the barroom, she limped out the door and into the street.

She was almost to her hotel when she spotted a face in the crowd. It touched something in the back of her memory, but she couldn't quite put her finger on it. It was almost an hour later, when she'd cleaned herself up and retreated to her room, that the face suddenly attached itself to a name.

She swore loudly, feeling furious that she hadn't recognized him earlier: Prime Lektor, former dean of Adopest University and onetime ally of Field Marshal Tamas, was a powerful, immortal Privileged who'd disappeared during the Adran-Kez War over ten years ago. What kind of terrible bloody luck did she have for him to show up here now?

Seeing someone like Prime Lektor in the same town as a god-stone couldn't possibly be a coincidence.

CHAPTER 27

B ellport is under siege."

Styke jerked awake, realizing he'd been nodding off at the reins, and blinked the sleep out of his eyes. The Mad Lancers stretched down the road in a column behind and ahead of him, with Jackal and his banner a dozen paces back and Ibana nowhere to be seen. Celine and Ka-poel rode together nearby, the latter teaching Celine her sign language.

Styke yawned and turned toward the woman addressing him. He didn't know her name, but she wore the crimson and blue of the Riflejack cavalry and she waited for an answer with a cool, professional air.

"How far out are we?" he asked, casting about for a landmark that he might recognize.

"Less than five miles."

Styke considered his options. They could swing down south, skirting Bellport and the Dynize Army and be well past them by noon tomorrow. But Bellport was their last chance to rest and resupply before heading out onto the Hammer *and* it was a good place to recruit.

And there was the matter of the traitor Valyaine. Perhaps he should just get that over with.

"Take me to Gustar," Styke told her.

Styke ordered a halt and rode ahead with the messenger, finding Gustar and a group of his dragoons hidden in a glen about two miles to the east of Belltower. Styke left his horse and climbed to the lip of the nearest hill, where Gustar was crouched among the shrubbery with a looking glass in hand. He offered it to Styke as he approached.

Bellport was a coastal city located at the mouth of a small, swift-moving river. Its port was built behind a tall hill that effectively protected the city from a seaward attack, and the north side was watched over by a stone fortress built by the Starlish almost two hundred years ago. The gun towers were outdated but effective, forcing an enemy army to approach from the south.

This seemed to suit the Dynize just fine. They were camped just under a mile south of the river, bombarding the suburbs and old city walls with artillery and the sorcery of what looked to be a single Privileged. Styke guessed the army at about five thousand infantry with a few hundred cavalry support. They were camped on the sandy floodplain, and he amused himself with the thought of a torrential rain carrying them all into the ocean.

Unfortunately, the weather was sunny and the ground dry.

"I can't imagine the garrison lasting much longer," Gustar said. "A day, maybe two at best." He pointed to a smoldering ruin in the corner of the city where the river let into the ocean. "That was their biggest south-facing guntower and it went down about two hours ago. Belltower has a few four-pounders on that hill over there"—he pointed again—"but nothing else outside the old fortress. Once they go down, the Dynize just have to cross the river."

"So you think they're done for?" Styke asked. From what he could see, he didn't disagree.

Gustar nodded. "Unless we intervene soon, the smart option is to head around to the south and be past them by tomorrow night. They'll be too busy securing the city to chase us—and they've only got a few hundred cavalry anyway."

Styke twirled his lancers' ring, considering. There was a lot of smoke rising from the southern suburbs, but the northern half of the city was still untouched and full of people he could save. "I don't want to leave an enemy behind us," he said. "The Dynize already have Swinshire. If we let them take Bellport, we'll be completely cut off on the Hammer."

To his surprise, Gustar smiled. "I was hoping you'd say that. Hit 'em from the rear and they won't see what's coming. I'm only worried about the Privileged. We don't have a powder mage to put a bullet in their head."

Styke handed Gustar back his looking glass. "Leave the Privileged to me."

The Mad Lancers swung south, using the hills beyond the floodplain as cover and coming up directly behind the Dynize position to slam into their supply train at a gallop. Styke gave the order to keep formation tight and only slow enough to kill anyone who raised a weapon. Then they came over the hills and found themselves less than a hundred yards from the rear lines of the enemy infantry.

Styke paused long enough to assess the situation, and was surprised to find Ka-poel riding up to him through the chaos they'd left of the Dynize train.

"You need to be back with our reserves," he said. "Find Sunin and Celine. Stay with them."

Ka-poel shook her head emphatically and showed him her slate. *Enemy bone-eye.*

Styke inhaled sharply. He was familiar enough with Privileged to know when to show caution and when to charge. But he was not familiar with bone-eyes beyond the ones in Landfall who'd kept the Dynize lines from breaking. "Will they be dangerous to our men?"

Ka-poel shrugged and spread her arms. *I don't know.*

Styke ground his teeth. "All right, change of plans. You're coming with me. Stay on horseback and stay close. We're going to kill the Privileged first, then run down the bone-eye." He flipped his reins and raced to the edge of the hilltop, where the Mad Lancers had just finished spreading out into a line formation. The old lancers were on the left flank, led by Ibana, with the Riflejacks on the center and right, Gustar out on their wing. New recruits were mixed in equally.

Styke rode past the old lancers and pointed. "Gamble, Jackal, Chraston, Ferlisia. Bring your boys and follow me. We have a Privileged to kill."

Styke took command of the center with about two dozen of the old lancers directly behind him and Ka-poel at his side. Down on the floodplains some of the Dynize infantry had just noticed them and were desperately trying to get the attention of their officers.

"Send 'em to the pit!" Styke roared.

Amrec leapt forward. They galloped down the hill, flying over the soft grass and leveling out on the plain. Mere seconds passed before he drew his carbine, fired off a shot, then exchanged the weapon for his lance. Carbine blasts went off all around him, and the Dynize lines turned in a panic, attempting to fix their bayonets.

They were too late.

The tip of Styke's lance tore through a woman's shoulder as she tried to raise her musket, and her companion fell beneath Amrec's hooves a split second later. The sound of the line being trampled beneath iron-shod hooves made Styke's heart sing, and he dug his knees into Amrec's sides.

They were through the rear lines in moments. Styke raised his lance, gesturing for the old lancers he'd set aside to follow him as he slowed and cut sharply mere yards behind his own left flank. Amrec leapt the bodies of crushed Dynize soldiers, and they swung out wide, beyond the lines of Dynize infantry that began to organize as the charge faltered.

Styke checked over his shoulder to see if Ka-poel was still with him, only to find her at his side. Her horse foamed at the mouth from the hard run, and her brow was furrowed with concentration.

"The trick to killing a Privileged," Styke shouted to her, "is to take them by surprise. Privileged are just like any other fool—in the middle of the battle they get tunnel vision. Any minute now someone is going to turn him away from his bombardment and direct him at the lancers. Our goal is to reach him before—"

Styke's words were cut off by a sudden jet of flame shooting across the battlefield. It was startlingly close and heading toward the Mad Lancer line where Styke had been mere moments before. Dynize and cavalry alike were consumed, and the air was filled with the screams of men and horses and the sickening smell of charred flesh.

"Before that happens!" Styke finished, sawing hard on the reins and directing his small squad of lancers back into the chaotic line of Dynize soldiers. They plowed the poor bastards down with the force of their charge, not even bothering to lower their lances. Styke caught the scent of brimstone on the wind and followed his nose. He soon saw the flash of white gloves among the teal uniforms and shiny breastplates. "Lances!" he bellowed.

His small entourage sprang into a V formation, lances lowering. The Privileged's bodyguard was turned toward the main attack, and they didn't see Styke's flanking maneuver until the last moment. The sound of horses hitting soldiers was an audible crack, and Styke saw a gloved hand flash upward and wave toward him.

His lance struck the Privileged in the left eye and came out the back of his skull, tearing the entire side of his face off as Styke's momentum carried him onward. Styke whooped loudly, laughing as blood spattered across his stolen breastplate and Amrec's mane. "Where is the bone-eye?" he shouted at Ka-poel.

Ka-poel's horse suddenly leapt out in front of Amrec, and Styke found himself following her as she clung closely to her horse's neck, weaving the creature expertly through lines of confused soldiers. He could smell the copper of her sorcery, trying to differentiate it from the other bone-eye's, but soon realized that he shouldn't have bothered.

Still clinging closely to her horse, Ka-poel drew a machete with one hand and leaned down, letting her speed carry the blade into the back of a woman's neck. The woman spun, blood spurting, and fell to the ground with a cry. Ka-poel immediately jerked back on the reins, and Styke had to do the same to keep from plowing into her. She leapt from her horse and straddled the woman, finishing the job with two blows from her machete.

The Dynize soldiers, who until now had been confused but not disorganized, broke with a suddenness that shocked Styke. They began to run immediately, throwing down their weapons and fleeing. Styke drew his sword and laid about him until there was nothing else to swing at, then took a moment to breathe.

Cleaning the blood from his face, he watched as the Mad Lancers crushed the Dynize against the river.

"Two hundred of ours dead," Ibana reported. "Twice that many again wounded."

Styke nodded at the number, pleased. He sat astride Amrec, flanked by Ibana and Gustar while the lancers mopped up what remained of the Dynize forces. As he'd expected, killing the

Privileged had been as simple as flanking the bodyguard. So few people were brave enough—or stupid enough—to charge directly at a Privileged that it was surprisingly easy to take them unaware.

The bone-eye, however, had been the breaking force. He remembered that particular sorcery from Landfall, how the Dynize had been impossible to break until enough of their bone-eyes had died. Their will had shattered with the same suddenness here.

"You know," he said to Ibana, "the Dynize at Windy River didn't break like this. They were tough bastards, even after Flint put them through the grinder."

"The army at Windy River didn't have a bone-eye," Ibana said.

"Right. Logically, they should have broken faster, like these guys did when their bone-eye died."

Ibana seemed to consider the conundrum. "Maybe they're trained very well. Naturally tough. A bone-eye strengthens their will but makes them brittle so that when the bone-eye dies, they are temporarily weak."

Styke turned to look at her, surprised by the observation.

"I've been giving this thought since Windy River," Ibana admitted. "A few years back I read a book on the effect sorcery has on the human mind. It was mostly incomprehensible rubbish, but I took away a few things."

"I'll be damned."

Ibana gave him one of her rare smiles.

"I mean," Styke continued, "I didn't know you could read."

Ibana leaned over and punched him hard in the shoulder.

Gustar finished taking a report from one of his cuirassiers and turned toward them. "A Privileged, a bone-eye, and an entire brigade shattered in exchange for a few hundred men? That's a damned fine trade, Colonel. Congratulations." Gustar's Riflejacks had taken the brunt of the Privileged's sorcery, but he, too, seemed very pleased with the results. "I think the boys have earned a day off in Bellport."

"I don't disagree," Ibana said.

Styke eyed the gates of Bellport. They had opened moments before, and he'd spied a small force riding out to greet them under a Fatrastan flag. "Strip the dead and wounded of supplies," he ordered. "Grab everything we can carry from the Dynize supply train. We'll camp here tonight and give the men leave in the city in the morning, then move the next day."

In the meantime, Styke had personal business to attend to.

CHAPTER 28

Michel sat on the floor of his room in the Merryweather Hotel in Upper Landfall. Since the occupation, the hotel had been taken over by midlevel Dynize bureaucrats unable to get a proper townhome near the capitol building. It was a posh place, far above his old pay grade, but he'd managed to use Yaret's name to secure a room there—and to take advantage of the fact the hotel was well guarded and unlikely to be infiltrated by Blackhats attempting to take his head.

The contents of Forgula's pocketbook were spread in front of him: seven Dynize ration cards, a bundle of cigarette rolling papers, a number of Fatrastan and Dynize coins, and a booklet filled with names and addresses on both sides of the ocean as well as a calendar of appointments.

It was the appointments that Michel had spent the last couple of days poring over. Everything in the book was written in Dynize shorthand and a sort of minimal cypher, and it had taken him and Tenik together two afternoons just to establish a working translation.

Michel stared at the calendar of appointments, reading over the last three weeks for the umpteenth time. He started from one point in time—the hour that Forgula met with Marhoush in Claden Park—and worked backward, trying to find a similarity between the three letters and two numbers she'd used to mark that appointment with any other appointment since the invasion. He was searching for a trail: evidence that Forgula had met with Marhoush many times in the past or would again in the future.

He finished his examination as the door to his room opened and Tenik slipped inside.

"Anything on Marhoush?" Michel asked, tossing the calendar of appointments on the floor.

"Nothing new," Tenik answered. "He's holed up in an old warehouse to the west of the industrial quarter. It seems he's being cautious since we raided his last hideout."

"Are we certain that he's staying put?"

"As certain as can be. One of our people saw his face less than two hours ago. He has people coming and going, but seems to have remained in one spot himself."

Michel snorted. "Damned fool. If he really thinks we're on to him, he should be moving every chance he gets. Staying in one spot makes it easier to find him. I've been telling the Blackhats for years that everyone should have some espionage training."

"I take it they didn't listen?"

"They wouldn't even let me give our actual spies enough training." Michel rubbed his eyes. They felt tired and bloodshot after spending so much time staring at paper. He needed to get up, go out onto the balcony—maybe even take a walk. He dismissed the notion. No time—and no need to put a target on himself. It had occurred to him last night just how much of a risk he'd taken by following Hendres himself. He should have pointed her out to some of Yaret's men and let them do the footwork. The more time he spent out among the populace, the greater chance he had of being recognized, even with his dyed hair and new mustache.

"Tell our watchers to keep their distance. I don't want Marhoush getting spooked. The sooner he moves, the more chance we have of following him directly to je Tura." Stifling a yawn, Michel wondered if he shouldn't go spend the next few days watching Marhoush's new safe house. He was, after all, the one who would recognize anyone else of importance.

There was just too much work to do.

"Any progress there?" Tenik asked, nodding at the calendar of appointments.

"Nothing," Michel responded. He picked up the book, tapping a pen against a bookmarked page. "We have her shorthand here for the meeting with Marhoush, and we figured out last night her system for marking names, places, and dates. But I haven't found a single match for Marhoush anywhere else in her calendar. She's either never met with him before or this was the only time she actually jotted the meeting down."

"And if it's the former?"

"If it's the former"—Michel tapped the pen against the page— "then maybe our first guess was right. Perhaps Forgula is attempting to turn Marhoush directly. She's not a traitor, or up to anything more insidious than recruiting an enemy. Which is exactly what we've been doing."

Tenik seemed doubtful. "Either way, Yaret wants to know."

"That's fair." Michel continued to tap away, considering his options. There might be something in this calendar that he missed—a hidden message jotted between the lines. Invisible ink. Even sorcery. But Forgula didn't have easy access to that kind of sorcery and this was, after all, just a calendar. She wasn't high-ranking enough to think it would be lifted by a pickpocket. This was probably a dead end.

He tossed the calendar aside and picked up Forgula's thin address book. This wasn't in shorthand or lightly ciphered, not like the calendar. It was simply a list of contacts and addresses, just like any government aide might carry with them. He'd flipped through it twice now and nothing had struck him as peculiar. But late last night, it had given him an idea.

"Do you have access to census records?" Michel asked.

"I do."

"I need the records of all the bureaucrats and civilians who came over from Dynize."

Tenik's eyebrows furrowed. "What do you need those for?"

Michel shook the address book over his head. "Because I want to compare her address book to the census records. If I can eliminate all the people who came with you from overseas, then I'll be able to tell who her local contacts are. From there, we can find out if any of them are known Blackhats and we'll have a new trail to follow."

Tenik walked over to the window, pushing aside the curtain and looking out for a few moments before answering. "Can't you differentiate between Fatrastan names and Dynize names?"

"In a pinch, yes. But I don't know every Dynize name, and you don't know every Kressian, Fatrastan, or Palo name. I'm not going to look for every single name—just the ones I'm curious about. It'll be a couple hours of work at most, and might save me a boatload of time in the future."

Or, Michel added silently, *I could just look for the latest entries in her address book.* But that wouldn't allow him to get his hands on the census data. He waited for Tenik to tell him he was being obtuse, watching carefully for an ounce of suspicion.

Tenik shrugged. "If you wish. There is a single book that lists every civilian that came over with the army. I can get a copy to you within thirty minutes. I'm not sure it'll be as helpful as you think, but I'll provide it."

"And someone to help me compare the names," Michel added, hoping it would allay any suspicion.

"Of course."

Tenik headed to the door, but stopped suddenly and turned to Michel. Michel swallowed hard, waiting for a sudden accusation, but Tenik had something else on his mind. "A warning to you, my friend."

"Eh?"

"Ichtracia has been asking about you. Your stunt with Forgula last night has piqued her interest."

Michel's throat began to feel tight. "She doesn't have better things to do?"

"Most of the Privileged are with the army," Tenik said with a shrug. "Ichtracia remains with the government because of her grandfather's wishes, but there isn't a lot for a Privileged to do in a new seat of government. Aside from the odd task that comes her way, she finds... other diversions."

"And you're worried I might be a new diversion?"

"Just warning you that she's been asking around, is all." Tenik raised his eyebrows. "However, I suppose everyone's been asking around about you. Before, you were a curiosity. Since you confronted Forgula, you've suddenly become very interesting."

Tenik left Michel alone with the contents of Forgula's pocketbook, which he spent the next little while glancing through once more before there was a knock on the door. A young woman arrived with the census data Michel requested. She was one of Yaret's Household clerks who'd picked up a little Palo and Adran, and they spent the rest of the evening comparing Forgula's address book with the census data.

The work was tedious. They marked each person as either Dynize or Fatrastan, then went back through and double-checked all of the names. Only thirteen—all of them written in at the end of the address book—were Fatrastan, and most of those were

readily recognizable sympathizers already helping the Dynize sta-
bilize the government.

Michel didn't much care about the information. It *might* be
useful, but his real goal was to look through the census data himself. He scoured it whenever his assistant didn't need the book. He
sorted through the tiny writing, poring over it like he might check
the books of a crooked accountant, looking for any sign of this
"Mara" whom Taniel needed smuggled out of the city. After four
hours he bought himself some more time with the book by order-
ing his assistant to triple-check the list that they'd made, and at the
end of the fifth hour he gave the book to her and sent her back to
the Yaret Household.

He stood by the hotel room window in frustration, watching as
the evening guard did their rounds. He considered his path to this
place, wondering at the idea that he was now working for a powerful Dynize minister, and he tried to imagine where Taniel and
Ka-poel were now.

He wished that Taniel was here. He had questions—questions
he hadn't known he would need to ask.

The first had to do with all the data he'd just scoured. Of the
thousands of civilians who had come over with the army to occupy
Landfall, he couldn't find Mara. And not just *the* Mara...but he
couldn't even find *a* Mara. It was as if the name itself didn't even
exist.

Which forced him to wonder what the pit he was going to do if
he couldn't even find this woman.

CHAPTER 29

The Yellow Creek jail was one of the few brick buildings in the city, positioned just behind the mayor's office at the end of a long street that terminated a hundred yards later at the base of one of the mountains. It was bigger than Vlora expected, with over two dozen holding cells guarded by a handful of deputies, all of whom kept a wary eye on Vlora as she was led down the hall to the last cell on the right.

Unlike the other cells, this one had several small windows, with real glass instead of bars, and a real bed and desk tucked into the corner. Taniel sat cross-legged on the bed, shoes off, jacket tossed over a chair as if he was staying in a hotel room instead of a cell. His brow was furrowed as he drew in his sketchbook, and he didn't look up until the cell door was unlocked.

"Afternoon," he said cheerfully.

Vlora paused in the doorway, noting that the guard had left the two of them alone. "Looks like you're living the high life in here."

"It's a cell for important people," Taniel explained.

"And you are?"

"A man with money."

Vlora took the chair and pursed her lips at Taniel. "And you mocked me for paying for two rooms at the hotel."

"Nobody's perfect." Taniel flipped the page in his sketchbook, then lifted his chin, looking down his nose at her. She remembered that look.

"You're not drawing me," she said.

"Of course not," he replied as he began to sketch.

Vlora let it go. "Do they know who you are?" she asked quietly.

"They think my name is Tampo." He paused to adjust the glove on his right hand, revealing a bit of red skin.

"And that?" Vlora asked, nodding at the hand.

"One Palo deputy knows who I am. She's a Daughter of the Red Hand and knows the passwords, so I can trust her, but I haven't been able to get much more than the city gossip and good meals. Speaking of which, I heard you met with the other big boss. Why do they call him Brown Bear Burt?"

"Has a big bearskin on his desk. Claims he got a lucky shot off at an Ironhook grizzly years ago and the name stuck."

"And Burt? It's an Adran name."

"No idea. Palo here call themselves anything they want. How did you hear that, anyway? The gossip in this city is out of control."

Taniel glanced up at her with a frown, pausing, before continuing his sketch. Vlora turned her face the other direction to annoy him. He didn't seem to mind. "There's ten thousand people crammed into a tiny valley in the middle of nowhere. Not much to do here besides poke your nose in other people's business. Did you find *it*?"

Vlora shook her head. "I've checked two of the big valleys and a dozen of the little ones. Been at it all morning, too. But there are a few things you need to know."

"What's that?"

"There's another powder mage in Yellow Creek."

Taniel looked up sharply. "Oh?"

"A man named Nohan. Claimed he was in the Starlish Cabal. Ever heard of him?"

"I haven't. Starlish, eh? They integrated their cabal, what, four years ago?"

"Six," Vlora corrected. "Privileged and powder mages, fighting side by side in a royal cabal."

"Times change." Taniel shrugged. "You met him?"

"He came on to me last night."

"And how did that go?" Taniel asked with a smirk.

"He's on Jezzy's payroll, but he suggested that the three of us team up and slaughter the entire city and steal all the gold we can carry."

"Enterprising."

"He sure seemed to think so. He didn't take my rejection well."

"I'm guessing you did it with your usual grace?"

"I called him a coward."

"Well done," Taniel said without a trace of sarcasm. "Sounds like it was warranted."

"It was, but it means that we have a powder mage to look out for. I tried to make it clear I wasn't his enemy, but he took the 'coward' bit personally and we beat the shit out of each other."

Taniel squinted at her over his sketchbook. "Oh yeah. I didn't notice that shiner when you walked in. So we have a rogue powder mage with a grudge in addition to all this other shit." He finally set down his charcoal and rubbed his eyes, leaning back in the cell bed. He let his gaze wander around his cell, his cool demeanor broken by a distasteful sneer. "This is incredibly inconvenient."

"I *would* appreciate help."

"I tried bribing the sheriff to see the judge earlier," Taniel said. "No can do. And she made it very clear that the moment I'm out of this cell, we won't be welcome in this town anymore."

Vlora quelled a rising frustration. "Meaning I have to look for this thing on my own? And I only have until you get out?"

"Sounds like it," Taniel said with an apologetic smile.

"You're the one with Ka-poel's damned compass in your head."

"Little good it's done me. I spent a whole night looking for the artifact. All I can tell is that it's here. I don't know where, though. One other thing…" He hesitated. "The sheriff says there's a good chance they'll try to hang me. The local judge has been trying to crack down on violence."

"Pit," Vlora breathed. She wasn't worried for Taniel's fate. She was worried that he would kill a whole lot of innocent people when they tried to carry out the sentence. The ticking clock in the back of her head just got louder. All she could do was hurry. She made a sour face, thinking back to the figure she recognized in the street last night. "What can you tell me about the Predeii?"

That got Taniel's attention. He closed his sketchbook and set it to one side, scooting to the edge of the bed. "That's not a question I want to hear," he said intently. "I don't know anything about them, not any more than you—powerful Privileged that were responsible for summoning the gods to give order to the Nine, then responsible for the chaos that occurred once the gods left."

"How powerful?" Vlora asked.

"Worth half a royal cabal on their own, is what Bo told me," Taniel answered. He tilted his face to one side, watching Vlora cautiously. "What aren't you telling me?"

"I saw Prime Lektor last night."

Taniel leaned on his fist, swaying to one side. "No," he breathed. "We can't afford to have them involved with this, too. You're absolutely certain?"

"I recognized him in the street," Vlora said, suddenly feeling less sure of herself. "It wasn't until a couple hours later that I realized where I recognized him from. I *think* it was him, but I won't be sure unless I see him again."

"And I'll bet my boots he'll recognize you if he sees you first."

Vlora swore under her breath. This damned city seemed to be getting smaller every day. First the spat between the big bosses, then a powder mage, and now a mythical Privileged older than her birth country. "If it *is* him, it can't be a coincidence."

"He's here for the stone."

"Of course. What else could it be?" Vlora asked with a shrug. "An ancient sorcerer doesn't just happen to show up in the little frontier gold-rush city where we're looking for an ancient artifact of great power."

Taniel looked like he swallowed a lemon. "We've got to find him. Shit, I wish Ka-poel were here. Prime Lektor might be more than even I can handle. I've fought one of the Predeii before and couldn't kill her." He paused. "*Why* would Prime Lektor want the stone?"

"Power?"

"He's an academic. Maybe he's trying to keep it out of Lindet's hands. Maybe he just wants to study it."

"That," Vlora said, "is too stupidly optimistic for me. We have to assume he's an enemy."

"Agreed."

"Do I try to put a bullet in his head?"

"If that'll even work," Taniel snorted. "Pit."

"You could get out any time you like," Vlora pointed out.

"With violence," Taniel admitted. "But yes. The city will close to us the moment I leave this cell, either by force or judicial order. I'll cool my feet for the time being, and see what kind of information my Palo friend can get me. I've got to be careful who I trust with the Red Hand information. I still have quite a bounty on my head."

"I'm going to look for Prime Lektor. If he's here, then he might already know where the godstone is."

"Be careful," Taniel warned, raising his finger. "We don't know what he's capable of. One of those Predeii carved through half of Tamas's powder cabal back during the coup."

Vlora remembered. Those people were her friends and comrades. "She took them by surprise," she said, hoping there wasn't too much hubris in her bravado. "I intend on taking him by surprise."

"And that powder mage?"

"Him, too."

Taniel scowled, his expression uncertain. "I should get out of here."

"No," Vlora said. She could do this. She *had* to do this. Taniel's help would be ideal, but she still didn't fully trust his motives. If she could make this victory her own, it would be worth so much more. "You can't attract attention. I'll find Prime and the stone by the time you're out of here." She stood up. "But I need to use every minute to do it."

Taniel took her hand, surprising her. "Vlora," he said seriously, "don't get yourself killed. There's more going on here than we know. My Palo friend says that the Palo Nation has a presence here, but he doesn't know anything else. If we can contact them, we might be able to get some help."

Vlora didn't know the first thing about getting in touch with agents of this Palo Nation. "I'm not exactly a welcome figure in the Palo community."

"They don't give a shit about the southern Palo. They only care if you can help them."

"And can I help them?" She *really* didn't like the sound of that.

"Maybe." Taniel seemed torn. "I'll see what I can find out from here. Just . . . be careful."

CHAPTER 30

Styke was greeted by the mayor of Belltower as he entered the old city gates the day after the Mad Lancers relieved the city. The mayor was an older gentleman with the dark skin of a Deliv, distinguished in tails and hat, with spectacles perched on the end of his nose. He wore a red sash proclaiming his title, and he was on foot surrounded by a small entourage of dignitaries dressed in their churchgoing best. As Styke rode through the gates, the mayor swept off his hat and bowed.

There was a part of Styke that reveled in his fame, that enjoyed the women, booze, and money his reputation had gotten him in his youth. But being thanked had always felt strained and awkward. He tipped his hat in return and gave a small wave to the dignitaries.

"You're Colonel Styke," the mayor said.

Styke glanced over his shoulder, hoping that Ibana would arrive with some kind of emergency that needed his attention. Ka-poel lurked on horseback a few dozen feet behind him. Other than her and Celine, there were only a few of his lancers riding in to see the city, and they slunk off quickly without making eye contact.

The cowards.

Styke lowered Celine to the ground and dismounted, handing her Amrec's reins. He shook the mayor's hand, hoping his discomfort was obvious enough that the group would bugger off.

"My name's Witbee," the mayor introduced himself. "Mayor Witbee. It's a pleasure to meet you, Colonel Styke, and I must immediately apologize that the city is in no shape to give you the reception you deserve." He gestured to his entourage. "These are all we could spare to come out and meet you. Everyone else is tending the wounded and putting out fires."

"No offense taken," Styke replied. "I'm not really one for receptions, to be honest."

The mayor charged ahead anyway. "You arrived in the nick of time, Colonel. We sent for help weeks ago and only just received word that the Third Army was on its way to relieve us. But they won't be here for days and..." His expression grew strained. "Well, we wouldn't have lasted much longer. The bastards were lined up for a charge when you arrived."

Styke resisted the urge to reply with *I noticed* and instead tried for a gracious smile, noting that Witbee had mentioned the Third Army.

"You charged a Privileged," Witbee continued. "Without any of your own, if I'm not mistaken. I've never seen anything like it."

"Privileged die like anyone else," Styke replied. "It's just a matter of getting close enough to put a lance through their eye."

The mayor tugged at his collar, his eyes fluttering as if he were unused to such bold discussion of violence. He stuttered for a moment, then said, "I'm sorry you and your men camped out on the plain last night. I sent someone to invite you in, but they returned without an answer."

"I sent them away. We had bodies to strip and wounded to tend to. Look, Mayor, I appreciate you coming out to greet me, but it's clear that you've got a lot of problems to deal with. I'm going to be blunt with you: Everything that I've heard says that you're one of the only cities on the west coast to survive the Dynize landing."

Witbee took a shaky breath. "I've heard similar reports. We've been discussing the possibility of abandoning the city and sending the people inland."

"With all due respect, that's a terrible idea," Styke said. "The Dynize are spread out, and Lindet's field armies are finally engaging the enemy. If the Third Army is already on their way, they'll need Bellport as a foothold in Dynize territory."

"This... this *is* Dynize territory now, isn't it?" Witbee asked, his expression fraught.

Styke pointed at the ground at their feet. "This is not Dynize territory, not yet. And I suggest you not abandon it. You've got what, a hundred thousand souls in Bellport?"

"About that, yes."

"Comb the city for fighting men, engineers, and labor. Conscript everyone you have to. Rebuild your gun platforms, even if you've got nothing to put on them—the Third Army will have extras." Styke wracked his brain for more advice, trying to remember the very same conversations he'd had with politicians during the Fatrastan War for Independence. The situation had been remarkably similar, except the Dynize had a *lot* more soldiers on the continent than the Kez did back then. He took the mayor by the elbow and pulled him aside, lowering his voice.

"A word of warning: The field armies are stripping the countryside for everything they can get their hands on—weapons, food, practical goods. If they arrive here and find Bellport in chaos, they're going to steal everything you have to survive the winter and leave you to rot."

"No!" Witbee protested. "The Lady Chancellor would never allow such a thing."

"The Lady Chancellor is leaving that up to the discretion of her generals, and I know the general of the Third Army personally. He'll strip you of everything he can."

"What can we do?"

"Organize the city. Rebuild those gun platforms, reinforce the walls, and dig trenches. Get every craftsman in the city working toward the war effort and when General Dvory arrives, he'll see a useful war asset rather than dead weight for him to strip of resources."

Witbee drew himself up. "I will do exactly as you say. I've served the good people of Bellport faithfully for eight years. I will rally them for all we have."

"And don't let General Dvory push you around. Tell him that Ben Styke is your friend and a city protector and that I won't stand for any mistreatment of Fatrastan citizens."

"Do you think it'll come to that?" Witbee asked incredulously.

"I hope not." Styke chuckled inwardly. If it did come to that, it would piss off Dvory something fierce. "If he continues to press, tell him that Lindet herself has guaranteed the city's safety."

"But she has done no such thing!"

"Consider me a mouthpiece of the Lady Chancellor herself," Styke lied. He clapped the mayor on the shoulder and turned to the retinue, raising his voice so that everyone nearby could hear him. "The Mad Lancers came to resupply in Bellport. We'll pay fair prices for what we need and won't take what you can't afford to spare. I'll allow my men a night's leave here before we move on tomorrow. If any of them refuse to pay for services or start fights, they will answer to me personally."

He continued. "We lost about two hundred men in that fight." He jerked his thumb over his shoulder. "We'll lose more to wounds. Anyone with courage and the ability to ride is welcome to join us when we leave tomorrow. If you don't know how to fight, we'll teach you how, and if you're looking to punch the Dynize in the teeth for what they've done to your families and homes, I guarantee you the chance." He nodded to himself. "That's all. Thanks, Mayor."

He returned to Amrec without another word, taking the reins from Celine and continuing on foot into the city. People stopped and stared as he passed by. He kept his head down and was left unmolested, but he could feel those eyes on his shoulders.

"How did I do?" he asked Celine.

"It was a good speech," she said, nodding in approval.

"I've never got on with politicians. Don't have the patience or the knack for obedience."

"My da used to say that a politician is just a money-grubbing whore who won't stoop to—"

"That's enough of that," Styke cut her off. "One of these days you're going to run out of things your da used to say."

Celine tilted her head to one side and reached up, taking Styke's hand. "He did talk a lot."

Styke spotted the lancers who had abandoned him to the mayor, as well as Ibana. The lot stood outside a gunsmith's, talking among themselves. "For all their need for circumspection, I've never met a thief who could shut up. Here." Styke gave the reins back to Celine and crossed the street.

Ibana greeted him with a nod, smirking. "How's the mayor?"

"I think I put him off with talk of violence," Styke replied. "But I prepped him for dealing with Dvory."

Ibana's eyebrows rose. "Dvory's coming here?"

"The mayor says the Third Army is a few days away."

"Do you want to wait for them?" Ibana had a glint in her eye, and Styke suspected that if he didn't kill Dvory fast enough for her, she'd do the job herself.

Styke shook his head. "He's in command of a whole field army. I'm not bringing that down on our heads right now. There will be plenty of time for gutting him when the fighting is done. What's going on here?"

Ibana gestured to the gunsmith. "We've got everything we need except replacement carbines. We're seeing if anyone has stock in the city."

"How bad is it?"

"We need a hundred. I'll settle for twenty-five. Smiths don't normally make carbines without an order, so we'll have to scrounge."

"Do what you can," Styke said, glancing over his shoulder. Ka-poel was still shadowing him, waiting in the street astride her horse. Seeing her, he was struck by a tale from his childhood—a Palo legend that spoke of a woman on horseback who rode into battle behind those who were fated to die a violent death. He thought of the stories he'd been told of Ka-poel and god killing. She would make a good angel of death.

"Are you going somewhere?" Ibana asked.

Styke pointed to a nearby barbership window, filled to the brim with playbills announcing various shows, poetry readings, cockfights, and other bits of entertainment going on around the city. One of them said, in bold letters, VALYAINE SORIS: FIGHTER EXTRAORDINAIRE. Beneath the words was the address for a boxing arena and a stylized, printed portrait of a man Styke recognized well.

"I'm going to go put a knife in another old friend."

CHAPTER 31

T here's been another bombing."

Michel tucked Forgula's address book underneath his menu and sat back in his chair in the café of the hotel lobby as Tenik slipped into the chair across from him. Tenik wore a grave expression, and Michel could instantly tell that something was different about this one. "Where?" he asked.

"The northern rim of Greenfire Depths. The bomb killed seven local Palo leaders and the minister of rations."

Michel didn't know the name of the minister of rations, but he did know the title. It was the woman in charge of making sure that everyone got fed—from the army, to the occupying civilians, to the Fatrastan and Palo citizens of Landfall. When Michel had asked who the most important people in Landfall were, Tenik had listed her title among the top ten—and based on what Michel had heard, she was good at her job. But that wasn't, Michel sensed, what was bothering Tenik. "She was an ally of Yaret, wasn't she?"

"A close ally," Tenik confirmed. "Our Households have been

friends for two hundred years. We were on the same side of the civil war."

"Shit."

"What's worse, her successor is her nephew. He's a capable young man, but he's back in Dynize. The fourth-in-command of the Household will have to step in, and *she* has never gotten along with Yaret."

Michel wondered how that would change the power dynamic. Clearly it was on Tenik's mind as well—though Tenik obviously had a better grasp of what this would mean. The fact that he was so gray-faced didn't bode well. "Does this have any effect on me?" Michel asked bluntly. It wasn't a question with any tact, but he'd found that Tenik responded better to directness than to dancing around a topic.

"I don't think so," Tenik said. "If anything, it just makes it more important that we find and stop whoever is conducting these bombings. Rumor has it that Sedial will free up some of his own Household to help with the search and give us more resources."

Michel quelled his natural suspicion. If Sedial was offering a hand, it meant that this had gotten serious. "No strings attached?"

"The minister of rations was well liked by everyone. Her Household will continue her work under her cupbearer, but efficiency will be lost." Tenik frowned. "No one wants ministers to die, not when we're in such a precarious position. Landfall is the hub of our invasion—Lindet has three field armies within a hundred miles. Our own armies are more than a match, but to guarantee victory, everything in the city must go smoothly."

Michel wondered, not for the first time, if Lindet had secret communications with the Blackhats here. Everything seemed just a tad too coordinated for the workings of a single Gold Rose and a skeleton crew of subordinates completely untrained for guerrilla warfare. "We know it's je Tura," Michel said.

"Knowing doesn't help us at all if we don't find him."

"Knowing will help us find him," Michel said with assurance. In addition to trying to discover Forgula's connection to Marhoush, he'd spent the last few days coordinating almost a hundred people in a counterespionage effort. Yaret's Household had rooted out dozens of Blackhat safe houses, turned a small number of Blackhats, and imprisoned hundreds more. But the bombings only seemed to intensify.

The only blessing, as Michel saw it, was that the occupied citizens wanted nothing to do with these bombings. Aside from a few radicals, most of the local leaders were decrying any violence that included civilians—and je Tura had made it very clear that he didn't give a shit who his bombs killed.

"I have to go," Tenik said. "I'll be in touch, but you might not see me for a couple of days."

Michel hid his surprise. Despite giving him quite a lot of power to hunt down his former compatriots, Yaret had left Michel with a leash—namely Tenik—that had been present for most of his time with the Dynize. Tenik disappearing for a couple of days would be the most freedom Michel had had since before the invasion. "What will you be doing?"

"Coordinating with the interim minister of rations," Tenik said unhappily. "And trying to convince her that it's best for her Household to remain close friends with the minister of scrolls. I have no doubt that at least one of Sedial's cupbearers will be attempting to convince her that a friendship with the Sedial Household would be of more benefit. Forgula might even be there."

A woman dead by enemy hands, and the dogs just fighting over the scraps. It reminded Michel why he considered spying a more noble profession than politics. "Anything I can do to help?"

"Find je Tura. Put an end to the bombings."

Tenik took his leave with those words, and Michel was once

again alone at his little table in the hotel lobby. He glanced around at the few others in the lobby. He was the only non-Dynize in this hotel, and ever since he moved in, people openly stared at him as they walked past—something he put up with just to get out of his room. From what Tenik told him, there were all sorts of rumors floating around: that Michel was a double agent who'd been working for Yaret for years, or that he was still a spy and taking advantage of Yaret's good nature, or even that he was half Dynize, half Palo—descended from some banished nobleman.

Michel did his best to ignore the rumors. Beyond punching Forgula in the face, he had little interest in Dynize politics. Results were what he needed.

He considered Tenik's mention of Forgula before fetching her address book from beneath his menu and heading upstairs to his room, where he found her calendar sitting on his bed. He flipped through the calendar to today's date. It was full of meetings and tasks without a single moment of free time. Between her old schedule and this new disruption, Michel very much doubted that she'd be returning home any time today.

There were all sorts of things Michel could do while Tenik was out of his hair, but he decided to do the most dangerous of them first.

Forgula's personal address was in a small strip of workers' homes in the Industrial Quarter. Unlike most of the Dynize bureaucracy, she had moved into an abandoned home in Lower Landfall, in a poorer area where many of the buildings were still occupied by their Fatrastan owners.

Michel scouted out the street for a few moments, checking for anyone who seemed particularly curious about his presence. At this time of day things were mostly quiet—a few old ladies hanging out the laundry in the street, a handful of children playing beside one of the industrial canals, but otherwise empty. The strip of homes where Forgula had chosen to live was a single building about eight homes long, each of them two stories tall, the whitewashed exteriors turned gray from the soot from nearby factories. Michel had been an informant in this part of town years ago, and he was quite familiar with this sort of block housing. It was mostly occupied by factory foremen—lower-class workers who needed to be near their work and could afford a little more space for a large family.

Michel walked up and down the street a few times before circling to the narrow alley behind the strip of houses. There was a gutter and rubbish pile back there, reeking of shit and rotten food, but there was also a raised brick walkway that accessed the barred doors of each of the houses.

The alley was abandoned, and Michel counted the back doors until he reached the address that coincided with the one written in the front of Forgula's address book. Standing on his tiptoes, he looked through the rear window. The place certainly *seemed* empty. Clearing his throat, he knocked loudly, waited sixty seconds, and knocked again.

Nothing.

He looked both directions, stepped up to the iron-barred door, and slipped a set of picklocks out of his pocket.

It took him three minutes to get through the iron barred door, another four to get through the actual door beyond that. He stepped into a well-lit rear hallway, the floor creaking beneath his feet. "Forgula!" he called.

There was no answer, so Michel began his search.

He wasn't entirely sure what he was searching *for*, but that had often been the case when he'd done this in the past. The house itself was rather nicely furnished; the furniture was fairly new, it had quality wallpaper, and there were small luxuries scattered through the rooms, such as books, mirrors, and nicer clothing that was definitely Fatrastan in origin. Most likely it had belonged to the mistress of a mill owner, someone who could afford the nicer things in life but wanted to stay near the factories.

Furniture askew, clothing lying out, and the occasional bit of jewelry lying discarded on a table told the story of someone who'd packed hastily to flee town. Only two rooms had been tidied: the sitting room and one of the bedrooms upstairs, and these, Michel decided, was where Forgula was living.

There were Dynize books on the nightstand, and uniforms and extra clothes in the closet that looked about Forgula's size. There were several notepads, and it only took a moment to compare the writing on them with the writing in Forgula's address book to confirm their likeness.

Once he'd done that, he checked each room with a steady, thoughtful eye. He looked for hidden nooks and crannies, disrupted dust, mismatched wallpaper—anything that would indicate a hiding spot for Forgula's valuables. He checked under shelves and sought gaps in the floorboards. Nothing seemed out of order, so he moved on to the more mundane: the bed, the wardrobe, and Forgula's sea chest.

He was careful to handle everything as little as possible. He memorized the locations of every item before moving something, then putting it back exactly as it was found. The goal was to be as thorough as possible without letting Forgula know that he'd been here at all.

The search took him less than half an hour, and it revealed almost nothing useful—though he did learn a great deal about Forgula. Letters from her father and little sister had come with her from Dynize, as well as tokens of affection and a stack of unsigned love notes that looked to be a few years old. Michel always struggled with this part of his job. Looking through the private parts of a person's life often revealed a more human side that he had to coldly ignore.

Only one item caught Michel's interest. It was a list of addresses filed away with a bundle of other papers in a hidden compartment of Forgula's sea chest. The addresses were most definitely in Landfall, and the paper looked fairly new. A brief check against the addresses in her booklet told him that this was not her standard list of contacts.

Michel returned the bundle of papers to the sea chest—sans the list of addresses—and made sure everything was in its proper place. One more quick search of the house, and he locked the back doors and slipped out through a window, closing it carefully behind him.

He couldn't help but be mildly disappointed as he left the Industrial Quarter on foot and climbed up the switchbacks to head back to the Merryweather Hotel. The list of addresses in his pocket might turn up something interesting, but it seemed that there would be no easy answers for Forgula's meetings with Marhoush. He couldn't help but decide that she was attempting to turn him— perhaps to get her own pet Blackhat and curry favor with her master, Sedial. If there was nothing sinister going on, he'd angered Forgula for very little reason.

He was getting near the Hadshaw Gorge when he got the sense that he was being followed.

Michel switched directions, heading down a couple of side streets before reaching the main avenue that ran alongside the gorge. He was careful not to look directly behind him—only stopping from time to time to check his pocket watch or look in a store window, trying to get some kind of look at whoever might be on his tail. If anyone was there, they managed to elude him.

His mood went from curious to uneasy, and he wondered if perhaps one of the Sedial Household or even Forgula herself had spotted him leaving Forgula's house. He'd wanted to spend the afternoon catching up with a few old contacts—the type of people Tenik would disapprove of him meeting—but he couldn't risk leading any Dynize to anyone who would raise suspicions. Perhaps he should head straight back to the hotel.

If Forgula had spotted him, though, Michel couldn't hole himself up with other Dynize. He took a sudden turn into an alley off the busy street and stepped up against the wall, waiting for anyone he recognized to pass him by. He slipped both hands into his pockets and fingers into his knuckle-dusters.

He waited for five minutes, then ten. He was just beginning to think his paranoia had gotten the best of him when he heard the sound of a pistol cocking behind him.

Slowly, Michel turned to look back into the alley. Hendres stood about fifteen feet away, pistol raised, her face expressionless. How she had managed to sneak up on him, he had no idea, but he tried to put together a quick explanation for his actions—anything that might let him talk himself out of this. "Hendres," he said.

"Michel." She breathed his name like a swear word.

"You don't want to fire that here," Michel said quietly. "You'll have soldiers down on top of you in a moment. Lower the pistol and we can talk. I'm not what you think I am." Slowly, so as not to risk a rash action on her part, he slipped his fingers out of his knuckle-dusters and raised his hands. "We should talk."

"No," Hendres said, "we shouldn't."

Michel saw the gun jump only a split second before something slammed into his chest. He jerked backward and slumped against the alley wall, where he stayed for a few seconds while Hendres watched him through the powder smoke. She turned and ran.

Michel frowned at the lack of pain. Had she missed? Had a misfire caused the bullet to bounce off him? He touched a hand to his chest, a few inches below his heart. His fingers came back crimson. There was a burning sensation, like having a hot coal against his skin, and it took Michel's suddenly foggy mind several moments to come to terms with the fact that he'd been shot.

And that he would probably be dead within a few moments.

He stumbled to the next street, walking along with a wall on his right, his fingers leaving crimson prints against the plaster as he tried to propel himself on. Each step felt like a thousand miles, but he barely managed to go two blocks before he fell into the rubbish beside a doorway, his eyesight cloudy and his mind confused. He thought he heard a voice somewhere behind him and wondered if Hendres had returned to finish the job.

Everything went black.

CHAPTER 32

Before heading down the main avenue of Bellport, Styke approached Ka-poel and let her horse nuzzle his hand. "Why are you following me?" he asked. "Don't you have sorcery to do somewhere?"

She rolled her eyes and went through a series of hand motions.

"She says that she's following you because you're her protector," Celine said, joining them with Amrec in tow.

Styke eyed Celine. "You picked that shit right up, didn't you?"

She learns very quickly, Celine translated for Ka-poel.

"What do you mean I'm your protector? The whole of the Mad Lancers is your bodyguard. You're safer out there."

Ka-poel pursed her lips and signed. It took several repetitions before Celine was able to translate a coherent sentence: *A bone-eye needs a protector. I am not incapable of defending myself, but I am far more dangerous if I don't have to worry about physical danger.*

"So go back with the lancers," Styke said, getting frustrated.

I haven't anointed the lancers. I have anointed you. Besides, Taniel has trusted you with me. Neither of us wants to betray that trust.

Styke noted the fond way she smiled when she signed Taniel's name. He spat in the dust. "What the pit do you mean by 'anointing'? Have you done any of that blood magic shit on me?" He thought of that moment in the town outside of Landfall just before the invasion.

Ka-poel regarded him coolly, but did not answer. This was not, Styke decided, the place to press the point. He didn't want to take her to task in public, and he *definitely* didn't want his men to witness him being stonewalled by a hundred-pound Palo woman. Besides, if she had put some kind of her magic on him, he would have smelled it. Wouldn't he have?

"We'll talk about this again. I have a man to kill. Are you two coming?" He climbed into Amrec's saddle and lifted Celine up after him.

"Are you going to let me watch you kill him?" Celine asked as they began to ride.

Styke sucked on his teeth. He *shouldn't*. He should turn around and leave Celine with Ibana. Better yet, he should hand her over to Ka-poel and tell them both to get lost. But he had the feeling that wouldn't actually work. Besides, he also had the feeling that he shouldn't tell a child about his plans to kill a man in the first place but that ship had sailed. "Just stay out of the way when the fighting starts."

Styke followed a stranger's directions across the city, eventually reaching a warehouse on the main thoroughfare just outside the old city walls on the north end of town. The warehouse's main door had been replaced by a colonnaded facade in imitation of the boxing arenas in Landfall, above which was an enormous banner bearing a likeness of Valyaine's upper body, fists held forward for a fight. The building had not been damaged by the shelling, the streets outside crowded with wounded and displaced citizens.

Styke left Celine with Amrec and entered through the front

door. He was surprised to find that it wasn't just the facade that had been remodeled: The entire inside of the building had been turned into a clean, well-lit arena, including boxes, bleachers, and snack stands. It could easily fit five thousand people, and from the busts and posters around the building, Styke gathered that there were shows every night. Valyaine himself, one of the posters proclaimed, was a feature every weekend.

The arena wasn't empty; it had been converted into a hospital for the victims of the shelling. Quiet moans filled the hall, coming from the countless wounded laid out on every surface. Surgeons and nurses rushed around, and Styke even spotted a woman in Privileged's gloves attending to the worst of the battered, filling the room with the brimstone smell of her sorcery. He breathed it in, enjoying the biting scent.

Styke almost backed out. He didn't need to fight in a hospital. But Valyaine was here somewhere. Styke could feel his blood begin to rise in anticipation of violence, and he caught the arm of a passing nurse. "I'm looking for Valyaine Soris," he said.

The woman looked him up and down, her eyes widening at his size. "I don't know where he is," she said. "But I'm in a hurry. I last saw him a few hours ago." She rushed off before he could question her further, leaving him empty-handed.

He plucked at his big lancers' ring, running his thumb over the skull relief and looking around the hall. Maybe, he thought, it would be best to come kill Valyaine on his way back through Bellport.

"Styke?"

Styke turned around to find Valyaine standing in the doorway, a load of fresh linen in his arms and a surprised look on his face. The surprise disappeared quickly, leaving behind something akin to resignation.

"Soris," Styke said, nodding slowly. He examined Valyaine in a heartbeat, taking in all the changes. Valyaine wasn't a tall man, easily a foot and a half shorter than Styke, but he'd always been well muscled. In the last ten years he'd grown positively enormous, with arms bigger around than Styke's and a chest that looked like it could catch a cannonball without splitting. He had a square jaw and short, jet-black hair, and he wore a businessman's suit and trousers. "This your place?" Styke asked, gesturing behind him.

"It is." Valyaine passed by Styke warily, handing the linens off to a nurse. He looked Styke up and down like a butcher prepping a piece of a meat, his eyes lingering on Styke's knife. "Heard you were still alive. Heard you saved Landfall."

"Something like that," Styke replied. He began to move slowly, keeping Valyaine in his field of vision, and they began to circle each other in the vestibule of the arena. "I heard you did a favor for Fidelis Jes a decade ago to buy you this." He gestured around the arena.

Valyaine took off his jacket and lay it on a nearby bench, never once taking his eyes off Styke. "Me? I got paid, sure. But I built all this myself."

"How much did he pay you?"

"Fifty thousand."

Styke scoffed. "Agoston got two million."

"I also asked for a favor from Fidelis Jes. I never cashed it in. Didn't see the need. I'm not the greedy shit Agoston is."

"Was," Styke corrected.

"Right. You do him with that big knife of yours?"

"I did." Styke tapped the underside of his jaw. "Put it through the soft spot here."

"You came across central Fatrasta. I imagine Tenny is dead, too?"

"Very," Styke lied.

Valyaine sighed. He didn't seem frightened or even all that put out. Just tired. "Dvory?"

"He's next."

"He's got a field army at his back, so best of luck with that." Valyaine's eyes fell to Styke's knife. "You gonna take it personally when I fight back?"

Styke almost laughed. That indignant anger now churned in his belly, but more than that, he felt *alive*, as alive as when he unleashed Amrec to a full gallop toward an enemy flank. "Traitor or not, I wouldn't begrudge a man a good fight."

"You wait here while I go get myself a knife?"

Styke snorted. Despite Valyaine's resignation, there was a light in his eyes. He, too, was looking forward to this. Styke made two fists. He didn't want this to go down like it did with Agoston. He wanted this to *last*. "We'll do this your way."

"Suit yourself." Valyaine rolled up the sleeves of his white dress shirt and flexed his fingers. They continued to circle.

"I always liked you, Valyaine."

"Yeah? Well, I always thought you were a wanker." Valyaine darted forward faster than Styke expected, his arms coming up in a boxer's stance and his right fist lashing out and connecting with Styke's chin in a powerful jab that snapped Styke's head back and brought tears to his eyes. Styke stumbled, raising his arms in defense, taking two more jabs to the ribs before he could fend off the attack.

Valyaine retreated, bouncing on the balls of his feet, fists held high. Styke copied the stance, remembering his days fighting in the barracks, well before the Mad Lancers. He swung at Valyaine's head, but the punch was too slow. Valyaine ducked beneath it, hammering his left side with a flurry of blows, causing Styke to double over—only to take a knee to his forehead.

Styke fell back against the wall. His eyes were blurry, blood leaking from his nose and mouth and streaming from Valyaine's knuckles.

"What are you doing, Ben?" Valyaine asked, dancing in front of Styke, feinting left and right. "Is this part of some path of vengeance? Is this some kind of redemption? Get out that big knife and end this thing. It'll go faster." He darted back in, pounding on the arm Styke raised in defense and then leaping back from Styke's counterjab.

He continued to talk. "Do you think you're some kind of hero? Rumor has it you've threatened to crucify any soldiers you find stealing from Fatrastans. Is that true?"

It wasn't, but Styke didn't see the need to correct him. It sounded like something he'd do.

When he didn't answer, Valyaine barked a laugh. "That's some hypocritical shit there, Ben."

"We never stole from the people we protected," Styke snapped. He pushed himself off the wall and brought his arms in. He closed the distance between them, attacking Valyaine with short jabs that the boxer simply slapped aside. Only one managed to land, hitting Valyaine in the cheek and sending him reeling.

Valyaine recovered and spat blood at Styke. "We stole from everyone," he growled. "You've got rose-colored spectacles, you big dumb asshole. If we needed something, we'd just accuse someone of being a royalist and take it from them. Maybe there was a veneer of honor to it, but never more than skin-deep."

The whole hall had grown silent, and Styke could feel the eyes of the doctors and nurses and wounded upon them as they continued to circle. He thought about his vengeance, and realized that to all these people he was just a big dumb soldier attacking their benefactor.

The vengeance was only in *his* head. But then again, that's all that ever mattered.

Valyaine came at him again, smashing fists against Styke's arms, jabbing his ribs. Styke swung hard and low, ignoring a blow to his face in order to land his own. He felt something crack beneath his knuckles, and Valyaine suddenly retreated again, holding his side.

Valyaine grinned. "Pit, I forgot how strong you are." He spat out more blood. "You know, Ben, it's been so long I forget what it was that Fidelis Jes said that made me decide to betray you. He prodded at all of us, you know—for over a year. He even tried to get to Ibana. Didn't anyone warn you?" He shook his head. "Nah, of course not. You don't warn Ben Styke. That's like warning a hurricane. What good would it do?"

Styke wished Valyaine would shut up and focus on the fight. This wasn't how it was supposed to go. This wasn't meant to be fun—not for him, and definitely not for Valyaine. This was just a man taking care of business. He swung with his left fist, letting Valyaine duck under it, following up with his right and grabbing Valyaine by the neck, lifting him and slamming him against the wall. Styke felt a kick against his knee and suddenly lost his balance. He gasped in pain as he fell, then felt Valyaine's fist slam into the side of his temple with the force of a warhorse kick.

Styke staggered to the side, seeing double, and turned back toward Valyaine.

"I've killed people with that punch," Valyaine stated with an almost maniacal laugh. "I never liked you, Ben, but I damn well respect you. You're a bloody mule. I love that. I love that you never go down. You know what? I remember what Jes said now—why I agreed to help him. Because he told me what it would be like having a monster like you roaming the countryside after the end of the war."

"That's it?" Styke demanded, trying to blink his vision back to normal. "That's all it took you to betray me? Some hypothetical image?"

"Hypothetical? Pit, Ben! What kind of shit did you smoke in the labor camps? I was *there*. I saw the terror that was the Mad Lancers. We were a goddamned force of nature. Cutting off the head was the only way to stop us." Valyaine shook his head. "I wish it didn't come to that. I wish we'd all just gone home, but instead we had to leave with the worst kinds of scars." He tapped the side of his head. "Agoston spent all his money to climb into the bottom of a bottle for the last decade. Tenny Wiles got himself a wife and buried his head between her legs. Worst of all, Dvory got put in charge of a whole field army as his reward from Jes. Between you and me, he never did care. I may dislike you, but Dvory...he *hates* you."

Styke's vision finally began to clear. "And you?"

"Me? It bothered me for a year or two. Then I forgot about it. Got a career. Made money. Started to help people in the community. I sate my bloodlust in the ring and I've only killed a few men doing it. Sometimes I go on a mala binge. Helps me forget about the things we did in the name of freedom."

Styke could see Valyaine settle his weight on his back foot, coiling like a snake ready to spring. He fell back a half step and when Valyaine leapt forward, he was ready. He caught the wrist of Valyaine's right arm and jerked him past, grabbing his neck and using Valyaine's own momentum to lift him clear off the ground. He spun, flinging Valyaine with all his strength through the arena doors.

The doors burst open, one of them snapping off the hinges as Valyaine stumbled through them and into the street, reeling until he finally collapsed in the mud.

Styke followed him out, removing his knife from his belt. To his surprise, Valyaine wasn't even unconscious. He lay in a puddle with about as much grace as a man could, looking back up at Styke through hazy eyes and laughing quietly to himself.

"What's so funny?" Styke asked.

"You," Valyaine said. "I always told Dvory that you would never die. He insisted you were already gone, that Jes had put you in front of a firing squad and a doctor pronounced you dead."

"And that's funny?"

"It's always funny when Dvory's wrong." Valyaine coughed and, slipping and sliding in the mud, slowly regained his feet. He eyed Styke's knife. "What's really funny is that you don't even know what you actually are. You always demand the closest loyalty from your own men, but you never give your own."

"I've always protected Fatrasta," Styke protested. He wondered why he bothered—he needed to step over and finish this with a swing of his knife.

"Bah," Valyaine spat. "A concept. You've never been loyal to a person. You've never listened to a set of orders without thinking about how you were going to disobey them. You've never been Commander Ben Styke, the officer that everyone else can depend on. You've just been that force of nature. They pointed you at the people they wanted dead and hoped you didn't come around and get them all killed." Valyaine looked at the knife in Ben's hand and raised his fists. "Let's finish it, big man."

Styke stared at Valyaine. He stared hard, letting the words rattle around inside his mind. He *needed* to kill Valyaine, to finish this whole thing off. He stepped forward, setting his foot for good purchase in the mud and took a swing.

Even as he went through the motion, he knew it was half-hearted. Valyaine knew it too. He stepped into the swing, catching Styke's weak wrist with a quick jab that made his hand go numb. His knife fell from his hands. Valyaine's next punch came all the way across the boxer's body and slammed into Styke's chest with immense power. Styke stumbled back, slipped in the mud, and fell.

He struggled to breathe, looking up at Valyaine. Slowly, Valyaine lowered his fists. He took one step to the side, picking Styke's knife out of the mud, then tossing it to him hilt-first. "I never wanted you dead, Ben. I just wanted things to end. You think about that real hard. Go slaughter Dynize until you swim in blood. If you still want more, you can come back here and gut me. I'll even open my shirt for you."

Valyaine turned around and walked back into the arena.

Styke struggled to his feet. He'd killed men before for walking away during a fight. He watched until Valyaine had disappeared, then limped across the street to where Ka-poel and Celine waited with Amrec. Passersby stared. He ignored them.

Celine had a strange look on her face, Ka-poel a scowl. Styke took the reins from Celine and realized that she'd probably never heard anyone talk like that to him—like an equal who was sick of his shit. She asked in a quiet voice, "Why didn't you kill him?"

It was an echo of the question she'd asked when he failed to kill Tenny Wiles. Styke sighed, knowing he was never going to hear the end of this from Ibana. *Because he beat me fair and square* almost came to his lips, but instead he said, "Because he wasn't wrong," and limped down the street with Amrec in tow.

Everything hurt—he hadn't been beaten that hard since the labor camp, and it wasn't a good kind of memory. He felt around with his tongue, making sure he had all his teeth, and gingerly touched his face. Broken nose. Split lips. Maybe a cracked rib. He still had a hard time breathing. He'd need a big supply of horngum before he left town.

They'd gone a few blocks when Styke suddenly spotted something out of the corner of his eye. He handed the reins to Celine, who still sat alone on Amrec's saddle, and limped down the street toward an old man he'd spotted leading a horse.

"You there," he said, tapping the man on the shoulder.

"Eh?" The old man turned, looked up at Styke, and did a double take. "What do you want?"

Styke did a quick circuit of the horse, looking at teeth, eyes, hooves, and legs while the man looked on, bewildered. "It looks like a midget Rosvelan draft horse," Styke said.

"Not bred that way. She's just a runt. Can I help you with something?"

"How does she do with noise?"

"What's this about?" the man demanded.

"Noise?" Styke said. "How does she do with it? Quick movements, large crowds, all that?"

"She does great," the man retorted. "She's a damned miniature warhorse, just too small for a soldier. What the pit do you want?"

Styke ignored the man's frustration. "Name me a price and I'll buy her right now."

The man looked around suspiciously before eyeing Styke for a long moment. "A thousand krana."

It was three hundred more than the horse was worth. "Done," Styke replied. "You bring her and any kit you have for her out to the Mad Lancer camp by nightfall. Tell Ibana ja Fles that Ben Styke bought a horse for the girl, and she'll pay you."

"I...I..."

Styke left the man standing there stuttering and returned to Ka-poel and Celine. Ka-poel had a small smile on her face, and Styke avoided looking her in the eye.

"Who was that?" Celine asked.

"Just some man," Styke replied.

"What did you want with him?"

Styke took Amrec's reins, patting Celine gently on the arm. "I wanted to buy his horse. She's yours. Should be there by the time we go to bed tonight."

The look of joy on Celine's face made him forget all about his broken nose, Valyaine, and the entire damned war. Unable to stop grinning, Styke led them back to the Mad Lancer camp.

CHAPTER 33

V lora caught sight of Prime Lektor again three days after
speaking with Taniel in the Yellow Creek jail.

Finding him was purely luck. Vlora was returning from another
fruitless morning of searching the nooks and crannies of the mountains surrounding Yellow Creek. The newsies on her normal route
had sold out of their papers already, so she went out of her way to
find a street corner where the boys still had some stock. She had
just found a paper and folded it over to read while she walked when
her gaze swept across the familiar profile.

Prime sat outside a café in the one small area of town that could
be considered posh—if one squinted a little. It was midday, and
he was enjoying a coffee, biscuits, and a newspaper while he faced
away from the sun.

Vlora forced herself to act casual, turning slowly to cut across
traffic and heading around to a nearby storefront where she
could get a good look at his face without crossing his line of
sight. Once she could clearly see the inkvine birthmark that cut

across the left side of his face, she knew he was definitely Prime Lektor.

Vlora waffled. A part of her wanted to walk over, pull up a seat, and ask Prime straight out why he was here. It was a foolish thought, one that she had no problem talking herself out of, and instead she circled around behind him and took a seat on a nearby stoop where she could keep an eye on him over her newspaper.

She only half read the articles as she watched the back of Prime's head. The news was all two weeks old, and was filled with rampant speculation regarding the war, Dynize military might, rumors of Lindet's assassination, and more. Nothing looked reliable and it frustrated her to no end, so she turned her attention purely on Prime.

One of the odd quirks of sorcery was that a powder mage could sense a Privileged, but a Privileged could not sense a powder mage. Vlora did not know if the same rule applied to the Predeii, but considering that Prime didn't just turn around and incinerate her, she assumed that it did.

The immediate problem was that, while she definitely recognized Prime Lektor, she could not sense his sorcerous presence. He was cloaking himself from any such scrying. It would make him difficult to follow or predict.

She tried to think of any possible reason for his presence in Yellow Creek—aside from the godstone. Nothing came to mind, and that left her with a number of pressing questions. What were his intentions regarding the stone? Had he already found it? Was he alert and ready in case he was found, or was he complacent in his power? There were no easy answers, which meant Vlora would have to find them the hard way, the dangerous way.

It was about thirty minutes before Prime folded his paper, finished off his coffee, and stood up. He was dressed as a frontier gentleman, with a tan cotton suit and matching top hat, a cane, and a pair of spectacles perched on the front of his nose. He surreptitiously took a look around before tucking the paper under one arm and heading down the street.

Vlora followed at a distance.

She didn't have to go far. Prime took a right at the next intersection and walked up to the front door of what passed for a townhouse in a frontier city. The building was a narrow two stories, a mix of wood and plaster construction with a sharply slanted roof and cheerful bright green shutters. Prime let himself in, leaving Vlora lurking at the corner and completely uncertain about what to do next.

She carefully cast her senses toward the townhouse, feeling around with a light, tentative touch for wards. There were all sorts of passive things a Privileged could do to protect a location. Doorknobs could be warded to stun or kill anyone who touched them, floors could inform the Privileged when someone had walked upon them, and whole buildings could be prepped to explode when entered. Wards were also, as far as Vlora was aware, next to impossible to hide completely.

Field Marshal Tamas had been an expert at detecting wards. He'd even taught Vlora how to pick a ward apart—something that most Privileged still considered impossible for a powder mage—but Vlora had never really caught on to the latter ability. The former, however, she'd grown quite good at.

Yet she sensed nothing, even when she poked around for the telltale signs of a ward that had been folded in on itself to hide it.

She was just beginning to wonder if she'd gone mad when the front door to the townhouse opened. She took a half step back, trying to look inconspicuous. Prime didn't even look up, staring at the front of his folded newspaper with a scowl as he walked briskly past her. She waited a few moments, then turned to follow him.

Had he already noticed her and was leading her into a trap? She tried to remember every detail about him. He was an academic, supporting Tamas during the Adran coup, and had apparently masqueraded as a succession of vice chancellors of Adopest University for hundreds of years. He might genuinely be absentminded, content that his power kept him hidden.

Vlora was deep in thought when she looked up to find that she was no longer following Prime. Her heart quickened and she doubled her pace, hurrying to the next intersection. She checked doorways and alleys for fifty yards. She even looked back down the street to see if he'd doubled back.

No such luck. He had disappeared entirely.

Vlora swore under her breath. This asshole could disappear, both in this world and in the Else. She couldn't see him; she couldn't sense him. He could be standing right behind her and she wouldn't notice it.

She doubled back around the block several times just in case she had missed him. After waiting for nearly ten minutes for him to reappear, she headed to his townhouse, where she walked up to the front door, took a hit of powder, and closed her eyes. In a deep powder trance she could hear footsteps, heavy breathing, sometimes even a heartbeat. She tried to focus on the house, ignoring the ambient sound of the street.

Nothing.

Searching his residence might turn up clues to the godstone's location. But if she hadn't been able to sense him disappear, that meant that he could create wards that she couldn't sense, either. Walking straight into his house might get her killed.

She waffled on the front step for a moment before noticing an old woman sweeping the steps of the next house over. The woman glanced up, noticed that Vlora was watching her, and leaned heavily on her broom. "What you selling?" she demanded.

The question caught Vlora off guard. "Excuse me?"

"The gentleman who owns that house doesn't like to be bothered. If you're selling something, you can tell me and I'll let him know when he's next in."

"Does he often buy things?"

"Never. But he likes to know who's knocking on his door. So you can either leave me your card or bugger off."

Vlora hesitated, trying to concoct some sort of story that wouldn't make Prime suspicious. Coming up with nothing, she tipped her hat to the old woman and made her retreat, heading down the street without a backward glance and frustrated that she'd not learned anything new about Prime.

She corrected herself on that last thought. She *had* learned two things: one, that Prime could disappear at will, and two, that Prime paid his neighbors to watch the house for him while he was out. If he was worried about being tracked down, it meant he was hiding something, and she was willing to bet it wasn't just his own sorcerous nature.

CHAPTER 34

The Mad Lancers left Bellport, heading west along the northern coast of the Hammer. They traveled slowly, sending out as many scouts as they dared and avoiding the larger towns and cities already flying the Dynize flag. They even stayed several miles inland to avoid being spotted by Dynize ships—of which, their scouts informed them, there were dozens plying the waters back and forth between Fatrasta and Dynize.

Styke kept to himself for several days, content to ride with the rear guard while recovering from the beating Valyaine gave him and teaching Celine how to handle her new horse. The creature turned out to be more stubborn than Styke had initially guessed, and would have found itself discarded with the rest of the extra horses had Celine not taken an equally stubborn liking to it.

Frequent reports came from Ibana with the vanguard. Styke read the reports and sent orders to the front. During the evenings he helped train the newest recruits—having picked up almost five hundred volunteers in Bellport—while Celine continued to learn Ka-poel's language.

On the fourth day of riding, Styke heard the distant report of artillery and made his way up the winding line of cavalry, joining Ibana with the vanguard over a mile ahead. She sat on her horse on a cliff top, eyes focused on something in the distance. Jackal, bearing the Mad Lancer standard, sat with her.

To the northwest, Styke was able to see the source of the cannon fire that continued to echo across the water. There was a small fortress, whose name had long since escaped him, positioned at the end of a long breakwater. It overlooked the space between the Hammer and an unnamed island, and it was exchanging a violent torrent of fire with a sizable Dynize fleet positioned in a half-moon around the fortress.

"I'm guessing," Ibana said without lowering her looking glass, "that you've been skulking with the rear guard the last few days because you failed to kill Valyaine?"

Styke glanced around. The only people within earshot were Jackal, Celine, and Ka-poel. Styke looked to Jackal, whose Palo freckles had darkened with all the time out in the sun. Jackal simply lifted his hands. This was not something he wanted to get involved with.

"I've been teaching Celine to ride her new horse."

Ibana snapped her looking glass closed and turned toward Styke. "I heard you let Valyaine beat the shit out of you."

" 'Let' seems a strong word. He's a champion boxer."

"And you have the biggest knife on the continent," Ibana retorted. "Why the pit did you square up fisticuffs against a champion boxer?"

"I wanted to see if I could kill him with my fists."

"It didn't work out. He betrayed you, and he's still alive."

"I can always go back and gut him later," Styke said, the words coming out a little more petulant than he'd intended.

Ibana fixed Styke with a long stare and then turned to Celine. "What's her name, sweetheart?" she asked gently, indicating Celine's horse.

Celine beamed. "Margo. She already had the name and I liked it, so I decided to let her keep it."

"That's a good name," Ibana replied. She nudged her own horse, quickly trotting around Margo before nodding. "Looks like a good horse."

"Ben bought her for me." There was an edge of challenge in Celine's voice, as if daring Ibana to question the man who would acquire a horse for a little girl. Styke almost laughed out loud.

He butted in before Ibana could get annoyed. "I haven't been hiding," he said.

"Good," Ibana said simply. She drew closer to Styke, letting her voice fall. She didn't look happy with what she was about to say, but she continued on. "You know it just as well as I do—the Mad Lancers ride on their reputation. On *your* reputation. You start sparing people who have betrayed you and people will think you've gone soft. The prospect of your knife is the only thing that keeps some of these bastards in line."

Styke sat back in his saddle, unsure how to respond. He remembered Agoston's blood running down his arms, and then sparing Tenny Wiles. "They start to get uppity and I'll set them straight."

"It's never come to that before. I don't want it to come to that."

Styke snorted. "Let me handle my vengeance the way I see fit."

"I will. It's just...a word of warning, that's all."

"Thank you," Styke replied.

Ibana nodded and rode off a few dozen yards, pulling out her looking glass to watch the distant bombardment. Styke turned to Jackal. "How has the ride been?"

"Easy enough," Jackal said. "Scouts are keeping us clear of Dynize forces. How is the rear guard?"

"Boring," Styke replied. He nodded to the distant fortress. "Do the spirits tell you how much longer that fortress will last?"

Jackal's eyes immediately went over Styke's shoulder, and it took him a moment to realize Jackal was looking directly at Ka-poel. "Are you kidding? Only the bravest spirits will come within a mile of her. I can always tell when she's getting near because they flee before she arrives."

"You hear that, blood-lady?" Styke called. "The spirits are afraid of you."

Ka-poel seemed entirely unimpressed.

"But it doesn't take the spirits," Jackal said, returning his gaze to the distant fort, "to see they're almost done for. There's six ships of the line out there and two brigades cutting off any support from the mainland. The fortress will fall within days." He gave Styke a curious look. "Are we going to relieve them?"

Styke glanced at Ka-poel. "Is the godstone in that fort?"

She shook her head.

"No," he told Jackal. "I'm not suicidal enough to charge two brigades in clear view of a supporting enemy fleet." Besides, he added to himself, they'd already resupplied at Bellport. "We'll have to swing around those two brigades. With luck, they'll be so focused on the fort that they don't even notice us."

Styke heard a sudden shout from down the road. He turned, curious, and was soon joined by Ibana. "What was that?" she asked.

"I'm not sure." Styke lifted Amrec's reins, spotting a dust cloud rising from a nearby hill, and a familiar old face suddenly burst into view. Sunintiel clung to her horse's neck, both she and her animal streaming tears from the hard ride, her wrinkled skin covered in a sheen of sweat. She stood in the stirrups, not bothering to slow.

"We've been ambushed!" she shouted. "Dynize cavalry from the rear!"

Styke whipped Amrec into a gallop. "Stay with Celine," he ordered Sunin. He pointed a finger behind him as he charged past. "And keep Ka-poel out of the fight!"

He and Ibana raced along the road, past the milling of confused cavalrymen. Styke came around the hill into the valley that contained the bulk of his forces, taking in the situation at a glance. Dynize dragoons had swept in from the southern end of the valley, crossing a small creek and opening fire with carbines on the Mad Lancers, who were still strung out along the road.

There were at least three thousand dragoons, with more coming over the hill, and they raked the lancers' flank with perfect precision, hitting them with a torrent of carbine fire in companies of a hundred before retreating out of range to reload. The lancers were in chaos—those that tried to fire back couldn't pack a big enough punch, and the few that charged were deftly avoided and gunned down.

Another wave of dragoons suddenly appeared at the other end of the valley, blocking a retreat along the road and engaging the rear guard with a withering fusillade.

Styke pressed Amrec harder, weaving among his confused troops. "Ibana!" he shouted. "Take the vanguard and swing around to their flank. They're not wearing breastplates. Hit the bastards with our lances!"

He continued on without waiting for an answer, galloping toward the rear guard and the fresh recruits being cut to ribbons. He passed Major Gustar, who'd just barely organized the Riflejack cavalry core enough to return fire. "Press them hard," Styke shouted, slowing just enough to get his orders out. "That hill they came down was easier for them to descend than it will be to go back up. Send your cuirassiers straight at their center!"

Styke was quickly past. He urged Amrec harder, watching as more of his cavalry fell to the enemy carbine volleys. The Dynize became bolder, pressing in on the rear guard, not bothering to retreat before they reloaded their weapons. Styke finally reached the rear guard, who were desperately trying to reload their own carbines.

"Blast the carbines!" Styke roared as he whipped past them. "Lances down! Charge!" He snatched up his lance, lowering the steel tip as he broke through the confused line of his own men and up the open road toward the Dynize.

Dragoons had come within ten yards and they seemed shocked to see him charging toward them wearing one of their own breastplates. A bullet whizzed past Styke's ear and he felt another slam into the breastplate, jerking him back in the saddle. He kept his hold on the reins and on his lance, leaning forward.

The closest Dynize fumbled with his carbine, dropped it, then tried to urge his horse to run in the opposite direction. Styke's lance clipped him in the side, tearing out four inches of flesh and several feet of intestine and burying it into the next dragoon. Letting go of his weighty lance, Styke drew his cavalry sword and urged Amrec forward, laying about him with his weapon.

Gore whipped from the rise and fall of his sword. Blood spattered his lips, but Styke didn't bother to check if it was his own or the enemy's. Their sudden onslaught turned to confusion at his charge, and still he pushed deeper, using Amrec's mighty chest to shove past the smaller Dynize horses.

Only upon turning to block the sword thrust of an enemy did Styke see that the new recruits had not, actually, followed him into the fray. Some of them stared at him dumbly while others fumbled for their lances. It wasn't until Jackal appeared, waving the skull-and-lance flag and charging forward, that they seemed to break out of their shock and attack.

A straight-bladed dragoon sword caught in the clasp of Styke's breastplate. He sheared off the arm holding it and discarded the blade, but the clasp snapped at the next impact of an enemy bullet. With one quick movement, Styke bit down on Amrec's reins and used his left hand to pry the other clasp off the broken breastplate. He swung it over his head and threw it at a charging dragoon, knocking the rider off his horse. Reins still between his teeth, he drew his boz knife and rammed it into the chest of a man whose mount had been pushed too close in the melee. He jerked it out and threw it overhand into the neck of a horse. The horse screamed, throwing its rider.

Styke finally fought his way to the top of the ridge, looking down at the road. It was covered with the bodies of men and horses—almost all of them belonging to the new recruits from Bellport, stragglers who'd fallen behind the rear guard. With a glance Styke could see how the dragoons had come out of the trees, catching them completely unawares and slaughtering them without a fight.

The glance also told him that he'd reached the very edge of this wave of dragoons—they had no more men attacking the rear guard. He whirled to rally the rear, to dispose of these dragoons and join Gustar and Ibana to fight their main force.

Something struck his shoulder just as he drew breath to bellow encouragement. He turned to see a dragoon charging him at full speed, smoking carbine being exchanged for a straight-edged sword. The rider didn't have time to fully draw her sword before her horse struck Amrec in the shoulder, sending both Amrec and Styke tumbling.

Styke barely managed to throw himself clear. Amrec fell on his side, legs flailing, finally righting himself and charging off before Styke could call to him.

The Dynize dragoon allowed her own horse to regain its balance before turning on a dime and pointing her sword at Styke and digging in her heels. Styke searched for his sword only to see it caught in Amrec's harness as the beast galloped away. He felt for his knife—remembered throwing it—and began to loudly swear at himself.

The dragoon leapt into a gallop, her sword held to her side as she swooped in toward Styke. He remained on her sword side for as long as he dared, then leapt in front of the charging horse and across to the opposite side. Before the dragoon could change her sword hand, Styke set the foot of his good leg and barreled, shoulder-first, into the soft side of the Dynize horse. Both horse and rider went flying.

The impact knocked the breath from Styke and nearly threw him on his ass. He barely stayed on his feet and ran toward the horse that, still flailing with pain, had his boz knife in its neck. He jerked the knife out, reversed his hold on it, and rammed the blade into the creature's spine with one quick motion, putting it out of its misery.

A shout of challenge was the only warning he got. The persistent dragoon leapt toward him, sword thrusting, and Styke barely parried the thrust with the blade of his knife. He charged forward, closing the distance, ramming his left fist into the dragoon's face.

She reeled back but did not fall, driving him off with blind swipes of her sword.

They both froze, staring at each other, giving Styke his first good look at his opponent. She was tall—not as tall as he or Ibana, but nearly so—and she had wide shoulders that reminded him of Valyaine. She was broad-faced with quick eyes and her red hair shorn to a finger's length. Her teal uniform had orange epaulets, which, Styke assumed, meant she was an officer. Over his shoulder he could hear Jackal urging the rear guard to finish off their Dynize attackers.

The dragoon regarded him for another long moment, her eyes flicking to her fallen cavalry, before suddenly turning and sprinting toward the closest empty saddle. She pulled herself onto horseback with incredible dexterity and was galloping back toward the edge of the forest before Styke could take a dozen steps.

He turned at the sound of a trumpet, watching as the Dynize

cavalry disengaged from the Mad Lancers and began to retreat. The lancers, for their part, were obviously badly mauled, and he was not surprised when Ibana did not give the order to follow.

He found the dragoon officer's horse where he'd shoved it over. The poor creature thrashed in pain with one leg broken and probably several cracked ribs. Styke calmed it as best he could and covered its eyes with one arm before putting it out of its misery.

He found Amrec and went back up the road in search of Ibana.

"That was a timely charge," he told Jackal as he passed.

Jackal waved back at him. "The spirits wouldn't forgive me if I allowed you to die charging an enemy army alone."

Styke found Ibana down in the valley taking stock of their—and the enemy's—losses. She was on foot, kneeling over a half-dead Dynize dragoon, trying to get the man to talk through a mouthful of blood. She left him be, snorting in disgust, then turned to face Styke.

"Find out where these bastards came from?" Styke asked.

Ibana shook her head. "He's not talking, nor is anyone still alive. We'll take a few captives and work on them later. Maybe give them to Ka-poel and see what she can learn."

"Maybe," Styke said. He wasn't thrilled with the idea of handing anyone over to Ka-poel. He wasn't entirely sure what she could do or how she could do it, but it sounded ... protracted. He did not like torture. "That retreat was organized. They weren't willing to commit everything to the fight, it seems."

Ibana kicked at a body at her feet. "Damn it. We've sent scouts in every direction. How the pit did they sneak up on us like that?"

"Send a few men to follow them," Styke said. "Not too closely, but ..." He glanced back toward the road, then in the direction they had retreated. "They came from the south, but they retreated to the west. Send a few men the way they came, too."

"Right." Ibana stalked off, barking orders, while Styke stared down at the poor bastard she'd been interrogating. One of his arms was hanging by skin and he had three stab wounds through his chest. He'd be dead soon enough.

He glanced up to the ridge, where well over a hundred of the new recruits lay dead or dying. He wondered about that Dynize officer. This ambush had felt strange. It had felt... personal. Were those blasted dragonmen behind it? Or was this something else?

CHAPTER 35

Michel was shaken awake by his own violent shivers. He lay on his back, staring up at blackness, a vague discomfort emanating from somewhere around the middle of his body. His first realization was that his entire body was trembling uncontrollably. No amount of effort could cease the shaking.

His second realization was that he could not move. There was not, as far as he could tell, anything *keeping* him from moving—nothing across his chest or binding his arms. His body simply did not respond to the commands. He could breathe. He could shiver. He could open his eyes and move his head slightly from one side to the other, though he did not know if his vision was dark or if he was merely in a dark room. Only a well of calmness from deep within—one he did not know he possessed—kept him from spiraling into outright terror.

He lay still for several minutes, attempting to get his bearings and gain control of his shivering body. He was unsuccessful in the first, and only mildly successful in the second. The problem, he realized, was that he was lying on something extremely cold. Cold and hard.

He cleared his throat, wondering if he could speak, and heard someone—or something—stir in what sounded like a different room. Footsteps followed, then Michel could feel a presence just out of his peripheral vision. Although he was fairly certain he knew the answer, he spoke anyway: "Am I dead?"

"You are not."

Michel let out a very soft sigh. The voice belonged to Emerald, which meant that Michel was likely lying on a slab in the bowels of the Landfall City Morgue. It explained the cold, as well as the darkness. It wasn't his first choice of a place to wake up to, but it certainly wasn't his last.

As if in answer to his thoughts, the dim light suddenly grew brighter, illuminating the stone ceiling that Michel had been staring at. "How do you feel?" Emerald said, sitting down beside him.

"I'm…not sure. I'm having trouble thinking, and I can barely move. I don't feel pain. At least, I don't think I do. My chest is very warm."

"That is your body *attempting* to feel pain. I injected a few drops of pure mala directly into your bloodstream."

"That explains a lot." Michel had spent his fair share of time on the mala pipe—in between jobs, of course—but he'd never quite felt this kind of sensation. He wasn't even aware mala could be injected like this.

"It was also several hours ago. If I had done so recently, you would have some trouble opening your eyelids."

"Right. I'd rather not do this again." Michel decided that freedom of movement might be preferred, even if it cost him a lot of pain. "How did I get here?"

"You collapsed less than a block from my door. A passerby thought you were dead and reported the body. You're lucky I was working, or one of my assistants might have just tossed you with the rest of the corpses."

Lucky. Right. "What was the damage?"

"You were shot in the chest," Emerald replied, his voice clinical. "The bullet lodged between your second and third rib. It was not difficult to remove, but you had lost quite a lot of blood by the time you were found. You've been drifting in and out of consciousness for two days."

Two damned days. Michel wondered how much had happened in just that time. He had a thousand questions, but bit them back. In due time. "Have I been on this slab since then?"

"Of course not. I had two of my assistants move you here about an hour ago so you wouldn't get blood on a bed while I changed your bandages. We were just about to move you back, actually. Too much longer and you'll catch hypothermia." Emerald leaned over Michel, his tinted glasses sliding down to the end of his nose as he examined Michel with calm, surprisingly blue eyes. "While you're here, you should try to eat something. I don't want you throwing up in one of our beds either. Hold on, I think there's still a little gruel left over from Horastia's lunch."

Michel listened to Emerald's footsteps recede, trying to come to grasp with what he would need to do to catch up on the last two days—and how he would deal with it all while recovering from a gunshot wound. He began to make a list in his head, shoving his way through the haze of the mala injection, trying to ignore the heat coming from his chest that, without the mala, would probably knock him out cold from the pain.

Emerald returned a moment later and gently put a pillow beneath Michel's head, then spoon-fed him a gruel whose flavor Michel could not place.

"Has anyone noticed I'm gone?" Michel asked between swallows.

"They have. Rumors have been spreading that you were shot and killed in this quarter, and that your body was tossed in the Hadshaw."

"Among who?"

"The Dynize. The Blackhats, for their part, are confident you're dead. They'd been shadowing you for days, waiting for you to be alone, and took your little expedition the other day as the perfect opportunity."

Michel licked his lips, trying to taste the gruel. Any sensation aside from the few this mala haze would allow him seemed suddenly important. "If rumors are spreading among the Dynize, they must have come from Forgula. No one saw me get shot except for Hendres. I wonder if she found me herself, or if Forgula told her where I've been staying."

"That, I don't know."

Michel realized how tired just eating and talking was making him. He had to focus the thoughts, ask important questions. "The name Mara—is it Dynize?"

Emerald seemed caught off guard. He paused with a spoon halfway to Michel's mouth. "It doesn't sound Dynize. Certainly not one I've heard."

"Then, what is it?"

"Gurlish, maybe? Could be Stren."

Pit. Michel threw a handful of silent curses toward Taniel for not giving him any more clues to accomplish this mission. He tried to think clearly—there *had* to be a reason for not finding anyone named Mara among the Dynize. Had Michel remembered the name wrong? Was it some kind of surname, or a nickname? He tried to consider other options, and kept coming around to the fact that he could not fulfill his mission if he could not even find the informant. So what did he do next? Did he flee the danger of the city? Or embed himself deeper with the Dynize?

"What else has happened since I was shot?" Michel asked. "Anything important?"

"Another Dynize minister was killed in a bombing."

"The minister of rations? She died before I was shot."

"I said *another*. It was a minor minister—road engineering, or something like that. He was inspecting a bridge about three miles up the Hadshaw and was killed in an explosion."

"Shit," Michel breathed. He wondered if it was another one of Yaret's allies and was suddenly struck with a thought. "Do you have my clothes?"

"Your shirt was a total loss. I have your jacket over here. Do you feel any nausea?"

"I'm fine. Look in my jacket pocket for a list of addresses and bring it to me."

Emerald set the bowl aside and disappeared from Michel's vision for a moment, before returning with the list and holding it where Michel could see. Michel squeezed his eyes closed, focusing his energy, and lifted his left arm as high as he dared. Emerald put the list between his fingers.

Half the paper had been soaked through with Michel's blood, making it impossible to read. But the top half was still intact, and Michel scanned his eyes across the addresses, trying to come up with some sort of pattern. "Kingston Street, where is that?" he asked.

"Lower Landfall, north of the plateau."

"And Gorin Way?"

"That's on the northern rim of Greenfire Depths."

Michel licked his lips. There *was* a pattern to these addresses. He could feel it, but what it was remained just out of his foggy-brained grasp. "What do all of these addresses have in common?" he whispered.

Emerald suddenly leaned over him, staring at the paper for a moment before sitting back down and offering Michel another spoonful of gruel. "They're the locations of the bombings that have been going on the last two weeks."

Michel's mouth fell open. "You're kidding me." He stared at the addresses, going over them again and again. He brought the paper closer to his eyes, noting a light pencil mark beside each address that he'd missed on his initial perusal. It was a number, seemingly nonsensical until he realized that it was the day of the month—this month and last—according to the Dynize calendar. Each day corresponded perfectly with each bombing at each address.

This wasn't just a list of addresses. It was the Blackhat hit list. Either Forgula had been given this so that she could keep herself out of harm's way, or it was a copy of a list of instructions she'd given to the Blackhats. Maybe even both. Michel's eyes had trouble focusing, his breathing growing strained.

"You need to relax," Emerald told him. "Otherwise you will set your healing back by days."

Michel tapped the paper with his thumb. There was an address right where the blood began to soak the paper, only half of which he could read. "What does this say?"

Emerald took the paper from Michel, studying it a moment. "Seventeen Chancellor's Court."

"And the number next to it?" Michel's hand began to tremble from the effort of holding up his hand.

This time, Emerald's study took almost a minute. He got up, went to the gas lantern in the corner, and held the paper up at several different angles. "I think it says eleven."

"The eleventh." Michel struggled against his own sluggishness to try to get to his feet. He barely managed to move his head off the pillow.

"What is it?" Emerald asked.

"Forgula is using the Blackhats to eliminate Sedial's enemies," Michel whispered. "That address is Yaret's Household. What day is it?"

"The ninth."

"Shit. I have to warn them."

"You're not going to get very far in your condition. You might be able to walk in two or three days, but..."

"Then *you* have to warn them," Michel hissed.

Emerald raised his eyebrows. "I don't have to do anything. Certainly not something that will put me or my people in danger." The words weren't said unkindly, but his tone was firm.

"Send a runner! Leave an anonymous note!"

"I will have no communication on your behalf with the Dynize," Emerald said. "I'm sorry, but it's too much of a risk. Messengers can be recognized or followed. To be perfectly honest, I haven't entirely convinced myself I'm not going to euthanize you and dump the body in the river so that you can't be found here."

Michel stared at Emerald, fear creeping in through the haze of the mala. His shivering, which he'd gotten mostly under control, suddenly returned.

Emerald continued with a sigh. "It is fortunate for you that I respect Taniel and Ka-poel more than I fear the Dynize. I will not chop you up while you sleep, I suppose, but I will also not do anything to risk any of my people. You can leave here once you can walk out on your own accord, but I will not involve myself in Dynize affairs." Emerald clapped his hands, standing up. "You need to rest. My assistants will move you back to a proper bed now. I'm afraid they're not used to carrying live bodies, so this may be slightly uncomfortable."

Michel didn't answer, trying desperately to come up with a way to convince Emerald to warn Yaret about the bombing. Yaret would die if his house was destroyed. Perhaps Tenik, too. Children would be caught in the explosion and, if it was big enough, dozens of Yaret's Household.

It wasn't until this moment that Michel realized he didn't want to lose Yaret. Not just for the mission but because he'd been the most understanding master Michel had ever served.

And he was a good man.

Michel was still trying to come up with something to say when two of Emerald's assistants put their hands beneath him—one under his shoulders, another under his feet—and counted down from three. They reached one and lifted, and all the warmth centered around Michel's chest suddenly burst into a brilliant lance of pain that flashed lightning across his senses.

Despite the pain, Michel could think of only one thing: Yaret was going to die in two days. And there was nothing he could do about it.

CHAPTER 36

V lora spent the next twenty-four hours attempting to catch
sight of Prime Lektor once more. It was, at the heart of it, a
game—Vlora spent every waking hour stalking the streets with her
hat pulled forward and her collar up, trying to find Prime Lektor
without him catching sight of her.

A dangerous game for certain, but it still felt like a game. She jumped
at every Prime-shaped shadow and could barely sleep for worry. Prime
was the key to all of this; she knew it in her gut. It seemed possible,
maybe even probable, that he already knew where the godstone was. If
she could follow him more carefully, he might lead her right to it.

She gave up late the next day, worried that she was becoming
too scattered in her search, and headed up to Little Flerring's place
in the hills. She found Flerring inspecting barrels of saltpeter as
they were removed from an ox-drawn wagon. Vlora waited until
the inspection was finished, then drew Flerring aside.

"Have you been able to find out about anything strange going
on around town?" she asked.

Flerring waved down the cart driver, slipping him several extra coins, before returning to Vlora and rubbing her chin. "You mentioned a madness thing last time you were here, right?"

"Taniel did. Apparently madness seized people at random if they spent too much time near the artifact."

"Not a lot of weird stuff going on," Flerring said thoughtfully. "Aside from the usual fights and killings and mining accidents. But a handful of miners up in Nighttime Vale have been hauled away raving mad over the last few weeks."

Vlora perked up. *This* was the kind of information she'd been waiting to hear. "You couldn't have mentioned this sooner?"

"I didn't know sooner. Just found out a few hours ago. Miners are superstitious by nature, and Jezzy has been paying the local doctors a heavy fee to keep quiet about the whole thing."

"Jezzy's territory, eh?" Vlora swore under her breath. Burt, she might be able to bribe or cajole, but Jezzy probably didn't feel all that kindly toward Vlora right now. "What can you tell me about the Vale?"

"It's a canyon northeast of here," Flerring answered. "Easy to miss, actually. The entrance makes it look tiny, but it opens up into a rather large valley. It would be a great spot for a summer home if there weren't five hundred miners living up there blowing the whole thing to the pit."

"Does Jezzy own the whole valley?"

"That she does. Apparently there's a real easy gold vein close to the surface. No one goes into that valley if they don't work for her."

Vlora considered the information, feeling at once jubilant and annoyed. In almost two weeks this was the first bit of solid intelligence she had. It wasn't guaranteed, of course. Miners weren't a stable lot, and madness could set in with this heat and dangerous work. But she would give it a thorough look, if she could sneak in past Jezzy's guards. She swore to herself, wishing it was Burt's territory.

"I need a favor," Vlora said.

Flerring frowned down the path leading back to the city as another ox-drawn cart trundled toward them, stacked high with barrels. "What kind of favor? I'm awfully busy right now."

"That artifact I told you about?"

"Yeah?"

"I need you ready to blow it up at a moment's notice."

"Now?" Flerring asked incredulously.

"Any time in the next week."

"Pit." Flerring hawked a wad of phlegm into the bushes. "I've got to cook up a special batch of blasting oil, if what you said about black powder is true."

"Right, your most powerful stuff."

"That takes time."

"Time I don't have."

Flerring eyed Vlora for a few moments. "Look, I work in batches, and I take orders. I started putting aside a little of the good stuff the moment you told me there would be a job, but if you want enough to crack through sorcery, you're going to have to wait in line. Jezzy, Burt, and eight independent mining companies are all expecting blasting oil this month. And they pay ahead of time."

"To the pit with all of them," Vlora said flatly. She cursed herself for not putting in an order properly the moment she laid eyes on Flerring.

Flerring rubbed her fingers together beneath Vlora's nose. "They pay ahead of time, and they pay in gold. Or cash krana. Either is fine with me."

"How about a promissory note from the Adran government?"

Flerring snorted. "A promissory note isn't gold."

"Gold won't keep all your permits up to date with the Adran government," Vlora responded. "I seem to remember your main headquarters being not that far outside of Adopest."

Flerring narrowed her eyes. "You wouldn't."

"I'm not," Vlora promised. "But I do still have friends in the government. I won't make bad things happen for you—I don't do business like that—but I *will* be there to make sure bad things *don't* happen to you. Catch my meaning?"

"So you're saying the next time some asshole minister tries to turn the public against explosives makers as a publicity stunt, you'll get involved?"

"Personally."

Flerring seemed to consider this. Over the years since the Kez Civil War, plenty of politicians had run for public office on the platform of demilitarizing Adro. Some succeeded, which was why Vlora had scooped up a whole brigade of Adro's finest who'd found themselves disbanded. Others aimed for infrastructure and logistics, hoping to shut down the powder makers and gunsmiths.

"All right," Flerring said finally. She made a shooing motion with her hands as the next cart of saltpeter arrived. "You give me your word, and a damned fat promissory note, and I'll make sure you have as much blasting oil as you need any time this coming week."

Vlora took that as a victory and returned to her hotel for dinner, taking a covert snort of powder as she entered the hotel great room and leaving a pair of coins on the manager's podium. She didn't like him, but keeping his palms greased might have its uses down the road.

She took her usual table and ordered whatever gruel the hotel kitchen had cooked up, sitting back and falling into her own head as she tried to work out her new strategy. She was going to have to reconnoiter Nighttime Vale, and it sounded like it was already heavily guarded because of Jezzy's gold mine. She briefly considered if Jezzy was working for Lindet directly—maybe Jezzy's men were excavating the second godstone, under the pretense of mining.

Maybe, she considered, Nohan was actually one of Lindet's agents and he was here to oversee the excavation.

Vlora tried to make the pieces work, but it didn't add up. Nohan was obviously a greedy git, and his suggestion that he and Vlora team up and steal all the gold meant he didn't know the real item of value hiding under his nose. Besides, Lindet seemed too heavy-handed to use this kind of subtlety. If she was already excavating the godstone, this whole place would be crawling with Blackhats.

Vlora put her head in her hands. *That* didn't add up, either. Lindet was heavy-handed, but she wasn't stupid. Working through intermediaries would keep her from drawing attention to the spot, and not tip off Dynize spies by sending an army of Blackhats up here.

And where did Prime Lektor fit into all this? Was *he* working for Lindet?

In short, Vlora didn't have any idea what was going on in this damned city. But she needed to find out, and quick.

She felt him before she saw him—a dark smudge on her senses, the feel of powder grains running down the back of her neck. Nohan entered the front door of the hotel a moment later. He wore short sleeves, showing off a number of bruises from their fight the other day, and an easy, friendly smile on his lips as he approached her table.

He sat down across from her, his pupils dilated from a powder trance. His eyes betrayed a brief wince as he moved, telling Vlora that he was still hurting from being thrown through a table. The knowledge gave her a brief stab of satisfaction, which disappeared almost immediately.

"I know who you are," he said in a low voice.

Vlora didn't answer him. She pushed aside her meal and leaned back, reaching slowly for the pistol at her belt.

He continued. "You're Lady Flint."

"That's preposterous," she scoffed.

"Don't play me for a fool," he spat, that easy smile disappearing in the blink of an eye. "The latest newspaper from Redstone has a bounty on your head and says your last location was just a couple hundred miles south of here." He kicked his chair back to rock on the back legs, looking angry but self-satisfied. "There aren't that many powder mages in Fatrasta. Certainly not many that fit your description. You're Flint."

Vlora didn't bother to deny it. He was too sure of himself—further denial would just make him more so. "So what do you want?"

He tapped two fingers on the table. "You know what you did to me?"

"Put you in considerable pain, I hope," Vlora said flatly, looking at the bruises on his arms. Her fingers wrapped around the butt of her pistol. She could try for a quick shot, but he was burning such a strong powder trance that he would doubtlessly be ready for it. Beating him to death in front of thirty witnesses seemed like it might not be the best option.

"No," he said. "I'm not talking about that. A fight is a fight, and I did try to kill you, didn't I? No, I'm talking about my letter."

"I have no idea what you're talking about."

He slammed both fists on the table, making her jump. "Don't play me for a fool!" he growled. "I wrote you a letter three years ago. I offered you my services—I offered to join the Adran Cabal—and you turned me down like I was some useless Knacked."

Vlora was bewildered. She didn't remember this at all. She got perhaps two hundred such letters every year, and almost all of them were hoaxes from madmen and disillusioned fools. A secretary usually sorted through them; then Olem examined those that remained. It was—

Her thoughts cut off as the name finally clicked. Nohan. The powder mage who got kicked out of the Starlish Cabal on accusations of treachery and cruelty. She could scarcely believe she'd forgotten the situation, because she'd written to the head of the Starlish Cabal herself to find out if Nohan had any real talent.

"You remember now, don't you," Nohan said, his eyes intent on her face. "I can't believe you forgot. Arrogant bitch."

"I forgot," Vlora said, "because you weren't worth my time."

Nohan exhaled sharply. "Not worth your time? You're the most famous powder mage alive, and I almost killed you the other day. How is that for not worth your time?"

"Killed me?" Vlora scoffed. "It was a damned fistfight. Besides, it's not all about skill. I turned you down because the head of the Starlish Cabal kicked you out for being a sadist." She leaned forward, seriously reconsidering beating him to death in front of witnesses. The Starlish Cabal had included a list of his crimes in their reply, and among them was the murder of children. "I know what goes on in a royal cabal. If *they* think you're a sadist, then Adom help your blasted soul."

Nohan stared daggers at her, and she silently willed him to flip the table and come at her. At least then she could kill him in self-defense. She might end up in a cell next to Taniel, but at least she wouldn't be chased out of town by the city deputies.

Nohan gripped the lip of the table, his fingers turning white.

Vlora looked away from him, as if he was beneath her very notice, hoping he'd use the chance to attack her. She swept her eyes out the window, barely noticing the passing traffic as she waited for him to make his move.

And her gaze landed squarely on Prime Lektor.

The Privileged sorcerer stood in the street, frowning, staring through the window directly at her. He was exactly how she remembered him, from the thoughtlessly rumpled clothes to the purple birthmark on his face. It was *definitely* him, and she could see in his eyes that he had just decided it was definitely her, too.

Vlora wrenched her attention away from Prime Lektor, preparing to throw herself onto the floor if he decided to unleash sorcery at her. Not that it would help. With so much warning, a Privileged of his caliber could destroy the entire block without breaking a sweat.

"Go on," Vlora grunted at Nohan. "If you're so bitter, see if you can take me." Her only consolation if Prime Lektor attacked was that Nohan would die in the same sorcerous conflagration.

Nohan remained frozen in place, and she could see in his eyes how much he wanted to leap at her. Sweat began to pour down Vlora's face, and she resisted looking back out the window. She couldn't take Prime in a fair fight on a good day, and she wasn't going to be able to take both him and Nohan. Might as well focus on one asshole at a time. She wondered if Nohan took her sudden nerves for fear of *him*. Laughable.

It felt like minutes before Nohan finally broke his stare. He got up, looking down at her with a sneer. "I don't know why you're here," he said quietly, "but I'm going to kill you and claim that bounty. Pissing on your corpse before I take it to Redstone will be the best revenge. Watch yourself, Lady Flint."

He strode out before Vlora could react, and she turned desperately toward the window once he'd left the building. Prime Lektor, however, was gone.

CHAPTER 37

The engagement with the Dynize dragoons had left the Mad
Lancers badly mauled. Unwilling to chance another fight,
Styke and Ibana agreed to retrace their steps along the coast for
two days until, late in the evening, they spotted Fatrastan flags on
the horizon.

Styke sat slumped in the saddle, tired as pit and feeling like he'd
been kicked in the head by a warhorse. He turned his eyes to the
eastern horizon, where he could see the edge of a Fatrastan camp.
Their flags waved in the breeze, torches flickering to life as the
sun went down. Styke watched the distant approach of one of his
scouts.

"I think I'm a hypocrite," he said, giving voice to something he'd
been considering for several days.

Ibana looked sidelong at him. "What kind of nonsense is this?"

He shrugged. "I came to the realization that I'm a hypocrite,"
he said with more confidence. He'd been thinking about what
Valyaine had said, sorting through his own memories of the War

for Independence all that time ago and realizing that maybe that treacherous bastard was right—maybe Styke was looking at his own participation in the war through the rosy lenses of the past. "I've always known I was a killer, a monster. But I never thought of myself as a hypocrite."

"And this is bothering you more than murder?" Ibana asked.

"Yeah. Yeah, I think it is."

"You're a strange man, Ben Styke." Ibana spurred her horse, riding out to meet the scout.

Styke exchanged a look with Jackal. The Palo bannerman shrugged. Styke sighed and rode out after Ibana, meeting the scout on a nearby hill. It was Ferlisia, one of the longest-standing members of the lancers. She snapped a salute.

"Did you talk to them?" Styke asked.

"Just briefly," Ferlisia reported. "It's the Third Army."

Styke nodded to himself. When he'd decided to pull back after that fight with the Dynize, he'd figured they would have to head all the way back to Bellport to find some relief. He hadn't expected to find the Third Army already out on the Hammer. They must have marched straight past Bellport without stopping.

Styke had a glimmer of suspicion that they'd been sent after the lancers but dismissed the notion. Lindet wouldn't send a field army of infantry to chase a highly mobile cavalry force.

She would, however, send them to secure the godstone.

Regardless, the Mad Lancers needed somewhere to lie low. "I'll go see if they'll let us lick our wounds inside their pickets," he said, lifting his reins.

Both Ibana and Ferlisia looked alarmed. "Sir, the commanding officer is—"

Styke waved Ferlisia off. "I know who it is. Dvory. That's why I'm going to ask myself."

"That's not a great idea," Ibana said in a low voice.

Styke looked over his shoulder at his column of lancers. They'd lost nearly half their number to death or wounds in the Dynize ambush. They didn't have healing Privileged or proper surgeons to deal with the wounded. They'd done so well and come so far, only to be blindsided by a superior cavalry force. Styke did *not* want to meet that force again without taking some time to recover.

"If Dvory betrayed you once, he'll do it again," Ibana said.

"Perhaps. He might not know I've been killing his old conspirators, though."

"He'll have passed through Bellport. There's no way he won't have gotten word from Valyaine. You damn well should have killed Valyaine when you had the chance."

"Yeah, I know." Styke wasn't thrilled about the idea of marching in there to ask for help from someone who'd betrayed him. But his meditations over hypocrisy the last few days had given him a more optimistic outlook than he'd expected. "Look, if those dragoons snuck up on us once, they can do it again. We need to recover, and this saves us having to go all the way back to Bellport. We get inside their pickets and we'll be safe until we can regroup."

Ibana pursed her lips, clearly wanting to argue.

Styke forestalled it with a raised hand. "I'll deal with Dvory. If I'm not back in two hours, head south and try to throw them off your trail."

He began to ride toward the camp without explaining himself further and tried to gather his thoughts. He wondered if maybe he'd known all along that he was a hypocrite, and that's what had truly kept him from killing Tenny Wiles. He wondered if maybe being broken by the labor camps had been a blessing to everyone around him, rather than the blow against the brave Mad Lancers that he'd always considered it.

He frowned into the setting sun at one point, only to see a small group of figures sitting on the horizon less than two miles away. They were all on horseback—four of them, if his eyes weren't playing tricks on him.

Those goddamn dragonmen, still plaguing his trail. Another good reason to spend a few days hugging a field army.

He was pulled from his contemplations by the sound of a horse whinny behind him. He turned in his saddle, a rebuke on his lips to send Celine back to the lancers.

But it wasn't Celine. It was Ka-poel.

Of course it was.

He waited for her to catch up, trying to figure out what he could say to send her away. Going to see Dvory was already a dangerous gamble. A wild card like Ka-poel might make things worse. But she'd already made it abundantly clear that he couldn't leave her behind.

"I think," he told her as she arrived, "that some dysfunction in the back of my brain silently tells me that I'm invincible." He wasn't sure why he shared the thought, but he continued. "Maybe I've had it my whole life. Maybe it was surviving the firing squad. Maybe it wasn't until more recently, when I survived that fight with Fidelis Jes. Or maybe it was something you put in my head with your damned blood sorcery. I don't really care, but I have the feeling that it's going to get me killed."

Ka-poel stopped beside him, watching him through half-lidded eyes.

"I was watching that sign language you're teaching Celine," he said. "I hadn't realized it before, but it looks like a jumble of Palo war signals and something else."

Ka-poel smiled coolly at him and nodded.

Styke felt pleased to have remembered as well as he did. He hadn't seen Palo war signals for over ten years, and even then he'd only picked up on the very basics while he was in the Tristan Basin. "Did Ibana tell you what I'm doing?" he asked.

Ka-poel made a series of gestures.

Styke shook his head. "I said I recognized it. Not that I understand it."

She pointed at him, then mimed hanging from a noose. *You're trying to get yourself killed.*

"I wouldn't say I'm trying," Styke said. He had a sudden worry that maybe he *was* trying to get himself killed and he didn't even know it. He'd always chalked his own courage up to a lack of fear, but maybe it wasn't so simple. "I'm not trying," he insisted. "We need surgeons and protection while we put ourselves back together. But Dvory might try to kill me. If he does, I intend on taking him with me. You probably should go back to Ibana until I sort this out."

Ka-poel pursed her lips and tilted her head. *That*, Styke understood. "Suit yourself."

Ka-poel put her slate away as they rode up to the sentries. One of them stepped forward, eyeing Styke and his horse. "State your name, rank, and business."

"I need to see your quartermaster," he said. "Then I need to see General Dvory."

"Name and rank?" the sentry demanded.

"Colonel Ben Styke."

The sentry's eyes widened. "Oh. Right. I, uh, better have someone escort you to the general."

Styke and Ka-poel were led through the camp. He was pleasantly surprised to find that the Fatrastan Army was significantly more organized than they had been during the War for Independence, with clean rows of tents and clearly marked regiments, companies, and platoons. It was the first time he'd been in a Fatrastan army camp in over ten years, and he felt more than a little nostalgia for the old days.

They were led to a large tent in the middle of the camp. Two guards stood at the entrance, bayonets fixed, and Styke was able to tell which one recognized him by the way the man straightened, inhaling sharply.

Their escort called out his name and rank and then went inside the tent, emerging a moment later. His face was pale. "General Dvory will see you now, Colonel Styke."

"That was quick," Styke commented dryly. "Stay here," he told Ka-poel, ducking into the tent.

Dvory was much as Styke remembered him—an unassuming-looking man with the dusky skin of a full-blooded Rosvelean. He was slim, of medium height with black hair and a plain face. At some point in the last decade he'd begun to wear spectacles. His bottom lip drooped slightly, giving most people the impression he was stupid, which, Styke remembered quite clearly, was not the case.

"Ben Styke," Dvory said, standing up from behind his desk. He folded his spectacles and set them on a book he'd been reading.

"Dvory," Styke replied.

"It's General Dvory now. You may call me *sir*."

Styke ambled over to the chair on the opposite side of the table from Dvory and sat down, listening to it creak angrily under his weight. Dvory was an honest-to-god real general. He didn't know whether to laugh or cry. Dvory had always been competent, but not "make me a general" levels of competent. Nowhere close. "Fat god-damn chance of that. You're welcome to try to have me beaten for insubordination. We'll see how that goes for everyone involved."

Dvory managed a pained expression and lowered himself into his chair. "I expected you sooner or later," he said. "Unfortunately, I expected the attitude as well. I heard you beheaded Fidelis Jes?"

"I asked to see the quartermaster," Styke replied. "I think it's ironic they brought me straight to you, considering you used to be one of my quartermasters. Yeah, I beheaded Fidelis Jes. He had it coming."

"I see." Dvory reached for a cigarette box, opened the lacquered lid, and plucked out a cigarette. He lit it with a match, inhaling deeply, and Styke thought he saw just the slightest tremble to his hand. "It's a pity," Dvory continued. "Fidelis Jes was a great man."

"He was a prick, and everyone knew it."

"Great men can be pricks," Dvory said. "Take yourself, for instance."

Styke interrupted with a snort. "You think *I'm* a great man?"

"Absolutely! You were, anyway. I understand you're a shadow of your former self, but you still have that attitude—that disregard for your betters that got you put in front of a firing squad." Dvory paused to smoke, looking over Styke's shoulder thoughtfully. "You've always been a pompous piece of garbage and yet...still a great man."

Styke ignored the insults, focusing on Dvory's careless appearance. Was he *trying* to goad Styke into attacking him? Or did he just assume he was safe in the middle of his army? Styke produced his most condescending smile. "Have you been practicing that speech in a mirror?"

"Excuse me?"

"The 'great man' thing. I bet you've been practicing that ever since you found out I killed Jes."

Dvory's eyes narrowed. He took a deep breath, ashing his cigarette into a half-empty glass of whiskey. Again, Styke noted that the carelessness of it seemed too performative. Dvory *wanted* Styke to think he didn't give a damn about him anymore. "Why are you here, Styke? Did you come to kill me? I heard Agoston disappeared. Tenny Wiles, too. Valyaine, though...he beat the shit out of you in Bellport. That must have been something to see. Have you softened in your old age?"

"I could kill you now," Styke mused aloud.

"And die by the hands of my guards. Not even you can fight a field army, Styke."

Styke leaned forward, listening to the chair creak. He drew his knife and planted the tip against the top of Dvory's table, spinning it. To his credit, Dvory ignored the knife and kept his eyes on Styke's face. But even with that bravado, he could almost hear Dvory wondering if the prospect of death would stop Styke from having his revenge. "No," Styke said, watching his knife spin before plucking it up in his hand. "I'm not here to kill you."

"Oh?" Dvory blinked in surprise.

"Of course not. We're on the same side, aren't we?"

"Are we?" Dvory asked. "No one reinstated the Mad Lancers. No one made you a colonel again."

Styke used his boz knife to trim his fingernails. "That's not entirely true. Lady Vlora Flint reinstated the Mad Lancers and my rank."

"A traitor with a price on her head," Dvory scoffed.

"A patriot who just happened to piss off Lindet," Styke said. "Regardless, I'm killing Dynize. That puts us on the same side. Or would you like to go back to Bellport and ask the mayor who arrived to save the city in the nick of time?"

"Ah," Dvory said, as if something had just occurred to him. "I wondered where the old goat got a spine. You put him up to it, didn't you? Told him not to let the army strip the city for supplies." He shook his head. "He's lucky we didn't need anything or I would have had him hanged." Dvory made a vexed sound in the back of his throat. "I should have *you* hanged for insubordination."

"Go ahead," Styke said, calling what they both knew was a bluff.

Dvory stubbed out his cigarette and scowled at Styke. "Don't think I wouldn't. Fortunately for you, I have strict instructions not to kill you or your men."

That did surprise Styke. He leaned back and put his knife away. "From who?"

"Who do you think? From Lindet. I saw her a month ago on her trip from Landfall to Redstone. She specifically said she wanted you left to your own devices unless you outright attacked a Fatrastan army." Dvory frowned at a spot above Styke's head. "Jes warned me a decade ago that Lindet had a soft spot for you."

"When he asked you to help separate me from Ibana and the others so he could execute me?"

"That's right."

"I just wanted to be clear on that point," Styke said. He considered lunging across the table. He could bury his knife in Dvory's chest before he made a sound. He might even be able to make it to the edge of the camp before the alarm was raised. But it wasn't worth the risk, not when he needed to look after his own. "You asked why I'm here. The lancers need a place to lie low for a couple of days. I want to do that inside your pickets."

Dvory looked like he'd been slapped. "Did you just ask me for help?"

"I did."

"Wait. I told you straight out that I betrayed you, and you turn around and ask for my help?" He sounded truly incredulous.

Styke resisted the urge to roll his eyes. "That's right."

Dvory stood up, pacing from one end of the tent to the other before retaking his seat. He rocked back and forth like a child unable to come to grasp with their emotions, then plucked up another cigarette. "Why should I help you?"

"Because I'm doing your job for you," Styke said. "Because patching things up with Ben Styke would be a damned good career move right now. Because you used to be a Mad Lancer and unless you're as cold as you're pretending, some of those people riding with me were your friends."

Dvory swallowed hard, but did not respond.

Styke sat forward and put his elbows on Dvory's table. He said in a quiet voice, "Two days ago, we were ambushed by a force of Dynize dragoons. They *ambushed* us. Me, Ibana, Jackal, all the rest. They took *us* by surprise. Now, I know you don't want to deal with a force of dragoons alone, not one skilled enough to sneak up on the Mad Lancers. They might not be able to crack a whole field army, but they can make your life miserable. But if you give us a couple of days to rest, we'll be on our way without taxing your supplies—and then I intend on hunting down those dragoons and butchering them. Like I said...I'm doing your job for you."

"We're heading west," Dvory said. "We move on tomorrow."

"We'll move with you," Styke said. "And sleep inside your pickets. You can use a few of the old lancers as scouts if you want."

Dvory seemed genuinely torn. He fiddled with the butt of his extinguished cigarette, his face looking like he'd just swallowed a lime. "If I allow this," he said, "are we square?"

"We're square." Then Styke reached across the table and shook hands with a man who had once betrayed him. He forced a smile on his face and tightened his grip just a little.

Ibana wasn't going to let him hear the end of it.

Dvory showed Styke out of the tent, and Styke was only slightly surprised that the initial two guards had become twenty, all of them with bayonets fixed and all of them pretending that they hadn't been waiting for some kind of signal as the two men exited. Ka-poel stood by a nearby torch, arms folded, flames dancing in her eyes. Her face was unreadable.

"Who is this?" Dvory asked, gesturing to her.

"My servant," Styke said.

"A Palo, eh? I heard your tastes had gotten...significantly younger since you left the labor camps."

Styke leaned sideways as if whispering to a friend, a smile plastered on his face. "Speak like that of my girl again and you will live out the rest of your life as a torso and a head in a flour sack."

A bead of sweat rolled down Dvory's forehead. "What are you doing out here?" he asked, quickly changing the subject.

"Asking for your help."

"No. Here, on the Hammer."

"Killing Dynize." Styke joined Ka-poel, touching her elbow

and pointing in the direction they'd left their horses. "Good-bye, Dvory. Don't forget to tell your pickets to expect my men."

When they were finally out of sight, Styke turned aside and spat into the grass. His mouth tasted of bile, his nerves shot, and he suddenly realized just how close he'd actually come to killing Dvory. Every muscle was sore and tight from the tension.

"I just asked a favor of a man who once betrayed me," he told Ka-poel.

Ka-poel pursed her lips, pinching two fingers together and thrusting them in front of Styke's face. It took several moments in the poor light to realize that she held a single human hair. It took him another few moments to realize the significance.

He barked a laugh. "Does that belong to Dvory?"

She nodded.

He felt a little of the tension leak off, and rolled his shoulders to loosen his muscles. "Leave him alone for now," he said. "You can keep the hair—it might come in handy. If I don't kill him for betraying me, I can still kill him for his smug, stupid face."

CHAPTER 38

Y ou look like you haven't slept in days." Taniel sat on the chair by one of the tiny windows of his cell, contemplating the gallows sitting just outside. His sketchbook sat in his lap, and he examined Vlora with a frown. Her hair was unkempt, her jacket dirty, and she could only imagine the bags under her eyes.

She leaned her head against the bars of Taniel's jail cell. "They both know who I am."

He frowned as she spoke. "Who?"

"The powder mage, Nohan. He put two and two together and called me out. Says he's going to kill me and take the bounty that Lindet put out on me."

"Can he?"

"Not in a fair fight."

"Right. Why didn't you just kill him when he threatened you?"

"Because I don't want to end up in here with you," Vlora replied.

"So buy him off," Taniel said, as if the answer were simple.

Vlora stared at Taniel, furious with him for suggesting it, and furious with herself for not just doing it in the first place. "I will *not* buy off a man who has tried to kill me. It's personal now—and I don't think he would take me up on it. Apparently we have a history."

Taniel didn't ask further, so Vlora didn't bother to explain. He sketched furiously, his hand moving over the page manically, and she could tell that sitting in this cell was bothering the pit out of him. "Who else knows who you are?"

"Prime Lektor."

Taniel's sketching stopped. He looked up, staring at the wall, then looked over at her. "You saw him again?"

"Twice more. Definitely him, even though I can't sense his sorcery. The first time, I tried to follow him and he disappeared into thin air. I know where he lives, but I'm not touching a Predeii's house. It's probably warded as tight as a king's palace. The second time I saw him—well, he spotted me first. Now he knows I'm here."

"That's not great," Taniel said with a frown.

Vlora rubbed her eyes. "Do we really know anything about him? Why does he want the stone? He's a scholar, isn't he? Maybe he's just studying it?"

"He's also part of the group that summoned Kresimir and caused the Bleakening," Taniel warned.

"But if we have our facts right, he didn't *want* Kresimir to come back the second time. He helped turn Adro into a democracy."

"We can't trust him." Taniel looked down at his sketchbook. He suddenly dropped his charcoal and ripped the page out, crumpling it and tossing it into one corner of the cell. Vlora raised her eyebrows. It was the first time she'd ever seen him destroy a drawing in anger—even the terrible ones from his youth. "I need to get out of here," he said.

Vlora didn't disagree.

"I can try to break out tonight," he said, "but there's a ton of miscreants in here and a heavy guard on them. I'll probably end up killing my way out." He didn't seem happy about this idea. "I don't like killing decent people, and the deputies here are probably the only ones in the whole city."

Vlora didn't like the idea, either. "We have to give it another week."

"You'll get killed," Taniel countered. "You can handle a rogue powder mage, but Prime is out of your league."

"I won't." Her mind raced. "I can change hotels and keep my head down. Flerring tipped me off to men going mad at one of the mining sites. If I can get inside, I might be able to find the stone; by the time I find the stone, you'll be out. We can deal with Prime and then bring Olem and the boys into town to claim the stone."

"It's risky," Taniel said slowly.

Once again, Vlora didn't disagree. But she could still move around the town freely, and she could still hide from both her antagonists. "Give me one more week," she said. "Then we deal with both of them together, and Flerring will have enough blasting oil for us to try to destroy the stone. Have you heard any more news from your Palo friend?"

"Not much that's useful. You really want to do this on your own, don't you?" he asked with a sigh.

Vlora wanted to tell him that she couldn't trust him anymore. She wanted to tell him that he was no longer human and that he was no longer the Adran patriot who had been a hero of two wars. She wanted to tell him that she *did* need to do this herself. "I want to do this without you having to kill decent people," she reasoned. "And without drawing any more attention."

"Even if it gets you killed?"

"I've fought worse."

"I know," Taniel said softly, "but you're my friend. I don't want you to die."

Vlora almost told him her thoughts, overwhelmed by a feeling of guilt over her mistrust of him. She bit her tongue. "I'm glad," she managed.

Taniel paced the cell. "The Palo Nation definitely has a presence in the camp, but I can't figure out how big. According to my Palo friend, their representative is an underling to one of the big bosses. Most of the Palo have aligned with Burt, so I'm guessing it's one of his lieutenants. If I can get word without raising any suspicions, we might have ourselves some allies."

"I would suggest," Vlora said, "not telling the Palo Nation about the godstones."

"I hadn't intended on it," Taniel replied. "Have you heard from Olem?"

"Nothing yet," Vlora said. "They can't be far off."

Taniel took a deep breath and fell onto the cell bed, arms outstretched. He still wore long sleeves and his right glove to hide his reddened skin. Despite his earlier claim of not needing much sleep, he looked tired, with deep crow's-feet at the corners of his eyes. She wondered what was going on with Ka-poel. Taniel claimed he could sense her, even at a distance. She imagined that was as stressful as it was useful.

Her own exhaustion—and separation from her lover and partner—were dragging at her. Her bruises hurt all the time; her body was exhausted from too little rest. She had to run a light powder trance and drink a bottle of wine just to think clearly.

Vlora turned to Taniel, remembering her thoughts about Prime from the other day. "You said the sorcerous compass Ka-poel gave you isn't working?"

"That's right," Taniel responded. He chuckled. "Compass. Right. That makes sense. Well, it's behaving like I've put a magnet underneath a real compass. I know that the stone is here, but it's not pointing in any direction in particular."

"Maybe that's Prime's doing."

"How?"

"Perhaps Prime is hiding the stone on purpose, to keep anyone from finding it until he's finished with it."

Taniel stroked the two-week-old stubble growing on his chin. "That sounds right. So if you find Prime again, you can follow him to the stone."

"I don't *want* to find Prime. I want to find the stone, then deal with him once I have you with me."

"That seems wiser," Taniel said.

Vlora pushed herself away from the cell glass. She felt like a wagon stuck in a muddy rut, unable to pull out of it even with her best effort. She had to get back to work before *she* went mad. "I'm going," she told him, holding up a single finger. "One week. You'll be out without having to kill, and I'll have found the stone."

"One week," Taniel agreed reluctantly.

Vlora left him there, ducking out of the jail and weaving into traffic, her eyes on the rooftops for the telltale puff of smoke from a fired rifle. By deciding to do this alone, she hoped she hadn't just proclaimed her own death warrant.

CHAPTER 39

Walking up the stairs of the Landfall City Morgue was the most painful thing that Michel had ever done.

He rested for as long as he dared—until early in the morning on the eleventh, when last night's injection of mala had finally begun to wear off. Pulling himself out of the bed in a dark corner room of the underground morgue was almost painful enough to put him on his back, to not care if the entire Yaret Household was about to die to a Blackhat bombing. But he managed to make it out of the bed and even find a bit of horngum in Emerald's laboratory before slipping out behind the backs of Emerald's assistants.

"Slipping," Michel considered as he climbed the stairs up to the street, "was probably a poor word. He dragged himself along the walls, then along handrails, up every excruciating step. Emerald had been very clear that he shouldn't move if he wanted to recover quickly—that leaving the morgue too early might put him back in it as a corpse. Emerald had also made it clear that he would keep Michel tied to the bed if he needed to.

But Michel didn't have time for any of that. If he didn't act, Yaret would die, and with him the Household. It would kill Michel's best chance of finding Taniel's elusive informant—and it would also kill people whom Michel had come to think of as friends.

Michel stopped on the second landing and bit off a piece of horngum large enough to make his mouth go numb almost instantly. It helped with the pain without dulling his senses, but he needed another bite after just two more flights of stairs.

He mentally detached himself from his body as he climbed, in a vain attempt to ignore the pain. It was something he did when he wanted to get into the right mind-set for a new job—when he had to become a totally different person. It involved floating mentally, a sort of forced high where he envisioned himself outside his earthly body looking in, trying to find a different perspective that would help him infiltrate the next mission.

In this case, he simply attempted to meditate, and he couldn't help but consider the complexity of becoming these different people—that the man whom his Dynize allies would call Michel Bravis was a different man than the Blackhats, or Taniel, would refer to by the same name. They were all still *him*, of course, but . . . not. He couldn't help but think of his mother, of deceiving her for all those years into thinking he was a loyal Blackhat when in fact he was still the Palo loyalist that she'd always wanted for a son.

He wondered if the guilt of that one deception was what drove him to keep climbing these stairs, even through the pain that cut past the vestiges of last night's mala and a healthy chunk of horngum. Perhaps saving the Yaret Household—people who had taken him in, given him trust, and defended him to their own allies—would somehow absolve him of all the instances of so-called friends that he'd betrayed in the past.

At some point, he realized, he would have to betray Yaret. He would add Tenik, the Household, and all of Dynize to the long list of people who wanted to kill him.

But not yet.

He finally reached the top of the stairs and froze, staring at the open door of the morgue's front entrance and Emerald, who had stopped with his foot halfway in, a loaf of bread under one arm.

"So you're going, then?"

Michel couldn't find the strength to speak. He nodded.

"You look paler than me. We have an elevator we use to bring the corpses up and down. I would have let you take it."

"I didn't think you were going to let me leave," Michel managed, taking strength from a surge of anger. An elevator would have saved him so much pain.

Emerald nodded solemnly. "I would have advised you stay. But if you're determined enough to climb five flights of stairs, I won't stop you." He tipped his hat. "Best of luck," he said, heading down the stairs.

Michel hated Emerald for the extra little skip in his step, then pushed out the door and into the streets. It took a moment for his eyes to adjust to the light and get his bearings. He would have to go directly to Yaret's House in Chancellor's Court. It was risky—either from running into Sedial's people or because he might get caught in the blast himself.

Walking on flat ground was easier than up the stairs, but Michel still found himself moving with frustrating slowness. Each step seemed like another mountain to climb, and whenever he couldn't find a wall to lean on, he was forced to concentrate just to keep from falling over.

The sight of a carriage rolling down the next street over nearly made him faint. He raised his hand, shaking two fingers at the driver, who pulled up and came to a stop just ahead of him.

"Heading home, sir," the driver told him. "I worked all night. No more fares for me."

"Chancellor's Court," Michel gasped. "Please, just one more."

The driver leaned over, peering at Michel. "You don't look so good." Carriages were not very common since the invasion. Most had been used to take their owners out of the city ahead of the Dynize. Those that remained had to get licensed with the Dynize government and install a large green sign on their side declaring their license. If Michel didn't convince the driver, he might not see another till the capitol building.

"I don't feel so good, either." Michel rummaged in his pockets and found two Dynize rations cards, as well as the card that Tenik had given him weeks ago that marked him as a member of Yaret's Household. He damn well hoped that the driver knew what it was. "Look," Michel said, "here's these. This card says I'm employed by the state. Take me and I'll make sure they pay you double."

The driver looked uneasy. "Look, fella, I don't want to get involved with the Dynize. Bad luck and all. But I'm heading that direction anyway. Give me the rations cards and I'll take you to Forlorn End."

Forlon End, if Michel remembered right, was just a few blocks from Chancellor's Court. "Done."

It was all Michel could do to climb into the carriage and collapse on the bench, where he clutched his aching chest and tried not to swear with each jolt and rock of the carriage. His breathing was shallow, his eyelids heavy, and he wondered what he was going to say to Yaret once he arrived. Convincing him to disrupt the House-hold and evacuate the street over a bloodstained list of addresses was probably going to be harder than it sounded.

He thanked the driver and climbed out at Forlorn End, before shambling as quickly as he could press himself down the street toward Chancellor's Court. He took a left down a narrow alley, intent on cutting across a handful of small streets to shave precious yards off his trip. He kept holding his breath, watching the sky, waiting for the blast of an explosion and a tower of flame.

Michel let himself through the garden of one of the townhouse mansions and came out into a courtyard less than a block from

Yaret's Household. The moment he stepped out of the garden, he regretted his shortcut.

His eyes caught sight of Forgula at the same instant she saw him. She stood with several members of the Sedial Household, talking in the street directly in the way of Michel's route. Michel swallowed hard, a cold sweat breaking out on the small of his back, his heart rate doubling.

Forgula tapped one of her companions and pointed, her face growing cold at the sight of Michel. The group turned toward him immediately, walking briskly. "Stay put, spy," she called to him.

Michel began to walk briskly in the opposite direction, hoping that the effort didn't knock him off his feet, and backtracked toward the next street over. He needed to get somewhere with witnesses—no, with *Yaret* witnesses.

He didn't know if Forgula had guessed that he had searched her home, or if she just wanted him out of the way, but he knew that if she caught him before he could reach a friendly Dynize, he would be dead within minutes. He risked a jog, looking over his shoulder to see Forgula and her cronies do the same.

He felt stitches tear in his chest and a shot of pain that blinded him for several moments. He nearly tripped and fell, stumbling into the mouth of an alley.

A handful of children playing in the mud caught his eye. He recognized two of them—definitely members of Yaret's Household— and he fumbled in his pocket for a nub of pencil and a paper. He scribbled three words, then signed his name. "You," he called to one of the girls in Dynize. "Take this to Yaret immediately. Run, and don't look back!"

The girl looked at Michel with some confusion before her eyes flicked to Forgula's group coming on behind him. She gave a quick nod, took the paper, and dashed off toward the Yaret Household. Forgula shouted after her, but the girl kept running.

Michel leaned against the corner of a building and wondered

if this was the best he could do. Forgula would be on him in moments. He reached toward his pockets for his knuckle-dusters, only to realize that both hands were soaked in blood. As was his shirt, and his pants. He was bleeding so heavily that Forgula wouldn't *need* to kill him.

He gave a soft laugh at how close he'd come to reaching Yaret, and resumed his walk. Behind him, he could hear the footsteps of Forgula and her people, which had slowed. They must have noticed his condition, realized that they could take their time. Michel forced himself to raise his head, looking around for some kind of salvation as he reached the next street corner and sought an ally.

No one caught his eye. He half bent, put his hands on his knees, trying to choke back tears of pain. At some point in his journey he had lost the rest of his horngum.

"Shit," he muttered to himself, and turned to face Forgula.

He was surprised to find that Forgula's group had stopped less than ten feet from him, and it took him a moment to realize why.

A carriage was parked on the side of the street. It was drawn by two brilliant black horses and had the black and red curtains of a Dynize diplomat. A familiar face was leaning out the window, watching Michel and Forgula.

It was Saen-Ichtracia, the Privileged who'd laughed when Michel punched Forgula.

Ichtracia appraised Michel with a single glance, then turned to Forgula. "You have murder in your eyes, my dear," she said.

Forgula's nostrils flared. There was an uncertainty to her stance that seemed at contrast with being waylaid by the granddaughter of her master. "There's a snake in our midst," Forgula replied. "I was about to crush it."

"Oh, come now, is that necessary? It looks like a stiff breeze would knock him over."

"Then it's a mercy killing," Forgula said. Her blackjack slid from her sleeve to her hand, and she took a step toward Michel.

Ichtracia tutted loudly, stopping Forgula midstride. "Michel, my little mongrel foxhead, what are you doing on this street? And in your condition? You should be smart enough to stay on the next street over."

Michel looked down at the blood now dripping openly from the hand he held over his chest. He used the last of his strength to force a smile onto his face, giving a small bow and grasping for the first thing that came to mind. "I was looking for you, ma'am."

"Oh? Whatever for?"

"To ask you to dinner." Michel had just long enough to see the look of fascinated horror on Forgula's face before he teetered and collapsed, facedown, onto the cobbles beneath Ichtracia's carriage.

"That is the third time this week I have passed out," Michel breathed. He lay in a pile on the floor of a carriage, looking up at Ichtracia as she stared dispassionately out the window. One of her footmen crouched beside him, holding his jacket tightly against Michel's chest. "It's really unpleasant."

Ichtracia remained silent, her eyes on something in the street, a troubled look on her face. Michel tried to read something from her posture and expression—why she had saved him, what her plans were, if she was going to help him—but came up with nothing. He couldn't focus through the pain coming from his wound, nor the great loss of blood. Instead, he found himself considering her striking features. A man could do worse than stare at her face as he died.

The carriage was moving, but Michel had no way of knowing in what direction. "Thank you," he said.

"Hmm?" Ichtracia looked down at him, her eyes cold, her thoughts obviously far away. "Oh, that." She snorted a laugh. "Having the chance to annoy Forgula is thanks enough."

Michel thought of the laugh when he'd punched Forgula back at the war game. Was there some kind of old rivalry between the two?

Past hatreds? Shouldn't they be on the same side? "I have to go to Yaret's Household," he said.

Ichtracia ignored him. "Tculu, will he survive long enough to reach the house?"

"He's still talking, ma'am," the footman replied. "I think that's a good sign."

"Saen," Michel said, trying to inject some force. "I have to get to Yaret's Household, please. I have to warn them."

Ichtracia's attention snapped toward him with a startling suddenness. "About what? The bomb?"

Michel's throat went dry. Ichtracia knew. She knew because she was Ka-Sedial's granddaughter, and Ka-Sedial had arranged the assassination. He had just stepped out of one fire and into a much, much hotter one.

"Oh, don't look at me like that," Ichtracia said. "I didn't put the damned thing there. You've been unconscious for about a half hour. Fifteen minutes ago, a bomb exploded, destroying Yaret's house. We heard the explosion, and word just reached us by courier."

Michel stared at her, trying to come up with a reply. Maybe she wasn't involved, but...had he been too late? Had that girl gotten his note to Yaret in time? "We have to go help," he whispered.

"Do we? Yaret isn't a friend of mine, and I've been given no orders to return and aid them."

Michel had no strength to feel grief, or outrage, or anything but the pain coming from his chest. He sagged, doing everything he could to keep his eyes open as the carriage finally came to a stop. The door opened, and at Ichtracia's order he was carried, none too gently, down the drive of a small estate and in through the front door. A candelabra was swept unceremoniously off a large dining room table and Michel was laid down in the middle, with Ichtracia standing over him like she was about to quarter a deer.

"Fetch me my tools," she told a footman before looking at Michel. "I'm going to do what I can for you," she said. "You've lost a lot of blood, but it looks like you've already been patched up once. If we can keep you conscious, you should make a full recovery."

"Are...are you a healing Privileged?"

"I am not." Ichtracia took a satchel from one of the footmen, set it next to Michel's head, and began to lay out tools. "My great-grandfather was a Privileged," she explained. "He pioneered a combination of sorcery and surgery that greatly increases a patient's chances of surviving. It is not nearly as effective—and much more painful—than healing sorcery. But it works." She pulled on her Privileged's gloves, the sight of which caused Michel to involuntarily attempt to get up and run. One of Ichtracia's fingers twitched, and Michel was pressed against the table by unseen forces. "Tculu," she said, "fetch Michel some whiskey from the cabinet. Give him a healthy swig, then put your belt between his teeth."

Michel could barely keep up. Ichtracia moved quickly, clinically, like Emerald but with a more refined sense of businesslike purpose. "Why are you helping me?" he asked.

Ichtracia looked down at him as if the answer were obvious. She put a hand on his forehead, her gloves soft to the touch, and wiped the sweat from his brow in an almost gentle manner. "I'll go to a lot of effort for a man who can make me laugh," she said softly. "Besides, you asked me to dinner. I may be a Privileged, but I'm not a monster. I'll never turn down a meal with an interesting person."

Any further questions were cut off by the footman pressing a bottle to Michel's mouth and pouring whiskey straight between his lips. He coughed, sputtered, trying to swallow as much as he could. The glass rim of the bottle was quickly replaced by the sour taste of the footman's belt being forced between his teeth.

Michel went bug-eyed as he felt sorcery hold him so tightly he could barely breathe. Ichtracia lifted a scalpel, examined it carefully, and then went to work.

What, Michel wondered as the cutting began, had he done to deserve this?

CHAPTER 40

Where are you going?"

Styke looked up from packing Amrec's saddlebags
and saw Ibana watching him from a few paces away, hands on her
hips, eyes narrowed. He checked to make sure a bottle of whiskey
was safely wrapped in the rearmost saddlebag, then tightened the
lashings to his bedroll. "I've got an errand to run," he said.

Ibana came around Amrec to stand beside him, looking concerned.
For three days they had followed in the shadow of the Third Army, drilling in the mornings and evenings and tending to the wounded. They
planned on heading back out on their own, first thing in the morning.

"What's this errand?"

Styke hesitated. "It's personal."

"It can't wait?"

"No. I'm just going a few miles. I'll be back before you're ready
to ride out in the morning."

Ibana didn't seem to buy it. "You're not doing something stupid,
are you? You have more people to kill?"

"Nope, nothing like that."

She gazed at him suspiciously.

"I swear," he added.

"Those dragonmen are still out there. Our scouts saw them the other day. If you go off on your own, they're going to kill you."

"That," Styke said, "is why Celine and Ka-poel are staying with you."

"Neither of them will stand for it. Pit, I won't stand for it. What are you up to, Ben? Why can't you tell me?"

Styke finished checking the saddle, then ran his hand along Amrec's flank, up his neck, and over his nose. Amrec nuzzled him gently. "Like I said, it's personal."

"Take an escort, at least."

"Not a chance. 'Personal' means not having fifty men with me. Besides, I'm more likely to lose those blasted dragonmen with just me and Amrec." He turned and fixed Ibana with a steady stare, waiting for her to continue the argument. He wasn't much for arguments and was satisfied to let her win most of them. But this . . . this was important. "If Ka-poel tries to follow me, you truss her up and throw her over the back of a horse."

"Do it yourself," Ibana snorted. "I'm not touching a blood sorcerer."

"Coward."

"Fool."

They stared at each other for a moment; then Styke pulled himself up into the saddle. "See you tomorrow morning."

He rode northwest across the Third Army camp and headed through their pickets on the far side, where it was less likely that anyone trailing the army would see him leave. About a mile out, he found a small river and rode down into the water, where he turned Amrec south.

"This is going to be real uncomfortable for you for the next couple miles," he told Amrec, "but you'll get carrots and sugar cubes when we make camp."

They stayed in the river for four hours, taking it slowly so that Amrec didn't slip. Styke hummed while his eyes scanned the riverbanks for Dynize scouts or dragonmen. He picked out familiar landmarks, dusting off hazy, long-buried memories and forcing himself to dig among them.

The light was just beginning to wane, the river becoming more dangerous, when Styke caught sight of a particular bend and a narrow, arrow-shaped boulder balanced on a knoll about twenty yards from the river. He directed Amrec out of the bank and took him up to a nearby grove, where he used an old shirt to carefully dry Amrec's hooves before leaving him tied to a branch with a feed bag over his nose.

Styke stood on the bank of the river for some time, watching the bats flutter overhead in the twilight and listening to the sound of crickets. He ran his hands over his face, taking deep breaths of the humid air.

He'd only ever been here three times in his life, but the place had a biting familiarity that threatened to bring tears to his eyes. Everything about the location was burned into his brain, from the mud of the riverbank to the moss on the boulder to the sound the breeze made as it rattled the leaves of the beech trees.

Taking one last deep breath, he finally turned away from the river and walked to the other side of the rock. He counted out thirty paces and found a big, white-sided beech. Bending over, he felt along the trunk until he found a set of deep grooves in the side. The letter "M," carved by a boy several decades ago.

Styke began to clear around the base of the beech, pulling away vines and slashing shrubs with his knife. It only took a few minutes to find the stone—a rectangular slab of white marble about the size of a bread box. He methodically cleared around it, then off to one side, where he kindled a small fire that cast just enough light so that he could continue to work.

Soon, the tiny grove was cleared of underbrush and the white marble scraped clean of thirty years of moss and grime. The edges were worn, the letters faded a little with time, but he could still make out the name "Marguerie ja Lind" and a set of dates. He knew what to expect, but he still let out a small gasp when he saw them, squeezing his eyes closed against unbidden tears.

He sat on his haunches beside the stone—for how long, he was not sure. He did not speak, or pray, or even think. His meditation was devoid of any direction.

After some time, he finally got to his feet and stoked the fire, laying out his bedroll across from the grave and leaning up against the big beech tree with the bottle of whiskey in one hand, a bag of sugar cubes in the other, and Amrec's nose nuzzling his ear every so often as he slowly fed him the cubes.

He watched the embers float on the heat above the fire and listened to the night noises until, sometime around midnight, they grew silent. Eyes closed, head back, he drew his knife and lay it across his knee before taking a swig of whiskey. Amrec snorted.

When he opened his eyes again, he was not alone. The man standing beside the grave was familiar. The sides of his head were meticulously shaved to leave a bright-red mohawk that was tied back in a knot over his left ear. His face was sun-hardened, the freckles thick across the bridge of his nose, black tattoos spiraling up his neck to touch his cheeks.

The dragonman did not look at Styke. He stared down at the gravestone, his brow furrowed. His duster was pulled back to show a bone ax in his belt, but he did not reach for it. In halting Palo, he asked, "Whose grave is this?"

Styke struggled to remember the dragonman's name. He was sure he'd heard it during his encounter with the group back in Granalia. After a few moments it came to him: Ji-Orz.

"It's my mother's," Styke told him.

"When did she die?"

The question was deeply personal, and Styke would normally have reacted violently to anyone asking after his mother. But somehow, here in the darkness with another killer, it seemed like a natural thing to talk about.

"When I was a boy." He tried to remember the dates on the stone. It was too dark to see them. "Thirty-three years ago, I think."

"Disease?"

"My father's drunken rage."

Ji-Orz's frown deepened. "What fueled his rage?"

"I don't remember. Something trivial, probably. He killed my mother and he went after my baby sister."

Ji-Orz glanced around, as if looking for another gravestone. Not seeing one, he moved to the fire and hunkered down so that he, Styke, and the grave created a three-pointed star around the flames. He stared at Styke, eyes unblinking. "I wish to know what happened, if you'll tell me."

The oddness of speaking so freely to a man who'd come to kill him finally caught up to Styke. He tapped a finger on the hilt of his knife. "Why?"

"Because I like to collect stories of people I meet."

"People you kill?"

"Sometimes. Not usually." Ji-Orz gazed into the flames, a brief smile touching his lips. "My mother told me stories, long ago. Before this." He tapped the bone ax hanging from his belt. "Stories are all I have left of her."

Styke looked down at the bottle of whiskey. "My mother used to sing. I don't have anything left of hers, though. My sister might. I don't know." He paused, considering the dragonman's previous question. "I murdered my father before he could reach my sister."

"Good." Ji-Orz nodded, as if patricide were a perfectly normal route.

"That drunken piece of shit," Styke continued, "rests in a mausoleum on the old family property. It wasn't right to put my mother in there with him, so I brought her here, where she grew up." Styke nodded into the darkness. "She was born in a cabin about a hundred yards from here. Just a rotten ruin now." Styke laughed softly to himself, remembering. "I was just a kid. Didn't even think to bring a shovel. I dug the grave with my hands." He still had tiny scars on his fingers where the rocky soil had cut them to ribbons.

He shook his head to dispel the memory, then took another swig of his whiskey. He wondered who would move first—he or the dragonman—and contemplated snatching up his knife. He looked at the gravestone, then at the dragonman.

"Are your friends sneaking up behind me?" Styke asked.

Ji-Orz shook his head. "We split up when we realized you were no longer with the army. I believe I'm the only one who found your trail."

"You probably shouldn't have told me that." Unless, Styke considered, he was lying.

"I do not want to be here." The words were spoken quietly but forcefully.

Styke sat up straight, watching the dragonman carefully.

Ji-Orz continued. "I fought on the wrong side of the civil war. Ka-Sedial's people murdered my emperor and brokered a peace. I did not accept *their* emperor, so I was disgraced. I spent years in the darkest dungeons. Forgotten, until Ka-Sedial found a use for me."

"The six sent after me," Styke asked, genuinely curious, "they're all disgraced?"

"Ka-Sedial is vain, wrathful, and arrogant, but he is not stupid. He would not waste six dragonmen on you—on a single person. But in the eyes of our people we no longer exist. He took the useless and found something for us to do. If we bring him your head, we are allowed to be people again." There was a faraway look in

Ji-Orz's eyes, and Styke wondered if this promise of freedom made the dragonmen reckless, or whether it made them more dangerous.

"Why are you telling me this?"

Ji-Orz looked at the gravestone and sighed. "Because I want you to know it's not personal."

"War is rarely personal."

"War is *always* personal," Ji-Orz said with an affronted expression. "The very act of taking the life of another human being makes it so. But this time is not—" He stopped talking, clearly frustrated. "Perhaps I don't get across my meaning. Ka-Sedial has our blood. Do you know what this means?"

"Vaguely."

"It means he can compel us, even across great distances. He can whisper in our ears and pry truths from our minds."

"That is...unsettling."

"It is rape," Ji-Orz said flatly. "But Ka-Sedial is not perfect. He cannot watch us all the time. And tonight...I will not fight a man on his mother's grave. I am a warrior, not a savage."

Styke wondered if this was all a ploy, if Ji-Orz said these things to get him to lower his guard. There was an earnestness in his face as he struggled to find the right words that compelled Styke to believe him. Yet there was still a doubt. He remembered Kushel's willingness to hurt Celine back in Landfall, and half expected a knife to come out of the darkness and slash his throat at any minute.

It did not arrive. Perhaps not all dragonmen were alike.

Several minutes passed in silence. Sitting forward, Styke shook the half-empty bottle of whiskey and handed it across to Ji-Orz. The dragonman regarded it for a moment before taking a swig. He took another, wiped his chin on his sleeve, and handed it back. He stood up, straightening his duster to cover his weapons.

"I will leave you to mourn, Ben Styke. Thank you for sharing your story with me. The next time we meet, I will attempt to kill you. I will probably succeed." He put a notable emphasis on "probably."

The dragonman bowed his head toward the gravestone and strode off into the darkness, leaving Styke alone. His passage was purposefully loud, sticks crackling as he walked, as if to tell Styke that he had, indeed, gone. Soon the crickets returned, and Styke settled back to watch the flames. Amrec nibbled at his shoulder.

"All out, boy," Styke said, showing him his empty hand, letting Amrec explore it with his velvety lips.

Styke finished the bottle and lay awake, staring at the flames while he waited for Ji-Orz's wrathful return, or for one of the other dragonmen to happen upon him. He did not remember closing his eyes, but when they opened once more, it was early in the morning. The fire was ash, his bedroll soaked with morning dew. Styke stirred from his spot and took a walk around the grove, examining the ground for sign of the dragonman hiding out nearby. He couldn't find any.

He finished clearing the last of the vines and brush from the grave and walked to the old, rotted cabin where his mother was born, casting its now-crumbled walls to memory. Returning to the grave, he bent to kiss the stone and then saddled Amrec. He left without looking back.

The column was already assembled to leave the Third Army by the time Styke returned. Ibana watched him arrive from horseback. Celine sat on her own horse nearby. Styke ignored Ibana and went to the girl first.

"Why did you leave me?" Celine asked.

"I had to do something alone," Styke said.

"I've seen you kill before."

"It's not always about killing," Styke explained softly. "I had to visit someone I love. Perhaps when this is over, I'll take you to visit her as well."

Celine seemed to sense the solemnity of his words. She gave an uncertain nod. "Ka-poel is angry you left her behind. So is Ibana."

"They can both damn well deal with it." He brushed her hair out of her face. "I should have taken you. I'm sorry. Next time I will." With that, he headed back to Ibana at the front of the column. He let her stare at the side of his face for several moments before letting out an irritated sigh. "Well? We've got Dynize dragoons and a godstone to find. Let's go hunting."

CHAPTER 41

Michel stepped down from Ichtracia's carriage, holding on carefully to the door until his feet were on firm ground. He wasn't entirely certain of his body, even after two days of forced recovering in Ichtracia's townhouse. Everything *seemed* to work, despite how sketchy her sorcery-and-surgery combination sounded, and he was in less pain than if he had just been stitched up again by Emerald.

Which didn't mean he didn't hurt. He looked up at the columned facade of the Landfall City Bank. It was an enormous building, over sixty feet tall with foreboding gargoyles perched on the decorated eaves, all finished in black marble. Last he heard, the bank had been ransacked and abandoned during the invasion and had sat empty ever since.

Now, though, half a dozen carriages sat out front, all of them bearing the black and red curtains of the new regime. A Dynize flag hung from the highest point of the roof, and he saw a steady stream of people coming and going. He couldn't help but wonder if

Ichtracia had fixed him up only to turn him over to Ka-Sedial to be tortured. He looked up at the driver of the carriage, one of Ichtracia's footmen. "Tculu," he said, "why am I here?"

"I just brought you to where I was told," the footman responded. He snapped the reins and drove off before Michel could question him further.

Two days locked up in Ichtracia's townhouse. Two days without any information from the outside world. It was worse than when he'd been stuck in Emerald's morgue, if only because he had no way of knowing who had survived the blast that destroyed Yaret's house, and whether he would emerge with any allies left among the Dynize. Other than Ichtracia, that was, though Michel couldn't consider her an ally. At best she was an enigma.

After his healing, they had exchanged less than ten sentences. And now? He was dumped outside the Landfall City Bank.

"Michel!"

Michel turned to find Tenik walking toward him from beyond one of the carriages. He couldn't help a smile, a wave of relief sweeping across him at the sight of a familiar face. "Tenik, I'm glad to see you alive."

"Perhaps," Tenik responded in a somber tone. "Come with me."

"What do you mean, *perhaps*?" Michel asked. Tenik didn't answer, turning sharply and striding away with a purpose that was incongruous with the laid-back man Michel had gotten to know. Michel was surprised at the brusqueness, and he slowly followed Tenik up the steps of the old bank and through the enormous front doors. Despite Michel's obvious discomfort, Tenik neither offered a hand nor slowed his pace. Inside, the cavernous main hall was a whirl of activity—men, women, and children seemed to fill most of the space and a vaguely organized sort of indoor camp, with tents and partitions splitting the room into thirty or forty smaller ones.

Tenik navigated the space with ease, and Michel had a difficult time keeping up. He paused in the center of things for a breather, only to look up and see Tenik waiting ahead, watching him with a cold stare that put Michel on edge.

They continued to the back of the great room and up two flights of steps to the bank manager's offices. Four Dynize soldiers stood watch outside, muskets shouldered. "Watch him," Tenik told them before slipping inside the offices. Michel felt their eyes turn on him instantly, and he shifted uncomfortably, wondering what he had walked into. There was something very wrong here, and it took him far too long to figure it out.

The realization hit him just as the door opened and Tenik reappeared: Everyone here thought that Michel was responsible for Yaret's death. He felt a trickle of sweat roll down the small of his back, and the behavior of Tenik—and the angry stares of the guards—now made so much more sense. This bank was the Household's staging point, where they'd all gathered to recover. Michel was the man responsible for this, or so they all thought, and he had little doubt who'd spread *that* rumor.

Tenik stood in the open doorway for a moment, his expression troubled, obviously trying to read Michel. For his part, Michel could do little more than sweat openly, knowing how pale and frail he looked. He knew what guilt looked like, and it wasn't all that different from a man trying to keep himself together when he is physically and emotionally empty.

"All right," Tenik said, "come in."

Michel stepped through the door and into the bank manager's offices, which he could tell in a single glance had been co-opted by whoever was taking over Yaret's position as the head of the Household. Michel wondered briefly how the line of succession affected the Name, and if Yaret would fade into obscurity, forgotten by all but a few dusty history books.

It was with some surprise that he entered a second doorway and found Yaret himself sitting behind the manager's old desk, leaning forward, fingers steepled, brow furrowed as one of his cupbearers spoke earnestly. At the sight of Michel, Yaret raised his hand, and the woman beside him fell silent.

There were four other people in the room besides Michel, Tenik, and Yaret. Michel recognized each of them as Yaret's top lieutenants. He tried to figure out who was missing and couldn't come up with anyone. Had none of them died in the bombing? His pleasure at the news—and the sight of Yaret alive and well—was tempered by the fact that everyone in the room looked at him with the same weighing, anger-tinged way the guards outside had. He was, he realized in an instant, on trial.

"Michel," Yaret said by way of greeting. "We're all rather surprised to see you alive."

Michel was about to answer that the feeling was mutual, but realized how bad that would sound before the words left his mouth. Instead, he just nodded. "I have the feeling I've missed a lot."

"Indeed. There are quite a lot of rumors swirling around about you right now."

Michel glanced at Tenik, but the cupbearer was clearly going to be of no help. He felt a spark of anger and grabbed on to it, using it to prop himself up in the face of silent accusations. He didn't know exactly what was going on, but he had a pretty good guess. He'd almost killed himself just attempting to warn them of the bombing, and here they were turned against him. "I'm going to guess that those rumors include my involvement with the bombing of your Household."

"Do you deny them?" Yaret asked.

Michel glanced around at the hostile faces. He'd begun to think of these people as his colleagues, Tenik even as a friend. He didn't deserve this. He was too tired, in too much pain. "Of course I deny it. You want an explanation for my absence the last week? Here it is." He launched into a quick summary of his adventures, starting with his search of Forgula's house, then his shooting by Hendres, and his recovery with Emerald. He finished with his attempt to warn Yaret about the bombing, and his time spent locked in Ichtracia's townhouse. He glossed over a few key details, like Emerald's name and occupation, but kept everything fairly true to reality.

Yaret and his people listened without interrupting, watching him carefully throughout the whole story. Michel ended with a sigh and, without being invited, took an empty chair from the corner of the room and dragged it over in front of Yaret's desk before collapsing into it.

"Ichtracia saved you from Forgula?" Yaret asked.

It was not the first question Michel expected to be asked. "She did. I have no idea why."

"She's taken a liking to him," Tenik interrupted, clearing his throat. "She has ever since Michel tagged Forgula at the war games."

Yaret snorted, burying a half smile, the closest thing to humor to enter this room since Michel's arrival. "No telling what's in a Privileged's head. Especially *that* one." He squinted at Michel, then suddenly produced a piece of paper. It was hastily scrawled with the words *Evacuate Household. Bomb.—Michel*. He set it in the middle of the desk so that Michel could see it. "That," he said, "is the only reason you're standing there right now, and not already handed over to the bone-eyes for questioning. Because of this note, we were able to get everyone out of the townhouse in Chancellor's Court before several barrels of gunpowder were detonated in the basement. The house was destroyed. The Household was saved."

There was a note of gratitude in Yaret's voice that made Michel's heart sing. He reined in his elation. This was still a trial, and it could still go bad.

Yaret continued. "Forgula has openly accused you of being responsible for the bombings that have taken place across the city. She and several witnesses claim you were present just before the destruction of my house. From your explanation—and from this note here and the witness of the child who brought it to me—you were attempting to warn us."

"I was."

"Good. Then I think we both see what Forgula is up to. Without evidence, though, Sedial will demand that I hand you over to the bone-eyes for questioning."

Michel glanced between the faces. They were all a little gentler, but cautiously so. He took a deep breath. "I'm sorry, sir, but I don't think you *do* understand what Forgula is up to."

"Oh?"

Michel produced the list of addresses that he had taken from Forgula's house. The paper was stained black with his blood. He handed it to Tenik, who examined it with a frown. "That," Michel said, "is what I found among Forgula's papers. It struck me as important at the time, so I confiscated it, but I was shot before I could give it a second thought. In my weakened state, I didn't grasp the significance of the addresses until the morning of the bombing, and that's when I attempted to reach the house to warn you."

"What is that?" Yaret asked Tenik.

Tenik's eyebrows rose. "It's a list of addresses—corresponding to every single one of the bombings, including the one that destroyed our house."

"You'll find that the handwriting matches the writing in Forgula's pocketbook," Michel said, trying not to sound smug.

Three of Yaret's lieutenants began to mutter. A fourth gasped openly. Yaret stilled them with a raised hand. "And?"

"I propose that Forgula has been working with Marhoush and the Blackhats. She struck a deal with them to kill as many of Sedial's enemies as they could. I have no idea what the Blackhats are getting in return, but it's clear from that list of addresses that she knew ahead of time where they would occur. I'd be willing to bet that Marhoush or je Tura has a matching list."

Yaret nodded at Tenik, who slipped out of the room without a word. Michel opened his mouth to ask where Tenik was going, but Yaret cut him off. "You're accusing Ka-Sedial of treason."

"I am," Michel said. "Forgula ran the errands, but it's too convenient of a pattern for Sedial not to have given the order."

"Would he dare?" one of the lieutenants asked.

Yaret tapped a finger against his chin, staring over Michel's shoulder at nothing, a scowl etched on his face. "Sedial has dared an awful lot. He would never risk the empire—if all of this is true, he probably has a plan to eliminate the Blackhats as soon as they've served their purpose. But he has never been above destroying his enemies."

"All of that was supposed to change with this war. We were supposed to be united," another of the lieutenants growled.

Yaret didn't answer him. Somewhere in the bank, Michel thought he heard a scream. He tried to ignore it. He was completely certain of this conspiracy now. It made too much sense, and it was clear from Yaret's body language that he wouldn't be hard to convince. Not with the evidence Michel had just put in front of him.

Yaret meditated in silence for several minutes, his eyes half-lidded in thought while his lieutenants avoided Michel's gaze. When the quiet had almost become unbearable, the door opened and Tenik returned just as suddenly as he left. He held a leather pocketbook—Forgula's—in one hand. He plucked the blood-stained address list off the table and compared the two, then nodded. "The handwriting is a match."

"And Marhoush?" Yaret asked.

"He's changed his story."

Michel perked up at this. "Marhoush is here?"

"You can tell him," Yaret said to Tenik.

Tenik nodded, then turned to Michel. "We brought Marhoush in the evening after the bombing and handed him over to our own Household questioners. His story has corroborated the story Forgula told us—that you are still a loyal Blackhat, spying on the

Dynize—but I just went to him with the story you told us and he broke down. He said that Forgula has been funneling the Blackhats supplies in exchange for conducting bombings at the addresses and dates she gave him. He even told me where to find a copy of that list you brought us."

Michel allowed himself to close his eyes and let out a sigh of relief. When he looked up, Yaret was smiling at him thoughtfully. "I'm glad you're still one of us," Yaret said.

Michel swallowed his guilt, pushing his real self deeper into the back of his head. "I'm glad I had evidence that Forgula is a lying sack of shit. What do we do now? Is this enough evidence to accuse Sedial?"

"I think it is," Yaret replied.

Tenik raised his eyebrows. "That will be dangerous."

"Dangerous or not," Yaret said with a shake of his head, "Sedial must be brought to heel."

Michel was hit with a sudden sense of foreboding. "Perhaps Tenik is right," he said.

"In what way?"

"That it's damned dangerous. *Too* dangerous. Sedial is the emperor's man, right? And he commands the armies and the Privileged? If we go after him openly—if we force him into the light—he may just crush us underfoot. It would be his only option."

"He tried to kill me," Yaret said quietly. "He tried to kill my Household. I will not let this stand."

"We won't," Michel assured him. "But I think I know of a way we can punish him without forcing a more deadly confrontation."

"I'm listening."

Michel took a deep breath. This idea would lessen the ugliness, but it would also make Michel another very powerful enemy. "When is the next public event where both Sedial and Forgula will be present?"

CHAPTER 42

Vlora did as she'd promised Taniel and changed hotels. She rushed a new order of clothes from a local tailor and changed her look, and generally kept her head down so that she could gamble her week on the only real chance she felt she had to find the stones: reconnoitering Nighttime Vale.

Flerring's description had been spot-on. The Vale was approached by a steep hill on the northern edge of town and entered through a narrow valley between two great pillars of stone. Because the Vale was entirely the property of Jezzy's Shovel gang, the valley was closed to outsiders and guarded by eight armed men at all times.

Vlora watched them for two days and nights, attempting to find some kind of chink in their routine that would let her slip into the Vale and back out again without being noticed. She grew more and more frustrated at the situation—the approach was out in the open, the guards were rotated in shifts without a gap, and every wagon that entered and left the Vale was guarded to and from the destination. According to a few old prospectors she asked, climbing around the other side of the Vale would take her four or five days.

She began to wonder if maybe Jezzy *was* in on the recovery of the stone—or if it was just that gold mines were more thoroughly guarded than some military armories. Bad luck either way.

On the third day she picked up a copy of the *Yellow Creek Caller* to find a surprising bit of information on the front page. The headline read MERCENARY ARMY MARCHES ON YELLOW CREEK. Below was a snappy story on the Riflejacks that said they were spotted in the region marching toward Yellow Creek. She returned to the newsie boy who'd sold her the paper and pointed at the headline. "Is this from this morning?"

"Yes, ma'am. Fresh information."

"Do you know anything else about this?" she asked.

"I don't think so."

Vlora fished a coin from her pocket and flicked it off her thumb. The boy caught it, looked over his shoulder, and took two steps closer. He spoke in a conspiratorial tone.

"Rumor has it the big bosses are frantic with worry. Each of them thinks the other hired a whole mercenary army to take their gold, and both of them are denying it. *I* heard that it was Jezzy who hired them. Supposedly the army's led by that Flint lady—you know, the one that the Lady Chancellor has put a bounty on?"

"I've heard of her," Vlora said cautiously.

"Well, everyone is arming up to protect their claims. The big bosses are forcing a production increase and offering huge amounts to anyone who carries a weapon. The guards are doubling. The mayor wants to close all the roads, but Jezzy and Brown Bear Burt want to keep them open to get their gold out. They say it's chaos in the mayor's office, and no one knows what to do."

Vlora left the newsie with an extra coin and strode off swearing under her breath. This was exactly why she'd come ahead of the army—exactly why she'd given herself an extra couple of weeks to try to find the stone before they were forced to bring in a few thousand soldiers and dig it up with violence. She originally thought that the town's defenses would be little more than an inconvenience, but now she wasn't so sure. Roadblocks in the harsh terrain could keep the Riflejacks from approaching the city for days or weeks, and when they finally arrived, they would have to deal with street-to-street fighting with people who thought they were there to steal the gold.

Vlora headed to the main street and checked in with the messenger service that she'd used to try to find Olem. The man behind the desk recognized her immediately and went to a locked box in the corner of the room, returning a moment later with a letter.

"It came yesterday," the clerk said apologetically. "We checked with your hotel, but they said you had left and not given them a forwarding address."

Vlora tipped the man and took the letter to the corner. She recognized Olem's writing immediately.

Progress has been slow. Took a circuitous route to approach from the east. News from Landfall. We are five days out. I fear word has gone ahead of us. Expect panic. We will hold at six miles and wait for orders.

"A little damned late," she said, lighting the edge of the letter with a match and letting it burn down to her fingertips. She did some quick mental math and decided that they were probably getting close to that six miles. Making camp six miles out could be good, though—it would give the city residents longer to worry about *why* they were here and who had hired them, which in turn would give Vlora more time to find the stone.

If the Picks and Shovels began fighting among themselves, the Riflejacks might have an easier time of mopping things up.

But none of this, she decided, was ideal.

CHAPTER 43

Michel sat in the hallway outside of the war game arena in the capitol building, listening as the cheering came to a great crescendo before tapering off into the general cacophony of loud conversation that he normally associated with the period at the end of a boxing match. He wondered briefly who won, before reminding himself that he didn't know who either of the players were, or most of the rules of the game.

Maybe if he stuck around here long enough, he would learn how to play.

Michel took a coin out of his pocket. He flipped it, caught it, and looked at the result. How, he wondered, did Tenik resist looking at that result every time? It was a natural human urge, wasn't it? To know how something ended?

Before Michel could ponder the question further, the doors opened and a stream of people began to pass him. No one seemed to really notice his presence, which, he decided, was probably for the best. He recognized most of the people either from the game he had attended the other week with Tenik or from figures he'd seen stalking these very halls over the last couple of weeks. The cream of the Dynize crop. If je Tura really wanted to cause some damage, he would toss a couple of grenades into that room during a war game.

Michel wondered if that would be on the list, eventually.

Michel spotted his target and climbed to his feet, body still hurting from Ichtracia's healing, the pain kept partially at bay by horngum. His hands shook slightly from a case of nerves, and he wondered why he was here rather than standing in a dark corner to watch the proceedings. He reminded himself that he had made plenty of accusations before. This was just far more public than he was used to. He would just have to get used to it.

"Forgula," he called sharply.

The people closest to him stopped in their tracks and turned, some of them doing a double take as they saw him. Forgula, her head bowed to listen to the words of a woman beside her, searched for the source of the summons until her eyes met his. All around her, the stream of people gradually ground to a halt.

Her lip curled slightly, but she bowed her head again and nodded to the man to go on, turning a cold shoulder toward Michel.

"You probably shouldn't enjoy this," Michel whispered to himself, stifling a smile. "Devin-Forgula a Sedial!" he barked.

Everyone had stopped by now. People were looking curiously between Michel and Forgula, the latter of whom finally pulled herself away from her companion and strode through the crowd toward Michel. She came up sharply, chin raised, glaring down her nose at him. "Shouldn't you be in a cell, spy?"

"Not me," Michel said, tapping the front of his jacket. She looked down, seeing the way he was dressed for the first time—a teal uniform, worn by ministerial servants on official business. It was similar to a Dynize soldier's outfit, though the cut of the pants was slightly different. This one had been tailored specifically for Michel just yesterday and it fit him rather splendidly. The jacket bore the crest scroll of Yaret's Household, and beneath that a small stitched cup.

"Why are you wearing that uniform?" Forgula demanded. She scowled at him, and he could see the first inkling in her eye that she knew something was off. "You have no right."

"I have a lot of right," Michel responded. "I saved the Yaret Household from a bombing. Hadn't you heard?" Michel knew for a fact that she *hadn't* heard. The last time she saw him, he was being carted off by Ichtracia just before the bombing. At his request, everything about his activities the last few days had been kept quiet. As far as anyone knew, Yaret had barely escaped the bombing because of an anonymous tip, and the Blackhat spy Michel Bravis was in Yaret's custody and being questioned.

"You didn't save them," Forgula said. She was uneasy now, lacking conviction. This had taken her completely by surprise.

Don't smile, Michel. "I did, actually. You remember that day, don't you? It was just earlier this week. You and your cronies tried to chase me down, even though I could barely walk. It's all right, though. Fortune smiled on me, and I still managed to warn Yaret about the bomb."

"You could only know about that bomb if you were the one to plant it."

Everyone was watching now, as if glued to the floor. There wasn't a sound within forty feet as people strained to hear the conversation. Michel was using his best Dynize, though he had to throw in a Palo word once in a while. He was certain that everyone was getting the gist. "Or," Michel said, "if I found this." He drew out the list of addresses he had stolen from her files. It was fragile from being caked with his dry blood, so he presented it to her in a stiff folder. She reached for it involuntarily, and he snatched it away. "This," Michel said, "is a list of addresses that includes—"

"I know what that is," Forgula hissed, glancing desperately at the crowd around her.

Michel went on in a louder voice. "It's a list of addresses that includes every location that has been attacked since the bombings started. It was found among your files last week, and is written in your—"

"Shut up!" Forgula said, grabbing Michel by the wrist.

"Unhand me," Michel responded coldly.

"Give me that." Before he could stop her, Forgula snatched the folder out of his hand and opened it up, staring at the list of addresses. There was a rustling nearby, and several soldiers took up positions along the edges of the hall, watching Forgula carefully. Michel almost wanted her to run, just to see what would happen. Yaret had ordered his men to be emphatic if necessary.

Michel took a half step toward her and lowered his voice so that only she could hear. "The thing is, if you're going to spread a rumor that I was shot by a Blackhat, you should consider the fact that there were no other witnesses besides me and the shooter—and you didn't hear about it from me. Also, having me shot by a Blackhat contradicts your story that I'm still working for them. Never cross your narratives and"—he tapped the folder in her hands—"never keep a copy of addresses where you intend to have people killed."

To Michel's left, a door opened and Tenik emerged with four more soldiers, taking up a position close enough to snatch Forgula if she attempted to attack him.

There was a sudden commotion, and then three emphatic clicks on the marble flooring. A corridor opened in the throng of people to reveal Ka-Sedial standing just inside the war game arena, a scowl on his face, quietly demanding to know what was going on. When his eyes fell on Michel and Forgula, he immediately began to stride toward them, cane in hand. Ichtracia stood just behind him, following with a curious look on her face.

Michel swallowed his nerves and glanced at Tenik, who gave an almost imperceptible nod. Waiting until Sedial was almost upon them, right as the Ka's mouth opened with a demand, Michel gave a quick, respectful bow and spoke first. "Great Ka, thank you for coming. We have a grave matter to bring to your attention."

Ka-Sedial glanced from Forgula to Michel to Tenik, the irritation on his face fading to something more neutral in the space of an instant. The old bastard knew a trap when he saw one, and he would wait to see how this played out before publicly castigating Michel.

Which was all Michel needed.

"What matter is at hand?" Sedial asked.

Michel bowed again. "By order of Yaret, we have come to arrest Devin-Forgula on charges of murder and treason." He half expected Sedial to bark a reply—to sweep in to cover for his cup-bearer. Instead, the old man simply lifted his chin and narrowed his eyes as if to say, *Continue.* So Michel did. "We have evidence that Devin-Forgula has conspired with enemies of the state in order to kill off her rivals among the Dynize." Michel so very much wanted to say "*your* rivals," but he kept to his script. This had to fall on Forgula's shoulders, and hers alone. "The bombings conducted by the Blackhats over the last few weeks were coordinated by Forgula."

"You have no evidence," Forgula said, finally finding her tongue. She snatched up the list of addresses and crumpled it, throwing it at Michel's face. "Just a damned bloody piece of paper."

Michel let the paper bounce off his cheek without comment. "We do, actually. We have a second copy of that paper found among the effects of a captured Blackhat. We also have the word of that Blackhat that you worked with him directly. And that, Great Ka, is why Yaret has asked for your assistance. We formally request a bone-eye inquisition of the Blackhat prisoner in question, followed by an inquisition into Forgula herself. We want to gain nothing but the truth, and we request that you aid us in that process."

To his credit, Sedial didn't even blink at the request. He remained silent for several moments, no doubt fully aware that the eyes of the Dynize upper crust were on him. He looked coolly at Forgula, then at Michel. "Of course," he said.

Forgula gave an anguished cry, lurching forward and snatching the sword from the Dynize soldier at Tenik's side.

"Stop her!" Michel cried.

Forgula leapt back, waving the sword once and looking Sedial in the face before taking it by the blade and pressing the tip to her chest and falling upon it. Her sobbing was cut short, body spasming as her weight caused the blade to pierce her heart. She slumped, then fell to one side with a thump, a pool of blood immediately beginning to widen around her.

Several of the crowd gasped. People attempted to step away from the blood. Ka-Sedial did not, so Michel didn't, either.

"I'm sorry, Great Ka," Michel said gently in the silence. "That was not at all how we wanted this to go." It was exactly how they wanted it to go.

And just for an instant, when he raised his face from the gruesome display, Michel could see raw fury in Ka-Sedial's eyes. Sedial knew this was what was meant to happen, and he knew that the message sent by this event came directly from Yaret—despite Yaret's absence. The fury was gone in the blink of an eye, replaced by the sad resolve of an old man. Ka-Sedial shook his head, tutting, before raising his voice.

"May Devin-Forgula's body be fed to the dogs," Sedial proclaimed, "and her name be forever struck from the records of the Sedial Household. May she be crushed and forgotten. Such is the fate of a traitor." His eyes landed on Michel's face on that final word, and Michel suppressed a shudder. He would not get out of this unscathed.

"That," he said quietly, "will not happen. Forgula will be remembered for what she was, and her crime publicized and recorded. Her name will be struck from your Household records, but not the public ones."

Sedial's eyes narrowed. "I make those decisions."

"I apologize, Great Ka, but you do not. The Ministry of Scrolls does."

"I see." Sedial settled both hands on his cane, shoulders slumped as if he was a man under a great weight, and gazed into Michel's eyes in an almost placid manner for a few moments before hobbling off. The crowd gave way before him, and Michel watched as he tracked Forgula's blood down the hall without seeming to care. Michel wondered if that was a metaphor for Ka-Sedial's whole career, and decided not to pursue the thought any further.

Slowly, the crowd began to move again. Conversation resumed, and people stopped staring at Michel or the body at his feet. A pair of soldiers approached, checking Forgula for any sign of life before lifting her by the hands and feet and carrying her off.

"That was well done," Tenik said.

Michel let out a long breath. He dragged his sleeve across his brow and dabbed the sweat off the back of his neck. "Pit, I never want to do that again."

"That's too bad. You did it well enough that Yaret might use you again in the future."

"I'm a spy, damn it. Not a constable."

Tenik tapped the cup insignia on Michel's uniform. "You're whatever Yaret needs you to be, cupbearer."

"Don't remind me."

Tenik gave him a small smile. "I will, and frequently. You still have a lot to learn."

"Don't I know it."

"Have we gotten anything from Marhoush?"

"The names of a half-dozen more safe houses and perhaps thirty Blackhats," Tenik answered.

"Do we know where je Tura is?"

"Marhoush has no idea. He *thinks* that je Tura uses the catacombs beneath the city to get around, but we've searched dozens of miles of that damned spiderweb and found little evidence of a giant network of Blackhat powder monkeys."

Michel growled in the back of his throat, frustrated. With Marhoush handed over to the bone-eyes, there would be no secrets left to learn—and he was their best chance of finding je Tura. "Keep looking. Send more men into the catacombs if you have to." He suddenly became aware that he and Tenik were not isolated in their conversation. He glanced over his shoulder to find Ichtracia leaning against the wall a few feet behind him, just out of the pool of Forgula's blood, watching him with a tight-lipped smile.

"I'll see to the body," Tenik suddenly said.

"Tenik, wait, I—" Tenik was gone before Michel could stop him, leaving him alone with Ichtracia. He turned, putting on his most charming smile. "Good evening, Saen-Ichtracia."

"Good evening, Devin-Michel a Yaret."

Michel felt goose bumps on the backs of his arms at the title. His smile faltered for a split second, but he didn't think Ichtracia noticed. "I'm sorry for the mess," he said.

"I'm not the one standing in it," Ichtracia said with a shrug.

Michel looked down to realize that he was, indeed, standing in Forgula's blood. He lifted one foot, looked around for somewhere to wipe it, then gave up. "What can I do for you, Saen?"

"I'm curious; did Sedial put her up to it?" Ichtracia nodded to where Forgula's body had been a minute before.

"Of course not. She acted alone, against her enemies."

"You mean the enemies of the Sedial Household. I'm not stupid, Michel, and I know who died in those explosions. None were allies of Sedial."

Michel licked his lips, glancing over his shoulder. The crowd had gotten out quickly, and he imagined that in a few minutes no one would be left but whatever poor sod of a soldier was tasked with cleaning up this blood. Most of the crowd had deftly avoided the pool, but the blood Ka-Sedial tracked down the hallway was smeared everywhere.

"Was it that obvious?" he asked.

"It will be after the gossip has gone around the city a few times," Ichtracia answered. "You showed everyone the math, after all."

"Good."

Ichtracia's eyebrows went up in surprise; then she smiled. "Oh, I see. Very clever. You want everyone to know that Sedial has broken the Dynize truce without actually calling him out in public. It erodes his power base without forcing him to respond immediately. Tell me, was this Yaret's idea or yours?"

Michel shook his head.

"Oh, I'll bet it was yours. Yaret is a very intelligent man, but he's not much of a schemer. You, however..." Ichtracia stepped over to Michel, putting her face just inches from Michel's to look him in the eyes. She was shorter than he by over two inches, but he felt as if she were staring down at him.

Michel cleared his throat. "I want to thank you again for saving my life."

"And how are you feeling?"

"Not fantastic. But it's better than being dead."

"Good. I suggest that you deliver on that dinner you offered me."

"I'm, uh, afraid that my favorite restaurant burned down during the riots." Michel thought that his mouth should be dry, his heart hammering, but to his surprise he found that he was calmer now than he had been ten minutes ago. Why would that be? Flirting with a Privileged was infinitely more dangerous than arresting an enemy of the state.

But, he realized, it was also more private. More intimate. This was what he knew how to do. A memory suddenly leapt to his mind, of watching his mother's cat play with a mouse for several days. When asked, his mother told him that the mouse was the safest critter on the block for as long as the cat found it entertaining.

"Your excuse fails to impress me," Ichtracia noted.

"Perhaps you have a chef at your townhouse?" Michel asked. Yaret was a fine master, but Michel had seen the fury in Sedial's eyes. He needed someone who could protect him right now.

Ichtracia cocked an eyebrow. She opened her mouth, closed it, then grinned. "I think you'll be a lot of fun."

Said the cat to the mouse, Michel thought. He linked arms with Ichtracia, falling in beside her. "Come, we must find somewhere to clean the blood from my shoes and pants."

CHAPTER 44

The Dynize dragoons appeared within hours of the Mad Lancers leaving the safety of the Third Army and harassed them all along the length of the Hammer for two more days. On the third, Styke called for a rest at midday and sent for his officers.

"Why are they riding my ass so hard?" Styke asked Ka-poel as he waited for his men to gather. Through his looking glass he watched a Dynize scout, wearing the now-familiar turquoise jacket and black pants of the Dynize dragoons. The scout was about three miles away and, from the way he was standing out in the open, clearly wanted to be seen. The Dynize were trying to get under his skin.

They were succeeding.

"Eh?" he asked, lowering his glass. "Why do they dog me? Did that prick of a Dynize commander order *them* after me as well?"

Ka-poel remained intractable, her face a mask of mild irritation, though whether that was directed at Styke, at the Dynize, or at their slow progress across the Hammer, he couldn't be sure. She finally shook her head. *I don't know.*

Styke made a vexed sound in the back of his throat. He'd been hunted plenty of times—the Kez had sent a whole field army after the Mad Lancers at one point during the war—but he'd never been ambushed so successfully as by these dragoons, nor followed so closely without his own scouts knowing exactly where the enemy was at all times.

He was struck by a thought that brought a smile to his lips. It was not *that* funny, but he soon found himself roaring, slapping his knee, bent double. When he was finally able to stand, he turned to find Ka-poel's facade broken and an expression on her face that clearly asked, *What the pit is wrong with you?*

"Ka-Sedial," he said, wiping a tear from his eye. "He must have been so incredibly pissed that someone crushed one of his dragon-men. When he found out I was a cripple...I can just imagine his face!" He made Ka-poel suffer through another round of chuckles, then gasped for breath.

Ka-poel smirked.

"I should write him a letter," Styke said. "Tell him that I killed another one. And that a third had her head blown off by a little girl!"

His mirth was interrupted by the arrival of Ibana and Jackal. Ibana had a fresh cut across her cheek from where a Dynize bullet had barely missed her face in a sortie less than three hours ago. They'd lost seven Mad Lancers and only managed to down two of the Dynize, and she was clearly not in a smiling mood.

"What's so funny?" she demanded.

Styke waved it off and forced himself to sober. "Nothing, nothing. Jackal, have you managed to wrangle any of your damned spirits so we can find out when and where these sons of bitches are going to hit us next?"

"I have, actually."

Both Ibana and Gustar adopted dubious expressions. Styke held a finger out to them. "Only interrupt if you have any better ideas," he said. They both remained silent, and he pointed to Jackal.

"There is one," Jackal said. "She was an officer until Ibana killed her two days ago—their equivalent of a lieutenant. She does not fear Ka-poel like the others."

Ka-poel seemed mildly intrigued by this. Styke asked, "Why not?"

"She will not say and I can't coax it out of her. From what she tells me, the Dynize are not…" He paused as if trying to come up with the right phrase. "They are not of one mind."

"Divided?" Styke asked. Ji-Orz had said as much, but it was interesting to have this confirmed by Jackal.

"They spent the better part of the last century locked in a bitter civil war. There were ultimately two sides and dozens of factions in each. She was a member of the side that eventually capitulated. She does not believe in Ka-Sedial's plan to unite the country by invading Fatrasta, and she did not want to be here in the first place."

"And that's why she's talking to you?"

"That, and she thinks her commanding officer is an asshole."

Styke wondered briefly if this whole conversation was more evidence that he had come unhinged. If someone had claimed to speak with spirits back during the old war, he would have sent them to the front of the next charge and hoped they either became a spirit themselves or got the sense knocked into them. "I like her," Styke said, referring to the spirit. "Does she know why they're after us?"

"That's not important," Ibana cut in. "Does she know what their plan is?" She gritted her teeth, and Styke could tell it annoyed her to ask Jackal a question for the spirits. Major Gustar remained silent, still looking skeptical.

"Their plan is to wear us thin," Jackal said. "They tried engaging us directly and lost more men than they'd expected. They will harass us until we reach the coast and then try to break us." He paused. "It seems they are not an ordinary cavalry unit."

"I could have told you that," Styke snorted.

"At the end of the civil war, they were the other emperor's body-guard. Or rather, they are what's left of his bodyguard."

"I'm being chased by four dragonmen and a damned imperial guard," Styke murmured to himself. "Ka-Sedial needs to learn to let things go." He cleared his throat. "How far are we from the end of the Hammer?"

Gustar spoke up. "A few days at our current rate."

Styke mused over the possibilities. "We could just ignore them until we reach the coast and they're forced to engage us."

"They'll bleed us dry," Gustar said. "We're down to less than six hundred able-bodied men. We could lose another two hundred in those days. My guess is they still have fifteen hundred left. That would leave us outnumbered nearly four-to-one."

"We've faced worse odds," Styke said.

Ibana put her hands on her hips. "I'll remind you again: We had enchanted armor. Not everyone is able to walk off every engagement they end up in, Ben."

Styke frowned, considering his cavalier attitude toward the deaths of others. He knew commanding officers whose hearts bled for every death under their command—Lady Flint was one of those. To some that was a weakness. Flint had turned it into a strength.

He turned his gaze to the west—toward the end of the Hammer and, if Ka-poel was to believed, their final destination. He wondered briefly at their end goal in regard to the godstone, whether they were to capture and hold it, or to destroy it, or to try to put it on a boat and sink it in the sea. He decided that was best left to Ka-poel. He, in turn, would take care of whatever killing needed done in order to get there.

His eyes fell on the sharp terrain. The geography at the end of the Hammer was a far different sight from the east coast of Fatrasta, where they'd begun. Gone were the plains punctuated by bogs, lazy rivers, and plantation houses. Even gone were the forests and rolling hills of central Fatrasta. The terrain through which they must now pass was a dense wood filled with steep ridges and deep ravines covered in hanging mosses. It reminded Styke of the sharp foothills of the Ironhook Mountains, but there were no mountains within hundreds of miles. The locals called it the Hock.

Superstitious people claimed that the Hock had been carved by a war between gods millennia ago. During his time in the labor camps, Styke had once been partnered with a geologist—one of those government-employed fellows sent to look for likely deposits of gold ore—who had insisted that this sharp terrain had been caused by immense mountains of ice creeping their way across the land tens of thousands of years ago.

Styke had always dismissed him as a lunatic.

"What will they expect us to do?" Styke asked, still staring at the edge of the innocuous-looking forest that marked the beginning of the Hock.

Gustar answered straightaway. "They have us heavily in numbers. They'll expect one of two things: that we'll make a run for the coast, in the mistaken belief we can find reinforcements from a Fatrastan fleet."

"Or?" Styke asked.

"Or that we try to hide in the Hock, shake them loose, and double back. They know that we know we're outnumbered and running out of options. They'll expect us to use the Hock as our chance to get away."

Ibana did not seem convinced. "There is a third option: that they know our reputation and expect us to turn and fight at the first opportunity."

Styke tried to put himself in the shoes of the dragoon commander. She was crafty enough to stay unnoticed all the way across the country and then catch them unawares in ambush. She also—so Styke assumed—had orders to kill Styke. Probably the same orders that Ka-Sedial had given those dragonmen. Would she go around the Hock and expect to catch up on the other side? Would she follow closely on his heels?

"Do we have scouts back from the Hock?" he asked.

"We do," Ibana reported. "There's just one major road to the coast. It has one relay station that's still manned by three Fatrastan troops, which means the Dynize have avoided the place entirely since they landed. So we shouldn't run into an army in there."

"And the dragoons haven't gotten ahead of us?" He looked back to where he'd spotted the scout to their east a few minutes ago, but they had disappeared.

"Absolutely certain of it," Gustar replied.

His two majors in agreement, Styke realized that rushing headlong into the forest had few consequences. "Bring me your scouts, some paper, and something to draw with. I want to know exactly what the terrain looks like before we head in."

Three hours later, Styke crouched in the underbrush at the edge of the Hock, looking out onto the road that his troops had passed through not long ago. He could see clearly for almost a mile before the road curved over a hill. It was empty and quiet.

Ka-poel lay beside him, using his looking glass to scan the horizon. Celine was somewhere a couple miles into the Hock with the camp and most of the horses. Ibana and Gustar were each about three hundred yards to Styke's left and right, respectively, lying in much the same position at the edge of the forest and waiting with bated breath for the Dynize dragoons to show themselves.

When Styke spotted the first scout, he rode not from the east but from the south. The rider came up just a few dozen yards from the edge of the Hock, riding parallel to the forest, peering into the trees as he went. Styke ignored the twinge in his leg and pressed himself lower into the brush as the rider came near.

The rider reached the road—an easy carbine shot from Styke's position—and stopped. Only a few minutes passed and he was soon joined by another rider from the north and then, crossing the distant hill and coming toward them, a third rider. They joined in conference for a few moments before the first and second riders headed into the Hock, following the trail of the Mad Lancers.

"Let them go," Styke whispered to Jackal. The command was passed quietly along into the forest.

Styke heard the clop of their hooves disappear and watched the third rider, who seemed content to wait.

Fifteen minutes passed, then half an hour, and then the two scouts reappeared to join their third companion. They conferred once again, and the third took off back down the road. "They'll report back to their superiors," Styke whispered to Ka-poel, "that we're camped roughly two miles into the Hock in an open hollow that would be easily ambushed. The rest of the army will be here soon. I want you to go back to camp and keep an eye on Celine."

Ka-poel gave him a thoughtful look and got to her feet, hurrying into the forest.

In less than twenty minutes, horses appeared on the horizon. They rode six across, carbines held sharply at the ready. Styke recognized the woman at their head—it was the same officer who'd slaughtered his rear guard and then tried to kill him last week. The column continued to snake down the road, extending for nearly a mile with room between the horses for them to maneuver. Styke guessed that they had a little under fourteen hundred riders, plus pack horses and spares.

They entered the forest so close that Styke could have thrown a rock at that officer. He crouched, his fingers itching to grab for his carbine, and waited the agonizingly long time until the end of their column had entered the forest before finally standing up.

The men around him climbed to their feet and followed him as they headed into the woods, following their tracks back to where they'd hidden their horses a few hundred yards up a slate-carved ravine that wouldn't easily show their hoofprints. He had just fifty men with him, but they were his very best—lancers who had been with him from the beginning. They reached their horses and donned their Dynize breastplates, mounting up.

"Send the signal," he ordered.

Jackal cleared his throat and hooted loudly. The call was carried over the next hill, and a few moments passed before it came back to them from both the north and the south.

Styke leaned forward in the saddle, waiting.

Two more sets of hoots eventually followed, and Jackal nodded happily. "They're in position," he reported.

Styke allowed a satisfied smile to cross his face and hefted his lance. "Wait until the firing starts," he said.

They did not have to wait long. Within minutes they heard the first stuttering report of a carbine salvo, followed by the screams of men and horses. Styke flipped Amrec's reins and allowed the horse to pick his way carefully down the winding ravine, followed by his fifty lancers.

A forest was, as these things went, a terrible place for cavalry to ambush cavalry. There was little room to maneuver for either side, and steep ravines meant an easy fall for a panicking horse. However, it was an excellent place for dismounted soldiers who'd had a chance to hide themselves to ambush an enemy cavalry force—and that's just the ambush Ibana and Gustar's men had performed.

Styke reached the end of the ravine and rejoined the main road just in time to see the panicking rear guard of the Dynize cavalry attempting some kind of counterattack. They were in utter disarray—a few had dismounted and leapt behind horses or into the foliage, looking for cover. Some scrambled about in a panic, reloading from horseback, and still others had attempted to charge their horses into the woods only to find themselves easy pickings on the steep banks.

A man with red epaulets stood in his stirrups, waving his carbine and shouting in an attempt to organize his men. Styke's lance clipped his arm, and Amrec's shoulder hit the rider's poor horse, sending both tumbling down into the ravine on the other side of the road. Styke and his lancers entered the thick of the Dynize dragoons, plowing through them with the momentum of a downhill charge, barely slowing to fight as they trampled or scattered everyone in their paths.

They reached a switchback, arresting their charge just enough to turn, and then continued on down into the ravine. The road became a mess of horses and men. Styke traded his lance for a cavalry saber and fought his way to the bottom of the ravine. The road leveled out, giving him a chance to regain momentum, and he and his men surged forward.

This went on for well over half a mile—fighting, climbing, charging, hacking. The road wound as much as any mountain pass over ridges and through narrow valleys. Dismounted lancers spread along the entire trail, firing from the high points and retreating up the inclines if the Dynize attempted to chase, while Styke charged through the middle of it to break up any possible semblance of Dynize cohesion.

He finally reached a long, straight bit of road, only to realize that he'd run out of dragoons to attack. The echoes of carbine blasts were all behind him now, and he searched the forest for the woman with the orange epaulets. There was no sign of her ahead nor evidence that she'd fled into the woods.

He joined the mounted lancers as they caught up with him, finding Jackal bloodied and sagging, the Mad Lancers flag flying from a broken lance in his outstretched hand.

"Wounded?" Styke demanded.

"I'll be fine." Jackal's eyes shone. "We ride through them once more?"

Styke assessed his riders. Less than half remained from the initial charge—more than he'd expected to make it. He flipped his reins and headed back down the road a few hundred feet, surveying the bodies of Dynize dragoons and the riderless horses running scared. He stopped twice to kill horses beyond help, and finished off several wounded dragoons. He found a few spots where hoofprints indicated that dragoons had fled into the forest, but still no sign of the woman with the orange epaulets.

He returned to Jackal. "We took a damned risk on those roads. I saw at least a dozen of us go down with lame horses. We wait here for Ibana and only head back if we hear a signal."

The signal—a trumpet's call—never came, and several hours passed while the blast of carbines became less and less frequent. Styke and his riders let their horses rest, tending to their wounds. Jackal had taken a bullet in the thigh. Styke's face was scratched to pit by branches, and his calf was sliced by a dragoon's sword. The same sword had cut a nasty groove down Amrec's flank, so Styke cleaned and stitched the wound. He inspected Amrec's hooves for cracks and tested his legs to make sure they hadn't been hurt charging up and down the steep roads.

It was beginning to grow dark in the hollows of the Hock when Ibana—still on foot—limped into sight. She was followed by a long column of dismounted lancers, and they continued on toward camp as Ibana leaned against the moss-covered stump of a fallen tree. She rubbed her leg, grimacing, and looked up when Styke approached.

"You look well rested," she said.

"I didn't want to send the horses back along those roads."

She waved him off. "That was the right call. How did it go?"

"I lost twenty-six riders. I imagine a few just lost their horses." Styke spotted one of his old guard carrying her saddle, walking with the dismounted soldiers. "How about you?"

"Seven dead."

Styke raised his eyebrows. "*Seven?*"

"Seven dead, about sixty wounded." A sly smile spread on Ibana's face. "We butchered the shit out of those slippery bastards. They didn't expect a damned thing."

"Did you make a count?"

"We counted eight hundred and thirty-some dead or wounded dragoons." She waved back down the road. "Ferlisia and her scouts are gathering all the good horses they can find and bringing them with."

"Their wounded?" Styke asked.

"Left where they lie," Ibana said dispassionately. "If their friends come find them, they might live. If not..." She shrugged.

Styke walked Amrec beside Ibana all the way back to the Mad Lancers camp. They'd left behind fifty men to set up tents and act as a guard, and they reported that none of the Dynize had come this direction. Styke found Celine, and the two of them watched while Sunintiel stitched the bullet graze on Ibana's leg.

"It was a good victory?" Celine asked.

"A very good victory," Styke answered. He felt strangely melancholic. As Ibana said, they'd absolutely slaughtered the poor bastards. Less than half of the enemy force remained—and if they wanted to press the issue, they'd have to fight one-to-one with the Mad Lancers now. That should have sent his spirits soaring, but something felt...off.

Perhaps it was the ambush. Anyone could have been caught with their pants down in the Hock. Styke liked a good ambush as well as anyone, but a straight fight always felt better to him. The enemy commander's greed had gotten the better of her.

He did the rounds, Celine by his side, checking in with the sentries and scouts and doubling their nighttime guard against an unlikely enemy regrouping before he headed to his tent. He lay back, using Amrec's saddle for a pillow, and was preparing to drift off when he realized what was wrong.

He didn't smell blood.

He found Ibana still doing her own rounds, startling her as he came out of the darkness. "Why aren't you wearing pants?" she asked.

"I was in my tent," Styke answered. "Have you seen Ka-poel anywhere?"

"Come to think of it, no. Not since before the ambush."

Styke flared his nostrils, breathing in deeply. The scent of her sorcery—which had become so ubiquitous over the last few weeks—was nowhere on the wind.

"You sent her back here, didn't you?" Ibana asked.

Styke recounted his footsteps. They'd been watching the Dynize scouts, and then he'd dismissed Ka-poel to return to the camp before the fighting started. There was no way she had gotten lost.

"Ben?" a voice asked.

Styke turned to find Celine rubbing her eyes.

"Go back to bed," he said gently. "Wait...did Ka-poel return to camp earlier?"

"Yeah, she got here just a few minutes after the shooting began."

Styke sniffed again. Still nothing. "Are you sure?"

Celine seemed to wake up fully, her expression growing startled. "Oh no."

"What?"

"I was supposed to tell you something when you got back. Ka-poel said she was going to find the Dynize camp."

"She *what*?" Styke and Ibana both asked at the same time. Styke ran to Celine's side, kneeling down beside her so their faces were inches apart. "Tell me exactly what happened."

"Nothing happened. She just told me to tell you she had gone to find the enemy camp. She needed information."

"How is she supposed to find the enemy camp if we haven't been able to for..." Styke trailed off. Pit. She must have picked up some bit of detritus that allowed her to track them. "What the pit are we supposed to do?"

"She said to come get her in the morning," Celine said.

Styke exchanged a look with Ibana. For a week they hadn't had any luck finding the Dynize dragoons, and the bastards had shadowed them for far longer than that. Finding their camp now, without Ka-poel's sorcery, might be next to impossible. He felt sick to his stomach at the idea of having ridden clear across Fatrasta only to lose the ward they were supposed to be protecting.

And he was mad as shit that she had just gone off without saying a word to anyone except a little girl. "We leave her," he spat.

Ibana seemed startled by the suggestion. "She's the whole reason we're here."

"And she damn well abandoned us. We're her bodyguard, not her valet service. We're not going to just come by and pick her up. These dragoons have caused us more grief than any cavalry I can remember and I'm not going to go looking for them." Styke was furious. He knew he wasn't thinking clearly, but he didn't care.

"Major Gustar will be spitting mad," Ibana cautioned. "He's here to find the godstone on orders of Lady Flint. If we abandon that mission, he'll take his Riflejacks and go."

"Let him." Styke squeezed his hands into fists, wishing he had someone to strangle.

Ibana remained silent. Her usual sour expression had been replaced by somber acceptance. "What will we do?" she asked quietly.

"Join the war. Head back and find something to fight. There's no need lacking for good cavalry."

"Ben," Celine said.

"What?" he growled. He caught her eye and forced himself to take a breath. "What?" he repeated in a gentler tone.

"You can't leave Pole."

"I'm not leaving her. She left us."

"*You* left the rest of the group on your own mission," Celine pointed out. "Just the other day."

"I told everyone I was going," Styke said. "I didn't just off and..." He squeezed his fists tightly until he could feel his ring biting into the skin of his finger. "This isn't the same thing at all."

Celine stood up straighter, fixing Styke with a scowl. "You're her bodyguard," she insisted. "She anointed you. I don't know what that means, but it sounds important. She just went to get information. We can find her and keep going." She folded her arms. "Or you can leave me behind, too. I'll go find her myself."

Styke would have laughed at the image of a child telling off a crippled giant if he wasn't already so angry. He forced himself to calm down, breathing evenly, trying to make himself think. After a few moments he strode off into the darkness.

"Ben, where are you going?" Ibana called after him.

Styke found Ferlisia playing cards with several of her scouts around a small campfire. He came up behind them, picking Ferlisia up by the back of her shirt and holding her at eye level. She blinked at him, licking her lips, while the others watched in silence. "Can I help you, boss?" she squeaked.

"No rest for the wicked," he told her. "Find me those dragoons— find me where the survivors are camping, and do it before daybreak."

CHAPTER 45

Vlora spent another day watching the Vale, only to see the guard double and the shipments become more frequent and more thoroughly watched. The next afternoon, she visited one of the local hardware stores for rope, and waited till dusk before setting out.

She took a long route, climbing the base of the mountain just as darkness fully claimed the valley and positioning herself about a hundred yards from the entrance to the Vale on a steep, but not completely impassable, part of the cliff that led up and over to Jezzy's territory.

She had two problems, the way she saw it: The first was that she had to climb in the dark, risking her neck on an untried route. Her second problem was that she had no idea what to expect on the other side: a steep scree that would be impossible to descend quietly, a gentle hill, or just a straight drop down into the Vale.

A strong powder trance heightened her vision enough that climbing in the dark was, while still risky, not as perilous as it might be to another person. She began her ascent quickly, visualizing the path she had laid out and climbing more by feel than by sight. She had just enough experience climbing to know that her route would be easy for someone carrying the right gear, and dangerous for an amateur. She used her sorcerous strength to bridge the gap by keeping impossible holds with two fingers, climbing over shelves, and in one case leaping straight up the side of the cliff for the next handhold.

She made it to the top of the cliff without incident, where she secured her two ropes. The first she dropped back the way she'd come, so the descent would be easier. The second, she carried with her to the other side of the cliff and looked down into the Vale.

Once again, Flerring's description was spot on. Nighttime Vale was a wide, secluded valley with a creek running through the center. At one point it might have been picturesque. But the trees had been ripped up, the creek diverted into gold-panning sluices, and the ground covered in debris and a forest of dirty tents belonging to miners. It was a whole different town up here, and it extended on for a good mile before winding its way up into the mountains.

Vlora picked out the guards easily. They wandered the tents in regular intervals, carrying torches and blunderbusses. Others perched up on the mountainside, guarding the entrances to the mines with rifles lest some enterprising miner slip down in to recover a lucky gold nugget. Security was tight, and once again Vlora couldn't tell if it was because Jezzy wanted to keep her most profitable mine safe or if she was hiding the excavation of the godstone.

The way down was steep, but not impassable. Vlora played out the rope as she went, giving herself a guide for getting back up, and proceeded as quietly as possible. She reached the bottom and then began to make a wide circuit around the miners' camp, keeping eyes peeled for anything that would have looked out of place in the other valleys.

Her first target was an open pit at the very opposite end of the valley. Creeping slowly, she slipped past a guard stand and down to the creek, then made her way uphill past the panning sluices and across what had probably once been a field of wildflowers. It was a muddy cesspool now, and she grimaced with each squelch her boots made.

She was able to reach the edge of the pit without raising an alarm, and knelt beside it as she peered downward, searching the depths for anything of question.

Nothing stood out, no sharp angles, no special equipment. She opened her third eye to look into the Else, and had no better luck. No color of sorcery. When she turned and swept the Vale with her vision, it came up with the same story. If there *was* sorcery at work here, it must be well hidden.

A previous fear crept into her thoughts as she studied the Vale: What if Prime Lektor was working for Lindet? Never mind the why or the how. The implications were terrible. He had the knowledge of thousands of years in his head, and Lindet had the ambition to use that knowledge. If they were working together for some reason, Lindet suddenly became a more dangerous threat than even the Dynize.

Vlora attempted to ignore the worrisome niggle and continued her circuit of the valley. She reached out with her sorcerous senses, each moment accompanied by the feeling that *something* was out there. Pinpointing the source of that feeling was like nailing down a shadow, and she was forced to attribute it to her imagination and keep walking. Stones shifted beneath her feet, and on one occasion a guard called into the darkness. But she managed to finish her search without raising an alarm, finding herself back up on the cliff with her ropes several hours after she'd crossed the cliffs.

Frustration gripped her. Nothing. Absolutely nothing. It was just a damned gold mine, without any secrets, and she had risked her neck and wasted her entire week on a gamble that the stone was up here. She wanted to kill something, errantly wishing that an alarm would be raised so she could fight her way through. She silenced the foolish thought and returned the way she had come, climbing her rope down into the next valley.

She returned to her hotel room, where she examined a number of cuts on her hands and forearms earned from climbing a cliff in the dark. She cleaned up and wrapped the cuts on her forearms. It was almost three in the morning when she finally rolled into bed, unable to think about anything except how mad she was.

In the morning, she would have to go to Taniel and tell him her gamble had failed. He would soon be released, and they'd have to hunt down Prime together, and if that failed? She would have no choice but to bring in the Riflejacks.

An army would bring Prime out of hiding, for certain. But would he slaughter them all before she and Taniel could kill him?

She was just drifting off to sleep when a sound brought her bolt-upright in bed. She looked around, trying to find the source of it. Nearly a minute passed before the sound happened again, and several seconds later she heard something different: the distant, familiar noise of a rifle shot.

Vlora saw the bullet holes in her wall the same moment she heard the shot. Her heart suddenly beating hard at the close miss, she gathered her things as quickly as possible and left her room, trying not to sprint. Nohan had found her, and he was out there taking potshots at her room like it was some sort of game. It was a damned good thing he was a bad shot. She tried to find him, reaching out with her senses, but at this range and without the rising powder smoke to guide her, it was an impossible task.

She left her horse in the hotel stable and crossed the city by foot. There was still plenty of noise at this time of night, with dozens of brothels and bars open for business to miners celebrating a good day or lamenting a bad one. Brown Bear Burt's brothel was one such establishment, and she slipped inside and looked up to the second level, where she could see Burt sitting at his desk in a robe and pajamas, cigar in hand.

"I need to see your boss," she told the Palo woman standing guard at the bottom of Burt's staircase.

The woman held up a hand. "It's after hours."

"He's right there," Vlora said in frustration.

"He doesn't take visitors this time of night."

Vlora thought about shoving her way past. Instead, she shouted his name. Burt looked up from a book and blinked at her. "Bella," he said to the guard, "let her up!"

Bella glared daggers at Vlora but let her pass. Vlora jogged up the stairs and joined Burt in his office, where he offered her a cigar. Something about his demeanor had changed since they'd last spoke, and he looked more cautious, eyeing her thoughtfully.

"Good morning, Verundish," he said.

Vlora didn't return his smile. "I'm here to offer you my services."

This seemed to catch him off guard. "Oh? At this hour?" He rubbed his chin. "What makes you think I still need them?"

"Because everyone is panicking over that army headed this way, and Jezzy still has that other powder mage on her payroll."

"True, true," Burt admitted. He puffed on the stub of his cigar and put it out, then leaned forward at his desk and began to fiddle with a new cigar, running it thoughtfully under his nose and breathing deeply as he watched her. "About that army," he said slowly. "What do you know about it?"

"Absolutely nothing," she said in a tone that she hoped would discourage any more questions. He obviously suspected something—with several powder mages in town, Nohan couldn't have been the only one to make the logical leap that they were related to Lady Flint's army camped nearby.

"Nothing?" he echoed.

"I know they're not here for your gold," she said, hoping that shut him up.

"Oh." Burt fell back in his chair, an obvious look of relief on his face. "Well, then. What sort of services are you offering?"

"I'm offering to kill that other powder mage for you. I want to duel him. Public, private, I don't care. Set up a fight, and dangle a wager in front of Jezzy. The powder mage will come—I know he will." Vlora chewed on her lip, hoping that Burt would take her up on the offer. Nohan was no longer a nuisance. He had almost killed her tonight, and she wanted him out of the picture completely before she and Taniel went after Prime Lektor.

Burt cut the tip off the new cigar with a boz knife he pulled out of a drawer, his eyes staring at the middle distance between them. Slowly, he began to nod. "What do you want in exchange?"

"I want you to tell your men to stand down when the Riflejack army marches through. They aren't here for you. I don't want roadblocks or fighting or any such thing." She was taking an awful risk admitting she was with the Riflejacks—any fool who had read her description in the paper would be able to figure out who she really was. But she had to take that risk. She was out of time, and she needed to simplify the conclusion of this mission as much as possible.

"You're confident you can kill him despite your wounds?" Burt asked, lighting his cigar. "Those hands look pretty banged up."

"Nohan and I have already crossed paths once. He came away worse for it than I did."

He tapped one fingernail against the blade of the knife. "I have no interest in getting in anyone's way," he said. "If the Riflejacks aren't after my gold, I have no problem with them."

"You know that Lady Flint has a price on her head."

"And an army of riflemen out there," Burt replied. "I'm not stupid enough to tangle with Adran soldiers. Besides, the bounty is nothing compared to what this valley makes me every week. I'll offer Jezzy a wager and a duel. You do some killing, and I think we'll part friends."

"I would like that," Vlora said. She felt herself relax, knowing that the end of this damned mission was almost upon her. She was probably going to get all her soldiers killed in a confrontation with an ancient sorcerer, she reasoned, but at least she wasn't going to have to rub shoulders with these people anymore.

CHAPTER 46

What have you been doing in here the last couple of days?"
Michel looked up from his studies, taking a moment
to pull his head out of long lists of family, Household, and regiment names and blink across the empty room to where Ichtracia
lounged on a divan in the sunlight. He thought, for the hundredth
time, of a cat playing with a mouse before the final kill, and forced
a distracted smile onto his face. "Do you mind if I call you Tricia?"
he asked.

Ichtracia raised one eyebrow. "Only if I can call you Mick."

"I'd rather not...oh, I see your point. That's fair." Michel
looked back down at the book laid out on the table in front of him.
He was in a dusty room on the second floor of the capitol building where Yaret's people had stashed most of the records they had
brought with them from Dynize. The floor-to-ceiling bookshelves
were packed with ledgers, and thousands more sat in crates or piled
up in the corners. Very little of it was organized in any useful way
and Michel had spent far too long just doing that. He considered

Ichtracia's still-raised eyebrow and remembered that she'd asked him a question. "I'm cataloging everyone that Forgula has worked with since the beginning of the invasion."

"That seems like an awful lot of work."

Michel squinted at her. She was right, of course. It was mind-numbingly boring; something that he would prefer to leave to a small army of clerks. But he couldn't just tell her that he was combing the army regimental records for someone named Mara. "This is something we'd do in the Blackhats," he told her. "We had a file on just about every enemy of the state, and it included all their contacts and family members. It helped us unwind conspiracies and root out cells of dissidents."

Michel had his own opinions on how useful those files actually *were*, but he needed the excuse to be up here, combing through all of these names.

"You should have someone else do that," Ichtracia said. She stretched on the divan, a casual smile on her face, watching Michel in a way that made it very clear what she thought he *should* be doing. He'd spent the last two nights at her townhouse and learned firsthand how *that* particular rumor about Privilegeds happened to be true. It had been a welcome bit of relaxation, for sure, but it had also been incredibly distracting.

She was damned distracting. She'd been lounging on that divan for twenty minutes, and Michel had read the same regimental record over and over again since she arrived. He couldn't stop glancing up at her, watching her face when she wasn't paying attention.

He caught himself watching her again, and rubbed his eyes. This search wasn't going anywhere. He'd looked through at least twenty thousand names and not a single Mara had popped up—not among the civilians nor the military. As Emerald had suggested, it wasn't even a Dynize name. He felt like his hands were tied; his whole purpose here was to find and extract this Mara, but he'd run out of places to look.

"There was another bombing this afternoon."

"I heard," Michel answered. "I imagine the Blackhats won't stop their bombings just because their Dynize patron has been cut off."

"Sedial is just biding his time, by the way."

Michel looked up sharply. Ichtracia was cleaning her nails, lips pursed. Switching from the bombing to Sedial so quickly seemed like a non sequitur, but she didn't look distracted. Michel said, "I'm not sure what you mean."

"That stunt with Forgula—he'll take it personally. He takes everything like that personally. Sooner or later—and I'm guessing sooner—he'll start asking Yaret why the bombings haven't been stopped. He'll ask why Forgula's death didn't put an end to the attacks, and why Yaret's pet Blackhat hasn't dug up his former compatriots yet."

Michel was more than aware of all this—or at least he'd surmised it. Having his suspicions about Sedial's anger be confirmed wasn't exactly comforting. "I'm looking," he assured her. "We have hundreds of people out trying to dig up je Tura's hiding spot. We've searched every safe house that I know about and looted all their caches. We've arrested nearly four hundred known Blackhats."

"And yet je Tura is staying one step ahead of you."

Michel pursed his lips, trying to keep a neutral expression. Ichtracia was friendly, even charming, but he had to constantly remind himself that she was a Privileged. All she had to do was put on her gloves and she could break him in two, so it was best not to snap at her when she needled. "I have no idea how. Je Tura will need dozens of men to conduct his bombings. He needs a network to supply the powder, make the bombs, and case his targets. We've scrubbed the city of his people as thoroughly as we damned well can and yet he still evades me." Michel sat back, grinding his teeth.

"Oh, don't look so put out," Ichtracia murmured. She rolled off the divan and crossed the room, coming around behind Michel. To his surprise, she began to rub his shoulders. "Look, I see what you're doing here," she said gently. "If you create a web of conspiracy around Forgula, true or not, then you'll be able to keep Sedial on the back foot. You can accuse his people, keep the other Households in suspicion of his motives, and perhaps stay ahead of him."

Michel felt himself stiffen up. Ichtracia's tone was helpful, but he couldn't help but hear a note of something sinister in her words. That was *exactly* what he had convinced Yaret he was up here doing, and Ichtracia had seen through it effortlessly. It didn't bode well for his long-term career in Dynize politics.

"What I suggest," Ichtracia continued, "is that you focus on the Blackhats. Even if you attack all his people, you won't get ahead of Sedial. He's been playing this game for longer than you and I together have been alive. But if you continue to add to your accomplishments, you will be harder for him to take his vengeance on . . . and he has been known to be forgiving to people who make themselves useful."

Michel tried to enjoy the back rub, pressing the back of his head against her chest. Rumors had it that Ichtracia and her grandfather didn't exactly get along, so maybe she really was on his side. Or perhaps she was lulling him into a false sense of security.

He pushed the book away from him, eyes closed, trying to form his own plans. "Do I have a future with the Dynize?" he asked.

Ichtracia's hands stopped moving. "Why do you ask?"

"Because I'm an outsider. I know what happens to outsiders. The moment I am no longer useful, I will be either forgotten or destroyed."

"You should have thought of that before coming to our doorstep." Again, the tone was not unkind, but in it she made it very clear that she'd be offering little sympathy. She paused, then let out a soft sigh. "You may," she said cautiously. "You're quite clever, though whether you're just the right amount to keep from being eaten alive remains to be seen. You're also useful. I've always thought of the Dynize as xenophobic, but next to you Kressians we're practically loving of other cultures." She let go of his shoulders and crossed to the other side of the table from him. "Put away the books," she suggested. "Come to the Foxhead Club with me for the rest of the evening."

The Foxhead Club was a bit of a joke among the Dynize. They'd taken an exclusive gentleman's club in the center of Landfall and turned out the Kressians, making it available only to Dynize and Palo upper crust. Michel wondered briefly if he'd be turned away, but imagined that no one would turn away the guest of a Privileged. He leaned forward, examining her face, wondering what time it was. Perhaps he *should* take a break. "Where do you fit into all of this?" he asked.

"All of what?"

"This." Michel gestured expansively around him. "Sedial. Yaret. The Households. Tenik told me that Privileged aren't allowed to be political in your culture. In Kressian culture they have their fingers in everything, and…" Michel trailed off, realizing that he'd let himself forget who he was talking to. When he was in the Blackhats, he probably would have balked at even addressing a Privileged, let alone speaking so candidly with one.

Ichtracia regarded him casually, tapping on the table with one long fingernail. "It is complicated, as you may imagine." She paused, frowning down at her hands, and for a moment Michel thought that perhaps her cool, collected mask had slipped. "Do you know about dragonmen?" she asked.

"I've heard the rumors."

"Dragonmen and Privileged hold the same position in Dynize society. We belong to the emperor. We are not people, nor citizens. We are tools. When we are needed, we serve without flinching, without questioning. When we are not needed, we are left to our own devices. We have no power of our own, not in a political sense, but we have a sort of power simply by being tools of the emperor."

Michel opened his mouth to respond, but found he had nothing to say. The idea of being a possession had never even occurred to him, and the slight crack in Ichtracia's voice when she spoke of it told volumes. "I..." He hesitated. "If you're a possession of the emperor's, and Sedial is the emperor's man on this continent, then..."

Ichtracia's slipping facade suddenly became cool and casual again and she regarded him with a dispassionate sort of annoyance. "I wouldn't worry too much about your own skin. Sedial may think he is the emperor, but he definitely is not. It's no secret that he and I do not get along. I have no intention of handing you over to him."

"I didn't mean—"

She cut him off. "It's all right. You want to know where you stand, and I won't begrudge you that. So here is this: I find you fascinating. You are an innocuous and boring person on the surface, but there are layers beneath your facade that I think I'd enjoy peeling away. I intend on playing with you for at least a few months before I cut you loose and move on to the husband of a minister or the daughter of a general. I will enjoy our time together, and I suspect you intend on doing the same. Do not expect anything more of me than you would a tool of the state, and I won't expect more of you than I would a spy who knows he needs someone to protect him from the lions among my people."

For a moment, Michel felt as if he'd been slapped. The shock was gone within seconds, and he found himself laughing.

"What's so funny?" Ichtracia demanded.

Michel reached out a hand. "Thank you for that. It's incredibly refreshing." She knew that he was using her to protect himself from Sedial, and she didn't give a damn. Somehow that knowledge relieved Michel, the idea that he wasn't hiding just one more thing from another person. "I'm sorry if I'm being rude, but you're far more pragmatic than I expected. I like that."

Ichtracia took his hand with a look of wariness. Slowly, that feline smile spread across her face. "Don't apologize. It's tiresome, and I don't want to find you tiresome quite yet." She released his hand and slid the ledger he'd been reading off the table with a clatter. "Your work is done for the night. Come with me to the club."

"Can I meet you there?"

"How long?"

"An hour."

"Don't keep me waiting." With a single glance back, Ichtracia strode from the room.

Michel waited for about ten minutes before cleaning up the ledgers he'd been looking through and then scrawling a quick note on a piece of paper and heading for the door. He stopped for a moment before leaving the room to look around at all the records, wondering how much longer he should continue with this farce. Ichtracia was right—he couldn't focus on looking through records anymore. He needed to focus on the Blackhats. He could abandon the idea of attacking Sedial through Forgula's associates, and also set aside his search for Mara.

At least for the time being.

He headed across town on foot, doubling back and waiting at intervals to be sure he wasn't followed, then headed down into Emerald's morgue, where he found Emerald standing over the open chest cavity of a cadaver, a length of intestine in one hand. He paused his work as Michel entered and shook his head.

"You obviously haven't been shot again. I hope you have a damn good reason for coming down here so soon."

"Can you get a message to Taniel?"

"Hmph," Emerald responded, setting down the intestine and resting his hand on the cold, dead forehead of the man lying on his workbench. "It's possible."

Michel pulled out the note he'd written and double-checked it, taking a deep breath. Perhaps it was his recent victory against Forgula—perhaps it was this new relationship with Ichtracia—but he felt like he needed to focus on his work for the Dynize. No more searching ledgers for a mysterious name. The note simply said:

Target can't be found. Need more information. Will remain in place. It was written in a cipher he and Taniel had come up with years ago. "Get this to Taniel. Any idea how long until I can get an answer?"

Emerald nodded at Michel to set the note on his workbench. "Two to six weeks. Maybe longer, if I have trouble finding him. I'll see what I can do." He sighed, clearly irritated, and pointed at Michel with a bloody hand. "You have to stop coming down here. If I hear back from Taniel, I'll find you and let you know. Until then..."

"Right, right. I'll be easy to find." Michel backed out and headed up to the street. He stopped, checking his watch and realizing he'd be half an hour later than he told Ichtracia. "I'll be either in bed with the enemy or in a shallow grave somewhere."

CHAPTER 47

Styke sat in the deep, oppressive darkness of the Hock, listening to the sounds of the forest and the distant snores of lancers in their beds. Unable to sleep, he'd found a spot on the edge of a ravine some fifty yards from the camp where he could see the smallest sliver of starlight through the thick branches overhead. Somewhere nearby, a critter stirred in the underbrush, approaching him slowly and fleeing when he shifted to get more comfortable.

His mind was a mess of conflicting thoughts as he considered the whole of his life for the first time since the labor camps and wondered if perhaps he was not the person he'd always fancied himself. He thought of Valyaine's statement about Styke expecting loyalty and obedience but never giving his own. He thought about Celine's defiance in defense of Ka-poel, reminding him that he would—and had—gone off on his own and just expected the lancers to be there when he returned.

It was one thing to be called a hypocrite by a full-grown man he intended to kill. It was a whole other to have that confirmed by a little girl.

Styke wondered if perhaps, all these years, even while losing himself in the labor camps, he had bought into his own legend: that of an unkillable monster, a force of nature. Maybe deep down he had begun to believe what people said about him.

He heard someone coming from the camp through the underbrush toward him. He could tell from the weight of the step and the way she moved that it was Ibana. She joined him up there, settling down next to him and pushing a skin into his hands. He smelled wine and took a sip.

"What are you doing up here?" she asked. "It's four in the morning."

"Couldn't sleep," Styke responded.

They shared a few companionable minutes in silence, handing the wineskin back and forth, and Styke felt a calmness come over him from Ibana's presence. They had not been this close—physically—since the war and it felt good to feel her hand brush his as they exchanged the wine. She'd been a guidepost since the beginning of the Mad Lancers, his levelheaded second-in-command, the one who would keep everything running even when he had to meet with Lindet or assassinate an enemy general or any of the other shit he got up to.

"I've been thinking..." Styke began.

"I've warned you to let me do the thinking." There was a long pause, and Ibana let out a soft sigh. "About what?"

"About being a hypocrite."

Ibana snorted. "Still? Is this because Valyaine called you one?"

"Celine did, too, just a couple hours ago. I think that I am, and I don't really like the feeling it gives me. I've always looked down on officers and politicians as hypocrites and cowards, and now, so long into this life, I realize that I am what I've always derided."

Ibana remained silent, so Styke continued. "I *am* a hypocrite, but I think I am too far along for it to be helped. To break my hypocrisy, I would have to swear allegiance to some higher power, or I would have to dismiss the Mad Lancers and head off on my own path. I am not willing to do either." He felt Ibana shake beside him, and it took him several moments to realize that she was laughing at him. "What the pit is so funny?"

She put a hand on his thigh and leaned over, and he was surprised to feel her lips against his cheek. She pulled away, wiping her sleeve across her eyes and chuckling. "You really think you're a hypocrite? I'll give you one thing: You *were* a hypocrite. Your double standard during the war was something we all decided to let slide because of who and what you are."

"So you discussed this?" Styke asked, incredulous. "Behind my back?"

"You think you're the only one to bad-mouth your superiors?"

Styke felt stung by the revelation. It was so simple. So stupid and obvious. Another hypocrisy. "What am I?" he asked.

"You're Ben Styke."

"Because you say I am," Styke insisted. He felt angry, confused. He was not used to delving this deep into his own insecurities. He had always trampled them underfoot, ignoring them like so much garbage, and moved on with his life. Why couldn't he now? The old way had gotten results, and he *needed* results right now.

"You're not just Ben Styke because we say you are, though I admit that the allegiance of the people who follow you gives your name weight," Ibana said thoughtfully. "You're Ben Styke because you always lead the charge. Because you can break a Warden's back and crack a dragonman's skull. Because you're big and strong enough to do whatever you want and yet you still have a sense of right and wrong. Even if it's a twisted one."

Styke stared through the darkness at his crippled hands, feeling the twinges in his wrist when he moved his fingers. He thought about how his doubt and pain went away when he wrapped his fingers around the lance and how all his other failings seemed to disappear when he charged into the face of the enemy.

"You're not a hypocrite, Ben," Ibana said. "You were, but you aren't anymore."

"I haven't changed."

"Haven't you?" Ibana demanded. "The old you wouldn't have spared Tenny Wiles or Valyaine. Definitely not Dvory. Not a chance. The old you wouldn't have sworn allegiance to Lady Flint. Seeing the way you look at her is the first time I've seen you truly respect a superior officer." She ticked off two fingers, then a third. "You took Celine under your wing, and you've always *hated* kids. Besides"—Ibana laughed again—"you didn't ask any of us to follow you. We came because we saw that you needed us—not because we needed you."

Styke felt his inner turmoil begin to ebb. "You're a better liar than I remember."

"No lies," Ibana said. "Maybe I dressed it up a little. But it's still the truth. And I still stand behind what I said before: We're here now, and we're all depending on you to remain Ben Styke. You can be a different man and still lead the charges."

"Do you think the men doubt me because I let Tenny, Valayine, and Dvory live?" Styke asked.

"Look, I know I gave you shit before, but to be honest…any grumbles that might have spread were silenced when we came upon you facing down six dragonmen," Ibana said.

Styke chuckled. "I didn't do that by choice."

"But you still did it. Not a lot of people see six dragonmen and draw a knife. Most will run. Pit, I'd run."

They finished off the wine, sitting in silence for some time before Ibana drew in a quick breath, then laughed softly.

"What?" Styke asked.

"It's Celine," she said, as if it were the simplest thing in the world.

"What do you mean?"

"I mean that all these things—these doubts, these changes— that have come over you, they're not because you faced a firing squad or spent a decade in the camps. They're because you have a child now."

Styke felt his face flush. "She's not mine."

"Oh, please. I've heard you refer to her as 'my girl.' You're not fooling anyone, least of all me. Celine is your child whether she came from your loins or not, and that's made you a different man." She turned toward him, and even in the darkness he could feel her piercing stare. "Tell me, do you fear death?"

"Of course," Styke scoffed. "Everyone fears death."

"There's a difference between being suicidal and not fearing death," Ibana said, "and the Ben I knew never feared death. So do you?"

Styke thought about it for a moment. Death was such an abstract notion: It always felt so far away, but he knew better than most that it could strike at any moment. He'd been within a knife blade of death on hundreds of occasions, and sometimes closer. When he said he feared death, it was a mechanical lie, said because that's what normal people were supposed to say. He had never feared death. Even when Fidelis Jes had cut him down, leaving him in a puddle of his own blood, he had not feared death. He had only feared leaving this world without taking Fidelis Jes with him.

And, he realized, he had feared one other thing.

"I don't," he said. "But I fear leaving Celine alone."

"I call it the same thing," Ibana said, sitting back. "Fearing your death because you won't go on living versus fearing your death because someone else needs you is just semantics. You fear for Celine, and I've never known you to fear. You look at her in a way you've never looked at a friend or a lover, including me."

Styke realized that he heard a note of hurt in her voice. He swallowed, uncertain of what to say, and decided to let it go. She had not meant for him to hear it.

He felt her hand on his thigh again, and her body shifted toward his; her face drew close. "Quiet the inner demons, Ben," she told him. "They've never been worth your time before, and they certainly shouldn't be now."

They were interrupted by the sound of hooves along the trail on the ridge above them. Ibana pulled away, and Styke listened as the hooves descended the road down into the hollow where the lancers camped. He heard a distant voice that he recognized as Ferlisia's call his name.

Ibana sighed, slapping him on the shoulder. "Go on. You've got work to do."

Reluctantly, Styke descended the ridge and headed into the camp. He found Ferlisia outside his empty tent, scowling at one of the guards. He put his hand on her shoulder, turning her around and gesturing for her to lower her voice. "Did you find them?" he asked.

"I did," she said excitedly. "They're camped about three miles from here. They're not trying to hide, but they picked a place that would be suicide for us to attack: a hill just inside the eastern edge of the Hock with steep sides and only one spot that horses could easily climb. They have lots of wounded men and horses."

Styke took a deep breath. Ka-poel would be there, no doubt. She was resourceful enough that she was probably still alive— unless the enemy commander had orders to kill her in particular. He lifted his head, seeing Ibana emerge from the woods. "Go find Jackal for me," he told her.

"Are we going to attack?" Ibana asked.

"Not exactly."

CHAPTER 48

Styke and Jackal were led to the dragoon camp by Ferlisia, arriving just before sunrise. Too late to work beneath the cover of darkness, he sent Ferlisia back to camp and he and Jackal huddled down in the Hock and waited and watched throughout the day.

The dragoon camp was much as Ferlisia described it: packed onto a long, wooded hill just inside the Hock. The hill was surrounded on all four sides by steep, rocky cliffs, between ten and fifty feet high, making it a solid defensive position against any force and doubly impossible to attack with cavalry. There appeared to be only one easy way up—a gentle slope pointing east less than two dozen feet wide and guarded heavily.

The cries of wounded men and horses could be heard throughout the day, and the occasional carbine blast sounded as they put down lame animals. It became abundantly clear that the dragoons didn't care if Styke knew where they were. Their defensive position was unbreakable by less than a brigade of infantry, and they knew that Styke didn't have that kind of firepower at his command.

Nor, they must have surmised, did Styke want to take the time to starve them off their high ground. The Dynize could wait for as long as their supplies held out, tending to their men. The ambush must have cooled their commander, making Styke doubly angry at Ka-poel for sneaking off. If she'd stuck around, the lancers would already be on their way to the coast.

Styke lay on his stomach in the underbrush about a hundred yards from the entrance to the hill, watching the dragoons change their guard as the daylight began to wane. Jackal lay beside him, apparently asleep, until his eyes suddenly opened and he got up onto his elbows, pointing at the hill.

"It's an old Palo settlement," he said.

"Eh?"

"I've been talking to the spirits. That hill. It was home to a village once. It's been a few hundred years, but there are some old spirits left hanging about. They fled because your bone-eye is there."

Styke snorted. The idea that Ka-poel could scare long-dead spirits still seemed preposterous. But at least it confirmed that she was, indeed, here. "Is she still alive?"

"According to the spirits, yes. It's hard to coax them to come this close to her."

"Can they tell us anything about the hill?"

"They called it the Castle, back when they lived there. Or their word for 'castle,' anyway. As long as they held it, their tribe could not be ousted from their land."

"What happened?"

"Brudanian soldiers. They wanted to clear the Hock so that trappers could use it. Lost half their regiment taking the Castle from the Palo." Jackal waggled a finger at the entrance to the Castle. "They tried to assault that and failed. Ended up putting ladders on the lowest cliff on the south side and overwhelming the occupants with sheer numbers."

"Show me."

Styke and Jackal pulled back beneath the closest ridgeline and took a long, circuitous route around the Castle. The dragoons had plenty of scouts, but they seemed to focus their efforts deeper in the Hock, at the halfway point between their camp and that of the Mad Lancers. Other than hiding on occasion, Styke and Jackal reached the south side of the Castle without issue.

The cliffs here were indeed the lowest—perhaps ten or fifteen feet of near-vertical rock. A single dragoon stood watch at the top, peering into the forest as darkness began to spread, cradling his carbine. Styke continued along the south side and looped around to the west, searching for better spots to climb the cliffs and finding nothing that looked promising. He returned to Jackal, falling onto his hands and knees to watch that one dragoon patrol the top of the shallow cliff.

"Do you remember the fortress at New Adopest?" Styke asked.

Jackal's placid face wrinkled, the hint of a smile on his lips. "I remember it."

"I'm not as spry as I used to be," Styke said. He wanted very badly to climb the cliff and do the job himself, but he did not have confidence in his own abilities to do so in silence. He shot a glance at the wound on Jackal's leg. "Are you?"

"None of us are," Jackal replied. "But I think I'm up to the task." He touched his leg. "This looks worse than it is, and there were a lot more guards at New Adopest."

Twilight was quickly upon them, and Styke and Jackal got to their feet. They moved slowly through the underbrush, careful not to make too much noise, until they were at the very base of the Castle cliff. The guard had changed, and another man now patrolled this small section, torch in hand.

Jackal waited until the guard had passed, and began his ascent, climbing the cliffside in almost complete silence. He shimmied up, grasping the old roots and reaching the top in less than a minute, just as the guard came back in his direction. Styke pressed himself against the cliff to hide from the light of the torch.

Silence followed, though Styke strained to listen for a grunt or a yell. A few moments later he heard a distinctive "Psst" and began his own ascent. He reached the top to find Jackal standing over the body of the sentry. Jackal stood stiffly, his posture all wrong, like a deer too scared to run.

"Everything okay?" Styke whispered.

Jackal nudged the body with his foot. "He just offed himself."

"What?"

Jackal came close, leaning in to whisper in Styke's ear. "I stepped on a twig. He turned to look at me and instead of shouting out, he drew his knife and slit his own throat."

The hairs on the back of Styke's neck stood up, goose bumps spreading on his arms. He knelt beside the body and found the guard clutching his own knife, still lightly convulsing as he silently bled out onto the dirt. Styke reached out to touch him but pulled his hand back, thinking better of it. He leaned over, putting his nose up next to the body. He took a deep breath, catching hints of copper.

He stood up to find Jackal's knife out, breath held, staring toward a pair of Dynize dragoons about thirty feet away. Styke held his breath, waiting for a shout, as the pair slowly approached them.

Styke readied his boz knife, preparing to spring forward when they got close enough, but was arrested when they spoke out in unison in perfect Adran. "You're wanted at the commander's tent, Colonel Styke."

Jackal's lips were pulled back in a snarl, nostrils flared. "I can't see a spirit for a mile," he said. "Even the ones I was talking to back in the forest have fled."

"Please," the pair of dragoons said again. "You're wanted at the commander's tent." Their words were mechanical, their backs straight and faces forward, though they stood at an angle to Styke and Jackal. "Follow us." They turned in unison and marched into the camp.

Styke kept his knife handy, looking at Jackal and seeing the whites of his eyes. He'd never seen Jackal this startled, not even facing down Privileged sorcery on an open battlefield.

"I've never seen anything like this," Jackal whispered. "Is this her sorcery?"

"I think it is," Styke said. "Or the sorcery of a bone-eye who wants us to think it's Ka-poel. But I didn't know the bone-eyes are capable of this kind of control." Hesitating just a moment longer, he followed the pair of guards into the camp, Jackal bringing up a reluctant rear.

The camp was quiet, with the occasional cookfire burning to coals and only a handful of Dynize up and about. None of them seemed to notice Styke and Jackal, and he wondered if they were also under some kind of sorcery or if they were just that inattentive within their own camp. He heard the occasional scream or moan from the east—the wounded from the other day's ambush—and they passed a corral in the open center of the hill where nearly three hundred horses were tied up for the night.

The two guards suddenly stopped in between a row of tents, stepping in different directions and gesturing for Styke to go ahead. He looked over his shoulder at Jackal, who still looked like an animal who wasn't sure whether to attack or run. With a shrug, Styke continued between the two guards.

There was a large clearing in front of a tent bigger than all the others around it—no doubt belonging to the company commander. A well-stocked fire and a handful of torches illuminated a macabre scene in the middle of the clearing. Two dozen Dynize soldiers— all of them wearing epaulets that marked them as officers—sat cross-legged in two rows on either side of the clearing. They didn't look up when Styke approached, or seem to move at all. They were so inhumanly still that he wondered if they were still alive.

Across from the tent stood the officer that Styke had brawled with when they ambushed the Mad Lancers a few weeks back. Her hands were clasped behind her back, her spine straight. She had the same expression as Jackal with eyes wide and lips pulled back, but hers was as strangely frozen as those of the men flanking her.

Years ago, Styke had been present when a gift had been sent from the king of Kez to then-governor Lindet of Redstone. The gift consisted of several life-sized facsimiles of Kez soldiers done up in wax. They were so well done that they looked like the real thing, until they began to melt in the Fatrastan heat. This scene had the same uncanny strangeness to it.

Sprawled in a camp chair like a bored queen receiving guests was Ka-poel. She lifted a hand in greeting to Styke, the other propped under her chin as she gazed at the dragoon commander.

Styke put away his knife and gestured for Jackal to do the same.

"I thought you were going to come for me this morning."

Styke nearly jumped out of his skin. The words came from the mouth of the commander, but they were spoken in perfect Adran and in a voice that did *not* belong to a burly, war-weary dragoon officer. The tone was soft-spoken, the voice a gentle soprano with a hint of a laugh to it. He looked at Ka-poel, who hadn't moved except to adopt a rather smug smile. He pointed at the officer. "Is that you?"

Ka-poel nodded.

Styke forced himself to relax. He walked down the line of frozen officers, leaning over to feel the soft breath coming from their lips and wave a hand in front of their eyes. He even pushed one over, watching him topple like a statue and remain cross-legged without so much as a flinch. Styke finished his examination by walking around the dragoon commander, examining her flushed face. Upon this closer look, he found her just as frozen as her men—except the eyes. They stared straight ahead, but there was life in them, and if he was forced to guess, he would say that she was still there, under the surface.

Styke wondered at this show of power. He'd been told that Ka-poel was more powerful than her fellow bone-eyes by several orders of magnitude, but that she was unpracticed. Could an enemy bone-eye do this to Styke? Could *she* do this to Styke? The answer to that second question was an obvious yes, and it made Styke's skin crawl.

He considered what Ji-Orz had told him earlier this week, likening the sorcery of a bone-eye to rape. The thought—and all these frozen faces—made Styke uncomfortable.

Jackal still stood outside the clearing, looking like he wanted nothing to do with any of this. Ka-poel barely seemed to notice his presence, and Styke waved him off. "Go back to camp," he told Jackal. "Tell Ibana that everything is in control here. We'll be back soon."

The words were barely out of his mouth when Jackal took off into the darkness.

"Will he be attacked leaving the camp?" Styke asked Ka-poel.

"No," she answered through the mouth of the commander.

"Do you have control of the whole camp?" he asked.

"Not exactly," Ka-poel said. "I have about a third of them. Enough to remain unmolested."

Styke walked around the commander once more, then over to Ka-poel. Despite her smugness, he could see she was uneasy. He wondered how much practice she had being up close and personal with the people she controlled. "We didn't find this camp until almost light this morning," he said in answer to her earlier question. "I didn't know you had things under control, so I didn't want to risk coming during the day."

Ka-poel pursed her lips, nodding as if this were a satisfactory explanation. "I'm almost done here. We can go soon."

Styke faced her, leaning over her until their faces were inches apart. "I want to know why you're here."

"Answers," she replied shortly. She was unintimidated by his size, returning his look coolly. Styke reminded himself that he was just as unintimidated by her sorcery. Disconcerted by it, yes. But it did not scare him, and he wanted her to know that.

"What kind of answers?"

That uncertainty that he had seen in her eyes suddenly came to the forefront. She scowled distractedly into the darkness. "The kind that I cannot get from anyone else but a Dynize officer," she said.

"Such as?"

Ka-poel did not answer. She sighed heavily, and Styke left her to stand in front of the commander. "Is she still in there?" he asked.

"Yes, she is. They all are, to different degrees."

"I want to talk to her."

Ka-poel's eyebrows rose. She shrugged, and a sheen of sweat suddenly sprang to the face of the Dynize commander, her eyes widening further, face tensing. "What do you want?" she snarled in Dynize. This, Styke realized, was her real voice.

"Who are you?" Styke asked in Palo. He repeated the question slowly to make sure she understood.

The sweating grew more severe. He wondered if she was struggling against Ka-poel's hold on her, and if it was possible to break it. "Can you force her to answer?" he asked Ka-poel, forestalling the answer by holding up a hand to Ka-poel and speaking to the officer directly. "No, wait. I don't give a shit who you are. Tell me why you're after me. Didn't Ka-Sedial think the dragonmen were enough?"

"Dragonmen?" the commander echoed.

"The ones who've been following me. They're not with you?"

The commander let out a hissing breath. "They're after you? If I had known that, I wouldn't have bothered."

"What do you mean? What do you know of them?"

"All I know is that six disgraced dragonmen were freed by Ka-Sedial after Landfall fell. They were given the task of assassinating a Fatrastan officer in order to redeem themselves in the eyes of the emperor. That's all I was told."

"So if you're not with them, who are you?"

The sweating intensified again, her eyes flicking from Styke's face to Ka-poel and back again. "My name is Lin-Merce," she said in a low voice. "And I'm here because you killed my sister."

"You weren't commanded to come after me?"

"No. I took my command and deserted the army."

Styke paused. Over the years, he'd had plenty of people come after him for revenge. He was, after all, a fairly prolific killer. But he'd never had someone abandon their post for the express purpose of vengeance. "And the consequences?" he asked.

"I can never go home." The voice came out in a whisper. Lin-Merce stared into Styke's eyes with more hatred than he'd ever seen in a human being, and he was suddenly struck by a rare moment of real compassion. She had given up everything for her vengeance. She had ambushed him; she had crossed swords with him. She'd even managed to outsmart him more than once over the last few weeks. Without Ka-poel's interference, she might have bounced back and still managed to kill Styke.

He could see in her eyes that she knew she was dead. She *knew* the power a bone-eye was capable of, and she clearly knew by now that Ka-poel was something special. But that hate was still there. Her whole body trembled as she fought for even a fraction of control so that she could strike at the man who'd taken her sister.

He wondered if he would feel the same about his own.

"When did I kill her?" he asked.

"She was with the cavalry you fought north of Landfall."

"When you first landed?"

"No. After your general fled the city. I was told you ran her down, trampling her beneath the feet of your horse like a dog."

Styke recalled *that* battle quite well. Windy River, Flint's men had called it afterward. The Mad Lancers had attempted a flanking move only to run into a superior force doing the same thing. The battle had been brutal, but the lancers had prevailed. "In battle," Styke said thoughtfully, "we're all dogs."

"She was everything to me," Lin-Merce whispered.

Styke gave a heavy sigh, walking around Lin-Merce and letting his eyes run over the lines of men sitting obediently, under the thrall of Ka-poel's sorcery. In another life, Lin-Merce might be him. These men might be Mad Lancers. And Ka-poel might be on the Dynize side.

"I have more to ask her." The voice came from Lin-Merce's mouth, but it belonged to Ka-poel.

"Every moment she lives is agony," Styke replied. "She doesn't deserve that."

"I don't care."

"I do." Styke stepped swiftly up behind Lin-Merce and took a solid grip on her hair. "You're the only cavalry commander who's ever gotten the best of me," he said in her ear, before drawing his boz knife across her throat. He pulled, going deep, the metal rasping along her spine, and he held her body as the blood soaked them both, until well after she stopped convulsing. Finally, he lowered her to the ground.

He knelt next to the corpse for a few moments before looking up at Ka-poel. "Oh, stop glaring at me," he told her. "You're like a goddamn child playing with ants compared to these. Either let them go, or let me kill them."

The glaring continued, and Styke stepped over the corpse and approached Ka-poel. "I know exactly what kind of a monster I am, but I don't approve of suffering. You can find your answers from someone else. She earned herself a quick death." He turned away, then thought better of it and swung back around to face Ka-poel. "If you have this kind of power, you should be using it to keep my men alive. You should strike first—not wait until we've taken such a damned battering. Figure out *what* you are, and be it. But don't toy with people beneath you, and don't waste the lives of my lancers."

He gave her one last long look and then headed back to camp.

CHAPTER 49

Michel was unable to stop thinking about how Ichtracia had the softest, most comfortable sheets he'd ever touched in his life.

He lay in her bed, staring at the ceiling, watching the late-morning light slowly inch across while he *tried* to focus on the Blackhats. Where was je Tura hiding? How had he arrested so many Blackhats without a single soul knowing where to find that asshole? How did je Tura keep conducting these bombings?

The questions kept running through his head, but he kept coming back to Ichtracia's sheets. She said they were some sort of rare silk from Dynize. Michel had slept on silk sheets once or twice, and he didn't remember them feeling anything like this. Even when he rubbed them between his fingers, it was like touching gossamer—ethereal, lacking any kind of substance. Like sleeping on the steam from a kettle in that split second after it had cooled enough to touch but before it had evaporated.

He glanced over at Ichtracia. She, apparently, had no problem sleeping until noon. She was still snoring softly, her face looking peaceful and pleased in that way of a child dreaming of something nice. She was, he'd decided, a genuinely pleasant person who happened to be a Privileged. Maybe not a *good* person. She spoke of killing and torture with the offhanded manner of someone who is well acquainted with both. But she was quietly charming in a way that almost made Michel forget about the pair of runed gloves in her breast pocket or next to the bed.

Michel slipped out of bed and headed to the window to watch the afternoon traffic. "You're letting yourself get distracted because you can't find the girl," he muttered to himself, glancing over his shoulder at Ichtracia's sleeping form.

"I'm protecting myself," he answered.

"And damn well enjoying it in the meantime."

"I can mix work and play," he insisted under his breath. "I've done it before."

"Not when there was this much on the line. You went off the road the moment you decided that punching Forgula in public was a good idea. You've become too exposed here—too known."

Michel sucked on his teeth, trying to come up with a rebuttal to his own accusations. Nothing came to mind. Back when he worked his way up through the Blackhats as an informant, he'd gone deep into enemy territory by joining separatist movements and rubbing shoulders with propagandists and gangs. He'd never infiltrated a damned government.

"Yes, you have." He laughed at himself quietly. "You're confusing Blackhat Michel with real Michel again. Your whole damn life is an infiltration. Do you think that the Dynize are any more dangerous than the Blackhats?" He briefly considered Taniel's warnings about the bone-eyes, but his thoughts were broken by a soft moan behind him.

He turned to find Ichtracia stretching languidly, giving him that cat-in-a-sunbeam smile that she seemed to use so often.

"What are you muttering about over there?" she asked.

"Work," he answered truthfully. He continued. "I'm trying to figure out where je Tura has gone."

"You're very focused."

"It's my job. I'm not allowed to not think about these things."

Ichtracia sat up, the sheets pooling around her stomach. She reached into the drawer of her nightstand and produced a mala pipe, lighting it expertly with a match and taking a long drag before holding it toward him.

"This early in the day?" he asked.

She let smoke curl out her nostrils. "One advantage to being a tool of the state is that I don't think about work. Once in a while I am pointed at something that needs to be destroyed or people who need to die and . . ." She made a "poof" gesture with one hand, then took another drag of the mala and set the pipe aside. Her tone was careless, but Michel thought he saw a tightness in the corner of her eyes.

"I'm taking your advice to heart," Michel said. "I'm going to ignore Sedial and focus on making myself useful to your government."

"*Our* government," Ichtracia corrected. "Or have you already forgotten your place, Devin-Michel?"

"Our government," Michel agreed. "Sorry, it takes some getting used to."

Ichtracia watched him with a soft smile, eyes half-lidded, and for a moment Michel harbored a fear that she could see through him into his secrets—that she'd caught all his tiny verbal mistakes and considered ulterior motives and already suspected him of being something more than either a Blackhat or a turncoat.

Ichtracia patted the bed beside her, and Michel took two involuntary steps forward before his ears caught the sound of a carriage coming to a stop in front of the townhouse. He backpedaled to the window and looked down to find a carriage with the red and black curtains of a Dynize dignitary. There were a dozen soldiers on horseback surrounding the carriage, and it didn't take long for Michel to find out why: A footman opened the door, and Ka-Sedial stepped out, knuckling his back while the footman ran to Ichtracia's door.

"Ka-Sedial is here," Michel warned, just two seconds before there was a hammering down below them.

"Shit." Ichtracia stashed the mala pipe and leapt from bed, snatching a silk robe from the floor. She threw it over her shoulders as she joined him at the window, looking down on her grandfather, and Michel was surprised to hear real venom in her voice. "I sent the damned servants away so I could enjoy you." The pounding continued, and she swore again. "Stay here, and don't you dare get dressed."

Barefoot and in just a robe, Ichtracia ran from the room. Michel listened to her footsteps down the hall and then the stairs. A moment later, he heard the door open underneath the bedroom.

He pressed himself against the wall, watching the group in the street outside. Sedial's bodyguard remained in their saddles while the footman returned to Sedial and gave a half bow. Sedial seemed to hesitate, and Michel couldn't help but think that if he had a rifle in hand, he could do more damage to the Dynize with a single bullet from this angle than all the work he could possibly do for Taniel for the rest of his life.

To his surprise, a second carriage pulled up behind Ka-Sedial's. There were no bodyguards, but Sedial gestured to the carriage as if it was expected. A Palo woman emerged, perhaps nineteen or twenty, and joined Sedial in the street. Taking her arm, cane in the other hand, Sedial walked toward Ichtracia's door.

Curious, Michel slipped on his pants and crept into the hallway, eyeballing the distance between the joists beneath the floorboards in an effort to avoid the creakiest parts of the floor. He could hear Sedial and Ichtracia speaking, but it wasn't until he was nearly at the top of the stairs that he could hear their conversation well. They spoke in quick-fire Dynize, making it a little hard for Michel to follow.

"...not to come here yourself. If you want me, send someone for me," Ichtracia was saying.

Sedial's voice was a little quieter, but there was a tone of irritated dismissal in his tone that sounded nothing like his public persona. "I'll visit you whenever I want. Are you worried I'll walk in on you with whatever slut you're riding lately?"

Michel nearly gasped at the strength of the language—he couldn't imagine *anyone* speaking that way to a Privileged.

Sedial continued. "There's no one here now, is there?"

"No, there's no one here," Ichtracia spat at her grandfather. "You're the one that's brought a stranger into my home. Who is this?"

Michel heard someone pacing. It was too slow and deliberate to be Ichtracia, and the sudden rap of a cane punctuated the footsteps. "I'm hearing rumors, Ichtracia, that you've taken in that Blackhat spy. I'll give you one chance to deny them, and all will be forgiven."

"Forgiven?" Ichtracia mocked. "You have absolutely no say over who I take into my bed."

"I do when they're enemy spies."

"He is a member of Yaret's Household."

"Even worse."

Ichtracia continued as if Sedial hadn't interjected. "He's handed most of the city's Blackhats over to us in a matter of weeks."

"He forced one of my people to commit suicide in public. Forgula was valuable to me."

Ichtracia barked a laugh, and Michel briefly entertained himself by imagining Sedial's face at being mocked openly. "You're pissed because he outmaneuvered her. Forgula was a bitch, and it was cathartic to finally see her get her dues." Ichtracia paused briefly, lowering her voice. "You were using enemies of the state to destroy your enemies *within* the state. You would execute anyone else for trying to do the same."

"*My* enemies weaken the state," Sedial growled, rapping the floor again with his cane. "Clumsy, foolish ministers like Yaret slow down our progress here."

"Ministers like Yaret keep the state together."

"I *am* the state!"

Michel was once again surprised to hear something like that so boldly stated, but he'd begun to get the impression that this conversation was a continuation of many more just like it. He heard Ichtracia give an angry sigh. "You're an old man hoping to leave a legacy of something other than blood before death finally claims you."

"You speak as if a legacy of blood is a bad one." There was a long silence, and Sedial continued in a softer tone. "I didn't come here to fight."

"Then what did you come for?" Ichtracia demanded.

"I came to tell you that you're needed down south. We have every Privileged in the city working on the stone, and they've made very little progress. Your help is sorely needed."

Michel shifted a half step closer to the stairs, listening carefully as the voices lost some of their heat. Ichtracia replied to her grandfather after a moment's hesitation. "I have told you before, I will not go near that thing."

"Even if I give you an order?"

"You are not the emperor, and the emperor made it very clear that I would not be forced to touch the godstone unless it was absolutely vital."

"It *is* vital."

There was another long pause, and Ichtracia laughed again. It was a bitter, venom-filled sound. "You can't undo what *she* did, can you?" Sedial did not answer, so she continued. "You have no idea how delicious that is," she said.

"Watch your tongue."

"Or what, you'll pack me off to be tortured? I know what pain is, you old lizard. I've had to stand next to you for more than ten minutes at a time, haven't I?"

Michel lay his head against the wall, eyes wide, wondering if Ichtracia had gotten so angry that she forgot Michel was up here. Surely she had to know he'd be listening? Even if he'd stayed in her room, he would have heard *some* of this.

Sedial took a measured breath and finally responded. "We will undo her sabotage. It'll take time, admittedly, but she is not as powerful as she thinks. Her sorcery is fumbling and amateurish, and when I catch her, I will teach her exactly what a bone-eye is capable of."

"Good luck with that." Ichtracia's tone told Michel that she wished Sedial anything *but* luck.

Another measured breath, taken with the long-suffering air of a man enduring untold indignity. "It doesn't have to be like this," Sedial said.

"Doesn't it?"

"No. You know I love you. You know I'd do anything for my Mara."

Michel felt every muscle in his body tense at the name. His breathing came short, and he tried to think. It *was* a name, he was certain. Wasn't it? A pet name? A reference to something else? It was the first time he'd heard the word used in any way in the Dynize language, and he wondered if perhaps he had just misheard a similar word.

Sedial continued. "I brought you a present, just like I did when you were a little girl."

Ichtracia snorted, and Michel suddenly remembered the beautiful young woman still standing down there in the room with them. "What is she, a slave?"

"Slave? No, we don't have slaves in the empire anymore."

"Then why would she be here by her own will? Surely she's figuring out right about now that you wouldn't allow her to live after listening to a conversation like this. Unless she's one of your spies, of course."

"Oh, come now. I didn't purchase her. I purchased the enormous debt that she owes some very bad people down in Greenfire Depths. She has agreed to be your plaything for as long as you want her around, after which you may send her back to the Depths or set her free or whatever you please. She *is* just your type, isn't she?"

"You think I want a plaything? How old do you think I am?"

"You always want a plaything. You've gone through dozens over the last few years. This one isn't allowed to talk back to you. I thought you'd find that quite satisfactory."

"What's the catch?" Ichtracia sounded like she was considering this offer, and Michel couldn't quite suppress his horror.

"Must there be a catch?"

"I know you better than anyone, you old lizard."

Sedial gave the amused harrumph of any elderly relative dealing with a difficult child. "Get rid of the Blackhat. Keep this girl as a gift, and I won't force you to go help with the godstone."

There was another long pause, this one nearly a minute, and Michel could hear someone walking around. He imagined Ichtracia doing a circuit around the "offered" woman, examining her like a man might examine a new horse. Ichtracia sniffed. "Do you want me to kill him?"

Michel's blood ran cold.

"I should make you do it yourself for being such a petulant little bitch. But no. Send him back to Yaret. I'll deal with him myself in time, but until then I don't need you mocking me by parading him around on your arm at the clubs and games."

"I'll consider it."

"You'll take it."

"Until you are my emperor—may all the heavens prevent that

from ever happening—I will not follow your orders. I *will* consider this offer of yours."

"Give me an answer soon."

"Leave the girl."

Michel imagined the two staring angrily at each other until Sedial suddenly rapped on the floor twice with his cane and left through the front door with a stride that seemed far too strong for a man of his age. Michel waited for just a moment before turning to creep back toward the room. He was stopped by the sound of a sigh.

"Can you talk?" he heard Ichtracia ask.

A frightened voice answered in Palo. "Yes, ma'am."

"Is what he said true? Did he buy your debt?"

"Yes, ma'am."

"That goddamn pig. Don't flinch away. I'm not going to take you to bed or kill you. Do you know where the army camps are to the west of the city?"

"I do, ma'am."

"Take this note to the guards at the camp of the Falcon Third Regiment. There is a man there named Devin-Cathetin, who I trust. He'll give you a job. Nothing you don't want to do, hear me? Go directly there, and don't use any of the carriages in the city, and don't go back to Sedial. I suggest you change your name and forget your friends and family if you don't want to end up dead. You can leave by the back door. Go!"

Footsteps fled down the hallway beneath Michel, and he heard the back door open and close. In the sitting room below him, Ichtracia dropped into a chair with a sigh. He slowly backed away from the stairs, heading back to the bedroom, where he found his shirt and boots and quickly began getting dressed.

He wanted to ask Ichtracia a thousand questions, but two burning bits of information kept his heart racing in a near panic: Would she put him out to please her grandfather, and was she this Mara person whom he'd been looking for this whole time?

He finished lacing his boots and looked up, only to find Ichtracia standing in the doorway with one arm up on the door, her robe open, another hand on her hip. Her eyes were puffy and red, her mouth turned down at the corners. Michel got to his feet and took a step toward her nightstand, with the Privileged's gloves sitting on them, wondering if she'd come up here to take her anger out on him.

"How much did you overhear?"

"Some," Michel said as innocuously as possible. "It was quite loud."

Ichtracia sniffed. "You were eavesdropping." She walked past him quickly, but instead of her gloves she retrieved her mala pipe and flung it at the far wall. It shattered, sending bits of glass, ash, and mala across the room. "You're a damned spy. If you weren't listening from the top of the stairs, I would think less of you. Well, out with it! What do you want to ask? Am I going to turn you inside out and hand you to Sedial?" She scoffed and crossed to the window, where she glared out into the street as if to be sure Sedial was gone. "Do you want to ask why I hate him? Come, I can see the damned question on your lips."

Michel tried to work some moisture back into his mouth. "Who is Mara?"

"What?" Ichtracia blinked at him, looking genuinely confused. Perhaps he *had* misheard the word. His inexperience with the language had defeated him, and now he'd asked a question that could arouse her suspicion. Too damn late now.

"Who is Mara?" he asked again. "I heard Sedial say the name."

Ichtracia still seemed baffled. This was certainly not the question she'd expected him to voice. "It's not a name." Michel's mind began to turn faster, trying to fit pieces into place in the hope that this new information might help him find Taniel's informant. Until Ichtracia continued. "It's not exactly a name. I'm Mara. It's an old word—a pet name that Sedial has used for me since I was a little girl."

Michel began to pace immediately, the near panic of earlier blowing into a full panic now. *She* was Mara. The goddamned nickname of a Privileged, and Taniel hadn't thought that either of those bits of information were important? Did he think that leaving out the Privileged bit was the only way to convince Michel to take the job? That otherwise Michel would have gotten out of the city as fast as his feet could carry him?

Because he was damned well right.

"Why do you want to know about that name?" Ichtracia asked, taking a step toward him.

Michel took the same step back, edging toward the door. He'd spent three days with her now, and he suddenly didn't recognize her anymore. It terrified him almost as much as those gloves sitting on the nightstand. "I have to go."

"What? No. Answer my question."

Michel glanced at the gloves, then at Ichtracia's face. "Yaret needs me right now," he said with more confidence than he felt, heading for the front door.

CHAPTER 50

It took a day to set up the duel. Vlora stayed in a back room of Burt's brothel, nursing the cuts on her hands and only leaving once, to send a secure courier to Olem with instructions to inch the army closer to Yellow Creek.

The morning brought a cold wind sweeping down from the mountains, chilling Vlora through her clothes as she stepped outside with an entourage that included Burt and fifty of his armed posse. Most of them were Palo, but more than a few were Kressian or Gurlish. The sun wasn't even above the trees yet, and traffic was sparse. Children lined the rooftops, watching them pass, and Vlora guessed that word about this duel had spread.

They walked down the main road, passing the hotel where Vlora had spent the first week of her stay. The fidgety manager stood on the stoop, eyes glued to the procession. They kept onward, finally turning off the street and entering a dusty park, where a public gallows stood ominously creaking in the wind. The corner of the park was full of tombstones.

Men and women lined the other side of the park, all of them similarly well armed, and they outnumbered Burt's people by at least a dozen. Nohan stood at the center of the group beside a dark-skinned Deliv woman in a corseted crimson dress. She was dressed more like a courtesan at a dinner party than someone out early in the morning to watch two people fight to the death.

Vlora leaned over to Burt. "Is that Jezzy in the red dress?" she asked.

"That's her." Burt puffed on a cigar. He wore a dashing brown suit, complete with cane and bowler cap, and he, too, seemed to be treating this as a matter of entertainment rather than dire consequence.

"Does she know what I am?"

Burt grinned around his cigar. "She has no idea. She bet her best gold mine against seven of my smaller claims without batting an eye. Either she knows something I don't, or she doesn't know that I know her man is a mage." He looked skyward, as if making sure the order of the sentence sounded right, then nodded to himself. "Whoever wins, this is going to be a lot more interesting than she expects."

So Burt was betting against the house. It didn't surprise Vlora, not much, but she was slightly annoyed at how cavalier he was about this thing. He might lose a handful of small claims, but she could be dead in ten minutes.

Vlora eyed the armed men. "Is this going to turn into a battle?"

"It shouldn't. The deputies are steering clear this morning, but nobody wants a real confrontation. This is just a bit of fun."

"And all the weapons?"

"Precaution."

Vlora eyed Nohan. He didn't look great. He still limped from their tussle, and his arms seemed stiff. He didn't look like he'd gotten much more sleep than she had—probably he'd been out hunting her each of the last few nights. She had little question that he was running a damned powerful powder trance.

Vlora was confident, but she knew that being too confident

could get her killed. This was a trained powder mage who delighted in killing. He was bigger, stronger, and just as fast. Even if she won, she was unlikely to leave this fight unscathed.

She tested the tightness of the stitches Burt's surgeon had redone on her arms, knowing that she'd probably rip them all out. Taking a powder charge between her fingers, she crushed the paper and reached up her sleeve to rub the powder beneath her bandages, feeling the fire as it reached her bloodstream. She took another charge and sniffed it, turning away from the others lest Jezzy see the act and try to cancel the duel.

She had Nohan out in the open. This had to end *now*.

Burt checked his pocket watch, then twirled it on the end of its chain. "It's time, ma'am," he told Vlora.

"Agreed."

She and Burt went to the middle of the park, where they were soon joined by Jezzy and Nohan. Jezzy gave them both a toothy, charming smile. "My friends," she began.

"Can it, Jezzy," Burt replied pleasantly. "This is the woman you tried to have killed when she wouldn't work with you."

Jezzy lifted her chin, looking down her nose at Vlora. "Is that so? The one whose friend killed poor Dorner? Pity, that. Dorner was always a loyal dog. Does your champion have a name?"

"Verundish," Vlora answered.

"Verundish." Jezzy rolled the name around on her tongue. "Nohan says he knows you. Is that true?"

"We have a history."

Jezzy's smile broadened. "I'm glad we're here to let you work out your problems. Do you know what Nohan is, little lady? He's a powder mage. You sure you want to fight him?" Jezzy scrunched up her face, wiggling her nose, her eyes smiling.

"Powder mages are all fluff," Vlora said, staring at Nohan. The bastard hadn't even warned his boss what she was up against. What a weaseling asshole.

"If you insist," Jezzy said. "Now, then, Burt. Are we agreed on the terms?"

"Your mine. My claims. Straight out bet with Kresimir and all gathered as my witness."

Jezzy's eyes flicked up to the armed men Burt had brought with him. "And no funny business?"

"None coming from me." Burt puffed on his cigar, then extended his hand. The two shook. He leaned over to Vlora. "Don't make me a poorer man, Lady Flint," he whispered. Then he retreated back to the other side of the park.

It was the first time he'd outright stated that he knew who she was. Vlora tried not to let it bother her, watching as Jezzy retreated as well, leaving Vlora and Nohan alone. She couldn't sense any powder on him, and had left hers with Burt. She wanted to focus on this without having to worry about him trying to detonate her powder, and he'd obviously felt the same.

"Just a couple of powder mages," Vlora said. "High as Gurlish sandriders with a pair of swords between them. This should be fun, don't you think?"

Nohan glared at her. "I'm not here for fun. I'm here to win back my pride."

"I'm not sure you had any to begin with," Vlora said, drawing her sword. Her mentor had always taught her to kill in cold blood—to set aside the quips and the insults and to let her sword talk for her. Vlora, however, was not Tamas. "You're an asshole, Nohan. You should just have accepted it and tried to rein in your lust for blood. You would have gotten a lot farther in life."

"What, working in your damned cabal?"

"You wanted to at one point. Now you're a bitter sword for hire, and you've been coaxed into a duel instead of sitting back and shooting at me from the other side of town. It was a good strategy. You should have stuck to it."

"You sure it was me who walked into a trap?" Nohan demanded.

Vlora let her eyes travel along the men standing on the other side of the park, then to the rooftops, wondering if perhaps she'd made an error. Was Nohan cleverer than she expected? Had he set her up? Or was this a last bit of bravado to throw her off her feet?

"Good-bye, Nohan," Vlora said, stepping forward.

Audible gasps rose from the watchers as the two crossed swords. Nohan leapt to the offensive, driving Vlora back with a series of thrusts that were almost too fast for the eye to follow. Vlora allowed herself to relax, drawing on instinct to parry and riposte, keeping her footing steady as she backed away. Their blades blurred in the morning sunlight, and dust rose around them from their footwork.

She continued to fall back. Letting an opponent tire themselves out was a time-honored dueling strategy, but that wouldn't work on a powder mage. At least, not very quickly. But she could let his fury build, keeping him at bay without striking back, and that's what she did as they circled the park. Within moments she could hear mutters, and someone said the words "powder mage." Bets were soon being shouted back and forth as the big bosses' underlings worked themselves into a frenzy.

Vlora parried a particularly powerful strike and was immediately forced to duck below a swing and throw herself to one side. Sweat began to pour down her face, and she focused harder.

Nohan managed to get inside her guard, nicking her right forearm. She answered by cutting off the tip of his nose, causing him to stumble back amid a flurry of curses. She followed him coldly, suddenly on the attack, moving with purpose.

He managed to parry several strikes in a row, but then she was inside his guard. She stabbed his right shoulder, parried a riposte, and stabbed him just below the ribs. His sword arm faltered, and she stepped forward and caught him by the front of his jacket, thrusting her sword through his heart until her hilt touched his chest.

She held him up, his body twitching, his eyes rolling as he died. After a few moments she pulled out her sword and let him fall.

The cheers, jeers, and bets quieted. The dust slowly settled. Vlora turned to Burt, who held his cigar between his teeth with a grin. His cigar was no shorter. The fight had lasted thirty seconds—maybe less. She turned to Jezzy, whose face was ashen, her broad smile gone. Jezzy took two steps toward Vlora, then stopped, hawking a wad of phlegm at her champion.

"You cheated," Jezzy spat.

The assembled crowd immediately erupted into chaos. Accusations flew from both sides. Burt held his arms up in alarm, shouting, "No!" over and over again, while muskets, blunderbusses, and swords were shaken angrily on all sides. Vlora whirled, her head spinning, her thoughts hard to focus after the euphoric adrenaline of the fight.

"Nobody cheated," she said to Jezzy. "Your man lost. Pay up to Burt, or everyone here will see you for a coward." She turned back to Burt, hoping he'd back her up, when she heard a musket shot.

Most people assumed that powder mages were infallible when it came to black powder, that they could stop every powder ignition and that any bullet that managed to fly would somehow miss them. This was, of course, a myth that Vlora had been disabused of from an early age. Any powder mage could be shot—all you had to do was overwhelm them, confuse them, or just take them by surprise.

She felt the bullet hit her in the back a fraction of a second after she heard the blast. She stumbled forward, falling to her knees, watching the surprise spread on Burt's face. Burt suddenly leapt for the ground, and the world erupted in violence as both sides opened fire. Bullets whizzed over and around Vlora, a soft undertone to the cacophony of powder blasts and men screaming.

Vlora struggled to open the button on the breast pocket of her jacket, only to remember that there was no powder inside. Her head was fuzzy, her thoughts confused. She felt a burning between her shoulder blades that she could not ignore.

All around her, men and women died. Weapons were fired, and it quickly became apparent that both sides had stationed people on the roof. The exchange grew more frenzied and wild, and Vlora forced herself to her feet and began to walk.

In the chaos and the dust and powder smoke, it was difficult to tell who was shooting at whom. She reached out with her senses toward the armed gang behind her, where Jezzy was being protected by her men, and detonated their powder with a thought. The kickback from touching off over three dozen sources of powder at once nearly caused her to pass out, but she pushed on until she fell on her knees beside Burt.

Burt seemed unharmed. He held his hands over his head, cigar crushed in the dust and cane lost as he pressed his face against the ground. She forcibly turned him over, searching his pockets for her spare powder cartridges and shoving them into her own jacket.

"Remember our deal," she growled, regaining her feet.

She detonated the powder of a trio of armed women on a roof across the street, ripping them—and the building on which they stood—in half. The exchange of gunfire continued, and Vlora wondered just how many men both sides had brought with them. Her ears ringing, she could make out gunfire from all over, extending well into the streets.

Both of these fools had brought their entire private armies with them.

She limped away from the park, back the way they'd come down the main street, snorting powder to quell the pain between her shoulders. She assessed the damage; her chest and the muscles of her back were tight, every step causing a spike of pain to bleed through her powder trance. She could still move her arms—though not as well. It would have to be good enough.

The acrid smell of smoke caught her attention, and she knew

immediately that it was not powder smoke. There was a fire some-where behind her, maybe even set by her own detonations, and she thought of all the slapdash wooden buildings crammed in together in the valley. Fire would spread damned fast. She redoubled her efforts.

The streets were full of people screaming and running. Vlora was jostled and shoved, but otherwise ignored. Some people ran away from the firefight; others called for a bucket brigade and ran toward the flames.

She reached Burt's brothel, fetched her pistol from Burt's office, and then went for her horse in his stable. A curious stable boy sad-dled the animal for a handful of pennies, while Vlora rested on a hay bale in the corner. Blood dripped down both arms, and when she finally regained her feet, the hay was crimson. It took the stable boy's help to get her into the saddle.

Vlora rode out of town, slumped in the saddle, trying to get as far away from the fighting as possible. This wasn't her war—this wasn't why she was here. She drifted in and out of consciousness, barely holding together enough to direct her horse up the road leading to Little Flerring's compound.

"What the pit is going on?" Little Flerring demanded from her vantage point above her cabin. Vlora tried to answer as she attempted to dismount, and only managed to slip from the saddle and fall to the ground in a heap.

The last thing she remembered was hands lifting her toward the sky.

CHAPTER 51

The Mad Lancers left the Hock—and the remnants of their dragoon rivals—and soon reached the coast. They skirted the city-fortress of New Starlight late in the evening, using a sunken road to slip by undetected. It wasn't until they were well past that Styke allowed himself to circle around the end of his army and gaze back upon the city, squinting through the fading light at Dynize flags flying from the turrets that had once flown the flag of the Fatrastan Army.

The city-fortress was not like anything else in Fatrasta. It was built on a wedge of land jutting off the northwest edge of the Hammer and guarded by a sloped curtain wall that cut the entire wedge off from the mainland and housed a small city—enough space for around ten thousand people. Inside that was the fortress itself, a towering knife of white stone, freckled with red, surrounded by seven mighty turrets, the largest of which was topped with an enormous lighthouse to warn incoming ships of the rocks below.

"Is that a castle?"

Styke turned to find Celine beside him, gently patting Margo on the neck. He sized up New Starlight, realizing that it looked far more like a storybook castle than it did the palisades or star-forts that dotted Fatrasta. "I suppose it is," he said. It wasn't a pretty castle, not by a long shot, but it had all the trappings of one.

"Who built it?"

"A Starlish duke," he told Celine. "He was one of the first serious explorers to cross through the heart of Fatrasta, and when he reached here, he enslaved the local Palo and made them build him this fortress. I think that was, eh, three hundred years ago?"

Celine's eyes widened. "It's stood that long?"

"There are older castles in the Nine, but it's a decent enough fortress." He pointed to the turrets. "Those are big enough to hold modern cannons, and the wall is sloped slightly, which helps take a pounding from straight-shot."

"Then why do the Dynize hold it?" she asked. "There's no sign of a battle."

Styke frowned at the fortress. She was right; there *were* no signs of a battle. The walls were undamaged, all of the turrets standing. "Sharp eyes." He pondered the question for a few moments. "The garrison must have abandoned it at the first sight of the enemy. Maybe when they heard about Landfall. Damned cowards." He resisted the urge to take a closer look. Even a poor garrison could have held New Starlight against an enemy siege—those towers would make short work of just about any fleet attempting a blockade.

But New Starlight wasn't his problem.

As they watched, a small, mounted force exited the curtain wall and rode east. Definitely Dynize soldiers. Styke remained until the sun was almost gone, searching the horizon for any signs of those dragonmen before turning Amrec to catch up with the Mad Lancers. Celine followed in his wake.

Their camp was a few miles south of New Starlight in a gentle valley large enough to hold most of their army but small enough for a scout to miss until they were right on top of it. As Styke and Celine rode in, the men were just beginning to set up their tents, and Styke proceeded to the other side of the camp, where he found Ibana, Ka-poel, Gustar, and a dozen Mad Lancers gathered around an opening in the hillside.

The opening had, until a few minutes ago, been hidden behind a boulder. The entrance was squat—no more than three feet by three feet—and held together by thick-cut timbers. It looked like the entrance to a tiny mine.

Styke handed Amrec off to a nearby soldier and joined Ibana. "Is it still intact?" he asked.

"We're finding out," she answered without looking away from the entrance.

Gustar knelt by the timbers, squinting into the dark hole, a half smile on his face. "A Blackhat cache, buried under a hill in the middle of nowhere." He shook his head. "How many people even know about this?"

"Five or ten," Styke said, kneeling next to Gustar and peering into the darkness. He could see a light, somewhere in the depths, bobbing around. "Lindet uses forced labor for this kind of thing so that word won't get out to the general public."

"What's it for?" Gustar asked.

"This," Styke grunted with a gesture toward their camp. "Lindet is a firm believer in being ready for anything. In addition to regular supply depots, she's got these caches hidden away all over the country— mostly in the less-populated areas. They're specifically meant to resupply an army. If this one is untouched, it'll provide us with canned food, wine, ammunition, and spare weapons to last weeks."

As if to answer the next unspoken question, the bobbing of the light suddenly came toward them, growing until the lantern was set aside and Jackal's head and shoulders emerged from the pit. Jackal grinned up at them. "Everything is there," he reported.

Ibana clapped her hands together. Styke couldn't blame her. They needed a bit of good luck after the last couple weeks of hard riding and fighting.

"Check the tins and barrels," Ibana ordered. "If the rats haven't gotten to any of it, give everyone a double ration of food and wine tonight."

"No drunks," Styke added.

"No drunks," Ibana agreed.

Styke got out of the way to let them work, and soon Jackal was overseeing a chain of men rolling out barrels and handing up crates to empty the deep cache. He watched them work for a few minutes, feeling suddenly tired from the events of the last few weeks. His body reminded him that he was no longer the Mad Ben Styke who could go a week without sleep and still fight a battle.

Looking around, his eyes fell on Ka-poel sitting on the hillside above the entrance to the cache. He was surprised to find her watching him, and when their eyes met, she got to her feet and walked away into the darkness.

Styke snorted. He still couldn't decide what he thought about what had happened last night. Walking into the Dynize cavalry camp unopposed, seeing all of those soldiers sitting cross-legged like they were waiting for a mummers' show in the park, unable to move or speak. The officer whom Ka-poel used as a mouthpiece. The memory floated in the back of his head like a bad dream, fuzzy on details, and he briefly wondered if he *had* dreamt it.

He continued to watch his lancers as they unloaded the cache for several minutes before confiscating one of their lanterns. He found Celine brushing down Margo with Sunin's help. "Finish that and come with me," he told her.

They walked into the darkness, lantern held high above Styke's head. Styke followed the coppery smell of blood sorcery, sniffing at the air every few moments until they found Ka-poel at the top of the valley, sitting on the ground with the contents of her satchel spread out across a rock. There was wax, bits of hair, tiny figurines, and sticks, dirt, and even some fingernails. It reminded him of the sort of non sequitur items his little sister used to collect as a child.

Styke set the lantern on the rock and sat down across from her, watching her face. She lifted her eyes to him for a brief second and squinted before returning her attention to a half-made wax figurine in her lap.

Styke patted his knee, letting Celine sit, then addressed Ka-poel. "What did you do with the Dynize cavalry yesterday?"

Ka-poel continued her work, finishing the figurine and gently pressing a dirty toenail into the soft wax, before brushing off her hands and lifting her gaze once more to him and Celine. She drew her thumb across her neck, then flashed several more signs.

"I killed them," Celine translated. "Just like you asked."

"Why did you keep them as long as you did? Why didn't you finish them sooner?"

"I told you. I needed answers." Ka-poel raised her chin, as if daring him to continue that line of questioning.

So he did. "And?" He drummed his fingers on the rock, looking over her assortment of disgusting knickknacks.

Ka-poel stared at him, her hands folded in her lap, before finally lifting them into the light of the lantern. "I have been trying to uncover my past," Celine translated. "When I was a child, my nurse took me from Dynize. I remember very little of that time—I remember a palace, and great halls, and I remember fleeing through the night and across the ocean in a small ship manned by sailors who knew they would die."

Ka-poel's eyes took on a faraway glint, her brow wrinkling with the telling. She continued. "My nurse took me into the swamp, and we joined one of the tribes there. She died very soon after from disease. Her death deprived me of my own history, and I have wondered who I am for over two decades."

"So who are you?" Styke asked. Her look was guarded, and he

knew that pushing too hard on a subject like this was likely to make a person button up for good. But he was still angry about the things he saw last night, and he didn't have the patience to be gentle.

Ka-poel waggled her finger, as if to say, *My story isn't done.* She continued. "My nurse sang me songs. I remember those. She called me a princess, and I always thought that was..." Celine struggled with the sign Ka-poel made, her small face scrunching in confusion.

"Hyperbole?" Styke suggested.

Ka-poel nodded. "I thought it was hyperbole. When the Dynize came, I had reason to suspect that perhaps...perhaps that wasn't the case."

Styke gently smoothed Celine's hair, watching Ka-poel's face carefully. She was normally stoic, sometimes bemused or playful. But she seemed genuinely troubled right now, and that set him on edge. She was too powerful to be troubled.

"A bone-eye has been calling to me," Ka-poel finally finished.

"What do you mean, 'calling to you'?" Styke asked, feeling goose bumps on the back of his arm.

"Sorcery," Ka-poel clarified.

"I gathered as much. But how? Does he know where you are? Is he able to track us?"

Ka-poel hesitated. "I don't know. I don't think so. But I was never trained in what I do, so there are many simple things that the Dynize bone-eyes are capable of that I am unaware of. So... maybe."

That didn't make Styke happy. Not even a little bit. Having someone like Ka-poel around—someone so powerful that they could take physical control of a company of cavalry—and have her admit that she had not mastered simple parts of her own sorcery was not only disconcerting, it was also downright dangerous.

"I have figured out," she said, "that this bone-eye can only call to me through shared blood." She paused. "Those lancers—well, their officers—I was asking them about the powerful bone-eyes who came over with the invasion."

"And what did you discover?"

"I am being called by an old man. His name is Ka-Sedial, and he was the one who came to meet your sister the day before their invasion."

Styke was on his feet before he knew it, towering over Ka-poel, fists clenched. "Be very careful what you say next," he said through clenched teeth. He could feel his heart hammering in his chest. The very idea that someone would discover that he and Lindet were brother and sister had never even occurred to him. Only *they* knew the secret, and neither was about to tell a soul.

His leap had sent Celine tumbling, and without taking his eyes off Ka-poel, he helped her to her feet and gestured for her to watch Ka-poel's hands.

"Sit down," Celine translated Ka-poel's next signs. "Blood is my business. You can't hide your relation from me." She sniffed, as if the smell of imminent violence coming from Styke was nothing more than an inconvenience. "I will keep your secret."

Slowly, Styke lowered himself to the ground.

"This is an exchange," Ka-poel said. "Do you understand? I keep your secret, and you will keep mine."

Styke tried to calm his pounding heart, remembering the conversation before his sister was mentioned. "This Ka-Sedial?"

"Yes. He is my grandfather."

"And what does that make you?"

Ka-poel smiled distantly, laughing to herself. "It makes me a princess. The Dynize emperor is my cousin."

Styke almost laughed himself. A damned princess, riding along with him. It seemed like something out of a fairy tale, yet so much of this already did. He wondered if it explained her power—if the Dynize royal family was stronger than most. "Why is he calling to you?"

"He is trying to be..." Celine struggled with the next word, and Ka-poel had to spell it out in signs. "Paternalistic."

"What does that mean?" Celine asked Styke.

"It means he's trying to be fatherly. Reaching out for a lost granddaughter." Styke didn't take his eyes off Ka-poel. "Are you answering?"

"I am not," Ka-poel said. "I may, tentatively, but I'm not sure if that will reveal our position. He knows who I am—he knows that I am that girl stolen away so long ago. But *I* don't know why my nurse stole me away. She took me for a reason, and I want to discover why. But if I ask him, he will lie."

"How do you know?"

"Because he may know who I am, but he does not know *what* I am. He does not know my power. I can see through his intentions like a pane of glass, and I know he wishes to use me."

Styke grunted. "I don't mind being used, but never against my will."

"I am of a similar mind," Ka-poel acknowledged.

Styke lifted his head, looking down the valley toward the soldiers unloading the cache. It was late, and he knew he needed to rest if they were going to ride all day tomorrow. "This thing," he said, changing directions and gesturing to the wax figurines and bits of detritus on the rock, "I suggest that you learn some... restraint. There is no reason to torture people at length."

"They feel no pain unless I make them," Ka-poel said, frowning.

"Physical, perhaps. But emotional? I looked into that woman's eyes. She knew she was being controlled and she tried with every fiber of her being to fight it. If you must do that to people, make it short. Suffering is needless."

"I had cause."

"We all have cause," Styke said with a shrug. "This bone-eye, Ka-Sedial. What will you do with him?"

Ka-poel looked down at the camp herself, her frown deepening.

"I will let him croon over the distance. I will let him wonder what I am up to. And in the next few days, I will find the godstone that he seeks and I will break it. Only then will I answer him, and I'll allow him to know what I have done." She smiled, an expression neither bemused nor playful. "Then I will demand that he explain why my nurse—a woman who loved me—felt the need to carry me off so long ago." Ka-poel's attention returned to the detritus spread in front of her, clearly a dismissal.

Styke left her with her figurines and headed back to camp deep in his own thoughts. Celine rode on his shoulder, clearly lost in thoughts of her own. "Do you understand never to speak of what you heard back there?" he asked.

"Yes," Celine responded. "I'm no snitch."

Well, at least her dad had taught her *something*. "Good. If you have questions, you may ask. But only when we are completely alone." He took her back to Margo and Sunin, then found Amrec and began the mechanical work of brushing him down for the night. He thought of Ka-poel's expression during their conversation, and of his own search for vengeance these past few weeks. He wondered if she had difficulty, trapped in her own body without a voice, unable to communicate beyond a bit of slate and a little girl's translations.

He finished his work and prepared for sleep. They would find this godstone soon, and it would be her work to destroy or disable the damned thing. And then, it seemed, she had questions of her own to answer.

Sorcery had never scared him. But he did not envy this grandfather of hers. Not when she finally turned her attention on him.

CHAPTER 52

Michel was so furious at Taniel that he couldn't think straight. He spent the night drinking at one of the few bars left in the city where he was fairly certain he wouldn't run into either a Blackhat or a Dynize; then the next morning he went to Yaret's new residence in the old bank. He stood outside, wishing he was still buried in a bottle of whiskey before running a hand through his hair and straightening the collar of his jacket.

Whatever was going on with Sedial, Ichtracia, or anyone else, Michel needed to finish what he'd started here in Landfall. Eliminating the Blackhats to the last man would make his chances of survival go up, so eliminate them he must. He held a large valise that he'd fetched less than an hour ago, and opened it once more to confirm the contents before heading inside.

He found Yaret and Tenik in deep conference in Yaret's office. Both men looked up as Michel entered.

"You look like you got hit by a carriage," Yaret said.

Tenik sniffed. "And you smell like a brewery. I know where je Tura is hiding."

"Oh?" Yaret asked.

Michel went to Yaret's desk, clearing off the papers into a messy stack and tossing them on a chair before opening the valise and producing an armload of two-foot-long cylinders. He opened one at random, discarded it, then another before producing a large roll of paper that he spread out across Yaret's desk.

"What are these?" Tenik asked.

"Maps of the catacombs beneath Landfall."

The two men stared at the paper in stunned silence. "Why haven't we been using these all along?"

"Because I didn't know they existed. The thought struck me at about four o'clock in the morning—Lindet was as good at keeping records as you, maybe even better. There are hundreds of miles of natural and man-made catacombs in the plateau. Most of the larger tunnels were sealed off decades ago, but there are plenty of entrances around the city."

"Yes, we know. We've been searching the damned things and haven't found anything."

Michel held up one finger. "I had two thoughts. One, that Lindet would have mapped those catacombs and stashed the maps in the Millinery library. They weren't important enough to take along, so they would have been left behind. It took me less than an hour to find them once I realized."

Tenik swore.

"My thoughts exactly. My second thought was that we've been looking for an operation—dozens of men moving around supplies and powder and sleeping in the catacombs and all that."

"Right," Tenik responded. "And again, we haven't found any sign of that."

Michel leaned over the table toward Tenik and Yaret. "*But we're not looking for dozens of men.* What if it's just je Tura? Maybe two or three others at the most?"

"There's no possible way he could have conducted all these bombings without serious help," Yaret protested. "He blew up my house!"

"A barrel of powder in the basement," Michel proclaimed. "I bet if you send someone to dig around in the ashes really carefully, you'll find a hidden tunnel that connects to the catacombs. Plenty of places in the city have them. Shopkeepers use them for storage. If je Tura is moving through those tunnels—if he has maps like these, or a seriously good guide—he could evade our soldiers indefinitely. Think about it. We would *easily* find evidence of dozens of men down there, but if he's carrying no more than a bedroll, a pack, and a lantern, he'll leave absolutely no sign of his passing."

"And the powder?"

"An off-the-books cache? A forgotten storehouse? I haven't met je Tura, but I've heard rumors that he's a strong son of a bitch. He could carry around a couple of barrels of gunpowder himself— certainly enough to set up in your basement."

Yaret snorted in disbelief. "You're telling me that hundreds of Dynize soldiers are being foiled by the work of one man?"

"With all the evidence—or lack thereof—it's the only solution we have left."

Tenik rubbed the back of his head, staring at the maps, looking as irritated as Michel felt. "So what do we do? He went off the schedule he arranged with Forgula the moment Forgula wound up dead. He's striking at random throughout the city. Do we just hope we get lucky?"

"Not a chance." Michel tapped on the map he'd rolled out. "We go in after him."

"But we've tried!" Yaret said in frustration. "We can't find him."

"We have maps now. We start at one entrance, we take in a thousand men, and we flush the bastard out like we would rats in a basement. At the very least we might be able to find his damned cache of powder. But if we're lucky, we corner him and catch him."

Yaret pursed his lips. "Four thousand."

"Eh?" Michel asked.

"Four thousand men. These tunnels are extensive and layered atop each other. I want at least four thousand men all searching them at once. A full-on manhunt."

"Damn," Tenik breathed. "We can't possibly…"

"We'll have to ask Sedial for manpower," Yaret said. Michel could see in his eyes that he was on board and determined. Only Tenik seemed skeptical.

"We can't trust Sedial's people," Tenik said in a hushed voice, as if Sedial himself were listening. "He won't want je Tura brought to light, lest he confirm that he was working for Sedial indirectly this whole time. It's another loose end."

"Then assure Sedial that we're hunting for the kill," Michel said dispassionately. "There aren't more than a handful of Blackhats left in the city. We can afford to shoot to kill when it comes to je Tura, and if Sedial thinks that evidence will die with him, then he'll give his help."

"And we lose a bargaining chip against Sedial," Tenik said unhappily.

"Is that more important than making sure more Dynize don't die to je Tura's bombs?" Michel asked.

After a moment of silence, Tenik nodded. "You're right. Yaret?"

"You have my full authority," Yaret said. "Begin the hunt first thing tomorrow. Get Sedial's help. Requisition every lantern in the city, and have our cartographers begin making copies of these maps. Go!"

Tenik was gone without a word, leaving Michel alone with Yaret. Without waiting to be asked, Michel sank into Tenik's chair with a sigh, a sudden headache appearing where his post-realization adrenaline rush had occupied his mind over the last few hours. He rubbed his eyes, wishing a pox upon all hangovers, and put his head down between his knees.

"You look in rough shape," Yaret said kindly.

Michel looked up. It was not a comment he expected from a superior. "Stressful day yesterday," he said, hoping it ended the conversation. He didn't want to explain the sudden conflict he had with Ichtracia, or the fact that he'd been eavesdropping on Sedial—though, to be honest, Yaret would probably enjoy the latter.

Yaret picked something off his shirt. "I, uh, heard you've been spending quite a lot of time with Saen-Ichtracia lately."

Michel hesitated a moment before answering. "She saved my life."

"And you show your gratitude by plowing her senseless for three days?" Yaret shook his head, then waved a hand at Michel to forestall a reply. "No, no. Don't explain yourself. That actually makes far too much sense when it comes to a Privileged. Forgive my crassness as well. Frankly, I'm more than a little delighted by hearing that someone Sedial hates has found his way into Ichtracia's bed, but I do like you, Michel, and so I think you should be warned."

"About the dangers of sleeping with a Privileged?" Michel asked, adopting a pained expression. "I'm not entirely ignorant."

Yaret's half smile disappeared, replaced by a serious look of concern. "No, by sleeping with Ichtracia. Not because of Sedial," he added quickly. "At least, not directly." Yaret shifted in his chair and sighed. "I won't insult you by explaining why we're here. The godstone, all of that. As a high-level Blackhat, I assume you know."

"I know a bit," Michel said slowly, wondering where this was going. "I know the godstone's purpose and that you want it. Not why you want it."

"Sedial ended our civil war by killing the rival emperor and then promising to reconcile both sides by creating a new god. *That's* why we're here. To bring peace to our country, we must resurrect the god that died to start our civil war. It was the only proposal that we could all agree on, so we spent well over a decade preparing to invade Fatrasta and seize the stones."

"What does this have to do with Ichtracia?"

"I'm getting to that. This was all Sedial's plan—his grand proposal. Many think of him as a great man for ending the civil war."

"And?"

"Ichtracia does not think he is a great man. When she was just a child, she accused her grandfather of murdering her family—her brother, her father, her sister. Officially, they all died to separatist assassins. Her accusations were swept under the rug, but she never recanted. Those rumors that she doesn't like her grandfather are wrong. She *loathes* her grandfather."

"Yet she still serves him."

"Because she is a patriot. She does not serve him, she serves all of Dynize. She knows as well as he does that bringing back our god is the best chance of reunification."

Michel held up one finger, trying to catch up with all of this. "I thought the godstones were used to create new gods, but you're speaking of resurrection."

"Of course. We brought his remains with us. Sedial is confident that the combined power of the stones, and of his bone-eyes, will bring our god back."

Something about that troubled Michel, but he wasn't entirely sure what. "So what does any of this have to do with me sleeping with Ichtracia?"

"Because Ichtracia has made a practice for over a decade of taking to bed anyone she thinks will annoy Sedial—generals, ministers, bodyguards. Half of his enemies in the capitol have gone through her rooms."

Michel frowned. "Should the promiscuity bother me? Because I'm a spy. Believe it or not, I've seen worse."

"Not really," Yaret said with a shrug. "That is expected of

Privileged. They are a force of nature in that way. But Ichtracia uses Sedial's enemies to annoy him and then she discards them. Many of those ex-lovers died under mysterious circumstances. Some even by Ichtracia's hand."

That was worrisome.

"Between Ichtracia and her grandfather," Yaret continued, "sharing the former's bed is doubly as dangerous as sleeping with any normal Privileged. It's something I wanted to warn you about personally."

Michel shook his head, trying to decide what he would do about Ichtracia. He'd spent much of last night in a drunken stupor trying to figure out why Taniel had left out so much information about "Mara," and his suspicions had begun to deepen. "I'll keep that in mind," he said.

"Good. I have use for you, Michel, and I expect you to have a long and fruitful career in my Household. Don't disappoint me."

Michel wondered how long that would actually be if he confirmed that Ichtracia was Mara and convinced her to leave with him. His heart hurt briefly at the idea of leaving Yaret and Tenik behind. He liked them, and he had grown into a place within Yaret's Household that, aside from the danger of Sedial, was actually quite fulfilling. He cleared his thoughts and plastered a smile on his face, getting up to look through the rest of the maps he'd taken from the Millinery. "I have the same hopes," he said.

CHAPTER 53

Vlora awoke in the darkness. She was immediately aware of the pain, crying out involuntarily. She gasped, choking on her own saliva, trying to make sense of where she was.

A light flickered into being and drew closer, and she was soon able to make out Little Flerring's face cast in shadows. Flerring laid a hand on her shoulder, pushing her down. "Moving is a really bad idea right now," she said.

"Powder," Vlora gasped.

Flerring withdrew, appearing a few minutes later. Vlora felt something pressed to her lips, and tasted the bitter sulfur of powder, then felt the grit between her teeth. The powder trance took effect immediately, running through her blood like fire, snuffing away a thousand pains until they were a dull throb in the back of her head. She forced herself to lie still and calm her breathing, letting the trance do its work.

"Better?" Flerring asked.

"Much," Vlora said. She tried to sit up, but the effort caused a sweat to break out on her brow without accomplishing anything. "How long have I been out?"

"It's a bit past one in the morning now. So maybe sixteen hours or so?"

"What's the damage?"

Flerring held a lead ball in front of Vlora's face. "That's the bullet I took out of your back. Embedded in the muscles back there. It didn't hit anything important, but I can't imagine you're going to have full use of your upper body for some time. I'm not a great surgeon, but I think I got all the pieces of your shirt and jacket out. Hopefully that'll help avoid an infection."

"You *think?*"

"I'm paid to blow stuff up, not perform impromptu surgery on powder mages. What the pit happened down there? I heard something yesterday about a duel, and then I woke up to see the whole damned city on fire."

Vlora tried to think. The powder trance was great at deadening the pain, but she'd experienced enough blood loss to leave her brain in a confused fog regardless of the powder. "I dueled Jezzy's champion—that powder mage I've been fighting with—and killed him. Jezzy accused me of cheating and then one of her boys shot me in the back. Once that gun fired, all pit broke loose. Jezzy and Burt's people all started shooting."

"I heard Jezzy's dead," Flerring said. "They're saying you killed her. Blew up the powder of the men standing beside her."

Vlora tried to feel bad about it—but it *was* Jezzy's man who shot her in the back. Likely on her orders. "She had it coming."

"I won't argue that. Her lieutenants are still fighting, though. There's armed gangs battlin' all across the city, while the poor bastard miners and businessmen are trying to put the fires out. Last I heard we lost most of Main Street and half the Gurlish quarter, and the fires are still going."

Vlora took a deep breath and held it, listening. They were a couple miles outside the city, but if she focused, she could still hear the occasional musket shot echoing across the valley. "Sounds like the whole city is tearing itself apart."

"I've got a pretty good view from above the cabin, and it *looks* like the whole city is tearing itself apart." Flerring got up, and Vlora heard the pouring of a cup of tea. "Here, drink this. It'll knock you back out."

"I can't," Vlora protested. "I've got to get moving. I need to contact my men. I need to find Taniel."

Flerring put her elbow on Vlora's shoulder, keeping her down, then forced her mouth open with one hand. "Drink," she ordered.

The tea tasted like horseshit and seemed to get everywhere but in Vlora's mouth. Flerring mopped up the spills and sat back while Vlora coughed, laughing. "I've got that promissory note, but I'd much rather take you back to Adro in one piece, sister. Is Taniel still rotting at the jail?"

"Yeah."

"I'll send one of my boys down. The deputies are gonna be working frantically to put out this wildfire you started. Shouldn't be too hard to slip him out."

Vlora almost protested that they needed him out legitimately, then discarded the thought with a sigh. What was the point? All their efforts at finding the godstone in secret had gone out the window. It was time for brute force. "Also, need you to send word to Olem. His scouts will have reported the fighting. He needs to know about Prime Lektor. If he brings the entire brigade in before we find Prime, it'll get everyone killed."

"I'll send a few of my boys looking," Flerring promised. "Until then, you need to rest."

"I don't have time to rest."

Flerring grinned down at her. "You're not gonna have a choice.

Not with that tea and all the blood you lost. You'll be out within minutes." Without another word, Flerring blew her lantern out and shuffled off into the darkness.

Vlora lay still in frustration, staring at the ceiling, wishing she could move. She might be wounded, but she could still think. She had to formulate a plan to find Prime and figure out what she was going to do if they couldn't destroy the stone with Flerring's blasting oil.

She was halfway through the second thought when she again lost consciousness.

When Vlora came to, it was once again light outside. The cabin was quiet and cold, and she guessed that it was still early in the morning. Outside, she could hear Little Flerring shouting instructions at her workers and wondered if Flerring was beginning to shut down her operation. It would make sense, of course. Even if order were restored tomorrow, the gold mines were probably going to be all but empty until the city could rebuild enough to support all these miners.

The pain was back. It wasn't bad, if Vlora didn't move. Or breathe. She could feel something soft beneath her fingers, and realized that Flerring had left her a powder charge. Saying a silent word of thanks, she managed to bring it to her mouth, breaking it open and sprinkling the powder on her tongue. Granules bounced off her lips and rolled down her cheeks, and she gave a sigh of appreciation as the trance kicked in.

Gradually, the hairs on Vlora's neck began to stand on end as she came to the slow realization that there was someone else in the room. "Who's there?" she asked, listening to the soft sound of breathing.

There was a creak as someone got up from a chair, then heavy footsteps. Vlora grimaced through the pain and forced herself to roll onto her side, expecting to find one of Flerring's workers keeping watch.

She froze at the sight of the man standing beside the bed. He was of medium height and heavy-set, with an aged, distinguished face marked by a purple birthmark that spidered across his bald head. He wore Privileged gloves on both hands, the runes gold and crimson, and frowned down at Vlora like a father might at a disruptive child.

It took all of Vlora's strength *not* to call out. Prime could kill everyone here before they had the chance to aid her. No sense in all of them dying. "Prime," she croaked, her throat dry.

"Little Vlora," Prime said. He dragged the chair across the room and sat down beside the bed, folding his hands in his lap. "I understand that you're Lady Flint now, is that true?"

"Yes."

"Seems like just yesterday you were a street tramp, taken in by Tamas." Prime snorted. "I've been following your exploits in the papers. First the Kez Civil War, then the Fatrastan frontier, then Landfall. Now I find you at the ass end of nowhere with a bounty on your head as if you're a common outlaw and not a war hero with your own mercenary army."

Vlora stared at the side of Prime's face, trying to read him. His expression was neutral, his face grandfatherly, and she grabbed on to the sudden hope that perhaps he wasn't here to kill her.

"When's the last time we saw each other?" Prime asked. "The Adran-Kez War?"

"Right before you ran," Vlora said coldly. She silently rebuked herself. She wasn't going to fight her way out of this—her only chance was to talk. Unfortunately, she was not good at talking.

"Ah, yes," Prime said, seemingly unbothered by the accusation of cowardice. "You have to understand, I'm not a violent man. I've never been good at war. And Kresimir was there! Pit, Kresimir scared me. You have no idea just how..." He trailed off, chuckling to himself as if he were relating a happy memory. "And then the god of the Nine was killed by mortals. If I'd known how that was going to end up, I might have stayed. But what's done is done. I moved on to other work."

Vlora was struck by a sudden memory of Prime Lektor visiting Tamas's house. She still had been an early teen at the time. Borbador hadn't yet been snatched up by the royal cabal. She and Taniel were not yet lovers. They were all just happy stepsiblings. Prime had visited for a private conversation with Tamas, giving each of the children sweets out of his pocket. She only now realized that he and Tamas were probably discussing the coup that they would perform against their king five or six years later.

Despite his grandfatherly look, despite his past loyalties and his current claim of pacifism, it was important to remember who—and what—Prime was. He had spoken with the gods and witnessed the creation of the Nine. He could snuff her out in an instant.

"So what are you doing here?" she asked.

Prime tsked quietly. "I was just about to ask you the same thing. This is an out-of-the-way place. You've been gallivanting around the city for weeks pretending to be a common hired sword. But your army is camped outside the city while you"—he pointed one finger at her, his hand trembling—"you have been looking for something."

Vlora tried to think of an excuse—any plausible reason for her presence here—but came up with nothing.

Prime continued before she could respond. "You're looking for the godstone. It's unfortunate, little Vlora. You lost one godstone to the Dynize on the plains south of Landfall. I will not allow you a chance at the second godstone. I will not allow anyone that chance."

"I…" Vlora blinked at Prime, trying to figure out what was going on inside his head. "I don't want anyone to have that chance, either."

"An interesting sentiment. I don't know who you're working for right now. It could be Lindet. It could be the Adran Cabal. Maybe you're working for yourself. But I will allow none of you to have the godstone. It is too dangerous to fall into the hands of mortals."

"And you think the Predeii are any more trustworthy?" Vlora spat before she could stop herself.

Prime seemed surprised by this. "What? Oh, absolutely not. If I knew where the others were—if any of them are alive—I would keep it away from them as well."

"I think," Vlora said, trying to focus her thoughts, "that we need to come to an understanding." If Prime was telling the truth, and he was indeed here to keep anyone else from finding the godstone, then they were fighting for the same thing. Prime could be a valuable ally if he could be convinced. She considered the ramifications and decided to tell him the truth. "Prime, I don't want the godstone used any more than you do. I fought for Landfall to keep the godstone out of the hands of the Dynize. I have a bounty on my head because I tried to arrest Lindet when I found out she wanted to *use* the godstone."

She continued in earnest. "I lived through that war. I saw it to the very end and I lost so many people I hold dear. I was a prisoner of Brude, and I saw Kresimir. Do you think I *want* more gods in this world? I'm here to destroy the damned thing!"

Prime sat back in the chair, looking troubled. He examined Vlora, tilting his head first to one side and then the other. "I've always been too trusting. I've always put my faith in people. That's why I spent so many centuries administrating a university in Adopest." His expression hardened. "But people have betrayed that trust too many times. I see the Dynize. I see Lindet. I see the ambitions of the cabals and the governments. All knowledge of the godstone must be erased."

"It's too late for that," Vlora said, reaching out to him. "The Dynize know. That's why they're here. *Everyone* knows. Everyone who matters. You can't hide it forever. Let me help you destroy it."

"I'm sorry," Prime said sadly. "I can't trust you. I wish I could, but... I'll make it quick." He raised his gloved hands.

"Wait!" Vlora pleaded.

There was a flash of movement out of the corner of her eye, and Vlora shied away, waiting for sorcery to burn the flesh from her bones. When she opened her eyes, she saw Prime sitting upright in his chair, a surprised expression on his face. Taniel stood behind him, a sword to Prime's neck. He held the sword like a garrote, with one hand on the pommel and one on the bare blade.

The blood pounded in Vlora's ears as she waited, helplessly wounded, for one of the two men to act.

Prime lifted his gloved hands. "Do you know what I am?"

"I know exactly what you are," Taniel whispered. "Do you know what *I* am?"

Prime frowned. "Is that Taniel Two-shot?"

"You've got an excellent memory."

"You died with Brude and Kresimir."

"My death was greatly exaggerated. Yours won't be if you don't pluck those gloves very carefully off your hands. I imagine you're very hard to kill, but I can decapitate you with a twitch and I will make sure all the pieces are scattered very widely."

Prime licked his lips, looking at Vlora ruefully. "Why don't you just kill me, then?"

"Because," Vlora told him, "I wasn't lying. We're here to destroy the godstone. We tried to destroy the one in Landfall but were unable to. If we all pool our knowledge together, we might actually be able to accomplish our mutual goal."

"You have five seconds to start taking off those gloves," Taniel warned. "Four... three... two—"

"Wait," Vlora said. "I need him to heal me."

"You what?" both men asked at the same time.

"I need you to heal me," she said to Prime. "I can't help in my state. I've got a bullet wound in my back and another on my shoulder. You at least need to take care of those so I can function."

"You would trust him to poke around inside your body? He was ready to kill you," Taniel said, his disbelief plain.

"If he's going to trust us, we have to trust him."

"I, uh, am not a very good healer," Prime said. "I've picked it up over the years, but I'm slow and not as thorough as a healer who has more power in the appropriate disciplines."

"Make do," Vlora said. She met Taniel's eyes. "Let him work."

Taniel relaxed, but he did not move. "All right, Prime. Get to work. We don't have much time, so focus on her back—and do a good job, hmm?"

CHAPTER 54

Vlora emerged from Flerring's cabin into the daylight, blinking to allow her eyes to adjust and reaching to scratch at the tightness that seemed to stretch across both shoulders and down her spine. Prime Lektor emerged behind her and, following close on Prime's heels, Taniel.

Vlora had been healed by Privileged on several occasions. The very best of them could make the experience only vaguely unpleasant—not unlike getting stitches from a skilled surgeon—and leave the body feeling a little stiff but good as new. Prime was true to his word in that he was not very good.

The process had taken him several hours. The bullet wound in her back was healed, true, but it felt as tight as a knot from riding a thousand miles in a badly sized saddle. The skin was taut and uncomfortable, and she would probably have to have it sliced open by a surgeon and rehealed sooner rather than later.

It was, she decided, still better than bleeding out. Or having to wait for months while she healed naturally.

"I warned you I wasn't very good," Prime said sullenly.

Vlora side-eyed the Predeii. There was a time when she had genuinely feared him, the way any teenager fears the headmaster of a university. That fear had changed when she found out his true nature and then...well, she'd never really come to grips with his abandoning Adro during the Adran-Kez War.

"It'll do," she said, rotating her shoulder and moving her sword arm. She could fight if she needed to, and that's all that mattered. "Where is the stone?" she asked.

"Nighttime Vale," Prime said.

Vlora swore. She'd scoured the Vale herself and seen nothing. Either Prime was lying or he had it hidden with sorcery. "You sure about that? I would have seen either it or your sorcery in the Else."

"I'm sure," Prime insisted, drawing himself up. His gloveless fingers twitched, and Vlora could feel his urge to reach into the Else. He still didn't trust them. "I'm not a novice when it comes to hiding sorcery," he said. "I hid in plain sight from the Adran Cabal for five hundred years. I can hide a bloody rock from some miners and a powder mage."

"That's fair. Stay here. I'm going to talk to Flerring."

Vlora found Little Flerring up in her largest workshop, overseeing the careful packing of black powder. The workshop was in chaos, tools strewn about, powder scattered on the floor as men hurried around with sacks and barrels. "What's going on?" Vlora asked.

Flerring glanced at her, then did a double take. "You should be in bed."

"I'm fine," Vlora insisted.

"You're not fine. You bloody well got shot." Flerring crossed the room and grabbed Vlora by the shoulder, pulling down the collar of her shirt to look at the wound. Her eyes narrowed. "There's sorcery here."

Vlora had no interest in explaining Prime Lektor's role. "Taniel arrived with an old friend. I'll be fine."

"Don't spill that, you twat!" Flerring roared at one of her men. "You're overfilling the barrels!" She turned back to Vlora. "We're packing up. The town is half-torched, and everyone is out for blood. I'm going to sell off what stock I can and get out of here before the Dynize come too far north. Fatrasta is too hot for my blood."

"The temperature or the conflict?"

"Both."

"Right." Vlora took Flerring by the arm, pulling her close. "That blasting oil. I need it."

"I don't—"

"I need it *today*," Vlora hissed. "We have a man who knows where the artifact is. I want it destroyed as quickly as possible. You've had your week."

Flerring looked toward her men packing her supplies and made a sour face. "I don't want to stick around any longer than we have to."

"Send your men ahead. You made a promise."

She could see the conflict in Flerring's expression. Flerring scowled, turning her head with a quick intake of breath, before finally speaking. "All right. I'll keep a few of my boys and all the blasting oil I've scrounged behind and send everyone else on. The location better be ready for blasting, because I don't intend on staying any more than a couple of days."

"Take all your supplies to the Nighttime Vale. I'll be waiting."

Vlora rejoined Taniel and Prime Lektor, and the three of them rode back into town, doing a long circuit around the base of the mountains to avoid the armed men prowling the streets and the bucket brigades still trying to put out fires.

"Who won?" Vlora asked Taniel as they crossed the entrance to a narrow valley. Nearby, a couple of drunk miners watched the town, passing a jug of grog between them and alternately weeping and giggling at some lost fortune.

Taniel looked up, deep in thought as he rubbed the cloth of

Prime's confiscated gloves between two fingers. "Brown Bear Burt," he said, nodding toward the center of Yellow Creek. "I understand you killed Jezzy with a controlled explosion. Not much to do for Burt but to mop up Jezzy's forces and put out the fires."

"I hope there's a damned lot of fires," Vlora murmured to herself. She wanted Burt distracted until they were well and gone. He'd promised not to get in her way, but the promise of a miner baron didn't reassure her.

"There were," Taniel answered, as if she had spoken to him directly. "But he also has a lot of men." A half smile crossed Taniel's face and he seemed to withdraw into his own thoughts again. Vlora leaned over and smacked him on the arm.

"What do you mean he has a lot of men? I thought Jezzy outnumbered him?"

Taniel blinked back at her. "Oh, yeah. That's what everyone thought. They also thought he was from Landfall."

"He's not?"

"He's not," Taniel confirmed.

Vlora's mind scrambled, trying to figure out what could be keeping Taniel distracted like this. Her thoughts went to the conversation they'd had riding into Yellow Creek three weeks ago. "Palo Nation?" she asked.

Taniel nodded. "I didn't know until I caught a glimpse of him on my way to find you. He's Palo Nation, and so is the army he's had camped up in the mountains until he brought them down to restore order last night."

Vlora felt her stomach lurch. "How big of any army?"

"About two thousand riflemen. The Palo Nation doesn't field real armies. They field highly organized groups of skirmishers armed with rifles that rival the Hrusch."

This was getting better and better. The Palo Nation had just taken control of Yellow Creek, leaving Vlora once more in enemy territory—and she *did* assume they were the enemy. Everyone was the enemy right now, because everyone wanted to get hold of the godstone. So much for Burt's promise. What *else* was he hiding? "We can't let them know about the stone," she said. She looked at Prime. "Your wards to keep the stone hidden, are they still in place?"

"No reason they shouldn't be," Prime answered.

"Are they looking for the stone?" Vlora asked Taniel.

He seemed to withdraw into himself once again, his face troubled. "I don't know. I don't think so."

"Then why are they in Yellow Creek? If they had the firepower, why haven't they seized control of the town before today?"

"It's not like them to act out in the open south of the Ironhook Mountains. I don't know what they're up to."

"I think I liked it better when you seemed to know everything," Vlora snapped, feeling her tension get the better of her. "Hurry up, old man," she told Prime. "We need to get a move on. I damn well hope no one stops Little Flerring on her way up here."

They continued on their circuit around the town and entered Nighttime Vale. A handful of Palo wearing dusters and holding rifles had replaced Jezzy's guards, but they were the only other people in the Vale and did not seem to notice the small party passing by.

"I've cloaked us in sorcery," Prime explained. "I always do when I come this way. It's best to keep the artifact hidden."

Vlora couldn't sense even the slightest hint of sorcery. The thought made her sick to her stomach.

Prime turned sharply after they passed the entrance to the Vale and led them up the side of the mountain, not more than fifty paces from where Vlora had crossed over the cliffs a few nights before. There was no construction here, none of the mining equipment or tents that were ubiquitous throughout the rest of the valley. There was just the foot of the mountain covered by a landslide of stone rubble from somewhere farther up the mountainside.

Prime stopped and pointed at the mountain. "It's difficult to see, but if you look carefully, you can trace the path of the landslide that deposited these stones here."

Vlora squinted up into the sparse cloud cover, barely able to see the peak through tufts of wispy white. If she squinted just right, she could imagine that the mountain's peak had once been more squared than pointed, and that one corner of that square had sheared off and tumbled all this way to rest in the Vale.

"The godstone," Taniel said, voicing the same conclusion that Vlora had just reached. "It was up there?"

"It was, yes," Prime answered. He looked at them sullenly, scowling at the gloves that Taniel still held in his hands. "You claim that you're here to destroy it. But it can't be destroyed. I've spent the last five years trying to figure out how to do so and came up with nothing."

"Have you actually tried to destroy it?" Vlora asked. "Or have you been studying it to further your own power?"

"I must study it to learn its weaknesses." Prime sniffed. "I have never been after power, my dear Vlora. I only seek knowledge."

Vlora looked at Taniel. "You remember what Bo likes to say about that?"

"Knowledge *is* power," Taniel quoted, giving Prime a sallow smile.

Without his gloves, Prime looked like nothing more than an overweight, cranky old man. He scowled at them both, then shook his head. "You cannot destroy it," he repeated. "I don't believe it can be done."

Vlora thought about all the black powder they had piled around the godstone in Landfall, only for it to cause not even a scratch. "We'll see. Take us to the damned thing."

Prime scoffed. "You think you're so smart, but you can't even see that which is in front of you. Dismount and take three steps forward."

Vlora did as instructed, feeling outward with her sorcerous senses for an illusion, or a trap, or anything. She could sense nothing, but as she took that third step, her vision seemed to shift. It happened so suddenly that it made her dizzy, forcing her to fall against a nearby boulder.

"Vlora?" Taniel called.

She waved him off and felt her eyes widen as she took in this new perspective.

The slope of old rubble was no longer there, but rather cleared away from her to the base of the mountain to create a flat work area upon which there was a small cabin, an outhouse, and a canvas canopy covering an obelisk that looked exactly like the one in Landfall.

Her breath caught in her throat, and the sight of the thing gave her a sense of foreboding that she hadn't felt since the end of the Adran-Kez War. Her chest was tight, her vision blurry. This stone—this *thing*—that had eluded her for the last month was suddenly here, right in front of her face, and she was speechless.

The obelisk lay on its side. It was not as large as the one in Landfall. Eyeing the dimensions, she guessed it to be around thirty feet long and less than four feet wide, tapering at the end. It was covered in ancient script that had been cleaned meticulously of all dirt and grit, and it was made of a light-gray limestone that made Vlora wonder if it was cut from the same stone as its larger twin back in Landfall.

Taniel and Prime joined them. Taniel did not seem as affected by the sight of the thing as she had been, though his breath did grow short. Prime merely scowled at it, like a man returning to a hated live-in relative.

"So they found you, eh?"

The voice made both Vlora and Taniel whirl, drawing their pistols. A woman had stepped out of the cabin and stood by the doorway, her arms crossed. She looked to be in her late thirties: a slim woman of medium height with a shaved head and an old scar that lifted the corner of her lip and crossed her cheek to her temple. Her arms ended in strange gloves that, upon closer examination, were unmoving bronze hands held in place by leather straps.

Vlora had never met this woman, but she knew exactly who she was from Borbador's stories.

She was another Predeii, personally responsible for the summoning of Kresimir during the Adran-Kez War. If Bo was correct, she was as much a catalyst of the war as Field Marshal Tamas. Vlora was *not* happy to see her.

"Hello, Julene," Taniel said, lowering his pistol.

"Two-shot," Julene purred. "It feels like we were hanging from Kresimir's ropes together just yesterday. How *have* you been?"

Taniel seemed neither perturbed nor particularly surprised to find Julene here. Vlora was both, and she kept her pistol raised for several seconds after Taniel had put away his. "That was ten years ago," Taniel said.

"When you've been alive as long as I have, Two-shot, a decade feels like nothing more than a long weekend." Julene's gaze fell to Vlora and she pursed her lips. "I told Prime he should have killed you the moment he spotted you in town. But he's a damned coward. What do you call yourself, Prime? A pacifist?"

"I went to finish her off," Prime snapped, "but this one showed up."

Julene took two steps toward Taniel, her nostrils flaring and her eyes narrowing. "Your blood witch is getting stronger," she said. "I can barely see the wards protecting you." She let out a sudden, half-mad, barking laugh. "Bad luck for you, Prime. You finally get up the guts to kill someone and the one powder mage in the world who can stop you happens to be about."

Vlora looked from Prime to Julene. "Some warning that you weren't alone would have been nice," she told Prime.

"You didn't ask," he responded.

Julene held up her metal hands. "I may be near immortal, but I'm not much of a threat. I still can't touch the Else."

"That only makes you slightly less dangerous," Taniel said. His casual manner was betrayed by the tension Vlora could see in his arms and the intensity of his gaze, like a dog with hackles raised. Vlora took a half step back. If this came to a fight, she was so badly outclassed that it was almost laughable. Taniel would be on his own against these two.

"We're here to destroy the godstone," Vlora interjected.

All eyes snapped to her. Julene turned her head to one side. "You what?"

"You heard me."

"I heard you. I just don't believe you. If you cornered Prime, you obviously know what the godstones do, and if you know, then you have no intention of destroying them. Mortals don't give up that kind of power." The wild look in Julene's eyes was suddenly gone, replaced by a focused gaze and a very distinct air of distrust.

"She's not lying," Taniel said quietly. "Both Lindet and the Dynize are looking for the damned thing. We intend on reducing it to rubble before either of them can reach it."

"You can't destroy it," Prime insisted once again. "It's too powerful. Kresimir made these things to last until long after all life on this planet is extinct. I can't even pick apart the simplest of the wards surrounding it, and I've been doing this for millennia!" Prime's voice rose in crescendo, and Vlora wondered if he truly had been trying to destroy the stone. He sounded frustrated as pit that even his powerful sorcery paled next to that of a god who'd been dead for a decade.

Julene had grown quiet, returning to her place in the doorway and watching Vlora and Taniel warily. "This is the work of a god," she said. "You would destroy it just to keep it out of the hands of others?"

"I would destroy it either way," Vlora said, forcing down her fear and fixing Julene with a look that dared her to question her resolve.

Taniel stepped between them, waving his hand in front of

Julene's face. "Everyone should calm down. If I'm not mistaken, and unless the two of you are lying through your teeth, we should all be on the same side. We don't want the godstone to fall into the hands of any of the local powers: Hence, it should be destroyed."

Vlora stared at Julene until the Predeii finally looked away with a sigh. "Agreed," Julene said.

"Agreed," Vlora echoed.

Prime still looked uncertain. "How do you propose we destroy it?"

Taniel looked to Vlora, and she suddenly felt foolish for her belief that the invention of a gunpowder maker from Adopest could do what thousands of years of sorcerous knowledge could not. "I intend on blowing it up."

"We tried that already, years ago," Julene said. "We piled several carts' worth of powder barrels on it and lit the fuse. It didn't do anything but cause a second landslide that we had to clear away."

"And we tried it on the godstone in Landfall," Taniel said.

"So why," Julene said with more than a hint of disdain, "do you think you can blow it up?"

Vlora remained silent, suddenly feeling overwhelmed and fearful. "We have to try," she finally said. "If we cannot destroy it, then we'll haul the thing to the coast, put it on a ship, and sink it to the bottom of the sea."

"And you expect to be able to do that with Dynize and Fatrastan armies crawling all over the countryside?" Prime demanded.

"With your help we could."

Julene scoffed again. "Don't look at us. I'm useless without my hands, and this coward might as well be. He'd rather pick up and run than raise his hands to cause bloodshed."

Prime's lip curled, but he did not dispute the claim.

Vlora looked to Taniel for reassurance, but he seemed just as uncertain as she felt. His brow furrowed, he walked to the godstone and ran his gloved fingers along the runes, shuddering visibly.

"I should have brought Ka-poel," she heard him mutter. Louder, he said, "Like Vlora said, we have to try."

"It'll be a waste of gunpowder," Julene stated.

"We're not using powder," Vlora responded, heading over to a rock and sitting down where she could watch the entrance to the valley. She ignored the others, taking the time to close her eyes and meditate.

It was almost three hours until a convoy of wagons finally appeared, with Flerring sitting in the foremost one. She said something to Burt's guards, money changed hands, and she continued on through the pass. Vlora went down to meet her and show her the way to the hidden godstone.

"Get working right away. We've got one shot at this, and then, if it doesn't work, we'll have to figure out another plan."

Flerring leaned down from the lip of the wagon. "I'll get to work," she said, "but you might want to head into Yellow Creek."

"Why?"

"Because four hundred Riflejacks just showed up outside the town and Burt is getting mighty nervous."

Vlora thought of the destruction and the rumors that must be swirling about her fight with the other powder mage. She then considered what Olem would do if he assumed her dead at the hands of a bunch of frontier ruffians. "Get started on the stone," she shouted into her shoulder, sprinting for her horse. "I've got to stop a slaughter."

CHAPTER 55

Vlora spotted her soldiers from the entrance to Night-time Vale. They'd taken up a position just on the edge of town, where they'd formed into two imposing ranks. Rifles were still shouldered, which was a good sign, but she knew better than anyone how quickly the Riflejacks could open fire from a ready position.

She wasn't able to see what they were up against until she was almost upon them. Galloping down the main avenue, she steered her horse through toppled carts across bloody cobbles—the aftermath of the fighting between Jezzy's and Burt's gangs—and arrived to find about three hundred hired guns and prospectors strung out across rooftops, shop fronts, and barricaded roads. There were about thirty yards between the Riflejacks and the city's would-be defenders. The Riflejacks had the numbers and the training, but the defenders held the high defensive positions. If this went south, it would go *very* poorly for both sides.

Vlora leapt from the saddle and crossed a short barricade to where Burt and Olem stood facing each other in the open space between the two forces. "Wait!"

Olem looked up with a surprised expression that passed quickly to relief and then stoicism. Burt let out a heavy sigh and gestured to Vlora as she arrived.

"See?" Burt said. "I told you she was fine the last time I saw her."

Vlora remembered lying in the dirt, facedown, after her duel with Nohan. "Fine" seemed like a stretch, but she let it pass. "Stand down," she ordered. "Both of you."

Olem regarded Burt with a long, thoughtful look, then swept his gaze across the assembled defenders. "We'll stand down when they stand down."

Vlora swore under her breath and turned to Burt. "This doesn't have to escalate."

"I'd really rather it not," Burt replied coolly. "The colonel here was just informing me that he would take apart Yellow Creek stick by stick to find you. I told him that was entirely unnecessary. You and I had a deal."

"And it still stands, right?" Vlora fixed Burt with a long, hard look.

"It still stands." Burt gestured to the city. "Thanks to you, and one of Jezzy's men getting trigger-happy, this town belongs to me." He scowled at Vlora, taking a step back to examine her shoulder and back. "The last time I saw you, you'd been shot."

"Shot?" Olem echoed. "I thought you said she was fine?"

"Fine-ish."

"Long story," Vlora cut Burt off before he could say anything else. "But everyone needs to back off before one of *your* men loses their nerve and this turns into a pitched battle. Olem, order the Riflejacks to fall back. Burt, will a half mile be sufficient to cool everyone's temper?"

"It will." Burt gave a magnanimous smile. "In the meantime,

would you join me for a drink? I think the three of us need to talk. Now."

"You don't remember me, do you?"

Vlora took a whiskey from Burt and glanced at Olem, uncertain. They sat around Burt's desk in the office above his brothel. The building was empty except for the three of them—everyone else putting out fires, sifting through the ashes, or fighting over Jezzy's unguarded claims. Vlora wondered why Burt wasn't out there overseeing the whole thing. "Have we met before?"

Burt offered Olem a cigarette and took his own seat, letting out a soft laugh. "We have. About twelve years ago."

"I only first came to Fatrasta a couple years back," Vlora said with some confusion.

"That doesn't mean I haven't been to Adro."

Vlora frowned. Palo were quite rare in the Nine. A decade ago they were still considered mysterious savages by polite society. "When?"

"Jilleman University," Burt said.

Vlora leaned forward, squinting at Burt's face. She searched her memory for a few moments before locking on to something. "I did meet a Palo. My first year. I don't remember his name, but..." She trailed off. Occasionally, a wealthy Palo chieftain would send a favored child to the Nine to get a Kressian education. Sometimes a whole tribe would pool their wealth to do the same. Vlora remembered one of the former—a boy, quite young with an optimistic face who'd paraded around in frontier buckskins and spoke Adran with an accent so bad it was laughable. She tried to reconcile that boy with the suave frontier capitalist sitting across from her.

Burt grinned, watching her face. "You do remember!"

"Your name wasn't Burt. I would have remembered that."

"No." Burt looked up as if searching his memory. "I don't even remember what I went by. Something unpronounceable."

"So you weren't really a chieftain's son?" Vlora asked.

"That, more or less, was true. Most of the details were either foggy or outright lies."

Olem stood with an unlit cigarette between his fingers. "Why the deception?"

"We'll get to that," Burt said, lighting a cigar before tossing Olem a box of matches. "First, you should know that both Lindet and the Dynize know that you're here, and why you've come. Lindet's Second Field Army was wiped out in three successive battles a couple weeks back, so she's in no position to send anyone after you. The Dynize, however, have five brigades on your tail. I'm guessing they'll be here in four days."

Vlora stared, openmouthed, at Burt. Olem scoffed. "You couldn't possibly know all that."

"I do," Burt said without a trace of smugness. "Lindet thinks she runs the messenger service along the mountains—and she does pay for most of it. But it's staffed by my people. The information carried along it reaches me before it reaches her. You," he said, pointing to Vlora, "were outed by her spies about the same time the Dynize destroyed the Second Army."

"You could have warned me."

"It wasn't convenient at the time," Burt said with an apologetic smile. "But it is now, and you're being warned."

Vlora tried to read Burt's face, attempting to come away with any real impression of the man. He was a blank slate, returning her gaze with a coolness that bordered on unsettling. "So you know why we're here?"

"I assume I do. You're looking for the godstone."

Vlora shared a glance with Olem before nodding slowly. "You're not a frontier capitalist, are you?"

"Oh, I'm very much a frontier capitalist," Burt responded,

looking somewhat hurt. "I've gotten to be filthy rich working this town." He gave Vlora a lopsided smile. "But you're right, I'm not just a prospector."

Vlora remembered her conversations with Taniel, and his search for a contact with the Palo Nation. "You're with the Palo Nation."

"I'm impressed you've heard of it."

"A friend warned me."

Burt snorted. "You mean Taniel Two-shot?" He scratched his head vigorously, squinting at Vlora through one eye until he was done. "I'll be honest, I don't really know what to do with him. Letting him sit in that prison for the last three weeks was the best decision I've made in years. I do *not* like someone like him running around unchecked."

"How did you know he'd stay?"

"Because he's a good man. We've met on several occasions, actually. Which was another reason I didn't want him to see me before I was ready."

"Are there any of our secrets you *don't* know?" Olem asked.

"I…" Burt pulled a wry face and leaned forward, spreading his arms across his desk. "A quick history lesson, my friends, and listen carefully because only a handful of Kressians have ever heard it: Fifty years ago, my grandfather ruled a midsized tribe in what you would call the Fatrastan Wilds. At the time, he had managed to unite dozens of tribes into a sort of loose coalition, not one of which had ever made contact with a Kressian. Until, that is, a young explorer arrived and made friends with my grandfather. The explorer wound up marrying one of his daughters—my mother."

"You're not fully Palo?" Vlora asked in surprise.

"I'm half-Adran," Burt said with a smile. "But I don't look it." He continued with his story. "My father was something of a Fatrastaphile—he loved everything about this continent, and colonial expansion was one of the few things that I've ever seen him get worked up about. Together with my grandparents, my aunts and uncles, and my mother, he began to make a plan for the future of his tribe, to protect them from the Kressian encroachment.

"Geography was our ally. Without inside knowledge, the Iron-hook Mountains are very difficult to cross, and the wilds beyond them are vast. For fifty years, no one has questioned the fact that Kressian explorers rarely return from their expeditions north. And for fifty years, no one in the Nine has questioned the wealthy, eccentric savages sent to learn at Kressian universities. You've gawked and laughed, but never thought twice. And during that time, we learned." Burt stopped, cleared his throat. "I've gone on too long, so here is a better summary: Beginning with my grandfather, the Palo Nation has studied you without being studied back. We have co-opted the best parts of your civilization. The tribes were united, the hereditary chieftain system replaced with democracy. We have become the thing that Lindet and all the rest of the colonial powers fear the most: natives who have modernized before we could be crushed underfoot."

A long silence hung in the air, and Burt took advantage of it to relight his cigar. He'd finished his tale with a measure of emotion, but it disappeared back into tranquility as he puffed up a storm of cigar smoke.

"Why are you telling us this?" Vlora asked.

Burt pointed his cigar at her. "Because I'm laying all my cards on the table. Because the Palo Nation won't remain hidden forever, and I, if you'll remember, am half Adran. I quite like Adro. It is the only democracy in the Nine, and I would like very much to lay the groundwork of an alliance."

Vlora felt like she'd been punched in the face. This was not what she'd expected when she came here looking for the godstones, not even in the slightest. Taniel's warnings about the Palo Nation were, in retrospect, not emphatic enough. "I think that our politicians would be amenable to the idea. But I'm not one of them."

"You're a damned war hero, an Adran general, and a member of the Republic Cabal. I can think of perhaps five people who would be more advantageous to have this conversation with. None of them are here, and none of them quite have your reputation for civility."

"I see. Consider me intrigued. But there are plenty of things to worry about before a formal alliance. Where do the godstones come into this? Or the Dynize, for that matter."

"The Dynize," Burt repeated, pulling a sour face. "They're one of the reasons we're having this conversation. If they win this war, they won't be satisfied with tall tales from over the mountains. They will explore north, in force, and they will do so with far more violence and organization than Lindet can manage. For all her intelligence, she's been holding together a house of cards by sheer willpower and has had no interest in pursuing rumors of our existence. I'm not convinced the Dynize will feel the same way."

"And the godstone?"

Burt frowned at Olem, then at Vlora. "We are a secular society. We have destroyed our idols, forgotten our gods, and we are better for it. My spies tell me that you and Lindet fell out because you wanted to destroy the stone, so I say this: By all means, destroy it. My government wants nothing to do with the damned thing. If we could have found it, we would have already removed it to the farthest reaches of our territory just to keep it out of Lindet's hands." Something must have shown in Vlora's face, because Burt lifted an eyebrow. "You've found it, haven't you?"

"And we're working toward destroying it," Vlora replied.

"Excellent." Burt stood up, clapping his hands together. "Can you do it before the Dynize arrive?"

"We hope so," Vlora said hesitantly.

"You have four days."

"Actually, we only have two. We have to destroy it, then get out of here before the Dynize arrive. The Dynize have instructions to take my head."

"Why?" Burt asked with disgust.

"Because I humiliated their general, or whatever he wants to call himself, back at Landfall."

"Ah," Burt said. "Nothing like a despot who takes things personally. The Dynize and Kressians aren't all that different, are they?"

"We all want to be the last ones standing," Olem commented.

"Now, that's just everyone." Burt raised his glass of whiskey. "You will have what help I can give you. The town is yours to billet your men, but as you suggest, you shouldn't tarry. Destroy the godstone or make preparations to move it immediately."

Vlora considered the offer for a moment, waiting for the other shoe to drop. Where was the price, or the betrayal? Was Burt seriously doing all this just to make a friend in the Nine? "You do realize that putting us up, even for a night or two, will earn the anger of the Dynize? If we leave, the town will be undefended."

"I know," Burt said with a sigh. "I've spent the last few years trying to take this town over by wile, to turn it into a beachhead for my country without Lindet finding out. Everything changed when the Dynize invaded, though. If they head our way, we will eject the prospectors and dynamite the passes. They might take the town, but my people will be safe up in the high places."

"Even if they have Privileged?"

"We are not . . . undefended when it comes to sorcery."

Vlora wondered what Taniel would say when she told him about this conversation. She would have to do it slowly, so she could cast his expression to memory. She stood up, putting out her hand. "We'll do our best to be gone well before the Dynize arrive. Thank you, Burt. And I hope this is the start of a long friendship."

CHAPTER 56

Michel sat on a stool, the only piece of furniture in a looted, upscale tenement apartment on the northwest edge of the Landfall Plateau. His eyes were closed, his mind wandering, as he considered the options available to him from this point out.

The apartment was, as far as Michel could tell, the nicest of Taniel's safe houses. It had tall ceilings and enormous, south-facing windows in the great room, and even a master bedroom with a balcony that looked off the plateau. At some point over the last couple of months it had been thoroughly tossed—a safe in the corner of the master bedroom had been ripped out of the wall, the furniture and silver stolen, and even the gas lines turned off and ripped out of the wall. It was the first time Michel had been to this particular safe house and he was more than a little disappointed to find it in this state.

But it did give him a place to think.

His whole mission with the Dynize was to snatch Mara—Ichtracia—and get her the pit out of Dynize territory. The fact that she was a Privileged made this more like trying to extract a rabid bear rather than an informant. Even if she was a normal person, all his old Blackhat routes were compromised. He needed a new escape route.

And he found himself less eager to use it than he had expected. The Dynize government was a viper's nest, with Sedial as the king viper ready to kill anything that moved. But part of Michel desperately wanted to finish what he'd started. Hunting down Blackhats had brought out a mean streak in him, a deep satisfaction at rounding up the people whom he'd helped to oppress Landfall for so long. Watching the way the Dynize treated the occupied city, and especially the Palo, had deepened Michel's hatred of Lindet's regime. Je Tura's indiscriminate bombings, his killing of women and children—these gave Michel a real urge to finally put him in the ground.

He bounced a coin on his knee, thinking about Tenik, and wondering if Tenik and Yaret would ever forgive him for disappearing right on the eve of finally clearing Landfall of the Blackhats.

"Guess we'll have to find out." Michel got to his feet, carrying the stool over to the corner of the great room. He set it against the wall, using it as a stepping point to lift himself onto the gaudy trim that went around the middle of the wall. He braced one leg on a hole in the plaster where someone had torn out a gas lantern, then kicked another hole in the plaster to get him up near the ceiling. He produced a knife, and began to stab through the ceiling until he hit something solid.

His legs trembled from the effort of bracing himself, and the half-healed gunshot wound in his chest began to burn. He quickly cut through the ceiling plaster and then used the handle of the knife to bash the rest of it until the ceiling finally gave way, a large metal box about the size of two saddlebags falling to the ground in a cloud of plaster dust.

Michel followed it down and cracked the seal on the box with his knife. He opened it cautiously, his face away from the lid until he was sure it wasn't booby-trapped, and finally took a good look at the contents.

He gave a low whistle. "Taniel, you were really damn ready for anything, weren't you?"

Michel found a large stable in the shadow of the plateau, a steady stream of carts moving in and out or parking in the street outside with loads of pumpkins or barrels or boxed uniforms for the Dynize Army. A sign over the door said HALFORD HAULING, and from what Michel had heard, the old man who owned the place had made himself a fortune just since the invasion by negotiating with some quartermaster to move supplies for a Dynize regiment.

Michel was dressed in a laborer's cotton suit—his favorite disguise—and walked straight in through the front gate of the stable with hat in hand. Dozens of workers repaired wheels, transferred cargo, or tended to horses, and no one seemed to notice him as he slipped into one of the cart-parking stalls and found a young man checking equipment in the corner.

The young man had thinned since Michel saw him last, five or six months ago. His wisp of a beard was still a disgrace, and he still had that plain face of someone who could disappear into the crowd, but he moved with a purpose and confidence that he had not possessed before.

"Hello, Dristan," Michel said, leaning against the wall beside him.

Dristan frowned and looked up at Michel, blinking a few times, clearly lost in his own thoughts. "Do I know you?"

"We only met briefly," Michel said, "but we have met. I heard you drive for Halford now. That's quite a step up from where you were before the invasion."

Dristan got a sort of worried look, staring at Michel sidelong like one might a long-absent cousin who'd come looking for money. "I think you have the wrong man."

Michel pointed at Dristan playfully. "That, I do not. The last time we saw each other, I was getting pissed at six o'clock in the morning in a pub in Lower Landfall."

The color suddenly drained from Dristan's face. He looked around quickly for anyone who might overhear, and he hissed at Michel. "Pit, I remember you now. You're the spy who was supposed to train me."

"I am."

"Well, you listen to me. You never came looking for me, so I got a good job with Halford, and they just gave me my own route, and I don't want nothing to do with anything spy business. The Blackhats are finished in this town, and I won't let you take me down with them. Hear me?"

Michel held his hands up. "I'm not trying to take you down with anything, Dristan. I just want to hire you for a single route."

"I just said I won't do anything for the Blackhats."

"I'm not with the Blackhats anymore. Pit, I changed sides just like old Halford, and the Dynize are making me rich. Ask around. There's plenty of gossip about a Blackhat turncoat."

Dristan eyed Michel with suspicion. "What do you want?"

"Like I said, I want to hire you. I just need someone to move a package for me."

"If you need something hauled, you go inside and talk to Halford."

"No, I won't. I want *you*. I already checked your route. You're taking supplies to the front about forty miles north of here. It's, what, a week round-trip?"

Dristan swallowed hard.

Michel continued. "Next time you go north, I want you to take two people with you. They can hide in your supplies, or ride out front with you, or however the pit you want to do it. Just get them past the Dynize checkpoints with that little official card I know you carry around with you."

"And what do I get in return? Are you going to blackmail me?"

"Not in the slightest. I'm not with the Blackhats anymore, and have no interest in forcing you to do anything illicit."

"That sounds damned illicit to me."

Michel gave a casual shrug. "Eh. It's more of a convenience than anything else." He produced a heavy little bag from his pocket and thumbed four shiny yellow disks, each about the size of a coin, into one hand. They were blank, without stamp or any national marking. He tossed one to Dristan, who caught it and stared for a moment before Michel said, "Solid gold. Ask a jeweler, if you want to confirm it. Four now, six when you get your passengers past the last checkpoint. And one more if you don't ask any damn questions."

Dristan continued to stare at the coin. "I could buy this whole stable with what you're offering."

"Right now," Michel said, "convenience is more important to me than gold. Do we have a deal?"

Dristan bit the coin, muttering under his breath. "I'm allowed to take whichever of the next four shipments suits me. You give me a day, and we have a deal."

Michel lifted one finger. "I'll have to get back to you on the day."

"You have big damn balls coming back here after storming out without an explanation the other day." Ichtracia stood in her bedroom, watching Michel through puffy, red eyes that told him she'd either been crying or smoking mala. By the smell, it was the latter. She wore a dressing gown and slippers, and a discarded dress on the floor told Michel that she'd recently returned from somewhere.

Michel gave her his most charming smile, fingering the small bottle of chloroform wrapped in a rag in his left pocket. "I apologize."

"I should turn you inside out."

The words had no bite to them, and Michel wondered if maybe she *had* been crying. There was a defeated tone to her voice. He immediately began to worry, hoping this had nothing to do with him. Perhaps she'd just returned from another fight with her grandfather?

"I came to apologize and give you an explanation," Michel said.

Ichtracia took a deep breath, and he waited for her to dismiss him without a word, but she let it out in a frustrated sigh instead. "I'd like to know why you left the other day. I could have used company."

That tone was full of more hurt than Michel cared to plumb, and he found himself shocked by the rawness of it. He circled around her toward the window, glancing out into the street. "Are we alone?"

"I sent the footmen out to get me dinner. We have a few minutes."

"Will you promise that you won't turn me inside out until I've explained myself fully?"

Ichtracia's eyes narrowed. She wasn't wearing her gloves, but Michel didn't know if they weren't in the pockets of her dressing gown. He touched the bottle of chloroform and wondered just how stupid he really was. "I promise," she said.

"I need to clarify something first. Your nickname is Mara, correct?"

"It is," she said through clenched teeth.

"Is that a common nickname?" He already knew the answer to that.

"Why would it be?" There was genuine anger in her eyes, and Michel moved on quickly.

"I need to know, because I'm here for a woman named Mara." Michel's heart began to hammer, and he wondered if perhaps he was committing suicide. If there was even the slightest chance he was wrong, he might be dead before he could reach the door.

"Look, I didn't come to the Dynize to get back at the Blackhats who betrayed me. I've never even worked for them—not really. I came to the Dynize because my boss told me to retrieve a woman named Mara and get her out of Landfall. He told me that she was in incredible danger."

Ichtracia's jaw tightened and she reached into her pockets, producing her gloves. Michel leapt toward her, hands out front. "Wait! You were in contact with a woman, probably with sorcery, until about a year ago. You spoke to her again perhaps"—he grimaced—"two months ago. She may have warned you I was coming, she may not have, but I was sent to get you out."

Ichtracia's eyes wandered the room, her brow furrowing, and the gloves slipped from her fingers back into her pockets. She took several steps over to the bed and sat down, staring at her hands for a moment before looking up at Michel. "I shouldn't have ever answered when she spoke to me," she said softly.

"But you did."

"Because she seemed to know me. I told her things—too many things—and I have betrayed my country."

This was not going well, not at all. "I don't know what you told her. All I know is that I was asked to get you out. Look, I had no idea you were the woman I was sent for until I overheard Sedial the other day. I've been looking in vain for Mara, only to find out I'm sharing her bed. *That's* why I left. I had to gather my thoughts."

"I see." Ichtracia's eyes focused on Michel. "You were sent to save me?"

Her voice took on an angry tone that Michel didn't like. "That's what I was told."

"From *what*?" she demanded.

"I have no idea. Danger. That's all I know."

Ichtracia leaned toward him. "You have nowhere to take me. These are my people. I never told the voice in my head that I wanted to leave. I just told her I didn't want war."

"Well, she thinks you're going to get killed if you stay in Landfall."

"And that's supposed to surprise me?" she asked flatly. Michel had the sudden realization that there was something going on beneath the surface that he knew nothing about. More information that Taniel had withheld? Or something new? "My whole purpose is to die."

Did she mean as a tool of the state? Michel took a half step toward her, lowering his hands until he could feel the bottle in his pocket. He grimaced inwardly. No, he was not that stupid. Beyond the danger of chloroforming a Privileged, pulling shit like that would destroy any trust that had grown between them the last few days. He realized, quite suddenly, that he couldn't do that.

"Who are you?" she asked him.

The question took him off guard. He considered a dozen lies, and discarded them. "You know most of it already. I really am named Michel Bravis, and I really was a Blackhat Gold Rose. But I truly work for a man called the Red Hand, and I infiltrated the Blackhats on his behalf. I was still maintaining my cover when he asked me to get you out of the city safely. My cover was blown by one of my fellow Blackhats, so I came to the Dynize."

"You're going to betray them. Us." She laughed bitterly. "I suppose you're not betraying us if you never really were one of us. Yaret *adopted* you into his Household. Do you know what that even means? He took a foreign spy under his wing."

Michel swallowed. That trust was long gone. "I'm not betraying anyone. I won't steal anything. I won't kill people. I'm not even looking for information. I'm here for you."

"Betrayal doesn't just involve murder, Michel," Ichtracia said. "This whole thing with you dismantling the Blackhats—it was a front?"

"It was." He hesitated before continuing. "It actually felt pretty good. I've had to work with those assholes for years while they torture and subjugate my people."

Ichtracia, through her anger, actually cracked a smile. "I knew you were interesting."

Michel watched her hands, waiting for them to dip back into her pockets for her gloves. If she went for them, he might have no choice but to tackle her and try the chloroform. He really didn't want to do that.

"All of that, just to get to me," she scoffed quietly. "I'm not leaving, Michel. I spoke with a voice in my head. I told her some information, sure. But I never told her I wanted to join some Palo freedom fighter off in the jungle."

Michel's heart began to fall. This was it. A complete failure to finish his mission and—surprisingly hurtful—the end of his relationship with Ichtracia. He would probably be dead in a couple of minutes.

"What will you do?" she asked.

"If you refuse to come?"

"Yes."

"I'll look for the next opportunity to leave. I'm not going to force you to come with me."

She snorted. "As if you could." In a moment of bravado, Michel tossed her the bottle of chloroform. She caught it, looked at the label, and stared daggers at him. "You were going to use this on me?"

"I considered it. I'm supposed to do a job. But I like you a little more than that. So if you don't want to come, I'll just tell my boss that I couldn't find you. If you let me walk out of here, that is."

Ichtracia passed the chloroform back and forth between her hands, then held it to the light to look at the liquid inside. "I've heard this is unpleasant."

"It's not enjoyable." Michel wondered if he should make a run for it. "Look, how about this: I stay here three more days. I help Yaret find that prick je Tura and put an end to the Blackhats in Landfall for good. If at the end of those three days you change your mind, I have a way for us to disappear. If not... then I'll go alone."

"I won't change my mind. These are my people, Michel. I have a duty to fulfill."

"Consider it." Careful to make no sudden moves, Michel headed toward the door. He was out in the street before he allowed himself to breathe again. Three days. Three ways this could go: Either he'd get out alone, he'd get out with Ichtracia, or she'd hand him over to be tortured to death.

What a way to live.

CHAPTER 57

W e've run out of land," Jackal reported.

Styke sat in his saddle, frowning at a grassy hill on the horizon. They were a couple days south of New Starlight and had reached the far southwest corner of the Hammer, where rolling hills of fallow fields stretched for thousands of acres in every direction, barren but for the occasional farming hamlet carving out a living in the poor soil. The farming hamlets had been abandoned since the Dynize arrival, and they hadn't seen another soul for two days.

Styke glanced at Ibana, who cocked an eyebrow at him and turned her horse around and rode back down the line, checking in with officers and making sure that the whole company was still together.

A few rows back and to one side, Ka-poel and Celine kept their horses close and spoke in Ka-poel's sign language, eyes on each other's hands. Styke joined them. "We've run out of land," he told Ka-poel.

The bone-eye dropped her hands and stared back at him before looking toward that same grassy hill on the horizon. Beyond it were the high cliffs of the Hammer and a steep drop down to the beach, and then the narrow ocean that separated Fatrasta from Dynize.

"Are we close?" Styke asked. "I want to find this thing and be done with it as quickly as possible. It's only a matter of time before a Dynize army picks up our trail. I . . ." He trailed off, noticing that Ka-poel's eyes did not leave the horizon. Without a sign, she flipped her reins and headed toward the coast.

Styke rolled his tongue along his teeth, feeling the myriad of old aches and pains that seemed to accompany every day at this age. "Where's she going?" he asked Celine.

"I don't know." Even Celine seemed confused, and Styke sensed that there was something wrong in the stiff way that Ka-poel rode.

He leaned toward Jackal. "Keep a close eye on her, and a hand on your carbine."

"You expect me to shoot her?" Jackal seemed surprised by this.

"I don't know what to expect. These godstones are unpredictable." He took a deep breath, trying to fill his nostrils with sorcery, but the only whiff he got was the scent of Ka-poel's coppery power. He waited, uncertain, for several minutes before finally heading after her. Jackal and Celine followed.

They reached the cliff tops, only to find that Ka-poel had abandoned her horse and taken a steep path down to the beach. Styke watched her pick her way through the rocks.

"Do we wait for her to come back up?" Jackal asked.

"Maybe the thing is on the beach," Styke grunted, swinging out of the saddle.

They descended to the beach and joined Ka-poel on the shoreline, who was standing with her shoes discarded and her feet in the surf. The water lapped at Styke's boots, and he watched the side of her face with a growing concern. Her expression was stonelike, devoid of her usual bemusement or defiance. Her eyes seemed distant, as if she were deep in some kind of dream. He breathed in again, trying to read her sorcery, but nothing about the coppery smell had changed.

Jackal clung to the base of the cliff, watching Ka-poel as one might watch a rabid dog. Styke wondered if Jackal knew something he didn't.

Celine kicked her shoes off and walked into the surf, too, gently taking Ka-poel's hand. Ka-poel responded to the touch mechanically, her thumb gently stroking the back of Celine's wrist, and Styke suddenly felt like an invader in a private moment. He clenched his jaw, letting his irritation overwhelm his discomfort, and stepped up beside the two of them. "What are you looking at, girl?" he asked Ka-poel.

Ka-poel's brow furrowed, and she lifted one hand and touched her thumb to her chest. Styke recognized her symbol for "I" and the hesitation that followed it.

"What is it?" he urged.

Ka-poel's hands moved. Celine tilted her head to the side, watching as Ka-poel repeated the short phrase several times in a row. Celine's face grew concerned, and she glanced quickly at Styke and then back at Ka-poel.

"What is she saying?" Styke asked, his mouth suddenly dry.

"It's . . . it's not here," Celine translated.

Styke felt a knot form in the pit of his stomach, irritation turning to disbelief, to anger in the flash of an instant. "What do you mean it's not here?"

Ka-poel spread her hands. *I don't know.*

Styke grabbed her shoulder, and she suddenly leapt away from him, stumbling through the surf and falling into a defensive stance, her passive face suddenly angry. That coppery scent grew stronger in Styke's nostrils, and he became very conscious of Celine standing between them.

"Whoa," he said gently, reaching out and taking Celine by the hand. He pushed her behind him, jaw tight, then set one hand on the hilt of his boz knife. "Explain."

Ka-poel looked from Styke to Jackal and back again, no doubt taking note of the carbine in Jackal's hands. There was something suddenly feral in her eyes that Styke did not like—that he had not seen before. Her gaze shifted slowly to Celine, and that feral look seemed to fade. She straightened; then her hands flashed, repeating the phrase from a moment ago. Then she continued.

"It's not here," Celine translated. "I was wrong. My... compass was wrong. This godstone is not in Fatrasta."

Styke resisted the urge to take a half step closer. "Then where have you been leading us?"

"Toward the godstone."

"You just said it's not in Fatrasta..." Styke trailed off, realization setting in. He turned toward the western horizon, staring across the ocean in the direction she'd been facing when they reached the beach. "The third godstone is in Dynize?"

Ka-poel gave a short nod.

Styke thought of all the soldiers who'd died to get them here—of the lancers who'd fallen, of the new recruits who'd been butchered by a vengeful Dynize cuirassier, and of his own wounds he'd gathered on the journey. He bit his tongue, hard, clamping down on his rage, and considered having Taniel Two-shot come after him if he staved Ka-poel's head in this very instant.

"How long have you known?" he managed when he finally allowed himself to speak.

"I have suspected for a few days."

"And you didn't tell me this back at the cuirassier camp? Or any time since as we rode deeper into enemy territory?"

Ka-poel's anger and defiance finally flagged, her gaze falling. "I needed to be sure."

"So... what?" Styke raised his hands, then let them fall at his sides again. He paced in the surf. "Your internal compass, this thing that's been leading as many as two thousand men across a continent at war, is off? By what? A thousand miles?"

"More like five hundred, I think."

Styke scoffed. Five hundred miles. He pointed to the ocean, finally taking that half step forward. "I can't ride my lancers across an ocean! Unless you're hiding something beyond that blood magic, I don't think you can do anything to change that. Can you?" He paused, feeling suddenly lost. All this time, all these lives. For nothing. "Can you?" he whispered.

Ka-poel shook her head.

Styke climbed back up the cliffs, leaving Jackal to keep an eye on Celine. By the time he reached the top, his mind was made up, his resolve strengthened. He found Ibana and Gustar waiting for him, while the lancers prepared a camp just beneath the rise of the hill, where they couldn't be spotted by passing ships.

"Pack it up," he said quietly.

Ibana's eyebrows rose. "Excuse me?"

"We're going back. The blood sorcerer was wrong. The godstone lies beyond the ocean."

Both Ibana and Gustar stared at him, working their jaws, coming to terms with this news. "Beyond the ocean?" Gustar asked, rubbing a hand across the stubble on his cheek.

"That's what I said, isn't it?" Styke couldn't feel anything but anger right now, and he fought the urge to go find Amrec, take Celine, and ride off before anyone could stop him. He wondered if he should just do that—if this dream of a reborn Mad Lancers was just a fool's errand.

He shouldered Gustar out of the way, heading toward Amrec. He heard boots behind him, and Ibana say, in a warning tone, "Don't meddle with him in this mood."

Gustar snatched him by the arm a moment later. Styke whirled, his boz knife coming to hand, and snatched Gustar up by the front of his jacket. "Pack," Styke ordered.

"Ben," Ibana warned.

Styke looked at Ibana, then lowered his eyes to Gustar. The Riflejack met the gaze. He could see resolve there, and questions, and a hint of fear. But Gustar did not shake or shy away. Styke set him down and shoved him, putting up his knife. He took several steps before the hopelessness seized him. It began in his chest like a spike of cold iron and quickly overwhelmed him, until his steps became staggered and he was forced to sit on the closest rock, his head falling into his hands.

"Pack everything back up," Styke said again. "Leave the bone-eye. She can find her own way back."

Ibana joined Gustar, and the two of them stared down at Styke. He could feel their eyes on his shoulders. "Back where?" Ibana asked.

Styke gave a half shrug, unwilling to raise his head. He'd seen plenty of men have a breakdown on the field of battle. He'd never experienced one himself, and the very idea of him sitting here fighting back tears, immobilized by hopelessness, almost made him laugh. He was Mad Ben Styke, and a ninety-pound woman leading his army astray had cut him off at the knees.

He wished Ibana and Gustar would go away.

"Back to Landfall," he answered. He gestured at Gustar without looking up. "We'll deliver you and yours back to Lady Flint. It's the least I can do."

"And then?" Gustar asked.

"And then we'll do what we do best. We'll slaughter our way back and forth across Fatrasta until either the invaders are dead or we are."

There was a measured silence. "That sounds...directionless," Gustar said gently.

"It worked for us before," Styke said.

Ibana sighed, pacing back and forth. Styke knew she would have words for him later, when they were out of earshot of the men. He wasn't looking forward to it.

"Well, sir…" Something changed in Gustar's voice, and Styke glanced up to find him standing at attention. "It's been a pleasure serving under you. I appreciate the offer, but the Riflejack cavalry will take our leave. Good day, sir." Gustar snapped a salute and spun on his heel, heading toward his men.

Styke exchanged a glance with Ibana. "What the pit is he going on about? Gustar! Get back here."

Gustar froze. Hesitantly, he returned to Styke, giving him a shallow smile and straightening his jacket where Styke had clutched it. "Yes, sir?"

Styke put his elbows on his knees, looking up at Gustar, fighting against his despair and shushing the little voice that told him to let Gustar walk away. "Where are you going?"

"To fulfill our duty, sir."

"What duty?"

"To escort Ka-poel to the godstone, sir. I was given very specific instructions by Lady Flint, and I intend on carrying them out."

Styke shook his head in wonderment. "Did you not hear me? The godstone is in Dynize. She can't lead us to it."

"We've come this far," Gustar said, brushing off Styke's words. "A little bit of ocean between us and our goal will hardly stop the Riflejacks. There aren't as many of us left as I'd like—five hundred, give or take a few dozen. That'll make it easier to find enough ships to commandeer to get to Dynize."

Styke pointed to the ocean with his knife. "You're going to commandeer a fleet and head to Dynize? Pit knows what's waiting for you there!"

"Not knowing what's over the next hill doesn't seem like something that would bother you, sir," Gustar said, managing to pull it off without the slightest condescension. Styke stared at him, wondering if maybe he had finally been taken by the madness so many had accused him of over the years. Gustar went on. "I've got orders, sir. Unless you have any other questions, I'd best go let the lads know that we're splitting off."

Styke waved him off, his feeling of hopelessness fouled by exasperation. He shook his head, and Gustar had gone about a dozen feet before Styke said, "Why?"

"Because I have orders, sir," Gustar said without turning.

"Bugger orders. You Adran pricks don't follow orders to certain death. Lady Flint isn't worth that. Nobody is."

Gustar stiffened. Slowly, steadily, he returned to Styke and squatted down in front of him, like a man about to explain something to a little child. He said, "Field Marshal Tamas was worth it. Lady Flint—Vlora, as most of us knew her when she was still a girl—she might not be quite there yet, but she will be someday, of that I'm certain." Gustar paused, as if choosing his words. "Styke, we haven't ridden across Fatrasta for you, or a blood sorcerer, or even for Lady Flint. We rode across Fatrasta because a god killed Field Marshal Tamas and tried to destroy our country. You may keep the truth of what we're *actually* doing here from yours, but I don't from mine. We faced the father god of them all on the battlefield, and we were nothing but rain in his eyes. Every one of us remembers that, and if we have to throw away our lives on the *chance* of preventing another piece-of-shit godling from walking this world, we will do so. Not for you, or your damned country, or to help you spread the carnage of your vengeance across the continent. We'll do it to protect our homes and loved ones. Lady Flint understood that. It's why she sent us out."

Gustar left Styke, returning to his cavalry. Styke watched him go with a frustrated sigh. His eyes went to Ibana, who just shrugged and followed Gustar without a word.

Styke stared at the ground, letting the tip of his knife fall to the dirt and slowly scratching it back and forth to create parallel lines. He knew he should be doing something, but he didn't know what.

Ibana would inform the men. Gustar would leave. The Mad Lancers would carry on.

He tried to tell himself that the godstone had been a long shot anyway. That even if they'd found it, there was no guarantee Ka-poel could dampen its power. That this whole mistake—this misled party, teetering on the edge of the continent—was Ka-poel's fault.

So why did he feel so strongly like a failure?

He felt a small hand on his arm. Celine took him by the wrist, forcing him to sit up, then moved his arm to one side so she could sit on his knee. He had a hard time meeting her gaze.

"Ka-poel is sorry," Celine said.

Styke didn't answer her.

"I don't think…" Celine trailed off, then took a deep breath. "I don't think she is certain of herself. She acts confident, but I think she scares herself."

"In what way?" Styke asked petulantly.

"Her strength. That thing she did to the cuirassiers in the forest—"

Styke looked up sharply, cutting her off. "How did you know about that?"

"She told me. She told me that she has controlled men before—even hundreds at a time—but that she's never enthralled them like that. She needed answers and took control of them, and she told me that it scared her."

"Why would she tell you this?" Styke asked, trying to decide if this was some sort of manipulation.

Celine didn't even have to consider the question. She frowned at Styke as if the answer was obvious. "Because she is lonely. I'm the only one she has to talk to. The soldiers are frightened of her, and you treat her like a tool. Her love is on the other side of the continent, fighting for his life, and she wants to be at his side, where she can protect him."

Styke thought of their meeting outside of Landfall, when he had accepted the commission in the Riflejacks and had sent out the order to gather the Mad Lancers. He had waited in that small town, wondering if his old comrades would come when he called, and she had appeared. She had smeared his forehead with blood and then vanished on the wind.

He touched his forehead.

Celine didn't miss the gesture. "She marked you."

"With her sorcery?"

"In a way. She says she will not try to control you. That she is not sure if she can."

"Then why did she mark me?"

"As her protector. Like Taniel."

"Why me?"

"Because you're one of the good ones."

Styke almost laughed. He shook his head, looking at Celine's earnest face. "I'm not one of the good ones, my girl. You've seen it with your own eyes. I'm no one's protector."

"But you protect Fatrasta."

"That's different. It's a continent, an idea, not a person..." He trailed off. "I'm not going to argue semantics with you."

Celine took his hand in hers. "You protect me. Back in the camps, and since. Sunin says that you would break a mountain over your shoulders to protect me, and I believe her."

Styke's eyes were suddenly misty. He dragged his sleeves across his face. "I would."

"So? Ka-poel is alone. You are all that stands between her and the Dynize. She may be powerful, but she is fragile, too. Halt the sea. Break a mountain. Be her protector, too." Celine leaned forward and kissed Styke on the cheek, then slid out of his lap and pulled on his hand in the direction of the camp.

Styke stared at the blade of his knife. "We should ride off. Tonight, when everyone is asleep. I can take you to the Nine and build us a house in the mountains and let you be a kid for a few years. This isn't a place for you."

"I know," Celine said seriously. "We can do that when this is over. I want you to teach me about all the horses."

"Shit," Styke said, climbing to his feet. The hopelessness still weighed him down, clutching at his muscles like a punch to the gut. He walked hand in hand with Celine, gesturing to Ibana to follow and heading toward where the Riflejacks were in the middle of repacking their gear. Ka-poel stood next to Gustar, holding her slate and bit of chalk. The two glanced up at Styke as he approached. Styke pointed at Ka-poel. "I'm still pissed at you. But I made a promise, and I'll damn well keep it. Gustar, the only place we're going to find enough ships to get to Dynize is New Starlight. Tell your men to set up camp. We'll need a lot of rest if we're to assault the fortress."

CHAPTER 58

I t's almost ready."

Vlora didn't acknowledge Flerring, not immediately. She was watching the preparations around the godstone from a safe distance—the other side of Nighttime Vale. She resisted the urge to reply, *It took you long enough.* Three days had passed since the Riflejacks had arrived and Burt had given her his blessing. Three of the four days that it would take twenty-five thousand Dynize infantry to catch up with them. They had gone well past their threshold of "make a clean escape" and had fallen to "hope the Dynize are sufficiently confused by the destruction of the godstone that we can slip away in the chaos."

Vlora finally turned her eyes to Flerring to find her vigorously scratching one arm.

"The thing makes my skin itch," Flerring explained.

"Right. That's why I've kept my distance. Is this going to work?"

"No reason it won't," Flerring replied.

"We packed its brother with enough powder to level a city without causing a scratch."

Flerring snorted. "See, there's your problem. You just cover it in black powder and light the damn thing, most of the explosive force will be lost going in every direction *except* toward the item itself. That's like trying to knock down a wall by throwing the artillery piece at it." She smiled across the valley toward the godstone, an expression that Vlora imagined had been on her face on more than one occasion while sizing up an enemy general. "No, we've used every ounce of blasting oil we had left. We turned it into a gel and applied it to the nooks and crannies. We've timed seven different explosions to occur in split-second intervals. This is top science, Vlora. God sorcery can eat my shit."

"I would rather not invite that kind of hubris," Vlora replied. Her soldiers were literally lined up outside of town, waiting for the order to head north double time if the godstone was destroyed. If the blasting oil had no effect, her second plan was also ready to be put into motion—all of her engineers standing by with the necessary equipment to lift the godstone onto a series of heavy-duty carts to drag it out of town.

And if that didn't work? Prime Lektor would bring the mountain down on top of the godstone and then stick around to hide it from the approaching Dynize army.

She had planned for everything—she hoped—and in a few minutes she would know what needed to happen next.

A fear in the back of her head told her that something would go wrong. That the Dynize, whom Olem's scouts had already spotted, would arrive twelve hours ahead of schedule. Or that the blasting oil would cause some sort of sorcerous backlash that would kill them all. Or that they'd be forced to run *with* the godstone and the Dynize would be upon them within days, slaughtering her outnumbered men.

"I don't believe in hubris," Flerring said, breaking the silence.

Vlora turned and looked at her, staring just long enough for Flerring to become visibly uncomfortable. "Please never say that again."

Her attention was pulled away by the sight of a group coming up from Yellow Creek. She didn't have to sniff powder to pick out the people in attendance: Taniel, Olem, Burt, Prime Lektor, and Julene, accompanied by several of Flerring's assistants. They joined Vlora and Flerring within a few minutes, and it quickly became clear that they'd been arguing for some time.

"It won't work," Prime Lektor said with a huff. "The powder of the combined Predeii couldn't crack one of those things two thousand years ago. Some damned gelled explosive won't do it, either."

Julene stood beside him, looking sullen and uninterested. She waved one of her bronze hands under Prime's nose. "Four of you together couldn't kill me, either. Then along came Kresimir and cut off my hands without breaking a sweat."

"That's different," Prime insisted. "That's powerful sorcery—the same kind of sorcery that's involved here. It only proves my point."

"And you've missed hers entirely," Taniel said quietly, rolling his eyes, "which is that nothing can be taken for granted."

Prime turned on Taniel, sizing him up for a moment in undignified silence. If anything, Taniel himself was living proof of that very statement. Vlora could see Prime swallow a pithy reply, and took more than a little amusement by the fact that Taniel could keep someone like Prime in check. "*You* think this is going to work?"

"I have no idea," Taniel replied. "I can certainly hope."

"Hope is worth nothing. We must plan—"

"We've planned," Vlora finally cut in, "as much as we possibly can. All we need is for you to do your part if the moment calls for it. Can we trust you to do so?"

Prime drew himself up. "I will do my part."

"The same way you stood up to Kresimir after he returned?" Julene scoffed.

Burt circled around the group and came up to Vlora's side, giving the others a skeptical look. "You're sure these are ancient sorcerers?" he asked quietly.

"I'm sure," Vlora replied.

"They've been complaining and squabbling like children since the moment I met them."

"They're just like that," Taniel said, turning his back on Prime and Julene. "The more you get to know the most powerful people in the world, the more you realize they're just that—powerful *people*. If it makes you feel any better, Kresimir was worse than either of them."

"No," Burt said. "That does not make me feel better."

Flerring continued to scratch her arms, looking more and more perplexed. "It's going to work," she repeated, with somewhat less confidence than before. She stared at Prime and Julene while she talked, clearly more uncomfortable with their presence than with even the obelisk she planned on destroying. "We're going to turn that thing to dust, then we're going to hightail it out of this city before the Dynize can catch up."

Vlora put a hand on Flerring's shoulder. "Just tell us when to watch."

"Just a few more minutes, it looks like," Flerring said. "My boys are triple-checking the detonators, and we'll be ready to go."

Vlora couldn't help the thumping of her heart and hoped that her anxiety didn't show on her face. What if Prime was right? What if it proved impossible to move the stone, and then he fled instead of hiding the stone from the Dynize? If the stone fell into Dynize hands, they would have possession of two of the three. She didn't know exactly *how* bad that would be, but there was a dark fear in the pit of her stomach that told her it would be catastrophic.

Her thoughts were interrupted by Flerring suddenly growing very still, staring across the valley, then waving back at someone. "We're ready," she announced.

Prime and Julene immediately ceased their bickering, and the group fell out into a line, watching curiously, until Flerring motioned to them. "You, uh, should probably all get behind those rocks," she told them.

"We're awfully far away," Taniel said doubtfully.

Burt was already following Flerring toward some boulders, and Vlora and Olem were right behind her. "Trust me," Vlora told him. "If Flerring says to duck, then we duck."

Within a few moments they were all situated under the cover of a pair of boulders, peeking out cautiously toward the godstone. Vlora turned her attention toward two of Flerring's assistants, who were still within throwing distance of the stone. They were, she realized, following a long cord down to the outlet of the valley before taking refuge clear around the other side of the rock faces that guarded the entrance to the vale. Vlora took a small hit of powder, watching carefully for a few tense moments before a bright flash suddenly flared from the assistants' hiding spot.

The flash whipped along the ground with astonishing speed, following the cord up toward the godstone. It sped across the valley, then up the path. The explosions were nothing like the eruption of gunpowder. Instead of a boom followed by inky smoke, there was an ear-shattering crack. As Flerring had warned, there were seven distinct explosions. They happened so closely to one another that even Vlora's sorcery-enhanced senses could barely tell them apart. Dust was sent in every direction, allowing Vlora to follow the force of the explosion across the valley as rocks scattered and leaves were blown off trees. She grabbed Olem and pulled him down with her, hiding behind the boulder while the entire side of the valley was peppered with stones thrown over a half mile away. A rock the size of her head struck just a few yards behind them, smoking from the blast.

"Holy shit," Burt said.

Vlora lifted her head to peer through the haze, trying to see what had happened to the godstone. As the air began to clear, she felt her heart fall. "Nothing happened," she said.

Beside her, Taniel was also squinting toward the godstone. He shook his head and suddenly lifted himself up and over the boulder, taking off at a run. Vlora was about to let him go when she saw what he must have seen—something *had* happened. Without a word to the others, she took off after him.

The whole group was gathered around the stone within ten minutes. Vlora walked around and around it, unable to stop grinning like an idiot.

The obelisk had been shattered into three distinct pieces. The smallest was the cap—a pyramid-shaped stone around four feet in diameter. The rest of the stone had broken in half, lengthwise, and the pieces now rested with about a two-inch gap between them.

Flerring slapped her hand victoriously on the capstone. "Ancient sorcery, meet modern science."

Prime Lektor stood back about twenty paces, staring at the godstone with a mix of fascination and horror, as if expecting the stone to reassemble itself at any moment. He seemed at a loss for words until Flerring spoke, to which he replied, "It's not exactly dust."

"It cracked along the seams," Flerring said, tracing her fingers along the break between the two halves of the main obelisk. "Just as planned. There were two deep grooves cut along fault lines in the rock, and we focused most of the explosion there." She tapped a section of the capstone where a large area of writing had been replaced by a spiraling fracture, much like glass in a window that had been shattered without falling from the pane. "It's true, all that oil should have turned this thing to dust. But considering how you were talking about that sorcery, I think we did pretty good."

Slowly, Vlora felt her smile fade. She took a step toward the stone and gently laid a hand on the surface. She felt a pulse, like the beating of a heart, touching her from the Else. It was an unpleasant feeling and she immediately wanted to wipe her hand off and leave this place at once. She forced calm. "I can still sense the sorcery of the thing."

"So can I," Prime Lektor said.

Taniel and Julene both confirmed it.

"It's faded," Taniel said to Flerring's annoyed expression, "but it's definitely still there. Do you think whoever built this thing planned for the possibility of it being broken?"

Vlora expected Prime to look smug, but the old sorcerer seemed baffled more than anything else. "It's possible," he said, "but they made it so strong that they must have thought it would survive anything. I doubt a god could crack it."

"Not even Kresimir could have conceived of a man-made force as strong as blasting oil," Julene said with a hint of wonder in her voice. She tapped her right stub against the capstone, examining it with a clinical approach. "Normally, when an object has been enchanted, substantial damage to it will unravel the enchantment. It may be that..." She trailed off. "Ah, I see."

"What is it?" Vlora demanded. Her anxiety was back, and she had gone from disappointment to elation and back again so quickly in the last quarter of an hour that she just wanted to know what the pit was going on.

Julene turned and smiled smugly at Prime. "Do *you* see it?" she asked.

With some reservation, Prime shook his head.

"Those fault lines in the stone are also fault lines in the sorcery. We couldn't see it, not when it was full strength. They must have bound the sorcery to the very grain of the rock. Helps make it stronger, but it also makes it vulnerable. The sorcery holding the whole thing together is like an outer layer. We broke through that with the blasting oil, leaving three distinct pieces of enchanted rock."

"So instead of having to deal with one godstone, we're dealing with three?" Burt asked flatly.

"Not exactly," Julene continued. She had perked up from her usual disinterest and had even grown excited. "It's not a godstone now, not nearly. The pieces are nothing compared to the whole. I think that it could be put back together, given time, but—"

"If we can separate the pieces," Vlora finished for her. Her mind was already working, pushing through a number of different plans. "Which is the most powerful piece?"

"I see it now," Prime finally announced. "'Power' is the wrong way of thinking about it. The two halves of the main trunk are where the meat of the sorcery is. But the capstone, though weaker, is used to connect them to make the three of them greater than the sum of their parts."

"That's all I need to know." Vlora turned to Burt, her heart racing. The moment she'd been waiting for—where she could see the next path she needed to take—was finally here. "You told us that you had made plans to take the stone north of the Ironhook Mountains if you could find it. Can you still do that?"

The question seemed to catch everyone off guard, including Burt. Taniel stepped forward before Burt could respond. "Are you sure about this?" he asked quietly.

Vlora ignored him. "Can you?" she asked again.

Burt eyeballed the pieces. "What do you need me to do?"

"I want you to take the two pieces of the main trunk and take them over the passes. As soon as you're north of the mountains, separate the two pieces. Send them to the farthest reaches of your territory, or beyond. I don't really care who ends up with them, as long as they are in two very different places."

"This is madness," Prime interjected. "We can't trust northern savages with even a fragment of the stone, let alone two-thirds."

Burt narrowed his eyes at the word "savages." "Then come with us, old man. You want to study them so badly, then we'll take you north with the pieces and you can make sure they're disposed of or hidden."

It was Vlora's turn to be surprised. "I thought you don't allow Kressians north of the Ironhook?"

"Like I told you before, the Dynize have changed everything, and we need to make decisions quickly. Besides, I have the feeling I know what your plan is, and I want insurance."

"What do you mean by insurance?" Taniel asked.

Burt pointed at Prime. "This one can hide the presence of the godstones. If he continues to do that, it'll give my people plenty of time to pull the two big pieces into the passes and dynamite them behind us. We'll be long gone before the Dynize Privileged can figure out something is up."

Olem, who had remained silent for this entire time, suddenly spoke up, fixing Vlora with a pained expression. "We're going to take the capstone, aren't we?"

"And lead the Dynize on a merry chase," Vlora confirmed, locking eyes with Taniel. "We take the capstone to the coast, put it on a ship, and we drop it into the deepest part of the ocean. And even if the Dynize happen to catch up with us, they'll wind up with just a fraction of what they need and no idea where the rest has been taken."

Olem considered the idea for a moment, and Vlora could see in his eyes that he thought it was going to get them all killed. He stared at the godstone, looking older than Vlora remembered him, and drawing out a pang of worry from her. "All right," he said. "But the Dynize are almost upon us. I'll have our engineers up here in half an hour and we'll be rumbling out of the town in two. We need to get as far away as we can before nightfall."

CHAPTER 59

Styke crested a hill and tugged gently on his reins, bringing Amrec—and the entire column behind them—to a stop in the middle of the road. He eyed the distant towers of New Starlight for a few moments, then swept his gaze across the rolling hills between his own party and the city-fortress before bringing his looking glass to his eye to get a better look.

"That's a lot more crowded than when we passed here five days ago," Ibana commented. She sat beside Styke, her comments no doubt directed at the army now camped at the base of the curtain wall that cut New Starlight off from the mainland. At a glance, and without a glass, any seasoned campaigner would put the army at fifty thousand men or more. "That's going to be a problem," Ibana added. "We can't break an entire field army, not by ourselves."

Styke kept the glass to his eyes, frowning toward the city and sweeping his gaze back and forth across the army camping outside it to make sure that his head wasn't playing tricks on him. "We may not have to." He handed Ibana the looking glass and sat back in the saddle, fiddling with his big lancers' ring.

Slowly, Ibana's mouth fell open. "Those are Fatrastan flags."

"Above the army and the city," Styke confirmed. "I'm not mad, am I?"

"Not about this." Ibana handed the looking glass back. "It's been five days since we passed here, and we very clearly saw Dynize soldiers manning the wall. Where did that army come from, and how the pit did they take New Starlight without a siege?"

Styke took off his ring, spat upon it, and polished it against his jacket before returning it to his finger. "I think that's Dvory and the Third."

"I knew we hadn't seen the last of him," Ibana grunted.

"Is this going to make our job easier or harder?" Styke asked, though he thought he already knew the answer.

"Harder," Ibana said. She swore, then continued. "If there is a fleet at harbor, Dvory isn't going to give it to us. But..." She trailed off.

"But," Styke picked up, "I'd damn well like to know how he got here so fast. And how he took New Starlight."

"Right. Do you want me to send Jackal?"

Styke felt uneasy. He felt that way a lot these days, dealing with Ka-poel and renegade cuirassiers and assassin dragonmen. But this... this felt different to him and he couldn't figure out why. The army was flying the flags of the Third. It was a whole field army, with Dvory at the head. He ignored Ibana's question and asked his own. "You think he sold himself to the Dynize?"

"Dvory?"

"Yeah."

"He's a slimy piece of shit, but there's no way he turned an entire field army. I know dozens of good, loyal soldiers in the Third."

Styke chewed on the inside of his cheek. "Get me Jackal. We're going to take a closer look."

*   *   *

Styke and Jackal approached the pickets of the army camped outside of New Starlight and were waved through with only a lingering glance and a curious whisper. They were soon among the tents,
riding down the main road that led to the curtain wall and the
city-fortress beyond it. Styke kept his eyes and ears open, keeping
Amrec at a walk, trying to shake the uneasiness that plagued his
thoughts.

The army was camped at leisure, sprawled and disorganized like
an army resting in the spoils of a great victory—though it was clear
that there had been no battle to take the city. Soldiers played cards
by the cookfires, set up ball fields out by the pickets, and stripped
the area of firewood and edibles.

"Are the spirits telling you anything about this?" Styke asked
Jackal out of the corner of his mouth.

Jackal looked just as suspicious as Styke, if not more so, and he
answered without taking his eyes off the camp. "The spirits are
fickle right now. Most of them have fled from Ka-poel's sorcery,
and the ones who haven't speak in riddles. They're . . . not helpful."

"What do you make of this?"

"I don't like it."

Jackal seemed to have nothing else to add, so Styke let him be.
Truth be told, he couldn't add any more himself. The circumstances of the Third Army's arrival seemed suspicious at best,
sinister at worst, yet there was nothing about the camp that spoke
to him of sedition or treachery.

As they neared the curtain wall, he saw a small group of men
gathered playing dice on a plank. One of them glanced up, did a
double take, then sprang to his feet and jogged toward Styke. He
was a thin, dark-skinned Deliv. He looked like he was in his forties,
with a touch of gray at his temples and a distinctive scar along his
left cheek. "Colonel Ben Styke?" he asked, falling in beside Amrec.

"That's me."

"Colonel Willen," the man introduced himself. "I saw you at a distance back near Belltower but I never got the chance to meet you. I'm with the Seventy-Fourth Rifles. It's a pleasure to meet you, Styke."

Styke pulled on the reins and turned to look down at Willen. "Pleasure is mine," he said slowly. The name sounded vaguely familiar, but he couldn't place the face. "Mind telling me what's going on here?"

"What do you mean?" Willen seemed genuinely perplexed by the question.

"I mean that five days ago, I rode past New Starlight and saw Dynize flags. I come back this way and the city is held by our side, without any sign of a struggle."

"Ah!" Willen's grin widened. "Well, sir, oddest bit of luck. I'll tell you, we weren't all that far behind—we arrived just yesterday morning to find the citadel completely abandoned. No ships in harbor, no spies hiding in the walls. Just an empty husk of a place stripped of supplies."

Styke leaned on his saddle horn. "You're joking." *No ships.* That would make it damned hard to get to Dynize.

"Not at all! I'll tell you, it's the damnedest thing. We had orders to take the city as quickly as possible, but it was empty."

"Do you know why?"

"I'm not one to question fortune, but..." Willen searched his jacket, produced a tin of tobacco, and tucked a wad into the corner of his mouth before continuing. "We came across half a brigade of Dynize cavalry slaughtered in the Hock—I'm guessing now that it was your doing—and our best guess is that the Dynize holding the city were spooked and decided to flee."

Styke bit his tongue, holding back a dozen reasons why the Dynize *wouldn't* have fled just because of some dead cuirassiers. He looked up at the nearby curtain wall and the high towers of New

Starlight beyond it, then glanced to the eastern horizon. "Perhaps," he said. "Perhaps not. Maybe they got wind of a field army on the way and decided they couldn't hold the fortress against it." It seemed like the only probable reason for abandoning New Starlight. Perhaps Styke was just being paranoid. "Tell me, did the Dynize spike the fortress guns when they left?"

"I'm not sure," Willen replied. "I can ask."

"Do so. Where is Dvory?"

"Ah. The general is in the citadel. His personal company is holding it."

"Taking the choice beds for himself, I suppose."

"A general's prerogative," Willen said demurely. "If you'd like, I'll take you to him."

"No need, I..." Styke hesitated, exchanging a glance with Jackal. "Actually, that would be wonderful."

"Hold on, I'll fetch my horse."

Within a few minutes, Colonel Willen was riding beside them as they headed toward the fortress. They passed beneath the curtain wall, which was staffed with guards from one of the brigades but not policed. The city-fortress within had been taken over by the army.

"All the buildings were empty when we arrived," Colonel Willen explained. "As far as we've been able to piece together, the city was abandoned by the garrison the very day that word came that Landfall had been taken. The people fled soon after, leaving it abandoned to be picked up by the Dynize."

"That's a shame," Styke said, watching a company of soldiers march past in the street.

Willen spat out a wad of tobacco. "Agreed. New Starlight isn't protected by sorcery, but the walls are strong and the guns powerful. They could have made a damned good stand against any sized fleet in the area. Pity, I say, but that's what we're here to remedy."

"What, exactly, are your orders?" Styke glanced sharply at Willen.

"They were secret until we actually arrived," Willen said. "But we were to march across the Hammer and take New Starlight as quickly as possible. Now, I believe, we'll garrison the city and use it as a staging point to cleanse the Hammer." Willen nodded toward the citadel. "General Dvory is meeting with all the brigadiers and about half the colonels right now. I imagine we'll have our next set of orders by tomorrow."

Styke debated his next options. If there were no ships here, then the citadel was useless to the Mad Lancers. His best bet might be to ride back to Belltower and use the good graces he'd earned with the city to commandeer a small fleet. In which case, he should turn around right now and ride back to camp. He didn't need Dvory getting overly curious about his goals.

"Why the urgency?" he asked Willen.

"Hmm?"

"You were told to march across the Hammer and take Starlight as quickly as possible. Why? Did you even bring enough artillery to take the citadel?"

"Only just—about the artillery, that is. We have a battery of twelve-pounders and six batteries of six-pounders. As far as the speed?" Willen shrugged. "The orders came directly from Lindet herself. One does not question Lindet's orders."

They reached the main door of the citadel only to find it closed. Styke rode Amrec right up to the door and gave it a shove. It was locked. He craned his neck, looking up to the murder holes for some sign of a guard detail.

"I say there!" Willen called, cupping his hands around his mouth. "I say there! Colonel Willen to see General Dvory. Open the doors!"

They were greeted by silence. Jackal rode back fifty yards, looking toward the top of the walls. "I don't see anyone," he shouted.

Willen scowled at the door as if he might open it by annoyance alone. "Everyone must be at the general's meeting."

"Strange," Styke muttered, feeling his uneasiness deepen.

They waited for a sign of life from within the citadel for nearly fifteen minutes until Willen finally shook his head. "I'll send men around to the other gates to find a way in," he assured him. "Dvory's damned bodyguard are too good to open the door, and they'll hear it from me. Can I escort you back to your men?"

"We're camped down the coast," Styke said. "To the east. I can find my own way back."

"Of course."

Styke raised one finger, turning Amrec this way and that as he examined the city-fortress. "How many scouts do you have out right now?"

"You'd have to ask a dragoon company."

"Do you have any dragoons attached to your brigade?"

"We do. My sister is their commanding officer."

"Do me a favor. Get them out into the countryside. The Dynize might have sailed away, but they might also be lurking out there somewhere."

Willen sucked on his teeth, obviously reluctant. "General Dvory gave the men an informal leave while we wait for our new orders. My sister won't be eager to send her boys out too early." He paused, looking up at the citadel. "I'll convince her," he added.

"Good."

Styke nodded good-bye and turned Amrec back toward the mainland. They were out of earshot when Jackal said in a low voice, "You told him we were camped to the east. You don't trust him?"

"I don't want Dvory to know where we are," Styke replied.

Ibana met them about a mile outside the curtain wall. "I was just about to come looking for you. Is everything all right?"

"I'm not sure," Styke said with the shake of his head. "I want you and Gustar to send out our best scouts. Scour the area."

"What are we looking for?"

"Dynize."

"A lot? A few?"

Styke glanced back toward the citadel one more time. He thought he spotted someone in a yellow jacket on the walls of the citadel, but by the time he found his looking glass the person had disappeared. "I don't know. Look for anything suspicious. No fires tonight. Tell the men to be ready to fight or flee at a moment's notice."

CHAPTER 60

Vlora sat on horseback, watching as rows of Riflejacks marched past her along the winding, treacherous foothills of the Ironhook Mountains. Less than fifty hours had passed since Flerring had cracked the godstone, and even with a swift departure from Yellow Creek they were only thirty miles or so east of the town. Supply wagons—and the big oxcart carrying the capstone—slowed them down, as did the rough terrain itself. Their only saving grace was that the men themselves were relatively fresh from days loitering outside of Yellow Creek.

But an army could only move as quickly as its slowest piece, and in this case it was the capstone. Sixteen extra oxen and a whole company of soldiers and engineers stood by to push or pull the wagon through mud or up steep embankments, to repair broken wheels or switch out tired animals. They worked with efficiency found nowhere else in the world, and yet it still wasn't enough.

"Where's Colonel Olem?" Vlora asked one of her aides, eyeing a particularly steep part of the road up ahead. The capstone would be along soon, and the engineers would have to deal with that hill, slowing down the whole army even further.

"I think he's coming up just behind us, ma'am," the aide answered.

Vlora acknowledged her response with a nod and headed back down the column, where she found Olem conferring with several of their engineers, walking beside them as he led his horse. She caught his eye and he broke away, mounting up and coming over to join her.

"We just had word from our scouts," he reported before she could speak. "The Dynize are coming up on us quickly—there's a full brigade just a couple hours behind us."

Vlora swore. "How the pit did they catch up so quickly? Didn't they at least head to Yellow Creek?"

"They didn't." Olem unfolded a hand-drawn map of the region and held it where Vlora could see. "As far as we can tell, they changed directions at this road here, heading to cut us off. Either they had better scouts than we expected or their Privileged were able to sense the capstone moving east and they made some quick assumptions."

Vlora tried to look on the bright side. "They've taken the bait."

"That they have. By the time they catch us, Burt will have the rest of the godstone up in the Ironhook passes. No chance of the Dynize following them up there."

It was, Vlora had to admit, a terribly satisfying thing to know that she'd outmaneuvered Ka-Sedial once more. It took an enormous amount of anxiety off her chest. However, she didn't need to remind herself that the Dynize could still slaughter her and all of her men. Saving the world from a Dynize god had been her first priority. Now she needed to get her people back to Adro in one piece, and Olem had not said "if" they catch us, but rather implied "when." "Do we have any chance of outrunning them?" she asked quietly.

Olem looked toward the engineers, his expression souring. "I think we can stay ahead of them if we keep moving, it's just that…"

"Don't lie to me," Vlora told him.

Olem glanced away, grimacing. "Dragging this capstone with us, we have no chance of staying ahead of the Dynize. As long as we're in the foothills, we can block the roads and keep them from flanking us, but as soon as we break out onto the plains, we'll be surrounded by five brigades of infantry."

Vlora tried to keep from spiraling into a well of despair. "I've gotten us all killed, haven't I?"

"I'm sure you'll think of something," Olem said confidently.

"That kind of pressure isn't exactly helpful."

"Hasn't stopped you before."

She wanted to slap that reassuring grin off his face. "If we live through this, my love, please make me retire."

"I'll do my best."

Vlora turned to watch as the cart with the capstone was manuevered up the steep hill on the road ahead of them, and was pleasantly surprised when none of the ropes snapped or the oxen stumbled. It was up and over the hill in just a few minutes, leaving her in a slightly more optimistic mood. She wondered what Tamas would have done in this situation, and realized she'd been with him in a tangle not so dissimilar during the Adran-Kez War. Had the odds been better, or worse? She couldn't quite remember.

"How hard will it be for the Dynize to get around us?"

"While we're on these foothill roads?" Olem asked. "Fairly difficult."

"Good. Tell the engineers I want them to keep that wagon going as quickly as possible, no matter what the rest of the army does."

"You intend to stop and fight?" Olem asked with surprise.

"'Stop' is a poor word for what I plan. We're going to bloody their noses a little, and see what kind of sorcerous support they have. Fetch me Taniel, Norrine, and Davd."

*   *   *

Vlora listened to the screaming of horses as she lined up her next shot.

Finding a proper line of sight in these foothills was next to impossible. It took climbing a tree on the next ridge over just to be able to witness the ambush the Riflejack rear had arranged for the Dynize vanguard. The ambush itself was in full swing—six hundred of her riflemen firing staggered volleys into a column of dragoons. The column went back down the valley for as far as Vlora could see, and had clearly not expected to run into the Riflejacks so quickly. Once the firing had begun, they had milled for almost a minute, the front line pushed ahead by the advancing column behind them, before charging up the hill toward her Riflejacks.

The dragoons died by the score in that charge, but Vlora forced herself to ignore them and kept her eyes on the column behind the battle. Her senses ablaze with a powder trance, she watched as word of the ambush was passed back beyond the curve of the next hill. She kept her gaze there, watching, waiting for the logical Dynize response.

It came within about two minutes. A Dynize Privileged, white gloves already on, appeared from down the column, his bodyguard shoving their way through the dragoons as he attempted to make his way forward to deal with the ambush. A Privileged of reasonable power could do enough damage to her rear guard to allow his dragoons to advance. If he had a lot of power, he might be able to brush them aside single-handedly.

Vlora had no interest in finding out. She braced the barrel of her rifle on the branch in front of her as she focused on the Privileged. She opened her third eye, letting out a small gasp as the world turned into a black-and-white landscape with a few pastel brushes of sorcery dabbed across it. The Privileged glowed brightly in the Else, forcing

Vlora to blink at the radiance. It took a few moments to notice that the Privileged had not come unprepared for this eventuality—that there was a half dome of hardened air just a few inches in front of him. It would be very difficult to punch through, and impossible to shoot around for all but the most skilled of powder mages.

The Dynize, it seemed, had learned from the battles they'd fought against powder mages.

Vlora shifted her attention to the woman sitting in the saddle just behind and to the right of the Privileged. She also glowed in the Else, and Vlora had seen enough bone-eyes by now to know them by their aura. The Privileged was focused on the battle ahead, no doubt trusting his shield of air, while the bone-eye seemed focused inward. Vlora had no doubt she was spurring on her soldiers, giving them the courage to charge uphill against her Riflejacks.

It was, so far, not working. Several hundred dragoons already littered the road, further slowing their compatriots. Vlora's Riflejacks worked with mechanical precision, firing staggered volleys into whatever came next. It was utter suicide on the part of the dragoons—unless, of course, they were simply buying time for their Privileged to reach the front and lend them a hand.

Vlora readjusted her grip, took a long, steady breath, and breathed out as she squeezed the trigger. As the bullet flew from the barrel of her rifle, she burned powder charges in her kit, adding extra strength to the shot so that it would soar straight and true across nearly a thousand yards of open terrain. As it approached the enemy, she nudged the bullet down and to the right. The bullet skimmed the outer layer of the Privileged's shield of hardened air and slammed into the bone-eye sitting next to him, snapping her head back and sending her tumbling from the saddle.

The Privileged whirled, watching his companion fall, right as a bullet tore through the base of his spine from the opposite direction. Another bullet killed the captain of the Privileged's guard, while two more bullets downed nearby officers.

Vlora allowed herself a victorious smile, glancing across the valley to where Taniel hid on the hillside opposite her. Somewhere to his left were Davd and Norrine, but Vlora didn't take the time to pinpoint them before turning her gaze back to the battle.

The Dynize faltered, the courage their bone-eye supplied suddenly gone. Some tried to flee back down the column, though there was no space for them to go, while others abandoned their horses and took cover in streambeds and ditches. Vlora found Olem standing with her rear guard, keeping them in check so that they held their ground. More than a few of them would want to press an attack, but Vlora had no interest in taking a single step back toward Yellow Creek.

The trap had drawn out the brigade's Privileged and bone-eye, and Vlora pulled a mirror out of her pocket, flashing it toward Olem. He nodded toward her, giving an order to pull back. Let the Dynize stumble over their dead and wonder when the next ambush would come. In the meantime, the Riflejacks would march double time to catch up with the capstone and continue their sprint toward the coast.

Vlora was just about to climb down from her perch when her preternatural senses picked up something she did not expect—not up here. It was the sound of hooves on gravel, as well as the jingle of cavalry kit. It was, alarmingly, coming from behind her.

She swung her rifle around and over a branch, shifting her position so that she could face toward the crest of the ridge behind her. To her surprise, she saw well over a hundred Dynize cavalry in their shining breastplates mount the ridge and fall into line. She swore to herself angrily, wondering what damned goat track they had found to be able to flank the Riflejack position. The dragoons hadn't just been buying time for their Privileged—they'd been buying time for their cuirassiers as well.

The charge was not an ideal one—through a screen of trees that hid the cuirassiers from the Riflejacks, across a tiny streambed, and then over a rocky field. Not ideal, but certainly possible, and with success it might be able to shatter her rear guard.

The cuirassiers finished falling into line, and their officer raised his sword.

"Piss and shit," Vlora growled. She dropped her rifle to the ground, hoping it wasn't damaged in the fall, and awkwardly pulled her pistol. Just as the officer lowered his sword, she pulled the trigger, floating a bullet fifty yards and, with an extra flare of powder, put a neat hole through his breastplate.

None of his cuirassiers seemed to notice him fall as they plunged over the lip of the ridge, charging through the screen of trees without a word, while the attention of the Riflejacks was split between shooting dragoon stragglers and preparing to pull back.

Vlora shouted for Olem across the valley, but the noise was lost among the screams of men and horses down on the road. She swore again, reaching out with her senses, and set off the powder carried by the six closest cuirassiers. The kickback of the sorcery almost knocked her off her branch, but the blast had the intended effect—causing the cuirassiers to falter, and Olem and the rear guard to look toward their left.

With her rifle dropped, Vlora could do nothing but watch as Olem shouted, waving his sword in the air as he kicked riflemen into a loose line and gave the order to fix bayonets. It came not a second too soon, as the Dynize cuirassiers slammed into the reeling Riflejacks. Vlora's heart leapt as Olem went down beneath the swinging sword of a cuirassier, and the line was broken by the sheer power of the charge.

Taking her eyes off the fight, she glanced beneath her and leapt from her hiding spot, hitting the rocky ground hard and rolling into a crouch. Fetching her rifle and leaving her hat behind, she sprinted toward this new battle, fearing the worst.

She reached the road in time to see the last of the cuirassiers pulled from his horse and butchered by angry riflemen. The length of their entrenchment was a scene of chaos, with horses and soldiers dead and dying in a hundred-yard swath. She could see in an instant that the cuirassiers had simply brought too few men. With an extra hundred they might have completely dislodged the rear guard, and even without them their charge had been devastating. Her rear guard was still reeling from the hit, officers attempting to organize their men back into ranks in case the dragoons mounted another attack.

A dragoon charge did not come. Vlora found Olem lying in the mud, blinking at the sky, his brow caked in blood. She dropped to her knees beside him, overcome by relief when his eyes immediately focused on her. "Are you all right?" she asked.

"I...I think so. Caught a horse's knee to the face. Does it look bad?"

It did. "You've had worse."

Olem struggled to stand up, and Vlora put her arm beneath his shoulder to get him back to his feet so that they could survey the damage. "The dragoons are pressing," Olem commented.

"Too many dead clogging the road," Vlora responded. "They won't be able to mount another charge at this point. All their cards were in that cuirassier charge."

"Pit, that scared the shit out of me. Damned good thinking, detonating some powder. Otherwise they might have hit us before we even saw them."

Vlora didn't feel as if she'd added much of anything to that fight. They should have seen that possible flanking maneuver and been ready for it. Frankly, she was furious with herself for overlooking it. "Looks like our boys are pretty mauled. We need to grab our wounded and fall back, double time."

"Agreed." Olem pushed Vlora away, testing his footing, then headed down the road shouting orders as if he wasn't still bleeding heavily from his forehead. Vlora grabbed a nearby infantryman, pointing at Olem.

"Find the colonel a surgeon. Make sure he gets stitched up within five minutes," she ordered.

Vlora spotted Taniel coming down the side of the opposite valley from her, his rifle slung over one shoulder. He stopped beside a dead cuirassier, watching one of the horses panicking in a nearby bush, before finishing his walk toward Vlora. "Those cuirassiers just came out of nowhere," he commented. "I was so focused on the battle, I didn't see them until you caused a ruckus with their powder."

"I barely saw them in time myself, and they were right behind me," Vlora responded. "I'm lucky one didn't spot me and put a bullet in my back." She shook her head, staring bleakly at the carnage one more time. This was supposed to be a way of discouraging the Dynize—clog the road, kill a few hundred of them, draw out their sorcery support, and then flee. Instead, the Dynize had managed to flank them in mere minutes. "Whoever is in command isn't someone I want to play games with."

Taniel remained silent.

"Pit," Vlora said softly. "Now we have wounded to haul."

"They'll slow us down less than the capstone."

"Yes, but we can ditch the capstone if we need to."

Taniel seemed surprised. "You'd really do that?"

"Burt has the rest of the godstone. The cap won't do them any damned good. If we need to drop it, we drop it."

"It might do them *some* good," Taniel said hesitantly. "It's still potent old sorcery."

"It's not worth the lives of my men," Vlora insisted.

Their argument was cut off by the arrival of one of Vlora's scouts. It was a young woman, dusty and glassy-eyed from a hard ride, her horse worked into a lather. The woman didn't bother to salute before barking out her report: "Ma'am, we've just caught sight of another Dynize army."

Vlora's head snapped up. "Where?"

"To our southeast. Two brigades, coming on quick. They're going to cut off our escape the moment we get out of the foothills."

CHAPTER 61

Thousands of Dynize soldiers flooded every known entrance to the catacombs in the Landfall Plateau at four o'clock in the morning. It was an impressive display, carried out with a precision that Michel found almost startling. Hundreds of copies of the catacomb maps were made in the course of just a couple of days, each one sectioned into squares drawn in different-colored ink and assigned to a company of soldiers. The companies were divided into platoons, each one of which was equipped with lanterns, pole-arms, pistols, swords, and a box of colored string that an infantryman would unravel as they searched the tunnels to mark that they'd passed through.

Michel watched as a platoon in their turquoise uniforms and steel breastplates hammered the lock off the iron-bar door in the basement of an old church not far from the capitol building and rushed down through the church's cellar of ossuaries and into the darkness below.

Michel held a lantern and a pistol, and he watched the last of the soldiers disappear with growing trepidation. He wasn't entirely certain which he feared more: cornering je Tura in some cave where a load of soldiers would die trying to bring him down or not finding je Tura at all.

"Claustrophobic?" Tenik asked.

"Not particularly," Michel answered, "but I am not made to go into a place without an easy exit, and instinct is a hard thing to overcome."

"If all these maps are right, we'll do just fine." Tenik was carrying a whole satchel full of those maps over one shoulder—all the originals that Michel had found in the Millinery. Not all of them had been copied—just the three with the most minute detail—and Michel wanted the rest on hand in case they needed to figure something out while they were deep underground.

"I am admittedly nervous about mass-produced maps done on the spur of the moment."

Tenik leaned toward him. "I can't disagree. But we pulled in all the regimental cartographers to get this done. They weren't amateurs."

"I sure to pit hope not. How did you manage to organize this whole thing so fast?" Michel glanced back up the stairs into the back of the church that they now stood beneath. He could hear voices up there: people shouting commands or asking for updates. The church was a sort of command center, and Michel and Tenik and the two platoons accompanying them were a "mobile" version of that command center sent to search the area directly beneath the capitol building.

A new squad of soldiers rushed down the stairs into the basement, squeezing in between Tenik and Michel and following their comrades into the darkness.

"Seriously, I'm damned impressed."

Tenik waited until the soldiers had all disappeared before answering in a low voice. "We got all this organized because most of these men know someone who's died to je Tura's bombs over the last month. Revenge is a powerful motivator."

They were joined by another squad, this one gathering around Michel and Tenik in the narrow space in the church basement. Michel glanced from face to face, noting the eagerness and hoping that none of *them* turned out to be claustrophobic. He took the satchel of maps from Tenik and looped it over his shoulder, then plucked one of them out, unrolled it, and turned it over on itself until he could hold it easily draped over one arm.

"All right," he said, "you've all been briefed by Tenik here, so I'll make this short: The capitol building sits directly over a series of chambers that probably date back to the old Dynize Empire. We're going to sweep those chambers, looking for hidden alcoves and nooks where a single man might hide." He swept his finger over a route he'd planned out in pencil, then asked Tenik to hold his lantern closer. "Be on the lookout for any indication that someone had been living down here: bedding, tools, gunpowder, even footprints in the dust. If the walls begin to close in on you, tell one of us and then trace the string back up to the surface. Got it?"

"Yes, sir," a dozen voices responded.

"Good."

Michel set aside the map and searched his valise for another—one of the older, more detailed maps that they didn't have copies of. He spread it across his lap and traced their route out one more time, making sure that they weren't going to miss anything by depending on the newer maps. The tunnels lined up with their plans admirably, and he was just about to roll the map back up when something caught his eye. It was a label on one of the dozens of chambers that they'd be searching, each of them marked by the cartographer with a single word in a language Michel wasn't familiar with.

It was labeled MARA.

The sight of the word made Michel's heart jump. "Let's go," he told the soldiers.

"Is something wrong?" Tenik asked quietly as the soldiers headed down into the darkness.

"This word here," Michel pointed. "What language is that?"

"Same language as the rest of those rooms, I'm guessing. Must be old Dynize."

"Do you know what it means?"

"Haven't a clue. Yaret might know."

The discovery troubled Michel as they followed their escort into the tunnels. He tried to shake it off, and had gone less than two hundred yards when he decided that perhaps he should rethink the answer to that *Are you claustrophobic?* question that he'd been asked a few minutes before. The tunnel they followed sloped gently downward, the rock slick with moisture and lichen, the light of Michel's lantern playing across the uneven shadows. It was so narrow that he could touch both sides and the ceiling without reaching.

Michel had always thought of the catacombs beneath Landfall as something akin to a sewage system—in that everyone knew they were there, but no one really liked to talk about them. Some people were afraid of tunnel collapses, others that they were haunted. Most agreed that it was best not to disturb the rest of the ancient dead.

They followed a zigzag pattern through a series of cross-halls and small rooms filled with ossuaries, full-blown tombs, and even bones packed into alcoves so tightly that not one of them could be dislodged. He reined in the soldiers every few minutes, moving slowly and consulting his maps by lantern light even though he had memorized their route. When it came to someplace as disorienting as the catacombs, he didn't want to make a mistake.

Their journey consisted of long stretches of moody silence, the soldiers tense and irritable, punctuated by the distant echoes of other searchers. After some time their squad vanguard finally called a stop, and Michel and Tenik were called up to examine an immensely heavy iron grate blocking their path. Michel pressed his face to the grate and noted the way the light from his lantern disappeared into the darkness beyond without revealing any walls.

"I've heard stories that the Kez sealed up a lot of these tunnels decades before I was born," he said. "We've reached the first chamber. Get to blasting."

One of the soldiers kicked at the grate. "It's solid, sir. If the room is still closed up, can't we count out the chances of them being enemy bases?"

"These chambers have more than one entrance," Tenik said. "We're going to do a proper job of this."

Michel retreated a few hundred yards back up the tunnel while the squad sapper worked. He listened to echoes coming down to them from a side passage, and once even saw the bobbing of a lantern. He wondered if je Tura was down here somewhere, having caught wind of the manhunt and desperately trying to avoid the searchers.

He caught Tenik's eye. "I've been thinking."

"Oh?" Tenik asked.

"We've been down here for over an hour and we've only seen one single other squad."

"So?"

"So there are four thousand soldiers searching these tunnels. I get the feeling the catacombs are bigger than we considered."

"Not much we can do about it now."

Michel thought about some of the maps in his satchel—the ones there'd been no time to copy. Many of them were half-finished, sometimes contradicting the more complete maps and other times hinting at the idea that there were tunnels that went far deeper, down below the base of the plateau. He wrestled with a fear that they'd just drive je Tura down into the farthest reaches without a prayer of catching him.

There was a distant boom, and Michel and Tenik headed back

to their squad to find the path ahead of them cleared—the heavy grate blasted along the edges and pushed off to one side of the tunnel. Michel ducked through the remains and into the first of the chambers, raising his lantern to get a good look.

Tenik gave a low whistle. "These aren't chambers, Michel. These are damned temples."

He didn't seem far off. The rooms were much larger than the map indicated, with vaulted, cavernous ceilings and a width that was large enough to accommodate most theaters. The floors were covered in dust, the walls slick. At second glance, Michel realized that it may very well be a theater or conference room of some kind, as apparent seating had been carved into about two-thirds of the room in a half-moon shape.

There was no evidence that anyone had been in here for a long time. Michel studied the floor, looking for footprints in the dust, mildly disappointed that he didn't find any beyond those of the soldiers who'd just entered with him. He crossed clear to the other side, where he found, per his map, a narrow tunnel leading to the next chamber.

"Chamber clear," one of the soldiers reported.

"Then we keep moving," Michel responded.

Michel and his squad searched chamber after chamber for hours. They moved methodically, following a path he'd laid out on his map so that they could search crisscrossing chambers without the risk of someone getting behind them. They found a dozen paths leading back to the general maze of the catacombs, most of which were still sealed off. Occasionally they came across one that had rusted through or been blasted in decades ago by looters.

It was almost noon when Michel checked his pocket watch and called for a halt in one of the larger chambers they'd attended. This one appeared to be some sort of communal living space, complete with old notches at regular intervals along the walls where torches might have been lit a thousand years ago.

Michel was exhausted and more than a little emotionally frayed. Even without any real excitement, he found the inky darkness battering to his nerves. The uncertainty was taking its toll, and every time they entered a new chamber, he wondered if they would trigger some ancient trap or encounter a collapsed tunnel or lose a man to madness in the claustrophobic area. Add onto all of that his exhaustion—they'd searched all through the night, for ten hours straight—and he felt ready to collapse.

"Do we have a depth?" Tenik asked him quietly. Michel could see the same exhaustion in Tenik's eyes, and took a moment to pull out his maps, looking carefully at the chambers. Decades ago a thoughtful cartographer had given a depth for each chamber, but many of the numbers were worn off, and Michel had no idea how accurate the legible ones actually were.

"Eighty feet below street level," Michel responded.

Tenik ran a hand through his hair. "Damn. It feels like we're so much deeper. I can throw a rock eighty feet."

Michel echoed the sentiment. To be so close to the city—probably just fifty or sixty feet below the basement floor of the capitol building—and yet be so removed from the world made him feel a little crazy. He looked around at each of the soldiers, wondering who would snap first, and curious if anyone from any of the other search parties had snapped already. He let his eyes fall to the box of string held by a soldier, forcing himself to remember that if he began to get twitchy, he could just follow that string right back to the surface.

It was just fine. No chance of being trapped down here.

"Do you think someone else has caught him already?" a soldier asked.

"If they have," Michel said, "they're supposed to send someone down our string to find us and let us know. But that could take two hours on its own." He cleared his throat and checked his watch. "We've got about an hour left until we're meant to head out. We're only about"—he unrolled his map and traced their path—"eight hundred yards from an exit." He pointed at the closest doorway into the next chamber. "We'll head in that direction. Don't worry, fellas, we'll be back in the sunlight before too long."

There were a few "yes, sirs," but most of them sullenly stared at their feet. Michel wasn't sure whether they were as frayed as he was from the oppressive rock or if they were tired and angry at not having found je Tura. He opened his mouth, trying to think of something to say to cheer them up, when a voice came to him from across the chamber.

"Sir," the voice echoed in Dynize. "I think I've found something."

Michel exchanged a glance with Tenik and got to his feet, heading across the wide space toward a lantern light off in the distance. He soon found a Dynize soldier standing beside a stone table of some sort, just a few feet from a separate exit that headed in the opposite direction from their planned path. She smiled tightly at him and nodded to the ground.

The dust outside the tunnel entrance had been disturbed recently, enough that Michel couldn't make out many single footprints, just a trail leading down into the darkness. Inside the tunnel, stashed behind the table the soldier stood beside, were six small barrels of black powder. Michel nudged each of them with his toe. All but one was empty. He knelt beside them, breath held, and turned the barrels upside down.

Burned into the bottom of each barrel was a single rose.

"These are from Blackhat storage," Michel said, eyeing the path into the darkness. He looked up at Tenik, then the soldier who'd made the discovery. "Ma'am," Michel said, "you may have just found Landfall's number-one enemy of the state. Everyone on your feet! There's been a change of plans!"

CHAPTER 62

Styke found Colonel Willen late the next morning as he rode through the gate of the curtain wall surrounding New Starlight. The camp appeared in much the same order as the night before, with everyone relaxed and playing games to pass the time, but Styke thought he could sense a tension among the men that hadn't been there before.

"Styke," Willen greeted him, riding up and falling in beside Amrec.

"Willen," Styke returned with a nod.

"Where is your Palo man?"

"Jackal? He's with my scouts."

"Good, good. My sister sent some of her best out last night, and more this morning. General Dvory assures us that the Dynize have abandoned the area, but I think having some of us out there will put the men at ease." Willen seemed anything but at ease. His jacket was unbuttoned at the collar and he looked like he hadn't slept well, with hair mussed.

"Has Dvory emerged?" Styke asked, nodding to the citadel.

"He has not." Willen grimaced and shifted in the saddle as he spoke. "Just messages. It seems that Lady Chancellor Lindet's orders have left the general staff in some confusion. They will remain in deliberation until they have come to a consensus as to what to do next."

Styke considered Dvory's assurances, as well as the lack of communication. He did not trust the bastard before, and he certainly didn't trust him now—but what could he be playing at? There was a whole field army here, holding a powerful fortress on the tip of the Hammer. He had put the army—who clearly were still loyal Fatrastans—in an excellent defensive position. If Dvory planned betrayal, what could he gain out here?

"So I can't talk with him yet?"

"You can't," Willen replied apologetically. "I'm sure that we'll have some sort of decision by the end of the night. Dvory is a persuasive man—the brigadiers will be lined up behind him before too long."

Styke nearly voiced his suspicions that Dvory was planning some kind of treachery, but decided to bite his tongue. Willen was an army man, and Styke doubted that he'd take well to an officer being slandered without evidence. But what evidence was there? Willen seemed nervous about the lack of communication, but he wasn't falling apart. "Did you ever find out if the Dynize spiked the cannon when they left?"

"Oh, I did at that. The cannon were not spiked. I'll confess, that has given me some confusion. It's the first thing *we* would do if we abandoned a fort to the enemy."

"Yeah," Styke muttered. "Me too." Louder, he said, "Are you familiar with this place at all?"

"Some. I was stationed here for a few months just after the war. My sister pulled some strings to get me transferred to Little Starland."

"I don't suppose you know of any way into the citadel?"

Willen tapped the side of his chin. "I don't. But..." He laughed to himself. "Actually, I do. There are a few sea gates out on the breakers. You can only reach them during low tide. The garrison uses them to clean detritus off the breakers and access the lighthouse out past the bay."

"Tunnels?"

"Dark, dangerous, and very wet."

"Can they be reached without a long swim?"

Willen considered this. "Might be. The north sea gate comes out on the mainland, but it's right into the rocks. Even at low tide, *those* breakers get hit hard enough to wash a man out to sea."

A bell rang high up in the citadel, turning Styke's head. He searched for the source of the sound, only to find it hidden from him by one of the towers. He breathed in deeply, the scent of the sea filling his nostrils. "Is there a storm coming in?"

"Might be," Willen replied.

"I'm going to check. Thank you for your help."

Styke snapped the reins gently, allowing Amrec to carry him away from Willen and toward the northern shore of the Hammer. He kept his eyes on the walls of the citadel as he approached, searching in vain for any sign of life.

The bell, he realized, had awakened something in him. He couldn't determine what, but there was a tightness in his chest that had nothing to do with his recent uneasiness. No, he felt a certainty—the certainty of a storm on the horizon or the violence of a battle—and with this certainty was a sense that he must act quickly. He forced the feeling down and proceeded to where the citadel met the earth and plummeted down into the ocean. Tying Amrec to a bush, he searched the underbrush until he found a narrow groundskeeper's trail that led down along the rocky cliff and then skirted the edge of the citadel all the way to the ocean. Fetching his carbine and knife, he headed down the trail.

It was a difficult walk, but by no means impossible. He passed a narrow bridge leading out to a low gun platform, sitting exposed and empty with three twelve-pound cannons protecting the harbor. He continued on and soon found his boots crunching along the gravelly shoreline. There was a narrow beach here, protected by the breakers, the sound of the ocean crashing against them drowning out anything else he might hear. He followed the beach along the foundation stones of the citadel and around one of the towers, then climbed up and over a boulder until he had a plain view of the docks beneath New Starlight.

The docks were not expansive—large enough, perhaps, for a handful of oceangoing vessels. They were tucked into a beach much like the one Styke had just crossed, protected from the open ocean by a stretch of man-made breakers. On one end of the beach a path led up into the citadel.

Styke looked for a way to reach the docks. A small boat might do it, if he could find one. Willen had been right about the ocean, though, and it was clear that even a strong swimmer would get dashed against the breakers at the base of the citadel. He eyed those breakers, following them along the course of the steep shoreline until he spotted a grate about fifty yards from his current vantage point.

The sea gate that Willen had told him about.

Styke was about to climb down to the breakers when something caught his eye. There was a ship coming in quickly, sailing in from the west. Styke squinted into the wind and was shocked to see that it flew the sunflower yellow of the Fatrastan flag. Settling back onto the boulder, he watched it come closer.

It was only when the ship was almost to the docks that he spotted more on the horizon. Ten, twenty. Maybe even more. There were frigates, transports, and ships of the line, all of Kressian design. He leaned forward, enthralled, wishing he had his looking glass with him. He had thought that the Dynize owned this coast, and as the lead ship came up to dock and dropped anchor, he tried to figure out how a fleet this size could materialize on the other side of the continent from Landfall.

There was a scrape of metal on stone, and Styke looked around sharply, searching for the source of the sound. He thought he heard voices on the wind, but when he could not find them, he turned his attention back to the ship coming in to dock. The minutes slowly ticked by and the wind picked up, the sky growing darker despite sundown being several hours away. Men scrambled through the rigging of the ship, rolling the sails, and a plank was rolled out.

Styke was just about to turn around and leave when he saw a familiar figure appear on deck.

Lindet.

"Oi!" he shouted, waving both arms. There was no response, and no one on the ship seemed to notice, his voice buried by the sound of the waves on the breakers. He looked once more for a way to the docks and didn't find one. Irritated, he hurried down from his boulder and across the hidden beach to the groundskeeper's path.

Lindet was *here*. No wonder Dvory and the Third had been in a hurry. This was some kind of damned rendezvous. All those ships out there—that was probably all that was left of the Fatrastan fleet. They'd picked up Lindet from the coast off Redstone and brought her down here to meet with the Third, where she could take command and sweep the Hammer clear of Dynize, just as Willen had said.

Styke almost laughed at himself for being such a fool. Dvory's secrecy was damned well explained away by this: Lindet didn't want anyone to know that she was taking the fight to the Dynize personally until she was on hand. He tried to figure out how this changed his own plans. The moment she discovered his presence, she would attempt to commandeer the Mad Lancers. If she found out about Ka-poel, that would...well, Styke wasn't going to let her find out about Ka-poel.

He was about halfway up the path when he passed the narrow bridge leading to the gun platform, and froze in place at the sight of some fifteen men—having appeared from seemingly thin air—working over the guns. They cleaned the barrels, brought ammunition up from a cache in the floor, and pointed to the distant ships. It wasn't the men themselves that startled him so much as their appearance.

Every one of them wore a turquoise uniform, a morion-style helmet, and a smooth breastplate. They had red hair and ashen freckles.

Styke changed directions in midstep and hurled himself across the bridge. He was among them before they even saw him, his knife flashing, and within the minute, he was coated in their blood and gore. Heart hammering, Styke looked toward the beach, only for his view to be obstructed by the corner of the citadel.

Goddamn Dvory *was* a traitor. This was Lindet's rendezvous, and Dvory had turned it into a death trap.

Somewhere far above him, there was a flash in one of the citadel towers and then the report of a coastal gun. More followed quickly, and Styke was suddenly all too aware that the Third Army was now sitting at the base of an enemy citadel, whose guns were being manned by Dynize. He wiped the blood from his face and began to run.

CHAPTER 63

Vlora rode past a field of the dead and dying, listening as their moans seemed to keep tempo with the clip-clop of her horse's hooves. Another reckless charge by Dynize dragoons, meant to do nothing more than slow down her column. At a glance, there were no more than a hundred of them—not even close to enough to do any real damage. Their horses had already been either put down or taken, and the Adran dead buried beneath simple stone cairns beside the road. The Dynize—wounded and dead alike— lay where they fell and remained ignored as the Riflejack rear guard marched past them.

She wondered if anyone had bothered to tell her about this attack. Perhaps. She was exhausted from days of forced march, barely able to sleep even when she did have the time. These attacks had come so frequently that they hardly warranted her attention anymore. They came at night, in the rain, even out in the open as the Dynize general sent his cavalry along every goat path and min- ing trail he could find to try to flank the Riflejacks—to try to trip them up and force the column to slow, even for fifteen minutes at a time.

She wanted to dismiss the attacks as a waste of the enemy's resources, but the truth was they were working. Despite the larger, more cumbersome army, the Dynize infantry remained just three hours behind the Riflejacks. Vlora felt like she could barely breathe.

Up ahead, her column snaked down through the foothills and onto a relatively flat plain, where the vanguard had pulled off to the side for a few moments' rest, allowing another company to take the lead of the column. She searched for Olem and was unable to find him.

The sound of galloping hooves made her turn to find Taniel and Norrine coming up the road from the west, covered in the dust stirred up by Vlora's infantry. Norrine wore a tired but satisfied smile, and Taniel held his rifle across the saddle horn. He pulled in next to Vlora and tapped on the side of his head. "That's all of them."

"All of who?" she asked.

"As far as we can tell, we've popped every Privileged and bone-eye in the Dynize Army. We've also killed half their senior officers."

"And yet still they come hard on our heels." Vlora had meant to say that in her head, but it came out without her even realizing she was speaking.

Norrine nodded. "They are . . . persistent."

Vlora looked back toward the dead and dying Dynize dragoons from the last ambush, unable to get rid of the weight of dread sitting in the pit of her stomach. "You've done well," she told Norrine. "Go find some chow."

Norrine headed up the column, leaving Vlora and Taniel alone by the side of the road. "I don't like the look on your face," Taniel said.

"I don't like the fact that we can't gain even an hour on these bastards. They won't slow down, even with their officers and sorcerers dead." She gestured to the dead dragoons. "They're throwing lives in front of us with as little regard as if they were tossing caltrops in a road."

"The zeal scares you?"

"It terrifies me. I have a little voice in the back of my head whispering every few minutes that we're all going to die on this blasted continent." She rolled her shoulders, trying to calm herself. "I'm not thrilled with the idea of dying, but there are worse fates. Dying, hunted like a dog...it feels like our campaign through northern Kez during the war all over again. Except this time *I'm* the one responsible for all these lives." She looked Taniel in the eye. "I don't want all these men to die here, Taniel."

Taniel's expression was grim. "You're doing the best you can."

She wondered at his plans. He wasn't an Adran, not anymore. He was stronger, faster, and sturdier than any normal human—even any powder mage—and when the Dynize finally trapped the Riflejacks and slaughtered them to the last man, Taniel would no doubt carve his way out and disappear into the hills, heading across the continent to reunite with Ka-poel. Vlora briefly considered grabbing Olem and attempting to run for it.

But who would she be if she abandoned the soldiers who so willingly sacrificed themselves for her?

Another thought crept up and touched the back of her mind. She flirted with it for a moment before shoving it to one side, where it waited, insistently, for her to consider it again. "I've got to talk with Olem," she told Taniel. She turned and followed Norrine up the column, riding past the dust-coated soldiers, down out of the foothills, and onto the wide field where the column ground to a halt for a brief rest.

Beyond the field was something that her maps called Ishtari's Crease. It was a great upthrusting of rock, as severe as a church's steeple, that ran north-to-south for about thirty miles. It varied between forty and eighty feet tall, and was occasionally broken by natural fissures or modern clefts blasted out for roadways. Beyond the Crease the land fell steeply down into an old-growth forest, beyond which one could just make out the distant plains that needed to be crossed before reaching the ocean.

Those plains had haunted her thoughts for days like a waking nightmare. Flat and open, with few defensible positions, the larger Dynize field army would be able to slow and surround the Riflejacks, cutting them to ribbons without the need of either tactical or sorcerous advantages. To outrun them, the Riflejacks needed at least a day's lead on their enemy. They had mere hours.

Vlora found Olem in a deep conference with the company's quartermasters. He spotted Vlora and broke off, coming to her side, where he gave her a tight smile. "We've sent the capstone on ahead while the column rests. Our scouts are telling us that we won't have to worry about being flanked by Dynize cavalry for a while—there isn't another place to cross the Crease for miles, so they'll either have to come straight up behind us, or wait until we're completely through."

There was a hint of suggestion in his words. It didn't take a military genius to see that the Crease was a tactician's wet dream. The road passed through a rocky divide less than twenty yards across, easily defended by a few hundred men, let alone a few thousand.

Quietly, so as not to be overheard, she said, "We're going to die whether we fight them here or out on the plains."

"The thought had crossed my mind," Olem answered.

"I'd rather not die at all."

"We can attempt to negotiate."

Vlora scoffed. "And give them time to catch up with us and maneuver? You remember the negotiation before Windy River."

"Things might have changed. We can try to give them the capstone."

"Somehow, I'm not sure that will be enough." Vlora eyed the

Crease. In another situation, she might have found it beautiful, in a rugged way. The cracked, broken rock was periodically flushed with green where a group of shrubs or trees had managed to eke out its existence. It wasn't, she decided, a terrible monument to make one's gravestone. "If we attempt a last stand here, how long will it take for the Dynize to find another crossing and come around behind us?"

"A day and a half for their cavalry. Two and a half for infantry." Olem paused. "There's the option of leaving a few hundred men to defend the pass. It would easily buy the rest of the army time to get a head start on the plains."

Vlora shot Olem a glare. "You think I should ask for suicidal volunteers?"

"I'm confident we could get enough volunteers to hold the pass." There was a glint in Olem's eye that Vlora didn't like.

"And I suppose you'd volunteer to lead them?" Olem clenched his jaw, but did not answer. Vlora knew him well enough to see that as a yes. "Out of the question." She paused. "How long do we plan on resting here?"

"No more than a half hour, then we'll send the vanguard through the Crease."

"Make it fifteen minutes. We need to talk again in ten, just over that ridge over there." She pointed to where the road passed through the Crease. "In private."

"I'll be there."

Vlora took her leave and headed along the column, her eyes searching the faces of her soldiers as they rested on the side of the road, jackets unbuttoned and packs thrown to the ground. The looks of exhaustion as she rode past them made her heart cry out with every salute and respectful "General Flint" that followed her.

The problem, she found, was that Olem was a far more popular person with the soldiers than she was. They respected her, for certain, but they loved Olem. And that made what she had to do next especially difficult. It took her a few minutes to discover a pair of faces up near the vanguard, and she dismounted and walked over to the two men lying a little off on their own from the main column. One was smaller, with a narrow face and thoughtful eyes, while the second was well over six feet tall and had the languid manner of a mastiff lying in the sun.

The two friends were former boxers who'd joined up with her during the Kez Civil War. She'd used them for dirty side jobs on more than one occasion. "Boys," she said, standing above them.

The big one, Pugh, squinted at Vlora from under his hat and then leapt to his feet with a snapped salute, kicking his companion, Dez, sharply in the ribs as he did so. "Ma'am!"

Vlora waited until they were both standing. "At ease, soldiers. I need a favor."

"Anything for you, ma'am," Dez responded.

"Anything?"

"You set up Pugh's mama with that good job in Adopest and you made sure my little brother didn't fall in with the gangs. That's worth a lot, ma'am."

Vlora gave them a tired smile. "First, I want you to answer a question with complete honesty. I will not hold any answer you give me against you in any way."

"Of course, ma'am," Pugh said.

"If I and Colonel Olem were both standing in front of you and gave you conflicting orders, whose would you obey?"

The eyes of both men widened. Pugh swallowed hard. "Ma'am?"

"Honest answers."

"I..." Dez said, "I suppose it would be yours, ma'am."

"You suppose."

"It would be, ma'am," he said firmly. Pugh echoed the sentiment.

"Good. Get some rope and meet me up on that ridge. Right there behind that boulder."

*   *   *

Vlora leaned against the boulder and watched as Olem, Dez, and Pugh together walked up the road toward her. She wondered whether this was a mistake, and forced herself to dismiss the notion. Sometimes, a thing had to be done to preserve lives. She wiped a few tears from the corners of her eyes and forced a gentle smile onto her face as the men reached her.

Olem was already concerned. She could see it in his eyes, though he didn't want to show it in front of the other two. "What's going on?" he asked her.

She jerked her head to the side, indicating the three men follow her behind the boulder, out of the sight of eyes of the army below them. Once they were secluded, she said, "Pugh, I would appreciate it if you would disarm and restrain Colonel Olem."

"What..." Olem managed, before Pugh slipped behind him and wrapped Olem in a bear hug that pinned Olem's arms to his chest. Dez jumped forward and took Olem's pistol, sword, and knife, before returning to Vlora's side. Despite their compliance, both men looked more than a little startled by the order, and clearly expected an explanation. "What's going on?" Olem asked through clenched teeth, his eyes full of anger and hurt.

Vlora took a shaky breath. "This is what's going on: In five minutes, Colonel Heracich is going to give the order to move out. He'll remain in command for the next two days, while Pugh and Dez quietly trundle you along with instructions not to let you out of their sight or allow you to speak with anyone. At the end of those two days, you will be released, and Heracich will relinquish command of the Riflejacks to you."

Olem began to struggle. "What the pit do you mean by all of this?"

"I mean..." Vlora heard her voice crack and turned away, unable to face Olem while she spoke. "I'm going to stay and defend the Crease," she said.

"What, on your own?"

"Yes, on my own." She glanced over to find Olem's eyes wide with shock. Pugh's mouth hung open. "It should give the Riflejacks time to get a lead on their pursuers."

Olem suddenly jerked backward, slamming his head into Pugh's chin. The big soldier reeled back, releasing him for long enough that Olem leapt for the road, clearly intent on heading back to the army to forestall this order. Dez tackled his legs, and he and Pugh dragged him kicking and struggling back behind the rock. Together they began to bind Olem. Dez stuffed a rag into his mouth.

Vlora squatted next to Olem as he was restrained, unable to help the tears that ran down her face as he glared at her. "I'm sorry," she told him. "I'm not going to let anyone else die for my ambitions—for my mistakes. Not the Riflejacks, and certainly not you. I know you're going to be angry. Please don't take it out on Pugh and Dez, or Heracich. They're only following my orders." She wanted to say a thousand things, but her stomach clenched so badly she thought she might vomit if she continued to speak. "I love you, Olem." She leaned forward, kissing him on the forehead, then stepped away.

"Keep him quiet until the army has made it twenty or thirty miles," she told Pugh and Dez. "And definitely don't say anything to my mages. If they ask questions, refer them to Heracich." She nodded at them, forcing a smile. "Thanks, boys. I hope I'll be alive to pay you back."

Olem was bound at their feet, his face red and streaked with tears. The two soldiers straightened and snapped salutes. "I wish it hadn't come to this, ma'am," Pugh said.

"So do I," Vlora answered.

"It's been an honor to serve under you," Dez said. "I know every man in the brigade would say the same. We'll never forget you."

"I appreciate it. Now, get him out of here before I lose my nerve."

CHAPTER 64

Michel followed the footsteps in the dust as the tunnel plummeted deeper into the ground. It passed through several more chambers, with no indication that anyone had stopped in any of them. At one point, Michel consulted his maps to see that he was within arm's length of the chamber labeled MARA on his map. He hesitated, peering at the dark doorway, wondering if an empty room thousands of years old would hold any secrets of value to his real mission here in Landfall.

"On the way back," he whispered to himself, and continued on with his escort.

He could sense the excitement of the soldiers. It was as if they'd been reinvigorated by the idea of catching je Tura, and they bit their lips and fingered their weapons. Occasionally one of them would joke about what they'd do to je Tura when they caught him.

They entered a new chamber—one narrower but significantly longer than the others, with walls lined with alcoves and carved tables. The momentum of his escort was suddenly seized by something that Michel caught sight of just a few moments later.

One of the alcoves had a bedroll in it. Michel approached cautiously, lantern held high, peering into the darkness. His heart suddenly hammered in his chest, and he imagined je Tura himself popping out from the very stone to stick a sword through Michel's belly. Beside the alcove he found a small seaman's chest, a lantern, several tins of spare oil, and a long, round leather tube that he immediately recognized as a map carrier.

He swallowed as he poked at the bedroll, his fingers uncovering the shine of steel.

"Can we be certain this is his hiding spot?" Tenik asked him quietly.

"Search down the hall," Michel ordered the soldiers. "Check the side passages. Don't go so far that you can't see the light of each other's lanterns, and stay in pairs."

Tenik drew his pistol. "You think he's here now?"

Michel lifted the bedroll to reveal, tucked to the back of the alcove, an old broadsword. It looked like something out of a museum, with two red gemstones fitted into a silver-etched hilt. The weapon was almost as long as Michel was tall. "Rumors have it that je Tura carries this damn thing everywhere. Rumors aren't necessarily true, but he might be nearby." He stopped, noticing that Tenik was peering at something in the darkness. "What is it?"

"Are any of our escort behind us?"

"I don't think so, why?"

"Because I swear I just saw a light in..." Tenik trailed off, and Michel heard a very distinctive noise that he'd heard on more than one occasion: the hiss of a quick-burning fuse, zipping through the darkness toward him.

"Everyone down!" Michel bellowed, shoving Tenik farther into the chamber and leaping toward the fuse, dropping his lantern as he attempted to stamp out the fiery little worm. It shot between his legs, and Michel whirled, jumped forward with foot extended, and slammed his head directly into the rock wall. He teetered and then tripped just as a blast erupted from the ceiling of the chamber.

Michel lay on the floor, ears ringing, a white flash of light embedded in his vision no matter how much he tried to blink it away. He moved one arm, then the other, hoping that nothing was broken and not entirely certain that he wasn't half-buried in a thousand tons of rock. "Tenik!" he called, his own voice seemingly small and far away.

Something stirred in the darkness. He *felt* it more than he heard or saw it, and he searched blindly for either his pistol or his lantern. There was a sound—again, as if from a great distance—and then a lantern flared to light. He blinked, trying to discern the light of the lantern from the light etched into his vision. It took him a moment to get his bearings; he lay against the wall of the tunnel, half-behind a stone table that seemed to have at least somewhat protected him from the blast. To his right was the string that led back the way he'd come. To his left was a pile of rubble from the collapsed ceiling of the chamber.

Michel finally looked up into the light, still half-dazed, only to realize that the lantern wasn't being held by either Tenik or one of the soldiers. The face behind it was old and grizzled, a Kressian face with black hair streaked with gray, pockmarked cheeks, and high-arched eyebrows that looked like they were locked in permanent surprise. The man grinned down at Michel, lips moving, and a voice from a mile away said, "My, my, aren't you a surprise."

"Val je Tura?" Michel asked, suppressing a groan. His recent gunshot wound hurt badly. He wondered if he'd torn open the stitches.

Je Tura walked over to the alcove and retrieved his sword. He drew it from the scabbard and lay it across his shoulder. The tip scraped the wall behind him. He sat down on one of the stone tables, head tilted to the side. "You've sussed me out. Are you that traitor spy, or just an unlucky Kressian conscript who just happens to have his very own escort of soldiers?"

"Would you believe me if I told you it was the second?" Michel still attempted to blink away the light of the explosion. He continued to feel through the rubble, looking for his own lantern, or his pistol, or some damned thing to defend himself with.

"I would not," je Tura answered. "I got a pretty good description of you from Hendres, and you about match the bill."

"How is Hendres?"

"Doing very well. Disappointed that you're still alive."

"I imagine she is."

"She won't be disappointed for long." Je Tura swung his sword off his shoulder. He was leaner than Michel would have guessed from the stories, though he was remarkably short for someone with his kind of presence. Michel thought he heard a groan from somewhere in the rubble, and je Tura squinted toward his handiwork. "The second charge didn't go off," he said. "Not sure if I got any of your friends. But it'll take 'em a while to dig through, and by that time I'll be long gone."

Michel's hand wrapped around a rock about the size of his fist. As je Tura stepped toward him, he hurled the rock with all his strength. It soared over je Tura's shoulder, bounced off the wall, and rolled into the dark.

Je Tura laughed. "Is that the best you've got, turncoat?"

Michel reached for another rock, but his hand touched smooth, polished wood. "No," he said, pulling his pistol out of the rubble. "This is."

The blast took je Tura full in the chest. Je Tura jerked back, staring down at Michel in disgust, then stumbling to one side. He dropped his sword with a clatter, then fell beside it.

It took Michel over a minute to get to his feet, ears still ringing.

Nothing seemed broken, but his whole damned body hurt. It took him well over a minute more to reload the pistol with trembling hands and step over to je Tura. He claimed the other's lantern and kicked the sword away from his hand.

Je Tura looked up at him balefully, clutching his chest, jaw clenched, not making a sound. Michel raised his pistol and aimed it at je Tura's head.

"Why'd you betray us?" je Tura demanded.

"You say that like I was ever one of you," Michel responded, his voice quiet lest someone on the other side of that pile of rubble overhear. "Don't get high and mighty with me, je Tura. You've been bombing public spaces for a month now. Killing children. Civilians. You're a piece of shit."

"You haven't seen what I've seen."

Michel considered pulling the trigger, not giving je Tura the satisfaction of a few last words. But his interest was piqued. "What have you seen?"

"You know about the godstone?"

"What of it?"

"You know what they're doing to try to get it working?"

"I don't."

"Well, civilians isn't even the start of it." Je Tura shifted, and Michel watched carefully to be sure he wasn't reaching for a weapon. He continued. "Blood sacrifices, turncoat. They're marching prisoners and orphans and every damn person they think won't be missed over to that great big obelisk and slitting their throats. They hang them like pigs to bleed every drop onto the surface and their Privileged and bone-eyes stand around. They chant and they wave their hands and they rub the blood all over the stone."

The hair on the back of Michel's neck stood on end. "Why should I believe you?"

"You didn't know, did you? I can see it from your face. These are the people you signed on with, turncoat. You think they call those foxhead magicians 'blood sorcerers' because they like the name?" je Tura laughed, sputtered, and coughed up blood.

"Are you the last one?" Michel demanded. "Is anyone else down here?"

Je Tura grinned at him, and Michel heard someone call his name through that rubble. "Go to the pit," je Tura told him.

"You first."

The echo of the shot made the ringing in Michel's ears worse. He checked to make sure je Tura was definitely dead, and went to the rubble where he noted a small space that revealed a bit of light coming through from the other side. "Is everyone all right?" he called.

"Tenik's in bad shape," someone answered. "The rest of us are fine. Je Tura?"

"He's dead." Michel looked at his hands, scraped and bloody, and wondered if he'd even be able to walk out of here. "Look, you need to stay put. I can't dig you out on my own. I'm going to head up and send down diggers and a surgeon. We'll have you out of there in an hour." He squeezed his eyes shut, trying not to think of Tenik buried beneath that rubble, body broken from the blast that collapsed the tunnel. "Shit, I'll have them send a Privileged. Hold tight!"

Michel hurried back up the tunnel as fast as he could manage, holding je Tura's lantern and following the string. He paused a few chambers over, looking toward the dark room labeled MARA on his map, then looking back toward his trapped escort. Swearing under his breath, he ran down that side passage and into MARA, where he held his lantern up high.

At first, the room seemed completely insignificant. It was neither the largest nor the most interesting of the chambers he'd searched. It was completely empty, perfectly spherical, and there was no adornment but torch recesses in the wall and a single stone slab in the center of the room. He almost turned and left, but something compelled him to step over to that slab. He peered at the dusty stone, noting a narrow indentation that ran around the outside of the slab and then spilled out at the end. It reminded him of the marble slabs in Emerald's morgue—the way they were designed to catch blood and funnel it to the feet of the body, where it could be cleaned up easily.

This did not look like a morgue.

With a final glance around, Michel rushed to the chamber where his escort had made their detour, then followed his maps toward the closest exit, praying that he wouldn't run into any more iron grates along the way. He managed to make it to the surface within twenty minutes, and within another ten he was at Yaret's headquarters. He babbled instructions, calling for Yaret to help Tenik, and then collapsed into a chair across from a table covered in the maps of the catacombs.

A whirlwind of activity followed. Teams of soldiers headed directly into the chapel catacombs, while others went to find the spot where Michel had surfaced. A Privileged was sent for. Michel remained numb, his mind barely working, his eyes still seeing the flash of the explosion and his ears still ringing.

It was several minutes before he realized that Yaret was watching him. "Je Tura is dead," he reported.

"You already told us," Yaret said gently.

"Oh. I forgot." Michel scowled, thinking of that chamber with the morgue slab that definitely wasn't a morgue slab.

"We'll get him out of there as quickly as possible. You did well coming to us instead of trying to dig them out yourself."

"I…" Michel didn't know what else to say, surprised at how distraught he was over Tenik's possible death. "I have a question. Tenik said you know Old Dynize."

"A bit," Yaret said, clearly caught off guard.

"Do you know the word 'Mara'?"

"'Mara,' 'Mara,'" Yaret muttered. "Oh, yes. It's the word for sacrifice."

"Could it be a room for sacrifice, too?"

"I suppose it could, yes. Why do you ask?"

Michel pushed himself to his feet. His valise of maps was still slung over his shoulder, but he couldn't organize the thought or energy to drop it. A thousand little pieces—information, half suspicions, and loose ends—suddenly clicked together in his brain. He thought of the godstone and of je Tura's claim of blood sacrifice, and what little he knew of Ka-poel's childhood. "I have to go."

"You're in no shape to go anywhere."

"It's okay, I'm not going far."

CHAPTER 65

Amrec's hooves hammered the ground as Styke flew through the chaos of the camp of the Third Army. Soldiers milled about, throwing themselves out of his way as he passed, and it was clear no one knew what was going on. Sergeants bellowed at their infantry to fall in line; commissioned officers screamed at each other in confusion. Styke slowed only enough to find Colonel Willen near the entrance to the curtain wall.

"What the pit is going on?" Willen demanded, looking up at the high towers now firing nonstop toward the ocean. "Who are manning those towers? What the pit are they firing at?"

Styke sawed at the reins, Amrec dancing eagerly beneath him. "Dvory has betrayed us. Those towers are manned by Dynize, and they're firing at a Fatrastan fleet."

"You must be joking." Willen was slack-jawed.

"Serious as pit. I just watched Lindet arrive. Dvory has captured her and now aims to sink her fleet. Unless my guess is wrong, he'll turn the citadel guns on the Third within moments and..." Styke trailed off, realizing that the citadel guns would only make a dent in the fifty thousand men camped so close. The Third had some cannon and scaling ladders, and though they'd lose thousands, they would still be able to take the citadel. Dvory wasn't that stupid. He had to have backup somewhere. "Your scouts! Have they reported anything suspicious?"

Willen began to sweat visibly. "One of the outriders just came back with word of a large Dynize force nearby. He didn't see them, just their trail."

"How far?" Styke demanded.

"A few miles off."

"Damn it all, get everything in order. Turn your guns and ladders on the towers and hit them hard and fast."

"Our generals," Willen objected, pointing at the citadel. Realization dawned on his face.

"They've either betrayed you or been betrayed themselves," Styke roared. "The colonels are in command now, Willen. Make it count!" He finally loosened his grip on the reins and Amrec was off like a shot, galloping through the camp and out onto the plains within minutes. By the time he reached the Mad Lancers' camp hidden behind the hills two miles to the south, the entire company had already packed and was on horseback.

Ibana and Gustar met him in the center of the gathered cavalry. "Starlight's guns are firing," Ibana called.

Styke answered with a nod. "Either Dvory has betrayed Fatrasta, or the Dynize have tricked everyone. Lindet is in the citadel, either dead or a prisoner, and they are firing on her fleet."

"Pit." Ibana gasped. "A shitload has happened in the last few hours."

"You have no idea. What do our scouts say?"

Gustar cut in. "There's a Dynize field army lurking out there. We think they screened themselves from us and the Third by circling the Hock."

"Shit." Styke wasn't sure whether *not* running into that army was a curse or a blessing. "They're going to smash the Third against the Starlight citadel while the towers pulverize their rear."

There was a long silence, and Styke listened to the report of cannon fire in the distance. With Lindet captured and the Third destroyed, the Dynize would have free rein through the Hammer. They could surge north, take Redstone and the eastern coast, and Fatrasta was lost.

"Do we help or run?" Ibana asked.

Styke looked from Gustar to Ibana. He could see that they both had just had the same thought as he.

"I wouldn't mind letting Lindet rot in a Dynize cell," Ibana mused.

"I can't disagree," Gustar grunted.

Styke tried to agree with them. Ten years in the camps. Torture, starvation, and hopelessness. Lindet deserved to reap what she had given him, but Styke also knew that without Lindet, Fatrasta was doomed.

And no matter how much she deserved it, he couldn't leave his sister to such a fate.

"Ibana, you're with me," he said. "Give me twenty of our best fighters. Wrap their carbines in wax cloth and make sure everyone has a good knife. Gustar, the Dynize will either arrive with the storm and attack at night, or first thing in the morning. Either way, I want the Mad Lancers to wait until the Dynize have engaged the Third and then hit them in the flank. Can you lead a night charge, in the rain?"

"That's suicidal," Gustar muttered.

"Can you?"

"I can."

"Good. You have command of the Mad Lancers. Ibana, tell Sunin to take Celine south and get her off the continent if the battle goes badly. Then find me my fighters. And bring me the bone-eye."

*   *   *

Styke, Ibana, Jackal, Ka-poel, and two dozen of the old core of the Mad Lancers galloped into the camp of the Third Army. Chaos still reigned as a heavy wind blew in from the ocean and the black clouds approached. Outside the curtain wall, officers attempted to form up their companies to face an as-yet-unseen enemy from the mainland, while inside the curtain wall crews attempted to bring their cannons to bear on the citadel towers.

Styke didn't spot Willen as they rode through, but he did see that the Dynize had finally showed themselves on the citadel walls. Sharpshooters on both sides exchanged fire, while gun crews on the interior towers worked to bring their own artillery to fire point-blank at the soldiers at the foot of the walls. A few courageous officers led charges with ladders, only to be raked by musket fire from above.

He rode past all of this, ignoring the mighty blasts as the citadel cannon opened fire, closing his ears to the screams of the Third as grapeshot fell among them like rain. He leaned into Amrec's neck, urging him faster, and listened to the pounding of hooves as they skirted the base of the citadel wall.

"Here!" he bellowed, leaping from Amrec as they reached the groundskeeper's trail at the north end of the citadel. His lancers dismounted, fetching their wrapped carbines, knives, and swords.

Ibana looked uneasily at the base of the citadel. "It's going to rain soon. It'll be damned suicide to scale this wall in good weather. Pit, Ben, we haven't scaled a wall for a decade."

"We're not scaling it," Styke said, wrapping his own carbine tightly and making sure his knife was secured at his waist. "We're going around and under. The wax cloth isn't for the rain—it's for the ocean."

Ibana took a half step back, her chin rising. "Pit," she breathed. "You want to fight your way *up* the inside of a fortified citadel?"

"That's what I said."

She looked around at their comrades. "We should have brought everyone."

"Too many bodies," Styke replied, throwing his carbine over his shoulder. "Jackal, what do the spirits tell you about what's inside?"

Jackal pointed at Ka-poel. "She's too close. I have one gibbering mad spirit sitting on my shoulder telling me we're all going to join him. The rest have fled."

"I always knew the dead were useless." Styke crossed to Ka-poel, lowering himself to one knee so that they were eye to eye. She regarded him coolly, her face placid, and he thought he saw a hint of violence in her eyes. "Can you help us in there?" he asked.

She tapped the machete strapped to her thigh.

"No," Styke said, taking his knife and stabbing his own palm with the tip of the blade. He put his knife away and dabbed at the blood, holding out his stained fingers to her. "This. Can you help us with this? Protection, strength, speed—can you give me anything?"

Ka-poel hesitated. Slowly, she reached out and touched his bleeding palm. She drew back, pressing the blood to her lips, then gave him a nod.

"Good."

Styke stepped to the edge of the cliff, looking down the grounds-keeper's path. Ibana joined him. "Are you sure about this?" she asked.

Styke thought of the times they'd charged into enemy cannonades or been unhorsed in the middle of a sea of bayonets. He thought of his old horse, Deshnar, and the power flowing through his muscles as they charged twenty times their number at the Battle of Landfall. He tried to wonder if he'd ever hesitated, if he'd ever shown the weakness that he now felt as he considered fighting his way through a fortress of Dynize.

"I'm certain," he replied.

Ibana met his eye. "Why? Lindet isn't worth this."

He remembered a time, as a child, that he'd been knocking at the gates of the pit with a fever. His baby sister had snuck into his room to put candies beneath his tongue, despite knowing their father would beat her if caught. "Not to you," he replied, and headed down the path to the ocean.

CHAPTER 66

Vlora sat on a stone to one side of the highway that ran through the crack in Ishtari's Crease, humming softly to herself as she drew a whetstone across the blade of her sword. Her jacket was neatly folded behind her makeshift chair, her pistols and kit on top of the small bundle. Her sword lay across her knees as she listened to the sound the whetstone made and watched as the Dynize Army emerged from the hills.

They snaked down onto the relatively flat bit of highway about a mile and a half from her position—a column of infantry six across and probably miles and miles long. Officers rode horses alongside the column, with a handful of scouts out ahead. From their formation, they were clearly not expecting a fight, and had ordered their men to march double time to try to catch up with Vlora's smaller force. Their advance scouts had probably seen her army continue through Ishtari's Crease and head down into the forest below.

She was running a light powder trance—enough that she could

see the moment one of the scouts spotted her. The column ground to a halt, officers were consulted, soldiers stared in her direction through looking glasses. She'd changed into an old pair of crimson trousers, so they probably wondered what the pit a single Adran soldier was doing out here alone.

She wondered how much time their hesitancy would cost them. Scouts were dispatched heading north and south along the Crease, no doubt looking for a trap. The general in charge of this field army had grown wary of her ambushes.

It made her smile.

It was almost a half hour until the column began to move again. It prowled forward, rolling toward her as inexorably as a boulder down a mountain but at a maddeningly slow pace. Though she tried to maintain her outward calm, her muscles cried out for the fight to start—for the beginning of the end. It reminded her of sitting in a theater next to Taniel, Bo, and Tamas, waiting for the most anticipated play of the season to begin while she clutched her handbill and hoped—in that way teenagers do—that the lead actor would look her way during the performance.

Every minute or so, Vlora took another hit of powder. She increased the dosage by a tiny amount each time, until her senses practically *hummed* with all the information flowing through them. She could hear the wings of every bug for two hundred yards, smell every flower, feel the tiniest speck of dust on the tips of her fingers. Her hands felt as if they were trembling, but every time she held them out to look, they were steady as steel.

She was so focused on the distant tramp of Dynize boots that she did not hear a single set of footsteps in the gravel behind her until they were almost upon her. She turned slightly, grasping the hilt of her sword. She wondered if a Dynize assassin had managed to sneak around her, or if Olem had escaped his ropes and come to try to talk her out of this.

"There are simpler ways to kill yourself, you know."

Vlora looked up at Taniel as he came to stand beside her. "Shouldn't you be with the capstone?" she asked.

"Shouldn't you?" Taniel's eyes were on the approaching Dynize column. They'd be here in less than ten minutes.

"I have other responsibilities."

Taniel snorted. "If you were facing down a company, I'd think you heroic. But you can't win this—not even a chance. There's a whole field army coming out of those hills and you will not stop them."

"I can slow them down."

Taniel was silent for several moments. "Enough to make a difference?"

"I wouldn't be here if I didn't think so."

"Look, the Riflejacks are a week's march from the coast. Then they have to find a harbor and ships to get them off the continent— if there even still is a safe harbor. If you gain them a few hours, it won't mean a damned thing."

Vlora lifted her sword, examining the blade for chips and flaws. It was in good condition, considering it had gone through several major battles with her. "Did Olem send you?"

"Nobody sent me. I caught wind and came myself. As far as I know, Olem is still trussed up like a pig per your orders. He's never going to forgive you for this, you know."

"I'm not terribly worried about that. And yes, I think a few hours will make a difference. My boys have orders to ditch the capstone if the Dynize get within five miles of them. Once the Dynize have both my corpse and the capstone, they're going to reassess this merry little chase. The northern Fatrastan coast is still Lindet's territory, and the Dynize will be hesitant to chase them too far. They might just decide to let the Riflejacks go."

"Are you sure they will?"

"I am not."

"And you're willing to throw your life away on that uncertainty?"

"I am."

Taniel gave an unhappy sigh. "Fine." Vlora expected him to turn and stride off with a huff, but instead he removed his gloves—revealing his red hand—and then stripped off his jacket and folded it up, setting it on top of Vlora's effects.

"What the pit are you doing?" Vlora asked.

Taniel didn't answer her. He undid his cuffs and collar, then rolled up his sleeves. "Do you remember when we first met?"

It was an odd question. Vlora frowned at Taniel, watching as he dabbed out a bit of black powder onto the back of his hand and snorted it. "I do."

"Do you remember the day Tamas adopted you?"

She forced herself to think back nearly two decades, picturing herself as a waif of a child, roaming the ins and outs of Hrusch Avenue, trying to survive between the uncaring streets and the cruelty of the orphanage. She'd met Taniel and Bo, and a cold-eyed gentleman whom she'd later come to know as Field Marshal Tamas. Vlora had gotten into some trouble, and Tamas had dueled a nobleman to save her life. He'd taken her in, given her a home, and trained her to be a powder mage.

"It's hard to forget. It was the most terrifying and the happiest day of my life."

Taniel gave her a peculiar look. "You've never been more terrified? With all you've been through?"

"I couldn't protect myself back then. I can now."

Taniel chuckled. "That's fair. I don't remember that day very well, but I do remember that night. Tamas took us all home. We had dinner together, back when we still did that, and I remember thinking how I'd never seen anyone eat so much. You didn't want to leave the table, and fell asleep with your face next to your third helping of cherry tart. Tamas carried you to bed, tucked you in, and then he brought us in to see you while you were sleeping. Do you know what he said to us?"

Vlora's face felt warm, her eyes moist. She blinked through a sudden haze. "No, I don't."

"He pointed to you and said, *This is your little sister. I want you both to promise me that you'll protect her, that the three of you will look out for each other even after I'm gone.*" Taniel squinted into the distance. "I didn't always get along with Tamas, but he protected the three of us until we could protect ourselves. Point being, I'm not going to leave you here to die alone."

Vlora felt the color drain from her face. She stood up, facing Taniel. "Don't do this. Don't try to guilt me into coming with you so that you don't have to die with me."

"I'm not trying to guilt you. I'm fulfilling a promise I gave my father." Taniel looked at her coldly. "And you *will not* deny me that."

Vlora sank back down to her seat on the rock, staring at her sword. Perhaps Taniel was right. This was an enormous mistake. She didn't mean to bring him into this, not when he had loved ones of his own, not when he had grand plans to change the world. She looked toward the Dynize column, the head of which was just a few hundred yards away. "It's too late to run," she whispered.

"That it is. What's your plan?"

"You ever see someone slice a baguette in half lengthwise to make a sandwich?"

Taniel's eyebrows rose. "Yes?"

"I'm going to slice straight down the column."

Taniel clasped his hands behind his back, smiling down the road. "I suggest you follow me in. I'm a little sturdier than you."

"I don't think I can keep up."

"Do your best."

"Right." Vlora stood up, sheathed her sword, and stretched her arms and shoulders. A handful of advance scouts rode on ahead of the column, coming straight toward her. They probably planned to pull her aside and question her while the column advanced past. Fine by her. She knelt down on the rocky highway, pulling four powder charges from her pocket and placing them between her palms, then raising her hands in front of her face as if in prayer. Eyes closed, she listened to the scouts ride up.

"You there," one spoke in bad Adran, "what are you two doing here?"

"I'm enjoying the view. She's praying," Taniel responded in Palo.

Vlora could hear the confusion in the scout's voice. "Where is your army?" She pressed her palms together tightly and ground them together to destroy the wrapping around the powder charges, then opened them up as if she were miming a book and buried her face between them, inhaling as hard as she could. Powder flooded her nostrils and mouth, granules like little specks of static as they touched her saliva and the inner membranes of her face. Her whole body *vibrated* with powder, every second seeming to take an eternity as her sorcery attempted to compensate for the barrage on her senses.

Tamas had always warned them about overdosing on powder— from either running a trance for too long a time or imbibing too much in one go. She'd flirted with the edges of her limits a few times, walking up to the precipice that would either make her powder blind or outright kill her. And now she ran up to that cliff and jumped off the edge.

Vlora's eyes flew open. She reached out with her senses, across the mile of Dynize infantry that snaked down the road. Every six rows, she detonated a single powder charge in an infantryman's kit. It took her less than a second, and within moments the column was overshadowed by powder smoke, the air full of the screams of the dying and the confused. She turned to Taniel and nodded.

The scouts were dead before they could voice another word. Taniel breezed past them, the very tip of his sword slick with crimson, sprinting into the head of the column with a speed Vlora had never seen before. He was upon them in the blink of an eye, his sword moving like the wings of a hummingbird, soldiers collapsing as he passed like some kind of avatar of death sweeping his scythe through the souls of the damned.

Vlora watched the dance for mere seconds before following him into the slaughter.

CHAPTER 67

Michel stumbled down street after street, ignoring the curious glances of the afternoon traffic and occasional Dynize soldier as he made his way to Ichtracia's townhouse. The heavy map-carrying case pulled at his shoulder, and he considered dropping it in the street but couldn't quite bring himself to do so until he reached the dead-end cul-de-sac where Ichtracia lived. He paused a few feet from the narrow garden path that led up to her front door, painfully adjusting his cuffs and collar. He tried to dust the debris from the tunnels off his shoulders, only to realize just how addled his head still was, and walked up to the front door. He knocked, fixing his most charming smile, and prepared to greet her footman. He *really* hoped that she would wait to kill him until he'd had a chance to talk a bit.

His smile disappeared as the door opened to reveal a man Michel had never seen before. He was enormous—easily six and a half feet tall—and as wide as a draft horse. Behind him, standing just inside Ichtracia's foyer, Ka-Sedial leaned on his cane. He eyed

Michel with the same sort of eagerness that a child eyed the display case of a candy store.

"I'm looking for Ichtracia," Michel said.

The brute snatched Michel by the front of his jacket before he could even think to yell. He felt himself swung around, held in the air like a doll and deposited on the floor of the foyer in the blink of an eye. The door shut behind him, and Ka-Sedial leaned over Michel, his kindly old face fixed with a gentle smile.

"Ichtracia isn't here at the moment," Ka-Sedial said. "But you have very good timing *and* very poor luck, Michel Bravis."

"I'm not sure what you're getting at, but it's not a great idea." Michel summoned all the bluster his aching head could manage. "I just put a bullet in the head of the man who's been bombing your people. Je Tura is dead, and within the hour every one of your bloodthirsty soldiers is gonna know I'm the man who killed him. I'm going to be very popular and—"

The brute leaned over Michel and punched him so hard in the jaw that stars swam in front of his face. His mouth numb, uncertain whether any teeth had been knocked out, Michel could do nothing but hang limply as the brute lifted him like a toy and carried him into the sitting room, where he tossed him unceremoniously into one of the chairs. The brute carried another chair over to face Michel, and Ka-Sedial took a seat, that gentle smile still fixed to his face. Despite his grandfatherly manner, his eyes smoldered with an entirely different story.

"I don't care," Sedial said. He raised one hand. "Don't mistake this for ingratitude, of course. I am pleased that je Tura is dead. He had far outlived his use to me. But your name will be forgotten long before you've finished screaming in my dungeons, so don't try to appeal to my very small regard for populism."

Michel stared at Sedial, uncertain what to say—uncertain if he could even speak. He didn't bother looking at the brute. The brute was just a fist, but Sedial was the man swinging it. Something had changed, and very recently, and Michel's luck had led him to stumble straight into Sedial.

"Shall we wait for Ichtracia to return?" Sedial asked. "Or should we continue this discussion now? Ah! I think I hear a carriage outside. Delightful—we won't have to wait long." He turned toward the door, raising his eyebrows. Michel heard the front door open. "*Mara*, my dear, please come in here."

Ichtracia appeared in the sitting-room doorway, an irritated expression on her face turning to shock at the sight of Michel. "What the pit are either of you doing here?" she asked in Adran.

"You know I prefer you speak to me in Dynize," Sedial chided.

"I'll speak in whatever I like, lizard. What are you doing here, and what happened to him?" She glanced at Michel. "I thought *you* were with Yaret. There's already a rumor going around that you killed je Tura personally."

Michel swallowed, wondering if opening his mouth would get him punched again. "I did," he managed.

Ichtracia's eyes turned to her grandfather. "Then what is *this*?" she demanded.

"My dear," Sedial purred, "your friend Michel is not what he seems." Michel resisted the urge to say, *She already knows.* Sedial continued. "While it seems that Michel managed to find our bomber, the *rest* of our sweeps through the Landfall catacombs were not entirely devoid of success. We pulled in three small cells of Blackhats still hiding down there. The first of those included a woman by the name of Hendres. I believe that she was Michel's ex-lover."

Michel felt his heart fall. He knew exactly where this was going. "I need to talk to you," he said to Ichtracia.

Sedial ignored him. "We didn't even have to torture her when she was brought to me. Within an hour, she had told me everything she knew about Michel. It seems that he doesn't work for the Blackhats, nor even for us. He works for a Palo freedom fighter by the name of the Red Hand." Sedial paused to examine his nails, waiting for Ichtracia to respond. Her eyes flicked back and forth between Michel and Sedial, but she said nothing.

"Ichtracia, I need to talk to—" Michel said, his voice stronger, but Sedial cut him off.

"This Red Hand has been set against both us and the Fatrastans for years. He's murdered our spies, even killed our dragonmen. Apparently he is a powder mage, though we still haven't managed to ascertain his true identity. I'm not even sure what his motives are, and I think you and I will have a long talk with your friend Michel to find out just exactly what information we're missing." Sedial turned to Michel, that grandfatherly smile disappearing. His eyes bore into Michel with a hungry intensity. "Well, Michel. Shall we begin?"

"Aren't you just going to take my blood? Force me to talk?"

"We will. Eventually. But I'm in no hurry. This way will be more amusing."

Michel fixed his eyes on Ichtracia while she, in turn, watched her grandfather as one might watch an adder. "Ichtracia," Michel said, "I know why he calls you Mara."

Both Ichtracia and Sedial stiffened. Sedial's lip curled. "You are not to address her," he said.

"He calls you Mara because you're his little sacrifice," Michel continued, talking quickly. "You're his backup plan with the godstone. If killing all those people doesn't force it to unlock its secrets, he's going to kill you."

Sedial laughed. "You're not telling her anything she doesn't already know. My granddaughter may be a sullen child still, but she knows her place." Despite the laugh, his voice held an edge of annoyance.

"It's sorcerous blood, isn't it?" Michel said. "It's stronger than regular blood. A *lot* stronger. He may sacrifice a Knacked or two, but that's probably not going to be enough. He has to have a

Privileged, waiting on his cue. Does the emperor even know that Sedial plans on using one of his tools that way?"

"Shut him up," Sedial said.

The brute stepped over to Michel and slammed his fist into the side of his head. A bright light shot across his vision, and he almost rolled out of the chair, but the brute caught him before he could fall. Michel spat blood at the brute, who didn't seem in the least bit bothered.

"Stop hurting him," Ichtracia said quietly.

"What?" Sedial and Michel responded at the same time.

"I told you to stop hurting him."

Sedial scoffed. "He's not your pet anymore, dear. He has betrayed the state, and he has betrayed you. You're not just going to watch as we cut him into small pieces—you're going to help keep him alive. And I intend him to remain alive for many, many months. Now, attend! Michel, tell me who the Red Hand is and why he opposes us."

Michel stared at Ichtracia. "I bet you weren't the first person he called Mara."

"His finger," Sedial said calmly.

The brute snatched up Michel's hand, pressing it against the table beside his chair, palm down. Michel attempted to fight, battering his fist against the brute's side and struggling to pull loose, but it was like trying to fight a marble statue. The brute drew a knife from his belt, slammed the tip into the webbed skin between Michel's pinkie and ring finger, and like a chef dicing a carrot, sliced off Michel's pinkie with a surprising crunching sound.

Michel screamed and lurched back as the brute suddenly let go of him. He clutched at his hand, blood fountaining from the little remaining stump of his finger. He pulled it to his chest, rolling in his chair, tears streaming down his face. He'd felt plenty of pain, plenty of times, but the sharp agony brought him near to throwing up.

"Let him bleed for thirty seconds," Ka-Sedial instructed, "and then sear the spot with your sorcery." He looked at Ichtracia. "Don't just stand there! Put your gloves on. If he dies tonight, I will take it out on you. You've had your fun with Michel. Now it's my turn."

Slowly, hesitantly, Ichtracia pulled her gloves out of her pockets and put them on. Through Michel's tears he could see the horror in her eyes and he gritted his teeth and tried to talk through the pain. "It was your big sister, wasn't it? The other one he called Mara. I bet she disappeared the night he killed your brother and father, didn't she?"

The brute's fist slammed across Michel's face, and this time it did knock him out of the chair. He landed on the floor, blacking out for a split second, blood from his hand soaking into the rug beneath him. He was suddenly lifted from the ground and thrown across the room, his body stopping mere inches from the wall. Nauseous, he tried to see through his pain and found himself held aloft by Ichtracia's sorcery on the opposite end of the room from Sedial. Ichtracia struck a pose, gloves on her hands, arms splayed like a child holding a toy away from their parent.

"What do you mean, *disappeared*?" Ichtracia demanded. She was staring at Sedial, but she was speaking to Michel. "I saw the burned corpses of all three of them. My sister is dead."

"Put him back here," Sedial said, pointing at the chair, his face screwed up in indignant anger. "I will take another finger every time he speaks without answering my questions."

Michel felt the sorcery around him tighten, and allowed all the pieces that had clicked in his brain to come babbling out. "Those burned bodies you saw were decoys. At least, one of them was. Your big sister didn't die in that fire. She was whisked away by her nanny, taken across the ocean by loyalists. She disappeared, and Sedial wasn't able to find her, so he killed some poor girl and burned the body beyond recognition."

"Shut up," Sedial growled.

Tears streamed down Ichtracia's face, but her jaw was clenched in determination, her eyes burning. "Continue!"

"You weren't Sedial's first choice, were you? He always knew he needed the blood of someone powerful to activate the godstones, and Ka-poel was destined to be a powerful bone-eye. That's why her nanny fled, that's why your father and brother died, so that she could get away. They knew, and they weren't going to let your grandfather sacrifice their kin for his ambitions." Michel spoke quickly, hoping he hadn't made any mistakes. He'd only realized any of this after his confrontation with je Tura and the realization that Sedial was sick enough to nickname his granddaughter "Sacrifice." That Ka-poel was a member of this family was only an educated guess...and if he was wrong, he was as good as dead.

"They had no vision!" Sedial shot to his feet, his composure completely gone. He shook his head, as if waking from a dream, and pointed at Michel. "How do you even know her name?" He gestured to the brute, who began to stride across the room to fetch Michel.

The brute suddenly stopped, a confused look on his face. He frowned; then his eyes widened a second before his head was suddenly stuffed into his own chest by invisible forces. His arms and legs followed, blood erupting across the room, and within moments Sedial's implacable henchman was an unrecognizable square of flesh the size of a small travel trunk, which was deposited at Sedial's feet. Ichtracia's expression hadn't changed through the entire event, but when her fingers stopped twitching, she said to Michel in a gentle voice, "You may answer my grandfather's question."

Sedial rocked back on his heels, and for the first time there was real fear in his eyes. Michel licked his lips. "I know because Ka-poel is the one who sent me here to retrieve you. She is married to the Red Hand, and she's the voice in your head—the bone-eye who has been communicating with you over the last year."

"Why didn't she tell me?" Ichtracia's voice came out as a squeak.

"I don't know. Maybe she wanted to tell you in person. Maybe she didn't know if she could trust you not to tell *him*." Michel nodded at Sedial. "But she didn't even tell me. I just figured the whole damned thing out an hour ago."

"Did you know?" Ichtracia asked her grandfather. "Did you know she was still alive?"

Sedial sputtered. "I had my suspicions. I knew she escaped with that bitch nanny and a few traitors, and I know that the dragonmen sent to Fatrasta to retrieve her never returned."

"But did you know she was here, alive, opposing you?" Ichtracia's voice rose in pitch.

"No."

Ichtracia squeezed her eyes shut. She drew a handkerchief from her pocket, one hand still raised toward Michel, keeping him fixed with his feet dangling above the floor. She wiped her eyes and nose. "I always know when you're lying, Sedial."

The old man was suddenly thrown backward, slamming into the wall with enough force to rattle the building and cause a shower of plaster to fall from the ceiling. He collapsed to the floor, moaning and cursing, and Michel was suddenly lowered to the ground. He almost fell himself, but was held on his feet by that invisible sorcery like someone propping themselves beneath his arms. Ichtracia strode across the room and delivered one vicious kick to Sedial's head, silencing his moaning.

A long, angry silence filled the room. Michel tried his best not to whimper, unsure whether he should look at Sedial or Ichtracia, and *knowing* he didn't want to look at the spongy bit of flesh that used to be Sedial's henchman. He clutched his hand, trying to stop the bleeding, trying to think through the pain. "Is he dead?"

"I'm a monster, but I will not kill my own grandfather."

"So what do we do?" Michel asked her. He tried to take a step forward, nearly collapsed, and decided to lean against the wall for a few minutes.

"We leave."

"When he wakes up, he's going to have every Dynize within fifty miles looking for us."

Ichtracia took a deep breath, chin raised. "You're going to get us out of the city."

Michel thought about Dristan and the stables, wondering if the kid had already left on his trip. *That* had been a risk back when he thought he could slip away quietly. Now that this had all happened—well, Michel wasn't entirely sure he could get out of Landfall without killing a thousand people on the way. "That's easier said than done."

"That's your next task," Ichtracia said with finality. "Get us out, and then take me to my sister."

CHAPTER 68

The ocean swelled and crashed, smashing against the breakers at the base of the Starlight citadel with a rage driven by the approaching storm. Styke paused to wipe the water from his eyes, only for the swell to slam into him once again, pummeling him against the rocks. He bent beneath the onslaught, his fingers gripping the icy stone, and forced himself to leap the next boulder and proceed over the breakers.

Somewhere above, the report of the cannons mixed with the thunder of the surf until they were one cacophony in his ears. He turned, waiting, grasping Ibana by the wrist and helping her over the stones, shoving her on ahead of him. He tried to see through the rising swell, counting the lancers still clinging to the rocks, and witnessed a wave hit Ferlisia in the back, slamming her into the rocks. When the wave receded, she was nowhere to be seen.

"Come on!" he bellowed, though he knew they could not hear him. "Keep moving!" He reached back and grabbed Ka-poel, lifting her bodily and shoving her along after Ibana before following himself. Out of the corner of his eye he saw the rising swell and snatched Ka-poel by the shoulder, pulling her beneath him, then braced his knees and arms against the rock as the wave hit.

The impact was a sensation like he had never felt, like being unhorsed in the midst of battle, then having the horse rear and fall directly on him—yet somehow worse. The force of the ocean shoved him, swallowed him, then threatened to pull him out to sea. His muscles flexed beneath the onslaught, his skin feeling as if it might burst, until the swell was gone. He shook his head and lifted Ka-poel, pushing her along before the next wave.

As quickly as he'd entered the vicious breakers, he was suddenly out of them again, climbing up on a stone shelf and turning to help the rest of the lancers as they emerged one by one, soaked and freezing, from the pitlike swell. Half of them had lost their carbines. A few had even lost their belts and swords. Little Gamble's arm was broken, and Jackal helped him to safety and set the bone.

Styke climbed along the ledge until he reached the sea gate. It was a heavy, iron-bar door like one might find in a dungeon. It was secured by chains thick enough to deter anyone lacking a smith's hammer.

"Belts!" Ibana ordered.

They tied the soaking belts together, then wrapped them around the iron bars closest to the rusted, salt-wrecked hinges. Styke stood at the front, flexed his forearms, and set his feet, passing the belt along the group.

"Heave!" Ibana shouted.

The hinges cracked.

"Heave!"

The door shuddered and pulled away from the stone, clattering off the ledge and down into the sea, nearly taking Styke with it before he pulled his knife and cut the belt beneath his hands. The knotted belts were untied and passed back, and the group quickly filed inside.

The corridor was dark and wet, cut out of the very rock upon which the citadel rested. Someone pressed a torch into Styke's hands. He removed the wax cloth from the end, and Ibana struck the match and lit it. Several more torches were passed along, and soon the corridor was illuminated in a flickering light. Styke pressed his palm to the stone, feeling the shudder caused by the firing of the guns. Somewhere above him, he heard a distant scream. He began to run.

The corridor was not long, and they soon emerged into a wider room—a pit at the bottom of a long, circular staircase, the base of which was littered with empty barrels, frayed ropes, shattered masonry, and corpses.

The corpses were not old, and the smell of them reached Styke's nostrils as he lowered his torch to let the light play upon their faces. They were two days dead, maybe less, and they wore the yellow jackets and pinned lapels of high-ranking Fatrastan officers. Styke only paused for a moment, a curse upon his lips. These were the missing brigadiers of the Third Army. They had died with knives to the backs and slit throats, and Dvory was not among them.

"Up!" Styke urged.

The circular staircase ended in a flat, stone ceiling, with the steps disappearing into a wooden trapdoor. Styke reached it first, pushing on the door. First tentatively, then harder, he pressed against it with his palms, attempting to lift it above him.

Ibana squeezed up beside him on the staircase and pushed. The door rattled some, but did not give. "It's barred," she told him.

"Willen could have damned well mentioned this," Styke growled. He shoved himself between the door and the top few steps, bending his neck and placing his shoulders against the wood. Taking a deep breath, he attempted to stand, shoving upward like a man lifting a sack of grain on his back.

The door held. He heard a creak, then a groan, and he continued to push until he could bear it no longer. He relaxed, taking a deep breath.

"We're going to have to go back out and scale the damned wall," Ibana said. "Lindet's going to have to damn well wait."

"Look for something down there to use as a battering ram."

"The angle isn't going to work for a ram," Ibana snorted. "This was made to withstand a siege. You're not going to break it."

Styke reset his shoulders and braced his hands and knees. He took a deep breath and pushed upward again. He strained, grunted, shoving until every muscle trembled beneath the strain.

"Ben, you're going to damn well hurt yourself."

Styke heard another scream far above him—a scream of pain, no doubt from a soldier wounded by a sharpshooter. In his mind's eye, though, it belonged to Lindet. He thought of all the years he'd spent in the labor camps, and he discarded them for the memory of a little girl tucking candies beneath his tongue when he was helpless, and he continued to push.

He felt something pop, a terrible pain spreading across his chest. He shoved harder, tears running down his face.

"Ben!" Ibana warned, but the voice seemed far away.

Something touched his bare skin. It was a hand, small and delicate, snaking beneath his shirt and tracing a trail with its fingernails up his spine until it was just below where his shoulders met the wood of the trapdoor. Through his foggy vision, he saw Ka-poel's face just beneath his left arm, her eyes once again young and mischievous. "What...?" he gasped.

The fingers tensed, nails biting into his skin. He felt a surge of strength, the smell of coppery sorcery filling his nostrils. His muscles bent and flexed, bones threatening to snap from the strain, and then a sudden *crack* and the release of tension as he surged upward. His momentum took him up and through the trapdoor, where he took several steps and collapsed on the cool stone floor of what appeared to be a large pantry full of beer kegs and sacks of grain.

He lay there, hand on his chest, as the Mad Lancers swarmed up the stairs to fill the pantry. His head pounded, his muscles on fire, and he heard Ibana distantly as she snapped orders. "Jackal, take these eight and open the front gates. If you survive that, head up and clear the towers. You four, see what you can do about the docks. The rest of you are with me and Ben."

Styke rolled over onto his back and gasped. Ka-poel crouched above him, her head tilted quizzically.

"That really hurt," he told her between breaths.

She touched her fingers gently to his forehead, then tapped a fingernail against his ribs. The pain was suddenly gone, the fire diminished. She tapped his ribs again and made two fists in front of his eyes, then pulled them apart.

"I broke a rib?"

She nodded.

He prodded the area gingerly, but felt no pain. "Did you heal it?" She shook her head.

Styke climbed to his feet, expecting the lances of pain at any moment, but they never came. "What did you do? Block the pain?"

Ka-poel pursed her lips and wiggled one hand back and forth. *More or less.*

"This is going to a hurt later, isn't it?"

She grinned wickedly.

"Pit." Styke stumbled to Ibana's side. "Where are we going?"

"Up, I assume," she answered, looking him up and down. "Pit, Ben. You just snapped an eight-inch beam of ironwood."

"A few other things, too. Come on, we have to find Lindet. Then I'm going to kill whoever is in command here."

"With ten men? I sent everyone else to try and open the gate. If Lindet is still alive, she'll be with Dvory. And he'll have his whole bodyguard with him. We need an army, Ben."

Styke unwrapped the wax cloth protecting his carbine from the water, then hefted his knife. He could still feel that pain deep in his chest, but it was a light buzz beneath Ka-poel's sorcery. His brain was on fire, his blood pumping. He felt like he was in his prime again, light on his toes and ready to grind stone with his hands. "We don't need an army. We're the Mad Lancers."

Styke caught a bayonet thrust on his carbine, turning the blade so that it scraped across the stone of the stairwell, and reached over to drive his boz knife through the eye of the Dynize soldier attempting to hold the hall. He lifted the spasming body and thrust it up the stairs ahead of him, using it as a shield as musket blasts made his ears ring. He reached the top of the stairwell and jerked his knife out of the soldier's skull, whipping it around to cut the throat of another as he passed and emerged into the great hall of the citadel keep.

Soldiers filled the great hall, turning bayoneted rifles and muskets on Styke as he entered the room. There were forty or fifty of them, a mix of Dynize with their morion helms and breastplates, and Fatrastan turncoats in their yellow jackets. Styke spotted Dvory at the far end of the great hall, and their eyes locked for a split second.

Dvory's face turned white.

"You didn't bring enough men," Styke shouted over the blasts of musket fire. A bullet slammed into his shoulder, jerking him back a half step and setting a fire of pain across an old wound. He ignored it, flipping his carbine over his shoulder and surging forward with his knife, carving into the Dynize.

His lancers flooded out of the stairwell behind him. They were down to eight now, after having to fight out of the kitchens and through the halls. Most of them bled from multiple wounds, clothes and faces soaked in blood, but the enemy fell back before them as if staring into the teeth of a thousand riflemen.

Styke sidestepped a bayonet thrust, feeling the sharp rasp of the blade across his ribs, and jerked the owner by the lapel onto his knife. He threw the body to one side and slashed, blinding a Fatrastan turncoat and leaving him to fall beneath Ibana's sword.

To one side, Ka-poel slid through the fighting like a snake in a den of rats. She stepped around bayonets and between gunshots, her machete in one hand and a long needle in the other. She thrust and sliced, and the men she killed didn't even seem to notice her until their blood splashed her black greatcoat.

"Dvory! Where is your army now, Dvory?" Styke's knife hand was slick with gore. He disemboweled a Fatrastan, then slid his knife beneath the breastplate of a Dynize and left the woman gurgling in her own blood. A pistol went off just over his right shoulder, and he felt the bullet take off his earlobe. He turned, skipping toward the owner of the pistol and cutting his throat, before returning to his march toward the traitor.

Dvory stood proud in his spot at the end of the great hall. His fingers gripped his sword with white-knuckled intensity, and he stared at Styke like a man staring down a charging boar. Styke wondered briefly if this was a trap—if Dvory had enough guts to fight him—before remembering that before all this the bastard had been a Mad Lancer. He had the guts.

Suddenly Styke was through the press of bodies, stumbling into the open. He took a deep breath, a growl in his throat, and felt the pain of a thousand tiny wounds. His jacket was soaked with blood and cut to ribbons, and rivulets of blood streamed down his neck. He licked his lips, relishing the pain, breathing in the stench of death, powder smoke, and sweat. He ignored the carnage of the battle still raging around him and took a step toward Dvory—only they existed now, and only one of them would leave this room alive.

Dvory shook his head. "You're a wreck, Ben. I've never seen you bloodier."

Styke hesitated. Dvory was too composed. He gripped his sword, his face was ashen, but he stared at Styke as if he expected to leave here alive. "You think I should change sides?" Styke asked.

"I think you should," Dvory answered. His sword remained in its sheath as Styke stepped closer and closer. "It's worked out for me so far." Dvory's pallor deepened, and a sheen of sweat appeared on his brow.

Styke glanced behind him. Only a few of his lancers remained standing. Ka-poel crouched over a wounded Dynize, fingers working the air before the man suddenly leapt to his feet with jerky motions and attacked his companions. Styke took another sidelong step, uncertain. Something was wrong here. "How has it worked out?" he asked.

Dvory attempted a smile. Styke could see now that his lips trembled. They moved, slowly, and Styke thought he heard a whisper. His hair stood on end as he realized that the coppery smell in the room was not all Ka-poel's sorcery. It belonged to someone else, another bone-eye.

"Where's Lindet?" Styke demanded.

"Here," a voice responded.

Styke skipped to the side, turning the blade of his knife just in time to catch the thrust from a short, powerful man wearing black leathery armor. As he deflected the thrust, he snatched the carbine from his shoulder and smashed it across the side of the man's face, snapping the butt just below the trigger. The man staggered to one side, shook his head, and righted himself.

A dragonman. And not just any, Styke realized as three more figures emerged from a hidden door to Dvory's right. The dragonmen he'd faced outside Granalia. Ji-Orz held Lindet by the back of the neck easily, his hand cocked as if ready to snap her spine with a flexed muscle. Lindet herself wore the same jacket and skirt that he'd spotted her in disembarking her ship. There were bruises on her face, but she looked no worse for wear. She lifted her chin toward Styke, as if unconcerned by the dragonmen around her.

The dragonman who'd attempted to blindside Styke took a step back, reassessing him, and licked his lips.

"Drop the knife or she dies," Dvory said, gesturing to Lindet.

Styke eyed Dvory for a moment, watching him tremble and sweat and tasting that smell of sorcery. "Are you really a traitor?" he asked Dvory. "Or did a bone-eye get his fingers in you?"

Dvory's tremble turned into an outright shake. "I told you to drop the knife." The voice that emerged did not belong to Dvory. It belonged to someone elderly, the accent biting and educated. Styke realized that Dvory's eyes were no longer on him, but directed over Styke's shoulder. He didn't have to look to know what had trans-fixed Dvory's attention.

"A bone-eye it is, then," Styke said. "Is it that piece of shit Ka-Sedial?" He gestured with his knife toward the dragonmen. "The one who sent these?"

"Ben, I didn't—" The voice belonged to Dvory for a split second before a look of annoyance crossed Dvory's face and the voice changed back to that of the old man. "We'll talk about your respect when you belong to me, Styke. Drop the knife or I kill Lindet. You won't let her die, will you? That's why you fought your way through all of these. For her." There was a flicker of a smile on Dvory's face. "Blood sees blood, Styke. Drop the knife, or I kill your sister."

"Your *what?*" Ibana demanded, stepping up beside Styke, her eyes wide.

Styke locked eyes with Lindet. He saw the corner of her mouth twitch upward and couldn't help but smile. A chuckle escaped his lips, and within moments he was laughing outright. He dropped his broken carbine and slapped his knee, then threw his head back in a roar. Across from him, her neck still in the grip of Ji-Orz, Lindet laughed with him.

Dvory stared at him in puzzlement. "What is so funny?"

Ka-poel stepped up to Styke's right. A dozen walking cadavers, their eyes blank, their bodies bloody, swayed behind her. She stared at Dvory, fingering her machete, and Dvory stared back. Ka-Sedial, it seemed, could be distracted.

"He's laughing," Lindet said softly, forcing Dvory to turn toward her, "because you have no idea who we are. Ben will save me if he can, just as I would him. But death? We've stared at our own deaths since childhood. You think to cow us with fear?" Lindet gave a warm, almost happy chuckle. "If you kill me, I am dead. I doubt Ben will mourn me long. I don't deserve it. But I *am* his blood, and he *will* avenge me." She paused, looking up into the eyes of Ji-Orz. "We laugh because whatever happens to me, the rest of you are already dead. Ben, kill them all."

Several things happened at once. The closest dragonman took a step toward Styke, knife thrusting, while a second dragonman broke for Ka-poel. A third jumped for Ibana.

Styke caught his opponent's thrust with his boz knife. The dragonman was ready for the counter and stepped close, drawing a second knife in the blink of an eye and ramming it, underhand, at Styke's side. Stepping into the blade, Styke felt it bite into his buttock, and the tip hit his pelvis. He wrapped his off arm around the dragonman's neck, pulling him against his breast, and squeezed with all his might. The dragonman jerked once, dropping his knife and slapping weakly at Styke's shoulder before slumping.

Styke cast the body aside as the third dragonman closed with Ibana. She fired her pistol point-blank, barely slowing her attacker, and drew her knife. Ibana was strong, but she was not as fast, and she fell back beneath three quick thrusts that threatened to overwhelm her. Styke swallowed the pain burning in his leg and leapt, tackling her assailant from the side just as he buried his knife between Ibana's ribs.

The dragonman squirmed beneath Styke, reached for another knife, and Styke bit off his nose and spat it in his face. He rolled off the dragonman and came up with his own knife just a fraction of a second quicker, burying it into the soft flesh just above the dragon-man's armor and sternum.

Styke turned to find that the second dragonman had cut through Ka-poel's ensorcelled soldiers with ease, and now pressed her violently. Styke forced himself to his feet, barely able to move, and took a step toward her.

"Don't kill her!" Dvory yelled in Ka-Sedial's voice.

The dragonman attacking Ka-poel faltered for a split second, trapping Ka-poel's machete with his own knife and turning his head just a fraction toward Dvory, as if in question. Ka-poel's other hand darted up, striking as quick as an adder, and rammed a long needle into the dragonman's eye.

Styke took a second step as the dragonman fell, and then stumbled down to one knee. He looked at Dvory, at the expression of horror on his face, then toward Lindet, who smiled softly in the grip of Ji-Orz.

"Kill her," Dvory ordered. "Kill Lindet, kill Styke, and bring me the girl."

Styke looked around the room. Everyone was dead or dying. Ibana clutched at the knife stuck between her ribs, struggling to breathe. Lindet was fodder for the dragonman. Ka-poel was quick, but she would not be able to handle Ji-Orz on her own. And Dvory still stood unwounded, unfluttered, his body being controlled by someone a continent away.

"Kill her," Dvory hissed.

Ji-Orz pursed his lips. There was no fear in his eyes as he looked across the carnage, but there was something else. His eyes met Styke's, and he gave a long-suffering sigh and let go of Lindet's neck. "No."

"What?" Dvory demanded.

"Your hold on me has broken. You are weak, Great Ka. You are spread too thin, and I am no longer compelled." Ji-Orz drew the bone knife from his belt, then a bone knife from beneath his jacket, and lay them both on the ground. "I'm tired," he said. "I'm tired of this. I'm tired of you. I've watched Ben Styke kill three dragonmen. *In all my life, I have never and will never see such a thing again.* I may fight him someday, but I refuse to slaughter an artist like this when he is barely able to fight."

Dvory straightened, his trembling intensifying. "You're scared of him?"

"I am a dragonman. We do not feel fear." Ji-Orz looked sidelong at Lindet. "But I respect strength."

"I will find you, and I will break you," Dvory said in a low, angry voice.

Ji-Orz inclined his head slightly. "I'll see you again, Ben Styke." Without another word, he was gone through the side door, out the back of the great hall.

Styke turned his gaze on Dvory, watching the struggle play out across Dvory's face in much the same way as it played out across that cuirassier commander Ka-poel enthralled last week. He could see the fight in Dvory's eyes and the sweat on his brow. He squeezed his eyes shut, then wiped the perspiration from his cheeks with the back of his sleeve. He gave a mighty shiver before looking down at Styke with someone else's eyes.

"You'll bleed out soon enough, Styke. No one survives those wounds."

Styke still rested on one knee, his head feeling heavy and his eyes tired. The dragonman's exit seemed to take the strength from his limbs, and he wanted nothing more than to lie down and sleep. He touched the bloody stone with one hand and tried to gather his wits before shakily pushing himself back up to his feet. He lifted his knife.

Dvory swallowed, looking from Styke to Ka-poel. His face took on an almost paternalistic expression. "Child," he said. "I've been calling for you. Why don't you answer? Kill them for me, and then join me in Landfall. You've locked the godstone, but I will unravel it sooner or later. With your help I can end this war quickly. We can put a stop to this bloodshed and unite the continents once more."

Ka-poel gestured emphatically.

"I don't know what that means. Why do you not speak? Are you mute?"

Styke lurched forward, grabbing Dvory by the arm as he began to draw his sword. He pressed the tip of his knife to Dvory's throat. "She called you a prick."

Dvory's lips drew back in a snarl, and suddenly Styke felt himself pushed aside. He staggered away as Ka-poel took his place in front of Dvory. She leaned toward him, searching his eyes as if looking through a looking glass at something far away.

"My child," Dvory whispered.

Ka-poel lifted her long needle and gently drew the tip down Dvory's cheek, gathering drops of blood as it went. She held it up to the light, and Dvory shifted nervously in front of her. She smiled at the man she saw behind Dvory's countenance, and thrust her needle into Dvory's eye.

The scream that issued from Dvory was not in his own voice.

Styke staggered toward Ibana, only for Lindet to rush forward, putting her shoulder beneath his arm and helping him the rest of the way. He got to his knees beside Ibana, leaning on one arm. Lindet took his knife and began tearing away strips of a dead traitor's jacket for bandages.

Ibana watched her work wordlessly, her eyes eventually traveling to Styke's face. "The guns have gone quiet," she muttered.

"So they have," Styke replied.

"You look like shit."

"So do you."

Styke looked down at the dragonman's bone knife still stuck between her ribs. "I'll survive. Will you?"

"I..." Ibana tried to shift, her face going white. "I don't think it hit anything vital. But it hurts like pit. We need a surgeon."

Lindet paused in her making of bandages. "Get me to the signal towers and I'll tell my ships that the citadel is ours. You'll be healed by sorcery by the morning. If you last that long."

Ibana stared at the side of Lindet's face. "I didn't see it before, but now I don't know why I didn't. Your sister." She snorted. "You have a damned lot of explaining to do, Benjamin."

Styke locked eyes with Lindet. He saw, for just a fraction of a second, Lindet's desire to make sure no one left this room alive but the two of them. He shook his head. She hesitated, then nodded. "Bandage yourselves. I'll send the signals."

Dvory's screams, in the voice of another, lasted for the rest of the night.

CHAPTER 69

Vlora wiped the gore from her sword, teetering on the edge of consciousness before a quick hit of powder brought her back from the edge. She leapt forward, sword in one hand and knife in the other, carving through a platoon of Dynize soldiers who attempted to hold her at the end of their bayonets. Sorcerous speed allowed her to slip through the gap between their blades, her sword flicking precisely. Her body moved mechanically, without the wherewithal for conscious thought, and she couldn't have said whether it was seconds or hours between the time she'd turned on that platoon and the time the last man hit the dirt.

Probably seconds. She *knew* it had been hours since the fight had begun, in the same way a man half-asleep knows when someone is trying to wake him up. Thousands lay dead behind her, littering the road back toward the Crease. Thousands more screamed from their wounds. She forced herself to ignore the savagery of it and press on, looking for the next throat to open with the tip of her sword.

The little part of her mind still able to function wondered where Taniel had gotten to. Most of the carnage along the road belonged to him—he was an impossible force, cutting a swath through the Dynize column with the same unstoppable power as a cannonball skipping across a battlefield. They were both up in the foothills now, killing their way through a second brigade of soldiers, and she'd lost sight of him at some point in what she thought was just the last few minutes.

Someone in the distance yelled to open fire, and bullets whizzed over Vlora's head or struck the dirt around her. One took a chunk out of her shoulder. She barely noticed it through her powder trance, but she reached out toward the sound of firing muskets and detonated the powder she felt in that direction.

A chorus of screams and a cloud of smoke rose from the ridgetop to her left, and the kickback from detonating all that powder literally knocked her off her feet. Her vision grew dark for a few moments and she wrestled with her mind to keep herself from losing consciousness.

Without even giving her body clear orders, she was back on her feet and sprinting toward a group of horsemen as they charged foolishly toward her down the road, horses leaping the bodies that Taniel had left in his wake. She reached out to detonate their powder, found none, and instead gathered all her sorcerous strength to leap into their midst with sword swinging. One thrust, midleap, cut the jugular of a dragoon. As she came down, she rammed her knife into the thigh of another dragoon, then landed in a crouch, sword swinging up to remove the leg of a horse that slammed into the ground behind her, rolling and crushing its rider.

Vlora barked a laugh and heard it tinged with mania. Nothing these assholes could throw at her could take her down. Not a thousand men, not ten thousand. She was soaked in the blood of their companions, coated in powder grime and dirt, her shirt half torn away and her hair a knotted mess of gore. She changed directions, pivoting on one foot to deal with the dragoons who had just ridden past her, and took a step forward.

At least, she tried to take one step forward. The leg worked, but her foot turned beneath her with a stab of pain that cut through the powder trance to hit her right between the eyes. She grunted, gave a half-hearted scream, and then felt the slashing point of a dragoon's blade cut savagely across her sword arm. Her fingers numb, the sword flew from her hand, and Vlora dropped to her knees.

It took her a few moments to assess the situation. During her jump, one of the dragoons must have sliced the tendons of her left foot. She could feel the nerves screaming out in pain through the dull ache of her powder trance. That other dragoon had done the same to her right wrist.

She laughed again and flipped her knife around in her left hand, attempting to force herself to her one good foot to take the dragoons' final charge.

Perhaps a dozen dragoons had made it past her. They turned their horses, swords held at the ready, and watched with uncertainty as she struggled back to her feet. All around her, wounded and terrified soldiers seemed to stare at her in the same way they might stare at a grenade whose fuse might or might not have failed.

Vlora detonated the powder of a squad of soldiers approaching from behind her. The act knocked her back to the ground and tore a gasp from her throat. One of the Dynize dragoons dismounted and took a half step toward her. His companions did the same. None of them had any powder on them, which meant that they'd been sent specifically to stop her. Perhaps even to capture her. Vlora reached out, gingerly feeling for every ounce of powder on the infantry within a half mile.

The sorcerous backlash of such a detonation would kill her. But it would keep her from being taken alive. Mentally, she held a match above that powder and prepared to set it off as her last living act.

"By the Mighty," one of the dragoons said. "I've never seen anything like it."

One of her companions shook his head. "The other one is worse. The general sent all of our dragonmen to stop him, and he cut through them like they were lambs."

"She tires," the first dragoon said, thrusting a sword toward Vlora. "The other one will, too."

The dragoons approached slowly, swords held at the ready. She could see the fear in their eyes—fear tempered by the smell of victory. She waited until one of them had come just outside of sword range and sprang from her knees, knife slashing. The dragoon was able to lunge back out of the way and Vlora stumbled on her useless foot and slipped in the gore of an infantryman, landing face-first on the hard-packed dirt road. She heard someone laugh.

"She's done," a dragoon said.

"Do you hear something?" another asked.

"Only screams. Should we try to take her alive?"

Someone kicked the knife out of Vlora's hand. She was grasped by the hair, her head jerked backward. She tried to stab the arm with her knife, then remembered it was no longer in her fingers. The feeble thrust of her empty hand was battered away. A foot planted itself in her gut, flipping her onto her back.

The pain meant very little through her powder trance. She wanted to laugh at them, that mental match still poised above all that powder nearby, but she couldn't quite summon the energy. *I'm dying*, she realized. She managed to get to her knees, the single action taking an eternity. Hands in her lap, she stared up at the dragoon who gazed down at her over the point of a sword.

She wished she could have spent one last night with Olem before she died. She wished that she could tell him once more that she loved him.

"She's gone," the dragoon said, tapping the side of Vlora's face with his sword. "Look at her eyes. We can take her back to the general, but I doubt she'll survive the trip."

"I'm not so sure. Look at her. She's cut to ribbons, but she's still fighting."

Vlora wanted to scoff. Other than her hand and foot, she'd barely been scratched. She let her head roll around, looking down at her body, before realizing that it was far from the truth. She'd been shot at least four times. Her shirt didn't even exist anymore, and her chest and thighs were a patchwork of bloody cuts that she hadn't even noticed in her bloodlust.

"Just take her head," someone said. "No need for the body."

The dragoon pointed his sword between Vlora's eyes, then raised it to one side with both hands. "It seems a pity," he said.

Vlora reached out with that mental match, using the last of her strength, only for nothing to happen. She blinked, surprised, then let out a resigned sigh. Her sorcerous well had run completely dry. There was nothing left to give. No final detonation, no blaze of glory. She licked the blood off her lips and tried to smile at her executioner.

The dragoon frowned. Blood began to run down his face, and it took Vlora several seconds to realize that a perfectly formed icicle had sprouted from his forehead. Odd, that. *There's no ice in Fatrasta in the summer.* Icicles rained down, slicing through the remaining dragoons before any of them could raise their swords.

Am I already dead? she wondered. *Is this the final fantasy that my body tells me before I give up the ghost?*

Something strange crept across the ground. At first, she thought it was a wave washing over the road. It certainly looked like a wave, but no water had ever been that shade of blue. A woman strode past her, hair tight in braids over both shoulders, wearing an immaculate crimson dress in the Adran style. She was wreathed in the same blue that washed over the ground, and Vlora realized that they were flames. They washed over and past that woman with a heat that hurt Vlora's face and barely even sizzled when it touched off the powder of dead infantrymen.

Dynize soldiers tried to run, but were consumed in moments, their bodies turned to ash where they stood. Vlora fixed her gaze on the woman, wondering who she was, though a part of her brain told her that she knew that figure well. Her eyes fell to the woman's hands, and the blue flame that sparked from them without gloves.

"You don't look so well, sister," a voice said.

Vlora tried to turn her head and found that she could not. Someone stepped around her, into her field of vision, and leaned close. Gloved hands touched her face gently, and the countenance of a man in his early thirties with auburn hair and curly sideburns smiled at her grimly.

"Borbador," Vlora whispered. "Are you dead, too?"

"Not last I checked."

"You must be. Otherwise you wouldn't be here to meet me on the other side."

Borbador gently slapped Vlora's cheek. "Stay with me here, my darling sister. You're not on the other side yet and I'd really rather you not head there when I've just arrived."

"You can't be here," Vlora protested. "I only sent for you a month ago."

"You think you're the only one who can write a letter? Taniel told me over a year ago that the Dynize intended to invade. I've been raising an army. Look, I can tell you about it later. I just need you to stay awake until Nila finishes mopping up a few brigades. It's going to take the two of us to keep you alive."

Vlora felt herself shaking, her powder trance unable to hold off the pain any longer. She trembled and wept, wishing any of this was real, knowing that it was the wishful hopes of a dying mind. "I missed you, Bo. I wish I could really say good-bye to you."

"Shush now," Borbador said, pulling Vlora's head against his chest. "Your family has come for you."

EPILOGUE

Styke stood at the top of one of the remaining towers of the Starlight citadel, leaning on the stone battlements as he slowly carved a horse from a bit of pine. His left hand still had a twinge from the firing squad despite two rounds of sorcerous healing over the last few months, and the pine slipped in his hand a few times as he worked. He sucked away the blood each time, enjoying the biting feel of the tiny cuts.

"I'm getting too big for wooden horses," Celine told him, dangling her feet off the edge of the tower.

"Who said I'm making it for you?"

"You always make them for me."

Styke held the horse up to the light, then shaved a bit more wood off each of the back legs. "You're an ungrateful little brat, you know that?"

Celine swung her legs around and crossed the tower to kiss him on the cheek, before returning to her spot. "You're getting better with the knife."

"Sorcerous healing will do that."

"I thought you said practice makes you better?"

"I used to be quite good at carving things," Styke answered, blowing wood shavings off the back of his hand. "I had to relearn how to do it with a crippled hand and a dull knife. Come to think of it, having something sharp on hand makes things a lot easier, too." He took the horse and walked over to Celine, holding it in two fingers and riding it across her shoulder, then holding it in front of her eyes. "What breed is he?"

"He is a she," Celine said pointedly. "And she's a Gurlish draft horse."

Styke frowned at the carving. "I was aiming for a Starlish draft, but it *does* look more like a Gurlish, doesn't it?" He set the carving next to her. "How is Margo?"

"We're getting used to each other."

"That wasn't an answer."

"Good. I like her a lot. She still starts when she hears a gunshot."

"She's a good horse. We'll train that out of her."

Styke paused, hearing the soft sound of footsteps on the stairs behind him, and half turned to watch Lindet emerge on the parapet. She stood straight-backed and formal by the stairs, her face once again unreadably haughty. She raised her chin at Styke, then let her eyes wander to Celine. There was a question there. He ignored it.

Celine climbed down from the battlements and stared up at Lindet. "You're the Lady Chancellor?"

"I am."

Styke put one elbow on the parapet and tried not to look interested in where this conversation was about to go.

"You don't look very dangerous."

"You don't look very interesting. Yet it seems Ben Styke has taken an interest in you."

Celine sniffed, unimpressed. "My da died in the labor camps. Ben protects me. He said he's made a habit of protecting little girls until they are big enough to protect themselves."

Lindet's eye twitched, and Styke rolled his tongue around his teeth in an effort to suppress a smile. "It seems our secret is out," Lindet said. "It's the talk of the entire Third Army. You know how I feel about tongues wagging."

"You can't control everything," Styke said.

"I can try."

"You can try. But you'll fail."

Lindet sighed, then crossed the tower to stand next to him, looking to the east, along the northern coast of the Hammer. "You're not worried about your reputation? Mad Ben Styke, brother to the ruler of Fatrasta? You're no longer a loose cannon, a force of nature. They'll know that you came from someplace. That your sister is the most powerful woman on the continent. Family connections tend to...dim the perception that others have of your accomplishments."

"I've never really given a shit what anyone thought about me," Styke replied, twirling his lancers' ring on his finger. "You're not worried about *your* reputation?"

"I sent my own brother to the labor camps for a decade." Lindet shrugged. "I think that goes rather well with my reputation." He saw the flicker of a smile at the corner of her mouth and rolled his eyes.

"I should throw you off this tower."

Lindet lifted her hand, placing it on Styke's arm. "I know. Your healing, did it go well?"

"It did, thanks." Styke instinctively rolled his shoulders, feeling the tightness from the healed cuts on his torso and the bullet wound in his shoulder. "Have you found the Dynize Army?"

"I have. They pulled back once your men threw open the doors of the citadel. It seems they didn't want to attack a field army *and* a fortress at the same time, and during a storm no less."

"Your ships?"

"I lost two to the storm. Three to the citadel guns. The fleet is in surprisingly good shape, considering the circumstances." She paused, her eyes narrowing as if something had pained her. "I...I would have lost the war if you had not come in after me. The Third would have been crushed, my fleet scattered, and my person either captured or executed. Thank you for that."

Styke remained silent. He couldn't remember the last time Lindet had thanked him for something. Not since childhood, certainly.

Lindet continued. "I have two gifts for you. The first is command of this citadel. Your lancers have earned some rest. They can get drunk off the nearby caches and sweep the coast of any Dynize landing parties. I won't take no for an answer."

"You want to put me in command of a city?" Styke asked flatly.

"A city without any people in it, yes. I'll leave a garrison large enough to man the walls, and your lancers. I think this is a good spot for you...for now. I'm going with the Third first thing in the morning, and we're going to sweep the Dynize off the Hammer. Once we're ready to head into the mainland, I will summon you."

Styke couldn't quite manage a thank-you. It was too obvious that Lindet was giving him the command so she could keep an eye on him. Not a lot of places he could go, sitting out here on the end of the Hammer. "What's the second gift?"

"The second gift is stored in a vault about seven miles southeast of here. You probably rode past it during your recent adventures."

Styke perked up, his heart quickening. "What is it?"

A self-satisfied smile cracked Lindet's face. "Your armor. All of it. Three hundred sets, plus another two hundred that I've gathered since the war. They don't all match, not like the originals, but I don't think that will matter to you."

Styke's mouth was dry. "I knew you were lying about destroying them."

"I knew you knew I was lying." Lindet gave a shrug, as if it didn't matter. "Tell me about the Riflejack cavalry among the lancers."

It was Styke's turn to be coy. "I picked up a few friends along the way."

"And your goals in this part of the continent?"

Styke gave her a thin smile.

Lindet rolled her eyes. "You're looking for them, aren't you? The other godstones?" She waited just a moment for an answer, then made a dismissive gesture. "The one on the Hammer. I'm guessing you didn't find it?"

"I did not."

"Good. You should keep your distance from the stones, Benjamin. You may be mad, but you don't want anything to do with them."

"And you do?" Styke asked, unable to keep the petulance out of his voice.

"Hmm. Tell me, where is the bone-eye woman who killed Dvory? What was her name?"

"I'm not sure what you're talking about."

All trace of emotion left Lindet's face. Her jaw tensed. "I've had my men looking everywhere for her, yet she seems to have disappeared without a trace. Your Mad Lancers are pretending she never existed."

"Odd, that. It's as if she never did."

Lindet snorted. "I'm leaving, Benjamin. You *will* stay here, and you *will* protect the coast from the Dynize. When I summon you, I expect you to have your armor and I expect you to have moved past this godstone nonsense. The stones will remain unrecovered until this war is won. Do you understand?" She turned on her heel and left the tower without waiting for an answer.

Styke leaned on the battlements, feeling tired, and watched the ships anchored out past the breakers. There were transports, ships of the line, commandeered merchantmen. It was, as he'd suspected, everything that Lindet had left in this part of the country. Now they crouched in the shadow of Starlight's guns, knowing they were the only protection against the roving Dynize fleets.

Less than a minute had passed before he heard footsteps again. They belonged to Ibana, and she joined him at the battlements immediately and glanced out to sea before fixing him with a sidelong stare. "I passed Lindet on the way up here."

"Yeah."

"Sister, eh?"

"Yeah." Styke didn't really much feel like talking about it. The conversation was going to be a long one, and very uncomfortable.

To his surprise, all Ibana said was, "That explains a lot. So what's our plan now?"

"Lindet has left me in charge of Starlight."

"She wants to keep an eye on you."

"That she does."

"So what will you do?"

"She also told me where my armor is. There's a vault seven miles from here. I want you and the lancers to head out immediately and fetch it."

This got Ibana's attention. A grin slowly spread across her face, and he could see a hungry look in her eye. "We have our armor back."

"That we do. We're going to wait until Lindet's been gone for three days. Then we're going to commandeer her fleet and invade Dynize. Sound good?"

Ibana straightened, a fierce grin on her face. "With our armor? That sounds wonderful."

ACKNOWLEDGMENTS

I have to start with thanks to my fantastic editor, Brit Hvide, and her guiding hand throughout the process of writing this book. Sequels are always tricky, and Brit stepped in as editor on the second book in a series without losing a beat. Thanks to my agent, Caitlin Blasdell, for her continuing support. She and her colleagues at Liza Dawson Associates help make sure I can keep writing for a living, which is one of the best gifts a guy can get!

Thanks to my wife, Michele. She sees every piece of mine before anyone else, and her fingerprints are all over the Powder Mage books. I couldn't dream of writing them without her help.

My appreciation goes out to my beta-readers, Mark Lindberg, Joshua Mulligan, Sam Baskin, Wyatt Nevins, and Peter Keep. Thanks to all the awesome staff at Orbit, who continue to help me put out great books. And finally, thanks to all of you for reading and continuing to support me! I couldn't do it without you!